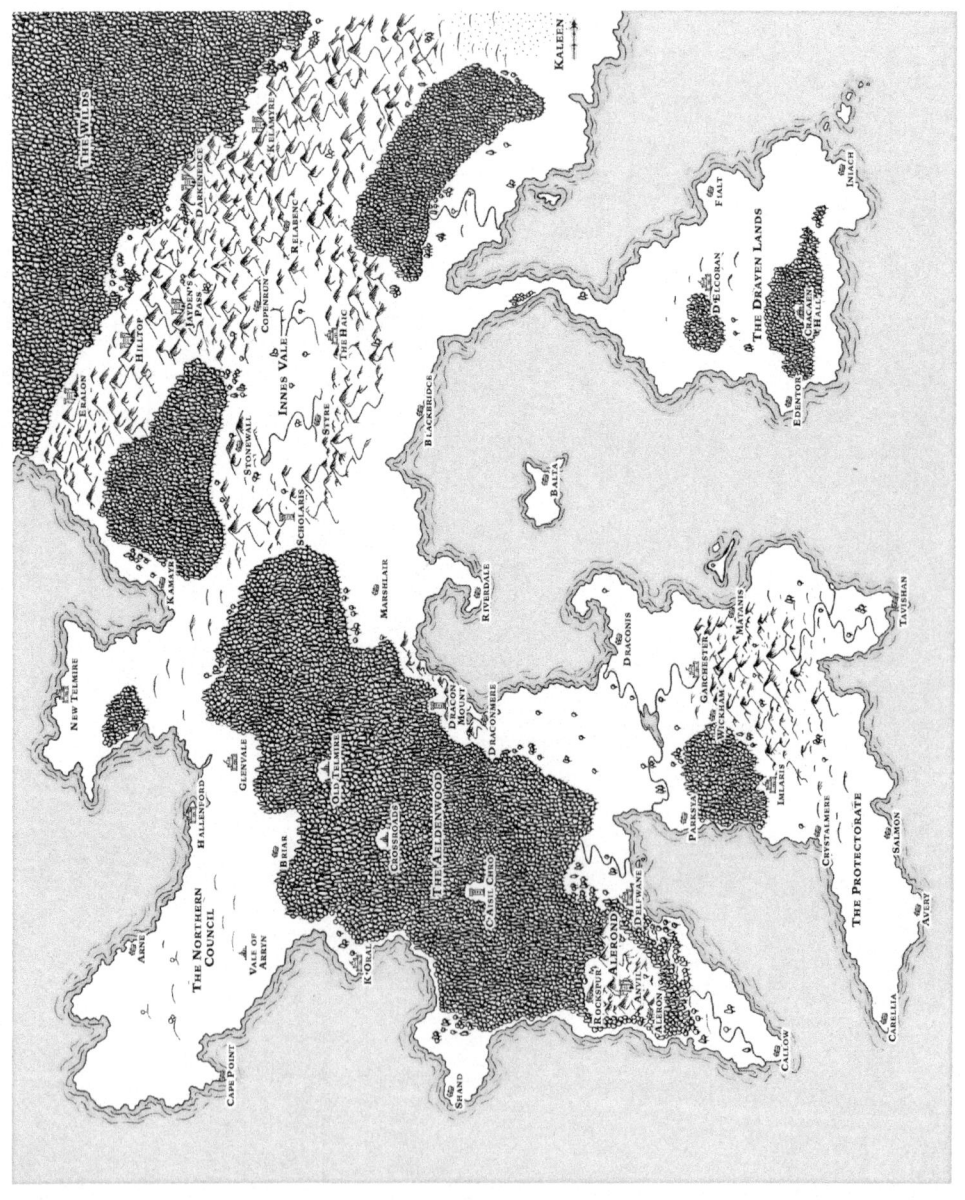

THE
MERCENARY CODE

THE SHATTERING OF KINGDOMS | BOOK I

EMMET MOSS

To those who stood by me, family and friends alike, whose support was unwavering and without judgement, I can never thank you enough.
You know who you are. I am blessed to have found your company.

To my wife. You are my rock. You never wavered in your support. I am a truly lucky man.

To Maas. You are the hardest working editor I know. Many times your passion kept this project alive.

THE MERCENARY CODE

"Upon the wind your voice whispers. Among the trees you walk within. Never will you abandon me, Aeldenwood."
—*Gorimm prayer*

PROLOGUE

The forest leaves rustled softly and a young wolf padded lightly across the clearing. Pausing to sniff the air, she detected a nearby scent too faint to be carried upon the wind.

Pacing in a small circle, she settled on her haunches and tilted her head towards an imagined sound. The air was suddenly quiet, and a feeling of apprehension arose in the ancient Aeldenwood.

A small grey squirrel crept forward with a large acorn bulging in its cheek. Glancing around suspiciously, the skittish creature nestled itself alongside the wolf's flank. Moments later, a large noble buck sidled up to join the pair, its healthy coat glistening a deep chestnut brown. The buck stared at the wolf while entering the grove with a majestic grace. Moving proudly to the center of the clearing, the stag waited patiently.

Ignoring the new arrivals, the wolf focused her large almond-shaped eyes on the thick undergrowth. Faintly at first, a stiff breeze began to stir, and the stoic trees of the old forest started to sway with the strength of the wind. Branches cracked violently as the rushing air increased in ferocity. Before long, a whirlwind swirled under the tall, wooded canopy. All three animals faced the torrent of air unflinchingly and remained steadfast.

Suddenly, at the height of its power, the windstorm ceased. Shattered branches crashed to the ground and clouds of leaves drifted back to earth. A flash of light penetrated the grove and illuminated the area with a radiant white glow. Expanding slowly, it grew in size and formed an oval-shaped archway. Completely opaque and standing no taller than an average man, the sculpted shape came to rest next to the wolf.

Sniffing the air once again, the animal stared expectantly at the portal while a figure emerged from within the bright depths of the strange shape. The large stag bowed its antlered head as the visitor brushed a long-fingered, greenish-brown hand along the animal's coat. Bending down on one knee, the stranger gently scratched the squirrel's furry chin. The squirrel chattered with excitement and darted up his arm, scurrying beneath the grey hood of his cloak.

He brushed a stray strand of white hair from his face and turned to acknowledge the excited wolf standing patiently by his side. A broad grin stretched over the delicate features of his face.

Calia 'na Brendwien. L'os delia Tel'ni, Greiyfois.

His lips did not move, yet the strange words could be heard by all gathered in the clearing. In response, the wolf raised her snout skyward and let loose a spine-tingling howl that echoed clearly throughout the ancient wood. The heartfelt cry had a musical tone that carried with it a tinge of sadness.

Overwhelmed by the greeting, the figure knelt down and embraced the wolf. Excited noises echoed from the edges of the clearing as forest dwellers, big and small, crept forward and welcomed the visitor. Turning a moment and whispering under his breath, he raised a hand towards the bright archway.

T'avoris na 'Geltilde. The clearing was plunged into semidarkness as the portal disappeared in a flash.

Without warning, distant wolf calls full of alarm rang out and an undercurrent of dread froze the members of the peaceful gathering. The she-wolf stood among the woodland animals and returned the call. With hackles raised, a menacing snarl replaced the warm, welcoming look she had displayed moments earlier.

Amidst the din, the stranger motioned to the assembled host and urged them to scatter. As quickly as they had appeared, they hastily returned to the safety of the dense brush. Only the wolf and stag remained by his side.

An ominous sound echoed to the north; the heavy tread of a great multitude moving at speed could be heard. Pausing only long enough to free a pair of long knives from his belt, the visitor bounded from the grove. Keeping pace by his side, the wolf returned the calls of her brethren. Attuned to the same howls, the figure turned sharply as if guided by the cries.

The thunderous rumble continued to intensify and followed in their wake as they fled. Branches cracked, trees splintered and animals scurried away as the horde continued its march. With the unholy sound in pursuit, the stranger proved himself fleet of foot as he soared nimbly over a number of sharply cut gullies with ease. His animal companion kept close upon his heels in full stride as they made their way unerringly to the east.

Yet still did the hunters close the distance.

Dark shapes appeared along the edge of the forest, and a rotting stench emanated from the darkness. Approaching a large clearing, the white haired figure paused to catch his breath. The young wolf growled at the nearest treeline, her teeth bared in a naked snarl.

With weapons in hand, the visitor murmured under his breath and a soft green glow filtered through the grove. His daggers reflected the light and illuminated the mass of shadows crouched on the edge of the clearing. Determined eyes surveyed the menacing creatures laid out before them. The shadowed beasts were barely visible as they moved along the periphery of the grove. He could see brief glimpses of their twisted bodies and gaping maws full of sharp glinting teeth.

Standing fearlessly, the strange man narrowed his eyes, lifted his blade, and beckoned his adversaries. With a roar that shook the foundations of the ancient wood, the horde swarmed forth from their hidden positions, a mass of heavily-muscled flesh with razor claws. The stench of putrid breath washed over him in a nauseating wave. Confronted by such a wall of mindless ferocity, he remained poised as his defensive position was overrun.

He cut a swath through the first row of shadowed hunters. Moving swiftly, he gracefully parried blows from all sides. The long daggers cut deep and many of the dark creatures fell with tendons severed and throats opened. Enraged by such an elusive quarry, the attackers trampled their own in a berserker rage. Only a single-minded hatred remained, and a determination to destroy the being that evaded their frenzied attacks.

At his side, the wolf fought in beautiful symmetry with each of his movements. With a violent ferocity, the animal attacked with the same calculated precision.

Crimson stains marred her beautiful white coat as she fought defiantly against the bloodthirsty throng.

For one brief moment, when the visitor's bloodied hands lost their grip on one of the blades and gore-splattered boots slipped on the growing pile of corpses littering the forest floor, the fate of the battle hung in the balance. The hunters found an opening and advanced on their prey.

The warrior struggled to maintain his balance as a hideous horned beast clamped its teeth down on his left shoulder. With jarring force, the creature's bite crushed bone and muscle alike. Grimacing in pain, the man drove his remaining weapon deep between the creature's dark eyes. Spinning to avoid another attacker, he tore his shoulder from the jaws of the dead beast.

Blood gushed from the wound and spilled to the ground. A dark stain soaked through his tunic. Grunting painfully, he paused to reclaim his fallen weapon and launched himself toward the remaining enemies with an unwavering look in his bright green eyes. Although pained by the fresh wound, he dealt death with every blow, and what had once seemed like a doomed final stand, became an unlikely victory. With practiced ease, the man silenced the wounded, his death strokes guided by mercy, even though his enemies would surely have shown him none.

Breathing heavily, the victor staggered towards the treeline holding his hand tightly against the gaping shoulder wound in a vain attempt to stem the bleeding. Falling to one knee, he tried desperately to regain his balance. After a moment, he too succumbed to darkness, his body crumpling to the earth in a motionless heap.

Her white coat tarnished with blood, the wolf raised her head and let loose a long, grieving howl. As night descended, the call was answered. Standing a silent vigil over the Aeldenwood's fallen visitor, she waited.

AUTUMN

3AE337

"With an ear-shattering shriek, the tree shuddered and fell forward, its limbs grasping for purchase, yet finding no succor. Gort Greatwood wiped the thick sheen of sweat from his brow and leaned upon his axe. A smile flickered briefly across his rugged features. For the fourth time that year, the Lumber had lived to tell the tale."
—Heartwood Tales, volume II

CHAPTER I

Briar - Northern Council

The inhabitants of the northern town of Briar slowly roused themselves after another bitterly cold autumn night. Frost rested lightly upon the earth in a thin sheet of immaculate white. Lazy smoke trails drifted from cottage chimneys near the center of town and early risers began tending to their daily chores. The pristine spire of the Church of Arne broke high into the crisp morning sky, and the Inn of the Black Boar stood proudly above the smaller establishments.

In the distance, there came a steady chopping sound from an immense stretch of woodland to the south. As far as the eye could see, large trees towered over the landscape like silent sentinels.

This was the Aeldenwood; and for as long as history in Caledun had been recorded, the forest had never seen a period of regress. Although merciless winters were common in the north, still did the majestic wood wear its lush canopy of leaves season after season. So it was and so it shall always be, said the people of Briar.

Alessan Oakleaf rose from his small bed, tousled his thick mat of black hair and tiptoed quietly across the wooden floor of his room. Dressed only in a pair of loose-fitting trousers, he shivered against the cold and pulled a heavy wool shirt over his head. Heading downstairs towards the Black Boar's common room, he paused to wake Wert, the boy responsible for tending to the kitchen fires for the coming week.

The inn had been busy the evening prior; the evidence of this being quite visible by the state of the main room. At a quick glance, Alessan spied an overturned table, a few broken chairs, many splattering's of food, and even a few items of clothing. He bent down and retrieved one of the cook's large iron crockpots that had somehow made its way out of the kitchen.

Mallory will be in a foul mood for the remainder of the day if she sees this mess, he thought as he set about his work.

From about the time he was barely four summers old, Alessan had followed the same predictable routine. He would light a fire in the large stone hearth, set the tables for the morning patrons, and sweep the large room to perfection. Monotonous though it was, he took pride in his work and aspired to show his mother how capable he truly was. As the increasing light of dawn began to peek through the windows, he stood back and surveyed his effort. Satisfied, he made his way through to the kitchen and nodded a stifled greeting to Wert.

Alessan donned his heavy woolen coat and headed out the back exit towards a healthy stack of logs that were partially stacked and ready to feed the roaring hearth fire. Blowing on his hands for warmth, he stopped to marvel at the tranquility of the new day. He rarely took the time to appreciate the unspoiled perfection of an early morning in Briar, but something about this late autumn day consumed him. The wind whispered gently in his ears, and he could hear the gentle cooing of the birds nestled high up within the inn's eaves. His boots made a clear crunching sound as they broke the icy crust of frost on the ground. Closing his eyes for a moment, he tried to forget the melancholy in his soul and the daily torment that he faced.

Curse this body, he muttered. *What did I ever do to deserve such a fate?*

Alessan was unlike the other inhabitants of Briar. He was known as a *ba'caech;* an old *Drayenmark* word for one whose body is unformed and weak. He was barely over five stones in height and had delicate stooped shoulders on a thin, bony frame. Though approaching twenty summers, in many respects he still bore the appearance of a child with his large dark eyes, wispy hair, and smaller build.

Underdeveloped though he appeared, it was his shriveled left arm that caused him the most anguish. During his birth, his father had struggled to free his mother's cord from its serpentine grip on the arm. With the flow of blood restricted, it had turned a sickly shade of blue even as it withered. As the rest of his body slowly recovered over time, his arm struggled to regain its strength. It remained weak and frail even to this day.

Looking down at his stunted body, he winced at the sight. He could walk, he could talk, he could sing and think as clearly as any, but he would forever be branded an outsider. Greater the anguish still, Alessan Oakleaf knew that he could never become a Lumber, and to the people of this small community, no greater shame could befall any son.

I'll never wield an axe.

The thought pounded in his head louder than any thunderclap. Glancing at the distant forest line, he could already hear the men of the village working at the edges of the great Aeldenwood. The constant thwacking sounds struck him like an arrow to the heart as he worked diligently at stacking the logs he would soon struggle to carry inside.

Over time, Alessan learned how to use his stronger arm to compensate for the weakness in the other and became quite adept at performing any physical task that he was given. These chores served to strengthen his good arm, allowing him to cast aside his doubts for small periods of time. Yet still he could not heft an axe.

"Alessan?" called a young voice from the open kitchen door. "Your mother is awake and she needs your help in the common room."

"On my way, Wert," he replied as he carried in the last of the extra fuel for the fire.

Pushing his way into the front room, he caught his mother's eye as she furiously scrubbed a side window. Shani Oakleaf had a welcoming round face and her long black hair was tied back in a tight bun. She had been beautiful in her youth, or so the town gossips often said, but the hardships of raising two children and losing a husband had taken their toll. Her skin sagged slightly under her cheeks and chin, while her puffy eyes didn't sparkle as they once had when Alessan's father was alive.

"For Arne's sake, Ally, you have to do better than this! You know the Sylvani arrive today and I'll not have them eating here if everything isn't perfect," she scolded. "Were you sleeping this morning while you did your chores?"

"No, Mother. I just knew we'd need a lot more firewood for the day, what with the soldiers arriving and needing extra in their rooms, and you know how it can take me a while..." He trailed off.

"Well don't just stand there gawking like a fool. Finish with the wood and go meet Varis at the stables. They need a good mucking."

He started back towards the kitchen where he had delivered the logs and she called after him. "And don't forget to sit for a moment and eat a good meal. Mallory will have a hot meal ready for you in a few minutes."

"Yes, Mother," he sighed and returned to his work.

ᙣ

High above the large stone mantle in the Black Boar Inn rested the axe that had once belonged to Darren Oakleaf. Sadly, it was a replica. The original blade had never been recovered. The immense head was double-bladed and etched with intricate silver tracings. Covering the thick oaken shaft above the handle was an elaborately carved mosaic crafted in the Lumber style. Woodland animals woven into tall trees travelled through the wood ending in the veiled face of a young woman. Next to this visage was a roving pack of wild dogs led by a beautiful she-wolf frozen in the tableau as she howled at a full moon. Within the moon, Oakleaf had placed the detailed carving of a small boy carried in the strong arms of his father.

ᙣ

A Lumber's axe is his legacy. It never leaves his side and, when needed, it could be handled with great force and precision. It hid nothing of the man who wielded it and was said to carry his loves, his fears, and even his dreams. Each was unique and was assigned to him for a lifetime. It was believed that each journeyman was granted the favour of Arne, for never in the recorded generations of Briar, had a master Lumber's axe been broken.

The crafting of each unique axe was a final rite of passage, granting its creator full status in the Lumbers' Guild. A yearly midsummer festival celebrated the young men who completed their training and were ready to begin their new lives on the edge of the Aeldenwood. During the commemoration, the massive axes were only slightly less adored than the men that carried them.

The Guild played an essential role in a region situated so close to the dreaded forest. The legendary woodsmen were revered for their dedication to their dangerous profession. The entire town of Briar revolved around the Guild and its members. The stores catered to their needs, many festivals celebrated their successes, and even the Church of Arne sang their praises. And when that unavoidable time arrived, the death of a Lumber was a mournful event shared by all.

Even the tale of the Guild's creation struck a chord in the hearts of the villagers. Nearly ten generations had passed since the people of Briar discovered that the Aeldenwood had started to encroach upon their land. Slowly at first, almost imperceptibly, the sparse treeline that dotted the southern horizon began its impending march. The loosely packed trees grew thicker and soon a wall of immense wood stood to the south.

The town legends told of a vanished race of tree people. Small in stature, the Gorimm were humanlike waifs who were said to have tended to the enormous trees in a bygone era, before mysteriously vanishing from the Great Wood. With their disappearance had come the terrible Gath; twisted creatures of nightmares that made a simple pack of wolves seem like a mere nuisance. None could compare to their malevolence and cruelty. And without Gorimm, the trees of the Aeldenwood had begun their slow advance across the land of Kal Maran.

The Kingdom of Farraine fell first to the inexorable march of the wooden soldiers. With the land overwhelmed by the forest, towns crumbled and were lost forever. The capital was abandoned last. The people of that fair kingdom were now refugees in the north, a family with no true roots and a terrible desire to reclaim their homeland. But every excursion into that ever blooming canopy of darkness, brought only death and destruction. For each tree that was felled, it seemed as though three would stand in its place only a day or two later. And so Farraine was lost, its people without a home.

To the south, the Dwarves of Alerond were expected to be the next victims of the strange and magical forest. The nation had lost the northern expanse of its land over the last hundred years as they tried desperately to hold back the fast-growing trunks of the Aeldenwood. For the time being, although besieged, the dwarves continue to resist.

And so, the Lumbers' Guild had been created, and the axes that hewed the majestic wood of the forest grew to become revered in the community.

Alessan let his gaze linger across the weapon as he chewed thoughtfully on a piece of hard bread. Memories of his father were often triggered by the axe. Sitting quietly he reflected on the happier times of his youth.

Mother had laughed back then and she had always danced during the festivals with father. He tore his eyes from the axe and contented himself with staring at the scraps of food still on his plate.

"Time to go, lad," wheezed an older man from the kitchen entrance, "the stalls need looking after."

Nodding, Alessan stuffed a last piece of buttered bread into his mouth and snatched his plate from the table. "Good day, Varis, always a pleasure to see your beaming face in the morning."

"I can't say the same, lad. Watch your mouth or I'll have you eating the dirt from the stable grounds," Varis snorted.

"In a good mood today, are we?" Alessan chuckled as he followed the older man through the kitchen.

Varis had worked at the Black Boar since the days of Darren Oakleaf's youth. His father had often told stories of the older man, to the chagrin, of course, of Varis himself. Born in the town of Bress, far north of the lands that bordered the Northern Council, his family came from a line of bordermen. From the keeps of the Iron Shield the tough bordermen heroically held back marauding bands of goblins and men of the Wilds.

How the man had wound up a house servant for the Oakleafs had remained a mystery. It seemed to most that the old man had always been there, quietly becoming a presence in the life of so many of the town's residents. Varis was crass and prickly on his best days, but remained a permanent fixture that Alessan would find hard to live without.

Toiling in the silence he had come to expect while working alongside the taciturn Varis, Alessan leaned his shovel against the nearest stall and headed outside for a brief moment of respite. The early morning bite of the wind had dissipated and the young man wiped the sweat from his brow.

He heard the approach of the Sylvani long before they reached the edge of town. The unmistakable jingle of harnesses and the metallic clang of heavy armor rang out along with the thunderous rumbling of hooves. While not a rare occurrence, the arrival of a mercenary company at the Black Boar often occurred in autumn. It was the time of year when the captains had finished their summer contracts and were now headed back to their winter camps.

"The Sylvani, no?" Varis asked as he leaned in beside Alessan.

"Aye. It's a new company. Crandle says they were formed after the battle at Baron Elburg's castle. Remnants of the defenders, he suspects."

"Bloody business, that battle. Many mothers lost sons and husbands that day," the older man frowned.

The Battle for Elburg Castle had signaled the end of last year's warfare, in the north at least. The Baron had made enemies among the nobility of Glenvale; rumours whispered of a forbidden lovers' tryst, and nothing short of his death would appease those in the capital city who had been wronged.

Led by Lord Darion of Hallenford, the armies of the council had marched on the castle, their intent obvious. The majority of the northern companies had been involved, as well as a small token force from the border fort of Eralon. The four week siege was bloody, the loss of life substantial, and in the end, the old Baron's head had swung from the gallows in Glenvale.

Captain Aachen Pragg had been contracted out by the Baron. By all accounts, his men had fought well; but the defenders had paid a high price in blood for taking the Baron's coin. The remnants of his men, as well as other decimated companies, had formed the small group now known as the Sylvani.

As the mounted soldiers came into view, the leader was easy to discern. Sitting high in his saddle, ornate cloak depicting the sword and shield tabard of the troop, the officer saluted the townsfolk who had come to welcome the warriors. The soldiers were a hard lot, scarred veterans who had seen many fights. Most sported wiry beards, braided in the mercenary way, as well as a large assortment of arms and armour. Weather-beaten faces, stretched taut by the exposure to the elements, did little to hide the steely-eyed gazes of men who had seen the horrors of war.

Alessan could tell they were older than most, what with the lack of smooth cheeks and fresh eyes. It was not surprising, considering the high mortality rate of raw recruits during their first full season of campaigning. It was the hardest year, so he had been told.

"He's no Captain Silveron," spat Varis, his stare locked on the gaudy officer who rode at the forefront of the column.

"No he isn't," Alessan returned to work as he spoke. "The Captain would never wear his ceremonial cloak in town. And besides, Gavin Silveron wouldn't have signed on with the Baron."

"That's right," Varis nodded. "He would have ignored the whole affair."

"Did you ever want to become a soldier, Varis?" Alessan inquired as he struggled to lift another heavy load of mud and manure.

"Never much cared for killing, lad."

"Really? I mean, wouldn't it be exciting to charge into battle swinging your sword? One day you could even have your name written in the annals of the Code."

"Exciting?!" Varis scoffed. "Are you daft, boy? War's no game. Most of those young bucks that run out on the field fail to realize that until their guts are hanging out or they're puking up supper after severing a man's leg. I never understood the glory of losing your friends and your own life for the love of money, nor could I ever entertain the notion of fighting to quell the petty squabbling of the nobility."

"It isn't always like that —" Alessan interrupted.

"Bah! Back in the days of the High King you fought for honour and the kingdom of Caledun. Now, they fight for money. It's why they're called mercenaries, lad!" Varis gestured in the direction of the Sylvani. "No loyalty, no honour, no purpose. Just slaughter."

Alessan deigned not to reply to the elder man's tirade and they slipped into a subdued silence. Swiftly, he cleared away the last area in the stables that needed dire attention. He knew it would be mere moments before the Sylvani handlers arrived to billet their mounts. His mother was sure to have seen to their comforts immediately upon their arrival at the inn.

Varis cleared his throat loudly. Turning to look the old man's way Alessan noticed that he had already replaced his pitchfork and taken off his heavy work gloves.

"Work's done, lad. We have time to wash up before your mother finds something else for us to do," he began. "And stop worrying about being a fighter, Alessan. You're not cut from the same cloth as those fools."

"Because I'm a *ba'caech*?" Alessan questioned.

Varis shook his head. "No, boy. You're too bloody smart for that kind of work." Seeing the stricken look on the young man's face, Varis softened his tone. "Listen, I know you don't want to stay here in Briar. By Arne, I don't blame you one bit for feeling that way, but you are no warrior. Leave here if you must, but find someone who will respect your gift with letters and numbers, and forget these dreams of wielding a sword."

"Sometimes I think those dreams are all I have left," Alessan answered wistfully.

"I won't hear any of that," Varis replied. "There's more to a man than a strong body. Your father knew that." Shaking his head, the old man shuffled across the yard, his gruff voice already calling out for Wert and Mallory.

☙

The Black Boar had long been famous within the region for its fine cuisine, namely its honeyed ham and thick spicy stew. For years, family recipes handed down in secrecy had kept the bellies of the patrons full and well satisfied. Apart from the food, a steady following had developed around a certain performer who resided within the inn's very walls.

Kayla Oakleaf was younger than Alessan by two summers. She was somewhat plain looking and would usually fail to attract a second glance when passed by in the market. Her face was pleasing and her figure slightly rounded at the hips but she was naturally shy. Despite her demure nature, every night that she performed at the inn was purely magical.

When taking the stage, the quiet young Kayla became an unforgettable vocalist. She would smile freely and blush at the applause. Many men would whisper to her promises of undying love upon hearing her sing.

Alessan had experienced the enchantment of her songs on many an occasion. He witnessed hardened battle veterans cry mournfully after a slow ballad. Later they would cheer themselves hoarse when a rousing jig would have the common room dancing with glee. Kayla Oakleaf sang like no other in Briar, and like no one else in all of Kal Maran, if some of the passing merchants were to be believed.

True to form, the inn was packed to capacity once it was announced that the young songstress would be appearing on stage that evening. The tables were over-flowing and the windows of the Boar were full of faces pressed up against the cold glass in hopes of catching a glimpse of their favourite minstrel.

Alessan tried in vain to push his way through the throng in the main room. He had two large bowls of steaming stew and several mugs of ale balanced precariously on his good arm. Hopelessly, he tried a second time to force his way past a packed table of thick-armed Lumbers. The giant men with tunics straining to contain their hefty physiques barely noticed the small figure struggling at their side.

Alessan's father was still considered a legend in Briar. Both a fearless worker and the strongest Lumber in town, he had been revered in the Guild. Darren Oakleaf's son was looked upon quite differently by the guildsmen. Deemed a failure imme-diately at birth, he was fated to remain so because of his appearance; no matter his intelligence, no matter his own self-worth. He was a *ba'caech,* and a *ba'caech* did not wield an axe in the Aeldenwood. And so, to these men of the Guild, it was as if he did not even exist.

Looking about for recourse, he spied a small opening behind two tables near the east windows. Slipping nimbly through the gap, he hurriedly delivered the order that had grown colder upon his tray. Never once did the company of Lumbers even glance his way. He slammed the mugs down on the table, sloshing the contents dangerously close to the rim. Muttering a quick apology, he scuttled off to gather his next round of orders. The evening was already proving to be a long one.

Thankfully, the crowd began to settle down. Friends, mothers and fathers quick-ly whispered for quiet as a white clad figure took to the small wooden stage near the fire. As always, Kayla was accompanied by Varis, the older man practically glowing due to the attention of the audience.

During the course of the performance, he would play a variety of instruments, from a beautiful mahogany lute, to a silver flute, and even a tiny piccolo.

"Thank you all kindly for coming this evening," she shouted above the din, "I would like to begin a little slower than usual tonight —"

"A jig! A jig!" roared a voice from the back.

"Shut your mouth, you drunken bastard!" came a brash reply.

Amidst a roar of laughter, Kayla waited patiently before signaling her companion to begin. As the first notes carried through the air, silence descended over her audience.

"'Bael and the Eldest'," Kayla announced, and then her voice soared.

> *T'was the Eldest who stood, full of malice and greed, cruelty and*
> *devilry, evil's true spawn.*
> *Aloft in its branches, death hung like a shroud, black was the wood*
> *that beat in its breast,*
> *Devourer of lands, keeper of souls,*
> *to the Aeldenwood went the Lumbers no more.*
>
> *But hither rose a champion, hero of yore,*
> *bound to no blade, no spear, no sword.*
> *Duty in love, and tied to his axe,*
> *came Bael the Mighty, the wielder of truth,*
> *and the roots of that forest did tremble.*

Kayla's lilting voice soothed the boisterous crowd. The epic was a town favourite, sung to children on cold nights as they lay huddled near the fireplace for warmth. It told the story of Bael of the Great Axe, the mythical Lumber who had done battle with an Elder tree of the wood, losing his life as he hewed the enormous monstrosity. There had been a time when even Alessan's mother had whispered the tale to him, but those days now seemed as far off to him as his dreams.

Using the relative calm of the customers as an unlooked-for boon, Alessan leaned happily near the back of the room. Closing his eyes, he settled comfortably against a wooden beam, listening, as was everyone else, to the haunting melody being sung upon the stage.

> *With a groan and a shriek, the Eldest did shudder,*
> *the wind did howl and carried its scream.*
> *Evil resisted and cried out in pain,*
> *its hold was lost on this world.*

In vain the wood cracked, dark heart cleft asunder,
*   sagging from strain, the Eldest could bear no more.*
Descending to earth, its shadowy spirit
*   took flight to the netherworld.*

Yet Bael of Briar, Lumber of old,
*   was terribly thrown by the fall,*
His body broken, he clung to his love,
*   the shaft of his weapon, the axe that was mighty.*
And so did he pass, with heart in his hand,
*   Bael of the Axe, great Lumber of yore.*

The crowd roared its approval as Kayla held the final note. A few customers shed a silent tear in memory of that Lumber, so powerful was the spell woven by her voice. In that moment, Bael of the Axe was more real than ever to all who had crammed into every nook and cranny of the Black Boar. Kayla nodded towards her many admirers, smiling in the firelight. Her eyes shone brightly and a warm flush coloured her pale cheeks. True to her word, her moving ballads soon gave way to romping jigs that had the floor of the old inn shaking.

After a lengthy performance, she apologized to the patrons and begged forgiveness when she declared that her night was over. The announcement was met with good-natured retorts, and the talented songstress returned for one last song before finally exiting the stage.

Alessan had a tremendous respect for his younger sister. She was one of the few people who accepted his twisted body for what it was; a burden, but by no means a reflection of who he truly was on the inside. They had spent much time together over the years, and he had cherished every moment. Alessan met her in the kitchen and wished her well, praising her performance and kissing her lightly on the cheek. Grinning, she hugged him tightly and headed upstairs to her bedchamber, her face still flushed from the excitement of the evening.

The Sylvani were as well-behaved as any men who came to the Black Boar, singing along to any tunes they recognized, and loudly cheering those they did not. Captain Pragg sat quietly beside an obese man dressed in a garish red and gold silk robe, his ample girth straining the fabric as he lounged across two wooden chairs. His meaty fingers were covered in rings of gold, each finding its match in a bracelet upon his wrists.

The pair remained in a spot by the fire for the balance of the evening, the soldier sipping slowly from a carafe of chilled wine, the merchant preferring the hearty house ale brewed locally in Briar. From his vantage point as a server, Alessan had long ago guessed that the Sylvani's partner could be none other than a merchant employer from Innes Vale.

If the Lumbers of Briar were looked upon in a strange and somewhat fanatical light by the people of Kal Maran, then the merchants of Innes Vale weren't far off from being vilified. Over the years, the merchant families of Innes Vale had profited from what many believed to be the misery of others. They profited on the trade generated by war. Each summer of warfare was looked upon by these cunning businessmen as just another lucrative venture, ripe for the taking. It was these men who had effectively cornered the market on everything concerning the supply and demand of a mercenary company. Their chokehold had allowed the Merchant's Guild to profit on a scale unimagined by earlier generations. Offer the right price and any of the Innes merchants could easily be bought; no loyalty but to themselves had ever been exhibited.

With such wealth and prosperity, came a reputation built around corruption, greed and needless waste. The merchants of the five Vale cities lived in such extravagance that it was hard to find respect from the hard-working and often deprived farmers and tradesmen in the rest of the land.

By Alessan's account, the evening had been a great success. Damage had been minimal and the customers free with their coin. *Mother will be pleased with tonight's profits*, he thought.

Shani Oakleaf had retired early at his insistence, and he suddenly realized how exhausted his own body had become. The hour was late and only a few patrons remained. The overweight merchant and two bookish men, likely belonging to his personal retinue, sat in one of the corner of the common room. A few soldiers lingered near the kitchen entrance looking somewhat unsteady after an evening of revelry. As he quietly went about clearing the recently vacated tables, Alessan could hear the conversation underway at the rear of the inn.

"This cannot be," the merchant exclaimed. "Valorius, I need you to check your figures once more. We cannot possibly need this much grain for the duration of the journey. This number seems obscene!"

"Master, I beg your forgiveness but both Vellix and I have accurately calculated the costs based on the price of feed in this backwater town," answered the thin aristocrat.

The three men were pouring over a scattered pile of documents while the portly merchant gnawed on a large drumstick. Passing close to the table, Alessan dared a peek towards the untidily scrawled list of supplies. In a brief glance, he could see that the merchant was correct; the numbers were far too high.

"Boy? Do you often stare at a man's private papers when you do your rounds? I have a mind to speak to your employer, regardless of the time." One of the men threatened.

Looking up into the beady eyes of the servant who smelled heavily of perfume, Alessan calmly replied, "My mother would be displeased with me if I let you wake her at this late an hour." Turning towards the large man he continued, "I beg your forgiveness, master merchant. I did in no way mean to offend you with my curiosity."

"You would do well to mind your tongue, as I'm sure you can ill afford to fight your own battles," sneered the one called, Valorius. He did not hide his disdain as he assessed Alessan's stature.

"Enough!" growled the big man.

Bowing slightly as he backed away, Alessan stared balefully towards the two retainers. Smiling at the two men, he turned his eyes to the merchant and spoke. "I fear I would be remiss in my duties as a good host, master merchant, if I did not inform you of a small discrepancy in your information. Those numbers are wrong and I fear you are being misled."

Raising his furry eyebrows, the big man shifted his weight and called him over. "A kitchen boy who knows his numbers? Explain yourself, young man. Be wary, if I find your answer lacking, your slight to my two servants will not go unpunished," he warned.

"I have worked in the stables for the better part of my life, sir. I know what type of feed is best for any horse, be they rugged draft horses, elegant stallions, or powerful war steeds," Alessan answered. "My father also deemed it important that my sister and I learn both our letters and numbers. I believe he thought that a man in my obvious predicament would need skills that could better complement my strengths."

"Go on, I'm listening," the merchant replied. Tossing his head in the direction of his accountants, he added, "Don't worry about these two, you can speak freely."

Alessan did notice the glance the large man directed towards his shrunken left arm. He chose to ignore it. "The Sylvani stabled one hundred mounts this morning. I know Varis mentioned your own personal escort consisted of eight draft horses and two geldings. The number on that list," Alessan said, stepping forward and pointing towards a sheaf of paper, "is enough to buy grain for an extra two dozen horses. I could have Marius, our storekeep, come by tomorrow and explain it all to you, Sir."

"Could this be?" the merchant questioned the closer of the two men.

"Master, I believe the numbers are correct. You possibly fail to take into account the discrepancy in prices between the Vale and here in the north," he stuttered in reply.

"Unless the coins in the Vale are all made of gold, there is no discrepancy." Alessan retorted quietly.

"Hah! You are a treasure and a clever lad at that!" The merchant roared. "No fear in your challenging tone, regardless of our well known reputations."

"It is true the merchants of the Vale are often frowned upon for their often extravagant behaviour when guests in our establishment, but I was taught better than that by my father," Alessan replied.

The merchant nodded slowly. "And a good man he must be."

"Was," Alessan corrected.

"Ah, I am sorry for your loss. No boy should grow up without his father to guide him, but you seem to have done well for yourself."

"Thank you, Sir – you are too kind."

"Nonsense, I am happy to have met you, young..."

"Alessan, sir," he replied.

"Well, Alessan, I look forward to our next encounter, but for now it is time for you to leave us. I obviously have sensitive matters that need immediate attention, but remember that Corian Praxxus owes you a debt of gratitude," the merchant finished with a wink and a grin. Turning to his two retainers, his smile faded quickly. "As for the two of you cutthroats, gather our things. I'll be dealing with you sooner than you would both like."

Alessan watched as the two men snatched the parchments from the table and hastened out the front entrance while Corian Praxxus berated them all the while.

It took the better part of an hour before the common room was as deserted as it had been earlier in the morning, long. The day had been long. Smiling to himself, but concerned about the scathing looks the two fops had hurled his way as they had left, Alessan knew he had best tread carefully until Master Praxxus departed the Lumber town.

Truthfully, it had felt glorious to challenge the two retainers regardless of the possible repercussions. The rush of adrenaline that had coursed through his body had seemingly banished the bone-weary exhaustion of the day. Unconsciously, he began whistling a song to the tune of "Bael and the Eldest", as he finished mopping the floor. Alessan yawned loudly as he worked and yet for that moment, he was happy.

"Many would have you believe that the problem with mercenaries is their loyalty, but I beg to differ. The only problem that I see, is finding a nobleman foolish enough to trust them."
—Captain Gerald Armsmater

CHAPTER II

Seracen Pass, Protectorate

Sheltered within the high walls of the Karipaal mountain range lay the Seracen Pass, a narrow passage cut into the verdant lands of southeastern Kal Maran.

Billowing smoke drifted skyward from a small circle of wagons stopped by the side of the well-traveled trade route. A modest campfire crackled and distant mutterings from those gathered echoed quietly off the steep canyon walls.

"Bloody cold out this evening if you ask me," grunted an armoured man as he walked up to join the small group gathered near the warm blaze.

"Aye, sergeant," nodded one of the soldiers in return. "But this late into the season in my village we'd be mighty happy it wasn't colder, sir."

"Bah! It is all on you. You are the fools who choose to live so far north," chuckled Sergeant Elswen. He blew hard on his hands to keep them warm. "I'll also bet you northern lads spend more time alone with horse blankets in the winter than you do with actual women!"

As with any remark the gruff sergeant found amusing, the men on duty laughed enthusiastically along with him. Garnet, the target of the evening's good-natured ribbing, chuckled as much as the next man. No soldier in the company wanted to offend the veteran officer. Elswen had been around longer than some of the new recruits had been alive. Why he had remained only a minor officer was a mystery to those who fought at his side. Strong-willed and tough as iron, the old soldier rarely discussed the life he had led with the other companies he had served. "That's all in the past," he would say when asked.

The southern mercenary company was named Pier's Brigade and Garnet gathered that it was no different than any other he could have joined. Taking a bite of hard trail bread from his pack, he attempted to change the subject.

"Any news from the westernmost front, Sir?" he asked. "Seems we haven't heard from Lord Yarr's messengers since prior to our rendezvous with the Lady Farraine's entourage."

Lord Gadian Yarr, a high-standing diplomat with the southern Protectorate, had assembled the largest contingent of mercenary companies during the recent summer. Reports indicated that he was heading towards Matanis on the coast, or otherwise hoping to exact retribution on the soft-hearted Duke Berry. It was rumored that the duke had already fled the mercantile port city of Garchester. As well as being the nobleman's residence, it had been hotly contested for the past three summer campaigns. The mineral-rich mines supported by the city were key resources that all nobles coveted.

"News may have arrived," the sergeant replied with a shrug.

"And what about the muster we saw near Garchester when we marched by? Lots of northern company standards were camped on the outskirts of the city." Another man questioned.

"Did it ever occur to you that the captain doesn't care what regular soldiers have to say about such things?"

"No, sir," Garnet replied cautiously. "I just thought I would ask since we're headed that way."

"Garnet's got a point, Sergeant," another soldier interjected. "We've all been kept in the dark on this one, and the Captain's not usually one to hold his cards so closely." The speaker held his boots in his hands, the soles roasting gently over the open flames.

Sergeant Elswen paused before answering the query and took a long pull from the flask off his belt. He grimaced as he swallowed a mouthful of strong cider. "Look, lads, I know nothing more than the lot of you. Captain Pier has seen fit to keep the details of this contract to himself. I'm not sure why, but I'll tell you one thing, for the pay we'll be receiving when this bothersome noble arrives at her destination, I'll not mind one bit if I know nothing but her name."

The men answered the officer with a chorus of ayes. Garnet stretched his legs, keeping them close to the heat of the fire. As exhaustion threatened to pull him to sleep before his watch was up, he was suddenly startled as an owl hooted noisily over his shoulder. Stooping to gather a handful of rocks, he launched them into the darkness.

"Cursed birds. Sometimes they can be as loud as the lot of us," he muttered to himself.

○8

The canyon walls that defined the Seracen Pass were not entirely natural formations. Immense jagged cuts clearly defined where labourers had once bloodied their hands as they painstakingly dug their way through the solid rock. In some instances, the terrain had worked in their favour. The current resting place where the mercenary company was bedded down for the evening was one such location. Only the northern elevation rose sharply into the night sky. The southern flank consisted of a soft green rise where a small herd of mountain goats slept soundly. Trees dotted the landscape, and more than a few groves generously provided firewood within easy reach.

It was on the edge of one of the smaller cliff edges that a slight movement gave a hint that someone other than the slumbering soldiers was in the vicinity.

"Orn and Bider are in position, sir," whispered a voice from the blackness. The signal had been received a moment earlier, the clear sound of an owl echoing off the canyon walls directly below where the mercenary sat perched.

From his left came a hushed reply. "Aye, I heard it as well. Let's head back to camp and inform the Captain." Standing grimly in the moonlight the soldier added, "Looks like we'll be finally whetting our blades this evening."

Silently, the two figures slid back from the canyon's rocky edge, mindful of the loose rocks that littered the ground. Any noise would carry far along the pass and a lapse of concentration could spell disaster for the company's well-laid plans.

CR

"Wren's Militia, the Black Watch and the Grey Rangers were the only northern companies in attendance," reported Brock. "There's a new command camped on the eastern side of the valley going by the name of the Red Band. They appear to be survivors of the disastrous siege of Crystalmere. A combination of at least three or four companies," he finished.

"Who's leading them? Not many were left after they lost the city in early winter. My squad was there when the prisoners were released," queried Ossric.

"Koren Blackern is the rumored leader. I believe he was a junior captain with the Kindred," Brock replied, his frosted breath clearly visible. The evenings were bitterly cold once the sun passed behind the valley wall to the west.

"Strange those companies merging into one. By Arne, those men hated each other! The city fell quickly, what with half the captains screaming curses at one another and the other half fawning over the damn nobles," continued Ossric. Taking a small stick from a nearby pile, the company sergeant poked absently at the coals of the cooking fire.

"They were quite desperate," Captain Gavin Silveron agreed. "We all know that the city was lost long before Lord Yarr's muster arrived," he added as he crossed the cramped quarters and donned his cloak. He shivered in the brisk evening air. "It was a hopeless battle."

"We were there, Captain?" asked Sergeant Fearan.

"Yes, we were" Gavin turned to his thickset officer who had recently returned from the west. "Continue with your report, Sergeant."

"Nothing much left to say, Sir." Fearan shrugged. "Duke Berry passed word that our company should head to Garchester after we complete this assignment. Seems he expects some sort of retaliation and wants a strong complement of men under his pay within the city."

"Thank you, Brock," Gavin nodded.

Looking around the modest officer's tent, the captain surveyed his men. With a full complement of two hundred soldiers, one hundred fifty of whom were veterans of at least two campaigns, Gavin had left only one of his officers back in Dragomere to prepare the company's winter base camp near the southern edge of the Aeldenwood.

The Fey'Derin, as they were known, did not follow the usual protocols of the other mercenary companies in the region. Most were bogged down with an over-abundance of officers which proved ineffective when decisions needed to be made quickly in the heat of battle. The Fey'Derin had adopted a command structure akin to those of the dwarven soldiers that fought, albeit rarely, on the battlefields throughout Caledun.

Captain Silveron carried only four officers, three sergeants and one lieutenant. Gavin chose to fight on the front lines with his soldiers, a decision that had earned him the respect of his men and one that offered him a better view of the tactical situation on the battlefield. Although thought by many to be a risky maneuver for a man of such rank, the Fey'Derin ignored the criticisms of others.

Gavin's gaze finally settled on his senior officer. Lieutenant Caolte Burnaise was a grizzled survivor in a career that often claimed its victims young and inexperienced. The seasoned veteran, with his scarred face looking more and more like beaten leather with the passing of every summer, had been with the Fey'Derin since their inception. Sitting cross legged, waterskin at his side, he scratched his long reddish-grey whiskers.

"I'll tell you lads what's going on. That bastard down in Imlaris is making his move." Looking directly at Gavin, the older man continued, "Gavin, we've had this discussion before. That priss Gadian Yarr has spent the better part of three years consolidating his power down in the south. With enough support he can, and will, declare himself bloody emperor."

"Cursed Arne! He'd have the rest of the land up in arms the moment it got out, Lieutenant," retorted Sergeant Fearan. "Pardon my words, Sir, but Yarr would be foolish to even try it."

"If a high king can be dethroned, what's to stop anyone from assassinating an emperor?" added Ethan Shade quietly. Leaning against one of the support poles, long wooden pipe dangling from his mouth, the youngest officer of the company pulled up a small stool and joined the group. "It doesn't make any sense, if you ask me, Sir. If Gadian Yarr hasn't solidified his power base, then anything else would mean a quick death."

"And if he has? He did take control of Crystalmere and the shipping industry last summer and has fought stubbornly for Matanis this year," Gavin declared.

"Then he has masterfully hidden the most incredible coup since the Shattering," added Ossric. "And Ethan, the old kingdom was overthrown nearly two hundred years ago. With the Code being enforced, Gadian couldn't field a command of his own. What man would dare anoint himself the next coming with a bunch of money-hungry mercenaries guarding his back?"

"Not exactly, Ossric. If he was optimistic that Imlaris and a few of the other southern cities... let's say Tavishan and Salman, would support his claim, then it would make sense as to why he nearly destroyed Crystalmere last year. Maybe he didn't get the right response from their nobility?" surmised the younger man.

"With the nobility in your pocket, maybe you don't need to worry how much your army would cost, Ossric?" added Caolte.

"It doesn't make sense. He'd need an army larger than is allowed under the Mercenary Code to hold anything once the north got wind of his ascension," added Gavin. "And let's not forget about Serian Rhone's reaction to such a declaration. The *Drayen* would have his clansmen up in arms seconds after he received any claim, rumored or not, that Gadian Yarr was now emperor of Caledun."

"Aye, Captain, my kinsmen would tear down the walls of Imlaris with their bare hands if that were the case," spat the older warrior.

Visibly frustrated, the Fey'Derin captain pulled on his leather gloves and adjusted his cloak. Rubbing his hands together for warmth, he let his gaze travel through the room, resting for a moment on each of his trusted companions.

"Well, we may as well resign ourselves to the fact that we have no idea what is going on in that scoundrel's mind. We need only concern ourselves with the contract at hand. Once we hear from the scouts, we'll decide whether we hit our targets in the pass tonight or tomorrow. Sergeant McConnal," Gavin turned to the towering man who still teased the ashes of the dying fire, "set up the watch rotation for the evening. If necessary, Ethan will relieve you and your men come dawn. For this evening, double the watch, standard sentries and perimeter as if for a wartime situation. One can never be too safe." Pausing for a moment, the young captain motioned to two of the men. "Caolte and Ethan, I want you both with me. We have time to review the plans for the Lady Farraine."

In mid salute, the Fey'Derin officers paused as two men ducked under the tent flap. The older man saluted the young captain and said, "Pardon the interruption,

Captain, but word had been passed that you were to be notified once the scouts had reported in. Bider has sent word that everything is clear."

"Excellent," answered Gavin. Turning to his officers as he stretched his tired muscles, he continued. "Gentlemen, a change of plans. Assemble your teams immediately. It's time we pay the Lady Farraine a surprise visit."

ଓ

"Arne's fury!" hissed Bider. His body tingled uncomfortably, just as it had earlier in the night. "That damn mage must be awake again."

"Aye, I feel it as well," replied Orn. "Let's head towards his wagon and see what we can come up with. If he shows any indication the spell is one used to search the countryside, we move now."

"Understood," nodded Bider.

Staying low to the ground, he followed the tall and lanky Orn Surefoot, the company huntsman and lead Fey'Derin scout. Bider's dark eyes probed the surrounding shadows. Based on the encampment's arrangement, he was confident that Pier's Brigade was not expecting any unwelcome visitors this evening. Only two pairs of sentries had been posted to each side of the trade route, and both were spending their respective watches chatting nonchalantly and playing cards.

The western sentries had paid dearly for their lack of discipline; their lifeless corpses now lay stashed in a dense thicket near the side of the road. Clustered close together, the groups of tents and supply wagons were easy targets for any nighttime invaders. A small group of men could easily contain any attempt by the slumbering soldiers to break free of an attack. Near the center of the campsite only a handful of men remained on guard duty. They remained huddled miserably around a small burning fire.

Only an oddly decorated wagon stationed near the edge of the site was reason for concern. Covered in a myriad of arcane symbols, strange in the eyes of the Fey'Derin scout, the wagon left Bider with an uneasy twinge in his stomach. It could only belong to a user of magic; a rebellious mage in this case. The Silveryn Order, long removed from the political arena of Caledun, had not sanctioned any involvement in this year's warfare. They rarely concerned themselves with the affairs of the greater world. Renegade mages were a rarity and their presence certainly meant trouble.

"There he is!" came Orn's urgent whisper.

Bider squinted as he scanned the edge of the brush behind the wagon. Although it took a moment for his eyes to adjust, he had no trouble picking out the shambling gait of a tall man wearing a dark robe. The small scout shook his head in disbelief as he watched the mage hitch the robe around his waist and squat down to relieve himself. The two Fey'Derin point men exchanged a knowing glance; Thaal, Elder God of Luck, had surely turned his eyes their way.

Crawling forward on his stomach and careful to conceal his movements and weaponry, Bider closed in on his quarry. When he was but a scant few feet behind his target, he rose stealthily from the grass and padded forward with speed. The sorcerer failed to hear the approach.

Bider's dagger sliced soundlessly across the man's throat and his leather-gloved hand closed over the unsuspecting mage's mouth. Gently cushioning the dead man's fall, he spun into a ready crouch with his eyes scanning once again for any unanticipated movement. Seeing nothing, he paused briefly to wipe his stained blade on the hem of the mage's robe.

"Must have been a heat spell that he was using," whispered Orn as he joined Bider behind the late mage's wagon.

"By Arne, as long as he didn't hear my approach, I really don't care." Bider replied. Sheathing his blade in a bandolier that crossed his chest, he peered cautiously around the corner.

Shrugging, Orn took a swig from a silver flask taken from a small pouch hanging on his belt.

"Put it away, Orn," warned Bider with a scowl, "you know what the captain thinks of that habit of yours."

"Yer no priest yourself, Bider," countered the veteran with a stare of contempt. "Just let me be."

"You know damn well that Gavin will see things differently. Put it away," replied the Fey'Derin soldier, a dangerous tone lurking behind his simple words.

Bider knew Gavin's opinion on the matter was important to Orn Surefoot, more so than the veteran scout would like to admit. The two Fey'Derin owed their loyalty to the man who paid their coin and both knew it would take a calamitous event to shake their devotion to him, coin or no coin.

Gavin Silveron had saved more men than he would ever take credit for. He had created his first company with little more than the castoffs from almost every company in the north. The veterans recounted stories to the new recruits, testifying to their own decrepit lives until rescued by the captain or his lieutenant, Caolte Burnaise. Even the greatest could fall from grace, so said Gavin.

Most men in the Fey'Derin remembered times when they had slept alone in alleyways or lay naked and bruised as they were beaten by ruffians. In this company, men were not ashamed by the past and Gavin ensured that they learn from it. Captain Silveron was hard and unyielding, yet fair and trustworthy; a combination that seemed to favour the men of the Fey'Derin.

For a long moment, both scouts locked gazes. Then, without another word, Orn Surefoot placed the flask carefully into an inner pocket and turned his attention towards a second wagon, this one quite ornate and obviously belonging to nobility. Delicate magenta fabric swirled softly near a curtained window and light music drifted idly from within.

After studying the disposition of the center guards, Orn seemed satisfied. Whispering over his shoulder, he crept forward. "Come on, Bider, the company will be here any minute and we wouldn't want to keep a lady waiting."

෮

"Ethan, you and your remaining Eagle Runners will be our support this evening. Stay mounted on the western side. I don't expect much resistance," said Gavin. "But stay sharp regardless."

"Aye, sir," the officer replied and slipped out of the tent.

"With their mage out of the picture, this should be routine, Sir," offered the large veteran Sergeant McConnal as he lumbered forward. Encased in a thick hide of steel plates, the officer shouldered his heavy broad axe and eyed his own assembled command. Ossric's Axemen were an imposing group. Armoured much like their commander, these grizzled and hulking men formed the backbone of the company's heavy infantry.

Nodding in agreement, the captain replied, "Aye, routine." Then, pausing for a moment, he raised an eyebrow as he tightened his worn leather belt and scabbard. "I thought routine a word that veterans frown upon, Sergeant?"

Grinning viciously in the moonlight, the big man laughed. "You must be listening to our campfire conversations lately, Captain. From now on I better mind what I say about you and Lieutenant Burnaise."

"Too late for that, you great lummox! But don't worry, we'll continue this conversation after tonight's engagement," added Caolte with a grin of his own. Turning to Gavin, the older soldier sketched a quick salute. "Everyone's in position. Once Brock's archers hit their tents, the smoke should cover our own advance. With Orn and Bider taking care of Lady Farraine, that'll leave Ossric to finish up. Those lazy sots will never know what hit them."

Keep my weapon safe, its edge sharp. Let my eyes not wander, focused must I be. Let the woods be calm, my enemies asleep.
—*Lumber Oath*

CHAPTER III

Briar, Northern Council

Morning came far too quickly to Briar, at least for the sleepy-eyed Alessan. His body rebelled as the light of dawn crept through the sides of the drawn curtains in his bedchamber.

Lying on his back, it took a considerable effort to instigate his terminally weak muscles into motion. Even the chill of the morning failed to invigorate his weary body. Thankfully, Varis had risen early and given him a much appreciated hand with the inn's daily chores.

A full cup of honeyed tea, and a large helping of eggs later, he felt much better, although it still pained him to move about. Such was the curse of his frail condition, not that he had grown up knowing anything different. He often wondered whether anyone else in Briar had ever experienced the same daily discomfort.

The gods certainly know how to play cruel jokes on some of us, he thought.

Spooning up the last of his eggs, Alessan watched as a nervous smooth-faced soldier strode in through the front entrance. The boyish mercenary looked barely old enough to enlist in a company, and seemed genuinely ill at ease. While he wore the colours of the Sylvani, his armour and company tabard were in immaculate condition. Alessan had met enough battle hardened veterans, with their well-worn regalia of often mismatched pieces picked from the field, to recognize a new recruit when he saw one.

The soldier was clenching a small scrap of folded paper in his right hand. From only a few tables away Alessan could see that it bore the official trade symbol of the Merchant Union of Innes Vale.

More out of curiosity than friendship, Alessan made his way over to the soldier. "New to the Sylvani?" he asked.

"Yes, I just finished training last week and with our numbers so low, well... here I am," the new recruit replied sheepishly.

"Has Captain Pragg given you a day of rest? I haven't seen any other Sylvani lurking about," Alessan asked. "It's a little early, but I'm sure our cook can have a hot plate of sausages ready in a few minutes."

"Oh no, I can't really," the mercenary replied. "Thank you all the same for the offer, but I'm not looking for a meal."

"Oh?" Alessan raised an eyebrow.

"I have been tasked with an errand for Master Praxxus. The company is drilling on the outskirts near Oakfeld Patch and I'm already running behind schedule," he replied hastily. "I'm to find a man named Alessan here at the Black Boar and deliver this message. Any chance you might know of him?"

"Aye, I'm quite sure I know who he is," Alessan chuckled. "I am the man you are looking for."

The recruit was somewhat taken aback, his eyes flitting over Alessan's stunted form. Alessan did his best to ignore the look, but in his heart he knew the difficulty in dismissing the constant barbs and stares often directed his way.

Offended for a brief moment, a touch of anger threatened to bubble to the surface. Somewhere deep within his spirit, those secret feelings were seething as never before. He turned his face away from the soldier, hoping to hide any evidence of his momentary inner struggle.

"Is there a problem, soldier?" Alessan asked after a lengthy silence had stretched out between them.

"No... no!" the messenger sputtered a reply.

"Did you expect someone different, maybe a Lumber, perhaps?" Alessan retorted.

Flushed with embarrassment, the young recruit thrust the folded missive into Alessan's outstretched hand. Then, mumbling a hasty apology, he fled the common room of the inn as if being chased off by wolves rather than a frosty stare. Watching him run off, Alessan shook his head in frustration.

At least he apologized. That, in itself, is a rarity.

ॐ

With the encroachment of the Aeldenwood, some of the oldest settlements now lay within the boundaries of the dark forest. Its steady advance was now a concern to all who inhabited the lands that were under guardianship of the Northern Council in Glenvale. Even with increases in the Lumber population, still did the trees of the Aeldenwood appear each morning, seemingly unstoppable even against the valiant axes of the trained woodsmen.

This had not always been true. For years, the annals of the Guild documented a slow, yet steady decline of the northern eaves of the forest. Since Alessan's birth, the imposing trunks had shot even higher into the sky. What had been but a pinprick on the horizon as a child, was now a tall black shadow as menacing as the darkest storm clouds.

The advance remained one of the land's most enduring mysteries. It was even recorded that eighteen years earlier, the archmage Tel'Caldron of Dragon Mount led an expedition into the heart of the forest. It was said he had been in search of the fabled Gorimm city of C'aisil-Chro. Tel'Caldron had entered the forest from the east with an impressive force of mercenaries numbering close to one thousand. They were never heard from again, nor would any trace of the doomed expedition ever be recovered.

The Silveryn Order has since refused dozens of similar appeals to explore the interior of the fast growing Aeldenwood. The mages of Dragon Mount contend that they continue to do all that they possibly can to find answers from their lofty perch in the Erienn mountain range. And yet for years now, no word has come from them, and still does the Aeldenwood grow.

Everything in a Lumber camp is built from the fallen trees of the Aeldenwood. It serves as a reminder to all who live within the stout wooden walls that the trees will pay dearly for every acre of land they swallow while the Lumbers still have breath.

Walking under the gates of Oakfeld Patch, Alessan craned his neck and took in the sights and sounds of the camp. The steady rhythmic chopping of the Lumbers was much louder than the distant continuous pops heard while in Briar. Long timber houses circled the perimeter with their walls touching the sides of the large settlement. A smithy and stables had been built near the center of Oakfeld Patch, with both buildings flanking a small church and meeting hall.

The outskirts of the Lumber fort were covered with bright and colourful tents belonging to the Sylvani. The mercenaries barely spared a glance as the young Alessan strode through their area. Most of the men were relaxing near campfires or tending to their equipment. One large officer was barking out a string of profanities as he supervised a training session near the center of the site.

Although the Black Boar often housed the officers of a company, the regular mercenaries were discouraged from staying directly in town. The people of Briar had learned over the years that drunken soldiers sleeping in town often caused problems. The well-mannered men of the Fey'Derin were an exception. With their base camp situated a day's ride to the north, they had always shown themselves to be a cut above the common soldier. Their officers, and especially the brooding Captain Silveron, had always expected exceptional behaviour while in town. Such respect did not go unnoticed.

Surveying the camp with wide eyes, Alessan could do little to stifle his excitement. Striding purposefully into the compound, he reveled in the earthy smell of freshly cut wood, the warm breeze on his face, and the incessant pounding of the Lumbers hard at work. Closing his eyes for a moment, he imagined himself carrying the weight of an axe in his hands. Breathing deeply, he lost himself in the wondrous vision.

His left hand clutched the missive that had arrived by courier that morning. It was an invitation to meet with the venerable Corian Praxxus here at Oakfeld Patch. Intrigued, and somewhat mystified by the offer, Alessan had begged his mother's permission to allow him to fulfill the summons. She was quite skeptical about the whole affair, but begrudgingly allowed her son to skip his chores and depart. She knew that it was not every day that a wealthy merchant from the Vale showed interest in a commoner from a small northern village.

Grabbing his favourite walking stick, Alessan headed out of town with his heart beating excitedly at the prospect of such an interesting rendezvous. He took the better part of the morning to arrive at his destination, as he preferred to stop and rest on a few occasions. His legs were far stronger than his arms, but they still required much coaxing.

Two Lumbers passed him at the gates, as did three mercenaries who were each carrying a large keg of ale. For once their reactions, or lack thereof, mattered little to Alessan.

"Alessan, well done! I'm glad you could make it," called out a familiar voice from the entryway of the meeting hall. "But had I known you would need to make the trek on foot, I would have sent a horse for you," Corian Praxxus frowned.

"It's no trouble, Sir. I enjoyed the walk," Alessan replied courteously.

The master merchant was dressed in a long burgundy robe trimmed with silver thread and lined with thick fur. Belted at his ample waist was a jeweled dagger, the ivory handle an obvious work of great craftsmanship. Alessan marveled at the rings the man wore on his thick fingers. More gold than he had ever seen in his lifetime rested upon those pudgy hands. Corian's greying hair and thick beard were heavily oiled with a heady perfume. Although not an unpleasant scent, the strong aroma made Alessan somewhat uncomfortable as he shook the merchant's proffered hand.

"I trust your mother approved of your journey, lad?" Corian asked, wrapping an arm around Alessan's thin shoulders.

"Yes, although she did need some persuading," he answered. "She asked me to pass on a greeting, and wanted me to inquire as to whether or not you would be dining with your entourage at the Black Boar this evening?"

Corian laughed heartily at the question. "She's quite the businesswoman, your mother! You can tell her I will most assuredly be dining in her fine establishment tonight, although it will be a solitary venture. Vellix and Valorius will not be joining me." Glancing towards a tall stack of chopped wood, Alessan spied the merchant's two aides piteously dragging heavy stumps over to a patiently waiting Lumber.

"Some penance was required after yesterday's unfortunate incident," Corian added.

"I see," Alessan replied softly. He continued to watch the miserable servants. He reflected on how often he had been on the receiving end of numerous insults while he laboured in the yard of the Black Boar. It would serve no purpose to celebrate their foolishness. Nodding as if in approval to his reserved reaction, Corian Praxxus motioned towards the entryway to the meeting hall.

The building served as the main hub of the camp. The Lumbers of Oakfeld Patch had decorated the hall with trophies earned by their many triumphs throughout the years. Large branches whittled by skillful artisans were mounted on the walls. Artwork portrayed Lumber legends hewing enormous trees, and carvings depicted the woodsmen as shining heroes of righteousness battling the dark, twisted trees of the ever expanding forest.

In the middle of the hall lay the Burning Hearth, a fire lit over four generations earlier and kept alive at all times with timber from the Aeldenwood. The tradition had its beginnings in Sycamore Grove, and soon carried forth to all Lumber strongholds. The eternally burning fire was said to represent the Great Wood's unrelenting march across the land. The Hearth was surrounded by long rows of tables where the men sat drinking and eating. The pungent odor of onion and potato stew, a Northern Council staple, drifted from a large pot bubbling over the fire. Captain Pragg sat in one corner with officers clustered around him, each one competing for a moment of his time.

Alessan looked towards the far end of the hall, his eyes settling on an ancient stump. The front portion of the old tree had been carefully removed, and the wood below polished to smooth perfection. Even at this distance, he could make out a number of the names burned into the wooden remains. Stunned, he was unable to breathe for a moment. At his side, the hefty merchant raised an eyebrow.

"You alright, boy?" Corian asked curiously.

Struggling to regain his composure, Alessan replied shakily, "I apologize, Sir. I'll be fine."

Patting him lightly on the shoulder, the merchant from Innes Vale smiled sadly. "I understand, son. Your father must have been a great man."

'Sorrow' was Oakfeld Patch's grieving tribute to their fallen heroes. When a Lumber died in the Aeldenwood, his name was inscribed upon the large stump in the meeting hall. Whether slain by denizens of the forest, or by the trees themselves, they were forever immortalized in the body of their enemy. It served as a reminder to all that the forest was an adversary never to be trusted.

"My father died near Burnt Elm" Alessan replied sadly. "His name was inscribed by my mother at that same camp. 'Anguish' is the name of the trunk that bears his name. Whenever I see a tribute, it's hard not to remember him."

They took a seat at the head of a long table near the Hearth, sitting in silence for quite some time. Corian Praxxus did an admirable job of looking in every direction but that of the solemn Lumber tribute. It took the arrival of a serving woman to return the merchant to good humour.

With food ordered, Alessan dismissed his solemn memories and looked expectantly at the wealthy man seated across from him.

"Why am I here, Master Praxxus?" he asked.

"All in good time lad... all in good time," Corian responded. "For the moment, enjoy the warmth of the Hearth, and the drinks our barmaid has brought us."

"I really can't afford it, Sir," Alessan replied sheepishly. He didn't want to embarrass himself in front of the prominent merchant, but his mother had no coin to spare for him as he hustled out of the inn earlier that morning.

"Bah! Your meal is on me, Alessan. You saved me quite a tidy sum, and it would be rude not to repay the kindness. You know, we merchants of the Vale aren't always what we are made out to be." He winked and took a long swallow of his bitter ale.

"I will admit, your generosity is surprising," Alessan answered cautiously, wiping foam from around his mouth on to his sleeve.

Corian chuckled. "I'm as greedy as the next man, but I'm not ashamed to repay a debt. Now eat up. We will talk of business only after you've told me more about your town and the history of these great lummoxes called Lumbers."

Alessan spent the meal regaling the merchant with tales of his life and the daily trials encountered by the inhabitants of Briar. He avoided any mention of his father, preferring to recount the legend of Bael of the Axe from his sister's song the previous evening. He followed that with the story of Gort Greatwood, his favourite since it was first told to him as a small boy.

"The Greatwood family has been around for generations and they've had more than their share of heroic axe wielders. But their greatest descendant was Gort. He carried a double-bladed axe, a gigantic weapon if the stories are to be believed. The day before his passage —"

"Passage?" Corian interrupted.

"Passage to manhood. It's a solemn ceremony that bestows the blessings of the gods into the steel of the Lumber blades. A young man, all alone on the night of the first full moon of the year, must take his axe into the very woods he will soon hew and ask for a blessing. It is said that the Gorimm are responsible for the magic that keeps the Lumber axes from ever breaking. The legend says that on the day before his passage, Gort found a large piece of silver, a moon stone perhaps, carved a recess into his axe shaft, and added the strange ore to his weapon. After his night in the forest, the axe he carried contained the purest silver, and the steel blade would glow softly even in the deepest darkness."

"Sounds like a mighty weapon indeed," the merchant commented.

"I believe it was!" Alessan avowed. "Many say it was magical and made Gort special, but his bravery made him legendary. In those times, a fourth Lumber camp was said to have existed far to the south of where we stand. Birch Copse was swallowed by the Aeldenwood, but in Gort's day he was based at that very stronghold. There had been a resurgence in Gath activity that year, and more than a few of the men treaded softly throughout both the day and night. Strange disappearances from the homesteads had riled up the inhabitants; gruesome murders had left only bloody trails into the surrounding woods."

Alessan continued, "Families began to flee the safety of their homes, and the stronghold was said to have been full near to bursting. Gort and a few of his stout comrades planned to put an end to the Gath menace. Leading the men out to his own homestead, they waited patiently for the creatures to arrive. Four days would pass before the Gath struck the farm," Alessan paused for a moment and looked across the table with a puzzled expression. "You do know what the Gath are, Master Praxxus?" he asked.

"Aye, I've heard of them; nightmarish creatures, terrible to behold and bloodthirsty to boot. Children's tales if you ask me, Alessan."

"Say what you want, Sir, but some would have you believe that they have returned to wreak havoc under the eaves of the forest. Or maybe they never truly left..." Alessan whispered.

"You tell a good story, lad, so finish it. Enough with this nonsense," Corian frowned, but Alessan noticed a moment of hesitation lurking behind the man's eyes.

"An epic battle raged around the homestead. As night fell, only the bright beacon that was Gort's great axe guided the Lumbers in their fight. The Gath were felled in obscene numbers, their bodies dismembered by the strokes of his men. As night deepened, Gort realized that the Gath's numbers would soon overwhelm his small band of survivors. Realizing that the creatures were attracted to the mysterious light of his axe, he made the ultimate sacrifice. Asking his remaining comrades to move inside, he barred the door to his humble cabin and ran into the surrounding woods."

Alessan paused and continued somberly, "The survivors of that day recounted his last hours. For a long time the glow of their friend's axe flitted among the trees, dealing death with every blow. The terrible howls and shrieks of the Gath rang out in the night. Near the break of dawn, a bright flash tore through the clearing where the men were barricaded in defense. With the flash came a sudden calm, and all sounds of the battle mysteriously vanished in a sudden wind."

"When morning came, no Gath remained near the house. Of Gort Greatwood, only his body was found. He lay surrounded by Gath, all horribly burned and slaughtered. No wounds marred his body, and he lay there as if only sleeping after the hard battle. To the dismay of his companions, no breath remained in him."

"A man to be well remembered," Corian stated. "And the axe? Where is it now?"

Alessan shook his head slowly before continuing. "Therein lies the greatest mystery. You see, his beautiful axe was never found. Many believe it was destroyed, while some worry that the Gath have kept it these long years somewhere deep within the Aeldenwood, a trophy to remind them of a hated enemy."

Clapping his hands in delight, the merchant congratulated Alessan on both his telling and the tale itself. Embarrassed by the praise, Alessan mumbled a quick thanks and buried his face in his own mug of ale.

Eventually Corian sighed and dug into one of his belt pouches. "Well, it seems the pleasantries are now out of the way, and it's down to the business at hand." Revealing a small leather sack, he tossed the bag on to the table. Hearing the unmistakable clink of coins, Alessan raised his head.

"Payment for your services," Corian said. "It should be more than enough to recompense your mother for her loss of labour today." Seeing Alessan's look of suspicion, the Innes Vale merchant opened the drawstring and poured the contents upon the table. "Go ahead, count it if you wish."

Having worked in the Black Boar for the better part of his life, Alessan could see that a small fortune lay upon the hard oak boards. Drawing a deep breath, he looked at Corian and asked, "And the service you require, Sir?"

"Young Master Oakleaf, I wish to go into the Aeldenwood. And for the money on this table, you're going to take me."

A registered company will be limited to a maximum of two hundred and fifty soldiers, of which only two hundred can be on active duty at any given time. The finalized roster, to be submitted at a formal Ca'lenbam, must include any company members slated for training. Rosters can, and will, be inspected throughout the yearly summer campaigns.

—*Mercenary Code of Conduct*

CHAPTER IV

Seracen Pass, Protectorate

Gavin Silveron walked slowly through the Fey'Derin encampment. He was pleased by the efficiency of the men, as they had followed his orders without fail. The camp remained on full alert, and the previous evening's battle seemed as though it had never taken place.

Tents were pitched in two neat rows and horses were cobbled in the rear. The main supply wagon, full of foodstuffs and expensive smithing equipment, was situated in between the officer's tent and his own private quarters. To the untrained eye, nothing seemed amiss. Any skilled scout who approached the site might notice the absence of a main cooking fire and the regular gathering of soldiers huddled around it. Instead, two smaller fires burned sparingly, one at each end of the tent lines. They were kept low so as not to needlessly blind the watchmen as they surveyed the perimeter.

From his vantage point on the western side, Gavin could see that only four men sat watch around the flames. The rest of the guards were sleeping until watch change. Shrugging off a chill, he paused and exchanged pleasantries with a number of sentries near the forest line. They were not surprised to see their captain up wandering this late in the night. In fact, they would have been more concerned had he not come by to share a steaming mug of tea. Gavin's restless nights were common knowledge among the Fey.

It had been nearly two years since the dreams had started, and with them came the nightmares. For months he had struggled to find peace after the setting of the sun, to no avail. The dark visions were interspersed with strange hallucinations almost impossible to describe. Although the company was aware of his troubles, only the officers knew the toll they had taken on their captain.

The nightmare was a recurring one, exact in every detail; every sound, every feeling, every object; all the same, no matter how often he experienced it. He would wake within an ancient forest, and sense that the trees themselves pulsed with a feeling of dread. As he walked through the imposing wood, his hands would brush up against the gnarled bark of any tree he passed. Intense feelings of loneliness and sadness would overcome him. These emotions were so poignant and melancholy that he could never suppress the tears. Such was how the vision always began, with that walk through the dark forest, his mind awash with the heartbreaking sentiments contained within those ancient trunks.

Although burdened by such suffocating emotion, he did not fear for his safety as he strode through the matted leaves that covered the forest floor. Only when he spotted the shadows darting at the edge of his vision, did his heart begin to beat rapidly. Twisted creatures roved the interior of the woods, slowly gaining ground as he raced through the tangled trunks.

Desperately hoping to escape his pursuers, he already knew the outcome of the chase before it began. A glimpse of the hunters confirmed his terrible fear; that it was the Gath that baited and followed him. The first claws would tear at his legs while their fangs dug deeply into his back, sending him sprawling to the ground. He could clearly remember the smell of the foul breath emanating from the beast perched upon his prone body. Grinding his face deeper into the earth, it choked the life from him as it tore his flesh.

And yet each time, as pure terror threatened to overwhelm his senses, he would glance to his left and spy a very different creature hidden in the shadows of a nearby tree. A thin figure, with dark eyes gleaming like twilight stars. Those eyes seemed to burn a hole in his mind, uncovering hidden secrets, his greatest fears, and his darkest desires. Suddenly, he would wake up covered in a thin layer of sweat, his heart throbbing in his chest, and a scream caught in his throat.

There was no doubt in his Gavin's troubled mind that in his dream he walked under the eaves of the Aeldenwood. With the fall of the High King, the lands of Caledun had experienced drastic changes. Gone was the ancient race of tree-tenders, the guardians of the Aeldenwood - the Gorimm. With the ancient guardians of the forest gone, it had given birth to creatures of horror and destruction. Without the guidance of the vanished people, the borders of the Aeldenwood grew rapidly out of control; a condition that worsened every year.

That vanished race, said to have once been beloved by all peoples of the High King, had been the caretakers of nature. Small in stature and of noble bearing, the histories spoke of their long silver hair, and bright welcoming smiles. They lived in the woodlands of Kal Maran, but often visited the cities of humankind. They were long of life, and had experience beyond measure. They were great craftsmen, architects, and practitioners of magecraft. They had often acted as the diplomatic voices of reason during the years of the great wars in the north. It was said that the High King's closest advisor and chosen confidant, had been one of the Gorimm.

History recounted that shortly before the death of the last High King, the Gorimm had retreated to their forest, forsaking those they had once nurtured. Many believed that the elder race had served its purpose and had elected to disappear into antiquity. Others believed that the decision was not of their own choosing.

In any case, Gavin Silveron thought, not a single Gorimm had been sighted in two hundred years. The strange people now resided only in shattered Caledun's fairy tales, with few drawings and paintings remaining of the elder race. Ancient relics said to have belonged to the Gorimm now gathered dust in temples, libraries, and houses of nobility. They were now but a wonderful tale to excite children as they dozed off sleep.

Pausing and waving at one of his men as he walked towards his tent, the captain of the Fey'Derin could not help but wonder, as he often had over these last few months, if the shadowy figure in his dreams could be one of the fabled Gorimm. He also questioned why he might be dreaming about them and was alarmed by the implications.

Shaking the disturbing memories from his mind, Gavin walked the perimeter of the camp. Pausing on the outskirts within shouting distance of the sentries, he gazed wondrously at the night sky. On such an autumn evening, so perfectly crisp and clear, he could lose himself in the silent beauty of the stars. Rare were the evenings that allowed such a peaceful and majestic view of the sky.

Just a few hours earlier he had led his men into bloody battle. How ironic that he, a man of violence and war, could find such solace in the tranquility of a starry night.

"Our ancestors look down upon us this night, Captain," came a gruff voice from over his shoulder.

"Yours do, my friend," he answered as his weathered lieutenant moved up to stand at his side.

"You would be surprised then, Gavin, were they to watch over you, the *Drayenmark*?" Caolte asked. Gavin had long professed to have forsaken any belief in the old gods. "I brought you some tea. Drink it. It will help settle your mind."

"I think there is little that will calm my thoughts tonight. I can't shake my dream any more so than I could the last time. It lingers…" Gavin answered.

"My people would say you have been sent a wondrous gift, a warning that will serve you well into your future." Caolte said, drinking from his own mug.

"Just as many of your people would say I was tainted by a dark power that will consume my soul, would they not? I would be *s'avelok*," Gavin replied.

"Tainted? Hmm, you have no reason to believe that."

The two men stood in silence for a long moment, slowly sipping their tea, and staring up at the clear night sky. The soft glow of morning had started to erase the stars hiding near the edge of the towering mountains where the company had camped.

"Have the bodies been removed?" Gavin asked, turning to face his senior officer and longtime friend.

"Yes. Pier's men were little more than a bunch of well-fed brigands. There wasn't much fight left in them once we eliminated their sentries."

"Casualties?"

"Twenty-eight, including most of his officers. That's unfortunate, but under the circumstances we can still barter well for Pier's release. We stripped their survivors bare, and the equipment should serve us well. Karn can do some modifications on the better weapons, but may just melt down most of the damned stuff," Caolte replied.

The Mercenary Code ensured the safe return of every officer in a company, regardless of their performance in a given engagement. A captain's reputation weighed heavily into the negotiation of the ransom payment the victors could demand. To wantonly kill or maim a captive officer was an offence of the most grievous nature. Common soldiers were rarely kept as prisoners. More often than not, they were relieved of all equipment and money, and released within three days. Most soon found employment at the next *Ca'lenbam*, the gathering that took place each spring before the summer's warfare commenced. With over three hundred registered mercenary companies, the Code was respected by all.

"And the Lady Farraine?" Gavin asked.

"Bider did give her one nasty knock to the head, but she'll be fine in the morning. Can't see how that noble wench will be happy to have been accosted by a lowly commoner, but I'm sure she'll listen now," the lieutenant rolled his eyes.

"I'll talk to her in the morning," added Gavin. "Until then, post two men at her tent entrance with orders that she not be allowed to roam about until after I meet with her."

"Yes, sir," Caolte nodded. Pausing as he headed back towards camp, the old soldier turned and inquired, "We strike for Garchester on the morrow?"

"Yes. Sergeant Fearan has the details. We'll leave at midday. No sense rushing out with Pier's Brigade shattered. The men could use the extra rest as once we hit the siege, I fear sleep will become elusive."

Lieutenant Burnaise nodded and sketched a quick salute. Kneading the taut muscles of his neck, Gavin turned back to the stars and enjoyed what peacefulness remained before daybreak.

ᬯ

The routine of yearly campaigning was at the core of a mercenary's life. Gavin had always enjoyed the morning drills and swordplay. Even as a new recruit in Black Company some ten summers earlier, the captain had developed an affinity for the exercises, and the aching of his muscles after a challenging session. His cares and worries were forgotten when he stepped out onto the practice field. His focus shrank to the simple parcel of land where he did battle. A skilled soldier performed well in practice and one who became lax in his drills became lax on the real field of battle. Rare were the times that distracted fighters came back alive.

Gavin had always toiled to instill that work ethic in his men, leading by example whenever possible. With the uncertainty of the coming siege still clouding his thoughts, he donned a practice vest and buckled a wooden sword to his belt. A session with the men always helped ease his troubled mind.

Because of the passion their captain exuded when it came to the practice yard, most of Gavin's soldiers were prone to the same excitement. It had become tradition among the men to challenge, and hopefully best, their captain. Gavin enjoyed the gamesmanship and encouraged his officers to join in the fun. Rarely did any real injuries result, and so most of the men did their best to attend the swordplay sessions.

"What's the wager today, Captain?" called out one of the men stretching near the edge of the clearing.

"I'm feeling like a lucky man today, Aren," Gavin flashed a grin. "I'll give two silver coins for a hit and a full ten for a defeat."

More than a few whistles rang out at the proclamation. Word, he knew, would quickly spread through the tents. Gavin began his own preparations, stretching and meditating amidst the sounds of the morning. As expected, it wasn't long before a crowd began to gather. He walked over to join Ethan Shade as Caolte started taking bets from the assembled mercenaries.

"How many are you taking on this morning, Captain?" Ethan Shade asked.

Gavin had met Ethan in the port city of K'oral. He had been on a recruiting mission with Ossric McConnal at the time, and had run into a problem with troublemakers in the Gilded Dragon, an inn of ill-repute. Granted, the large and often boisterous McConnal may have been at the root of their confrontation, but it mattered little. Ethan, fair of face and looking more like an aristocrat than a fighter, had come to their aid brandishing a thin rapier with both an entertainer's flair and a veteran's skill. Ethan had been exceedingly drunk at the time, and was barely able to stand once the last man fell to their blades.

Impressed and somewhat charmed by the flamboyant aristocrat, a friendship had soon blossomed. Now, some three summers later, Ethan Shade, once an intoxicated gambler, was a changed man. He had taken the opportunity Gavin had presented to him very seriously and was now a responsible and well-spoken officer. Reared as a noble, the second son of a well-to-do family, he had been neglected most of his life, cared for by the family servants more so than by his parents. Ethan had taken well to the rigid rules of the mercenary company, and even more so to the familial atmosphere it bred. Dressed in an immaculate long black coat, his grey and blue tabard underneath, Ethan Shade looked as ready for a gala feast as he did for a fight.

"I'll take four on my own, but if you're up for it, we can do this together."

"Heh, we might have to up the ante. We can't have the men losing so often without providing incentive enough to fight," the quiet man grinned.

"By the gods, Ethan, I can't afford any more!" Gavin protested with a smile.

"Whenever you're ready, Sir," called out one of the men he had greeted earlier. Five men, all veterans of at least two campaigns, stood ready and eager to challenge the two senior officers.

Although Ethan was an excellent swordsman, the Fey'Derin captain surpassed him in skill. Gavin Silveron had often been called a master, though he refused any such accolades. He taught his men patience and focus; not fanciful attacks and risky parries. Too many had died trying to create openings where none existed.

Amid good-natured insults from the crowd, the two men took to the field and were quickly surrounded by the six challengers. The rules of the contest were simple; to be tagged twice meant defeat. Tagging another combatant could mean anything from the disarming of a weapon, to a sharp blow to the head, although such dangerous hits were frowned upon.

Dropping into a protective stance, Gavin placed himself at his companion's back, guarding Ethan's flank. If he guessed correctly, the other soldiers would hope to overwhelm the two immediately by closing in quickly from all sides.

Surprisingly, the soldiers were content to probe their defenses, each taking turns pressing a short attack. Gavin and Ethan repulsed the quick bursts with ease, content to wait them out. Finally, once a hearty chorus of hisses were showered upon the combatants from the crowd, the six men struck as one.

The Fey'Derin were highly trained, and their battle skills were renowned across all of Kal Maran. Few companies boasted such a well- rounded ensemble of skilled warriors. Gavin was immediately thrown backwards, nearly colliding with his partner. Fighting on the defensive, he parried desperately to the left as two blades snaked into his range. Sliding his blade along the second man's thrust, he used the flat of his sword to land a numbing shot to his attacker's hand. Cursing and grunting in pain, the weapon fell from the man's nerveless fingers. Using the disarming to his advantage, Gavin frantically twisted to his right, dodging a third soldier's slash and delivering a strong kick to one of his first attackers.

Risking a glance at Ethan, Gavin saw that the noble had been struck in the leg. The officer limped slightly and was favouring his right side. Thinking quickly, Gavin charged the men, giving Ethan a moment to recover as they exchanged sides. With one man still disarmed, Ethan could better protect his wounded leg against attacks from his left.

Gavin's charge, as all in attendance would swear around the fire that evening, was flawless. With a quick succession of strikes, the deftly moving captain had defeated two of the three men, leaving the third desperately looking for a way past his guard. The maneuver was not without risk, as it had left him open on both flanks if Ethan were not able to cover his back.

Ethan upheld his end admirably, and the combat was over within a few moments. Gavin greeted the roar of approval with a curt nod and salute.

Ethan was the consummate entertainer. Flourishing his blade, he bowed deeply from the waist. Then, amidst the cheering, he flashed a few moves with his blade, saluting smartly to his commanding officer and partner.

Laughing at the spectacle, Gavin returned the salute and firmly shook each of the challengers' hands, graciously accepting their congratulations. Pausing for a moment, he dug into his belt pouch and tossed Darren, the soldier he had disarmed, twelve silver pieces, two to each man earned for the hit on Ethan.

Watching the men joyously congratulate each other brought back fond memories of his first few seasons in Black Company. Gavin could still remember challenging his sergeant to a duel, hoping that he could break through Caolte's guard and score a hit.

Life was far less complicated as a recruit, and Gavin often wondered how different things would be had he never fought at Parksya's Ridge. Too many companions had been lost in that battle, and too many good officers he had come to trust and admire had fallen. Strangely enough, that battle garnered him some renown, as well as a promotion, but not a day went by that he did not miss the many men who died on that blood-soaked field.

Learning to deal with the aftermath of combat was a skill Gavin continued to work hard on improving. Even after his many campaigns, losing any man, from officer to recruit, was extremely difficult. Momentarily lost in the memory, the captain failed to hear the heavy footsteps of Sergeant Brock Fearan.

"Captain, I believe we have a pressing matter that requires your attention," coughed the officer.

Turning to acknowledge the man, Gavin spotted a bright scarlet handprint that glowed red on Brock's face. "Is it safe to assume that the Lady Farraine is in a welcoming mood this morning, Sergeant?"

"She slapped me when I informed her that we had only one choice of meal here in the camp. She seemed angry that we didn't have a menu, Sir," he finished with a growl.

"Seems like our lady friend may find things a bit difficult until we arrive in Garchester. I'll wash up quickly and speak with our guest. Until then..." Gavin caught the quickly retreating form of his partner from the contest, "Ethan will entertain her. He certainly knows how to court a lady."

"Gavin, you can't be serious?" Ethan groaned. "I need to have the Eagle Runners out within the hour, if we are to be on schedule for departure."

"I'm sure Orn will see that all the necessary preparations are made," Gavin replied. Ignoring the man's look of bewilderment Gavin pressed, "I'll be no more than a quarter of an hour, Ethan. See to it that the Lady Farraine feels welcome in our humble camp."

"You worthless piece of common slime, I'll have you know that I am the Lady Aria Farraine, eldest daughter of the Duke of Telmire and the last known ancestor of the family of Ki —"

"And the long-time consort of Lord Dalemen of Avery," Gavin finished slyly. Enjoying the sudden discomfort of his guest, he pressed his advantage. "The very same man who now leads his mercenary contracts against the city of Garchester, the home of my own employer, Duke Furnael Berry."

"I fail to see the importance. With whom I spend my private time is my own business, and it is far beneath a simple captain to have any interest at all in the private affairs of a noble lady," Aria spat back, her words dripping with scorn.

The noblewoman's tent was in a state of complete disarray. The wash basin, Gavin's own, had been thrown the length of the room, while the serviceable bedroll and cot had been overturned. Several plates of food, along with their contents, had been strewn about as if caught up in a midwinter storm. Even the Lady Farraine herself seemed quite disheveled. Her night clothes were wrinkled and dirty, the hem was torn, and the silk straps that held her ample bosom seemed about to snap. A pile of fancy clothing that Ethan had saved from her wagon were the only items in the room that had not been treated with disdain.

"Allow me to explain," Gavin answered calmly. "Your intimate business is very much my concern. Knowing the particulars of Lord Dalemen's whereabouts, his connections, and his loves, is of the utmost importance to my employer."

"Speak plainly, you bastard! I'll not stand here in such indecency and have you talk circles around your motives for assaulting my personage," Aria roared in return.

Gavin smiled patiently, "As you wish, my lady. It would seem very unlikely that your consort, Lord Dalemen, would wish to put you in harm's way, would it not?"

"My lord would never tolerate such an act."

"Well then, if Duke Berry were to have you as his noble guest within the very walls of Garchester, would your lord not be remiss if he showed no reluctance to fight against the very man who holds your life in his hands?"

A horrified look dawned across the woman's face as she realized the importance of Gavin's suggestion.

"By the gods, you would use me as a pawn?" she breathed quietly.

"When outnumbered, Lady Farraine, a man must do what he can to tip the balance in his favour. With your Lord Dalemen hamstrung by your capture, ther leaves far fewer able-bodied men left to throw into the siege. Duke Berry now holds the trump card in this year's game of war."

"He wouldn't dare..." she whispered.

"But he already has," Gavin replied. "The moment you arrived in this tent, the game changed. In the case of Lord Dalemen, I would hazard a guess that it is not in his favour."

"Captain Pier will not stand for this injustice. He was well paid to be my escort, and he will return to rescue me. His life will be forfeit if he does not," Aria replied in defiance.

"The company with whom you travelled is no more. Captain Pier is also one of my captives. His head may very well roll for the failure of his contract, but for now he is my prisoner, and will be ransomed as per the laws of the Code."

"The damned Code won't spare him once his failure is known," she smiled wickedly. "I can assure you that I will enjoy making him suffer."

Gavin shrugged.

"Almost as much as I will enjoy watching you suffer, Captain Silveron," Aria Farraine added with a stare that held such hatred that even the staunch mercenary had to wonder at what atrocities this noblewoman would happily commit in the name of vengeance.

He allowed his eyes to narrow and as he addressed her, "You would do well to remember your place. I am a patient man, but am known to possess a temper. Do not push my limits."

"I will expect a meal befitting my status, commoner," she said as he collected a scattered cup and plates, and made his way towards the tent entrance.

Refusing to acknowledge her with another look, he paused and spoke softly over his shoulder, his voice sweetly imitating the deferent tone servants used when addressing a noble.

"I trust my lady has enjoyed her morning meal. It is a long time until we dine again, but I'm sure you knew that, even as you proceeded to throw your fare about the room, much like an impudent child."

Incoherent screams followed him out into the cool morning air as he considered the coming journey. A week in that woman's presence would do little to warm his heart.

ഇ

There were few things Bider enjoyed more than scouting. As an Eagle Runner under the command of Sergeant Shade, the young thief had spent the last two years ranging about the countryside as a company scout. Bider worked best alone, and he thrived on the thrill of the hunt. This morning though, things seemed bound to remain dull.

With the enemy easily defeated, he expected that Gavin and the other officers wanted a clear path into the western foothills of the nearby mountains. Across that land of rolling hills and lush green valleys, lay the city of Garchester. Near Garchester sat an invading army bent upon the removal of the Fey'Derin's current employer, Duke Berry.

At least some excitement lay in the prospect of a dangerous assignment once they arrived at their destination. Until then, the company scout sighed and sat down on a small cliff face overlooking a small babbling brook. Turning to survey the area, he watched as his mercenary comrades climbed slowly through the pass he had traversed earlier in the day.

The Fey travelled light. Whereas many companies burdened themselves with an odd assortment of retainers, family members, and useless equipment, Captain Silveron would have none of it. Families were to be left at home, regardless of how long the company planned to be on duty. Distractions they were, Lieutenant Burnaise would comment, and he was one to talk, having left his wife and children up north during all of his many campaigns.

Finishing their first tour in the south, Bider suspected a milder winter was in store for the company this year. The southern climate was beautiful compared to the harsh, cold weather of the north. Snow was not a rarity, but the winter rains clogged up roadways worse than even the thickest snowfall. Reminded of the slogging spring journey south earlier that year, Bider wished for a short moment that he could drown his worries in a bottle of spirits.

More than two winters ago, Captain Silveron had found him belly down and bleeding like a stuck pig in the port city of Shand. Why Gavin had decided to show him mercy after he had tried to slice the money pouch from another Fey soldier was still a mystery. What Gavin had seen in the scrawny ill-fed runt and thief, he had yet to say.

It had taken more effort to break his thieving habit than it had to become a soldier. The unflinching restrictions of the company had earned Bider more than a few harsh reprimands for his behaviour.

To the end of his days, Bider would be grateful. One of the Captain's odd quirks, was his refusal to accept the name the small thief had earned during his years as a sewer rat in the port city. One of those first nights, beset by shakes and convulsions attributed to his bad habits, Gavin had given him a new name - Coren D'Elmark. To this day, Gavin would only address him as Coren, never Bider. The Fey merely laughed when he had first inquired about the man who led them and his curious ways. "Figuring out the Captain," he had been told, "was about as easy as marrying a noblewoman if you were a commoner."

"Daydreaming, Coren?" called a familiar voice from below.

His eyes locked with the very man he had been musing about. Bider answered with a grin. "I was just trying to watch the birds, Captain. Too bad you brought the company this way and scared 'em all off. Just plain rude, you know?"

Gavin's glared at the scout.

Amidst laughter echoing from the soldiers within earshot, Bider bounced to his feet and saluted sharply. "I'll be sure to warn you about them next time, Sir. You can count on me."

With that, he disappeared over the cliff edge and headed east, easily outdistancing the slower moving column. With any luck, they would be in Garchester within the week. Until then, it seemed that watching birds may be the only pastime available.

Comprised of a chain of well-built fortresses, the Iron Shield proudly defends the northern borders of Caledun from the scourge of the goblin tribes present in the Wilds. Without the resilient sword arms of the border guards, the northern expanse of the kingdom would lay ripe for the conquering.

— Ilias Bertram
The Histories, Vol XI

CHAPTER V

Darkenedge, Iron Shield

The wind blew fiercely across the cold stone ramparts of the keep while the Wilds lay hidden in the distance by an ever-deepening gloom of falling snow. Winter seemed destined to arrive early this year, much to the chagrin of those who called the northeastern reaches of Kal Maran home. The strong weatherworn walls of the structure held firm against the coming tide, as they had for each and every bitter winter that had come before.

From his lofty perch high atop a sentry tower, Leoric D'Athgaran clutched his cloak tightly around his sturdy frame. Leather gloves lined with fur were unable to keep his fingers warm. Only a few hours into his watch, he could feel the chill penetrating deep within his bones. It was not without reason that the people of this region feared the turning of the seasons.

Releasing the hold upon his cloak, Leoric grimaced and tried to rub some warmth into his frozen, numb fingers. Scratching idly at his beard, a common facial feature that men of the region sported with pride, the soldier watched a clearing to the left of the keep.

An open field lay just at the edge of his range of vision. This was due mainly to the reduced visibility in such a storm. As he had expected, bulky dark shadows were gathering in the spot where his eyes were trained. Fighting back a rush of anger, he kept his focus even with snow swirling all around him, and counted the figures as accurately as possible.

Only fifteen tonight, he mused as the small gathering stood stoically against the weather. Time slowed to a glacial pace, and his tired eyes strained to keep watch.

As a slight brightening in the east pierced the overcast sky, Leoric watched the figures slide back into the shadows, heading deep into the treacherous Wilds. Sighing heavily, he shrugged his shoulders in order to dislodge a fresh patch of snow from his ice-covered hood, and welcomed the scraping tread of footsteps from the stairwell below.

On time, and carrying a steaming mug of sweet-smelling cider, a cloth-swaddled man appeared around a corner. His face was a mass of dark whiskers, growing nearly to his eyes and his shaggy mop of hair seemed better suited as a stallion's mane. Stuall was anything but pretty, but he would be the first to tell you how much warmer he was in comparison.

Beaming, the man greeted Leoric with a hearty slap to the back. "Bloody cold out last night, eh?" the man laughed cheerfully.

"I can barely feel my feet this morning," Leoric answered grimly. "They would be foolish to attack on a night like this, goblin or no."

"Were they back again? Buggers must be truly dim-witted to stand about in weather like this. Even my old sire knew better than to go outdoors in a late autumn storm, and we all know how crazy my old man was," Stuall exclaimed. "In any case, you'll need to report it to the watch Captain, same as always."

"I'll go before I break my fast and head to bed for the morning. No sense leaving it unattended to," Leoric nodded, preparing himself for the long trek from the tower to the barracks.

"That's why I like you, Leoric. You always know when things need to get done. It saves me time knowing that you'll take care of things that the others find bothersome," Stuall grunted as he leaned out over the tower's edge and downed a healthy swig from his wooden goblet.

Leoric smiled weakly and wished the man a good morning.

Only two days remained before the watch changed and he received a much needed repose from sentry duty. Engaged for the last fortnight, he was looking forward to spending time with the other men in the evenings, a privilege the sentries unhappily evaded while on duty.

By the time he arrived at the watch captain's office, a semblance of warmth had begun to seep back into his ice-cold bones. His cloak, a welcome companion during the previous evening, was now a hindrance. The frozen snow had begun to melt and it had started to weigh down the heavy wool covering. Dislodging some clinging chunks as best he could before entering the officer's quarters, Leoric saluted the young man sitting behind a large oak desk.

"D'Athgaran - Crow's Tower sentry, reporting in."

"Good morning, Leoric. Can't believe the weather we're having. It's a wonder you still have all your digits this morning."

"Coldest it's been this season," he answered. The young officer of the watch was good-natured when compared to the drill masters of Darkenedge. As with most of the desired posts in the frontier keeps of the Iron Shield, they were usually bestowed to the youngest sons of minor nobles in the hope that they would earn some valuable experience commanding men. A second or third son from a minor House wasn't destined for much beyond a middle officer's ranking or mercantile placement, but exemplary duty in the Shield could lead to a future commanding along the expanse of the border.

"I take it you must have something to report if you came here before breakfast and a well-earned rest?" the officer asked.

"Yes, it seems as though our *friends* aren't quite as bothered as they should be in this weather. At least a good dozen, maybe even fifteen, watched from the east last night. That makes eight days now, foul weather or not," Leoric reported.

"Strange and very unsettling. I'll note it down in the log and have Marshal Aram review this afternoon. You aren't the only sentry to report sightings last night. It could mean that our visitors are up to no good."

"The men have been talking about a raid. Any truth to that rumour?" Leoric asked, signing his name at the bottom of the evening logbook with a fine quill.

"You know I can't comment, D'Athgaran," the young soldier replied. "But I do know the commanders are meeting later today," he added with a knowing glance.

"Understood. I'm off to thaw out these old bones of mine. Have yourself a good day, Sir," Leoric saluted.

"Only two evenings left before you are relieved, soldier. Don't go enjoying that morning nap too much now."

Chuckling to himself as he headed towards his chambers, Leoric stopped only momentarily to grab a small plate of sausages and a cup of hot tea. Devouring the food in only a few bites, he peeled off his wet garments, pulled on a clean pair of trousers, and contently snuggled into his warm blankets.

That eighteen other men were busy rousing and preparing themselves for the coming day mattered little to him. As far as he was concerned, within the hour, the room would be his. If there was one bonus to nighttime sentry duty, it was the silence of his sleeping chamber during the day. Pulling the jumble of blankets tightly around his body, Leoric soon fell asleep.

❧

The afternoon came far too quickly.

> *"I'd kiss a girl with eyes of green,*
> *I'd kiss a girl with eyes of gold,*
> *I'd kiss a girl with any coloured eyes,*
> *but it's you I'd rather hold"*

> *"I'd love a girl with —"*

"I swear by all the gods Angvald, if you don't shut your cursed trap and Christian doesn't stop that screeching, I'll rip out both your tongues and feed them to the wolves!" roared Leoric from his warm bed. Staring balefully at the heavy-set culprit strumming a small lute and a swiftly retreating smaller man, he leapt out of his once-inviting cocoon.

"Leoric, my apologies," Angvald replied sheepishly. "We didn't see you there."

Listening to the thickly accented reply, Leoric growled and shot the man a second glare.

"Now, now, we didn't mean to disturb you," Angvald continued, his thick fingers plucking a few strings on the instrument. "Now look, you've gone and scared my singer."

"Christian will get over it. You, on the other hand, had better remember this moment when you're on sentry duty next month," Leoric said as he pulled a tunic over his shoulders.

"Ah! You're not one to back down from a fight are you?!" the big man bellowed. "I like that in a man."

Angvald hailed from distant Kaleen, a land of large men, larger appetites, and an abundance of both sun and sand. The nation of Kaleen had long remained detached from the affairs of greater Kal Maran, although the occasional visitor, curious as to what the greater world offered, would spend time within the Kingdom of Caledun.

The Kaleenians were known as the barbarians of the east, tribal by nature, and much akin to the goblin tribes that bordered the mountain range to the north. Hemmed off from the rest of the land by the mighty *Volkstall* Mountains, the people of Kaleen remained a mystery to most, and few travelers from Caledun had ever been granted permission to enter their closed borders.

Angvald insisted that he was a musician at heart, even though he had arrived in Darkenedge two summers earlier hoping to train with the men of the Iron Shield. An accomplished warrior and an avid drinker, the foreigner had found himself accepted by the strange crew that lived and guarded one of the gateways to the west.

Including Darkenedge, five keeps protected the passes through the mountains into the prosperous Vale of the Innes merchants, and the territories of the Northern Council. The rugged northern expanse was sparsely populated and only Hilltop boasted a companion city of a size that rivalled some of those found in the more forgiving regions of the kingdom.

Gritting his teeth as the biting wind sent chills through his body, Leoric wasn't surprised. Born in a small village near the border of the *Drayenmark* holdings to the southeast, it had taken him several winters to adapt to the harsh climate. Even so, rare were the days in which he didn't long for the temperate south.

"Any more news about a raid?" Angvald rumbled, strumming a few final notes before reaching for the lute's case.

"The Marshal is meeting with some of the garrison captains late this afternoon, but I've no real idea what's going on," he replied. "I do know our neighbours had another squad out on my watch again last night. Can't see how the Marshal can ignore that."

"Those goblins need to be taught a lesson, if you ask me," the Kaleenian spat.

"I might agree but I'm sure of one thing..." Leoric said.

"What's that?"

"The Marshal surely won't be asking you," he answered with a laugh. As Angvald's deep bellowing voice erupted in mock anger, Leoric finished lacing his boots and headed out into the hallway.

With most of the day gone, his stomach reminded him that it was time for his first meal. Glancing out one of the keep's numerous tall windows, he judged it less than two hours until sunset. Soon after darkness fell, he would be making his arduous trek up into the Crow's Tower for another miserable stint on duty. No officer could rightly complain about a sentry's performance; that is until they spent a fortnight staring out into the cold Wilds with nary a sensation in their extremities.

Dispelling the depressing thoughts from his mind, Leoric made his way swiftly through the corridors of the lower keep. A heavy, tasty aroma drifted through the passage closest to the great hall; stew if his nose did not deceive him. Thick home-made bread, perfect for dipping, would go a long way in helping him forget his upcoming shift in the tower. With luck, Frengold and his assistants had been busy cooking up a feast while he slept.

At this time of day the hall was nearly empty, another small perk belonging to those on nighttime duty. Without the usual jostling for position and space while trying to devour a meal, he would be able to eat comfortably.

Only a handful of other men were present, most from other companies in the keep. They sat at the long wooden tables that were spread about the large chamber in an orderly manner. He assumed they had drawn night duty for the month and although they were all stationed at Darkenedge, Leoric didn't recognize any of them. The keep itself housed over a thousand men with a few outlying garrisons totaling additional fighters in the hundreds. The commanders of the Iron Shield fortresses had long ago learned that any unprotected settlement quickly became a target for the marauding goblins.

Silently nodding at those few men who acknowledged his arrival, Leoric used a large wooden ladle to fill a bowl with steaming stew from a blackened pot near the hearth. The tantalizing aroma wafted into his nostrils as he spooned the thick broth into his waiting mouth. If guard duty did anything for a man, in the very least it increased his appetite.

Suddenly a loud horn broke the relative silence of the chamber, and curses erupted from nearly every man hunched over their meals. Angrily shaking his head, Leoric pushed his bench away from the table. All men of the Shield knew how much the commanding officer of the keep frowned upon tardiness. The horn call summoned all able-bodied soldiers to a general muster, and the officers would expect the presence of all within minutes. No excuse was ever deemed worthy, nor warranted.

Leaving his half eaten meal, he walked briskly through the central passageway of the keep and passed into a large open courtyard. Briefly scanning the crowd for his own company, he made his way over to the gates. It was the usual gathering point for his comrades, and sure enough, familiar faces greeted his arrival with words of welcome. Slipping smartly into position, he nodded curtly towards his sergeant.

"Nice of you to join us, D'Athgaran," Sergeant Alleran mused. "I was beginning to wonder whether sentry duty had finally addled that small brain of yours."

"Good afternoon to you as well, Sergeant," Leoric sketched a small bow. "The brain's fine, but thank you all the same for asking."

"Stop acting the fool," the veteran growled although he smiled. "Just be thankful you weren't the last to arrive. I swear by Arne, if it's Darius again, I'll have him scrubbing pots for the rest of his life."

Within minutes every man not injured, sick, or on duty, stood at attention near the gates. As was the custom for a general muster, military dress was not required. Most of the soldiers wore a simple tunic and trousers with the odd few who had been drilling in the training yard still bearing their padded armour. Although the rule held true for a common soldier, the same could not be said for the officers of the keep. Watching the commanding officers on the raised platform at the front of the crowd, Leoric wondered if they slept in their uniforms. The always crisp outfits sported the black and gold trappings of the borderlands.

Marshal Aram was an aged warrior who possessed the unmistakable air of an expert commander. His manner was strangely out of place in the harsh surroundings of the rugged border keep. At first glance, one would expect someone more suited to a noble's court, than the solid stone walls of Darkenedge. He had held command of the keep for over thirty years; making it more than half his lifetime. Slowly smoothing his long white moustache that drooped well below his chin, the old soldier surveyed the assembly in silence.

Flanking the Marshal were the other senior officers; the aristocratic Quartermaster Siff, and Captain Stone, the senior man of rank. Both men were well-respected and honored almost as much as the Marshal. The soldiers of Darkenedge had little to complain about despite their difficult task. They were well fed, well paid, and apart from the brutal northern winters, they were well situated. Leoric supposed most of them despised their drill sergeants, but for the officer corps, only respect was given.

As a hush settled over the assembly, Marshal Aram's strong baritone voice boomed loudly for all to hear. Leoric came quickly to attention and added his own voice, as he always did, when the Creed of the Iron Shield was spoken:

> *Stone shall be my home, my protector, my savior.*
> *Strong shall be my sword, part mind and spirit.*
> *Serve the border, shall I, with full commitment.*
> *Defender of lives, and livelihood, have I become.*
>
> *Leave no man.*
> *Leave your fears in your past.*
> *I will show courage and loyalty. I will be true to my command.*
> *I am a keeper of the Wilds, a warrior, a comrade.*
> *I am a borderman, and I fear no evil.*

Since the fall of the last High King of Caledun, those words had been faithfully spoken aloud whenever the men of the Iron Shield gathered together. The oath spoke to the bonds of brotherhood that existed between the proud men of the borderlands. Many had ill-favoured backgrounds and some had once given up hope on a life that had treated them so poorly.

Leoric sighed as he delivered the final few words, closing his eyes as memories of his own past rushed through his mind. He tried to shake away those old feelings, long since buried, and hopefully forgotten. *Could he ever really leave his old life behind...?* He took a moment to compose himself, and turned his attention towards Marshal Aram and the words his commander was shouting.

"— threaten our borders. The savages flaunt their newfound freedom and strength. They tread in our fields; they walk to the very gates of our homes. It is time we showed them the true mettle of the Iron Shield. It is time they feared the bite of northern steel. Once more, we shall ride into the Wilds, and claim territory that the enemy has occupied!"

A resounding cheer erupted from those assembled. Leoric was always impressed by the Marshal's skillful rhetoric. His manner of speaking did much to sway the men. To a new recruit, it must have seemed as though the soldiers of Darkenedge had long sat idle behind their walls of stone, biding precious time against the slow approach of the goblin hordes.

And yet, here instead was a man of action, a leader who would no longer tolerate the insults and attacks on the courage of his troops. Despite his old age, it often appeared as though he was leading his men out into the Wilds for the very first time. Leoric stifled a small chuckle. It would not do for his sergeant to see him laughing at any officer, let alone the commander, but it was difficult not to when you knew these patrols were a monthly excursion. Even during the harsh winter months, the men of Darkenedge left the warm confines of the keep to patrol and raid the goblin settlements to the east.

"Shouldn't be our company that's called today," whispered a man to his left.

"We fought this summer, but I'm not sure Gadey's men are at full strength yet after the casualties they suffered in that blasted ambush," Leoric returned with a nod.

"Aye, you might have the right of it, but I still believe Captain Pont's company would be up before ours."

Leoric shrugged. "Makes no difference anyways, Wilt. If we don't go out this month, we'll be out when the weather turns. Would almost be a blessing to patrol the forest edge now, rather than when the snows are deep."

"You know me, Leoric, I'm never in a mood to go out and get killed by a savage, snow or not," Wilt replied.

Leoric turned his attention back towards the front and listened as the senior captain detailed the watch reports for the past month. He didn't realize someone was calling his name until a hand fell hard on his shoulder.

"D'Athgaran, are you deaf?" Sergeant Alleran hissed in his ear. "There's a lad from the Watch offices whose been calling your name for a bloody minute. Pay attention, or the next time I'll box your ears like you're a child!"

"Aye, Sir," Leoric responded sheepishly. He caught the eye of the man seeking his attention. The junior officer he had spoken with that morning motioned him over. When a Watch supervisor sought you out, one would be better served not to be found.

"Sorry to bother you D'Athgaran, but it looks like we're short two on the roster. The cold weather lately has a few men off their feet with the grippe. I already pulled Caleb out of his covers earlier this afternoon, and I'm afraid you're next on the replacement roster," the young officer said apologetically.

"You can't pass me over this time? I barely had time to eat before the general muster was called." Leoric asked.

"Sorry, soldier. Take a few minutes and visit Ferngold in the kitchens. Tell him I sent you and he'll set you up real nice for doing us this favour. Understood?"

"Yes, Sir," he replied dejectedly. Waving briefly to his sergeant, Leoric turned towards the keep and headed in towards the kitchens. Muttering silently to himself, he knew that within moments, all the heat from his bones was bound to seep back into the cold stones of the Crow's Tower.

The night watch, even at the best of times, could be long and hard. There were periods during the summer when the blistering temperatures threatened to exhaust the sentries on duty. Leoric had never been so lucky. By mid of night, the winds from the north were howling and tore forcefully at the heavy cloak that he held desperately close to his body. Biting snow stung his frozen cheeks, and his fingers had long since gone numb.

He rarely thought of anything but the inviting warmth of a hearth when faced with such elements, but try as he might to dissuade them, old demons scurried through his mind. Visions of his lost daughter and wife refused to grant him peace of mind. Such nights crept up out of the darkness only a few times each year, but arise they did.

He made vain attempts to bury the hardships of his old life, a life he now pretended never existed. He avoided speaking about his family or past with any of the men at the keep. A good borderman always respected a man's silence. One never questioned the reason a man came to the Iron Shield, and for that Leoric was grateful. Only he knew that Darkenedge had saved his life. If only it could have saved the lives of those he had so desperately loved.

Lost deep in thought, he failed to notice the arrival of two heavily cloaked men.

"Foul weather indeed, D'Athgaran," grunted the taller of the two visitors. "What say you to some warmth and a few hours of sleep?"

Leoric turned towards the soldiers. Even in the snowy darkness he could make out the sharp-nosed features of Edan Alleran.

"Sergeant?" he sputtered.

"Come on. I need you rested in the morning. You've got one free pass on sentry duty this cycle, so you had best enjoy it. Trent here is going to take your place. He's from Pont's command," the stalwart sergeant motioned towards his companion.

Still confused, Leoric followed the officer. "I don't understand, Sir? Sentries never get the night off."

"They do when their company leaves in the morning. Can't have tired men patrolling the Wilds now can we, soldier?" the tall veteran grinned.

Ebin Longshackle... Saron of Elmen Vale... Murran Blackwood... Fallon Birch...
— *'Sorrow', Lumber Grieving Tribute*

CHAPTER VI

Oakfeld Patch, Northern Council

"Master Praxxus, you don't understand. It's not that I don't want to bring you into the Aeldenwood, it's just that, by law, I cannot," Alessan pleaded.

Corian Praxxus would hear no arguments as he was determined to visit the legendary wood, whether anyone agreed with him or not. For the first time since meeting the merchant, Alessan detected a stubborn edginess in the man's voice; one that hinted at his true nature. He understood then that this was someone who rarely failed to receive what he wanted, or demanded, for that matter.

"The Lumber's Guild set the law, sir. Only Guild members have permission to enter these woods. Only the southern King's Road can be used by outsiders and that lies twenty leagues to the southeast. What you ask is simply not possible," Alessan explained once more.

"And what measures are in place that would stop two men from wandering under the eaves of the forest?" Corian retorted.

"Well... none I guess, but we would be in violation of the Lumber Code."

"The same Lumber Code that gives the people of Briar the right to ignore you because of the body you were born with?" hissed the man from Innes Vale.

Pushing back his wooden bench, Alessan stood up and started walking away. "This conversation is over, sir. Don't pretend to know what I feel. You insult me no less than do those fools who sit at the far end of this hall," he replied in anger, and directed a cold stare towards the merchant.

What bothered Alessan was not the merchant's choice of words, but the fact that his own thoughts had, on occasion, mirrored those of the businessman. More often than he cared to admit, he had bitterly cursed the laws of the Lumbers and all they represented. Being an outcast had taken a larger toll on his confidence than he was ever willing to admit.

"You know as well as I, Alessan, that you dream of walking under the boughs of that forest as much as I do" he said. "I apologize for my lack of tact, lad. Now come, let's discuss our little adventure."

Glancing around the meeting hall, carefully avoiding 'Sorrow' while doing so, Alessan gauged the reactions on the faces of the Lumbers who sat nearby. Not one of the men had even turned an eye in their direction. As far as these men were concerned, a greedy merchant and the town's *ba'caech* were of no interest. Why he might have expected anything different, Alessan could not say. Maybe a small part of him fervently hoped that someone actually cared.

Letting his shoulders slump forward, he mustered up some semblance of a smile and rejoined Corian at the long table. "Alright, I'm listening."

Corian Praxxus was right about one thing in particular; there was no doubt in Alessan's mind that he yearned to walk in the Aeldenwood. Lumber blood flowed through his veins, and the same passion and love of the natural world lived within him.

To the south, growing larger by the year, loomed the immense mass of trees. As a child, his father would bring him on occasion to the forest's edge. A few times, Darren Oakleaf had allowed Alessan to explore inside the boundaries of the forest, always cautioning his son about the dangers lurking within the deeper recesses of the wood. How many times since his father's tragic passing had he dreamed of returning to walk amongst those ancient trees?

Early that day, they had left Oakfeld Patch on foot and had set out to the north. When he was certain that they had not been followed, Alessan turned and guided them eastward. Before long, they had reached the edge of the wood. Towering above them were trees that soared higher than the eye could see. Corian showed none of the apprehension that Alessan tried desperately to hide. Full of questions and eager to touch anything at hand, the portly merchant headed immediately to the edge of the forest.

"Unbelievable, lad. Simply incredible!" Corian exclaimed as he ran his hand along the trunk of a particularly gnarled tree. "Strange to think that such majestic creations evoke such terror and unease among your people."

"You act as though you have no trees in the Vale, Master Praxxus," Alessan replied.

"Oh we have trees, but none such as these. The Vale is lush and green, but relatively boring," he replied. "The *S'Kairn* mountain ranges are beautiful in their own way, but rather barren. Now these trees are truly a wonder to behold!"

Making their way a little further south, the unlikely duo headed deeper into the shadowy gloom of the Aeldenwood.

Alessan sat down heavily on the edge of a small stream. Kneading his cramped muscles, he breathed a sigh of relief as the soothing pressure washed away some of the pain. He was determined not to show any weakness in front of the merchant. Surprisingly, he found himself warming to the big man's open and boisterous commentary. He was drastically different from the usual citizen of Innes Vale, and for some strange reason, the favour he garnered with Corian Praxxus had become quite important to Alessan. Although he could detect something darker lurking beneath the big man's jovial nature, Alessan understood better than most how to maintain a suitable façade. He did so each and every day.

They had walked the better part of a league into the forest when they came across a cheerful stream, upon whose banks they now rested. Corian was off a ways, happily following the noisy little brook as it wound its way further towards the heart of the mighty forest.

Leaning his walking stick against the nearest tree trunk, Alessan bent down, cupped his hands, and dipped them into the frigid stream. The shock as the cold

water splashed across his face was exhilarating. Tiny rivulets of the icy liquid continued to slide down the small of his back as he wiped his face dry on the hem of
his travelling cloak. Shaking his head to clear the dampened hair from his eyes,
Alessan rose to his feet and immediately locked eyes with a strange figure across
the stream.

For a moment he thought his vision deceived him; but after wiping his eyes with
the back of his hands, the man was still standing there upon the banks. He was
unlike any man Alessan had ever seen; deeply tanned, but with a strange greenish
tint to his skin that matched the foliage surrounding him.

His long hair was white, almost silver, and cascaded a fair ways down his back.
A few colourful feathers, much akin to those that the *Drayenmark* used, were
woven within the locks. His body was slim and slightly taller than Alessan, who
barely reached above five lengths. His fingers were long and slender, and his
wrists were covered with an odd collection of wooden bracelets. He was dressed
in a brown material that looked like leather, but something about the way it settled against his skin seemed out of place. There was a jagged tear in his cloak near
the shoulder, and he was favouring the left side of his body, cradling that arm
against his body.

Mystified, Alessan turned his attention to the stranger's face. Sleek white eyebrows matched the man's hair, and an elongated jawline with high cheekbones gave
him the enlightened air of a noble. Even from a distance, Alessan could make out a
strange, complex tattoo that surrounded the man's left eye, trailing down most of
the cheek. It countered his refined look, and conveyed a wilder, savage edge to his
overall appearance.

But it was his eyes that held Alessan transfixed.

Two uncommonly vivid green orbs stared at him. They held Alessan paralyzed,
no matter the expanse of space that separated the two men. They shone like precious jewels, pure emeralds of indescribable beauty.

Alessan was frozen with indecision. It was as if the entire forest was waiting on
the reactions of the two men facing each other. He noted the sudden absence of
sound, the clarity of the water, and how the surrounding trees seemed to defer to
the strange being, their wooden limbs bending as if to bow. And yet, still did Alessan's gaze return to those stunning eyes.

I drakan'is or in burin.

Alessan swore that no word had been uttered aloud. The strange sounds seemed to have materialized from within his mind. Suddenly terrified, he tried in vain to will his body into motion. He felt panic rising within his stomach, churning uncomfortably, and his heart frantically beating within his chest. His breath began to catch in his throat, and yet still no sound issued forth from his lips.

Kar indin Caledun.

Trying hard to suppress the crashing wave of terror threatening to overwhelm him, Alessan shook his head apologetically as he tried to reply. The words stretched out impossibly from his mouth, but he was finally able to speak. "I don't understand. Your words make no sense to me."

A brief flicker of knowing crossed the man's features. Raising his hands slowly, his lips moved as if muttering something under his breath. For a moment, the paralyzing fear lessened in Alessan's body.

A tortured soul you carry, came the voice inside his head, clearly understandable. *I beseech you not to worry, you are in no danger. I seek only the High King of Caledun.*

"There is no High King, and only a shadow of the former Kingdom of Caledun remains," Alessan replied, confused by the topic of conversation. "Where once the king ruled there are now only trees, and so it has been for two centuries."

The High Seat of Magnach, Caledun?

The words expressed a touch of desperation. An overwhelming sense of sorrow was suddenly conveyed through the simple thought and an unbearably deep pain struck Alessan's body without warning. He was whelmed to his knees, his eyes watering and his heart dangerously aflutter.

"There is no Caledun, please..." Alessan heard himself plead from far off, "stop the pain."

The agonizing throbbing ceased immediately. Clutching his chest while gasping for air, Alessan was surprised by the light touch of hands upon his back mere moments after the numbing ache had struck. The figure crouched at his side, an embarrassed and worried frown written plainly across his visage. His eyebrows were deeply furrowed, causing lines to crease the man's forehead. The jewel-like eyes stared at him intently.

I beg your forgiveness. I had forgotten how powerful my peoples' skills could be to a human. Rest child, for I would have no harm come to you.

The light touch of the long greenish fingers transmitted a feeling of warmth to his ravaged mind and body. The healing flow traveled quickly through his entire frame, cleansing the remaining spasms of pain that had ricocheted through his insides.

"Who are you?" Alessan managed to utter.

My people call me C'Aelis and I seek the king.

"I've told you, Caay-liss," Alessan repeated, his tongue tripping clumsily over the strange pronunciation of the man's name. "There is no true king. Besides the duke in Glenvale, there is only the self-proclaimed king, the mad Serian Rhone of the *Drayenmark*. And he is king in nothing but name."

Aaah...the Drayenmark, mused the voice. *Are they still the keepers of the truth?*

"Keepers of the truth?" Alessan frowned. "The *Drayenmark* are clansmen, nomads who roam the eastern wildlands."

Much has changed with our absence, the man spoke as if he was alone. This close to the stranger, Alessan realized that the man not only favoured his left arm, but that it was wrapped in a sling fashioned of vines and leaves. Dried blood covered his shoulder, the heavy stains old and brown.

"You're hurt," Alessan commented. Turning to dig into his pack, he pulled out a small root and offered it to C'Aelis. "Here take this, it will help to clean your wound. My father used to bring them home whenever mother hurt herself in the kitchen. Just chew a piece —"

Mash it in your mouth and apply it to your wound and it should deaden the pain as well as speed up the healing process, smiled C'Aelis. *I may have spoken out of turn. Perhaps things have changed less than I first believed.*

Carefully shifting his damaged arm, the man exposed a terrible wound. All along the jagged edge of the gruesome tear, Alessan recognized the light purple residue of the *F'elan* root.

"You know of the *F'elan* root? I thought it something of a secret within the Guild," questioned Alessan.

Gently replacing the dressing, he nodded. *I know not of your Guild, but of the root I am well versed in its properties.* C'Aelis' slight smile seemed to hide some deeper meaning.

"You must be from a faraway place if you know nothing of the Lumbers' Guild," Alessan exclaimed nervously. "Come to think of it, that wouldn't surprise me in the least. Where are you from, anyway?"

Lumbers' Guild? C'Aelis wondered, ignoring the question about his origin.

Suddenly a peculiar light shone in the entrancing eyes of the small man. Slowly extending his good arm, he reached towards a small sapling that grew at the stream's edge. His long spidery fingers spread out like a fan, lightly brushing the young tree trunk. An almost imperceptible shiver rippled through the earth and trees in the area.

Alessan watched the serene expression that had settled over C'Aelis' features dissipate. It was replaced with a look of such sadness that Alessan unknowingly reached out towards him, aching to ease some of the burden that this strange man obviously carried. Why he cared, Alessan could not say, but rarely had such strong emotions swept through his soul. As Alessan touched his arm, C'Aelis flinched and his hands broke their contact with the small tree.

They slay the woods. They kill the brothers and sisters of the earth, yet they know not how much pain they cause. They do not understand that it is not their fault. They only fight for freedom. Repeatedly nodding his head, the shaken man seemed confused. *What have we allowed to happen?* C'Aelis stumbled backwards. Alessan watched in stunned silence, as a tear slid down C'Aelis' smooth cheek.

Finally finding his voice, Alessan asked, "Understand what, C'Aelis? What do you mean?"

But C'Aelis had vanished.

ഗ

Alessan's return to the Black Boar that evening brought a slew of queries from his mother. The coin he brought back served only to increase the barrage of probing questions about what had transpired at Oakfeld Patch that day.

"I worked on his accounts, Mother. After he realized I knew my numbers and was honest enough for his liking, I checked and rechecked his totals," he lied.

Alessan was never comfortable being dishonest, but his visit to the Aeldenwood had to remain a secret. The members of the Lumbers' Guild would surely enforce a harsh penalty for such a transgression were they to find out. He had no desire to face those consequences, and truth be told, he had enjoyed his adventure with Master Praxxus. Yet, his encounter with the strange woodsman had left him puzzled, and that worried him much more than anything his mother could say. Of the stranger, Corian Praxxus knew nothing.

"I don't like feeling bought, Alessan," his mother said. "But if you were doing honest work, I can't very well be mad at the man."

"Even if he needs help again?" Alessan added.

"We'll see, son," she answered. "For the moment you need to earn your meagre keep from this old woman. Get changed and help Varis clean the upper floors. A second merchant caravan is set to arrive early tomorrow morning, and I'll not have the place looking like a sty."

"Yes, Mother," Alessan smiled while making a hasty retreat.

Corian had concocted the story hoping that Shani Oakleaf would allow her son the freedom of a few more visits out to the camp that month. So far, the wealthy merchant's plan seemed to have worked beautifully. By the end of autumn, Corian would be heading northeast towards the capital of the lands ruled by the Northern Council. After resupplying in Glenvale, the master merchant planned on braving the long overland route south to sell his wares far from the semi-frozen trade routes of the north.

By nightfall, every bone and muscle in Alessan's body had decided to complain. Not used to such physical exertion, he could barely keep the orders on his carrying tray as he served the many guests in the common room. He put on an energetic and cheerful outward appearance, as he did not want his mother to grow suspicious of his behaviour. A man who spends his day working on accounts is not someone who should be physically exhausted. Quietly thanking the gods that the Sylvani had not been given leave to drink in the inn this evening, he finished his chores relatively early and headed up to his room. Collapsing on his mattress with nary a thought to undressing, he fell asleep instantly.

Alessan Oakleaf dreamed that night. He did so almost every night, often about his hopes for the future. He would sometimes be a Lumber, or even fighting as a mercenary captain in the summer wars. With increasing frequency, he had also started to dream about some of the young ladies who lived in or around town. A small notebook at the side of his bed held the memories of everything except those particular dreams. This night, the strange visitor named C'Aelis was the focus.

He found himself in the Aeldenwood, striding purposefully along a marble path that he knew did not really exist. The trail was flanked not by wild and twisted branches, but instead by straight and proud trees that stood like guards on either side. In his hand he held a jeweled dagger, the golden blade glittering brightly in his grasp. The soft-spoken voice of the mysterious C'Aelis whispered inside his mind. Falling to his knees, Alessan clutched his head as pain ripped through his thoughts, much like it had earlier that morning. His vision clouded over, and he was threatened with a loss of consciousness. As darkness descended, he thrashed about, and the golden weapon fell from his tingling fingers.

He awoke in a small stone chamber filled with candlelight throwing shadows play-fully against the ancient stonework. Glancing around the room, he was struck by the sad disrepair of the furniture. Old parchments covered by thick layers of dust sat on sagging shelves, and a grand oak desk was arranged in the center of the room. Ales-san stretched his taut muscles and strode over to a small window. Staring through it revealed an impenetrable darkness, and he was taken by the smooth stonework ledge that rested beneath his fingers. Straining to see something in the gloom, he missed the soft tread of footsteps closing in behind him. As a hand came down to settle on his shoulder, he spun around and loosed a scream.

Opening his eyes in a panic, Alessan sat bolt upright in his bed. He heard his scream tail off into the air. Shivering uncontrollably, he peeled off his shirt. Damp with sweat, he tossed the top into the far corner of his bedchamber. Clutching his sides, he tried to stop the shaking as he reached for his notebook. He took a moment and scrawled a brief description of the unsettling dream.

Getting up, he made his way across the cold wooden floor and donned a new shirt. Still shivering, he turned away from his bed with sleep far from his mind, and trudged downstairs towards the now empty common room.

Hoping that Mallory had left a pot of stew out near the fire, Alessan glanced out a side window as he tiptoed quietly down the creaky stairs. He judged that it was still a few hours before dawn. As expected, the common room was empty of any customers. The fire in the great stone hearth sputtered weakly and, with minimal effort, he was able to ignite a healthy blaze that was soon crackling. Disappointed that no pot hung from the iron ring above the hearth, he was content to place his feet close to the comforting warmth.

Why had he been so rattled by such a dream?

There were no creatures of darkness, no beasts with fangs, no wolves, or bloodthirsty hounds. Besides the incredible pain that had pierced his mind, a pain that he attributed to C'Aelis' strange speaking talent, his dream had been somewhat unremarkable.

So he had walked on a forest path and looked about a small chamber. What of it? Confused, he leaned back against one of the wooden tables in the room.

"Can't sleep, Ally?"

"What? —" he stammered. For a brief instant, he had been immersed in the dream once more. The startling voice jogged his memory, setting him on edge for the second time that evening.

"It's only me, silly," giggled Kayla. His sister gave him an exasperated look as she walked towards the table, two steaming mugs of cider, and a long piece of hard bread balanced precariously in her arms. "Well don't just sit there, Ally, grab the mugs, please. Careful," she added, "they're very hot."

"Sorry," Alessan apologized sheepishly.

"Why are you so jumpy tonight? You looked like you were on your last legs before you even started working this evening. I notice these things you know," she said, taking a seat beside him and pulling a woolen shawl tightly around her shoulders. Cupping the mug of cider between both hands, she sighed and closed her eyes.

"Just a bad dream is all," he replied, carefully sipping his own drink. "Yourself?"

"Every once in while I just can't sleep," she shrugged. "Seems the harder I try to sleep, the harder my mind works at keeping my eyes open." Kayla gave him a side-long glance. "So tell me about this dream. It's been a long time since you've been unable to sleep because of a nightmare."

"You're right, but back in those days, father was always..." Alessan trailed off. An awkward moment of silence followed his reply. The death of their father had been hard on both of the Oakleaf children; but if it had served any purpose, Darren Oakleaf's children had grown extremely close. Leaning her head against his shoulder, Kayla closed her eyes.

"It wasn't really a nightmare, Kay, just one of those weird dreams that can leave you feeling different."

"I have those sometimes. You probably wrote it down in that silly notebook of yours though, right?" she chided him. The notebook had been a fiercely contested item when the two siblings were younger. Kayla was forever finding new ways to discover and hide the cherished book. Had she not kept a small journal of her own thoughts, Alessan may never have seen his beloved journal again.

"Kayla, do you believe in the old legends?" Alessan questioned.

"The ones I sing about?" she replied.

"I mean all of the legends. Bael, Gort Greatwood, the Under Wars, or even the stories of Queen Eris of Magnach," he answered. "I used to think they were all real people at one time or another, but now I wonder if they are only fanciful tales."

"I know that when I sing about Bael, Eris or even the Gorimm, I can feel something channel through my body. It's an energy, and I take strength in those powerful feelings. I like to believe that it is the audience and their belief in the story being told that gives me such a sensation."

"But do you truly believe in them?" Alessan pressed.

Kayla took a moment to consider her answer. Alessan smiled as he watched his sister's round face crinkle as she weighed the matter carefully.

"I believe they all have some form of truth to them. I hope they *are* real. I know they can't all be stories simply made up to entertain children."

"No, I guess they can't," Alessan whispered and hugged his sister close. Sharing the shawl with her brother, Kayla snatched the last bite of bread.

They chatted quietly about a great many things that night, but Alessan found it hard to push the dream completely from his unsettled mind. As the feeble grey dawn heralded the coming of a new day, he crawled back into his bed. And though he slept, a deep and restful repose remained elusive.

Companies must be registered at the onset of every season. Failure to comply will result in the refusal of contract rights for the upcoming Ca'lenbam. Grievances proving that unforeseen circumstances delayed registration can always be submitted at said Gathering.
—*Mercenary Code of Conduct*

CHAPTER VII

Garchester, Protectorate

D arkness... impenetrable... menacing...
 Once again, the nightmarish terror assaulted him as he slept.

Spinning, Gavin could feel the hot breath of his pursuers through the tangled maze of undergrowth, yet he could not see them. There was only darkness, and it beckoned him from beyond. He could sense his thoughts being shredded like fine parchment. His muscles were cripplingly contorted, and he lost his balance as he tried to run. The creatures arrived, filled with unyielding hate, and with deadly fangs exposed. He screamed and was consumed by the black void...

Gavin awoke with a start, his heart hammering in his chest. Breathing heavily, he assessed his surroundings in an instant, sighing softly once he realized he was safe. He had escaped the horror for another night.

Turning his head, he was comforted by the usual sounds of the company ready-ing for breakfast. The clang of pots could be heard, as well as the voices of men who had pulled morning duty. Usually a chore delegated to the greener recruits of the company, this morning at least things had changed, and gruff veteran voices pierced through Gavin's haze of sleepiness. Ethan had, as ordered, placed veteran warriors on the early shift, giving his squad a good night's rest in case they were needed that morning.

Cocking an ear to the proceedings, Gavin heard nothing untoward, and walked over to the small wash basin Caolte had left in the tent. Splashing water over the entirety of his head, Gavin shivered as the cold shocked him fully awake. Donning the company tabard over expertly crafted chainmail and snatching a pair of leather gloves, the Fey'Derin captain stepped out into the sunlight.

"Morning, Captain," called out several soldiers. Each snapped a sharp salute and returned promptly to their chores. Gavin sighted Caolte and Brock seated by one of the fires; the older clansman was whittling away at a piece of wood, the younger officer deftly sharpening his sword. He called out a greeting, accepting a mug of hot tea and a hard biscuit as he joined them.

"She's getting colder these days," said Gavin around a mouthful of food.

"Bah! If we were near Marshlair this time of year, you'd be slogging through ice and mud whilst freezing your toes off," exclaimed Caolte.

"Still warmer down south than up near the Shield," Brock added. "Does this look sharp enough, Captain?" he passed his weapon down to Gavin.

Thumbing a finger up and down the length of the blade, he nodded and smiled. "T'is fine, Brock. I also wouldn't be familiar with the climate of the Iron Shield."

"Why's that, Captain?"

"Honestly never been there, Sergeant. Furthest north I've travelled would be near the mountains. I stayed there for a few days while running an escort for Black Company," Gavin replied.

"Black Company was your first, eh Captain?"

"Yes," he paused thoughtfully. "It was a long time ago."

"Back in your younger days?" added Caolte, winking at Brock. It was an ongoing company ruse to heckle the captain about his age. Although most men deemed he had lived almost thirty summers, Gavin had never revealed the truth. It was common knowledge among the soldiers that when the Fey were founded, now five summers past, Gavin Silveron had been the youngest mercenary to ever lead his own company.

Shaking his head at the laughter that rippled around the fire, Gavin finished his biscuit. A comfortable silence, one that only soldiers who have spent years campaigning together could appreciate, settled over the site. Even in the cold of the morning, somehow everyone was warmed by each other's company. Such was how this strange collection of men, all failed mercenaries before rising to fame in the Fey'Derin, lived and enjoyed their second lease on life.

"Is Coren around this morning?" Gavin asked.

Scratching his moustache, the older lieutenant finished a long drink of steaming tea before answering. "Bider? I sent him out earlier than usual. You know how he gets when we approach the cities."

"A little excited today, was he?" added the Fey'Derin captain.

"A little! Hah, he was practically humming with energy," Caolte replied. "I told him we needed an idea of what we're coming up against. He'll be busy sniffing around every rock and pebble this side of the city. I don't expect he'll be around until we break at midday."

"Are we anticipating trouble today, sir?" Sergeant Fearan inquired.

"No, no, Brock," Gavin shook his head. "Garchester won't be under siege until later this week. Not even Gadian Yarr can move men that quickly. With the Lady Farraine in Duke Berry's pocket, we'll have far less to defend against."

ଓଃ

With one hand shielding his eyes from the sun, Bider scanned the countryside. The sheer canyon cliffs had fallen off, only open fields, already harvested for the upcoming winter, greeted his gaze. Far off in the distance lay the outer walls of Garchester. From his vantage point atop a large outcropping, the Fey'Derin scout could make out heavy movement clogging the roads leading to the city. Large caravans, many overloaded with a myriad of household objects and supplies, crawled relentlessly forward. Families on foot were trying their best to slog through the muddied roads, parents urging their smaller children to keep up. For a city the captain expected to fall under siege, there seemed to be an urgency to the actions of all those seeking entry.

Bider frowned as he watched a small group of soldiers race furiously through the refugees. Even from such a distance, he could easily denote the telltale signs of men who had recently seen battle. Standards fluttered raggedly in the wind, blood stained the armour of the riders, and an obvious desperation lay in their attempts to push through the steady stream of travelers blocking their way.

"Why do they look behind?" Bider wondered aloud.

Plaintive cries, faint but relatively clear, drifted into hearing range. Concerned, Bider scanned to the west once more. It was now apparent that Garchester may not be as safe as Captain Silveron had first believed. Barely within view, he spied the beginnings of a skirmish between defenders of the city and another company of soldiers wearing scarlet and black, their banners displaying a snarling wolf-like beast. Within moments, panic ripped through the packed throng, and refugees scattered while the battle raged furiously close by.

Bider paused to count, as best he could, the numbers involved in the battle and sprinted off. He reached his tethered horse as the clanging tones of the city alarm bells rang out over the fields. Urging his mount into action, he crouched low over the steed's mane. He knew the captain would want answers if the Fey'Derin were to respond in enough time to make a difference.

Speeding back in the direction of his company, it wasn't long before Lady Farraine's slow-moving wagon came into view. Ignoring the soldiers calling his name as he tore through the procession, Bider headed directly to his superior.

"The city is under attack, Sergeant!" he reported as he pulled up hard on the reins. Ethan Shade commanded the vanguard this morning, and his Eagle Runners were currently out on patrol. This mattered little to the flamboyant sergeant, turning confidently to the man at his side.

"Aton, alert the outriders. I want the Eagles assembled here quickly. Also, send word down the line and ask the Captain to come forward immediately. Understood?"

Nodding in reply, the mercenary raced off. Ethan addressed Bider. "Seems like Yarr might have a trick or two up his sleeve."

"Not sure, but I know —"

"Save your breath, Bider," Ethan interrupted, "No sense in you telling your story twice. Let's wait for the Captain."

"Aye, sir," Bider replied.

* * *

Captain Silveron looked anything but pleased as his mount raced to the front of the column. The company had already halted their advance, and a flurry of activity now replaced the quiet calm of the morning. Soldiers equipped their armor and checked their supplies as the alarm bells from Garchester now reached their ears.

"Report, Coren," Gavin commanded, the remaining officers also reigning in their mounts.

"A strong force has attacked what can only be the city's rearguard on the east road. Duke Berry can't have more than a few dozen men out there at the moment."

"Numbers on the attackers? Hazards?" Ossric demanded.

"Could be a whole company," Bider replied. "Over three hundred refugees in the vicinity, with little to no weaponry. They're panicked and scared. I counted at least fifty to sixty attackers with one standard in the mix. I don't recognize them."

"What is this standard they carry?" Caolte asked as the officers continued to ready for battle.

"Black and scarlet tunic with either a wolf or coyote as their figurehead," he answered.

"Bah! That's no wolf, Captain that has to be a hyena!" Sergeant McConnal interjected. "And we all know what that means - Khali and his bloody Reavers."

"Reavers?" Bider queried.

"Yes, Coren," Gavin responded, "Not good news at all to hear of them, for they are no friends of ours." A dark look glinted dangerously in Gavin's eyes as he continued, "Sergeant Fearan you have command while I'm gone. If anything should happen to me, make sure the Lady Farraine arrives safely in the city. Duke Berry will know what to do with her. Ossric, Ethan and Caolte, you have one minute to rally as many soldiers in your squads as possible. We ride out immediately."

As the officers turned to leave, Bider caught a short exchange out of the corner of his eye. The captain paused to grip Sergeant McConnal on the arm, giving the big man a stern look.

"We travel light, Ossric. We need speed, not power right now. You'll get your chance to settle your score with Khali, but I need you to be in control. Understood?" he whispered sternly.

"If you insist." Ossric grunted his reply.

Adjusting his leather armor as he turned to meet up with his fellow Eagle Runners, Bider considered the men he would soon face in battle. Khali's Reavers were well known to those who had been following Captain Silveron for years. The feud between the two companies was quite interesting, but Bider knew he must deal with the matter at hand. *Survive the battle before you, or you will become history,* he chided himself.

Finished with his preparations, Bider rode out with Sergeant Shade and Orn Surefoot. They raced west with less than one hundred mercenaries. Surely it was enough men, the scout hoped, to turn the tide of the skirmish near Garchester.

෬

Leaning low over his mount, Gavin was angry for underestimating the capabilities of his enemies. It was a rare mistake, but the gnawing guilt of the error hit him in the pit of his stomach. He remembered all too well the last time he had been overconfident. There were far too many gravestones belonging to his friends to easily forget.

Dispelling the painful memories, he caught the hard stare of his most senior officer; Caolte Burnaise knew exactly what he had been thinking. The veteran campaigner gauged the thoughts of others with an uncanny surety that bordered on the arcane. The only thing Caolte loved more than his wife, was battle; and into such a fray, the Fey'Derin now rode.

Giving his companion a confident nod and adding a shout of his own, Gavin bore down on his horse while surveying the men clustered tightly around him. They wore looks of grim determination, with eyes focused on the terrain ahead, and anxious to wield sword, axe, and bow. His gaze paused momentarily on any soldier with a nervous expression. With a simple glance and brave nod, he projected to each man his overall confidence. Gavin believed with certainty in the great value of each and every man.

With deadly speed, the lightly armoured Eagle Runners under Ethan Shade's command engaged the enemy. Following closely behind and bracing himself for the first blow, Gavin drew his blade and wielded it with a tight grip. Even as it cut deeply into the side of a scarlet clad rider, he was quick to assess the tactical situation.

There were many soldiers, mainly on foot, circling the terrified refugees, shielding them as best they could. Duke Berry had reacted promptly to the incursion made by Khali's Reavers. Yellow clad soldiers continued to pour forth from the city gates, defiant as they struggled through the mass of people desperately seeking the protection of the high city walls.

Blocking a slash from a nearby attacker, Gavin spun to his left and whirled his blade skillfully across the assailant's unprotected throat. Turning away from the torrent of blood that followed, the Fey'Derin captain rode to the defense of three men who fought beside the fallen body of one of their own. Charging two enemies from behind, Gavin and two of Ossric's Axemen broke through the ranks, giving one of them time enough to sling the fallen man over the side of his horse. Barking orders, he sent the wounded man towards the city, one of his comrades leading the escort.

The Fey'Derin pushed forward, connecting with what remained of the city's rearguard. Exhausted soldiers fell into step behind a wall of Fey'Derin steel. Realizing that they would soon be overwhelmed, the scarlet and black clad attackers hurriedly formed deeper ranks. They fought on, and slowly began to give ground as their wounded were shuttled to the rear.

As fresh Fey'Derin continued to ride hard into the clash, Khali's men turned and fled, their opportunity to inflict any more punishment on the refugees was now lost. Caolte and Ethan led the Eagle Runners after them at pace, inflicting few casualties, but ensuring a full retreat.

Acknowledging his men with sword held high, Gavin raised his voice in a triumphant shout. A roar of approval erupted from the soldiers. Noticing the powerful Ossric at the edge of the field, Gavin dismounted and joined his officer.

"A good accounting of ourselves, Captain!" the big man clasped forearms with his commander.

"That it was. Khali won't soon forget the blood debt we owe his men," Gavin paused to wipe his long sword on the hem of a fallen Reaver's cloak.

Ossric smiled through his thick, braided beard, "The lads and I will see that it is paid. They're fortunate I got off my horse or I'd still be hounding them with Ethan and the Lieutenant right now."

"In any case Sergeant, you have wounded to attend to," Gavin commented. "And remember, I need your temperance in command on the field, not vengeance."

"Aye, sir," the sergeant mumbled his reply.

"I'm heading directly to the keep. I need to inform Duke Berry that his prize will be arriving soon. With the enemies encroaching, he'll want to know that his bargaining stake is safe. Organize the men, and I'll meet you at the gates as soon as I can," Gavin said as he pulled himself back into the saddle.

"Should I inquire about our lodgings or assume we're in the northern quarter as before?"

"Assemble at the gates and escort the lady to the keep if I haven't returned."

Ossric chuckled, "I've never had the privilege of being a noble's escort before, Captain."

Gavin waved to his sergeant, turned his mount, and rode towards the chaos clogging the roadway into Garchester.

ᙡ

Furnael Berry was one of the last remaining nobles of old blood in the south of Caledun. That he had attained the title of duke, honoring a tradition long abandoned by the present leaders of Kal Maran, was unexpected and made him something of a firebrand.

With the Shattering of Nations had come swift persecution against the conspirators involved in the assassination of the High King. Most of the nobility, once a generous complement of dukes, earls, viscounts, and barons, were stripped of their titles and simply disappeared.

In that terrible time of anarchy, not even the men who had orchestrated the king's downfall wished to give the appearance that they meant to lord their power over the common man. The men of the north had eventually lapsed in their persecution, naming in the present-day many of their city leaders after the codes of the old nobility.

In the Protectorate, the alliance of southern city-states governing the resources of their rich countrysides, remained opposed to the dictates of a forgotten era; except, of course, for the erstwhile Berry family.

As Gavin made his way through the winding streets of Garchester, he noted the preparations the duke had taken in protecting the city. Soldiers wearing the soft yellow tunics of the House of Berry were numerous and alert. Large stacks of arrows could be seen leaning against almost every crenel along the outer wall, and the harsh clangs of the smiths surpassed even the raucous cries of hagglers and shop owners. Duke Berry had not been idle these past summer months.

Deeper into the city, he determined that the gates to the keep were well guarded. Sharp-eyed soldiers manned the walls and flanked the gateways. Ignoring the dangers within could also spell disaster. It would not be the first time a siege was averted if the reigning nobleman was to fall to an assassin's blade. The leaders of Caledun, north and south alike, used whatever means necessary to increase their territory and wealth. Little trust existed between these men of power across the land.

The guardsmen were cordial as he gained entry to the audience chamber. The duke had obviously given word that Gavin was to be allowed entry immediately. Although based near the northern town of Briar, Gavin had spent enough summers down south to have garnered his company some amount of favoritism. He had fought for Duke Berry during the past two seasons, which meant that his infrequent visits were mostly tolerated by the house guards.

Gavin entered the long greeting hall with its beautiful tiled marble. Banners of old hung from the rafters, depicting the various Houses that had once proudly ruled over the region. Garchester had an illustrious and bloody history. Continuing with the reign of the Duke Berry, the city had seen its walls stormed six times, yet breached only twice.

Conscious of his ringing footfalls, Gavin entered the cavernous meeting room and recognized some of the men and women gathered near the large chairs from which the duke usually conducted his business. In the far corner of the room were two beautifully carved ebony thrones, their likeness once adorning every city within the land of Old Caledun.

The High King's thrones were stunning to behold, immaculately carved, and possessing an exquisite ebony polish. Sadly, they were fewer in number than they had once been. Once again, following the breaking of the nations under the High King's rule, many cities threw down the seats of their one-time leader, a final defiance to his rule. Others though, left them alone, worried about old wives tales that spoke of curses against those who would further defame the rightful king.

In any case, Gavin knew that few now waited for a rebirth in the kingship, few even cared. With only the mad King Serian Rhone of the *Drayenmark* a true descendant of the old line, there remained little hope for change.

"Captain Silveron! It is good to see you once more," boomed a loud voice. "I owe you my thanks for your timely arrival."

"There is no need, my lord," Gavin replied with a short bow. "Your men had things under control, even as my company arrived. Khali incurred casualties that will delay the coming siege."

"You know you are a tough man to please, my young Captain. One day I'll get you to accept when I offer you my thanks," Furnael Berry declared with a smile.

The duke had seen well over forty summers, but still looked a man half his age. His family line was long-lived and his thick mop of raven black hair showed not even a streak of grey. Furnael was tall and sturdy, his stature owing to the soldier he professed to be. Gavin respected Berry's ability with the blade but it was his tactical genius that had garnered the boisterous nobleman much acclaim.

"So tell me, was Pier's Brigade where I hoped it would be?" the duke inquired knowingly.

"Aye, my lord," Gavin replied. "We attacked at night and slew as few as possible."

"And the Lady Farraine?" The duke asked in a whisper.

"She is well. One of my officers will be arriving with your guest later today. She is unharmed, but extremely disagreeable," Gavin reported.

"Hmmm, yes." Furnael retorted. "That woman is a snake even on the best of days. I owe you a great deal, Captain."

"The bounty price will be more than sufficient, my lord. And we have already agreed upon the fee for retaining the Fey'Derin's services for the duration of the siege, have we not?" Gavin asked.

"Always the mercenary, right Silveron?" the duke commented. "Everything is ready, and the documents are awaiting your signature. They are in your quarters."

"The same arrangements as before?"

"Of course."

"And my men?" Gavin added.

As the question was asked, a squat man with only a few remaining wisps of white hair left on his head, touched the duke lightly on the arm. "If I may, my lord?" he asked.

"Of course, Gerant, of course." Duke Berry smiled agreeably.

"They are to be billeted in the eastern quarter. There are new barracks there that should easily accommodate your soldiers. If they need any medical assistance, just send word to Captain Morase at the central gates."

"Thank you, Chancellor Gerant."

"You are most welcome, Captain Silveron," the older functionary replied. Frowning, he continued, "I'll remind the servants to set out a clean set of clothing for you, sir."

Gavin nodded politely in the man's direction. "You are too kind, Chancellor, and it would be doubly appreciated."

"Now, I'll expect to see you at dinner," Duke Berry stated. "There are a few men I want you to meet, including a few captains whose services I have managed to procure in the last few days. I'll want your assessment at the war council later this evening."

"Understood, my lord," Gavin replied with another slight bow. As he left the hall, he gave a nod to a few officers waiting to see the nobleman. Three northern companies, in addition to his own, were already in attendance. It seems that friends in the south are becoming harder to find for the flamboyant Duke of Garchester, Gavin mused.

☙

That evening, Gavin stifled a chuckle as he entered the keep's council chamber. Duke Berry was rubbing at a bright red imprint that had recently appeared on his right cheek. It was apparent that the Lady Farraine had met with the resident Lord of Garchester. That the tall noble had been on the receiving end of another one of the woman's tirades was no secret. More than a few of the hardened soldiers in the room had trouble focusing on anything other than the fresh mark while addressing him that day.

Duke Berry valiantly ignored the looks and concentrated on the collection of maps covering the immense wooden council table. As Gavin entered, the noble looked up and motioned him over with a wave of his hand.

"Captain Silveron, thank you for joining us," he said as he gestured towards the two men at his side. "I would like you to meet Alvin Draven, captain of the Helmsmen and Duncan Sledge, captain of the Red Falconers."

Gavin greeted both officers with a vigorous handshake. "Pleased to meet you, gentlemen."

"Along with the Fey'Derin, and my house soldiers, we are currently the leaders of close to eight hundred men," Furnael Berry commented.

"And the armies of Lord Dalemen? What can we expect of their deployment?" Gavin asked.

Sifting through a thick stack of parchments, Captain Draven withdrew a detailed list of company names and troop numbers.

"At the very least," he began, "we can expect nearly twenty-two hundred. If the remainder of the other companies near the bottom of that list actually arrive, we could be facing three thousand enemy soldiers."

"He has ten companies? How can he afford so many?" Gavin exclaimed as his mind registered the new information. The cost of that many men would be enormous. Most battles throughout the summer pitted three to four companies per side. Employers simply could not afford the price to feed and supply that large a force.

Furnael shrugged, "Although Lord Dalemen is fronting these armies, Gadian Yarr is funding the better part of any fees owed. As we all know, his coffers are deep."

"His influence hurts us as well. He has required less men in the east fighting near Matanis this year. Few companies dare to stand against him. That city is weak, with only a token defense beyond what the Grey Rangers and Herod's men can provide," Gavin added.

"Will it hold?" Captain Sledge asked.

"I believe it might," Furnael answered with an uncertain grimace. "Lord Baleford is leading the defense. He's a capable tactician, but he'll be hard pressed. He can expect high casualties and that means we may lose more allied companies before next spring's *Ca'lenbam*."

"Forcing Dalemen out of this fight would be a severe blow to both his numbers and morale. It would certainly make Yarr look far less shrewd," Captain Draven offered.

"How severely?" Gavin pressed.

"It would cut his force in half." Duke Berry responded after a moment spent pondering the situation. "To save face, he will not allow any company with ties to his money draw blades while his consort is in mortal danger. At least eleven hundred would stand down."

Gavin followed the duke's assessment. "Those men would stay in the vicinity, but until her Ladyship is released, Lord Dalemen is effectively neutralized."

"Will they still attempt a siege with such a loss?" Captain Draven asked. "Our soldiers would be at an advantage."

"Have no doubt, Gadian Yarr wants this city and he wants it badly," Duke Berry cursed. "I hold more than a few resources he'd like to see fall into his lap, including the mines along the *Karipaal* range. I also hold the key to the defense of the east. If he hadn't slipped those men north around the Caeronwood so late in the summer, only the Seracen Pass would have been open through the mountains, and I would have strategically blocked it with my own men."

"Seems like bad business to attack, knowing your allies may very well be slaughtered." Gavin frowned.

"He'll attack no matter the cost. He needs Garchester if he wants to control the east. The west is already under his sway, but I'll be damned if I let a man get that powerful," the duke avowed. "There hasn't been a noble with such power in nearly two hundred years, and if someone doesn't stop his march across the Protectorate territories, he'll stand uncontested."

"Well then, it seems we have no choice in the matter," Captain Sledge said. Reaching into the pile of maps on the table he smiled grimly as he pulled one and placed it before the other three men. Gavin nodded his approval as they looked over a detailed map of Garchester.

"Gentlemen, we have a long night ahead of us," Furnael sighed, looking in turn at each of the captains under his employ. "We can assume that the siege will begin tomorrow. There is the final defense of the city yet to plan."

The sun's rays were already spreading across the fields next to Garchester as Gavin stumbled into his quarters. Hoping to steal a few hours of sleep before he was needed once more, the Fey'Derin Captain slowly pulled his boots from his feet. Sitting quietly on his bed, he glanced briefly out the small window of his chamber and out across the very same road his men had fought upon a day earlier. Only a few scattered rags and blankets remained where, not so long ago, hundreds of terrified labourers had nearly lost their lives.

Comforted by the silence, Gavin rested in his bed with one arm covering his eyes in order to block out the bright morning sun. Sadly, he knew that the new dawn would bring none of the same peace. Instead, there would be the chaos of war and the death of many. Drifting off to sleep, he tried his best to hang on to the serene moment. Only the gods knew if it was to be his last.

Of quiet days and glory, they stand the test of time. Alone amongst friends, of the tenders they yearn.
—Unknown

CHAPTER VIII

Briar, Northern Council

To Alessan Oakleaf, the Black Boar had suddenly become a much smaller place. The stout wooden passageways and busy common room that had once loomed so large, now seemed quaint and cramped. One visit to that beckoning world so close beyond the gates of Briar, had produced in him a bubbling impatience.

Alessan found it strange that a place so important to him could so easily be cast aside. Now, when he picked up a mop or slogged through another day in the stables, it wore down his constitution. Each command barked by the cook, and every whispered assurance from his mother, drove him to frustration. He was no longer content in taking in the rich aromas drifting through the rooms and hallways of the inn; smells that used to elicit many fond memories. He wished only for the sweet fragrance of moss, fresh grass between his toes, and the brisk bite of wind on an autumn afternoon. He longed for a refreshing drink from one of the streams along the edge of the Aeldenwood. Above all else, Alessan Oakleaf wished fervently for his freedom.

With his mind awakened by the new experiences made possible by Corian Praxxus, Alessan took every opportunity to join the master merchant at Oakfeld Patch. His mother continued to believe that he was being paid to work on the man's accounts, and so he did, to a certain degree. Corian spent the day lecturing Alessan on the art of mercantilism, and revealing many of his strategies and goals. That Praxxus was business savvy was never in doubt, but Alessan quickly realized that he genuinely liked the man. He was boastful to be sure, but not unkind in his demeanor, as the merchants of Innes Vale were often portrayed. He encouraged Alessan to ask questions about the trade, and seemed delighted with the opportunity to teach a willing student.

Although wealthy beyond belief, Corian Praxxus listened to what Alessan had to say. And so, the *ba'caech* from Briar, someone who had never been accepted by the Lumbers, was filled with pride whenever a Sylvani messenger arrived with a small pouch of coins and a missive requesting his presence. Both his mother and sister grew suspicious as his time with the merchant increased. Yet seeing him truly happy for the first time since his father had passed, they would always agree and grant him permission to leave.

Although Master Praxxus had become somewhat of a mentor, Alessan still pondered the encounter in the Aeldenwood with the peculiar figure by the water's edge. C'Aelis had spoken to him through the very thoughts in his mind, and he yearned for answers. *Could the long-forgotten Gorimm have returned? And if so, why? Where have they been since disappearing so long ago?*

These questions gnawed at him while he slept, consumed him during his menial tasks, and tugged at him whenever he walked under the eaves of that Great Wood. Praxxus, to his credit, noticed the curious behavior, but Alessan refused to elaborate on his worries. Other than the brief and carefully worded conversation with his sister after the incident, he had spoken to no one about the mysterious meeting. Sitting with his feet dangling lazily in the water of a newly discovered stream, Alessan tried his best to push aside the constant thoughts.

"You have that serious expression on your face again, lad," remarked Corian. The oversized merchant lay floating on his back, stark-naked in the waist deep water, and basking luxuriously in the sunshine. Alessan shook his head, trying in vain to dispel the white-bellied image from his mind. He could see that Corian was apparently not embarrassed by his ample girth.

"Just thinking about how my mother and sister are getting on without me, Master Praxxus. It's not usual for me to have missed so many days of work. Come to think of it, in a given year, I can't say I've ever missed so many," Alessan replied.

"Your mother is making a tidy little profit off me, young Oakleaf, so don't fret too much. She knows as well as I that I'll be leaving soon enough, and things will return to normal," he replied.

"What if I don't want everything to go back to how it was?" Alessan asked quietly. "What if I want to be more than just a stable boy?"

"Now what do you mean by that?" the big man pressed.

Shrugging his shoulders, Alessan dropped his eyes to his lap and muttered a quick, inaudible reply.

Standing up abruptly, Corian Praxxus drew himself out of the water, his naked form dripping profusely as he towered over the younger man. "Now see here, Alessan Oakleaf. If I have taught you anything, by the gods, I hope I've taught you to stand up and make your voice heard!" the merchant barked.

"Your problem isn't that no one respects you, it's that you refuse to be heard. You cower in a corner, pretending to care about what those bloody Lumbers think, but you don't have the stones to say or do anything about it! Oh you'll complain, that's for sure, but that's all you'll do! You've a sharp mind in that body of yours, and you refuse to be anything but what others have already deemed your lot in life!"

Stunned and angered by the passionate words, Alessan rushed to his feet, planting himself firmly in front of Corian Praxxus and looking him straight in the eyes. "I believe you have no right to tell me what is wrong with my life!" he hissed menacingly. "You can't possibly understand."

Laughing sarcastically, the merchant continued, his bulk quivering with every word. "You think everyone grows up with respect and a good life?! Do you honestly think you're the only boy ever to grow up with adversity, Alessan? Listen to yourself for a moment."

Alessan looked away, and Praxxus continued in a quieter tone. "You've had a tough life, I'll give you that, but I was born into a poor family. I never let my family's lack of wealth stop me from attaining my own dreams. I wanted to travel the world, and so I have, from the fortresses of the Iron Shield, to the far off deserts of

Kaleen. But *I* made it happen, boy. *I* clawed, *I* scratched, *I* fought and pushed myself through all of the barriers, and who's to say you can't do the same?"

"I'm not you, Master Praxxus. I can't do it alone," Alessan slumped back down near the stream's edge, his hands clasped tightly together.

Grabbing his robe from the shore, the Corian covered himself and sat down heavily at Alessan's side. Breathing deeply, he put a large arm around Alessan's thin shoulders. "I never said I did it alone, Alessan. There was a time when I needed help, and you know what?"

"What?" Alessan whispered. "I asked," he replied quietly.

"Asked?"

"Aye, lad, I asked for help," Corian Praxxus replied.

༄

Alessan had always been attuned to his dreams. Being a heavy sleeper, he had somehow tapped the uncanny ability to clearly remember his nightly imaginings. Beginning when he was a young boy, he faithfully kept a journal at his bedside. Filled from cover to cover with strange and exciting stories, he had painstakingly recorded everything in as much detail as possible.

As he grew older, and the despair of his frustrating life started weighing him down, his dreams seemed to darken. Clouded by inner doubts and turmoil, he had lost the ability to remember them, and it had been some time since they were at the forefront of his mind. Now, since meeting the silver-haired man in the woods, the clarity of the nighttime visions returned.

For three consecutive nights, he dreamt of C'Aelis. They were not exact recreations of that afternoon by the water's edge, but they were remarkably similar nonetheless. In each of the dreams, he spent his time wandering under the eaves of the Aeldenwood with the stranger.

He was calm and more relaxed than he could ever hope to be. His body felt stronger, and the daily aches and pains that were second nature had receded. His arm was still shriveled, but there was a healthy glow to the skin that was surprising. And walking beside him was C'Aelis, the slight impish man offering a supportive arm as Alessan struggled to avoid slipping on the thin layer of frost that coated the ground.

The Aeldenwood was beautiful. The ancient gnarled trunks of the large trees dominated the area, each and every one unique. Alessan was sure that every tree had a fantastic story to tell. The ground, although lightly dusted by the weather, was soft and yielding as they tread upon it. Oddly, the deepest cold of winter never penetrated the strange woods.

The contempt for the forest, shared by all the people of Briar, seemed absurd when surrounded by such serene beauty. In the distance, the gentle rushing of water could be heard, the sound soothing and, regardless of the temperature, inviting. All around them, life was abound. Be it through a thick piece of dangling brown moss, or the defiant green leaves fighting off the approaching winter; the forest was alive.

Both travelers found a large boulder to sit upon. They rested and enjoyed the bold rays of sunlight making their way through the thick canopy of leaves looming overhead. Alessan was certain that they spoke as they often stopped moving and stared intently into each other's eyes for long periods of time. And yet, he could remember nothing of what was said. In that moment of the dream, he was a disconnected spectator, a presence flitting about the edges of the trees, hoping to glean some knowledge from the two figures he observed.

And with every vision there came a moment of panic, a disturbance in the surrounding forest that heralded the end. Darkness would creep up menacingly, and a chorus of wolf howls would shatter the peaceful scene. Fear would overtake him, and he would awaken.

Not long after his first visit to Oakfeld Patch, disturbing rumours began making their way to the Black Boar. With the details discussed in hushed tones, many Lumbers wore grave expressions that bespoke of tragedy. Bran Elmwood, a well-respected man and member of the Guild, had gone missing. An excursion to his homestead was planned by members of the Guild in the hopes that they would find Bran unharmed, but many held little hope.

Stubborn Lumbers who refused to give up their family homes, even after the Aeldenwood had encroached upon their fields, were often never seen again. For generations now, the Aeldenwood had claimed not only Lumbers, but entire households. Rare were the cases where any sign of the disappearances were unearthed. It was as if they had simply vanished, with nary a word to their neighbours, relatives, or friends.

Alessan was certain Bran's disappearance did not bode well for the region, or himself. His mother would be hard pressed to let her only son travel to Oakfeld Patch on the heels of such dark tidings. If there was one thing Alessan had come to expect from his current employer, it was the man's insatiable curiosity. Now for the first time since meeting Corian Praxxus, Alessan was afraid of where that curiosity might lead.

Not surprisingly, a note arrived early the next morning. The clean-shaven Sylvani recruit passed on the message while wearing a bored expression. Alessan assessed that the soldier would rather be doing anything other than delivering messages like some errand boy for the wealthy. Yet he was relatively polite, and the small sack full of coins was exactly as promised. Watching the messenger leave, Alessan fought hard to suppress his old dreams of one day becoming a soldier himself; a mercenary destined to gather fame and fortune on the battlefields of Kal Maran. Shrugging, he let the foolish daydream pass.

Corian was waiting for him near the Burning Hearth. The big man lay seated in its shadow, a long, thin wooden pipe sent smoke drifting lazily up towards the ceiling. As always, Alessan spared a quick glance at *Sorrow*, with its names emblazoned upon the ancient wood. The merchant seemed lost in thought. His lips were pursed slightly around the end of his pipe, and his eyes held a faraway look.

Gently sidling up near the man, Alessan cleared his throat before speaking. "Pardon me, Master Praxxus, I hope I'm not disturbing your thoughts, but I felt compelled to inform you of my arrival."

"Eh?" Corian murmured. "Oh, it's you, young Oakleaf. I was startled there for a moment."

"My apologies, sir," Alessan replied.

"No, no, don't apologize. You know, you can never leave an old man alone with his thoughts for too long. Do so and he's sure to wander a long ways down that path before all is done," Corian stated.

"Sound advice, sir."

"I'm not so sure that you'll be remembering that bit of advice anytime soon, you young rascal!" the merchant bellowed. Pausing to put away his pipe, he pulled himself to his feet. Stretching loudly, he jerked his head towards the tribute Alessan was trying to avoid.

"They carved that fellow's name in the trunk this morning. I've never experienced anything like it, what with nearly a hundred men here chanting and speaking soberly on his behalf. It was almost spiritual," he finished solemnly.

"To the people of my town, and others along the northern edges of the forest, it is very spiritual. Our reverence for the Lumbers is something every man, woman, and child in Briar considers to be essential, Master Praxxus," Alessan replied.

"You are a strange folk, Alessan," Corian said with a sad smile. "But you are also a brave and noble people. I grew up in a society where your standing and accumulated wealth defines you. In my travels, I have seen few lands, with the exception of far-off Kaleen, that stray from that basic tenet. And yet here, in the middle of the Northern Council territories, I find a small town that has built their faith around the axe, and that Great Wood."

"We're not really worried about politics and the like here in Briar. We chop down trees, and that's about all," he replied.

"That you do, lad that you do!" Corian smiled, a mischievous twinkle in his eyes. "And that brings us to the matter at hand."

"The matter at hand?" Alessan was puzzled.

"Seems that since that Lumber fellow went missing, everyone's on edge," the merchant began. "No one wants to answer any of my questions regarding this strange disappearance, and so I deem it's necessary to find out myself."

"How do you mean, Master Praxxus?"

"Well, to begin with, you must know the whereabouts of this man's homestead, do you not?" Corian pressed.

"I do," Alessan hesitated. "It's not far from the larger stream we visited only a few days ago."

"Excellent!" Corian exclaimed, "That is where we shall find our answer. No one disappears without a trace, Alessan."

It took a moment for the man's words to sink in before Alessan burst forth unexpectedly, "Are you mad?! By all accounts, a whole family has ceased to exist, and you want to go trudging about the woods on a hunt for whomever or whatever took them?"

"You can choose to take such an attitude, young Oakleaf, but I'm only curious," the big man huffed with disdain. "I promise I won't do anything drastic, and in any case, you are my guide. As your employer, I am reminding you of who pays your mother a tidy sum of coin..."

Defeated, Alessan grabbed his walking stick and headed for the doorway. Turning to don his warm woolen cloak, he glared at the merchant. "Coming, sir? We have a ways to travel and you know how slow I move."

ଔ

The Elmwood homestead lay nestled next to a small riverbank. Where once the view from the stout wooden cottage would have carried all the way to the river's edge, there now towered a multitude of thick trees. The tall trunks of the Aeldenwood choked the old farmer's fields, and almost nothing remained of the old barn that had once housed the livestock. The trees had grown almost to the walls of the cottage, yet they seemed to shy away from anything built by the hewn limbs of the forest. It was as if the forest was aware of the house's origins. The cottage itself was of a simple design; one floor high, it was well-built and serviceable. The people of Briar were not known to be skilled architects.

The two men spent the first hour carefully trudging through the woods near the house, hoping, as Corian suggested, to find some trace of what may have transpired. As Alessan had already concluded, their time was being ill-spent. Undaunted, the merchant suggested they enter the house itself. As the two travelers approached the rear door, Alessan suddenly felt the hair on the back of his neck rise. Catching a hesitant look creasing Corian's features, he spun around and squinted at the surrounding trees.

"I felt it too, lad," Corian whispered at his side. He had removed a long knife from his belt and held it outstretched in his hand.

"There is something in the woods, but what, I'm not sure..." Alessan responded, keeping his voice as low as possible.

"We'll circle the cottage. I'll go left and you to the right. If you see anything call out, and keep calling until I arrive," Corian instructed.

Nodding, Alessan slid noiselessly to the right side of the building. A strange terror gripped his heart and pressed painfully on his chest. Struggling to catch his breath, he turned around the corner of the cottage, and was sure he heard a muffled thump from nearby.

"Master Praxxus?" he hissed. "Master Praxxus?!" Fighting to keep his rising panic in check, he scanned the trees once more. Were those dark movements flitting among the old trunks of the forest? Biting his tongue to quell a scream, he spun, limping quickly towards where he had last seen his companion. Nearing the rear of the cottage, a shadow launched itself from the side and drove him to the ground. As the air exploded from his lungs, he tried desperately to scramble to his feet.

Stay down low, Alessan of the Oakleaf Clan. If you value your life, you must do as I say!

Shocked by the voice speaking in his mind, Alessan lifted his head from the earth, straining to catch a glimpse of C'Aelis; for he had no doubt it was the same voice. "My friend is somewhere close by. I need to find him," he whispered.

Your friend is stunned, but otherwise unhurt. He is stubborn, and I was left with no choice but to help him find a safe place in which to hide.

"Why are you here, C'Aelis?" Alessan asked, and then added the question that burned in his mind. "Did you take the Elmwoods?"

I hunt those that harmed your countrymen. You are in pain, Alessan, but within you there is a care and strength of which I can only marvel. There is much my people must atone for, and yet there is so little I can do...

Unable to control himself, Alessan let out a sob that wracked his small frame. He felt a soft hand gently grip his shoulder. That simple offer of comfort allowed him to catch his breath and turn to look directly in to that same stunning pair of emerald eyes he remembered. Once again, he found himself lost in those green orbs, pulled deeply into the brilliant swirls of colour that seemed to move within each eye.

You are strong, Alessan. I humbly request your pardon once more for opening my mind to you. I have become forgetful of my own strengths.

"Can I get up?" Alessan asked.

No, my friend. I must go now, but give me your word that you will remain here until the sounds of the forest have returned. Only at that time may you leave, until then you remain in danger.

"But what do you hunt?" Alessan asked.

In response, C'Aelis dropped to one knee and touched a finger to Alessan's temple. Immediately, a series of visions invaded his thoughts like a windstorm over the deserts of Kaleen. Dark twisted bodies, guttural sounds, and red eyes flashed through Alessan's battered mind. The visions raced by, too numerous to count, and then suddenly they were gone. Spinning around, he caught a glimpse of the green-cloaked figure slipping noiselessly through the trees.

I must have your word, Alessan of the Oakleaf Clan... the words echoed in the air.

After a moment's hesitation, Alessan replied softly, "You have my word, C'Aelis."

The two men spoke little as they returned to Oakfeld Patch that day. Corian had almost no recollection of the events, and believed he had fallen and hit his head. A bump the size of a small egg had materialized near the top of his balding crown of grey hair. Alessan caught him stealing worrisome glances towards the forest's edge during their sojourn home. It was apparent the master merchant was not being entirely truthful.

It was far past nightfall when Alessan arrived back at the inn. Although aching and exhausted, he paused to tidy up the common room, and sweep the floor of both the kitchen and the foyer. Adding a few logs to the large stone hearth, he wearily trudged up the stairs to his room. He was sound asleep the moment his head touched the soft pillow.

გ

Three days later, Corian Praxxus and his entourage left Briar. Of the encounter near the Elmwood homestead, he would say little. Alessan believed that C'Aelis had been in contact with the man, for without his timely arrival, whatever had lurked in the surrounding woods would surely have claimed both men as prey. Trying to broach the subject with Corian had proved impossible, and resulted in more than a few heated exchanges.

Corian's caravan was headed northeast with a small company of Sylvani. They hoped to reach Innes Vale before the passes through the mountains became too treacherous to travel. The wealthy entrepreneur had sold all of his present wares, and remained determined to restock and head south for the spring. It would mean a risky winter voyage, but the dangers of such a journey did not seem to bother the businessman.

Alessan watched sadly as a dozen Innes Vale wagons slipped quietly out of town. A light dusting of snow had fallen the previous evening, and looking around at that pristine beauty, Alessan felt at peace. Although the merchant had ignored his plea to join the caravan, Corian had winked conspiratorially when asked when they would meet again. Alessan trusted his new mentor; a man who had taught him to examine his burdened heart, and find comfort in who he really was.

Raising a hand in farewell, Alessan smiled as the vociferous merchant waved back, his ample girth nearly throwing him off balance as his wagon mired for a moment in the mud. They had exchanged only a few brief words of parting, words that, upon reflection, Alessan found wholly inadequate for the time they had spent exploring the Aeldenwood together. Yet Corian had seemed preoccupied, and Alessan did not want to distract the businessman. He grudgingly had to admit that the man from Innes Vale had probably met more than a few ambitious young men over the years. Alessan was worried he had been no different.

Leaning heavily on his walking stick, he stood a silent vigil until the procession had become little more than a dark smudge on the horizon. With the sun glistening brightly off the newly fallen snow, Alessan sighed and turned away.

With the Black Boar feeling so unfamiliar these days, it took Alessan far longer than usual to get his chores attended to. By mid-morning, although the large common room hearth had been lit and the stables swept, there were a number of cleaning duties that still needed his attention. With both Varis and his mother on the prowl, Alessan did his best to avoid both the kitchen and the main foyer. After the second dressing down by Varis, for what the older servant called shoddy work, Alessan could take no more. Seething, he slipped through the kitchen as quietly as possible, and headed towards the servants stairwell.

Muttering under his breath, Alessan climbed the stairs to his room and slammed the door. Even before slumping into an uncomfortable chair, his mind registered a folded piece of gold-embroidered parchment laying on his bed. Reaching out slowly to grasp the paper, Alessan could feel his heartrate rapidly increase. Steadying a shaking hand, his eyes darted about the room before he dared open the letter. His eyes scanned the words written upon the single page of parchment.

Young Oakleaf,

You did not think I would leave without saying goodbye, did you? Corian Praxxus would never show such a lack of manners! It is hard for a man of my talents to invest in another man's career. My business is, and will always be, the most important thing in my life. My children, my wife, my friends — they are all secondary when it comes to making money. It is simply, for better or ill, who I am.

And yet in you, Alessan, I sense an ambition, a drive that reminds me of my youth. I respect such ambition, and yet am afraid of any who could one day be my competitor. Do you have the desire to make of yourself what you wish? That is an answer I cannot give, but can definitely offer to influence.

You asked for my help, and after much thought, I have decided to honour that request. Upon my return, I will expect you to be ready to set out for the southern lands of the Protectorate. We will be spending at least two years down south, so do not take this commitment lightly. You will be a servant in my entourage, treated no better or worse than the others, and our camaraderie will cease to exist. I want you to learn from me, not to become my friend. Business is business.

Expect my arrival by your Winter Festival. Your mother will be paid a large sum upon my arrival in compensation for your services.

Until next we meet, young Oakleaf.

Master Corian Praxxus

Shaking with excitement, Alessan clutched the letter tightly as he read the page over and over again. It all seemed so surreal. He was to be given a chance to make something of himself, and he would not let this opportunity pass him by. Alessan leaned back dreamily in his chair, his thoughts racing with a multitude of ideas and goals. He was bursting with excitement and full of promise.

And yet later that evening, as sleep continued to evade his frantically preoccupied mind, Alessan found his thoughts turning back to the strange encounter near the Elmwood residence. When his mind should be full of visions of the south with its lush vineyards and rolling plains, all he could think about was C'Aelis. *Two times now they had met, and yet, what secrets lay behind that piercing emerald gaze? What lurked among the trees of the Aeldenwood? And what lay behind the terrible sadness in the strange man's soul?*

Alessan knew he had been shown a glimpse of something evil when he had pressed C'Aelis about what he hunted, but the images in his mind were jumbled and incomplete. Excited as he was about his employment offer, Alessan's thoughts remained preoccupied with the mysterious Aeldenwood, and the man he now believed to be a Gorimm.

He slept poorly that night, tossing in his sleep as he had when nightmares of his father's death had plagued him as a child. Twice he awoke in terror, and although his hands quickly reached for his old journal, he recorded nothing; he had forgotten the dream. Judging by his sweat-soaked bed sheets and quickened heart, he wondered if forgetting was not all that terrible.

Contractual obligations are binding. Once a captain sets the company seal upon an employer's parchment, it completes the agreement for both parties. The details of all prior negotiations and offers are private and must be held in the strictest of confidence. Failure to do so may result in breach of said contract.

—*Mercenary Code of Conduct*

CHAPTER IX

Garchester, Protectorate

The fourth day of the siege found Bider and Orn sitting atop the ruined remains of a small apothecary. The shop lay in the shadow of the eastern wall, and it had paid the price for being situated so close to the gates. An immense boulder, launched from one of the many catapults arrayed against the besieged city, had crashed through the roof of the small store. Bider wondered if the owner had been inside at the time.

Fortunately, the casualties had been minimal during first few days. Gadian Yarr's forces seemed content to remain at a distance and maintain a seemingly endless barrage from their engines of war. Most buildings located between the large outer wall and the inner walls of the keep had seen serious damage. Anticipating his enemy's tactics, Duke Berry had long ordered the populace to move inside the city's interior walls. Yet he could do nothing for their houses and workshops, except hope that they would be spared.

The Fey'Derin's multiple squads allowed for versatility in their deployment, and the company was largely spread out by task. Ethan Shade's Eagle Runners were stationed near the eastern gate, and spent their time patrolling the walls and fortifying the inner defenses to protect against a possible breach. Sergeant McConnal and his Axemen were holding the main gatehouse alongside the duke's heavy infantry units. Lieutenant Burnaise had joined Sergeant Fearan and his Footmen to the south.

"Hey, Orn," Bider said. "Any reason why they don't attack? It's been nearly four days since we've arrived, and still they only pound us with stones."

"They might still be smarting from their earlier losses, Bider," Orn grumbled a reply. "I can tell you one thing though, Duke Berry is surely despised by those assembled outside."

"By all accounts, Lord Dalemen hated him even before this latest incident," Bider repeated what he had heard from one of the duke's soldiers. "Something about an argument in the council chambers of Imlaris. With his consort in Berry's hands, his patience must be wearing very thin," he added.

"Aye, you might be right," Orn agreed. "In any case, with little more than half an army able to fight, their commanders must still be debating the best course of action. Winter's not so far off, and it would be quite idiotic to continue the siege once the snows hit."

"How long do you judge we have to hold?" Bider asked with some concern in his voice.

"At least two weeks, three would ensure that snow will be on the ground," the Fey'Derin scout replied after a moment's thought. "Let them try sleeping while not able to feel their fingers or toes. Trust me, it's not pleasant and their morale will suffer."

Pausing to survey the devastation around the high outer wall, Bider wondered if anything would remain for the victors if the barrage continued for much longer. It would be a shame, in the end, to defend only a decrepit shell of a city.

Finishing the last few bites of his midday soup, Bider heard the unmistakable dull thump as a siege engine launched another stone missile towards the wall.

"Incoming!!" screamed a soldier from the upper watchtower.

Throwing his wooden bowl and spoon to the side, the small scout dove immediately to the ground. With his arms clutched tightly around his head,   he clenched his teeth and awaited the inevitable. Most veteran soldiers swear that hiding from a barrage is pointless. If a stone is destined to fall within your radius, no amount of protection will keep you alive. However, being a thief for the early part of his life had taught Bider to trust his instincts. In this case, they screamed for him to lay flat, throw his arms up over his head, and hope for the best.

Not twenty paces behind where Orn sat and Bider lay prone, a terrible crash sounded. When the dust settled, two large stone pieces lay entrenched in one of the small houses. It was severely damaged, and the weakened support beams buckled under the added weight. A few soldiers who had been resting nearby, ran quickly towards the crumbling structure. Bider cringed as the beams gave in and the roof came crashing down. He could only imagine how some of the inhabitants would react after losing everything they had once owned.

"Don't know why you bother panicking like you do," Orn exclaimed. He was still calmly spooning up the remains in his own bowl of soup. "You young soldiers are so jumpy. I would bet you a month's pay that Sergeant McConnal would never flee such a volley."

Shaking his head, Bider brushed off his uniform, bending over to recover two daggers that had fallen from his bandoliers. He was content in knowing that if another giant stone came his way, he would gladly find himself in the dirt once more. There was no sense in playing games with one's fate.

Shortly thereafter, a company of city guards arrived and started gathering volunteers to help move the rubble. Both members of the Fey'Derin joined in the cleanup, pushing aside as best they could the larger pieces clogging the road. Eventually, the pathway was cleared, and both scouts returned to their post atop the outer wall.

Accepting a mug of water from one of the guardsman, Bider's gaze wandered over the assembled enemy troops camped beyond bow range on the outskirts of the city. At least a thousand men lay to the west, another four hundred were guarding any attempt at a sortie from the south gate. A dozen distinct banners flapped in the strong wind, with each company standard easy to distinguish from Bider's elevated vantage point. He studied the banners, and counted only one northern company among the groups to the south. Most were unfamiliar him, and his eyes settled uneasily on the symbol of the black hyena belonging to Khali's Reavers.

Nudging Orn, Bider gestured out towards the standard. "What's the story behind the Reavers?" he asked. "You've been around since the early days of the Fey'Derin."

"The Reavers are a bad lot," Orn said, spitting over the wall. "A very bad lot."

"That's what I *know,* not what I want to hear," Bider pressed.

Orn gave his companion a deliberate once over before answering. "Over the last century or so, there have been several unspoken rules in our profession," he began, "One, is to always minimize casualties of the innocent, especially women and children. Another is to always accord captured officers fair and just treatment. Although such rules were never written into the Code, mercenary companies don't take kindly to torturers —"

"So Khali's men tortured officers?" Bider interrupted with alarm.

"If you're going to interrupt, I'll stop right here and now," Orn growled. "Now are you going to shut that trap of yours or not?"

"Yes, sorry." Bider answered timidly.

"As I was saying, there are several actions that are widely frowned upon. The last revolves around a company's base of operations during the winter months. Be it a temporary encampment, or a permanent home city, it matters not. You leave the men and their families alone. There's plenty of time for killing when the spring arrives."

Pausing to take a long sip from his ever-present flask, Orn shot Bider a suspicious look. "You won't say anything to the Captain now will you?" he glared.

"Not as long as I hear this story..." Bider responded carefully.

"Well, it was three seasons ago, the year before you came on as a recruit, and the company was staying south for the winter. It was the first time the Captain chose not to take us back north to Briar, instead planning to stay near the eastern edge of the Caeronwood. Sergeant Fenton and the Lieutenant left the autumn campaign early with our newest recruits and built a relatively comfortable camp for the men. Rumours began to swirl by season's end that a few southern companies had been contracted out later than the usual, and many mercenaries across the region speculated at what might be developing. Seems a few of the nobles in the Protectorate territories held the northern companies in some contempt, deeming them unfit to fight in southern lands."

"But the Code states that the whole of old Caledun is fit for any company to do battle," Bider retorted.

"That's right, but it doesn't mean it sits well with some of the noblemen hereabouts. The Code isn't perfect, and men's hearts can be easily twisted, even by the most mundane of things," Orn continued. "After the Battle of Cobourne, where the Fey'Derin fought for Lord Erion Brawn, word escaped that an early winter bounty was out on our company. It seems the Captain's choice of employer over the years had angered certain factions, most notably Lord Yarr and his ally Duke Garius of Imlaris."

"I'm not familiar with that name." Bider said.

"He paid a large price to spearhead the campaign against our recruits. They hit the camp before we could muster our strength and warn them. That twelve of the fifty-six men survived, including Lieutenant Burnaise, is something of a miracle. It was a slaughter, and our young men had no chance. Bran, that big brute of an Axeman, still sports a nasty scar under that beard of his, but at least he survived, unlike many of his friends."

"And it was Khali's men that attacked?" Bider hesitated to ask.

"Aye, it was. They showed no quarter. Women who had arrived from the north or sweethearts from the nearby towns, it mattered little. Khali's men murdered them all. Sergeant Fenton died trying to protect his young son and wife," Orn replied gloomily.

"The Captain was cold that day. He showed no emotion, and yet we all knew he was hurting. His vengeance was swift and as unmerciful as the unjust attack. He mustered half the company and ambushed Garius as he travelled between cities. No one walked away from that battle unscarred. Captain Silveron ignored the man's pleas for mercy and took his head, sending it in a box to Gadian Yarr. Then we travelled north, taking a winding road through the *Erienn* mountain range, passing by Dragon Mount and the Silveryn Mages."

"And the Reavers?" Bider asked, entranced by the sorrow etched in the storyteller's words.

"We fought them the following season. Sergeant McConnal nearly destroyed their vanguard single-handedly, and the Captain, well he was both terrifying and awe-inspiring to behold. We haven't seen those bastards in well over a year now, and it's all any of us involved in that ambush can do to hold our tempers in check. There's a reckoning still to come. The Captain swore on those dead men that he would kill the man who coldly slaughtered those innocents, and if I know the Captain, that day is coming." Orn hung his head as he finished, staring solemnly at the ground.

A long moment passed, and Bider felt a pang of guilt knowing that he had reopened old wounds. Ignoring Orn as he took a second and then third pull from his silver flask, Bider slipped down the stone staircase and left his friend alone with his thoughts.

ଔ

"This is the second letter that has arrived since we delivered our terms to that scoundrel," Duke Berry swore as he brandished an official looking parchment. "That bastard wants his lovely mistress back in his arms immediately! Does he think I'm a fool?!" the nobleman asked.

"They'll attack on the morrow, my lord," Gavin replied immediately.

"How so?" Captain Sledge asked, a befuddled look upon his face.

"In the eyes of the nobleman, he has requested the release of Lady Farraine two times. Two times he will have been refused by the barbaric Duke Berry, a demon-spawned kidnapper," Gavin replied with a smirk. "He knows that any more delays in attacking could spell disaster should the weather take a turn. He has done all that he can up to this point and will now watch from a distance," he finished.

"Sound thinking, Captain," the duke nodded appreciatively in Gavin's direction. "If you have deduced the truth then we must look to our defenses. How stand the walls in respect to the heavy bombardment we've suffered these last few days?"

"Captain Draven?" Gavin asked the commander of the Helmsmen whose company was stationed along the southern wall.

"They are well supplied, that's for sure," the officer began cautiously. "They haven't let up the pounding on our side since last morning. The wall seems sound, but I worry about how much it can withstand before a section merely crumbles under the feet of my men. I'll be honest, my lord, the damage is considerable."

"The city damage has been quite extensive," Captain Sledge nodded in agreement. "The lower town, and anything within the vicinity of the eastern and southern walls, has taken a dreadful thrashing. Our men have done their best to keep the streets clear, but after this morning's attack, I have more wounded than I desire under our present circumstances."

"Yes, I've seen the lower city with my own eyes gentlemen, and we can only hope to defend the lives of the citizens. We knew there would be damage, so let's focus on what we can do to better prepare ourselves for tomorrow," Duke Berry sighed.

"Is there a chance we might hit their siege engines?" Captain Sledge offered.

"They are well defended and situated near the center of the encampment. It would be a tall order to get within striking distance of those damned catapults... but not impossible," Gavin replied.

"How so?" Duke Berry asked.

"The Fey'Derin couldn't do it alone, but Lieutenant Burnaise and I were exploring this same subject earlier with a few of my scouts. If a diversion could be created, some men could sneak safely into the enemy camp. There are enough mercenary companies mingled out there to use as cover as they slip through the lines."

"And this diversion?" the Helmsmen captain inquired.

Pointing to one of the maps laid out on the table in the council chamber, Gavin indicated a location to the rear of the southern camp where the main body of the enemy was positioned.

"We know that supplies are paramount to their success here at Garchester. With one unexpected winter storm, the advantage shifts to us as we lay warm and safe in the city. Although it would be difficult to stem the supply trains that replenish the garrison, one quick feint could draw enough attention away from where I'd send my men. If we can turn as many eyes as possible to the rear of the camp, we might have one opportune moment to strike the siege engines."

"A feint is possible, but those men would have to be on mounts. How else would they return to the city before their escape route is cut off? You are asking my men to commit suicide—" Captain Sledge bellowed angrily.

"I would never ask that of any man, let alone an entire company," Gavin responded. "The soldiers will be well provisioned and would strike hard and fast. Once the supply station is in disarray, they flee to the south and away from the combat. Upon reaching the treeline, they could turn east and head to the foothills," Gavin finished.

"I would commit no fewer than twenty," Duke Berry commented while studying the map intently. "But no more than thirty. We need able bodies here in the city. Still, this opportunity to disrupt their operations is one we can ill afford not to attempt."

"I will commit some of the Falconers, my lord," Duncan Sledge offered confidently, "But I will need to discuss with my officers who will be chosen from the company, as well as who should lead the endeavor,"

"We must strike tomorrow night. As the sun falls, I'll send my men over the wall. The Eagle Runners will need some time to get in to position," Gavin replied.

"Your numbers, Captain?" Duke Berry asked.

"Six or seven, my lord. Ethan Shade will be in command."

"Alright," the duke nodded in agreement. "We have scant time to prepare, gentlemen, so let's not waste any more of what we have. You will still need to meet with your officers, and the night grows short."

ᙘ

"Word's been passed that with the morning comes an attack," Orn crunched on a piece of hard bread, crumbs sprinkling down through his thick moustache.

"I guess they've finally tired of launching those cursed stones and want to get rid of us the honorable way," Bider replied with a chuckle.

"Don't take it too lightly," Orn answered ominously. "They'll be out to spill blood; be wary it's not yours."

Orn Surefoot had spoken true. At the first light of dawn, Gadian Yarr's troops gathered beyond the walls of Garchester and began their march towards the city. Surrounded by the loud footsteps of hundreds of soldiers stepping in unison, the enemy army advanced while the catapults continued to bombard the city in advance of the main attack.

Bider watched in dismay as two guardsmen to his left were smashed by a large stone that landed atop the outer wall, crushing both men in its path. Bravely trying to settle his nervous stomach, he stood firm at his post and took heart in the courage of his Fey'Derin companions. The archers atop the wall loosed their first volley and a storm of arrows rained down on the attackers as they closed in on the walls. With muscles tensing, Bider drew his two long daggers in preparation for what was to come.

The first enemy wave reached the wall with a roar, stepping over many bodies pierced with arrows and bolts as they made their final approach. Bider rushed forward when the expected ladders touched the top of his wall, joining the other soldiers in pushing the heavy wooden steps from the ramparts. The sheer numbers were overwhelming, and a multitude of ladders were quickly moved into new positions. With great speed, the first enemy soldiers scaled the walls and joined the battle in full.

Bider soon lost all sense of time. His world was reduced to the few bloodied feet surrounding him. He thrust his blades outward and stabbed ceaselessly at the attacking men. He struck with swift precise strokes that demonstrated his exceptional skill in wielding the two blades. At his side, Orn Surefoot swore loudly and taunted the enemy mercenaries as they raced towards him. Buoyed by this brash audacity, Bider lent his voice to the rousing shout of the stout defenders as it echoed over the battlements.

Messengers rushed between defensive positions, valiantly delivering messages to officers and subordinates when needed. By midday, word arrived that a portion of the eastern wall had been breached by a timely catapult barrage. Enemy soldiers were pouring into the city as the defenders, Fey'Derin soldiers included, attempted to close the breach and regain the initiative.

Archers continued to rain death down upon the advancing foes from their rooftop positions, but for many hours, the battle to the east seemed to hang in the balance. A company of Helmsmen were pulled from their assigned wall in order lend aid. Orn and Bider soon found themselves hard pressed to hold their own defensive positions.

As the day progressed, Bider strained to lift his weary and cramped muscles, as he fought desperately to keep fresh enemy soldiers at bay. Worried about the fate of the wall, the sudden reappearance of a company of guardsmen bolstered his spirits. With another roar, this time with his voice hoarse and raw, Bider pressed forward.

A strong hand gripped his shoulder as he moved towards a hole in the lines.

"We've earned a rest, lad," Orn Surefoot said, the man breathing heavily. The scout spat blood from his swollen lip but was otherwise unhurt. "The reserves will carry the fight while we get water and food. We're no good up there if we can't lift our blades."

Nodding wearily in return, Bider gratefully followed the Fey'Derin scout down the long flight of stairs that would take them to safety.

By late afternoon, the eastern breach was under control, and the forces of Gadi-an Yarr began an orderly retreat. The arrival of Sergeant McConnal and his platoon of heavy infantry had eventually turned the tide. The inexperienced city guards-men, all brave but wholly inadequate at holding the opening in the wall, had taken grievous casualties. Yet they had garnered a new amount of respect and admiration from the mercenaries whose livelihood it was to fight. During the chaos of battle, eight of Ossric's Axemen fell, and another half dozen were sorely wounded. It was a small price to pay for the safety of the inner city and control of the outer walls. Of Bider's own squad, a half dozen had fallen, with many more wounded.

Bider was faithfully cleaning his daggers when word passed through the ranks that some of the company's Eagle Runners had been called to the main command tent. It had taken one of the messengers an extended period of time to deduce the whereabouts of a certain Coren D'Elmark, as he had never heard the name before. The scout was known as Bider within the company and was addressed as such by all — except the Captain.

Captain Silveron had situated his command post in a large three level tavern slightly beyond the enemy's catapult range. The Northern Steel was a reputable establishment, and even Bider had to admit they served a seasoned boiled cabbage that made his mouth water. The slight soldier straightened his company tabard before entering the side dining area currently being used as a meeting chamber.

Giving a slight nod to the other men gathered in the room, Bider took a seat near the window. The stately chair felt somewhat strange beneath his weight. The wood was a rare type of red oak, and he imagined the cost of that piece, let alone the other dozen or so chairs clustered nearby, more than surpassed the largest amount of coin he might ever lay claim to. Shifting slightly in a sorry attempt to make himself more comfortable, he gauged the other Eagle Runners in the room.

Rayn and Garett were both new recruits, and their nervousness was easily discerned by their eager, shifty eyes. They sat quietly, but exuded an uneasy energy that Bider could identify from his own experience as a new mercenary. Embroiled in a siege such as this would be memorable for the two men — if they survived.

Directly across the table was a man Bider knew well, as only two years earlier they had been recruits together. Bron was a tall, rapier-thin man who possessed a stoic grace that impressed most. While not a strong fighter, he excelled in plans of stealth and uncommon tactics.

At Bron's side, idly puffing a black pipe, was Alec of Derry. A veteran of three companies and over a dozen years of mercenary service, the middle-aged man was rude, gruff, and generally abysmal to be around. His disposition aside, he was a talented archer and shrewd swordsman. The simple fact that he had lived through so many years of campaigning was a testament to his skill on the battlefield. As Bider caught Alec's eye, his stare was answered with an intense, calculating glare from the man.

It didn't take long for Captain Silveron to arrive with Orn Surefoot and Sergeant Shade at his side. "Good evening, gentlemen. I am glad to see you are all here and on time," the Captain said with a hint of a smile. "If only I could get such results from my officers," he added. Amidst the good-natured laughter that followed, most of the nervous energy in the room dissipated. As was customary, Captain Silveron spent little time with pleasantries when pressing business needed attending. "We are calling this little nighttime endeavor 'sleepwalking,' so I assume you men are all ready for a long night's work?"

"Yes, sir," they all replied in unison.

"Good," Captain Silveron replied with a nod. "We are working on a joint venture with the Falconers. Captain Sledge will provide a squad of thirty riders who will head out at deepest night and attempt to disrupt the enemy's southern supply lines. This mission is nothing but a ruse; a feint designed to distract. Understood?" The officers agreed, and Sergeant Shade, after a signal from the Captain, moved forward.

"The Eagle Runners will use this diversion to strike the catapults. We'll use oil and any other supplies we can collect. We plan to slip over our walls near mid of night. That should leave us plenty of time to infiltrate their weak perimeter and blend into that mess they call a camp."

"Uniforms and equipment, sir?" Alec asked.

"You'll each be assigned a partner for this mission," Orn stepped forward, tossing a large bundle of clothes upon the table. "Each pairing will be wearing a tabard that matches a company from Lord Yarr's levies."

"But there's seven of us, Orn..." Rayn stated nervously.

"I travel alone," the lanky veteran replied with a menacing snarl.

"Orn has other objectives and may need his space," Sergeant Shade added hastily. "The rest of us have only one goal — the catapults. You will have torches in your packs, but otherwise wear only what you would while walking among the Fey."

"It is imperative that no alarm sound before the Falconers exit the city and ride for the rear of the army. Anything that brings attention to the center of that camp will compromise the entire plan. I don't need heroes out there, I need survivors." Captain Silveron added with authority. "I'll leave the minor details to Sergeant Shade, but I wish you all well. Safe journey to you, always," he finished.

That simple phrase had become something of a company watchword. The Captain had often spoken these words before sending men into battle, or on the eve of a siege much like this one. Company lore believed it to be an ancient blessing that the kings of old imparted upon their warriors, but Bider shied away from accepting too many of these veteran tales. Regardless of its roots, the young soldier always felt comforted by the saying. Standing with his companions, he answered his commander proudly, "Safe journey to you, always."

⁂

Ethan Shade was the first man to slide noiselessly over the edge of the rampart. Without hesitation, the nimble officer launched himself over the crenel and down the thick rope, sliding quickly to the base of the wall, his hands burning from the friction. One by one, the remaining six soldiers followed their commander.

Hitting the ground with a soft thump, Bider joined the sergeant and whispered luck to the other members of the sortie. Crouching low, the deft scout watched as the company broke into pairs and headed off into the night.

Pausing to adjust his tabard and cloak, Sergeant Shade motioned him forward. They wore light blue and red tabards, matching a southern company named the Corsairs who were camped on the far side of the assembled host. Both men knew it would be best to avoid a chance encounter with a member of that group and so chose their route accordingly.

It took longer than planned to carefully cover the distance between the city wall and the first set of perimeter guards. Pulling dark cloaks tightly around their bodies, the two Fey'Derin slipped through the lines without notice. The captain had predicted as much, Bider mused, following his companion past two guards sitting quietly by a small cooking fire. No one in the camp expected a surprise attack from anyone stationed safely behind the strong walls of Garchester.

The men in the camp were organized, yet extremely complacent. As Ethan and Bider made progress towards their goal, they no longer attempted to remain unseen. In fact, in order to blend in, they paused at several campfires and chatted quietly with men who were trying to keep warm. On one occasion, Sergeant Shade surprised Bider by offering one group of soldiers a taste of spirits from a small, black flask pulled from within the folds of his cloak.

And so, as the night slowly slipped by, the two Fey'Derin crossed into the inner camp, where the now silent war engines were amassed. Unlike the outer perimeter, the inner camp was heavily guarded, and twice they were challenged by alert guards who declared the area off limits.

Frustrated by their inability to gain access beyond the final sentries, Sergeant Shade signaled to Bider, and they took a seat beside the nearest canvas tent. Gentle snores could be heard, and the officer shook his head. "I hope the others have fared better. I can only assume that the center of camp is the most difficult in which to gain entry, or else the others may be in serious trouble," Ethan whispered.

"The western catapult range seemed almost deserted, sir. If anyone can find a way into that compound, it will be Alec," Bider replied.

"That bastard can bluff his way through anything," Ethan answered. "He'll have those sentries running with their tails between their legs before he's done."

"But it doesn't change our own predicament," turning an eye to the sky, Bider looked concerned. "I judge we have very little time before the Falconers sortie. We need to be ready."

"I have an idea, but it will involve some stealth, and more than a little bit of luck," the officer suggested. "If you're up for it."

"That I am, Sergeant, just tell me what to do."

A short time later, Bider confidently approached a third set of sentries. It was a pairing the two Fey'Derin had avoided up to that point. The scout's cloak was thrown back over his shoulders, his company tabard easily distinguished, even in the dim light of the torches perched nearby.

"What can we do for you, soldier?" asked the first guard, a tall thick man with a large broadsword strapped across his shoulders.

"I have received a summons by my sergeant to attend to him here. I believe he needs my help with some supplies for our catapults on the western line," Bider replied without hesitation.

"I'm not sure we have anyone from your company here, friend," the same man replied cautiously. "Company and name?"

"I fight for the Corsairs and Sergeant Shade is my squad leader."

On cue, from the darkness behind the two men, a tall figure suddenly appeared. Pointing behind the sentry, Bider smiled. "Why here he comes."

"Blasted recruits are all the same!" Sergeant Shade howled. "You send a summons an hour ago, and yet still the young pups don't arrive! And where is Drew? I specifically requested that ox of a boy, not some half-pint like you."

Bider did his best to look terrified. "My apologies, Sergeant, I was just following orders... I was told we only needed a few tools to work on our catapults."

As Ethan continued to berate Bider, the two sentries stared on in disbelief. The Fey'Derin sergeant reached forward and pulled Bider after him and into the compound. Neither of the guards were anxious to step forward, and they seemed more concerned that the officer's rage was focused on his young charge and not directed at them. Within a few moments, the two Fey'Derin disappeared from view.

Ethan and Bider breathed deep sighs of relief as they passed outside the final sentry's line of sight. Whispering a few words of good fortune to each other, they split up and advanced stealthily towards the large shadowy outlines of the catapults.

Kneeling beside a large tent, Bider gently placed his pack on the ground and carefully slid out several oil soaked torches and a small cask. Assessing his surroundings, the young scout judged it best to soak the furthest two catapults first and then carefully make his way back to the supply tent he was now crouched beside.

Moving adeptly through the shadows, he approached each siege weapon and carefully doused the heavy wooden crossbeams with oil. Once the preparations were complete, he would strike up a torch and light each catapult as he raced along the edge of the compound. He hoped that the Falconers sortie would confuse the enemy long enough for each blaze to fully ignite, as well as allowing for his hasty escape. Captain Silveron's planned chaos meant that timing would be critical.

Fearing he had only moments to spare, Bider slipped into the supply tent. He could hear the mumbled conversation of a few enemy soldiers perhaps fifty paces beyond the next tent. As his eyes adjusted to the darkened space, he gasped as he noticed what lay in front of him. Cask after cask of lantern oil and other stored fuels were stacked within the tent.

Quietly breaking open two barrels, he poured the oil out towards the tent flaps and carefully continued the flammable trail back to his original hiding spot. Barely holding back his excitement, he bounced lightly on the balls of his feet. Glancing at the sky repeatedly, he knew that time was short. All was ready, and he was prepared to dash towards his first target. He had only to wait for the signal.

It seemed an eternity to Bider before the first screams and shouts of alarm carried through the night from the rear of the camp. Men were yelling orders and sleeping soldiers struggled to their feet, their bedrolls quickly forgotten. Lighting his small torch, he sprinted forward. Following his planned route, and touching off the fires much quicker than even he thought possible, he returned to his hiding place.

In that short amount of time, he watched as not only his catapults lit up the night sky, but several others on each side of the camp burst into flames. A small fireball shot skyward to the west, and Bider guessed that Alec of Derry was the likely catalyst behind such a blast. Turning quickly to his remaining task, he crouched low and dropped his torch directly on the thick trail of liquid that led into the supply tent. Turning his back to the trail of fire, he tore off towards the edge of the camp, the thought of escape now foremost in his mind.

Without warning, an enormous blast of hot air propelled him forward. Bider looked down only to realize that he was flying rapidly through the air, tumbling like a falling leaf in an explosion of his own making. As the ground rushed up to meet him, the Fey'Derin scout was plunged into darkness.

The War of Iron saw the keeps of the Iron Shield nearly beaten into submission by an overwhelming number of goblin soldiers. Briefly united under a single banner, the goblin armies of the Wilds numbered in the tens of thousands.
—*Trent Gorian Histories, Vol. XII*

CHAPTER X

The Wilds, Northern Wilderness

The Wilds are filled with mystery, cold beauty, and danger. It is a land that refuses to be tamed by the toil of men. The very trees and earth rebel against any sign of encroaching civilization. It is a land of wild beauty, a reminder of the way things once were, and perhaps always meant to be. Its dense forests, rocky landscape, and many rivers, have rarely encountered the footsteps of humankind. No man-made trails exist beyond the sparse dirt pathways located on the border and under the protection of the fortresses of the Iron Shield.

Game is plentiful and varied, with creatures rare in the south living within range of many of the borderland keeps. Deer and elk roam freely in the fields, yet darker creatures, shadowy shapes in the night, dominate the thoughts of the families that live nearby. When one speaks of the Wilds, it is to speak of the unknown.

Although few men have ever lived long in this uncharted wilderness, one race moves freely about this untamed land. Goblins of the north, bitter enemies of the men of the Iron Shield, call the Wilds their home. They are a thick-bodied race, tribal in nature, with dark green skin and a savage lust for violence. They are fierce in battle, and even more dangerous than a ravenous pack of wolves when threatened. Most wear animal pelts and bone necklaces, and their close-cropped, dirty white hair is strangely luminescent. So little is known about their culture and race that many men, especially the nobles of the Northern Council and the Protectorate, refuse to deem them civilized. Yet it is the men of the borderland patrols that often raid and burn entire villages belonging to these tribes. The long-held belief that the goblins are a dangerous threat and need to be quelled holds true, even to this day.

Leoric D'Athgaran didn't care what others thought of the goblins, he had only his own beliefs — he hated them. The borderman had seen first-hand the savagery they had exhibited time and time again in battle. He had confronted them on multiple occasions, coming perilously close to their tattooed and painted faces that unleashed inhuman screams. He had been witness to their grisly ritual of beheading, watching them don the bleached skulls as trophies. He had seen them in action, and he loathed them; but truly he knew that deep within himself, he feared them.

Such thoughts ran through Leoric's mind as he mounted a dark grey horse, gently guiding the beast into line. He was patiently waiting for the Marshal to arrive and lead them out into the wilderness. Looking around at the gathered men, Leoric could easily discern all those who had already experienced a patrol.

An excitement surged along the entire line, but the veterans were far more subdued. Many of them sat quietly on their steeds, serious expressions locked on their worn faces. They, as well as Leoric, knew the gravity of the situation. These men had fought the savages of the north and knew all too well the dangers ahead. An experienced warrior of the Iron Shield knew better than to underestimate a goblin war party.

The newest arrivals, on the other hand, could barely contain their enthusiasm. Most chatted incessantly, or checked and rechecked their weapons for the tenth time that morning. They would become harder men after meeting their adversaries. And if they did not, it would mean their death.

With the light of dawn behind them, the armed procession of two hundred men set forth. Marshal Aram commanded to start, but the patrol planned to split up once the forest border was reached. Both groups followed a single winding trail that carried them closed to the edge of the Wilds.

The three day journey would culminate with their joint arrival at Sharpe's Point. The famous battlefield, where Arion Sharpe had defended a small hilltop camp against a horde of goblins, was shunned by the barbaric creatures. The Marshal often told tales of that heroic defense, being an young officer at the time. He reminded his men that the goblins could not contain their fear of defeat, hence why they avoided the legendary battle site.

Leoric thought differently. Why, if you were a goblin, would you return to well-defended natural terrain when you could choose an attacking point more to your liking? Such had been the case, the borderman reminded himself, when Pont's company had been ambushed en route to that very same location. There were enough men slain on that day to serve as a grave reminder of the unforgiving nature within the creatures of the Wilds.

That first day, Leoric rode as a member of the rear guard, his broad shouldered friend, Angvald, walking briskly at his side. He had quickly learned that the men of Kaleen frowned upon the steeds of the east. As far as Angvald's people were concerned, a warrior fought with the ground firmly beneath his feet. And so the foreigner was content to walk alongside the riders, debating politics and philosophy endlessly with the men of the company. Compared to the last fortnight spent alone and miserable atop the towers of Darkenedge, Leoric welcomed the conversation and good-natured ribbing that resulted from a few heated discussions.

At the end of the first day, Captain Napat broke from the main column and headed southeast with half the command. The Marshal remained with Leoric and his companions, turning slightly to the north, and leaving the trodden path that served as a final indicator of the world of men. Without the guiding trail, the main patrol made slower progress, but they steadily continued their journey deeper into the forest.

Rising at first light the following day, Leoric joined Sergeant Alleran near the front of the column. The sergeant elected to send scouts out to the north and the east. The Marshal was adamant that they not be the victims of an ambush. Not an experienced tracker, Leoric reluctantly dismounted and followed a small group of men into the woods.

Believing in every soldier's right to explore all disciplines of combat, the companies of the Iron Shield excelled in training their men to the paramount of their abilities. Strengths and weaknesses in various skills were noted by the officers of the border keeps. Yet each man was trained in all areas of battle doctrine; including everything from unarmed combat, to tracking, to wilderness survival. And so, although not thrilled at the prospect of creeping quietly through the snow-covered woods, Leoric was aware of what needed to be accomplished.

By mid-morning he joined his sergeant atop a loose outcropping of bare rock overlooking a deep valley. Accepting a piece of trail bread from the officer, he gratefully slumped down into a sitting position. A strong biting wind blew at this height, and Sergeant Alleran raised his hand as Leoric was about to speak. A curious expression crossed the veteran's features, and a sudden frown washed over his worn countenance.

Confused, Leoric sidled forward and looked to the valley below for a clue to the sergeant's concern. For long moments the two men were frozen like statues, their bodies taut and facing north.

Far off in the distance there drifted a sound above the wind, faint and yet distinct. It was a cacophony of noise that any of the border soldiers would recognize even in their sleep, so often had they been subjected to it. It was the clamor of a training yard with its ringing clash of steel weapons, and the abrupt cries of warriors engaged in their drills. Sergeant Alleran recognized the sound as well, and his face was grim. The patrols had failed to report evidence of any war camps or cohesive army units in the area. Leoric deduced that the existence of such a training facility could only mean one thing — the goblins were preparing for war.

The sergeant motioned him forward as he quietly slipped his mace out of the belt loop where it hung. Leoric had a sudden feeling that eyes were watching them as they continued to creep forward over the rock. The sounds continued to carry alarmingly over the trees and small cliffs of the Wilds. It took the men until late morning before they topped the final rise that garnered them a clear view of their objective.

A shiver swept through Leoric as he peered down over the edge of the tall escarpment where they were perched. Far below, sprawling across the entire length of a massive clearing, was an armed goblin camp. Hundreds of figures were spread about the area. All were hard at work.

Some trained with bows, others at close combat, and from a distance the border-men could make out two large tents where the distinct clanging of metalwork rang out. The trainees wore an assortment of armor types and had adorned their protective pieces with slashes of bright colors. A simple detail, yet Leoric noted it immediately, sensing that it could be the most telling observation gained from their discovery.

For ages, the goblin tribes of the north remained fractured and divided, spending as much time killing each other as they had raiding the human settlements in the south. Over many years of warfare, the men of the Iron Shield had learned to discern goblin tribes by the colours they displayed in battle. Never before had any boderguards discovered a settlement or raiding party that consisted of mixed tribal members. Yet here in the camp beneath Sergeant Alleran and Leoric, were hundreds of the creatures wearing a variety of different shades.

"The markings, sir," he whispered, carefully pointing towards the vast open area that served as the main combat arena. "At least a dozen, if not more."

"Fourteen, D'Athgaran," Sergeant Alleran answered. "This does not bode well for the Shield."

Again Leoric felt as though they were being watched as he continued to stare down into the clearing. Scanning the surrounding forest proved futile; as far as he could tell, the two men were alone. The feeling remained and glancing towards the trees, he was startled as the sergeant grabbed his arm.

"Relax, soldier, we've seen enough. The Marshal needs to hear our report and learn what we may be facing this coming spring."

"Spring?" Leoric asked as the two men slowly backed away from the edge of the cliff, disappearing into the thick brush from where they had emerged.

"Attacking in the winter wouldn't make sense. And besides," the sergeant added, "they aren't ready. They aren't working on tactics down there, only the basics. I gather they have only just started their preparations." Catching Leoric's puzzled expression, the officer continued, "The edges of the clearing have been freshly cut, I could see the new stumps even from this distance. The grass in their main training area is still green, hardly what you would expect if hundreds of goblins had tramped across the earth for any length of time. I doubt they expected the Marshal to send out a patrol this late in the year and assumed they would have little trouble keeping the camp safe from detection."

Impressed by Alleran's keen eye, Leoric slipped the mace back into the loop on his belt as he followed the borderman south back towards the measured pace of the travelling column.

Marshal Aram was incensed that the goblin tribes had begun preparations for war. That the long-time commander of Darkenedge was surprised by a unified force of the savage creatures was call for concern. For well on thirty seasons, the Marshal had defended the settlements near his keep. Never had any inklings of a tribal alliance surfaced among the savages. The goblins, simply put, were never expected to exude any kind of civilized behaviour. To Marshal Aram, a man who had crushed many a war party, the thought seemed preposterous.

The numbers to the north also dictated a harsh new reality — there would be no raiding on this patrol. Their numbers, well-trained or not, were far inferior to what the border commander needed to safely attack. Even a disturbance of the goblin training program could cost the Iron Shield far too many lives. With the certainty of war laid plainly before him, the Marshal knew that every man who could wield a weapon atop the walls of Darkenedge would be worth far more than a man riding into battle in these accursed woods.

With regret, Marshal Aram ordered the column south, and deeper into the woods, in order to avoid any chance of discovery. Sentries would be posted that evening, their numbers doubled as an added precaution, and the entire patrol would head west the following day. The safety of the keep was of paramount importance, as was the responsibility to alert the other border keeps regarding the perilous situation. A unified goblin nation with months of preparation time may not match the Shield's battle prowess or discipline, but their numbers alone could tip the balance.

The company increased their travel speed, but the need to cross a few deeper streams caused serious delays in their movement. By nightfall, the patrol had gained far less ground than planned. Even Leoric agreed that to remain so near the goblin camp was tempting fate.

Scouts had spent the better part of the day disguising their travel as best they could. Regardless, they all knew if the trail were discovered with such little distance behind them, they could be overrun that night.

Leoric was thankful to have pulled first watch. After spending so many late nights staring into the frigid darkness from the Crow's Tower, he found the enclosed woods almost comforting. The cold wind barely pierced the thick tangled growth of the forest, and he remained far warmer than he ever would have believed. His sentry duty passed by quickly and uneventfully. He had heard no break in the eerie quiet of the night, and had detected only one brief glimpse of movement — a small red fox running nimbly atop the thin crust of snow.

After his replacement arrived, Leoric stopped by the center of camp and greedily gulped down a steaming mug of hot cider. He was surprised when the Marshal had given permission for a small, albeit well-sheltered blaze to be built for their comfort. The Marshal, as always, seemed to fear little, even with the gravity of the situation so clear after today's unexpected findings.

Finishing his cider and a small meal, Leoric sank gratefully into his bedroll. Pulling his woolen cloak tightly around his body, he listened to the soft murmur of the men on duty near the fire, as well the strange creatures chirping and rattling in the night. He was soon fast asleep.

ଓ

"You know this place isn't so bad. I mean, it's eerie and a little unnerving at night, but all in all not so menacing as the stories have told. It was actually quite beautiful when we rode beside that river this afternoon with the sun glinting off the snow and water. I could al —"

"Oh shut your mouth, Darius," whispered one of the men dicing to his left. "And keep an eye out there. If you're talking, you can't be watching."

"So shut up!" added another. The men around him laughed.

The perimeter guards were stationed a good distance from the main camp. Marshal Aram had posted four sets of men for the evening, but at this moment, two pairings were embroiled in a low stakes game of dice. Staring deep into the forest gloom, Darius Morten returned to his duty, doing his best to ignore the continued chuckling and barbs sent his way.

He was a recent arrival to Darkenedge and the younger bastard son of a minor noble from the south. Most of the men were aware he had been sent away as a form of exile, keeping him far away from the prying eyes of his father's estranged wife. Darius, on the other hand, believed that he had been sent north in preparation to one day inherit the command of his father's armies. Darius Morten was not known for his intelligence.

He did, however, take the responsibility of his profession quite seriously. Standing guard in the darkness, he stared intently into the forest. His eyes had adjusted quite well to the night's gloom, and for the second time in the last few minutes, he thought he had detected movement directly ahead. A large ancient and gnarled tree might offer great cover had someone been attempting to sneak up on the borderland guards.

"Warren! Warren!" he whispered out of the side of his mouth. "I need your advice on something."

The large soldier looked up from his game and sent Darius a look of hatred. Swallowing nervously, he tried a second time. "Warren! There is something moving out there."

"Bloody hell, Darius! If you've interrupted my game for nothing, you're dead," came the reply. Reluctantly, the big soldier pulled himself to his feet and came to stand at the young man's side. "What did yo —"

In quick succession, three arrows penetrated Warren's body; one in the neck, leg, and chest. Gurgling with pain, the man collapsed to the ground. As Darius raised his voice in alarm, a second volley whipped through the night air. Shocked, he fell forward, pierced through by three black-feathered shafts. As his lifeblood slowly leaked out on to the forest floor, Darius watched in horror as dozens of black shapes ran past him towards the camp.

Two long ragged screams interrupted Leoric's dreams. The borderman immediately bolted to his feet, kicking his bedroll aside and frantically diving for his weapon. His defensive instincts, ingrained through countless hours of training, took over. Taking a deep measured breath, his hand closing over the worn leather grip of his mace, he joined a gathering of men in the center of the camp. Wearing little more than his leather breastplate, leggings and boots, he gazed sheepishly at the fully armoured Sergeant Alleran standing confidently in front of the uncertain men.

Dark figures were already writhing on the outskirts of the camp, and Leoric strained to discern friend from foe. The inhuman screeching of the goblin raiders pierced the night, and more than a few bordermen cringed at the horrific sounds. Clearing his thoughts long enough to pull a leather breastplate over his bare chest and place a helmet upon his head, Leoric hefted his mace and joined the battle.

The outer perimeter defenses had fallen. Goblins swarmed under the trees in a mass of chaotic movement. It reminded him of a boiling mob of angry ants streaming forth from their hill to attack unwanted visitors.

Leoric dodged to his left as a dark shape leapt at him from the abyss. Spinning to face his adversary, he balanced his mace lightly in his grip. The goblin wore a crimson pelt, and its skin was covered with a black soot that made the large whites of its eyes gleam. In its hands, it carried a long, thin serrated blade. Leoric paused for a brief instant as he realized the weapon was already dripping with human blood.

With an ear-shattering scream, the creature lunged forward. Allowing the goblin's momentum to carry it too far, Leoric sidestepped the charge and swung his mace down upon the back of the monster's head. The resulting crack at the base of its skull left him no doubt that this enemy was dead.

As he turned back towards the fray, a heavy blow landed squarely across his back, driving his feet out from under him. He managed to remain on his knees, but was stunned as he dropped his mace and tried desperately to reach towards the assailant on his back. Pain lanced through his side as the creature slashed into his hastily donned leather armour. Realizing his dangerous predicament, Leoric bucked and spun, furiously trying to dislodge the beast before its next blow landed.

He felt a burst of strength as his fingers gained purchase in the thick hide of an animal pelt. Even as the goblin sank sharp teeth into his neck, tearing at the muscle, Leoric dove forward and sent his enemy sprawling over the very top of his head. The goblin was quick to recover from being flipped onto its back, but Leoric had already moved in for the kill. With a crushing blow, he bashed the goblin's twisted right leg. As the creature screamed incoherently in pain, he swung his mace in a wide arc, making contact directly with its face and pulverizing the bones with a loud crunch.

The camp was quickly overrun. Only a small circle of soldiers fought as a cohesive unit. Not surprisingly, Marshal Aram was in the center, his loud commanding voice barking out orders in a vain attempt to repel the attackers. With relief, Leoric spotted the giant Angvald among the defenders. His friend's large frame was bare except for a loose pair of breeches and his boots, but with his double-bladed axe in hand, Leoric was certain the man was better protected than most.

Quickly dispatching two more goblins, Leoric knew that his life might depend on whether or not he could reach a stronger defensive position. Ducking quickly into a tent, one of the few that was not aflame, he corralled a set of leather greaves for his exposed legs. Adding a discarded shield from the corpse of one of his comrades, he finally felt adequately protected.

Unfortunately, the battle looked grim. Although the main body continued to hold firm, it was obvious to Leoric that his friends would soon be overwhelmed. Even now, at the edge of the fighting, he could see the terror in the eyes of those that remained. The Marshal had underestimated the goblins and was paying dearly for his arrogance.

Realizing that a significant part of the engagement had passed him by, Leoric knew he faced a difficult choice. He could either attempt to wade through the frenzied ranks of the enemy and reach the temporary succor of the defensive circle, or he could slip into the forest and attempt to bring word to Darkenedge that foul things were afoot in the Wilds. The training camp they had seen earlier that morning was proof enough that the goblins could be massing on the northern front for the first time in nearly a century.

Weighing the two options, Leoric looked grimly towards his companions and silently wished them well. Then, hefting his mace in one hand, the shield in the other, he slipped into the trees. Above all else, Darkenedge needed warning.

The sound of the battle carried loudly through the forest. Even with the camp long behind him, Leoric could still hear screams and the clash of arms. With pride, he realized the Marshal was putting up an epic fight against the nearly insurmountable odds. Once again, a swift pang of guilt struck him in the pit of his stomach. Shaking his head in the hopes of dispelling the feeling, he calmed himself by believing that the others would understand. If the Iron Shield fell, the lands of the North would be ripe for the plundering.

It was while crossing a small, knee-deep stream that Leoric first detected a set of eyes upon him. A tingling at the base of his neck warned him that he may very well have been seen leaving the battlefield. In a small clearing up ahead, three shapes suddenly emerged from the dense shadows of the large trunks. Leoric felt all his confidence seep from his body as two more goblins stepped out on the path behind him. Blood dripped from their naked blades, yet he could also see that two of his opponents sported bloody wounds of their own.

He was surrounded.

Loosing a wild scream of his own, Leoric took the battle to them. Swinging his mace with vicious fury, he was determined to take as many of the creatures to the afterlife with him as possible. Savagely bashing aside the short blades and daggers of the goblins, his berserker attack was rewarded with the sickening thud of his mace crushing bone. With a determined scowl, he watched the stricken goblin collapse to the ground, cradling a shattered arm and shoulder.

Leoric drew the encounter out, but the final outcome soon became evident. Although he had dealt severe damage to two of the goblin warriors, so too did their steel blades bite deep into his exposed flesh. Bleeding from more than a few minor wounds, Leoric felt the fatigue creeping into his muscles. The loss of blood made his mace feel heavier than the largest of axes, and his shield arm now drooped dangerously low. Spinning desperately to avoid a dagger thrust, he slipped to his knees. In desperation, he tried in vain to regain his feet. His legs, soaked now with rivulets of blood, refused to respond.

In a rage of frustration, Leoric spat at his enemies. The three goblins grinned wickedly and swooped towards him like vultures ready to consume their prey. Raising his mace in a final attempt at bravery, Leoric barely felt the explosion of pain as it ripped through his head. Pitching forward onto his face, the darkness overwhelmed him.

I have formed strong bonds with these men, having never forsaken my own company. Grudging respect I give to few, and in this business of soldiers for hire, I have learned to trust no one.
—Captain Gerald Armsmater

CHAPTER XI

Garchester, Protectorate

Gavin was standing atop the shattered ruins of the south gate when a tremendous roar threw him flat. Lying prone, he chanced a brief glance out across the enemy encampment. With a look of admiration, the Fey'Derin captain watched a large plume of fire lift off high into the night sky. The smaller coil of flame that had ignited to the west was a tiny blaze compared to this mighty conflagration.

A state of chaos reigned among the enemy soldiers stationed near the catapults. Gavin smiled with satisfaction as he pulled himself to his feet — the engines of war were burning. Some, it seemed, had exploded with many pieces now strewn across the battlefield. Far to the rear, the faint cries of battle could still be heard. His ears were still ringing from the blast that had shaken the walls of Garchester. He could only imagine how the soldiers in close proximity to the explosion were dealing with the aftermath.

Catching the eye of the solid Ossric McConnal, Gavin gave him a silent nod indicating that all had gone well with their gamble. The plan had worked. How his Eagle Runner squad had devised a way to create such a magnificent blast, he knew not, but he'd be damned if he wasn't going to ask Sergeant Shade the moment of his return.

It was near dawn, and the long night's sky was finally lightening to a soft grey, before anyone returned. The survivors of the small force stumbled through a guarded postern on the north side of the city. Gavin and Caolte had arrived earlier and were waiting patiently for the Fey'Derin to return.

Orn Surefoot arrived first, the veteran scout clutching a wounded shoulder that was bleeding heavily. Word filtered through the team of messengers that a high-ranking captain in the enemy camp had been assassinated. With a tired but content expression on his face, Orn reported that his mission had been successful.

Gavin greeted each man with hearty thanks and sent them immediately to the healing quarters; not even one had returned unscathed. Rayn returned alone, as did Garett. Their partners, Alec and Bron, had fallen in the fighting near the catapults. Lastly, faltering as he carried a man draped unceremoniously over his shoulder, Ethan Shade arrived. Covered in black soot, his clothing torn and ragged, the Fey'Derin sergeant grimaced as he passed through the small gate.

"Coren?" Gavin asked dejectedly, his eyes lingering on his officer's burden.

"Bider should be fine, Captain," Ethan stifled a weak chuckle. "He set off that pretty explosion I'm sure you witnessed. He must have hit a supply depot of lantern oil or something of that nature. He flew no less than thirty feet through the air once the fires started."

"And he's not dead?" Caolte asked incredulously.

"He landed on some sacks of grain. They must have cushioned his fall. Luckiest bastard I've ever met," Ethan winced as he allowed a guardsman to take the small scout from his arms. "He's unconscious and possibly damaged his arm, but he'll survive."

Caolte and Gavin slung the exhausted sergeant's arms around their shoulders. As the three men celebrated their good fortune, Gavin paused a moment to mourn Alec and Bron, who would never return. *Even in victory*, the Fey'Derin captain cursed to himself, *there is heartache.*

ભ

A bright light shone in his eyes as he came to, and although Bider desperately tried to move away, his body screamed out in agony, forcing him to remain immobile.

"Relax you fool, no need to get all fidgety on account of the sunshine," a familiar voice came from his bedside.

Bider sighed as he watched Ethan Shade step to the large bay window and pull a thick burgundy drapery across it. With the sun thankfully dimmed, he struggled to get into a sitting position. Believing that the change would relieve the pain that pulsed in his back proved to be a mistake.

"It feels like I've spent a month getting worked over by a gang of Sergeant Mc-Connal's men."

"Well you did learn to fly for a moment or two," Ethan Shade joked. "That cache you set afire did an army's worth of damage to the center of that camp. You ought to be proud of yourself."

"Aye, well it seems my misplaced visions of grandeur will be keeping me out of the fight for a day or two," Bider complained.

Passing the scout a cup filled to the brim with cool, clear water, Ethan shook his head and laughed. "A few days, Bider?! You've been recovering for the better part of six. It's a wonder that you're even alive. I'll be damned if I can explain it."

"Six days?!" he exclaimed in disbelief. "But how goes the battle? Do we still hold the outer wall?"

"The Captain was down on the field this morning discussing terms with a few of the enemy leaders. We're following the procedures for a transfer of prisoners just as the Code dictates."

"What happened?" Bider asked.

"The battle was hard fought, and twice we were pressed to hold breaches through which the enemy swarmed, but hold we did. Mind you, with most of their catapults gone, they could do little besides storm the very walls we defended. It was a slaughter. Lord Yarr wanted this city, no matter the cost. His contracted men took severe casualties, some southern companies have less than half of their men left, others are no longer," the man replied.

"And I missed it all." Bider said with regret.

"You did your duty and can take heart in that. We lost Alec and Bron that night, but struck what may very well have been a fatal blow to the enemy. You did well,

Bider," the officer gently gripped his foreman. "The healers say you'll need another day in bed before you're up and about. We have some time remaining before we head north to camp, so rest up."

Still frustratingly weak from the ordeal, Bider merely nodded. As Sergeant Shade reached the chamber door, a thought suddenly leapt to the forefront of his tired mind. "The company, sir, how did we fare?" he blurted out.

The Fey'Derin officer leaned briefly against the open door before turning and answering. "We lost thirty-three. Most fell as Captain Silveron himself led the charge that retook the southern gate after the second breach. The men fought bravely."

"And the Captain?" Bider whispered, almost fearful of the response.

"Captain Silveron is fine," Sergeant Shade replied. "He tore through the enemy like nothing we've ever seen before."

"He's a good man our Captain, and a skilled one at that," Bider commented. "And he leads as though we are more than mere paid men."

"The Captain, as much as he'd like us to believe otherwise, is no mercenary," Ethan replied with a thoughtful expression crossing his lean and refined features. "Every contract we've signed, and every deal he's brokered, has always been for the common good. Even when we fought four years ago alongside Lord Darion of Hallenford, the north having risen in revolt against the belief he had murdered his wife, still did Gavin never hesitate in siding with the besieged nobleman. When the truth came to light and the man's son was condemned as the culprit, there were few who were proud of their actions," he said, his voice filled with sadness. "Yet, the Fey'Derin could hold their heads high. In all that he does; from finding us washed up and alone, to choosing to give us a second chance, the Captain has proven he is by no means a simple man. And above all," Ethan Shade winked, "he is no mere mercenary."

With a few words advising the injured scout to sleep well and get some rest, the officer slipped quietly from the room. Alone with his thoughts, Bider nestled himself deeply into the cushions. One day, he hoped, all of his questions surrounding Captain Silveron would be answered.

CB

A day later found Bider walking gingerly among the remains of the enemy encampment. Tents, bedrolls, clothing, and myriad of other items lay scattered about. Searching the clutter carefully, most soldiers tried to find something of value from which they could profit.

The Mercenary Code of Conduct forbade any looting, be it of a city or camp, until all the terms of surrender and prisoner exchange formalities were concluded. Once completed, the victors were granted the ability to pillage the remains of the enemy area. This often involved a great deal of underhandedness and a fair amount of corruption, especially among mercenaries of different companies. As with all things, the Fey'Derin were expected to represent the company to the highest standard.

Knowing that he was in no condition to participate in the rummaging, Bider was pleased to be simply walking outside and breathing in the fresh air, albeit a light smoky smell still remained. Staying cooped up in bed for another day, especially for a young man of his nature, had proven to be nearly impossible to endure. And so, although his ribs still pained him, the scout had gingerly made his way out of the confines of the keep.

The scars of his nighttime attack were still present on the battlefield. Bider looked wondrously at the small crater that now stood in place of the supply tent he had inadvertently used to destroy the surrounding area.

He now realized his sheer good fortune in surviving an explosion of such magnitude. Yet the surrounding fields and roads had remained relatively unscathed. The siege had been relatively short, and the people of Garchester were already beginning to return to their outlying homesteads in the hopes of regaining some semblance of normalcy before the winter arrived.

The city itself had taken a severe beating. Many buildings lay crumbled or damaged, pieces of their wooden or stone exterior strewn haphazardly around the damaged roads and homes. The walls, Bider realized with chagrin, were barely standing in some places. The incessant pounding of the siege engines had weakened the southern and eastern walls. From his present vantage point, he could see large cracks running the length of some surface areas. Broken crenels and two destroyed towers lay near the base of the battlements, a stark reminder of the long repairs that would be needed in order to prepare the city for future defense.

As Bider eased his battered body onto a wooden bench, he marveled at the resilience of the townsfolk. Heads were held high, regardless of the devastation that surrounded them. Having never before experienced the sheer destruction that could result from a siege, Bider was grateful he had lived to see another day.

"Sergeant Shade mentioned you might be up and about this morning, Bider," called out a soldier carefully threading his way through the mess, arms overflowing with weapons and small pieces of armour.

"Good morning, Garett," Bider smiled and waved at the young, blond haired recruit. "It's good to see you."

The Eagle Runner breathlessly dumped his booty on the ground and joined Bider by the stones of an old fire pit. "I wouldn't miss this loot for anything," he added.

"That's right. This is your first, isn't it?" Bider remarked. "It always feels good to realize you've been on the side of the victors, doesn't it?"

"It certainly does! Oh, the Sergeant asked me to inform you that the squad has collected a separate set of items for you and the other wounded. He has your coin in the officers' quarters in town when you have a chance to stop by."

"Much appreciated," Bider replied.

Company policy always supported soldiers wounded during an engagement. For the first time in his brief mercenary career, Bider finally knew what is was like to be one of the injured, and he was genuinely pleased by the generosity of his fellow companions. Having your service recognized by the rest of the company did much to strengthen the bonds that already existed among the Fey'Derin.

"How do you feel today?" Garrett asked.

"Sore," Bider responded with a wince. "But I'll live. How about your arm?"

Garett had taken a deep cut to his forearm while attempting to evade capture during the raid. The healers had administered what help they could, but the recruit would need time, as Bider had, to fully recover from his wounds.

Rubbing the wounded limb, Garett shrugged before answering. "The healers saved the arm, but I'll have a scar for the rest of my days. It's still weak, but I feel stronger every day."

"Good to hear," Bider said encouragingly, clapping the young man on his good shoulder.

The two men talked quietly about the battle as the sun continued to roam across the sky. Around midday, Bider helped Garett collect his items and headed to the

city. With luck, Sergeant Shade would be in town. Receiving coin called for a bit
of a celebration.

଎

The large chest thudded loudly on the beautiful marble floor of the audience hall.
The jingle of coins echoed like tinkling bells over the dull boom. The elderly Chancellor Gerant reached into his thick ceremonial robes and pulled out a small silver
key. With a solemn bow, the dignitary presented it to a waiting Gavin Silveron.

The audience hall was almost empty. Despite the importance of their arrival
and prowess in battle, few nobles of Garchester cared to show respect to the mercenaries who had shed blood so that their homes would be spared. Such is how it
always was in the aftermath of battle, especially a siege of this nature.

Duke Furnael Berry was present, having recently met with the other captains
hired for the defense of his city. Both the Helmsmen and the Red Falconers
had performed admirably, being well paid for their troubles. Gavin spoke briefly with both officers before entering the hall himself, wishing them both a safe
winter. They had been solid mercenary commanders, but neither had shown
much ingenuity or flexibility when under duress at key moments during the
battle. Watching the two men leave, Gavin was struck suddenly by the realization that he wouldn't consider either of them for any post of authority over
his own men.

Returning to the task at hand, Gavin smiled at Gerant, a man he had grown
fond of during his years working for the duke. Flanked as always by his officers,
Caolte looking more and more uncomfortable in his ceremonial garb, and Ethan
practically noble in his own; Gavin was suddenly filled with pride. Once again, his
men had done themselves proud, and his officers had led with confidence, skill, and
courage. Also, dressed in his formal company cloak and attire, an outfit he rarely
wore, Gavin nodded respectfully towards the Chancellor and accepted the offering
with a soft word of thanks.

"Everything has been counted by my hand, Captain Silveron, including an added percentage befitting the risk that your men chanced by executing your bold
nighttime strike," Gerant said.

"I'll send the extra to the families of the fallen. I am humbled by your generosity, Lord Berry," Gavin replied.

"Nonsense, Captain Silveron. You need not be humbled in any way for the service you have provided. Once again, your men fought valiantly and with honour, a trait I believe that is fast becoming a rarity among the mercenaries of this age. You have a rare talent, young Silveron, and one I will continue to covet," Duke Berry answered.

Entertained by the reference to the debate regarding his perceived loyalties, Gavin replied in a blithe tone. "I have rejected your offer of service how many times now, my lord?"

"Three," the duke answered heartily. "And I'm sure it will be a dozen more before I finally crack that stubborn head of yours, Captain!"

"At least that many, my lord. But your continued efforts do wonders for my confidence!" Gavin added.

Stepping down off the raised dais near the seat of his office, Furnael Berry clasped Gavin's outstretched arm in a soldier's handshake. Forearm gripping forearm, his beaming face suddenly took on a serious tone. "Watch your back, friend. You have made many enemies this year, Gavin, and I'll not have you grow lax during the winter months."

"You too have made a bitter enemy in Lord Dalemen among others, and I'll remind you to be cautious in your dealings this winter. Although Lady Farraine has now been safely returned, she is one who will not soon forget her imprisonment. Gadian Yarr has also been halted twice now in subsequent years of warfare from attaining his most sought after goal. He'll not sit idly by while you strengthen your position," Gavin replied.

"Gadian Yarr has only been delayed, Gavin, we both know that," the duke replied earnestly. "This year we've lost more friendly companies than ever before, and my list of allies grows thin. I may find myself seeking refuge in the north before I know it."

"All we can do, sir, is continue to fight against that tyrant. Yarr is filled with a lust for power and does not intend to leave any alive who refuse to follow his lead in the Protectorate. We must use this time to alert the north of his intentions."

"Bah! The Northern Council fights only amongst itself," Duke Berry scowled. "You left that region because you knew, as well as I, that a united

North might prove to be an obstacle that Gadian can't overcome. But that group of squabbling nobles may only bring ruin down upon our heads. If they react too late to the threat, it will matter little."

"All we can do is try, Duke Berry," Gavin replied resolutely.

"I will look to your arrival at the *Ca'lenbam* with anticipation, Captain Silveron. Stay safe and watch your back. If you ever need anything, anything at all, don't hesitate to make contact. I need you alive."

Gripping the duke's forearm one last time, Gavin nodded and intoned the phrase that had become so familiar to his own men. "Safe journey to you always."

CƷ

By morning, the Fey'Derin were ready to leave Garchester. The men of the company wore fatigued looks as they rode silently through the slumbering city streets. More than a few of the men had spent some of their rich findings in the taverns and brothels that had reopened following the retreat of the enemy. Strict rules forbade certain company members from partaking in some forms of merriment, namely the consumption of spirits and ale. With the checkered history of many of the members still fresh in his mind, Captain Silveron expected nothing less than the best behaviour. Although some soldiers slipped through the cracks, on the whole the company respected their commander's wishes.

Orn Surefoot, of course, was still drunk and in a stupor by the time Sergeant Fearan and Lieutenant Burnaise tracked him down at one of the seedier establishments. Orn's longstanding battle with drink was the single biggest hindrance to a promotion of his rank. The dark glare that Gavin sent the scout's way would have burned through the heart of any other man.

In Orn's case, he screamed expletives that made even some of the hardest veterans cringe in dismay. Orn would pay dearly for his rebellion once the men arrived at *Galen'hide*, their encampment and intended home for the next few months. Captain Silveron was notorious for his punishments, and the old huntsman would rue the words he spat towards Gavin once the cloud over his mind had dispersed.

And so the Fey'Derin left Garchester, the vanguard leader Sergeant McConnal setting a steady pace that soon left the battered walls of the city far behind. The company had completed their fifth year of warfare and were anxious to spend some well-earned days resting and preparing for the next campaign.

They passed along the western edge of the Caeronwood, Bider marveling once more at the beauty of the trees. He had grown up in the foothills and mountains of Innes Vale, and had always shown great interest in the woods. Of course the Caeronwood was nothing compared to the mysterious Aeldenwood, but until they arrived north along that great forest's edge, his strange curiosity for the shadows that lurked under the eaves of those large trees was sated.

Fifteen days after leaving Garchester, Bider and a few of the Eagle Runners were sent out ahead of the main party to scout the land. In keeping with a five-year ritual Caolte Burnaise had initiated with the founding of the company, it was time to test the new recruits.

A new mercenary needed a full year of training before they were considered ready to embark on their first contract. The Fey'Derin chose their forty to fifty men in the spring, spending the entire year working them into fighting shape. One officer, usually on rotation, was charged with the weighty task of forging a competent force from the amateurs. This year, the task had fallen to Sergeant Eör Rockfar.

As Bider crouched in a small bush near the top of a slight rise, he fondly remembered his attempt to search and find the invading Eagle Runners during his tenure as a recruit. The scouts under Sergeant Shade needed to get one man to the sturdy wooden wall of the encampment before an alarm sounded.

The recruits, of course, had been told that the company would be arriving sometime this week and were expected to be wary and alert. Three of the five years had seen the victory handed to the Runners. Bider's complement had failed miserably in their duty when the lanky Orn Surefoot nonchalantly appeared in the meeting hall, took a seat beside two surprised soldiers, spooned himself a large bowl of steaming soup, and proceeded to consume it.

Sliding forward while keeping prone and as invisible a target as possible, Bider brushed aside a handful of snow that had fallen on his head from the leaves above. Already winter had sunk its teeth into the land. A native of far harsher climates further to the north, Bider ignored the slight chill that gripped his body.

As he inched closer to the camp, he could see movement to the south. From his vantage point, he spied one of his fellow men creeping skillfully along the edge of some shrubbery that had yet to bend against the weight of the newly fallen snow. The soldier was closer to the objective than he would have expected. Straining to see who it was that moved through the snow cover, Bider gasped, recognizing the smooth movements and sheathed blade poking up nonchalantly from beneath the man's cloak as he slid forward. Captain Silveron had joined the game.

Although surprised by his discovery, Bider could do little but grin in appreciation at the sheer audacity of the man. The captain must know that if he were to be discovered, there would be no end to the barbs and jokes from the men. With glee, and more than a little admiration, Bider watched Gavin not only arrive at the wall undetected, but also slip over the wooden rampart and into the camp itself. Within minutes a bell clanged loudly from the center of camp. Bider pulled himself to his feet and waved as other Eagle Runners appeared from concealed positions on the outskirts of the camp.

As he joined Garett and a few other friends at the base of the ramp that led into camp, he laughed at the exasperated looks the new recruits had on their faces. And there, just inside the gate, was the captain. Beside him stood a short, barrel-chested man, who seemed nearly as wide as he was tall. His greying beard was scragglier than usual, but the dwarven Sergeant Rockfar was a welcome sight.

Each man paused to congratulate Captain Silveron as they passed under the archway, chuckling at the merry glint lurking in his eyes. The captain was a hard man, often quiet, and to see his broad smile was something special. And so, Gavin Silveron greeted Bider and the cheerful Eagle Runners.

"Welcome to *Galen'hide*, gentleman. Welcome home!"

WINTER

3AE337-338

Aer, the fundamental catalyst used and manipulated by magekind, is pure energy. As proven by the First Age experiments of the Archmagus Tel'Contell, it is the source of power from which all living things borrow, and the basis for all life in Kal Maran.

— The Silveryn Doctrines, Volume I

CHAPTER XII

The Shield Edge, Sanctuary of the Silveryn Order

Tel'Andros looked in horror at the mangled bodies that lay scattered across the forest floor. They were little more than children; their smooth faces once alive with the curiosity and wonder of youth. Yet now, under the eaves of the Aeldenwood and within a few feet of the Shield itself, no breath stirred from the eight small corpses.

It's impossible that this has happened.

In fact, it was a tragedy of the worst kind; a culling of the increasingly rare talent that the Silveryn Order travelled the expanse of Kal Maran to discover. Every year their numbers dwindled, and every year the Shield continued to weaken.

Running his hands along the surface, Tel'Andros pondered the reality of its waning strength. The Shield looked like a shimmering wall of silvery blue water rising from the terrain. The magical barrier reached high into the sky, eventually fading from view as it disappeared into the clouds. An electric tingle quivered beneath Tel'Andros' fingertips, and the sensation caused his muscles to twitch involuntarily. The feeling was harmless to a mage of his abilities. Unlike most of humankind, a Silveryn mage could walk through the barrier as easily as a man might walk beneath a cascading waterfall.

Although his mind wandered, the harsh reality of the present tragedy forced him to face the grisly matter at hand. With trepidation he returned his gaze to the slain novices. The three girls and five boys had barely seen a dozen summers, and now they would see no more. Kneeling down beside the closest body, Tel'Andros struggled to maintain control of his stomach as it roiled and tossed uncomfortably. The girl's body had been savagely torn apart. Her left arm hung limply by a thin shred of bloodied tissue, while the hand itself was completely missing. Her soft brown robe was a tattered mess, and deep slashing wounds crisscrossed her torso. The girl's neck was tilted awkwardly to one side, and the right half of her throat had been ripped out. Dark crimson blood had poured from the gash, seeping into the newly fallen snow. Reaching out a trembling hand, Tel'Andros gently closed the young girl's eyes and whispered a quiet prayer beneath his breath.

As he moved towards the next victim, he suddenly recalled her name — Tari. She had been a soft-spoken girl with a beautiful smile. Pausing to look at her tortured body one last time, it was all he could do to control the terrible sadness that welled up inside of him. It would serve no purpose to weep now for the fallen. There would be a time and a place for mourning. For now, the mages of the Silveryn Order needed to exact their own measure of vengeance; those responsible would face justice.

As he crouched near the next victim, this one a tawny-haired boy, he heard the soft rustle of robes as someone approached. Ignoring the new arrival, he gently closed the novice's sightless eyes. What remained of this child was nearly impossible to describe. *The pain he must have felt before his passing...*

"Pardon my intrusion, Tel'Andros, but you asked me to inform you if we found the remains of Ir'Roland."

Slowly returning to his feet, Tel'Andros turned to face the speaker. "Thank you, Sasha. If you would be so kind," he motioned towards her.

"Of course, Magus," she responded immediately, her eyes desperately trying to avoid the slain children. Walking next to the shimmering wall of the Shield, she led him towards her find.

Less than a hundred paces from the site, the Archmage Roland lay in a pool of his own blood. His gold-trimmed robes were reduced to rags, the remaining pieces barely covering his battered frame. Roland's command and understanding of Aer had been both profound and impressive. His murderers cared little for such details. Most of his face had been viciously slashed by claws belonging to creatures unmerciful in their savagery. Breathing deeply, Tel'Andros carefully extracted the man's hood from behind his shattered skull and covered as best he could the gruesome visage.

Unlike the carnage near the young novices, there was clear evidence that Roland had not fallen easily. The burned bodies of at least a score of Gath lay scattered throughout the area. The destroyed forms were a welcome sight to Tel'Andros, suddenly overcome by a dark flash of hatred. *Such senseless violence...*

For many years now, the Order had been losing strength, while its enemies multiplied. Where once the halls of Dragon Mount had been filled with enthusiastic laughter and the excitement of youth, now there remained only cold stone and empty corridors. Few people cared to send their children to the once hallowed halls of the Silveryn Order. With regret and a slight tremble of fear, Tel'Andros recognized that losing eight novices was a severe blow. Still, this was a stark reminder of the importance of the Shield and the commitment required by the mages to fend off the unnatural forces that threatened their borders.

The vicious Gath had first pierced the magical ward that summer. The Council believed such a feat to be impossible for such mindless creatures, and yet the leaders of the Order still refused to admit that a second force must have played a role in the breach. The Archmages were silent regarding the dark rumour circulating among the rest of the mages in Dragon Mount. They refused to acknowledge the obvious secret known by all; that only renegade mages possessed the skill and the power to rend the Shield. They, and only they, could be responsible; but Tel'Andros knew the cost of forcing the issue with the Council.

Looking down at Archmage Roland, his body mangled and broken, Tel'Andros realized that matters were quickly slipping out of control. Regrettably, Ir'Roland had been one of the many who had dismissed his suspicions regarding the Fallen as foolishness — and now he was dead.

"He fought well, Magus," sounded a voice from behind. "The Gath will think twice before attempting another raid through our defenses."

Tel'Andros ignored the new arrival as he brushed some dirt from his robes, staring balefully at the twisted carcasses of the terrible beasts. He suspected that the First would be unimpressed by the report she would soon receive detailing today's slaughter. The Gath should never have been able to breach the barrier, let alone attack with such strength and ferocity as to slay one of the Order's highest ranking mages.

The black-armoured soldier waited patiently to be addressed. Tel'Andros knew him well. He was the Koriani Third, and Andros was pleased that the elite guard from Dragon Mount had sent one of its finest to investigate the tragedy. The First would be wise to consider this a matter of the utmost urgency.

He was clad in the customary garb of the Order's private guard, including black leather armour embossed with a slash of silver at the sleeves. The warrior looked grim in the weak morning light.

Tel'Andros soon realized that the forest behind him was crawling with soldiers, most crouching to better observe the bloodied ground.

"Deowyn, I will need your men to scour the forest immediately. If any of the Gath remain in the area, I want them hunted down," Tel'Andros ordered in a calm yet menacing tone. "Ir'Roland did cast his distress spell only moments before he fell. He died here hoping that the creatures would consider him the only threat so that his young charges could escape. Something must have gone terribly wrong..." he trailed off.

"My men are already tracking fresh Gath movements along a trail to the west. If the creatures can be caught before they leave the boundaries of the Order, they will be destroyed," Deowyn replied confidently.

"And your take on the battle site, Third?" Tel'Andros asked.

"I believe you are correct, Magus," the soldier nodded sadly. "Once the archmage discovered the Gath within the boundaries of the Shield, he reacted to protect his pupils."

"But..." Tel'Andros prodded. He could tell that an unspoken addition to the Koriani soldier's hypothesis was forthcoming.

Clearing his throat, Deowyn continued. "All signs indicate that the mage was the last of the party to be slain. The placement of the Gath bodies," he indicated with a gauntleted hand, "is consistent with a battle being fought towards the clearing, not away from it. The Archmagus was trying to return to the clearing, not flee from it."

"But why?" Tel'Andros asked, confused by the suggestion. "Ir'Roland would have known that the children, as much as his counsel had always been valued, were more important than his own life. The novices are the future of the Order."

"He did so because he was not the target," Deowyn averted his eyes. "The children were."

A light drizzle began to fall, penetrating the thick forest canopy overhead. Lifting his face to catch the cold rain, Tel'Andros closed his eyes and shivered. It took a moment to realize that it was the Koriani guard's comment that had caused the sensation, and not the rain.

The children... He agonized in silence.

Here we are again old friend,
a journey's rest, a road, an end.
In darker times, we will wander,
to tear the fears of men asunder.
A yarn of glory, love, and pain,
a warm respite from pouring rain.
For t'is my calling, passion, and way,
as my mistress, your songs I'll play.
— 'The Lute', Shenro Taleweaver

CHAPTER XIII

Briar, Northern Council

The blizzard tore through the shuttered and empty streets of Briar with a ferocity that worried even the hardened old-timers.

For three days and three nights the winds howled, and the snow fell as a thick blanket on the northern town in amounts never before seen. The shrieking gale hampered sleep, and many grew short of temper. For a folk that thrived upon the outdoors even in the dead of winter, the forced confinement had many a family arguing and fuming with each other about everything.

Even the Lumbers, regarded as the hardiest of men, were forced to endure a certain incarceration of their own. They were trapped miserably within their camps and away from their families. By the third day of the storm, the townsfolk were carefully monitoring their wood piles for fear of running out of fuel. It was fire that warded off the deadly cold that managed to slip through the cracks of the homesteads in Briar.

In the Black Boar, Alessan's world had been reduced to two simple chores: stoking the fire and monitoring the large black pot dangling over the flames.

Even his mother's inn, a well-built and well-maintained establishment, felt the cold bite of the incessant winds and driving snow. Early on the second day, Alessan and Varis had painstakingly covered each and every window in the large common room.

His mother wanted to block out as much of the storm's chill as possible. Alessan wondered how some of the outlying homes were faring in the midst of such a powerful blizzard.

Local business had been slow, but the arrival of a large merchant caravan returning from the south kept the common room partially full, if not a little boisterous. With nowhere to go, the men and women of the party had chosen to drink themselves into a stupor. Even now at the crack of dawn, three men diced in the corner with an almost empty bottle of spirits at their side. A few of their companions lay sprawled across one of the wooden tables, with their snoring clearly audible from the far end of the room.

As always, Alessan was overlooked as he struggled to carry an armful of dried logs through the mess and clutter. Carefully avoiding the majority of the dishes and food strewn about the floorboards, he reached the hearth with a sigh of relief. His body, but especially his weakened arm, tended to throb painfully when the colder weather settled in for the season. Rubbing his arm for good measure, he headed back to the kitchen.

His mother would be expecting him at the breakfast table. It was a rare treat to be able to eat together with Varis, his sister, and his mother, as they were almost always busy serving the customers. With the common room still in use, the Black Boar's workers had some time to pass before the remainder of the merchant party retired. His mother decided that cleaning the room could wait.

"Did I hear voices coming from the front, Ally?" his mother asked as he sank into one of the wooden chairs at the small dinner table.

"Yes, Mother," he nodded, reaching for a steaming homemade biscuit. "There are still three of them awake and dicing. The others are... sleeping," he added, taking aim at a crock of butter.

"Are they still drinking?" Kayla frowned.

"One of them has been drinking since he arrived," Varis cut in. "Nothing much to do while cooped up I suppose. Not my choice these last few days, but a popular one around town I'd be willing to bet."

"Quite a disgusting display of behaviour if you ask me," his sister replied.

"But one that fills the coffers and pays for our food," Varis answered.

"Let it be. We've seen worse, and I'd rather speak of something else besides the storm and our guests," Shani Oakleaf said, passing a thick slab of cooked ham to the old man.

Alessan noted the tired expression on his mother's face. It had become quite common to see her this way ever since he had mentioned the prospect of leaving with Corian Praxxus. She appeared defeated, he realized with chagrin. Although a hard woman, harder after the death of his father, Alessan had been raised in a loving household. His mother had never beaten them, nor had she demanded more from her children than could be expected. She seemed to believe that should Alessan depart, he would never return. She was saddened by his enthusiasm to leave his family behind. A stranger, she had argued one night, had earned his trust and confidence more easily than those who had loved and accepted him all his life.

He knew what she meant by the remark. He was a *ba'caech* in the eyes of the world; half a man who could do little to support either himself or others. Without the Black Boar to run after her death, Alessan knew she feared for his future. It was a loving and realistic response for the son she had sheltered since his birth. Strangely enough, although he dare not speak such thoughts, Alessan was confident his father would have supported his desire to see the world. Twice now, those very words had been dangerously close to the tip of his tongue. Turning away when his mother was angry had always been the best course of action; and when speaking of his dead father, it was the only course to follow.

"Karli Burnaise is expecting soon," Kayla said, breaking Alessan's train of thought.

"The Fey'Derin lieutenant's wife?" his mother asked.

"Yes, I met her in the market last week. Some say it could be twins with the size of her belly," Kayla commented.

"That will be her seventh and eighth, no?" Varis asked. "Seems the *Drayenmark* are of a hardier stock than you and I. That woman must have seen close to forty-five summers, and yet here she is ready to bear twins! Wasn't much I wanted to do at forty-five except eat, drink, and sleep," the man laughed, glancing at Shani.

Frowning at the older man, but with the hint of smile tugging at the corners of her mouth, Shani Oakleaf slapped the man on the arm. "Varis! I swear, one of these days you'll claim the last shreds of my children's innocence!"

"Hah! Too late for that don't you think?" Varis joked.

Enjoying the comfortable talk at the breakfast table, Alessan felt a twinge of guilt. Listening to the natural banter that flowed so easily between them, he could do little but smile. Looking around the table, he realized he would miss his family and friend dearly. Life, as much as he complained about it, could be far worse, but his heart truly sought to be outside the confines of Briar. For the moment though, being home was just fine, just fine indeed.

In the hopes of entertaining their increasingly miserable tenants, Kayla sang that night in the Boar. She took to the stage with confidence, even when faced with the reality that many of the intoxicated customers sitting before her failed to possess even the slightest control of their actions.

The wine and mead flowed steadily throughout dinner, and even the well-travelled Varis was skeptical of the mood. A rowdy crowd could spell trouble.

Not being aware of the young singer's talent, it took the better part of two haunting melodies of times gone past before the merchants settled quietly into their seats. They were astounded by the clear beauty of Kayla Oakleaf's voice.

> *To stay faithful, a bond of brotherhood was spoken,*
> *An'Darim heroes and many a tale told.*
> *Honour and glory for the heart of a kingdom,*
> *courage and love for a life not their own.*

> *An'Darim! An'Darim! Where can you be?*
> *Your people are gone, and their need so long past.*

> *A country divided, and your standard carried by the wind.*
> *Who will endure the burden of a nation?*
> *Who will be the shield guard to defend the downtrodden?*
> *Who will bury the dead and pray for new light?*

An'Darim! An'Darim! Why are we left so alone?
Mighty were you, and true was your sword.

Across rivers, forests and meadows of old,
through rain and snow once came your cry.
On steeds of glory you once rode till the dawn,
Fear in our enemies, the heroes of song.

An'Darim! An'Darim! Where shall you go?
No king and no glory, yet the Drayen still suffer.

Ease the pain of a people forever changed,
Strength in each other and beliefs long held sacred.
Alone we now remain, your company forever passed,
but we hope for a change, a return to times long gone.

An'Darim! An'Darim! What shall we tell the child?
The one who believed, and now walks alone.

As the last words carried clearly through the stunned silence of the room, Alessan wondered if he had seen his sister perform for the last time.

She had chosen a strange tune for her final song. It was a heartfelt ballad dating back to the dark years after the Shattering. The An'Darim had been the king's own guard; a personal company of elite soldiers that had disappeared after their liege lord was slain. Disgraced by failure, some said; others were convinced they had been betrayed by one of their own.

Penned by Shenro Taleweaver, a bard of some renown hailing from the southern regions of a land now consumed by the Aeldenwood, the ballad was a call for their return, a plea for sanity amidst the slaughter and discrimination of that terrible time. The An'Darim had never returned, and scarcely any trace of their history remained. With the passage of so many decades, the tale lived on in song. Alessan was touched by the heightened emotion contained in that last lingering note. His sister, he marveled, had a way with music that could pierce the hardest heart and soften the darkest soul.

As he settled into bed that evening, Alessan was overcome by a mounting nervousness over his impending departure. The letter Master Praxxus had left for him nearly five weeks ago lay on his small night table. The neatly folded parchment was his reminder of the opportunity waiting for him. He was determined to prove his worth to the wealthy man who had unexpectedly become his mentor. Although his mind was seldom completely at ease, for the first time in his young life, Alessan believed that he could find success outside of Briar.

He was only mildly surprised when he awoke to find himself walking through the forest. His dreams had become meticulously detailed; the smells, the sounds, the feelings. It seemed as though he could control the environment to a greater degree each time he dreamt of the fabled woods. He could even sense an energy emanating from the trees, the earth, the air, and the water.

As a boy he had never been naïve. At a young age, he had lost the opportunity to enjoy what it meant to simply be a child. Burdened by his twisted body, Alessan had often prayed that one day he would awake as if from a long dream. *Wishful thinking from a sad child*, he thought...

Having been subjected to punishment and torment from the healthy growing boys of the town, Alessan knew all about his frailties. Yet when he walked beside the immense trunks of the forest and touched the gnarled bark, he felt more alive and capable than he had ever thought possible. There was no pain in his dreams. His arm was still shriveled and weak, but the throbbing discomfort was gone. He walked proudly along the trails of the ancient forest.

Alessan could sense that he was striding upon one of the older paths in the Aeldenwood. Since meeting the stranger called C'Aelis, he often experienced variations of the dream he had first dreamt in late autumn. He had since decided that the man was not human, but could only be one of the long vanished Gorimm. Moreover, he believed that the connection made with the visitor on the riverbank had resulted in these prescient visions.

The many trails of the Aeldenwood were the centerpieces of his dreams. On some occasions, he found himself sitting in a dilapidated stone building; other times, he sat in a beautifully furnished study admiring books and ancient manuscripts. C'Aelis sometimes appeared, but rarely acknowledged

Alessan's presence. So vivid and intense were the dreams, that they become permanent memories.

Sometimes there would be nightmares. They would often take the shape and form of twisted abominations lurking in the shadows between the trees. The world would become dark, and the hideous creatures of the woods would hunt him, pin him down, and rend the very flesh from his body.

On those nights he would wake screaming, his terrified cries often bringing his sister to his bedside. She had noticed a change in him, but Alessan was thankful for her silence. Apart from his arcane reference to the Gorimm that late autumn night, she had avoided the subject. If she did ask about C'Aelis, he would be hard-pressed to lie to his sister. Having grown up for so long without their father, the two siblings had forever leaned on each other for support; to deceive her simply felt wrong.

When he awoke screaming early the next morning, body taut and eyes wide open with terror, she remained quiet once again. But the look in her eyes revealed that her patience was rapidly coming to an end.

ᘓ

Two days later, the storm broke. The people of the north shook themselves from their wintery slumber and returned to work. Huge amounts of snow were cleared from the streets, and the sound of hammers were clearly audible that first morning as men worked tirelessly to repair the damage caused by the high winds.

Varis spent the morning collecting broken shutters and patching up those that could be saved. Alessan assumed the older man would need help cutting the new ones and so took to his daily chores with zeal in the hopes that his mother would grant him permission to work outdoors. After so many days trapped in the inn, the fresh cold air would be a welcome respite.

Alessan was sweeping a thick layer of dirt from the back storeroom when word arrived that a large caravan from Hallenford had weathered the blizzard at the Fey'Derin encampment to the north. Master Corian Praxxus, true to his word, headed the convoy. According to the messenger, the caravan was due to arrive the following evening. The Black Boar was cordially asked to be their host with a special request that the Lady Kayla Oakleaf grace the common room with her beautiful voice. The request was gladly accepted by the young songstress.

လ

In silence, Alessan watched the large procession as it arrived. The main room and suites shone like new. The kitchen was prepped, and Varis was dressed in his finest clothes. The women of the household wore festive dresses in honour of the occasion. The arrival of such a large group would set the inn further ahead than usual when it came to counting their earnings for the year. The Boar had always done exceptional business, but with the high profile merchant staying for a second time, even Alessan's mother could smile in anticipation of the rich rewards. An honest day's work was nothing to be ashamed of, she would always say.

The wagons started rolling into town from the northeast not long after midday. Alessan had only a few moments to watch as they made their way through the town's recently cleared roads. There remained some time before the arrival, as their pace was slowed considerably by the deep drifts left behind by the great storm. Extra wood was still needed in the kitchen if the cooking was to go smoothly that evening.

And so, some hours later, the Black Boar was left spotless due to their hard work. Alessan stood somewhat patiently near the entrance, his mother having set him on watch for Corian's arrival. His nervousness was obvious, and he began to fidget as the minutes dragged on. His palms were sweaty, and his tight collar added to his discomfort. And then, with a great amount of zeal, the door to the inn was thrown open.

"Young Master Oakleaf, it is a pleasure to see you once again!" boomed Corian Praxxus, surveying the room. "And the place looks simply wonderful!" he added.

Alessan smiled broadly as the big man, bedecked in exquisite gold and silver jewelry, entered the Black Boar. His clothing was made of the finest silks available on the market, and his crimson winter coat was trimmed with thick white fur belonging to the rare Kelamyrian lynx.

He looked heavier than he had at his departure in late autumn, with a rounded belly of girth bulging out even further than Alessan remembered. His boisterous nature and exuberant personality remained perfectly intact. Walking over to join him at a table near the roaring hearth fire, Alessan realized he had genuinely missed the curious man.

"The pleasure is all mine, Master Praxxus."

Seeing Alessan waiting cordially upright near the table, much as an employee or servant might do, Corian waved impatiently towards the wooden bench. "Come, come, and sit. Until tomorrow morning, I'd prefer to pass on the formalities and enjoy a drink with a friend."

"My apologies, sir." Alessan replied as he took a seat.

"No matter, lad, no matter. But on the morrow, as I've already mentioned, things will change. You will be one of my bookkeepers, at least for the coming journey."

Reaching across his ample chest and unbuttoning the clasp that was holding his cloak in place, Corian smiled. "Enough of business, Alessan, I have need of a fine ale to quench my thirst, and I have still to pass on greetings to both your mother and sister. No one will ever contend that Corian Praxxus of Innes Vale is an unkind and rude guest!"

Word spread quickly throughout town that Kayla was to sing for the guests at the Boar. Everyone was proud that it was not the arrival of strangers that brought the townsfolk to the inn, but the talents of the young woman from Briar. Strangers were passing moments; some good, some bad, and infinitely less important to a town that boasted only a few hundred souls.

The night was a resounding success. Kayla sang, accompanied by Varis, and the crowd enthusiastically applauded each and every one of her renditions. They danced and sang along to familiar tunes; they drank and roared their approval at others. After hours of harried work, Alessan found himself seated across from Corian with a welcome mug of ale gripped tightly in his own hand.

"Is everything is settled with your mother, Alessan?" Corian asked. The merchant was on his third plate of mutton and showed no signs of slowing down. Alessan had been given permission to sit with his new employer for a few minutes, as long as it did not interfere with his serving duties. Although unhappy with his choice, his mother respected the need to speak with the merchant.

"Yes," Alessan frowned.

"She still thinks I will be the death of you then?" he inquired. "She's still angry," Alessan nodded.

"Women can be such pains," the merchant chuckled. "Sometimes you need to ignore their reasoning and worry about yourself. Who cares really?"

"I am his mother, Master Praxxus, and trust me, I care," responded a menacing voice from behind him. "It is my job and responsibility to worry about my child. I need no other reason for my anger, and I believe it is quite clear that Alessan has ignored my request to remain at the inn until he is older. Do not patronize me by explaining to my son, *my son*, how a woman thinks!" Shani Oakleaf slammed two new pitchers of ale down hard upon the table, turned without another word, and headed back through the packed crowd.

At that moment, Alessan wished he could crawl beneath the table and remain hidden for the remainder of the night. Corian fared little better against the motherly assault. Red-faced and obviously embarrassed, the merchant refused to make eye contact with anyone.

"I believe I should get back to work, sir. With the size of the crowd this evening, it's hardly fair that I spend more time chatting with the guests than serving."

"Aye, that seems best, lad. I'll see you in the morning," Corian replied. "And remember..."

"Yes?"

"You work for me now. Friendships often get in the way of business, but I may need advice on occasion. When I do, I'll seek you out."

"I'm sure you'll know where to find me," Alessan answered, shaking the man's hand before slipping through the crowd towards the kitchen.

Exhausted, Alessan reached his bedchamber well after mid of night. Despite his excitement about the upcoming journey, for one night at least, no dreams or nightmares pierced his veil of sleep.

മ

The caravan was immense; comprised of two dozen large wagons, each one packed to the brim with a multitude of items destined for the marketplaces in the southern expanses of Old Caledun. Twenty pack mules, all heavily laden with even more accessories to be sold in the south, waited impatiently in the snow that morning. The naturally stubborn animals sniffed at the snow while watching their handlers warily. Two larger covered wagons were placed near the center of the train, their ornately painted doorways a sure sign of wealth and prosperity. Gold trim adorned the outer frames of both the rolling carriages. One belonged to the venerable Master Praxxus while the second housed a robed figure that rarely exited the confines of his stately quarters. Alessan had only glimpsed the man for a brief moment when he had stepped out to speak to Corian Praxxus.

The Sylvani milled about in ordered confusion. Many of the mercenary soldiers took the time to recheck their packs. To leave something behind prior to such a journey would be to lose it forever.

The Sylvani had prepared for a lengthy stay down south. Captain Pragg calmly answered questions from various officers in the company, pointing here and there while riding up and down the line to ensure everything was in order. The mercenaries, after an extended stay near Oakfeld Patch, were as anxious as anyone to head south and into the warring Protectorate. They would arrive in time to attend the Gathering in the spring, and they were anxious to see what contracts would be offered for the next summer of warfare.

With nearly sixty members of the caravan's entourage and the combined hundreds of the newly formed Sylvani nearby, Corian Praxxus bellowed orders with an air of such superiority and arrogance that Alessan found himself glad he wasn't responsible for the planning of the journey. The large merchant accosted any who reported a delay or problem concerning the eventual departure. Seeing the entrepreneur in action, Alessan wondered briefly if he could ever command with such conviction and passion.

Corian remained aloof as the company prepared to set forth. The camaraderie of the previous evening would be the last for some time. Upon his arrival that morning, Alessan had been issued a simple green tunic and dark trousers. His new uniform was sturdy and well-made; a little fancy compared to his usual attire, but acceptable just the same. He was treated with the same respect as every other man reporting for duty that morning. Although he caught several eyes warily watching his preparations, Alessan felt confident that his frailties would be viewed as insignificant. If Corian Praxxus determined that there was merit behind your service, most of the caravan workers took that as proof enough that you belonged.

An hour before the sun was to rise that day, everything was ready. The departure, so long delayed by the brutal storm of the previous week, slowly began. Mules snorted and stamped their hooves, horses neighed and pushed forward into the deeper drifts that remained, and the wagon drivers whooped and called out instructions to their horses. The chaotic din of noise was like nothing Alessan had ever heard.

Pausing at the entrance of the Black Boar, Alessan hurried inside. Clustered together near the entryway stood his mother, Kayla, and Varis. Fighting back a rush of emotion, he gripped the older man's hand firmly. The often pragmatic and unemotional man pulled him fiercely into a tight hug.

"You stay safe, Alessan. Watch your back, remember your place, and do us proud. I have no doubt that you will," Varis whispered as they held each other.

Nodding in reply and realizing the impact his departure was having on the longtime employee of the family, Alessan addressed his sister.

"You know you can't go off into the world and forget who you are or where you came from, Ally," she said, hugging him close.

"I won't," he replied, his voice strained by the effort of the goodbye.

"I made you something, a reminder of the people who care for you in this backwater town." Kayla reached into the pocket of her apron and retrieved a beautifully crafted bracelet of wooden beads intertwined with a supple cord.

Alessan accepted the token with gratitude. He turned the bracelet over and caught his breath when he saw the images engraved on the back: his sister's musical note, his mother's heart, and Varis' clenched fist. And yet the fourth symbol, his father's axe, made his heart flutter. Smiling at Kayla, he held her tightly one last time.

"Father would be proud of you, Ally," she whispered, tears rolling down her round cheeks.

And finally he stood before Shani Oakleaf, the mother who had so desperately wanted her son to remain safe in her home, protected by her strength and love. Her eyes were moist as she pulled him fiercely to her chest.

"You can still back out, Alessan," she said.

"You know I need to do this, mother. I need to see what lies out in the world for me. Briar has never fully accepted me. They decided I lacked the strength to be respected," he answered.

"They know nothing," Shani whispered as she let him go, tears falling freely between them.

"Maybe they do know nothing, but one day I'll return and I'll prove it, I'll show them their mistake," he said with conviction.

"Don't do this for spite and revenge, lad," Varis interrupted, his hand resting lightly on the young man's shoulder. "Do it for yourself."

"I will," Alessan answered, and after turning one last time to embrace his mother, he headed out the doorway of the inn he had known as his home for his entire life.

Limping painfully in the deep snow, he forced his tired and aching body to move quickly. Catching up to one of the wagons, he accepted a proffered arm of help and climbed aboard. Leaning out and around the corner of the cart, he waved enthusiastically at his mother and sister. Fighting back another wave of emotion, Alessan Oakleaf turned around. He faced forward with a determined gaze, looking out at the snow covered fields that surrounded the small town.

Briar was now a part of his past.

The Wilds are infested with a sickness that sends my stomach into re-volt. There is no order, no sense of sanity in this untamed land. It is such a waste to watch the savages we call goblins, the only inhabitants of this place, miss the opportunity that lies so clearly before them. The warring clans of this barbaric race disgust me.
—Baron Ely Stone 'The Uncharted Lands'

CHAPTER XIV

The Wilds, Northern Wilderness

L eoric D'Athgaran wanted to die.

The words reverberated in his weary mind for the third time that morning. He struggled to maintain some semblance of reason even as he forced his beaten and nearly naked body to continue moving. Leoric raised his head and stared at his captors with an unwaveringly spiteful glare. At his feet, the emaciated form of a young woman lay on the ground, shielded for the moment by his own haggard frame.

For his arrogance, the thick end of a staff cracked across his already swollen face. Staggering under the force of the blow, Leoric rubbed his jaw and spat blood from his mouth. The woman had recovered enough to grasp his outstretched arm and struggle back to her feet, her thin pale face looking graciously into his eyes. With a dull, throbbing pain now radiating from chin to temple, he responded to her with as much of a comforting look as was possible under the circumstances. Truthfully, Leoric wanted to die and be done with it. *It would be so easy...*

Although he had long since lost track of the passing days, Leoric judged by the bitterly cold air and increased snowfall that nearly a month had passed. It was hard enough to keep track of his own muddled thoughts, let alone focus on the passing of each day. Only the never ending torment of this accursed journey warranted any consideration. It had become almost unbearable, and no amount of training had prepared him for this kind of struggle.

His body ached from minor wounds obtained in battle, and his stomach growled due to the measly portions of food they had been allotted. Most of his welts and bruises were received defending some of the helpless prisoners. Sleep was a luxury he could barely remember; a fantastical dream of a past he had once lived. His left eye was swollen shut going on two days, and his left wrist was contorted in an odd position. The fact that he could still use the hand was the only good news he could relate since his capture.

Shuffling his feet, he watched the men and women lagging near the rear of the line. Leoric prayed they would reach their destination before it was too late. The line, regardless of his efforts, continued to grow shorter.

When he had regained consciousness after the battle, Leoric found himself bound tightly and thrown into a tent with a dozen of the men from Darkenedge. Those first moments were filled with denial, and thoughts of a heroic escape were already swirling in the minds of those assembled. It was agonizing to now realize how distant such an escape had really been.

By the end of that first day, two men were dead and the rest of the group was stripped bare except for their boots and filthy loincloths. Had it been high summer, he was certain they would have left the area in bare feet. With a blatant disregard for the weather, they were given nothing else to protect their exposed skin. Although the temperature was strangely tepid for such a northern expanse of Kal Maran, still the prisoners suffered. By the end of the first week, most sported frostbitten patches of skin that were blackened and numb.

The nights were terrible for all. Huddled together with a few dozen unwashed bodies, Leoric could only wonder why fate had decreed such a punishment. Modesty had been thrown aside weeks earlier, and the scantily-clad group used each other's warmth to pass the night. Everyone had trouble sleeping, and most nights were spent tossing and turning uncomfortably. Yet still did they trudge onward.

Catching the eye of his friend Angvald, the Kaleenian met his stare with a look of steady conviction. The big man was bringing up the rear, hoping that his presence and great strength would lend confidence to the weakened stragglers. Tragically, some could not be saved. Noticing a small waif-like woman only a few steps in front of Angvald, Leoric read the brutal truth lurking in his friend's eyes. *Elanor would be the next to fall.*

At the outset they had numbered thirty-two; now, only eight remained. The price of exhaustion, starvation, and infection was all the same. Death shadowed each and every one of the survivors, harassing them and mocking their weak attempts at avoiding the inevitable. It lurked not only in the darkness of the forest, but also in the depressed emptiness of their minds.

Angvald and Leoric stood as two of only four remaining soldiers. A young recruit named Drake and the veteran Halas completed the small group of fighters. Drake limped painfully near the rear of the line, his leg stinging from a recent beating. He displayed courage and resilience to the others, but the haunted look in his eyes betrayed his actions. He was near collapse, so near in fact, that Leoric moved to his side in order to lend him comfort.

Halas, on the other hand, was battered almost beyond recognition. Leoric had counted himself as one of the rebellious souls who still carried themselves with whatever small amount of dignity he could sustain, but Halas sought death with glee. He was downright hostile to his captors; inviting every beating with a smile, every flogging with laughter. The man refused to give in to his goblin captors. It was only a matter of time before his body was so broken that he had been left for dead somewhere in the uncharted Wilds.

The other prisoners were peasants who had been living simple and comfortable lives before the goblins raided their settlement north of the border fort. This goblin activity was far more calculated than the men of Darkenedge had anticipated. The hardy northern folk continued to fight bravely for their lives in captivity.

Elanor and Shale were two farm women who struggled to keep up the brutal pace set by their captors. Shale was the young woman Leoric had protected as she lay exhausted in the cold snow. Stephen and Merias were the final two country folk;

men of uncommon stock who spoke little, and yet trudged forward resolutely in the face of such malice.

Leoric worried about the older peasant's state of mind. Stephen had taken to mumbling in his sleep; seemingly caught in the memories of a better time. He held conversations with the night sky; his eyes shut fast against the current surroundings. Stephen spoke as if his wife and children were present; he even spoke aloud to his dead mother. Each day it seemed to take the man longer to break the fugue that clouded his thoughts. He would not last much longer if the situation worsened.

Leoric often wondered if the goblins were playing some vile joke on the prisoners; walking them in circles and laughing at their pain. Trying hard to disregard this idea, the borderman pushed onward.

Later that day, with weary and frozen muscles, Leoric stumbled in the deep snow. Falling to his knees brought a welcome respite for his tired legs. Overcome with relief, he closed his eyes and let the weak sunshine of the afternoon wash over him. He could hear birds singing in the trees and the gentle rushing of water of a nearby stream. The sound of swishing branches swaying in the light breeze comforted him. *So peaceful... so quiet...*

"By Olaf of the Hunt, you are not going to die on me now!" swore Angvald as a pair of thick arms wrapped themselves around Leoric's upper body. Unable to combat the enormous strength that his friend still possessed, Leoric snapped opened his eyes.

"Don't give me that look you fool!" the big man spoke harshly. "I need you, and so do the others."

Pausing to look at the rest of their sorry column, he was surprised to see the rest of the prisoners helplessly watching the exchange. They wore sad looks that struck him with a profound grief. Nodding grimly at Angvald, a pair of goblin savages approaching with staves ready to be used, Leoric steadied himself and stood to his feet.

Dying would be too easy, he thought.

ഗ

By morning, only seven remained.

Elanor had died in her sleep, bundled between Merias and Shale. Seeing the body lying on the cold ground, her eyes vacant and staring at what only the gods knew, Leoric feared that eventually they would all perish. Staring at the frozen corpse, he wondered how long they would last. *If they all fell… would anyone care that they were gone?*

An intense beam of sunlight cleared the edge of the clouds and pierced the tall trees bordering the small clearing. The bright white snow shimmered like a sea of diamonds. Watching the sun rise and noticing the peaceful expression on Elanor's face, Leoric was struck by a lingering memory.

Alanna D'Athgaran died on a warm summer's morning. The sweet scent of lilacs covered the smell of death in the bedchamber. The curtains were drawn, but from an open window drifted the clear outdoor sounds of that beautiful day. He could still remember the cheerful chirps of the bluebirds, the chatter of the large red squirrels, and the subdued hush of the wind.

Swathed in many blankets, Alanna lay peacefully on the bed. The fever had worsened during the night, and yet for this brief moment, her face was serene, her breathing deep and unlaboured. The night had been hard on her tired body, and the chills remained. She was a tall woman with eyes of clear blue and hair the colour of desert sand. She was everything most lovers dreamt of, and she could have chosen any man to be her husband.

Somehow she had seen something special in the face of a bumbling farmer who shied away from the town gatherings and fairs she so loved. She was graceful and elegant; a woman with a noble beauty that far outshone the other ladies of the town. Never arrogant, Alanna held Leoric's heart in her hand from the moment he laid eyes upon her. He had lost count of the number of times he begged the gods on high to allow him to endure her suffering. He wanted so much to take away the poison that had defiled her, and grant her the peace that she so deserved. Take me instead, he had prayed…

She was brave when faced with her mortality. Even in those last few hours with the fever raging, she made attempts to smile and assuage his fear and sadness. He was amazed by her indomitable will throughout her lengthy battle. The clerics had given her days to live, and yet here she lay, albeit fragile and weak, almost three months later.

For all he tried to do, Leoric could not stop the inevitable. In the early hours of that final day, she smiled and held him close. Alanna whispered one last time in his ear as he cradled her body gently in his arms.

"Watch over our baby, dear heart. Maya will need your strength. Promise me you'll keep her safe. And my love... know that every time you look at her, a piece of me smiles back."

They were her final words; and the only promise she had ever asked of him, lay broken for almost three years.

Sadly, Elanor's body had been left behind. No hymns were sung to appease the gods for her wandering spirit; no holy man spoke a prayer in her honour. As the others had been discarded by the merciless creatures, so too, was she.

Days later, they came to a vast river. The roar of a mighty waterfall could be heard to the south. Struggling to remember the partially charted maps he had examined of the Wilds, Leoric could not recall ever seeing a river this large on any of the old parchments. He knew now that he was in a land where for centuries no man had travelled.

Standing on the riverbank, he imagined himself diving silently into the cold inviting water. Enjoying a moment of peace, he sat down on a large rock overlooking the waterway. He cleared his mind of the boiling hatred and overwhelming despair that had threatened to engulf him over those past few days.

Turning to watch the goblins, he was struck by their paradoxical nature. They were beastly, and yet displayed a degree of civility that leaders of the Iron Shield had so often dismissed. Their clothing was more than simple animal skins, and their terrible battle trophies built from bones showed a high degree of craftsmanship. Under their pelts they wore simple homespun breeches and tunics. Leoric had met the savages many times before and had never seen them dressed in such garb. He could do little to shake the notion that there was something sinister afoot with the tribes in the Wilds. The new cooperation was cause for concern, and here he felt as though he were seeing a different breed of the enemy.

The creatures laughed and joked together, much like the men of Darkenedge did each and every day. It appeared as though they were comrades and not the greedy isolationists Leoric had once believed. He continued to watch his captors closely, hoping to glean some small advantage that could be exploited. He had clearly assessed their strength and discipline, and found few weaknesses. Their brutality was extreme, and their hatred of humankind drove them. *Would he and the others have treated the goblins differently had the roles been reversed?* He preferred not to pass judgment on his fellow man, but he doubted there would be much sympathy for the enemy.

"They're in a good mood today, Leoric," said Angvald in his deep baritone. Raising an eyebrow in response to his friend's comment, Leoric's eyes widened when he saw what was being offered. Two bright red apples glistened in the man's hand. "It's not every day that we eat something other than stale trail bread."

"Thank you," Leoric answered graciously. "It's a blessing made all the better because it was unexpected."

"Aye, you have the right of it. In my land this would serve as a small reminder that, regardless of our dire predicament, things could still be worse," the Kaleenian replied.

"How so, Angvald, how so?" Leoric countered.

"We could be dead," he replied solemnly. "Our bodies left untended in the wilderness. Abandoned without hope of ever having the rites of passage evoked. Abandoned into the afterlife with no guide to reach the halls of our forefathers."

"I am not a spiritual man, friend. You know that," Leoric replied wistfully. "I sometimes believe that those gone before us may have found peace, while we must endure."

"My people believe that death chooses you at your birth. All that is left for you is to walk your own path. Whatever your choices in life, that path will eventually lead to death's predetermined door."

"And do you believe this as well, Angvald?"

"I would stake my life on my beliefs. Would you?"

"I lost my faith a long time ago," Leoric muttered quietly. "I trust only in my own will to survive."

"Every man can lose his way. To some it is but a test. Perhaps you need time to find yours," his friend replied. Then, with a thoughtful expression creasing his tanned face, Angvald took a large bite of his apple.

The two men leaned against the outcropping for a long while, enjoying a rare break from their ordeal. Leoric was thankful for the silence after their conversation. He was not yet ready to speak about the past and what had brought him such pain and suffering. The same thing that had broken a set of beliefs he had once believed in so strongly and followed so devoutly.

A light fog was beginning to settle over the water, and Leoric's attention was again directed towards the riverbank. The pause in travel, it appeared, was never intended. Their captors awaited something from the opposite shore. Angvald was the first to spy a small dark shape moving slowly over the choppy waters.

With trepidation, Leoric watched as a wooden ferry built from rough timber logs and bound with strong twine approached. As the craft drifted closer, the unmistakable shape of more goblin guards, most of them hard at work steering the raft through the fast current, materialized from out of the fog.

The goblin captors herded the prisoners together along the rocky shore. They straightened their armour and stood at attention while waiting for the large raft. Their mannerisms at that moment reminded Leoric of a young Darius; the boy always so intent upon making a good impression. Yet he had always found a way to cause a problem and bring about the ire of Sergeant Alleran. Leoric paused when he remembered that Darius lay dead upon the forest floor; cold and lifeless for over a month now.

Little time was lost on pleasantries as the craft docked against the shore. Immediately after the two goblin parties met and exchanged guttural words, Leoric found himself pushed onto the slick floor of the wooden vessel. Large enough to accommodate the ragged band of prisoners as well as both groups of goblins, Leoric was surprised when only the pilot guards on the raft remained with them as they continued north.

Midway through the passage, Leoric caught Angvald's eye as he was leaning heavily against one of the vessel's railings. Sidling nonchalantly up alongside the support, Leoric joined the Kaleenian.

"I caught wind of something those bastards said when this band landed on the western side," Angvald whispered through clenched teeth.

"You speak goblin?" Leoric exclaimed. Upset by the near outburst, it was a long few moments before Angvald could reply.

"I've listened to them for long enough now," he finally explained. "Walking at the rear gave me a chance to catch some phrases that were repeated or accompanied by a laugh or a curse. It helped keep my mind focused."

"Fascinating." Leoric whispered. "I still have much to learn from you. Did you hear anything of value?"

Angvald grunted, "It seems as though the Marshal escaped the ambush. Somehow the old veteran ran free with a small company and headed to the rendezvous point with the rest of our men."

Weeks earlier, the report Angvald had brought forth regarding the battle was grim. They had both been captured before the combat ended and were skeptical that the defenders could have held out for much longer. Even though the remaining men had travelled a fair distance and used the terrain to the best of their advantage, the numbers had simply been overwhelming.

The news buoyed Leoric's flagging spirit. At least he knew the fortress would be forewarned of the coming tide, and preparations would be made for a likely attack in the spring. His brothers in arms would exact revenge for the men of the Iron Shield lost in the ambush.

"I can almost imagine Sergeant Alleran at the Marshal's side," Leoric gave his friend a slight grin.

"There's no way he'd let the goblins take him down," Angvald coughed, trying his best to cover a chuckle. "And if they did, they'd receive such a tongue lashing before he died that I'd bet none of the savages would ever forget it!"

"The Sergeant did have a certain way with words," Leoric smiled.

"They've also been repeating a strange word that I don't even begin to understand, but have come to believe refers to a place, possibly a town," Angvald added.

"Our destination?"

"Aye, I believe so. Strange though, they speak the word with a reverence. If not a place, it could possibly be a king, or perhaps a general of some sort."

"Do the goblin tribes even have a royal family?" Leoric mused. "In any case, what is this word?"

"*Lok'Dal hie.*"

It took the better part of the day to cross the rapidly moving current of the immense river. With the short winter days upon them, the light quickly began to fade as they landed on the far shore and once again began to trudge forward on foot. Although well-rested compared to recent days, most of Leoric's muscles had seized up.

By nightfall they were only six, and the march stopped for the night. As he devoured his daily piece of bread, Leoric realized with some surprise, that they now trekked upon a cobblestone road and not the uneven forest floor. Mystified by the change, he had an uneasy feeling lodged firmly in the pit of his stomach. He sensed that their journey would soon be coming to an end. As he bedded down and pressed in closely to the warm huddled bodies of his companions, he wondered about the meaning of the strange word Angvald had overheard during their travels. *What could it mean?*

By mid-afternoon the next day, with the sun shining brightly above, the gruff soldier from Darkenedge was given the answer to his question. Standing atop a steep cliff, he gazed at the green valley below. With a sense of foreboding, Leoric D'Athgaran looked down upon *Lok'Dal hie.*

Company salaries and bonuses fall under the discretion of the company captain. In an effort to increase the tenure of a member, and as a show of good faith, it is understood that each soldier will be entitled to mandatory leave, or a subsequent rest period, between contracts.
—Mercenary Code of Conduct

CHAPTER XV

Galen'hide - Sanctuary of the Silveryn Order

The fire crackled as Gavin read the long awaited words written so carefully on the parchment he held in his hands.

Dearest Beloved,

How long has it been since last we set eyes upon each other? Would that you had stayed north for the winter. I hope that this letter finds you well. News has arrived from the merchant ships on the coast, and I can only assume you fought for Lord Berry again this summer. By all accounts, the duke held the city once again.

My father seems unimpressed that Lord Yarr has gained so much control in the Protectorate. I'm afraid your warnings have fallen upon deaf ears. Instead, he has continued to entertain the greedy, self-absorbed men of the courts with my impending marriage. He sees only political gain where he should be seeking happiness for his

*daughter. I know his allies are using me as a pawn to gain favour
with the enemy, but I would be wed to none other than you, Gavin.*

*Reginald has since informed me that both the barons Welch and
Haldwell have made offers concerning alliances that would benefit
my father's interests. I fear time has grown short, and I reflect daily
on what would happen if I was ever to make public my feelings for
you. A great man like my father would shudder at the thought of his
'noble' daughter in the arms of a mercenary captain. The commoners
have long been considered beneath the rulers of the Northern Council.*

*I miss you so much, Gavin; your smile, your touch, your voice. Can
it be that two people could fall so madly in love and yet never be
granted the pleasure of the other's company? I can only pray that the
gods are merciful and hear of our plight.*

*Please pass on my regards to the others. Tell Caolte I am proud he
will be a father again so soon. Ethan's father took ill in the fall, but
has since recovered. There is not much in this world that can defeat
Lord Shade. Ossric, I'm sure, is miserable. That he can't find an
excuse for battle in the dead of winter must be driving him mad!
Be safe, dear heart.*

I am yours, Gavin Silveron, always and forever,

Danys

Gavin sighed. Receiving mail from Danys Ford rarely came without a cost. The
joy of reading the words expressing her love for him was tempered by the realization that they could never be together. Their worlds were so different that in the
eyes of her family it would be a crime for a low born mercenary to engage with the
daughter of a duke. And so it was that the only woman he had ever truly loved was
among the class of people that he was unable to marry. Nobility married nobility,
and that was the end of it.

Lord Angelo Ford was the most powerful man in the Northern Council. Although his influence paled in comparison to the expansive reach of Gadian Yarr,

still did his word hold favour with the nobility. As with the south, the concerns of the populace were largely ignored. The nobles looked only to themselves.

Frustrated, and realizing he would not be seeking the comfort of his blankets any time soon, Gavin donned his thick cloak and stepped out into the crisp air of the winter night.

Life for the soldiers had regained some sense of normalcy. After another successful campaign fighting for Duke Berry, the company had been resting quietly for the past month. Loud clanging from the smithy's shop rang out every morning, and the training yard was always crowded. Upon their arrival, Gavin had allowed the men to spend a few days in town, the nearest being a small backwater place named Gamewood. It was no city, but it boasted two taverns, an inn and a brothel.

Once the merriment had concluded, the Fey'Derin officers returned to the business of training and upkeep of the company. The daily routines the recruits had tried so desperately to forget returned, and yet there was only a smattering of complaints about wood gathering, cooking, cleaning, and of course, winter night duty.

Gavin relished these times; periods of rest where he could actually sit back and reminisce on the year. It was a profession that rarely allowed time for pause or reflection. The young captain was satisfied with the minimal loss of life this year. The men had performed admirably under duress, and the new arrivals, now well trained and soon to assume their new commands, showed great promise.

The stout Eör Rockfar had his troubles dealing with a few of the more stubborn men, but had resolved every issue with tact. It had taken a monumental sacrifice on the dwarf's part to remain at the base camp for a summer. Eör was proud of his battle prowess, almost as much as Ossric McConnal. The two warriors took great pleasure in dueling on the practice field; the towering Ossric with great axe in hand, and the stout yet powerful Eör wielding a heavy iron mace. Those contests were something to behold, even more so than his own, Gavin thought, but far less successful in coin for the loser. He was thankful to have another few years before he needed to ask the dwarf to remain behind once again.

It was late in the night, and the camp was quiet. A few men walked the walls, their eyes scanning the countryside for movement. In this freezing weather it was normal to expect the men to move about as much as possible. Keeping warm was crucial with the cold winds sweeping over the low hills. *Galen'hide* was on a small peak bordering the edge of the land claimed as a sanctuary by the Silveryn Order of Mages. A fort built of sturdy logs hauled up from the nearby Aeldenwood, it stood in the foothills of the *Erienn* range with towering mountains beyond soaring high into the eastern sky.

Clasping his heavy cloak at the neck, Gavin climbed the stairs and headed towards one of the fort's tall wooden towers. Inside, he knew he would find Caolte Burnaise puffing on one of his long-handled wooden pipes whittled from discarded wood. Sure enough, as he finished his short climb up the ladder, Gavin accepted the outstretched hand of his long-time friend.

"Another sleepless night?" Caolte commented with concern. He turned his gaze immediately back to the countryside once he had pulled Gavin up from the ladder. The arrival of a friend was no excuse for failing in his watch duty. Neither did being on guard warrant the absence of his pipe, Gavin noted.

"I'm starting to wonder if I've forgotten what it means to sleep, Caolte," Gavin answered. "Danys sends her greetings, and her congratulations as well."

"Karli wrote that she believed it might be twins this time," the *Drayenmark* soldier answered proudly, a fatherly glow radiating from his face. Although often absent due to his chosen profession, the veteran doted over his three boys and three girls, whenever the chance presented itself.

Gavin took no offense that the man eagerly awaited the turning of the seasons. With the spring, Caolte would attend the *Ca'lenbam* before heading home north to his family. The latest group of new recruits would be his only charges for the upcoming year.

"I'd best watch you and that wife of yours, old man," Gavin chuckled. "Before long you may have the numbers to rival our company. What will I do when the Burnaise family comes to claim its place in the leadership?"

"Bah! You just worry about finding yourself a woman of your own before you bother me about my brood." Caolte joked. "You wouldn't even know how to bed a woman, let alone make twins!"

Reacting with mock indignation, Gavin playfully shoved the man with his shoulder. Even before completing the movement, he sensed the tautness in his lieutenant's arm.

"Hsst! Movement to the left," the clansman whispered urgently.

Peering into the night, Gavin spied three dark shapes crawling slowly along the parapet towards a pair of company guards. Before he could react, the two Fey'Derin sentries fell to the stealthy attackers' blades. The two officers leapt from the tower to the wooden walkway below and raised the alarm.

"Awake! Awake! Assassins on the wall, assassins on the wall!" both men shouted.

As they landed, Gavin watched two shapes run from the interior of his quarters. Yelling at the slowly rousing men in the adjacent barracks to watch the ground, Gavin registered the incoming glint of a naked blade.

Instinctively, he rolled forward and dodged the deadly thrust of the outstretched dagger. He heard the whiff of the slicing blade whistle in his ear, passing within a hair's breadth of his temple. Caolte was several paces behind him and had not been so lucky. A painful grunt followed by a loud thud announced the clansman's heavy fall.

Leaping to his feet, Gavin reached for the dagger hidden in his boot top; it was missing. Cursing himself for his carelessness, he could picture it lying atop the small chest stored in his quarters. Unarmed and vulnerable in the darkness, he had only to buy time before help arrived. Two other assassins now closed in on his location. The Fey'Derin captain glanced at the fallen veteran and quickly assessed Caolte's condition; he was still breathing. Knocked senseless and bleeding only a few yards away, Gavin moved to protect his fallen friend.

These were trained killers that would stop at nothing to finish a job, unconscious man or not. Bouncing lightly on the balls of his feet, he eyed his opponent. The black-garbed attacker waited patiently for his companions. No sense in attacking alone when you could control the fray easily with three to one odds, Gavin thought.

Realizing he had little time left, he went on the offensive. Weaving as he charged, he managed to slide under the assassin's guard, though the maneuver cost him dearly. Pain lanced across his unprotected ribs as he blocked the second dagger thrust and twisted up and behind the assailant. Applying weight to a pressure point slightly below the wrist, Gavin barely paused before snatching the falling weapon and slicing the man across the neck. Blood spurted wildly, splashing his face with gore.

Ignoring the blood trailing down his side, he glanced hopefully towards the now awakened barracks. Men were running to his aid, but even from a distance he could see other sentry guards lying flat and motionless on the walkways. As the next two black-armoured intruders closed in, several arrows flew past the chaos. One of the men staggered forward, two shafts protruding from his back.

The second man expertly gauged the battle and launched himself over the side of the wall. Gavin scrambled towards the spot and watched as his enemy landed lightly upon his feet and tore off into the darkness. Swearing profusely in the dark, Gavin watched as Ethan Shade, bow in hand, reached his side and vaulted over the edge with three Eagle Runners in tow. Bloodied dagger in hand, Gavin pressed his free hand to the wound in his side and slumped to the ground beside Caolte. The man's pulse was strong, his breathing deep. Even so, Gavin insisted the men tend to the fallen officer before any time was spent on his own injuries.

Sitting with his back to the wall, Gavin shook his head in disbelief. Someone must truly want him dead to send assassins from the Guild his way. They didn't work cheap. Puzzled and exhausted, Gavin knew one thing for certain; death had come to the Fey'Derin that night, and retribution was now the next order of business.

&#x03;

The Aeldenwood was a real forest, a forest of old, Bider thought as he examined a light depression near a patch of tall grass valiantly protruding from the snow. The trees were ancient beyond compare and he had the sense of walking under a green sky, verdant and timeless. Dangers were ever present, yet Bider could spend hours uncovering secrets the dark wood hid so convincingly. It was incredible to think that the lost kingdom of Farraine, with its towns long since abandoned, lay buried beneath this twisted woodland. That curiosity alone was reason enough to hike deeper into the forest.

He turned his head back to the task at hand. Assassins from the previous night, their target clearly Captain Silveron, were of greater importance on this winter morning. Six attackers, all skilled and commanding a hefty price for their services no doubt, had been employed in an attempt to strike at the very heart of their company. The Fey'Derin had apparently alarmed the elite of the Protectorate enough to warrant particular attention during this usual period of rest for the mercenary companies across Kal Maran.

Early that morning, Bider and the bulk of the Eagle Runners were sent out to scour the countryside for clues that might lead to the remaining attackers' whereabouts. Lieutenant Burnaise, his arm bound in a sling, fumed at any mention of the enemy's escape. Based on the accounts of several witnesses, two of the six had evaded capture, with each heading in a separate direction in the hopes of throwing off an organized pursuit. Captain Silveron issued explicit orders to take the men alive, but after hours of fruitless searching, Bider was unsure they would ever be found.

The assassins of the Thieves' Guild were notorious for both stealth and subterfuge, as well as the price they charged for their services. Only the rich and powerful could afford to use the resources such a fell group offered. It was rumoured that the Guild had ties to most of the dominant noble houses in the land. Even the mad Serian Rhone of the *Drayenmark* was said to have an agent that lived in the Thieves' Den. Bider was one to know; his history as an amateur thief was a story he had done well to keep hidden from the rest of the company. The Fey'Derin were all reformed men, but there was little love lost for a man who had once spent his evenings mugging and stealing.

Clearing his mind, Bider re-examined the mark he had found. Leaning closer to the impression, he snapped his fingers and waved Garett over. Pointing towards a second indentation, he pulled the young man in close.

"This one's been sloppy. He might be tired or wounded, I'm not sure," he said with some urgency. "I have the trail, but I'm not sure how old it is yet. I need you to go see Sergeant Shade and pass on my findings. Tell him to send someone back with you, no sense taking chances if we can take them down easily." Nodding, Garett turned and quickly made his way back towards the camp. With luck, Bider mused, he would not be gone for longer than a quarter hour.

At first the trail was difficult to see, and progress was slow. As he continued to follow the markings, Bider realized that the assassin's tracks were quite fresh. Almost no effort had been made to cover the path, and the assailant was obviously worried about his potential escape. He was convinced that his quarry was nearby.

The clear tracks had been the clue. No Guild member of this stature would panic; these were soldiers who could take down their prey with ease. One lone scout would certainly not register as a threat to the person hiding nearby. *Kill the scout quickly and then blend back into the environment...*

Bider was confident with his blades, but he was no pompous fool. In a stand up duel, one on one, he would be no match for a member of the Guild. He could only hope Garett had found someone quickly and would return with numbers. He had no desire to die today.

As he crouched by a large oak, a soft rustle came from his right, an accompanying whistle of air following instantly thereafter. Bider was already moving, but still he was too late. Wincing, he threw himself on the ground behind a small thicket. Closing his eyes tight, he grimaced and clutched the bone handled dagger hilt entrenched in his shoulder. Had he moved any slower, the blade would now be lodged in his throat.

"Do we really need to continue this charade, little one?" the assailant spoke from the shadows.

Bider spun around, desperately trying to spot the location of the voice; a very female voice, he noted. This woman toyed with him, but his plan was to delay his death temporarily so as to give Garett and the others more time. He needed to save every precious moment.

"A continuation is all I can offer, m'lady," he called back. "Once your dagger missed, I knew that the battle was joined. Would that you had given me some fore-warning," he added.

"Cute, but by the mere fact that you still breathe is proof enough. Otherwise I'd be emptying your pockets as you lay choking on your own blood," she replied.

"I'm glad you like me," Bider said, stalling further. He pulled the blade painfully from the wound and was quick to staunch the bleeding with the ripped sleeve of his tunic. Tying a rough tourniquet, he struggled to his feet with his eyes continuing to scan the forest. Reaching down and grasping the discarded weapon, Bider whistled in appreciation. "Nice blade by the way."

"Enjoy it for the next second, wee one, because it's mine," the assassin spun around a tree some ten paces to his left, arm cocked and ready to release a second missile. Caught off guard, it would be almost impossible to evade the throw. Believing she had been positioned directly ahead, he had set his stance in response to a threat from that location.

She's too good.

As the black-garbed killer's arm reached its apex, a sudden movement from behind caused the slightest hesitation. In shock, Bider watched a tall, green creature the size of a man reach out and swat the woman aside. She flew through the air as though weightless, tumbling to the ground some distance from where she had been standing.

Utterly fascinated by what was unfolding, Bider watched as the creature made entirely of earth and grass, crushed her in its arms and withdrew into an area of dense brush. As quickly as it had appeared, the creature vanished.

"Coren, are you all right?"

Still shaken by what he had just witnessed, Bider was surprised to see Gavin Silveron crouching at his side. "I think so," he stammered.

"We cannot remain here, Coren, it isn't safe. Can you travel?" the captain asked impatiently, his eyes trained on the space where the assassin had been standing.

"Yes, and Captain did you see that?!" Bider exclaimed. He could barely breathe, and his heart thudded loudly in his head. Accepting a hand from his commander as well as a clean strip of cloth for his arm, Bider locked eyes with the man.

Gavin Silveron turned his gaze away. "I saw nothing," he replied.

"But the assassin..." Bider whispered.

"She must have tripped and fallen into a hidden chasm. These woods hide many treacherous things," Gavin replied with indifference.

Stunned by the denial, Bider took a moment to collect himself before turning to follow the Fey'Derin leader. Still uneasy from the strange conclusion to the attack, the small scout nearly walked headlong into one of the ancient trees. *The Aeldenwood took that woman's life, but by the gods, how could you explain it? And why would the captain turn a blind eye?*

Cß

"If I leave for Dragon Mount, I only show my fear!" Gavin hissed as he surveyed the five men gathered around the table. "Am I to turn tail and run like a coward?"

"Is it better to worry about your pride than your life, Gavin?" Caolte retorted hotly. "I'll have you know this isn't an attack like Khali's."

"Don't you dare bring talk of that incident into this room. It has no bearing on the present!" Gavin retaliated sharply.

"I would beg to differ, Captain," Ethan interjected. "The last time our enemies used that mongrel Khali in an attempt to strike at the Fey'Derin's foundation. The only difference this time lies in the manner chosen to bring about the same result."

"I agree." Eör Rockfar nodded. "They used assassins; Guild assassins, no less. Where once they hit our youth, now they target our leader." The gruff dwarf tugged absently on his braided reddish beard as he finished his statement.

Exasperated, Gavin shook his head. "But unlike before, I can guarantee I'll not find a trail to Gadian Yarr's or Lord Dalemen's estate, nor will I be able to strike back. The Guild has always kept their motives hidden."

"Why focus on vengeance, Gavin?" Caolte asked earnestly. "We have identified the enemy. Next year's warfare may very well decide the future of the land, and Duke Berry will need every ally he can muster."

"And why are we so important?" Gavin paused and looked at the officers around the table. "Why do I need to stay alive? I could enter Imlaris and have a fair shot of killing that bastard Yarr, if I so chose. Why should I sit here and bury more men and leave the culprit alive to scoff at our sorrow?"

"Gavin, if there is one thing that will tear you apart, it is the blame you take on for each fallen man," Eör replied sadly. "Those soldiers on the wall last night knew what they risked by joining the company. They were proud of it, and damn proud to serve with you. Don't pity them. They were Fey'Derin, and they died with honour."

"I don't often speak against you, Captain, nor against revenge," Ossric's deep voice reverberated from the folds of his thick beard. "You know how badly I want to see the fools from Khali's band of murderers suffer for their brutality, but I believe the others here speak the truth. From the moment you pulled me out of the sewers in Avery, I knew you were different."

"Ossric..." Gavin sighed.

"No, no, just let me finish, Captain. The recruits need to complete the ritual, we all know that, and so what better reason exists than to have you lead the party north?"

"We'll double the watch and keep veterans on the walls. If the Guild strikes again, we'll be ready," Sergeant Brock Fearan added.

"Speak with Ir'Wolien while you visit. The old man will be glad to see you after so long," Caolte said, his eyes sparkling as the Silveryn Archmage's name was uttered. Only Ethan caught the flash of anger that briefly crossed Gavin's face.

"It seems you've already decided." Gavin said, his gaze slowly travelling to each member sitting at the table.

"That we have, Captain. It's in the best interest of the company." Ethan Shade replied.

Realizing that he was handily outnumbered, Gavin's head slumped down onto the rough wood. "Do I dare ask what time I leave?" he mumbled.

"I'll have my recruits ready by the break of dawn. A four day march will do them some good," Eör smiled, clapping the captain on the shoulder. "We'll see you in the morning, sir. Do try and get some sleep."

The other men joined in approval and wished him goodnight. For the first time since the Fey'Derin's inception, Gavin realized how exceptional his men had truly become.

The effect of the Aeldenwood's supernatural growth will be far-reaching. Vital trade routes connecting the various regions of Old Caledun and Farraine will be severed. An era of isolation will result; an era that, I believe, will curb our world's advancements and limit our cultural evolution.

—*Tel'Lianne, 'The Aeldenwood Mystery'*

CHAPTER XVI

King's Road, Northern Council

Corian Praxxus had selected a dangerous route for his caravans. With the encroachment of the Aeldenwood over the past generation limiting the central trade roads, an increasing number of merchants were more than likely to pay the extra coin and board a vessel on the coast. Disappearances continued to mount among the convoys electing to follow the once safe passageways through the Great Wood. Very few merchants remained who chose to risk their livelihood for what appeared to be an easier and cheaper journey.

In regards to Corian's business interests, there was the tantalizing prospect of increased profit. The trip through the forest was considerably less expensive. There was no extra cost for hiring a ship and its crew, no sea sickness, and no lengthy travel diverting his wares far away from their eventual destination. With the arrival of winter, he also counted on the thick eaves of the Aeldenwood to serve as protection from the elements. Snowfall was rarely heavy in the supernatural forest, and

Corian wasn't fond of the bitter winds and icy waters of the sea.

And so, at the risk of his own safety and that of the whole entourage, Corian Praxxus from the Innes Vale was willing to attempt passage on the old King's Road. The route was key to the bulk of all trade in Caledun back in the time of the High King. Historians often compared it to a river current, with goods moving constantly, and the well-worn path teeming with activity.

In the dark years of decline after the king's death, the road remained one of the few passageways connecting the northern and southern peoples of the old kingdom. For reasons unknown, the path remained relatively free from the invading woodland that so indiscriminately claimed land in all directions. Some speculated that the Silveryn Mages were involved in what seemed to be some sort of magical protection.

Alessan was eagerly anticipating their arrival at the famous roadway, yet in the pit of his stomach was also a feeling of dread. Although the Aeldenwood was anything but welcoming, he still wanted to tread the same path spoken of in the histories of Caledun.

They would also be passing through the forgotten land of Farraine, a one-time neighbour and ally to Caledun during the rule of Darion Lordares. Although the capital city of Telmire had been abandoned only a short generation earlier, the kingdom was no more. Farraine had been ruled by a royal family of its own, one that could trace its roots back as far as Caledun's kings of old.

On occasion there had been war and strife between the lands, but when in need, both had supported the other. In 3AE329, the Northern Council ceded a small parcel of land near the northernmost tip of their holdings to the surviving members of Farraine's royal family. New Telmire was little more than a refugee town at that point, but the foundations of a new capital city had slowly taken shape over the past decade. The youngest daughter of the last king would rule one day, but for the present, a regent had been appointed until the girl reached maturity. Alessan was convinced that passing along the borders, and even within ten leagues of the old capital, would surely be a sight to behold.

Slowed by the terrible road conditions and the size of the column itself, the trip along the northern edge of the Aeldenwood was both tedious and treacherous. On more than one occasion, impertinent pack mules, as well as problems with various wheels and hitches, caused the convoy to grind to a grumbling halt. Well sheltered by the unsettling trees of the forest, none of the men wanted to spend any more time in the cold than was absolutely necessary.

Three or four times daily the wagons would get stuck in muddy ruts, putting additional stress on the metal fastenings already replaced once by the caravan smiths. The wind howled mightily, and some of the horses drawing the wagons proved more stubborn than those Alessan had worked with in the stables of Briar. Nearing the end of the fourth day, he wondered whether he could survive the physical toll his body was being forced to endure. His muscles ached terribly, and yet he complained little and slept as best he could in the cramped quarters of his covered carriage. In the Lumber community, Alessan had long ago learned to curb his tongue, all too aware that he would be judged harshly for calling attention to his frailties.

For the time being, he worked alongside a trio of handlers, all of whom drove a wagon and supervised the care of a half-dozen mules. Two of the men rarely spoke to him, but then Seamus and Domhnall barely spoke at all. Half mumbled grunts were the norm for the two northern men who, if Alessan had understood correctly, had been working as merchant handlers for the most of their lives. Neither was married, and their favourite topic seemed to be the beautiful women of the south.

The last man, the lead driver, was the complete opposite. Fingus O'Neill was a gravelly-voiced man who possessed not only the most intimidating arms Alessan had ever laid eyes on, but also held the dubious distinction of being the biggest talker amongst the caravan folk. Fingus loved the sound of his own voice. He talked incessantly about the wildlife, his own life, his home town, his dreams, religion, and of course, women. The middle-aged man was excited by the fact that Alessan had not heard any of his stories. Ignoring the insults hurled about by the other men, Fingus delighted in telling the new arrival everything and anything that came to mind.

Surprisingly, Alessan really didn't mind. Growing up in the sleepy confines of a small community, he enjoyed hearing of far-off places and strange people. As the two men worked tirelessly to free another wagon from the ice that morning, he realized that he rather liked Fingus.

ᘖ

"So this is the King's Road..." Alessan said on the sixth day, the column trudging forward under the trees. Craning his neck to watch the foliage cover the sun, Alessan was unable to suppress a shiver of anticipation.

"It's only a road, lad, so don't be getting too excited," Fingus grinned from his seat. "Looks like any other road I've travelled, smells like any other road, and has holes and ruts in it just like any other road I've seen — so I don't know what the fuss is all about."

"But it's the famous King's Road!" Alessan replied enthusiastically. "Aren't you the least bit excited?"

"I don't want to speak for the other men, lad, but there are quite a few things that get me worked up, and trust me, they don't have anything to do with this road," Fingus shook his head. "Now a woman, or a fine bottle of brandy... that would get any man's blood racing!" he guffawed.

Realizing that these men cared little about where they were, Alessan resigned himself to enjoying the moment quietly.

"If yer wonderin', we're headed to the Crossroads," Fingus replied as he chewed thoughtfully on a long twig. "With luck, and if the weather holds with this here roof above our heads, we can expect to make camp sometime by week's end."

"I heard Seamus bellyaching all morning about the place," Alessan remarked.

"Seamus is all worked up about the spirit stories some were telling last night. It seems as though his stones aren't half as big as he might have let on," Fingus laughed.

"Is it a town?"

"T'was an old waystation back in the days of the king," Fingus snorted. "Merchant caravans would often spend a night, and some tales say that on occasion even the Gorimm visited the place. With the passing of years, the old buildings have crumbled, and the stop is uninhabited. Some companies passing this way have heard strange things in the dark, but I think they're just letting fear take hold...that or the drink!" the driver howled.

"Have you ever been there before?" Alessan pressed.

"Aye, a long ways back in my career," Fingus answered. "I might've been close to your age, and probably had the same look of excitement. This was before the roads down south became treacherous and the rumblings of the Gath. All I know is, I never heard any sounds, nor did I see anything. That's all the proof I need," Fingus spat the end of his chewed stick off to the side, "In any case, the Crossroads is a place that's fine passing through, but it's no place to make a home."

Alessan remained quiet and mulled over the conversation. Excited by the prospect of seeing another new place in the wider world of Caledun, he passed the remainder of the day wondering what they would find when they arrived.

∞

More often than not, the mood of the camp was jovial once the men had settled down for the evening. It was then, Alessan quickly learned, that a world from which he had been so carefully sheltered, reared its ugly head. Alessan was mildly familiar with both drinking and gambling, although he had never been overly fond of either of the two vices. Three days after leaving town, he had swallowed more burning spirits and dark mead than he had consumed over the course of his entire young life.

Working with stubborn mules while nursing a queasy stomach and splitting headache proved to be an unwelcome exercise. Alessan also learned about the mysterious women who paraded around camp. Having grown up in a relatively quiet and respectful village, he had never been privy to the seedier side of life, one that involved gambling, drunkenness, and ladies for hire.

The women who followed along in the column were tall, thin, and even in the cold, scantily clad. They wore expensive jewelry, and the intense smell of exotic perfumes permeated the air all around them. They were striking to behold, with darkly painted lashes covering glittering eyes that beckoned any man who would dare steal a glance. Alessan blushed when he learned they could be bought for a price, and that there was little they regarded as taboo.

On one of the first nights of the long journey, Fingus caught Alessan in the middle of a lustful stare. With a smile, he educated the younger man in the simple rules that governed any dealings with the ladies. Having never garnered any attention from any women back home, Alessan spent a few days agonizing over the intense thoughts now invading his mind. With chagrin, he knew it would only be a matter of time before he attempted to satisfy his growing urges. Although stunted in growth, Alessan maintained the same strong desires of any young man, and as with all young men, he often fantasized about being with a woman. That the rest of the men in the convoy had all experienced the pleasure of a woman irked him, and being determined to fit in, he soon made a decision.

One night, fed up with the merciless ribbing of his companions, Alessan made his way into the area frequented by the women and haggled briefly with the towering man who guarded them. After settling on a price, he was directed towards a small wagon and ushered through the doorway.

The carriage smelled of a heady perfume that Alessan had often noticed while walking alongside the column. The interior was quite plain, with the walls empty except for a few gauzy drapes that provided some measure of privacy.

"Good evening," said a woman languishing in a mass of pillows and exquisite silk sheets. "My, aren't we a young one tonight?" she commented as he entered through the door.

She was very thin and looked only slightly older than Alessan himself. Her hair was dark and tied in a tight knot at the top of her head. Her bright blue eyes shone when he extended his small bag of coins.

"I'm not as young as you might think," he replied sullenly.

"I really don't care how old you are, and don't worry, I'll be gentle. Now take off those clothes and come to me," the woman purred.

Alessan had never been as uncomfortable with his frail body as he was at that very moment. Glancing down at his bony frame and shriveled arm, he wondered whether any woman could ever come to love him. Would he be forever satisfied with women who would gladly service a man in exchange for coin?

"Well then, are you going to stand over by the entrance for the rest of the night?" the woman asked as she lay back in the thick covers, her clothes now discarded next to the bed.

"No... no, no, ma'am," he stuttered, moving slowly towards her.

"Good," she smiled. "You can leave the coin near the door. Blow out the lantern as well, and I'll show you what a woman can do for you."

A rush of excited nervousness rippled through his naked body. His heart pounded loudly in his breast, and for a moment it was all he could do to stop himself from
fleeing the sparsely decorated wagon. Pausing a moment to calm himself, Alessan
finally stepped forward, blew out the lantern, and plunged the room into darkness.

၀၃

As the newest member of the entourage, Alessan was usually assigned the most un-
favourable of chores, the worst being the collecting of suitable firewood. The eerie
tales involving the Aeldenwood served as reason enough for many of the handlers
to avoid venturing too far into the strange forest. The King's Road was easily wide
enough to accommodate the large merchant wagons, and most traders elected to
stay huddled with the column. Superstitions, it seemed, played upon on the minds
of those working for the demanding Corian Praxxus.

Alessan found it ironic that although he had left the drudgery of his old life, here
he was collecting wood for a fire, much as he once had every morning in Briar. Nine
days out from his homestead and things had changed far less than he would have
supposed when first leaving on the journey.

Finding some amusement in his predicament, he set to his tasks with the same
care he had shown back in Briar. His father had always stressed the importance of
working hard and being proud of what you had accomplished by a day's end. *The
true measure of a man*, the big Lumber often said, *can only be found in the pride of
that man's work.*

With the Crossroads only a day away, the men and women huddled close around
the fires, enjoying the warmth in the midst of another chilly night. Although somewhat milder under the large canopy of the forest, the nights were still frigid. A
warm fire went a long way towards warding off the cold, if only for a while. Spring
still seemed a far-off dream.

Squinting in the failing light of another long day of travel, Alessan was collecting what dead wood could be found along the old road. With one bundle quickly
returned, he glanced at the branches providing the leafy roof overhead. Faint sunlight strained to pierce the thick foliage. The days were much shorter here in the

Aeldenwood, what with the forest itself shedding a gloomy darkness over the entire journey. Alessan realized, as he stooped to collect a thick branch that lay at his feet, that he missed the open sky and the feeling of freedom that came with it. For all its wondrous and uncommon beauty, the Aeldenwood was stifling.

Cradling the wood under his weak arm, Alessan walked deeper into the forest, his mind wandering while a tune whistled from his lips. As he bent over to retrieve some fresh kindling, he could sense the unmistakable presence of another creature.

Straightening from his crouch, he turned and carefully gauged the surrounding treeline. His body stiffened with apprehension as he caught a flash of grey flit between two trees. Placing his bundle of wood down on the forest floor, he kept his eyes fastened on the closest trees. He quickly brandished one of the sticks, this one as long as his arm and plenty thick if it needed to be used. Long seconds passed before the dark shape moved once more, the bulk of its body hidden by a thick stump.

Alessan tightened his grip on the makeshift club as the other inhabitant of the wood took a step out into the dim light. Dark eyes peered out from a thick wintry coat as a young wolf carefully padded forward. Entranced by the animal's calm demeanor, Alessan quelled his mounting fear, willing himself to remain in place. The animal showed no sign of agitation or fear of man, traits common to the wolves that prowled near Briar and other Lumber towns of the north.

As the creature sank down on its haunches, Alessan caught a clear glimpse of the long and ragged wound decorating the wolf's left flank. As if in reply to his discovery, the young animal twisted its greyish white head and carefully licked at the injury.

The wound is healing well. She is stubborn, but brave. Your concern is admirable though, Alessan Oakleaf.

Mesmerized by the strange animal, Alessan had completely missed any sign that someone had crept up to stand nearly at his side. Turning to acknowledge his mysterious acquaintance, he frowned.

"You know you could warn someone when you approach, C'Aelis."

My apologies, Alessan, but I was making no effort to hide my presence, a hint of amusement laced the words. *I fear my dealings with your kind are quite rare these days.* Turning towards the wolf, the Gorimm beckoned her forward.

You have nothing to fear. Greiyfois is a dear friend of mine; a steadfast companion while I attempt to set things to right.

"Can you speak with her as well?" Alessan asked.

Of course I can. It is no different than when I seek counsel with the trees, the rocks, the water, or the earth. We are all part of the living world, Alessan; yet some refuse to see what is plainly visible.

"Talking to the trees, huh? You are different, that's for sure," Alessan replied with a shrug. "She's beautiful, but what happened to her side?" he asked, looking at the long gash.

The Gath have become terrible foes, the Gorimm responded. *She was loath to let one of them take me to my ancestors. It is like I said, she is stubborn.*

"Incredible..." Alessan breathed.

Greiyfois thanks you for the compliment. However, she considers your scent particularly offensive. Ruffling the thick fur around the wolf's head, C'Aelis laughed heartily. It was the first audible sound uttered by the strange man in Alessan's presence.

"She can understand me?"

To a certain degree, yes, with a little help from me, C'Aelis nodded. *She is also very good at reading our features.*

Alessan let the rest of the tension slide from his body. Sitting wearily upon the ground, he looked once more towards the Gorimm. The man looked exhausted, his usually graceful posture had a slight stoop at the shoulders. His silver hair was damp and mashed against his forehead, the thin tendrils dangling limply down the contours of his face. Oddly, his garments were heavily stained and mud-splattered.

"So have you spoken to any others?" Alessan asked after a moment.

I have been far too busy, C'Aelis replied. *The outer wards have needed resetting, and my travels have opened my eyes to the gravity of this world's condition. Where once my people had friends, I now fear speaking with any until my work is complete.*

"Why me, then?" Alessan questioned. "I've seen you more than once."

Call it fate if you want, young Oakleaf. Mayhap the gods above see some use in our exchanges, brief though they may be. Of course, maybe it is all just luck, a haphazard meeting of strangers. Regardless, I am glad to find you well.

"You, on the other hand, look terrible," Alessan replied with concern.

I would be lying if I didn't agree. It is a small price to pay for the transgressions of your forefathers, C'Aelis trailed off.

"Transgressions?"

It is of no matter at the moment. You need only be concerned about the direction in which you travel.

"I have no choice in the matter, C'Aelis. We are heading to the southern Protectorate."

The way is closed, Alessan. The King's Road is far from safe, the Gorimm warned.

"And the Crossroads?"

The Crossroads will be your death, if your companions so choose. I have come to warn you of the Gath. They move quickly to surround your patron's entourage. It will be a harvest like those creatures have not seen for many summers.

"Harvest?" Alessan whispered.

They will destroy you all, Alessan, and this time there are far too many for Greiyfois and I to deal with. You must turn your column north and seek another route.

The conviction of the sending caused Alessan to shiver. "I have no influence here, C'Aelis. Master Praxxus won't heed any warning from me, or from anyone else for that matter!"

Then you are already lost, Alessan of the Oakleaf Clan, C'Aelis replied sadly.

"What?!" he cried in despair. "Then come with me, C'Aelis. Come speak to the man. He can't ignore such a warning if it comes directly from you."

I cannot. The people of this shattered world may react quite violently and out of fear. This is a place of legend and foreboding among your people.

"I didn't react that way," Alessan replied in exasperation.

I believe your life experiences have tempered your judgment of others. I know from your thoughts that you have always frowned upon those who judge on appearance alone. You are different, Alessan, C'Aelis added with a warm smile.

"But —"

I also believe that my fate does not lie entwined with that of the men and women you travel with. It is your task, if you are willing, to speak with Corian Praxxus. He knows me, Alessan. He has seen me twice now. Once when we met near the banks of the Da'fil, and also when I fought near the homestead of your people. He will believe —

In mid-sentence, C'Aelis suddenly jumped to his feet. Greiyfois growled deeply and immediately raced off into the woods.

The Watchtower! The wards have been activated! The words screamed through Alessan's mind, the pain whelming him to his knees. Crying out, Alessan looked at C'Aelis and saw a panicked look within his emerald eyes.

My apologies Alessan, but I must go. Ancient wards have been reactivated, wards that should never have been touched. Keep heart, and do what must be done to convince the merchant of my warning.

"I will try," Alessan responded with uncertainty.

If all else fails, ask him about Inigan.

"Who is Inigan?" Alessan posed the question, but C'Aelis had disappeared. Sinking to his knees, he put his head in his hands and closed his eyes.

Wondering how he would approach the coming dawn, he suddenly wished he was back at the Black Boar, safe from all the hazards of the world. His sister would be readying herself to entertain the guests, and the gruff Varis would be at her side, skillfully working his cherished lute. Familiar faces and familiar times flashed as if in a vision, and he found solace in the memories.

Alone in the woods that night, Alessan Oakleaf from Briar cried softly. Only the trees of the Aeldenwood stood vigil over his suffering, silent witnesses to a young man's fears and self-doubt.

The Shield is unlike anything I have ever seen. I cannot help but wonder at the reclusive mages who created such a wondrous thing. It is an artifact birthed during the mighty Age of Legends. I also ponder about the future of ruined Caledun. That such powerful magic can be wielded by one faction sets my nerves on edge. What the Silveryn mages could do if they so decided...
—Lord Crispin, *The Explorers, Volume III*

CHAPTER XVII

Erienn Mountain Range, Sanctuary of the Silveryn Order

Bider knew exactly why he had been designated part of the support company on the expedition to Dragon Mount. He didn't like the reasoning behind it one bit, yet despite his injury, here he was riding his mount northeast through the foothills of the *Erienn* mountain range.

They had seen something that day in the woods north of the *Galen'hide,* but Gavin Silveron denied the truth of the matter. According to the Captain, the assassin had tumbled off one of the rocky ledges that dotted the Aeldenwood and disappeared into the rough foothills below. For the first time since joining the company, Bider found himself doubting his brooding captain.

Bider expected most of the men would laugh and ignore the impossible story. The Aeldenwood was unsafe because of the Gath, but the idea of a walking mound of earth and vegetation was preposterous. Captain Silveron's corroboration would bring immediate credibility to the tale, and possibly unsettle the men. For that reason, and that reason alone, Bider continued to hold his tongue and avoid his commander.

And so, with his arm in a sling for a few days now, he slumped wearily in his saddle. The trek to Dragon Mount had been a yearly tradition for the new recruits of the Fey'Derin. As far as he knew, the Fey were the only mercenaries who dealt with the secluded mages of the high mountain. The Silveryn Order had long ago pulled their forces from the battlefields of Kal Maran, citing the use of magic in battle as immoral, dishonourable, and a perversion of the study of magecraft. Over the past century, the Order had slipped even further into obscurity. Once a thriving place of culture and education for new mages, it now struggled to find novices to join each year. The halls of Dragon Mount, some whispered, now held more ghosts than living beings.

There was a time when the Silveryn mages had acted as advisors and courtiers to noble families all across the land. Along with the Gorimm, the long-lived practitioners of the arcane held positions of honour and great influence. With the Shattering came drastic changes, and the respected archmages came to be seen as threats, a hold-over from times of old. In those dark years after the fall of the king, hundreds of mages were hunted down and fell to the sword. In defense of the Order, the Silveryn mages closed their borders, and now covertly seek out only those born with the power.

The purpose of the company's current journey was ultimately one of protection, albeit a certain amount of discomfort would need to be endured by the newest Fey'Derin recruits. The soldiers were to receive their mark, a magical tattoo cast into the skin and fused with living energy. When a spell was cast, the mark would react, sending a clear signal to the bearer that magic was active in the vicinity. It was this talisman, Bider recalled, that had warned Orn of the approaching mage working with Pier's Brigade. Although somewhat effective at protecting against minor charms and wards, the tattoo acts as only a warning and is not a magical shield.

With the growing number of renegade mages in the land, Bider was glad to have the charm. Gently rubbing his chest, he grimaced as he remembered his own branding. The visit to Dragon Mount was the final initiation at the end of a Fey'Derin recruit's probationary period. Once completed, the veterans had a duty to welcome all into their brotherhood.

Bider scanned the sky and cursed at a large gathering of slow moving dark clouds, harbingers of another blasted winter storm. He twisted in his saddle and donned a second thick cloak. No sense freezing to death with the journey only just begun.

Gavin was aware he had lost the trust of the soldier fast becoming one of the Eagle Runners best scouts. Coren D'Elmark was also one of the few men Orn Sure-foot seemed to have a connection with. When the two scouts were paired together, Gavin could see that Ethan rested comfortably in the knowledge that the one-time thief would keep the problematic Orn under control.

Coren had started giving him dark stares, as well as doggedly evading his every attempt to talk the matter through. He could see that that the scout was wrestling with what had transpired in the forest. Regardless of the cost, Gavin was determined to keep the event under wraps. Caolte, for one, would have too many questions regarding the strange creature's appearance. The captain and lieutenant had a long-running debate over the Aeldenwood's many dangers, and Gavin had no desire to renew the quarrel.

More disturbing than the encounter in the wood was his long-delayed return to Dragon Mount. For four years he had sent various officers with the recruits, each time finding one trivial reason or another to pass on the important journey. It seemed a lifetime since he had last walked the brightly lit halls of the Silveryn Order stronghold.

He slept poorly that first night and refused to even try on the second. Rubbing his tired eyes, Gavin watched as the column left the rugged foothills and entered the high mountain pass that would lead them to the mysterious Shield and beyond. His return was certain to spark a new debate regarding his future. If he had learned anything from his dealings with mages of the Order, it was that once they had designs on your fate, there was little one could do to break free from their clutches.

Three days into the journey saw the company approach the fabled Shield. The shimmering wall of magic ensured the safety and privacy of the Order. Cast twenty years after the treachery at Magnach, and the subsequent murder of the king, the mages had erected the barrier with the promise of only a temporary separation from the rest of the kingdom. The years slipped into decades and the Shield had become as permanent a fixture in the land as the continued growth of the Aeldenwood.

A long-robed figure greeted them from the inside of the glowing crystalline energy field. Words carried through the barrier as if it did not even exist. Gavin noticed the look of surprise written plainly across the mage's features. Smiling, Gavin disembarked from his mount and embraced the man.

"It's good to see you, Andros," he said as the shocked mage held him tightly.

"I thought we would never meet again," the mage responded warmly. "It has been a long time for you. And it's Tel'Andros now, Silvares."

"A mere blink of an eye to a man of your esteemed prowess," Gavin said. "And it's Silveron now, Tel'Andros, Silvares no longer."

"You left behind your name?" Tel'Andros expressed with alarm as they turned to address the soldiers.

"If you claim to be my friend, then leave it be. I was serious when I told Ir'Wolien that I would play no part in his elaborate schemes. We can discuss this later," Gavin warned.

"Understood, but you would do well to curb your tongue. There are many who retain the ill will birthed by your departure. The First will want to see you once word reaches the Koriani barracks. Her reaction will be... unpredictable, I'm sure," Tel'Andros answered with a hint of concern in his voice.

Gavin watched as the mage invoked a spell that would allow the passage of the Fey'Derin through the shimmering wall of energy. The chant was spoken in a language few had heard before — the old tongue. The dialect was nearly extinct in the world of Kal Maran. The dark years of rampant pillaging, unrest, and destruction, had cost the people of Caledun dearly. Recorded histories of the time were scarce, and the Order had always lamented the loss of knowledge suffered after the Shattering. In many ways, they sought to protect the knowledge that remained.

With the spell completed, the Fey'Derin company passed into a region unchanged for over two centuries. It was a vision of the old world; peaceful, untamed, and pure. The lush, green foliage was more vibrant, and the sky above was a piercing blue unlike any the soldiers had seen before. Even the air felt different, consuming the place with an otherworldly presence.

"You have grown since we last met, Gavin," Tel'Andros said, the column slowly winding its way up the steeper trails of the *Erienn* range.

"It has been a long time, if we are to count by the years of the Order,"

Gavin replied. "You, on the other hand, look exactly the same."

The mage looked thoughtful for a moment as he chronicled the elapsed time. "Seven years, nearly eight, have passed in the greater world. You were a scrawny youth who thought himself a man," Tel'Andros laughed.

"How fares the Order?" A sad look from the mage caused Gavin to pause. "What has happened?"

"Recently, the Gath struck us a terrible blow. Ir'Roland and his novices were slaughtered near the edge of the Shield," Tel'Andros replied mournfully.

Aware of the Order's many struggles, Gavin was certain that such a tragedy was unprecedented. "But why were they outside the protection of the Shield? Ir'Roland should have known better."

"The Shield was breached."

"How?!" Gavin exclaimed.

"The Gath must have been assisted, but no one will even entertain the thought that someone could be behind the attacks. It was the third time, in the last year no less, that evidence has proven the Shield is failing," Tel'Andros finished.

"And Ir'Wolien? How did he take the news?"

"His granddaughter was among the novices, a talented young girl who had all the makings of a master," the mage shook his head sadly. "The Archmagus wanted revenge, but the Koriani had no luck tracking the raiding party. Deowyn was recalled before the creatures could be overtaken. The First feared an ambush."

"She may have been correct," Gavin speculated. "This only increases my need to speak with Ir'Wolien," Gavin said, catching the gleam in the mage's eye. "Don't get excited, old friend, I have no intention of returning. This is but a temporary stay."

"Brynne isn't going to like it..."

"Leave her out of this," Gavin replied harshly.

Tel'Andros was silent as they continued on the path the Dragon Mount.

ᴄʒ

High, white stone balconies shone brightly as the Fey'Derin arrived at the base of the Dragon Mount citadel. Robed men and women walked across spectacular arched bridges spanning the cliffs and canyons of the mountainside. Vast open windows were clearly visible on all sides of the lofty stone peaks.

The main gate of the citadel was flanked by two natural waterfalls, their light spray landing refreshingly upon the wearied travelers. Bider watched in awe as a small collection of brown-robed children sat in one of the fountain pools near the entrance. The six children floated peacefully above the surface, their eyes tightly closed in concentration, and their robes barely an inch from the water. At the pool's edge, a middle-aged woman spoke quietly to the students, observing each child's every move.

The front courtyard served as more than just a showpiece. The young scout noticed with some trepidation that the number of Koriani, the Order's elite soldiers pacing the walls and higher balconies, had been doubled. The sentries were wary, their bodies taut and their senses heightened. Recent events had put the guards on edge. Not one of the soldiers had turned to follow their arrival. The Koriani had eyes only for the wilderness beyond their home. An uncomfortable omen, Bider decided, as he dismounted and stood at attention with the rest of the company.

"Bider, you have command of the Eagles and the new recruits while I'm gone," Sergeant Ethan Shade ordered as the men awaited Captain Silveron. The commander was busy greeting a group of mages excited by his return.

"Pardon me, sir?" Bider stammered as the enormity of the sergeant's statement settled over him.

"You have command. Get the men settled and have all the recruits report to Kaleris Square on the morrow. The Captain, Sergeant Rockfar, and I, have been summoned to meet with members of the Council later today. It seems the Captain carries some weight here, although I can't understand why," Ethan muttered.

The tradition had always been that no Fey'Derin soldier could enter the citadel proper. The men had always been billeted near the entrance to Dragon Mount, just as they would be on this visit. For an invitation to be issued to Captain Silveron revealed an elevated status rare among outsiders.

Bider snapped to attention. "Aye, sir. I'll look after the men and have everyone ready and accounted for. When can we expect your return?" he asked before the hawk-nosed man could slip away.

"I'll be there for the ceremony, as of course will Sergeant Rockfar," Ethan replied. "His men will want to know that he'll be present for the casting," with a smile, he gripped the scout on the shoulder. "You'll be fine, Bider, but watch Orn, will you? Keep him out of the drink. The last thing Captain Silveron wants to hear is that Surefoot has embarrassed himself and the company."

"Yes, sir," Bider replied hesitantly.

୭

Under normal circumstances, a member of the Order or a distinguished guest would have to book an appointment with the Archmagus Ir'Wolien far in advance. Gavin suspected that his presence at Dragon Mount would command the greatest of attention, and Ir'Wolien would be forced to grant him an audience. Pushing open the ornate silver doors to the elder mage's audience chamber, Gavin's expectations were confirmed. He had only to endure a few hours of waiting time before being admitted.

The chamber itself was beautiful. A high vaulted ceiling reached far overhead with intricate columns flanking a carpeted path leading to a raised marble dais. The wall behind the large ebony desk and silver backed chair was constructed entirely of majestic windows.

The man sitting behind the writing desk was elderly, and unlike many of the mages who walked the corridors of the vast mountain complex, his age showed. Ir'Wolien had been the head of the Council for the entirety of Gavin's life, and many decades before. His hair was entirely white, and his face sported a thin white beard that drooped far below his chin. He was dressed in the ceremonial garb of his office, a green and silver robe that conveyed both wisdom and grace.

Bowing low at the foot of the raised platform, Gavin met the man's stony stare with confidence. "It's good to see you, Ir'Wolien."

"It has been a long time by your standards, Silvares," the man replied, inclining his head towards the young mercenary.

"It's Silveron now, Archmagus. When I left the mountain, I left my old name behind," Gavin said.

"Nonsense, you are Silvares. I'll not be party to such a ruse," the mage replied.

Ignoring the slight, Gavin attempted to change the subject in hopes of avoiding a confrontation. Speaking with Ir'Wolien had never been an easy task.

"Something occurred in the Aeldenwood. I am confident you may be able to shed light upon it," Gavin began.

"Now what seems to be the problem? Did the trees convey their sadness again and unsettle your brooding heart?" the older man asked with an unmistakable mocking tone.

"I saw something," Gavin said through clenched teeth.

"And what did you see, Silvares? Did the shadows scare you as they did when you were a child? You know there wasn't a day that went by that I didn't hear of what your mind 'saw' in the Aeldenwood."

"It was an Earth Fiend."

"An Earth Fiend?" Ir'Wolien took a sharp breath in surprise. His face clouded over and the dismissive attitude was instantly gone. "You were attacked then?" the Archmage questioned.

"It was an assassin from the Guild," Gavin answered.

"Then it is as we first believed..." Ir'Wolien exclaimed. "The wood was reacting to the threat of the assassin...protecting you... You have made powerful enemies while in the world. It goes without saying, then, that you have also made powerful friends, no?"

With that comment, Gavin realized that little had changed in the years since his departure. His carefully contained rage rushed to the fore. With a snarl, he answered, "You're twisting this event into one that benefits your own, Archmagus. I can see the look in your eyes. I will not be used!" Gavin countered.

"For once, Silvares, think of how important your life is, think of what you might mean to the land. That the wood reacted as it did reveals the stirrings of long dormant Gorimm powers."

"That's the problem, Ir'Wolien, you lie to yourself every time you speak those words. The Order wasn't thinking of the land, they were thinking of the power and influence they would command if the plans of the Council came to fruition. My life and the results of your lust for power had no bearing on your discussions —"

"It is my duty to keep the Order strong, fool!" the old man snapped. "Why is it so wrong that we look to benefit from the situation? Why is it so wrong to wish for a strengthening of the Order? If you are handed an advantage on the battlefield, do you opt to throw it away on account of the moralities involved? I should think not!"

"My men have free will. You strove to take mine away from me, to subvert a child!" Gavin yelled.

"I merely wanted to shape your future, to guide you in making the right decisions. I offered you knowledge, and I —"

"That knowledge spelled your doom," the soldier interrupted. "Could it not be that the gods were pulling strings, advocating on behalf of free will by allowing my access to the Hall of Records? There are so many ifs that I care not to explore what may have been. I chose to leave because there was a world that offered me a chance at a life unhindered by your expectations."

"It is your duty!" Ir'Wolien replied defiantly.

"We both know it also belongs to another. That he is beyond your power to influence only strengthens my resolve to bring about change by following the rightful laws of the land," Gavin shouted.

"Laws made by bloodthirsty fools who tore a kingdom apart and murdered a great king? Have you truly strayed so far from the path we once taught you?" A long silence stretched out between the two men after the question was posed. "Why have you returned home, Gavin? Is it only to renew an argument already years old, or to torment an old man who wishes his people not fall into obscurity?"

Frustrated, Gavin shook his head and took a step forward. "I needed information and some counsel, Ir'Wolien, and knew nowhere else to turn."

"Then ask of me what you will. I don't care to argue with you anymore," the mage sighed heavily. "We are both stubborn men, more alike than you would care to admit, Silvares," he added.

"I spoke with Tel'Andros this morning and he mentioned the recent tragedy that befell the Order. I need to know if the Aeldenwood is safe," Gavin asked.

"He was a good man, a strong ally, and an even better friend," Ir'Wolien bowed his head. "Did you know that Ir'Roland was one of your few supporters when you appeared before the Council those many years ago? He saw merit in your words."

"I never knew..."

"That is because you rarely listened. But why do you ask about the forest? Do you plan to visit that dreaded place?" the Archmage asked.

"I believe something has changed in the forest," Gavin said. "My dreams, as well as the appearance of the Earth Fiend, have led me to believe that the answers I seek may be found within the Great Wood."

Ir'Wolien raised himself from his chair and clasped his arms behind his back. Turning to look out of the beautifully crafted window and into the valley below, he took his time before answering. "The Gath roam in ever-increasing numbers. They seem more intelligent, even organized. I am beginning to wonder where some of my old colleagues have gone and fear the troubles they may have awoken."

"The Fallen?" Gavin whispered.

"Yes. The renegades have proven themselves to be more powerful than we anticipated, and perhaps now they tamper with the forces of evil that inhabit the Aeldenwood. Only a few of us know what transpired at the time of the *Gorath 'ni D'eralok* and the warnings of the wood infecting the land. The Fallen may be unwilling pawns in a greater plan."

"Then all the more reason for me to journey there," Gavin answered with conviction. "But I need to know what precautions to take," he pressed.

"A night or two at the south watchtower will be safe enough. I will send Tel'Andros with you," Ir'Wolien immediately raised a hand to stop the retort set to fly from Gavin's mouth. "And don't argue with me. I need no spy to inform me of your plans. I could read your thoughts well when you were a child, Gavin. Don't presume that I cannot read you as easily right now."

"Thank you, Ir'Wolien. Tel'Andros' presence will be tolerated for the time being, but please don't attempt to renew the games of old. Remember, I deduced your plans once before," Gavin smirked. "And don't be so quick to assume I won't uncover any new ones."

Giving a slight bow to the Archmage, Gavin turned and made his way towards the chamber's exit. The massive stone doors boomed and echoed in the cavernous hall as he pushed them open. Passing into the corridor beyond, Ir'Wolien called out with a question that almost caused him to stumble.

"Have you spoken with Brynne?" Ir'Wolien called out.

Gavin continued his march away in silence.

The leader of the Silveryn Order chuckled and yelled one last parting shot of advice as Gavin strode quickly down the long hall. "My daughter will be displeased that you haven't sought her out. Be smart, young Silvares, and find her before she deems it time she found you."

After extensive research and first hand observation (often in fear of losing my own life), I can now effectively prove the existence of fourteen distinct clans among the goblin tribes of the Wilds. Why scholars believed for so long that only eight existed remains a mystery.
—*Callum Andware 'Savages in the Frontier'*

CHAPTER XVIII

Lok'Dal hie, The Wilds

With a sickening thud, Leoric felt the club connect with his exposed midsection. Bracing himself against the pain, his body sagged in the arms of his captors.

Sabak! Gulok! One of the jailers roared.

Spitting blood in reply, Leoric struggled to stand, his strength faltering. At his feet, partially shielded by his solid frame, lay the quivering form of a young girl. Even through his swollen eyes, he met her terrified stare with what he hoped was a reassuring one of his own. Already, her left cheek had reddened, the result of a heavy-handed blow from one of the goblin guards standing beside them.

"Not problem... yours!" the officer said in crude common tongue as he directed the two flanking brutes to pull Leoric upright. On occasion, the goblins of *Lok'Dal hie* resorted to speaking the common language as a way of making their displeasure clear to their captives.

"She is a child!" Leoric answered as calmly as possible. He could feel a rising tide of rage welling up within. The sight of Rosa sobbing and curled defensively into a tight ball served only to fuel his anger. "She was hungry. If you fed us well enough, you wouldn't have this problem."

"Food is lots... need no more, only for us!" the green skinned soldier replied menacingly. Grabbing a fist full of Leoric's hair, the goblin pushed his head down near the young girl's, "Next time, girl die."

Uttering a series of sharp commands in the guttural goblin language, the patrol leader had Leoric abruptly dropped to the ground. He felt the cold stone floor against his face and could still hear Rosa crying at his side. Between wracking coughs, Leoric managed to roll over on to his back and reach out a hand to the young girl.

"Rosa? Are you alright? They're gone, there's nothing to worry about now," he called out to her. After a long silence, Rosa turned and acknowledged his gentle ministrations.

"I'm sorry, Leoric," she sobbed.

"Hush now. I know you were hungry; you just need to be careful about what you take from the stores. They know everything that our fields produce, down to the last carrot, it seems."

"I'm so sorry!" Rosa wailed in return.

Leoric carefully cradled her in his strong arms and slid into a sitting position with his back to a large wooden crate. "Rosa, you must to listen to me. I need you to find help."

"No, please, no! They'll get me!" she cried. Leoric watched her collapse to the floor, her small body shaking fearfully.

"Rosa, listen. Find Angvald and bring him here. I need help to return home. I know you're frightened, but I need you to be a brave girl. I need you to do this for me. Can you find help, Rosa?" he pleaded. His mind was already wandering, a dreadful pounding bringing flashes of darkness to his eyes. He felt like he may soon pass out, and with enough blood loss, his life would be in danger.

Encouraged, the girl stood up and brushed the dirt from her filthy dress. "I will get Bear for you, Leoric."

Mustering a smile at the mention of the large Kaleenian, Leoric sent her away. Lying there alone, he reflected upon how drastically his life had changed.

Weeks earlier, he had looked upon a scene of such glory and wonder that he thought he was dreaming. There upon the edge of the cliff face, deep within the uncharted Wilds, Leoric looked down at a city that seemed to have been transplanted from the legends of old.

Built of some unknown purple-hued stone, the walls, towers, and buildings of *Lok'Dal hie* gleamed brightly in the sunlight. Thin spires, hundreds of spans high in the least, towered above ramparts that reached high above the fields and rivers of the surrounding countryside. Raised in a small town, Leoric was struck by the uncommon number of buildings reaching numerous stories into the air. In the north, only a rare few possessed the wealth and desire to build so lavishly, and yet here he bore witness to an entire opulent city.

Glenvale, the unofficial capital of the northern reaches of Old Caledun would have been swallowed whole had it been placed behind the enormous walls of *Lok'Dal hie*. The city itself was divided by three sets of walls, each one larger and more impressive than its predecessor. The buildings, Leoric noted as he scanned the incredible sight, also showed a marked increase in both size and detail. The closer he looked towards the center of the city, the more clearly defined were the distinctions between areas.

Cobblestone streets crisscrossed large open-air plazas while tall majestic trees and fountains added colour and variety. Attempting to decipher the maze-like roadways, Leoric could discern no immediate pattern, and yet he could not shake the feeling that the architects of such a magnificent design must surely have had reasons to build in this manner.

The architecture itself was unlike anything Leoric had ever seen. Even the smallest buildings were comprised of sweeping arches, intricately detailed columns, and large windows. Many of the taller towers were topped by long spires that stood rigid against the high winds, a feat that belied their frail appearance. The crafters of such a place had been masters of their trade, of that there remained little doubt. But how had a race of people Leoric had long considered savages, been the artisans of such an architectural wonder? Even Imlaris, the seat of power in the south, would pale in comparison to *Lok'Dal hie*.

In the center of it all was a castle perched upon a natural incline in the terrain. With an impressive array of towers and thick, purple stone walls, the city's fortress appeared impregnable. 'I wouldn't want to be in the army that tried to assault this place', Angvald had commented when joining him atop the cliff.

Apart from the formidable inner defenses, an outer wall of the same strange material surrounded the acres of cleared woodland that had been turned into farmer's fields and irrigation canals. From his vantage point on the cliff, Leoric could discern small figures toiling the land, their bodies appearing as little more than tiny ants on the horizon.

Yet, however wondrous the city was, the sight below caused Leoric to shudder. He was afraid, very afraid. What hope could the remaining men of Darkenedge have against a people that lived in a city such as this? The fractured goblin tribes, now reunited, would sweep across the fortresses of the Iron Shield like a blistering winter wind; savage, brutal and merciless. How could his people have been so blind?

Shifting his body to alleviate a stabbing pain in his side, Leoric was desperate to walk those cobblestone roadways of the goblin city. Instead, he found himself toiling in the shadow of the great outer wall, guarded day and night by the captors he now loathed.

The surviving members of their small party had become farmers and miners. Their skills in the life they had left behind now playing a crucial role in determining their fate within the goblin work camps. After weeks of hard labour, Leoric now viewed the dreary compound as his new home. Having spent his youth on a farm, he had been selected with the other men and women who knew the trade to work the fields. Angvald, on the other hand, made a daily trek into the very cliff face of *Lok'Dal hie* to work as a labourer in one of the many mines dotting the massive precipice of stone.

♋

"Leoric! By the gods, you have to stop doing this."

With a wry grin, Leoric left behind his troubled thoughts and stared up at the big man from Kaleen. Angvald's thick, braided beard bounced vigorously as he shook his head. With his dark burly hair like that of a rough pelt, it was easy to see why he was known by some as Bear. At his side stood Cara and Benoit, both wearing looks of concern.

"They were beating her, Angvald, a mere child!" he answered, accepting his friend's hand. "I won't stand for it."

"You won't be well enough to stand if things continue, Leoric," Cara muttered, gently dabbing a wet cloth over the two fresh wounds on his face. Sadly, she possessed the same careworn expression of the other captives at the farm.

"They went easy this time. I think H'erok is beginning to take a liking to me," Leoric joked.

"You're a fool," Cara replied with a frown. "A noble fool, but a fool nonetheless."

"How's Rosa?" he inquired as they crossed the field and headed towards the main farm house.

"Apart from the bruising, her mother says she'll be fine. No telling what may have transpired had you not arrived," answered Benoit as he slipped his shoulder under Leoric's other arm to help support the injured man's weight.

Benoit, his nervous twitches ever present, managed a weak smile as he gave the news. A scholar, and the only true pacifist among the prisoners, he was most troubled by the face of such wanton violence and brutality.

"With all that she went through, that wee girl has shown that she has a warrior's spirit," Angvald added.

"She has yet to see her seventh summer, and it's a wonder she isn't dead. We all know the penalty for stealing," Cara said.

"Leoric has paid the price for defending her," Angvald commented. Pausing for a moment, the tall warrior studied Leoric's battered body. "Never thought you were a pretty man in any case," the Kaleenian bellowed.

Wincing due to his bruised ribs, Leoric joined the others in a rare bout of laughter, even though it was at his expense.

ᘓ

The men and women lived in two separate rooms of an old farmhouse in the makeshift labour camp. Although it had seen better days, remnants of the magnificent home still remained. Its enormous size was rare enough, as it could easily accommodate the thirty prisoners. A high sloping roof and curved tresses marked the unique design that struck Leoric as both beautiful and somewhat eerie. It was an uncomfortable feeling staring up at the ceiling and realizing that you now lived in a home where you did not belong. All of the owners of the building's past were now lost in time.

The rest of the compound was a replica of a dozen similar camps, or so Angvald had been informed while working with in the mines. One large warehouse was used for storing the harvest, while a large farmhouse and a few smaller residences were reserved for goblin guards, child-bearing women, and favoured captives. The only source of water, other than the muddy streams and canals that dotted the land close the city, remained a large stone well at the center of the camp. The water was clean enough, somewhat brackish, and did not always quench the thirst.

After the grueling trek from Darkenedge, Leoric was thankful for every small thing, regardless of its simplicity or lackluster appearance. Each captive had two sets of frayed clothing and a worn pair of thick-soled boots. Even now, weeks into his stay near *Lok'Dal hie*, Leoric still suffered from numerous sores on his feet. Without the provided boots, he may not have been able to work and would likely have been moved from the farm.

The nights were terrible. In the darkness of the sleeping rooms, many would be lost in memories and far-off dreams of freedom. It was at night that the children cried softly, and even some of the men would shed silent tears in remembrance of lost loved ones. No one on this journey had arrived at the camp unscathed by tragedy.

Leoric struggled each evening with the demons of his past; the haunting memories of Alanna and his lost daughter, Maya. In the dark of the night, when he drifted on the edge between a veil of blissful sleep and the cruel waking world, he could imagine himself back at home. He would feel the presence of his family so near, so comforting... And yet as desperate as he might dream, he knew that that his past life was no longer real. He had lost everything and now he dreaded the long days and nights spent in the shadow of *Lok'Dal hie*.

To pass the time, many of the adults often congregated in the last common room in the house that remained unoccupied. Their goblin captors allowed some independence within the homestead, and nights spent dicing and talking amongst themselves alleviated some of the oppression and boredom.

Leoric usually joined Angvald, Cara, Benoit, and an older gentleman named Auric near the large fireplace. Of the three new faces, it was Auric who caught Leoric's attention. The old man, balding on the top of his head, but with long wispy grey-hair down the sides, was dangerously emaciated. He revealed that he had been a captive of the goblins for well over a dozen years. Leoric was shocked that Auric could still muster the strength to rise each morning, knowing full well the drudgery that awaited. Yet the eccentric old man carried himself with steadfast confidence, and there was a surprising twinkle in his bright blue eyes. Although Auric refused to speak of his life before his capture, something lay hidden in those eyes that Leoric was determined to unlock.

"Another day done, another bruise to prove it," Angvald cursed, sliding down the long wooden bench where they met each evening. The two friends spoke quietly of the workday, Angvald complaining bitterly about the back-breaking labour of the mines, while Leoric sympathized with him. Working outside, especially in the uncommonly mild temperatures of the deep Wilds, was nothing to complain about. Knowing full well he was one of the lucky men living in the relative comfort of the compound, Leoric always did his best to diffuse any talk about his bearable labour.

As Angvald related another story, one Leoric was sure he had heard countless times before, his attention was momentarily drawn to the front door. Accompanied by his ever-present entourage of camp bullies, in sauntered Joram Eldrin. The swarthy dark-haired man claimed his usual seat near the fire, a table routinely set aside for the uncouth ally of the goblins.

Upon their arrival, Leoric and Angvald had quickly assessed the influence Joram possessed in the camp. According to Cara, he had become a favourite of the goblin guards; a stooge that benefited greatly from those very connections. It was not uncommon to see Joram drunk on whatever spirits he had obtained from their wardens. Leoric could only guess at what cost such items were obtained. The simple fact that the man shared an entire residence with only a few of his thugs and their women stank of bribery. What information or services Joram provided remained a secret, but such favouritism would surely have come at a heavy price.

Within moments of sitting down, Joram was surrounded by a group of fawning admirers, as a man of his influence could offer protection and favours. He soon initiated his nightly game of dice. With few pleasures and amenities allowed within the walls of the house, dicing was always encouraged.

An hour passed, bringing with it full darkness. The days, Leoric noticed, seemed longer than in Darkenedge. It was yet another oddity of the Wilds, another in the increasingly long list of differences between this untamed region and that of the Iron Shield. At the front door, he watched as a small cluster of women arrived. In their midst, walked Kieri Greydale.

Once a citizen of Holdfast, a small village a few days travel north of his old fortress, Kieri carried herself with impressive poise and grace. Of average height with a slender and shapely frame, she possessed a dazzling smile. She worked in the same four fields that Leoric sweated over each day. The two had become friends, and behind her grey-eyed gaze lurked something that Leoric found captivating.

Kieri sent him a quick wave as she settled down on the bench beside Joram; he was intently following the dice and barely acknowledged her presence. Averting her eyes from Leoric's, she nestled in closer to the camp scoundrel.

Leoric could do nothing but continue his stare. Her light brown hair, clipped neatly at her shoulders, bounced playfully around the contours of her face. Even from a distance, he could see a yellowish tinge near her left eye that darkened her otherwise pale skin tone. A momentary flutter of anger swept through him as he glanced towards Joram.

"Wipe the scowl off your face! Do it now if you want to stay among the living," Angvald said in a low angry voice meant only for Leoric's ears. "You keep stealing looks at the lass and I'll start believing you have a death wish."

"I don't know what you're talking about," Leoric replied sullenly.

"Bah! It's as plain as day, you fool." Angvald hissed. "Whenever you two are near one another, you wear your feelings out in the open."

"She looks at me, as well," Leoric commented. It was strange being drawn to a woman again. For longer than he cared to remember, he had remained faithful to the memory of his wife, lost to an illness he was powerless to combat. He had loved her dearly, just as he had loved his daughter.

"Aye, that she does, but she belongs to Joram, not you."

"She doesn't belong to anyone," Leoric growled.

"I'm sorry, Leoric, but here in the compound, she most certainly does." Pausing to take a sip of water from his glass, Angvald leaned in close. "How do you know that bruise she sports isn't because of all of those looks?"

Irked by the implication, Leoric locked eyes with his friend. "Speak plainly, Angvald. If you have something to say, don't play games with me."

"Fine!" Angvald replied hotly. "We both know that Joram holds all the power here —"

"Through fear and intimidation —"

"The method matters little," Angvald countered. "All that matters is that, in the case of our little society, Joram can make rules, but he can also break them. If he thinks for one minute that his woman desires the company of another man, he will kill her... or you."

"He wouldn't dare," Leoric scoffed.

"Why not?" the big man continued. "We've been here but a few weeks and already people have sought your help and attention. You've taken beatings for two children, however misguided those actions may have been, and it hasn't gone unnoticed."

"I acted as I felt I needed to. In both those cases they w —"

"It doesn't matter!" Angvald interrupted. "Sometimes I wonder how a man as humble and naïve as yourself could ever have survived this long," the big man paused before continuing. "Leoric, if Joram sees you as a threat and if you don't step lightly, you'll soon be as lifeless as those we left in the Wilds."

Leoric peered intently at the water that swirled in his mug. Accepting his friend's tacit response to an argument that had become something of a nightly ritual these last few days, Angvald leaned back and carefully spread his large, calloused hands above the welcoming warmth of the fire.

Cara arrived shortly thereafter, her eyes were wet with tears as she approached the table. Following a step behind her, the wizened Auric's gaze was also somber.

"What is it?" Leoric asked. Auric turned to stare into the fire as Cara slumped wearily onto the worn wooden bench.

"Stephen has died," she said through tears.

"Oh no..." Leoric whispered. "How?"

"You all know his visions were worse this week. He was more delusional today than I had ever seen him. Before falling asleep, he asked me to remember him," Cara recounted. "I thought nothing of it until I arrived home tonight and went to check on him. He died this afternoon in his sleep. I think he decided it was time to let go and never wake..."

"Does Merias know?" Leoric said after a momentary silence.

"Yes," Cara replied. "He's with him now. I believe he wanted to be alone."

Merias, one of the other men who had survived the journey east with Leoric and Angvald, had spent the better part of his free time caring for the troubled Stephen. The two men had known each other before the goblins had raided their small village for labourers. For Merias, Stephen represented that tangible link to his past, a past the sick man had so desperately attempted to cling to. The death would diffi-cult for him.

"He has gone to join his forefathers," Angvald spoke passionately, his deep voice filling the uncomfortable silence that had settled between the four. "In that we must be glad, for he is now protected by those who have gone before him."

"To have lived through the journey only to succumb now seems so sad... so wasteful." Leoric said, his own eyes briefly tearing up. Putting an arm around Cara, he held her close. Losing anyone reminded the small band of captives of how few they truly were, and how their lives now consisted solely of this makeshift family.

"Stephen asked of us one thing; to remember him," Auric said, his body facing the blazing hearth. "I believe to honour his memory, we must honour his dying wish." Moving with a unique grace, the greybeard wiped a thin hand across his eyes and turned to join his friends. Clasping the man lightly on the shoulder as he made room along the bench, Angvald smiled sadly in the firelight.

The four companions, strangers only weeks before, spent that night lamenting their loss. They did so quietly at first, and then knowing that the spirit of the dead man would approve, they joked and told stories of what they knew of him. Leoric laughed that night and wondered privately what stories would be told at his pass-ing, and more importantly, who might be left to tell them.

Awaken sentinels, you keepers of the earth,
Arise o' breaker of oaths, bringer of death.
Sleep frigid north, slumber and die,
Fear the silent dark, the night, the eyes.
—Ir'Kaleris 'Kaleris Prophecy', 12:2

CHAPTER XIX

Sanctuary of the Silveryn Order, Dragon Mount

Despite Bider's best efforts and the help of the rest of the Eagle Runners, Orn Surefoot was drunk by sundown. The lanky hunter was found passed out in a stable only a few roads from the inn where the Fey'Derin were lodged. Bider had made an error in judgment when he sent some men out into the streets to scour the area for the man. The head scout had opted to hide closer to the inn than expected.

The small town near the Silveryn citadel boasted a few favourite spots that Orn was known to frequent. Sure enough, a tavern on the far side of the town confirmed Orn's consumption of an excessive amount of spirits.

Looking pitifully at the comatose man lying at his feet, Bider was worried that the company officers patience was rapidly wearing thin in regards to Orn's disruptive habit. The drunkard stank of something unholy. Bider was quite sure that Orn had passed out in a pile of manure, some of which now adorned the better part of his clothing. Covering his nose in an effort to quell a gagging reflex, Bider prodded the man with his foot. Orn failed to respond immediately, and so Bider called in the two recruits waiting outside the stable. He had them load Orn onto the rear of one of their horses and return him to the barracks at Dragon Mount.

Captain Silveron would not be pleased. There had been severe repercussions after the debacle in Garchester, and Gavin would surely be angered by this latest blunder. Well aware of the Fey'Derin commander's serious nature and emphasis on discipline, Bider suspected Orn would be feeling the results of this latest ill-fated binge long after the drink left his clouded mind.

Bider had also claimed the silver flask, Orn's constant companion, hiding it in a pocket sewn into his cloak. The captain would want to know its whereabouts. Bider had no choice but to make his report to Sergeant Shade in the morning, and he feared that only the gods could help the slumbering man now.

∞

"Where is he?!" Gavin snarled as he stalked into the barracks.

As one, a group of newer recruits rose and fled the room. The dark look on the captain's face spelled doom for the man who lay slumped in a corner of the chamber, his clothes still soaked with vomit and stained from his previous evening's adventure. Accompanied by both of his officers and a terrified Bider, the Fey'Derin captain confronted Orn directly.

"Get up, you drunken bastard! Get up NOW!" Gavin ordered, approaching the recovering hunter. No trace of the young captain's usual patience remained. Even Ethan Shade took a step backward, watching the proceedings with some degree of fear.

Orn, to his credit, attempted to lurch to his feet. Unfortunately, he staggered about ungracefully. Painfully the others witnessed the struggle.

"What can I do you for, sir?" Orn stammered as he clutched a bedpost for support. His free hand pressed lightly against his temple as he attempted to straighten his clothing and brush some of the dirt from his trousers.

"I have tried to look past your failings, Orn, but this time you've gone too far. Not only have you disgraced the company name, but you obtained drink against a promise you knew I would be honour-bound to keep," Gavin seethed, his temper barely held in check. It was common for the scout, once in a drunken stupor, to completely forget his actions. Today, it seemed, was no different.

"Not sure what you mean, Capt —" Orn replied sheepishly.

Gavin's roundhouse right hit the man before he could finish his reply. In shock, Bider watched as the soldier flew backwards, landing heavily on the stone floor. To his knowledge, Gavin had never struck another man of the company in anger.

With a look of utter disbelief, Orn rubbed his jaw and wiped a thin trail of blood that was now dripping from the corner of his mouth. "Captain?" he whimpered.

"I don't want to hear it, Orn! I don't want excuses. I don't want reasons. I don't want to hear anything! And I swear if you talk out of turn once more, I'll spit you on my sword without thinking," Gavin warned.

"Gavin, let's talk about this," Sergeant Rockfar attempted to interject, the Dwarven warrior gently laying a hand on the captain's arm.

Spinning, the Fey'Derin commander addressed the much smaller, but stronger dwarf. Through pursed lips, he asked Eör, "Sergeant, are you familiar with the Koriani custom of a Blood Challenge?"

"No, sir, can't say that I am," Eör replied uncomfortably.

"By Arne, no..." whispered Sergeant Shade from where he crouched, offering the fallen Eagle Runner a hand at regaining his feet. Ethan Shade had gone completely pale. Bider looked on nervously and awaited the explanation.

"A Blood Challenge is what the Koriani use to lay claim to a rank of leadership within their order. The battle involves a duel that can only be decided by the drawing of blood on three separate strikes. This is no duel fought in the training yards across Old Caledun. This is not about wooden swords and good-natured fun." Gavin continued. "People die fighting these challenges. The Koriani show no mercy. If you leave yourself unprotected; you will die. If you make a mistake; you will die. If you miss a parry; you will die. They are masters of many styles of combat, true students of the art of war. They could cut our company apart as if we were nothing but a passing breeze," the Fey'Derin captain finished. A stunned silence settled over the men. No one attempted to meet the burning gaze of their captain.

"Who did he pledge, Gavin, and why would they accept a drunken man's oath?" Sergeant Shade asked.

"I have friends here, Ethan, but I also have enemies. They know I am honour-bound to accept a pledge initiated by one of my men. Whether by trickery or not, Orn has played right into their hands," Gavin replied.

"But simply speak with the Koriani!" Ethan begged. "They will understand that a terrible mistake has been made."

Gavin shook his head stubbornly before answering. "The laws of Dragon Mount protect the challenge. I cannot, in good conscience, break the law while I remain a guest in the Silveryn house."

"Then who was pledged?" the officer asked a second time.

"All four of us. We must all face the Koriani in separate Blood Challenges. Orn, Ethan, Eör and I." A shocked silence followed the captain's words.

"By the gods, I was drunk!" exclaimed Orn. "They can't do this!"

"Exactly, you were drunk," Gavin said coldly. "For your insubordination, Orn Surefoot, I leave you with two choices if you survive your duel. One, you can return to *Galen'hide,* renew your oath to me, and forfeit your place in the Fey'Derin as a veteran until I find you worthy to walk among them once more. Or two, you leave the company never to return. This charade has gone on long enough."

"Captain, please..." the veteran pleaded.

Bider could see the pain in the man's eyes. Never before had the company witnessed their captain give up on a member. Some left after a year of service, returning to their families after realizing that theirs was not a mercenary life. Others had faced severe punishments for their disobedience and since been reformed as solid company soldiers while many never left. And yet here was Orn, a veteran who long ago should have achieved the rank of officer, desperately pleading for another chance.

Gavin Silveron ignored the plea and calmly turned to face Sergeant Shade. "Orn Surefoot is an Eagle Runner no more. I will need you to commandeer his uniform and steed. Pay him what he is owed for his service. He is to leave the barracks immediately and must find his own lodgings for the evening."

"Gavin..." Sergeant Rockfar tried to intercede.

"It is the only way, Eör," Gavin responded confidently. "If the Fey'Derin are truly where his path leads then he may return when I see fit, but I will brook no further argument in the matter."

With that, Bider watched as Captain Silveron walked away from Orn, who was left quietly sobbing on his knees.

⚬

The branding remained the primary reason for the Fey'Derin's yearly visit to Dragon Mount. Once again, the casting was a success, and the enchantment was now rooted within the labyrinthine tracings of the tattoos worn proudly on the chests of the new recruits.

The procedure was relatively simple, but as Bider knew from his own experience, excruciatingly painful for the full minute the imbuement took place. Over the years, the subject of the tattoo had become a closely guarded secret among the men of the company. The charm was not overly powerful, but served as an important first line of defense when facing practitioners of the arcane. As with the successful nighttime raid of Pier's Brigade, Bider had received forewarning of the mage at work in the enemy camp.

It was Captain Silveron that had first starting tracking the steady rise of renegade mages in battles across the land. As a means of protecting his men against the growing trend, he had reacted accordingly. Although the cost was rumoured to be significant, Gavin requested no coin from any recruit undergoing the procedure at the Silveryn Order's mountain home. Around the campfire, and especially among the company veterans, the marking added to the mystique of their captain.

By day's end, Bider had made sure that all who had passed out from the pain — a common reaction to the magic's blistering sting — were resting comfortably in their quarters. Drained by the day's activity, he joined the morose sergeants for a late night tankard of ale before settling in for the evening.

⚬

The early hours of dawn found Gavin brooding in a spacious gallery overlooking a beautiful garden. Although winter had arrived, many flowers still bloomed in Dragon Mount as though it were spring. The emotions that raged within him were best dealt with alone. Here in this peaceful place, he could even begin to forgive the actions of the man he so desperately wanted to save.

For years, he had selected members of the Fey'Derin on the basis of his own internal compass. He was gifted with the ability to discern in each person some measure of integrity and potential. Orn Surefoot had all the makings of a brilliant officer, and yet still did he struggle with old demons; demons he could not so easily deny once he had consumed enough drink.

Gavin wondered if Orn would survive the morning. The scout had never been an expert swordsman, and the Koriani were ruthless towards fools who believed themselves to be their equal. Gavin knew first-hand the arrogance that existed within the ranks of the Order's soldiers.

Engrossed in thought, Gavin nearly missed the hush of movement that signaled the arrival of a second presence in the gallery. A delightful scent wafted over him, carried by the light breeze. The fresh smell of lilacs brought back a rush of memories and he turned to greet the newcomer.

"I knew I would find you here," said the woman. "You never did sleep easily, Gavin."

She strode from the shadows, her dark eyes bravely matching his silent gaze. She was lithe and graceful, with a long green gown that flowed freely around her shapely figure. Golden brown hair fell across her shoulders, and a thick strand curled playfully along the contour of her face.

"I could never sleep, Brynne, because you often found an excuse to keep my eyes open," he smiled playfully. "You look beautiful," Gavin added, rising to his feet.

"And you look older," Brynne replied, tracing her hand lightly along his chin. "You are wiser, Gavin, but I sense a deep sorrow. You have seen things..." They stared at one another with only the sound of the wind breaking the nighttime calm. After a long moment, they embraced and held each other.

Brynne Wolien, daughter of the most powerful man in Dragon Mount, the very same man Gavin had fought with that afternoon. The two had spent much time together, their pasts inexplicably linked. As he held the woman in his arms, Gavin fought back a tide of memories he had once thought bested by the passage of time. He realized now that Brynne's presence was the pivotal reason he had refused to return to this place he had once called home. Gavin's thoughts also turned to another...

"Why has it been so long?" Brynne finally whispered, pulling back and staring at him with a pair of accusing eyes. Suddenly, her hand darted forward and connected soundly with his cheek. "So much has changed, and yet here you are like a vision from my dreams, acting as if there is no distance between us."

"I'm sorry, Brynne, truly I am. I needed to break away from the suffocating walls of this place," he explained.

"You didn't even say goodbye, Gavin!" she responded angrily. "You left on the eve of my petition to become Second; a petition you refused, and you thought I wouldn't be affected?"

"Brynne, please, that's all in the past now. I can't explain what I did. Know that I had but one moment to decide my path, and so I chose to leave."

"I will never understand you, Gavin Silvares. Just as I will never understand your soldier's behaviour yesterday evening," she replied.

"It's more complicated than it seems," Gavin suggested.

"Word reached us here in the mountains of your exploits over the past few years," Brynne replied, a hint of pride in her voice. "I have always been watchful of the soldiers you send for the branding, and yet I could never understand what you were trying to build with these men you employ. They are a haphazard lot who appear better suited to dirty backwater towns than your company."

"I sense things about the men I choose. It's the only the answer I can give," Gavin muttered.

"But this man is a drunkard!" Brynne exclaimed. "And yet you *chose* him. Your judgment may not be as refined as I once thought."

"Orn Surefoot is a drunk, but he is also Fey'Derin," Gavin retorted, his voice now dripping with venom. Her rebuke had touched on his own frustrations. "Don't presume to tell me how to run my company, or how to handle punishment. Orn will serve his sentence, and I need no interference from the Koriani, or the Order!"

"You, of all people, Gavin, must witness the rabble that fights in the fields across Caledun. You, who could have led us, must surely realize the superior doctrine and discipline of the Koriani."

"I willingly gave up that path, Brynne, and you would be surprised at the character and courage of this 'rabble' I choose to lead. They are brave and loyal and I warn you to ware your tongue where the Fey are concerned," he hissed.

Taken aback, Brynne studied his face before responding. "My apologies," she said dismissively. "You are aware that your men will most assuredly die tomorrow."

"As might I," Gavin replied. "But I offer you a choice to help spare the two men who had no say in their pledges. For Orn and myself, I ask for no mercy. For Eör Rockfar and Ethan Shade, I would ask that you allow another to fight in their stead."

"And why do you believe that I have the power to speak on your behalf?" Brynne asked.

"Because you are the Koriani First, and the decision is yours alone," Gavin replied.

Brynne Wolien had been a superb warrior when Gavin left Dragon Mount for the northern reaches of Old Caledun. In the intervening years, he had remained interested in the inner machinations of the Koriani. His officers had relayed a fountain of knowledge each and every time he returned from the mountain fortress. Gavin knew that the beautiful young woman facing him had challenged the last First over a year ago. That unfortunate man's corpse now lay buried with honour deep within the mountain.

"You never fail to surprise me..." she whispered, lightly touching his tender cheek. "I would have been proud to be your Second."

"Let it go," Gavin replied coldly and shied away from the touch. He could not trust himself in the matter of this woman he may have once loved, and might still.

"And who would you have replace your men? Who will you choose to sacrifice in their stead?" she mocked.

"I will fight two battles for you. A higher risk to my own life in return for the safe passage of my men."

"My father may not approve of such a request," she mused.

"You are the Koriani First. Is the choice not yours? That is, unless the Council now controls the matters of the sword, as well as the arcane?" Gavin provoked. He expected that an affront to the woman's pride would clinch the matter.

"Fine," Brynne replied hotly. "But there remains the choosing of the combatants."

"I leave that task in your capable hands," he smiled. "You know as well as I that the Koriani will be very interested in such a contest. They will remember my skills with a blade and will be curious to see what the world has done to them."

"And Surefoot?" she asked.

"Orn has chosen his own fate. On the morrow, the gods will decide whether he walks from the yard."

"Then it is decided. The morning may very well spell your end, Silvares," she nodded formally. Pausing a moment longer, Brynne Wolien walked gracefully away from Gavin, leaving him with a final word.

"I would have gone with you," she said without turning around.

"I know..." he replied after she had disappeared from view.

⅓

Bider arrived early at the battleground with the rest of the Fey'Derin. The field bordered the edge of the town in a clearing weathered by the tread of hundreds of soldiers. What little grass remained was flattened down into the earth, and the cold weather had left the field hard and well-suited to the fast movements of a duel.

Bider was surprised by the incredible number of Dragon Mount citizens arriving to watch the dangerous spectacle. The mages were gathered together with looks of superiority clearly written across their features. The stone-faced Koriani soldiers were impressive in their black uniforms. A large ragtag collection of artisans, farmers, and labourers had also arrived to witness the duels. Without realizing it, the Fey'Derin soldiers had pressed together, each grey-cloaked man finding comfort in the presence of his companions.

Word was circulating in the crowd about a change in the usual format. Bider and the others reacted with dismay when told of the bargain the captain had brokered. Orn and Gavin were to fight, but Ethan and Eör had been spared. Captain Silveron was a master with the blade, but battling two Koriani of the First's choosing would likely be an impossible task to overcome.

Bider's thoughts were interrupted as Gavin and Orn Surefoot arrived. Thankfully, Bider noticed, the scout appeared sober. They were accompanied by several Koriani guards and a young woman of striking beauty. It was this woman that stepped from the procession into the clearing and addressed the assembled host.

"May the gods watch over the men who will do battle this day," she cried out. "Three strikes for the victor. May their clash be just and mercy left behind. A Blood Challenge has been issued, and you shall all bear witness!"

The crowd roared its approval, the Koriani especially lending their voices in support of the coming fight. The Fey'Derin on the other hand, Bider was pleased to see, held their tongues. They stood stoic and silent, knowing full well the stakes on this cold grey morning.

"First Challenge! Orn Surefoot against the Koriani Seventh." Brynne announced, the named combatants taking to the field.

Orn was surely overmatched. The talented veteran had never been one to enjoy the lure of the training yard. He was a scout; stealthy, agile and capable with a variety of weapons. He was known for his prowess with the longbow, but was by no means as skilled with the sword he now held in his right hand. He had opted to forgo a shield and instead carried a long knife in his left hand. From experience, Bider knew it was the weapon Orn felt most comfortable wielding.

His Koriani opponent was a tall whip-thin man who bounced lightly as they circled each other. He wore light leather armour and brandished a long sword that looked deadly in the morning light. His movements expressed a sense of speed and seasoned dexterity. Bider expected him to be deft with his blade, and hoped that Orn would do well to end the battle as quickly as possible.

Orn immediately attempted a few searching thrusts that were easily deflected as the men circled each other for the third time. After another turn, the scout grinned at his counterpart like a man with nothing to lose, and backed away from their dance. He lowered his weapons, and yet his eyes never strayed from his enemy. In rapid response, the black-garbed soldier launched himself forward in a dazzling blur, hoping to take advantage of his position.

It is a wonder that Orn survived that first assault. The second weapon served him well as he desperately parried the flashing long sword, but he could only hold off for so long, and first blood went to the Koriani. As the two men disengaged, it was apparent that one of the blade's thrusts had slipped past Orn's guard and scored a hit along his side. His grin was replaced by a grimace, and a dark stain soon appeared along his ribs.

The next few minutes passed quickly as Orn played a defensive game, scarcely keeping his opponent's sharp blade from striking his body. Twice he pushed forward and lunged towards an opening in the Koriani's defenses, and yet both times his attacks were blocked. During the exchange, a second slash had opened a long gash across Orn's right leg, and the Fey'Derin scout struggled to maintain his balance.

With a sinister look in his eyes, the Koriani Seventh pushed his advantage. Bider struggled to comprehend Orn's resilience. The scout should be dead, and yet he parried the incoming flurry of blows successfully and retreated. He was breathing heavily, and the first wound bled freely, soaking his side and hampering his movement. His opponent showed no mercy, and Bider looked on with concern, knowing full well the soldier could finish off his friend almost at a whim.

Orn dodged the first two swings of the next attack and moved inward to counter with his knife. The crowd watched the maneuver and realized the older scout, if he could block the Koriani's descending swing, may very well be able to slide past the guard and strike true. As Orn pushed off the hard muddy ground, his wounded leg finally gave out and he stumbled. The thrust that should have been blocked glanced off his sword and bit deeply into his shoulder. With a cry, Orn Surefoot toppled to the ground.

"Third blood!" Captain Silveron yelled immediately. The Koriani soldier had paused with his sword raised high above his head, clearly intent upon finishing the fallen scout.

"By the gods, he played your game and survived!" the captain declared.

Brynne Wolien locked eyes with Gavin, and for what seemed like an eternal moment, no sound other than the heavy breathing of the two combatants could be heard. Finally, the Koriani First acquiesced, motioning her warrior away from the defeated Fey'Derin.

"As you wish, Captain," she offered slyly. "In any case, yours is the battle we have all come to witness." Turning to the assembled crowd, she called out triumphantly, "Second bout: Gavin Silvares of the Fey'Derin challenges the Koriani Fifth!"

The captain was dressed in his company leathers and carried only his long sword. He held no shield nor had he opted to wield a second weapon. Speed, Bider surmised, would be essential for the upcoming contest. Gavin's eyes betrayed no emotion, and his focus was only on his opponent.

The Koriani Fifth was a hulking man, dark-eyed and calm in the face of such danger. He held his much larger blade securely in his hands. The broadsword would be slower than the captain's, but would deal a greater amount of damage were it to make contact.

As the two men met each other and initiated the first few searching thrusts, it was clear that both soldiers had spent significant time training over the years. The Koriani Fifth would likely have bested any of the Fey'Derin with the possible exception of Lieutenant Burnaise and Sergeant Shade. The man was quick for his size and immediately pressed his height advantage over his smaller opponent.

The captain was graceful on his feet and dodged the first few blows as if performing an intricate dance. He used lightning quick jabs with several feints in the hopes of catching the larger man off guard. He was easily the faster of the two, and looked to exploit his adversary's lesser dexterity. With a loud cry, the Fey'Derin company cheered as Captain Silveron slid past an overextended slash and scored the first hit of the bout.

Gavin could hear the rumble of discontent among the assembled Koriani faithful as his blade found flesh. The wound, albeit a minor one, was well placed. The slight gash across the Fifth's arm would bleed down his bare arms and wreak havoc on his sword grip. A bloody hilt would mean an extra advantage over the course of the battle.

Gavin didn't recognize his Koriani opponent. During his years spent at Dragon Mount, he had familiarized himself with the majority of the power players of the fortress, and yet he could not place the warrior who once again attacked with a calm ferocity. The right to claim the title of one of the Koriani Ten was an honour hotly contested. The man before him had great skill, but was untried. Ultimately, he fought well, and had obviously been trained for just such an occasion.

Gavin often argued that the Silveryn Order's soldiers were exceptional students of war, but had never received the practical experience required to mold them as a unit. They fought as individuals, a characteristic that would doom them in open warfare where the rules could change in an instant. Great soldiers could break under pressure, and even the most talented and skilled swordsman could be overwhelmed by a score of middling opponents. The Koriani, Gavin expected, would be lost if they ever chose to enter the mercenary battles of Caledun.

The battle raged back and forth across the field with both men attacking and defending in a blur of speed. Gavin's experience came to the fore when he noted the slight dip of the Fifth's left shoulder before he attacked to the right. Timing his move with the Koriani's feint, Gavin spun, bypassing the outstretched stab of the broadsword and slicing the man deeply across the back as they switched sides. A second cry of dismay echoed from the crowd. The Koriani Fifth was the favourite against this upstart captain from the North, and much coin had exchanged hands in wagers. Others, Gavin noticed, reacted as expected once word revealed who this captain truly was. Silvares was a name known to all at Dragon Mount.

Gavin gambled on a reverse parry, allowing his blade to slide down the length of the opposing broadsword until both hilts were tightly locked. Without hesitation, he withdrew a hand and reached forward as if in an effort to pull the Koriani's sword from his grasp. The Fifth, clearly the stronger of the two men, ignored Gavin's right hand and shifted the full weight of his mammoth frame in an attempt to overwhelm the Fey'Derin captain's weakened grip. Continuing with the surprise tactic, Gavin dropped his sword and the sudden loss of counterbalance threw the Koriani off kilter. Taking full advantage of the opening, Gavin quickly drew a small dagger from his belt and traced the knife along the warrior's unprotected flank. Blood welled up from the wound as the Fifth tried to maintain his balance.

"Third Blood!" Gavin called out.

Amidst a chorus of boos and curses from the locals, Brynne stood up and raised her hands in a sign for calm and order. Eventually the yelling subsided. Once silent, she motioned the second combatant forward. "Final Challenge. Captain Silveron of the Fey'Derin versus the esteemed Koriani Second!"

An excited murmur rippled through the mob as a broad-shouldered muscular man with a dangerous tint in his eyes entered the clearing. Gavin recognized his opponent immediately, discerning that this next duel would be hard fought. Enias Traihelm was only a summer younger than Gavin, and the two men had often sparred together as they had both risen through the Koriani ranks. They had never been friends, but there had always existed a mutual respect between the two.

Enias was cruel, ambitious, and handled all manner of blades with deadly speed. As the Koriani Second approached, Gavin stole a glance at Brynne. She refused to acknowledge his stare, and with that, Gavin knew that no mercy would be shown if the upper hand were to fall to his opponent. He expected Enias would view this fight as an opportunity to remove any and all doubt that he was the better fighter.

Gavin had witnessed this unbounded ambition in the young soldier in the past. It had led to the unfortunate death of several recruits on the Koriani training grounds of Dragon Mount. It was just this prejudiced approach that had struck Gavin as dangerous behaviour within the closed ranks of the Silveryn Order's protectors. They would kill their own without delay.

Stretching his shoulders to alleviate some stiffness, Gavin maintained a defensive stance as the Koriani Second hunted for an opening. With a snarl, Enias gave way to his impatience and charged forward. With a sharp clang, the two blades hammered together and the battle was joined. Bider had observed Captain Silveron defeat dozens of men in training yards across the land, and yet he had never witnessed the exceptional skill on display this day.

Enias was like a snake unleashed, coiling his position and then releasing a venomous strike. He darted ahead while keeping low, and for a moment, Gavin teetered on the edge, his sword repelling a series of hard thrusts that sent him reeling. The elation of the first victory was all but gone as the men of the Fey'Derin company realized what was now at stake.

Glancing down the line, Bider caught the stern looks of concern marring the faces of the remaining officers. Ethan Shade looked quite ill, his face pale and hands clenched nervously at his side. Beside him stood the stout Sergeant Rockfar, calmly fingering the hilt of his own weapon. The Dwarf's eyes were locked intently on the pair of combatants in the clearing. With an uneasy shudder, Bider turned back to the fight.

Well into the extremely well matched contest, both men had scored only minor wounds against each other. Enias had struck first with a glancing blow as Gavin had tried to roll away after a near miss. The wound was trivial, but blood did trickle from the captain's shoulder. The successful attack drew lusty cheers from what had been a nearly silent crowd. As the roars of approval increased, the captain dodged a heavy overhead blow and smashed his fist into the face of the Koriani. Pressing his advantage, Gavin initiated a string of attacks, forcing Enias to parry the whirlwind of blows. Bider watched in awe as the man spun and deflected each successive stab of the captain's sword.

The battle stretched on. Each man traded blows, countered attacks, and attempted everything from thrown dirt to elaborate feints. Bider was keenly aware that time was not on his commander's side, what with the first duel exhausting some of his stamina. With mounting trepidation, he could see how desperately Captain Silveron needed every brief moment of respite offered.

By the gods he is fast, faster than when we last crossed blades, Gavin thought as he parried another hard slash from his opponent. His lungs burned, and his arms were beginning to tire from the relentless pace of the contest. Lulling his enemy into a false sense of security, Gavin refused to hide his encroaching fatigue. *Let his confidence rise*, the mercenary thought, *and I will strike one last time.*

Throwing back another flurry of blows, Gavin waited for Enias to continue to press his attack. Once the man committed, he sidestepped and slew-footed the Koriani. The crowd uttered a collective gasp of astonishment as Gavin's blade came crashing down in what surely would be the decisive strike. And yet somehow it was blocked, the force of the blow shattering the weapon near the hilt. A piece of the blade pierced the edge of Enias' eye, lodging a mere inch from the socket, the shard drawing blood and scoring a second strike for the captain. Gavin wasted little time holding his shattered weapon and instead returned to his dagger. In a final attempt to end the duel, he stabbed downward towards the Koriani's stomach.

But the downed soldier recovered quickly and stabbed back with a dagger of his own pulled from his boot top. With cries of pain both men fell backwards, a dagger imbedded to the hilt in Gavin's thigh and his own knife protruding from the Enias' midsection. Blood poured forth from the wounds as each man wrenched out the blade.

"Third Blood," Gavin cried out, his voice hoarse with fatigue. He fell to one knee and quickly tore a strip from his tunic in order to bind the dripping wound on his leg. At his side, Enias pressed a hand against the gash in his stomach in a vain attempt to quell the blood pooling around his hands. Several Koriani guards dressed in ceremonial black ran out onto the field in order to tend to his wounds.

The Koriani First signaled Gavin's victory and the crowd of onlookers were stunned. Men and women who had moments earlier been clamouring and roaring their approval, uttered nary a sound. Although keeping the joy that leapt in his throat contained, Bider could barely believe that the captain had regained his feet. Blood darkened Gavin's tattered company tunic, and yet with unbelievable strength of will, the wounded Fey'Derin leader limped towards Ethan Shade and the mage Tel'Andros, both men standing shoulder to shoulder near the edge of the clearing.

"I will need a new sword, Sergeant," the captain said as he studied the broken hilt he had reclaimed from the ground. It was all Ethan could do to nod and numbly receive the shattered blade from his commander's outstretched hand covered in rivulets of fresh blood.

"Sergeant Rockfar, is the company ready for departure?" Captain Silveron called down the line.

"Aye, sir!" replied the taciturn Dwarf, his gruff rumble leaving no room for objections from the surrounding gallery.

"Excellent, move us out. We have a long ride home," the captain said as he staggered through the crowd. The assembled soldiers parted like a sea of tall grass in the prairies of the *Drayenmark* holdings. Gripping the reins of his horse tightly in one hand, Gavin pulled himself into the saddle. Without a glance behind at his fallen challengers, Brynne, Tel'Andros, or the lanky Orn, Gavin rode away towards the gate.

As the Fey'Derin wound their way through the town, they spoke only in hushed whispers. With a final look and wave towards the wounded but still breathing Orn Surefoot, Bider paused to dig into one of the saddle bags before he himself joined the slow moving column that made its way down the cobblestone road and into the wilderness.

With a smile, he hefted the silver flask high in the air and called out to his friend. "I'll return it when you arrive at *Galen'hide!*"

Soon after, Bider exited the gates of Dragon Mount with the rest of the Fey'Derin company. He desperately hoped to see the old scout once more.

The esteemed Duke of Telmire, Lord Kirion Wales, had at one time predicted that the waystation for weary travelers known as the Crossroads would become one of the greatest cities of Caledun. Less than two decades would pass before the first cities of his nation succumbed to the advance of the Aeldenwood.

—Tel'Arena, 'The Fall of Farraine'

CHAPTER XX

The Crossroads, Aeldenwood

Alessan spent the better part of the morning gathering his courage for the inevitable conversation with Corian Praxxus. No matter how often he played out the imagined dialogue in his head, he knew his words would be met with sarcasm and derision. Corian loved money, and the trip through the Aeldenwood meant increased profit. For the boisterous master merchant, that was reason enough to risk the dangers of the dark wood.

And so Alessan found himself in Corian's opulent quarters. Truthfully, he welcomed the break from his duties working around the caravan's foul smelling and ornery mules. The merchant's space was a veritable palace compared to the cramped carts and worn pallets used by the teamsters. Beautiful draperies covered the large windows, lush gold-trimmed cushions adorned two large sofas, and the flatware that balanced precariously upon a beautiful wooden table was of pure silver. The total value of Corian Praxxus' carriage alone could very well finance a lesser merchant's train in its entirety.

Alessan ignored his plush surroundings and focused instead on the work ahead. Corian's accounting records were quite lackluster in certain aspects, something Alessan found very odd knowing his employer's eye for each and every detail concerning his business ventures. It was apparent that the previous manager of the man's affairs had done a poor job. This might explain the current absence of both Vellix and Valorius, the two retainers Alessan had embarrassed when leaving for Glenvale the previous autumn.

"How go the figures, boy?" asked the large man as he maneuvered his enormous girth through the small entryway.

"Well, I've managed to clean up the latest batch of records you passed my way, but there remains some inventory inconsistencies between your master copies and those submitted by the Fisherman's Bottle in the Haig. And that doesn't even begin to scratch the surface of the three companies you deal with in Relabeng," Alessan paused as he searched briefly through a pile of red-marked parchments. Holding up a long piece of paper carefully crisscrossed with a myriad of newly inked red numbers, he passed it to Corian. "Ah, here it is. Miner's Pick, Gidion Hall, and the Farmer's Market. Something just doesn't add up..."

Scanning the page with narrowed eyes, the big man shifted his weight and sat down heavily on the nearest sofa. "Bah, I always expect some skimming off the top, you know," he growled. "But these numbers are obscene. There will be some hard questions asked to certain men I trust, and by Arne their answers better be to my liking."

"I'm sorry, sir," Alessan said quietly.

"Don't you apologize, young Oakleaf! There's no shame in being an honest man, although in a trade that employs few of them, we had best keep you my secret," Corian laughed.

"Well, that's all I can look at this afternoon, Master Praxxus. Fingus will have my hide if I haven't returned for my shift with the reins. He's good-natured as long as he's had his afternoon nap," Alessan began organizing the dozens of scattered documents.

"Ah, I can appreciate your work ethic, lad. Very commendable indeed," Corian answered. "We should arrive at the Crossroads this evening, and if time permits, you are welcome to dine late with me along with my aides."

Catching the panicked look that briefly flashed across Alessan's features, the merchant reached out to steady the young man. "Alessan? What is it?"

Shaking free from the merchant's grasp, Alessan tried to pass off the slip, but Corian would have none of it.

"There's something you aren't telling me, Alessan Oakleaf, something that is obviously weighing on your mind. Now out with it."

"I'm not sure it'll do much good, sir. I think —"

"Enough!" Corian interrupted. "I said out with it."

"Well... it concerns the events at the Lumber household." Alessan began cautiously.

It was now the merchant's turn to turn pale. Leaning back heavily into the plush pillows on his seat, Corian met Alessan's searching gaze.

"Go on, lad."

Clearing his throat, Alessan stammered over his first few words. "Well, you should know that I had a visitor the other night after we called a halt to the evening."

"On the King's Road, or at the homestead?"

"Here in the Aeldenwood. On the road, I mean." Alessan clarified. Knowing full well how foolish his next words would sound, he nevertheless pressed on. "The man who visited me was the very same man who saved our lives in the wood that day. I believe he is of the Gorimm race."

"I know not what you speak of," Corian answered brusquely.

"But you do, sir!" Alessan exclaimed. "C'Aelis came to deliver a warning. Even now as we approach the Crossroads, so too does a large group of Gath. If we cannot turn the train northward, we will be overrun!"

"Madness! You speak madness, Alessan."

"He spoke to you, Master Praxxus. He told me so." Alessan continued desperately.

Corian Praxxus surged to his feet, his face a bright scarlet red. Alessan retreated against the rear wall of the carriage. The dangerous tint in Corian's eyes terrified him.

"Don't presume to tell me what I have done, or what has happened to me!" Corian shouted.

"We have to turn the train around," Alessan said, cowering before the large man.

"We will do no such thing! Our profits lie to the south, and it is to the south we shall continue."

"Inigan." Alessan whispered quietly. "Inigan..."

For a brief moment, as his words pierced the red mist of rage that surrounded Corian, Alessan was sure he would be struck. With a look of murderous anger, the merchant raised a clenched fist. "How do you know that name?"

"C'Aelis told me."

Corian's eyes opened wide with shock, and as quickly as his temper had flared so too did all the menace retire, leaving in its wake the pale face of a tired and distraught man. He slumped back into his seat, his hand reaching for a goblet of wine. Clutching the glass, he downed the drink in one smooth gulp. Wiping a hand across his fleshy lips, he finally looked towards Alessan.

"Sir?" Alessan prompted.

"Inigan is my daughter," Corian offered sadly.

"I'm sorry. I meant you no disrespect. It's just that C'Aelis warned me that our time was short. I couldn't remain silent."

Corian shook his head, "We will speak of this further, Alessan, but I need some time to think. We will camp at the Crossroads tomorrow evening and then, after consulting the Sylvani, I'll make a decision." He raised his hands quickly in an effort to ward off any protests before speaking with finality. "The decision is mine to make and I'll hear no more from you. You've made your thoughts on the matter clear. Understood?"

Alessan nodded in agreement.

"And you will breathe no word about what has transpired here. Friendship will not save you if you do, lad," Corian finished and turned away.

As Alessan left the carriage, he stole a final glance inside and saw the merchant from Innes Vale deep in thought as he gazed longingly out one of the side windows.

CB

The Crossroads appeared suddenly out of the mid-morning gloom. A thick fog swirled around the caravan as the partially ruined buildings materialized from the mist like a ghostly mirage.

It was larger than Alessan had at first imagined. The Black Boar was Briar's only inn, and yet here in the middle of the Aeldenwood, he made out the remains of two large inns in close proximity. The sagging buildings, albeit in terrible disrepair, still managed to dominate the trading stopover. Combined with a number of old shops and taverns, Alessan marveled at the size of the waystation.

As the caravan approached, even the tall spire of a Church of Arne appeared to tower over the nearby buildings. Fingus cackled like a man possessed as he watched the look of awe on his young riding companion's face. Alessan was so swept up by the mysteriousness of the moment that he wasn't bothered one bit.

As night fell, Alessan worked diligently at brushing down the animals and helping to shore up some broken timbers that the men were using as tethering posts for the pack mules and horses. All around him men and women were settling down for a quiet night's sleep. The pace had been hard over the past week, and although a few small groups drank and talked loudly near newly lit fires, most of the workers preferred to grab what extra rest they could.

Alessan's attention was only half on the task at hand as he kept constant watch on the foreboding treeline. Beyond the long abandoned structures, the darkness was absolute. His attempt to convince Corian Praxxus to turn the column around had proved to be futile. The Sylvani guard watch had been doubled, but the column wasn't alerted to the potential of a Gath attack.

Alessan desperately wanted to speak with Corian. Twice that evening he found himself pacing frantically within view of the man's large wagon. He wanted to plead once again and ask the merchant to flee north. A terrible sinking feeling had settled in the pit of his stomach, and somehow he knew that impending doom awaited the caravan.

Sleep was long in coming, and he tossed restlessly upon his bedroll. It was well past mid of night when he finally succumbed to weariness and nodded off.

Pure dread swept over him before he was even fully awake. Screams and cries of alarm carried from a distance as Alessan struggled into his clothes and woke his sleeping comrades. He could only wonder if the Gath had arrived to claim their harvest. Pausing only long enough to confirm that Fingus had risen from his drunken slumber, Alessan threw a cloak around his thin shoulders and leapt down from the wagon.

A scene of utter chaos greeted him.

Furiously rubbing his tired eyes, he watched as two Sylvani soldiers were brutally torn apart. Two black creatures remained crouched over the still twitching bodies. They were gruesome to behold; their bodies a mass of twisted bone and corded muscles. Their dark skin glistened in the firelight as they fed upon the still warm flesh of the slaughtered mercenaries.

In horror, Alessan realized that Corian's confidence in the protection the mercenary company could offer had been terribly misguided. In the face of such a ferocious surprise attack, the Sylvani were no better off than the labourers who huddled with fear inside the numerous wagons.

C'Aelis knew. He tried to warn us... Alessan's terror was overwhelming.

Already veteran soldiers were being overrun, even as the younger recruits fled for their lives. The officers tried to shout their orders over the din, but to no avail. The swarming Gath were everywhere, their talons rending flesh and armour as easily as cutting through dry parchment. Even the most determined of the soldiers could not resist the sheer number of creatures.

Alessan watched with revulsion as the beasts threw themselves brutally upon their prey. Many of the travelers had already dashed into the night, their weapons discarded in flight and comrades quickly forgotten. The bonds of brotherhood could only carry a man so far. The darkness of the dense wood encircling the Crossroads beckoned them all with the slim hope that they might live to see another day.

Many of the creatures had stopped to feed, allowing some of the men from the caravan to evade notice. Fingus mouthed a string of curses as he took in the scene and Alessan doubted if running was even worth the effort. They had invaded foreign territory, and the Aeldenwood, so careful in hiding its dark secrets, was exacting revenge for their arrogance. Corian Praxxus had ignored all warnings and allowed his caravan to continue along the King's Road. The price for such vanity was now being paid in blood.

"By the gods, boy, it's as if we'd strayed into a doorway to the Burning Lands." Fingus said. His wrinkled gaze was frozen and his eyes failed to hide a feeling of utter horror.

As Alessan turned to acknowledge his companion, a spray of blood stung his eyes. In shock, he watched Fingus fall to his knees while clutching his severed neck. Diving hurriedly under the nearest wagon, Alessan closed his eyes as another creature leapt on the driver and pinned him down. He shut his eyes tight and turned away, but could do nothing to block out his friend's shrieks.

For a long moment, Alessan awaited his own death. When he finally opened his eyes, he could do little but stare as the monstrous Gath continued to tear through the beleaguered ranks of the Sylvani and merchants alike. He watched as the oft-maligned Captain Pragg valiantly tried to rally a score of recruits near the center of camp. His gravelly voice could clearly be heard above the chilling screams. Against such overwhelming odds, Alessan doubted that much could be done. Would their defense only delay the inevitable?

The Gath continued to show little heed for their own lives as they threw themselves fanatically at the divided ranks of the Sylvani. The soldiers, accustomed to the ordered turmoil of a battlefield, could barely keep their defensive lines in check, let alone attempt any serious push to solidify their position. A multitude of fanged creatures boiled over from the surrounding wood, and as C'Aelis had warned, the denizens of the Aeldenwood showed no mercy for the trespassers of their shadowed realm.

Alessan jumped as another body, this one a young girl of maybe fifteen summers, crashed to the ground. He stared as a lithe and twisted Gath landed heavily on her chest, its claws sinking into her slight shoulders. Already wounded and in near hysterics, she lay paralyzed beneath the beast.

Fighting back his own mounting fear, Alessan imagined his own sister lying helplessly beneath such a creature and found a seed of courage he thought lost to the terror of the night. With a scream of rage, he charged forward. Spying a broken wooden spar from beneath Fingus' body, he grabbed the makeshift weapon, and ignoring the fiery protests of his crippled arm, swung with all of his might.

With a tremendous thud, the wood cracked across the side of the Gath's head and knocked the beast to the side. With a deafening shriek of pain, the creature rolled across the forest floor and lay still. Trembling, Alessan took no chances and brought his makeshift weapon down a second time, crushing its skull.

He turned back towards the girl he was trying to save. "It's all right," Alessan gasped. "That thing is dead... it can't hurt you anymore."

As he approached, the girl began to scream. She tore at her own hair and spun away from his outstretched arms. He watched helplessly as she staggered off into the darkness. Fear had claimed her, body and soul.

He turned back to survey the raging battle and searched for anyone who might be able to provide safety. Aachen Pragg was nowhere to be seen amongst the surrounded Sylvani, and sadly the crumbling defense of the small pocket of mercenaries buckled under the next wave of attackers. It was only a matter of time before the line would disintegrate and all hope would be lost.

Having little choice but to enter the dark forest, Alessan laboured through the broken-down buildings of the ancient Crossroads. Frantic screams echoed in the night as he limped away. With the ominous treeline mere paces away, a cold chill gripped his heart. Blocking his passage were three Gath feeding on a body.

Crouched over the fallen soldier, the three creatures snapped and fought with each other over the choice portions of their quarry. Alessan couldn't pull his eyes from the ghastly spectacle and found himself unable to move. As one of the smaller creatures was thrust violently aside by one of its brethren, he stood there helplessly as the beast finally took notice. With a low growl the Gath dropped into a crouch, its sinewy muscles tightening in anticipation.

Valiantly clutching his improvised weapon, Alessan braced himself for the inevitable charge; one he knew would surely overpower his weakened body. As the Gath pounced, its jaws opened wide and delivered an accompanying screech. He closed his eyes and desperately swung the spar with all of his strength. Stumbling as the weapon made no contact, he clenched his teeth and braced for impact.

Opening his eyes, he saw the Gath writhing on the ground at his feet with four blue-shafted arrows embedded in its chest. Spinning around, Alessan caught the quiet hiss of wind as a second flurry of arrows whistled past his ear and struck the remaining creatures. With shrieks of pain, the two Gath lurched forward and collapsed, their blood soon mingling with that of the slain mercenary.

"Arin and Daghan, forward positions! Lorne, remain next to me along with Master Praxxus," rumbled a deep commanding voice.

"I want Master Oakleaf to stay with me, Caleb," came a familiar voice, as Corian Praxxus stepped from the shadows of the nearest ruin with a dark look in his eyes. "And give him a decent weapon for Arne's sake."

Stunned, Alessan's legs nearly gave out with relief as Corian, accompanied by four Sylvani, strode up to meet him. By their grim looks and bloodied tabards, he could tell the soldiers had already seen their fair share of fighting.

"H — how?" Alessan stammered, numbly accepting a bloodied long knife as a new weapon and dropping the makeshift one.

Corian smiled sadly and replied. "The gods must be watching over us, lad. I was in no better position myself until Sergeant Holt found me. I watched Grianne and Ella torn apart and could do nothing. It makes no sense to me why I was spared."

"But..."

"All that matters, Alessan, is that we are still breathing, and I mean to take full value of this opportunity," Corian replied, a large meaty hand coming to rest briefly on Alessan's small shoulder.

Sergeant Holt, a man who looked as gnarled as any of the ancient trees that stood in the Aeldenwood, took no chances as the small company entered the forest. He sent the two scouts ranging ahead to scour the area for any signs of the attackers. Screams continued to filter through the trees as they made slow but steady progress along a narrow path that followed the contours of an eastern shallow gorge.

As the sounds of battle finally grew faint, the Sylvani officer called a short halt. Only intermittent screams pierced the weighty silence as the six men huddled together to keep warm. A quick survey of their supplies produced little in the way of sustenance. Food and water had been the least of their concerns while fighting their way free of the creatures. The thought of grabbing supplies had never even entered Alessan's mind.

"We wait only to catch our breath," Holt uttered, obsessively wiping down his sword. Although the veteran soldier had dealt relatively well with the events of the last hour, even he could not hide his discomfort completely. "Come morning, we'll find our bearings and look to do some hunting. Small game should be enough to keep us alive, and I'll warrant not one of you fancies stopping for a longer hunt," he continued.

"Not with those demons chasing us, sir," Arin replied.

"Then our course is clear," Corian agreed. "We move on in a steady pace and stop only when necessary."

"Aye," muttered the others, silence once again settling over the beleaguered group.

 C3

Hours would pass before any sound of a possible pursuit would reach their ears. At first, only a faint rumbling was felt in the ground, nearly imperceptible. As dawn broke, and a slight lessening of the darkness enveloped the tall trees, the distant tread of heavy feet soon became clear. Pursuit, it seemed, was not going to be easily shaken.

For the second time in less than half a day, Alessan struggled to his feet and forced all thoughts of his body's limitations from his mind. To slow the group would mean death for everyone. He was still distressed by his failed rescue of the young servant girl and shook his head in an effort to clear his mind. Yet he forged onward, with eyes focused intently on the large back of the master merchant.

Heartened by the quick progress the small group was making, Holt called a brief halt with the hope that both Corian and Alessan could find some measure of renewed strength before continuing. Corian looked positively ill, his face flushed and breathing laboured. The man's extravagant clothing was torn and stained, while sweat poured down his forehead.

Surprised, Alessan realized that he was making out better than the large merchant from Innes Vale. Although aching severely in both legs, his fear of the Gath pushed him forward. The thought of being overtaken by the terrible creatures was enough to keep his exhaustion at bay and his feet firmly moving.

Regardless of their pace, it soon became clear that the Gath were rapidly closing the distance. With dawn finally bringing a dim light to the forest, the group sensed that their time had run out. Frustrated at the inability to shake their pursuers, Sergeant Holt stopped the group near a series of large boulders.

The terrain led to a sharply cut ravine that seemed a worthwhile place to make a stand. Two men could block the entrance to the gulley while a large outcropping would allow a third man, armed with a bow, to take advantage of the higher ground. And so, with the sounds of pursuit drawing ever closer, the Sylvani took their places, each man's face painted with exhaustion.

Long agonizing minutes passed before a scream of pain broke the silence. Arin came running into view, his bow and quiver held tightly in his hands.

"Here they come, men," Caleb Holt growled. "If we're to go down, let's make them pay dearly for every inch of ground they claim."

As expected, the Gath showed no qualms in launching themselves into the

waiting blades of the Sylvani. Strategy aside, the ferocious creatures nearly trampled one another to reach them. As Arin reached his position on the high ground,
the sergeant and the tall, lanky Lorne brandished their blades. Clutching his own
long knife, Alessan stood beside Corian, both of the inexperienced men on the
watch for anything that managed to elude the others. If all worked according to
plan, Daghan would begin a quick rotation between the seasoned warriors.

With unmatched fury, the Gath swept into the area, their assault relentless
and merciless.

"Hold steady! Watch your flank, soldier," the Sylvani sergeant instructed as
the wave hit.

In those first few chaotic moments, it was a marvel that the two Sylvani did not
fall under the solid wall of fangs that threatened to overwhelm them. Alessan was
impressed by their poise under the tense circumstances. Both Sylvani held their
own, and their blades bit deep and often. With a steadied calm, Arin fired missile
after missile into the tangled mass of attackers from his position overlooking the
entrance to the gulley. The mercenary focused on landing strikes that would either
debilitate the enemy or kill them outright.

"Three moving towards the rock face!" Daghan called out, the perceptive soldier
carefully picking out movements behind the lines. With alarm, Alessan spied the targets moving quickly in an attempt to bypass the small group's defenses. A few seconds
later, Arin had dealt with the intruders, each corpse sporting blue-shafted arrows.

As the men switched positions, they began to tire. Daghan, a sure-footed scout,
slipped on the blood-soaked terrain and barely avoided a gruesome fate. With sweat
pouring off all four men, their confident parries became strikes of sheer desperation. Only their training and reflexes allowing them to survive for even a moment
longer. The Gath numbers did begin to dwindle, and Alessan's hopes were rekin-
dled. He realized that with only a score of the creatures left alive, there was a chance
that the small band could survive.

But as the toll of the fallen began to mount, the bodies further blocking the
incoming Gath, Lorne cried out in pain, his blade falling to the ground. In a flash,
Daghan leapt forward as a stopgap and Corian pulled the wounded soldier back to
safety. With a grimace, Lorne peered at the long gash. That it bled heavily wasn't
the only problem, for without another warrior to help hold the line there would

be little for the defenders to do. Grunting in pain, the seasoned mercenary directed Corian's placement of a makeshift bandage.

"Ware the sides, Alessan! It won't be long now before they flank us," warned a voice from behind. Arin jumped down from his perch, his now empty quiver of arrows lying discarded on the rocky ledge.

Alessan nodded and tore his gaze from Lorne and Corian. As if on cue, the forms of two small Gath, spider-like with skin the colour of ash, clambered along the side of the natural rock formation. Shouting a warning of his own, the young man from Briar braced himself for an attack. With shrieks of rage, both creatures leapt towards them. Awkwardly twisting to the side, Alessan grimaced as his blade slid across the side of the nearest creature. Black blood flew wide as Arin also reacted to the attack, his long sword embedded deep into the second Gath's chest.

"Cursed Arne... what is that?" breathed Corian, staring out across the battlefield.

Turning to follow the big man's gaze, Alessan nearly lost the meagre contents of his stomach. The creature now striding into the clearing had not been present during the massacre at the Crossroads, or if it had, Alessan had surely never set eyes upon it.

It was taller than the other Gath by a good four or five feet, had unsettling beady eyes, and its thickly corded body was heavy in the chest and neck. It had strangely swollen and clawed hands and feet, along with a glinting row of bloodied teeth. These were as nothing compared to the sharp needle-like spikes that adorned the creature from top to bottom. The mammoth creature's skin was a different hue than that of the smaller Gath, pale and white as opposed to ebony. The small group watched in fascinated dread as those Gath that could not get out of the beast's path were trampled outright, their crushed bodies left twitching on the ground.

Sergeant Holt turned briefly to make eye contact with Corian. "Master Praxxus, I believe it's time you took your leave. Take the boy with you and don't look back. We Sylvani will hold for as long as possible."

"You'll do no such thing, Sergeant," Corian replied emphatically.

"It's in accordance with our contract, Master Praxxus," Holt gasped, preparing to face the monstrosity that approached. "I'll be damned if with my dying breath I don't uphold the Code."

"He's right, sir. It's our duty," Lorne agreed, his long knife clutched firmly in hand.

"Forget the Code, men. We need to run, and run now!" Corian shouted.

"There are far too many who die without honour in our profession, and I'll not be one of them," Sergeant Holt proclaimed.

With a disbelieving shrug, Corian caught Alessan's eye. "May Arne watch over you all," he said before fleeing into the forest. Alessan followed, taking one last look at the valiant mercenaries.

Arin let out a defiant cry as he launched himself towards the waiting arms of the huge monstrosity.

Silent streets and cobblestone roads, Darkness reigns where light did shine. Only an empty hearth remains, Where music once played.
—*Shenro Taleweaver, 'Fallen Farraine'*

CHAPTER XXI

Lok'Dal hie, The Wilds

Angvald Helmmarson was born into a family of fishermen and sailors. Although most of the land in Kaleen was barren desert, the coastal areas next to the sea were lush and bountiful. Those who didn't farm the land worked the water instead.

He grew up in modest surroundings but never found reason to complain. There was always plenty of food to go around, although it didn't compare to the variety he would enjoy later on his many travels. Life wasn't always easy, but only fond memories remain of his childhood.

His people were divided into fiercely loyal clans, born of distinct family lines. Dozens of these tribes held sway over the vast land. Kaleen was unfettered by the trappings of nobility, and begat no kings in its long and bloody history. Instead of noblemen, family patriarchs quarreled incessantly over land, food, and simple luxuries.

Frerr Helmmarson, Angvald's grandfather, ruled over the familial lands for as long as he could remember. It would remain that way until his passing, when Angvald's father would assume the mantle of leadership. Frerr fought bitterly with rivals from nearby holdings in his youth and had made something of a name for himself. He also built the seaside home where three generations of the family still lived. As the third eldest son, Angvald had the freedom to pursue his own interests, and although a keen fisherman and astute warrior, he decided to leave the family stead before his fifteenth summer.

He spent time in many of the lands of Kal Maran, with stops in far off Valence, ruled by a council of Lords, to the Shattered Isles, a collection of disparate islands that many believed were the remains of an ancient and powerful empire. The young Kaleenian had studied the arts and loved music, especially his beloved lute. He even spent a year in one of the strange monasteries of the Kann, a reclusive religious sect.

He eventually settled in the northern reaches of Old Caledun, making his way to the fortresses of the Iron Shield and enlisting for three years of service at Darkenedge. With his thirty-eighth summer fast approaching, he met Leoric D'Athgaran.

Something in the other man's nature had drawn the exuberant foreigner to the quiet borderman. The sadness behind Leoric's eyes struck Angvald deeply, as he had grown up knowing the importance of family. It took some time before the guarded Leoric opened up to him about his past, but Angvald eventually learned about the heartache his friend tried so hard to keep hidden.

As their friendship deepened, Angvald discovered how determined Leoric was to move on. Although still reeling from his devastating loss, Leoric began to shed the heavy burden he had carried for so long. During this healing process, Angvald realized that Leoric D'Athgaran had become part of his family and part of that special circle he could call on regardless of the need.

Leaning heavily against the doorway to the farmhouse the prisoners called home, Angvald covered his yawning mouth with a large hand. Whether his friend Leoric wanted to admit it or not, the man had made himself a target in the camp. Only a fool could miss the besotted glances that he exchanged with Kieri. That she was embroiled in an ugly relationship with Joram was not his business. Rather, he thought grimly, it had not become his business *yet*...

Prideful bastards like Joram didn't take kindly to such insults to their manhood. Leoric, whether by choice or not, had drawn Joram's ire the moment Kieri had first waved in his direction. Cara was perhaps the only other person to see the look of hatred that crossed the drunken man's face.

And so, for the second night in a row, Angvald chose to keep watch over his sleeping friend. It was rare these days for Leoric to even fall asleep at all, and he would be damned if he would let anyone disturb his rest. Joram would make his move; Angvald was sure of it. Until that unknown moment, he would wait and ensure Leoric's safety.

ങ

On occasion, Auric would lead wagon trains from the surrounding camps into the strange city for trade. The trips would usually last a few days depending on the amount of supplies and how quickly the men could unload. Leoric decided that the prospect of staying at least one full night in the mysterious *Lok'Dal hie* was reason enough to join one of these excursions for the first time, regardless of the heavy lifting involved. If the bony Auric could survive the effort, he knew he would be just fine.

Climbing into the driver's seat of Auric's wagon, Leoric took his place at the reins. Having experience on a farm helped enormously when dealing with the stubborn draft horses. They were likely acquired through raids, as Leoric had yet to see many of the beasts. The goblins had shown little interest in learning how to deal with the animals. They seemed perfectly content to allow their captives to train them as they saw fit.

On this day, the caravan was headed out of the farm laden with meats from that week's slaughter. Leoric had joined the wiry driver in the lead wagon, listening to his incessant banter with little interest. As they continued along the muddy path, he realized that he was nearing almost two months in captivity. With a mild winter wind blowing lazily in his face, he imagined what it would be like to be a free man.

Leoric was hard pressed to rein in the swelling excitement he felt as the wagons steadily approached the colossal walls of *Lok'Dal hie*. The city walls towered over the carts as they moved under the protection of their long shadows. Leoric was astounded by the rampart's perfectly smooth appearance. It was like gazing at a wall of shimmering purple glass. Up close, the walls appeared to be tinted red near the extremities and a far deeper purple within the solid mass. He had never seen or heard of such architecture in all of Kal Maran.

The gates themselves were mammoth pieces of stone, standing a full ten men in height. They were the largest gateways Leoric had ever seen. Passing beneath the archway, the borderman couldn't shake a feeling of insignificance.

Entering the city proper did little to alleviate the sentiment. The city streets were broad and made of smooth stones. Tree-lined avenues, wider than any he had ever seen wound throughout the city. White marble fountains dotted the cityscape with clear flowing water filling the pools. Most of the fountains were topped by animal statues of incredible detail.

But it was the city buildings themselves that fixated his attention. Surprised, Leoric struggled to understand what he was seeing. The houses, many of them multi-storied, appeared more careworn than he would have expected. It soon became obvious, as the wagons wound their way through the outer city, that many of the buildings were abandoned, their exteriors showing wear not uncommon to some of the deserted towns of Old Caledun.

The goblins are visitors to this place, Leoric thought. *They are no more welcome here than is humankind.*

Until now, he had believed that the goblin tribes of the Wilds had created such a false impression of their people, a savage nature carefully crafted to hide brilliance unseen among humans. Now it was apparent that they were only scavengers, opportunists who had found a city long abandoned.

But what of the people who had built this magnificent city?

He then saw something that gave him pause. At first he believed it was a mirage, a trick that his weary mind must surely be playing. He stared at the tall form of a robed man.

One human in a city of goblins? Leoric wondered.

The man wore a silver-trimmed robe and carried himself confidently, almost arrogantly, in full view of more than a dozen goblins. Here was no culled and meek captive. Straining to keep an eye on his target, Leoric caught a glimpse of the man's face as the stranger passed from view. A sharp-nosed profile was little to go on, but something to ponder. *Who and how could a human have penetrated the city? Was he the last owner, the builder of the ancient city? Something altogether different?*

Leoric continued to wonder as Auric led the wagons over a long stone bridge. The span crossed the banks of a river, one that must surely have been diverted from one of the numerous mountain trails of the wilderness. Not only an aesthetic addition to an already startling achievement in architecture, the water also served as a secondary barrier in the city's defense. It was baffling to envision the sheer number of soldiers it would take to not only attack, but defend the metropolis.

Once clear of the water, a small squad of goblin warriors arrived to escort the men through a second gate. Here, in what Leoric imagined was the inner city, goblins were far more numerous. The streets were alive with noise, the harsh dialect of the wilderness race still indecipherable.

Houses here were in better repair, although the ebony wood that adorned the damaged buildings near the outer wall had been replaced by the lighter oak of the surrounding area. Small goblin children played raucously in the streets, and besides their physical differences, Leoric found that they were quite similar to human children.

Not far beyond the gateway to the inner city, the journey came to an end. Passing into a large compound near an immense warehouse, Leoric followed dutifully behind his companion, stopping the wagon near a large ramp that led into the building itself. With a sigh of regret, he turned his gaze to the task at hand and tried hard to forget the myriad of questions that rattled around in his troubled mind. There would be time to think once the work was done.

The unloading went much as he had expected. As shadows lengthened across the yard, Auric showed no signs of his age. The older man carried the food stores without so much as a grunt of exertion. They worked in silence, which suited Leoric, and although they had made a significant dent in the supplies, by day's end there was still much to do. Excited by the prospect of remaining a night within the strange city, Leoric joined Auric inside a small, partially damaged building off to the side of the warehouse. The older man had already started a fire and was happily humming to himself when Leoric approached.

"I emptied the last of your wagon into the back room," Leoric said, stooping to enjoy the heat from the flames. "That only leaves a few hours of work in the morning."

"Aye, we did well," Auric grunted. "You work much faster than some of Joram's fools who come along for the ride."

"I'll take that as a compliment, old man," Leoric smiled.

By nightfall, tired and sore from the day's hard labour, the two men settled in relatively early. They spoke little, and Leoric soon drifted off to sleep.

A rough, calloused hand clamped down hard on his mouth, causing Leoric to jolt awake in terror.

"Hsst! It's only me." whispered an unmistakable voice in his ear. Looking up into Auric's blue eyes, Leoric frowned. "I needed to make sure you wouldn't make any noise," the man replied with a sly smile.

"Why?" Leoric questioned as he struggled to free himself from his blankets. As best he could tell, the night was barely half over.

"I want to show you something," the old prisoner replied. Then, motioning for Leoric to follow, he crept silently out the entryway and across the warehouse grounds. With his curiosity mounting, Leoric decided to follow.

Three times while travelling through the neglected buildings and abandoned causeways, Auric warned Leoric to be quiet. He reluctantly followed the man's instructions in the hopes that eventually the purpose of the nighttime sortie would become clear. The two men skulked carefully through the city, avoiding the areas populated by the goblin inhabitants. Leoric noticed that Auric treaded the way with confidence. *This is definitely not the first time he's walked this route.*

For a quarter hour they picked their way through the streets, always careful to avoid areas lit by the moonlight. Then, with a deft signal from his guide, Leoric hurried across a final open courtyard and in through the doorway of a tall stone tower.

The building was musty, and a heavy cloying odor hung in the air of the lower floor. The front foyer of the tower had seen better days. Two once decadent tapestries hung in tatters along the north wall, their bright colours long faded. Of the original pattern, nothing was recognizable. The wooden furniture had decayed over what must have been a long period of time. Even so, Leoric was struck by the elegant craftsmanship of each corroded piece. Curtains had been eaten by moths, and some of the rooms appeared to have been ransacked. Leoric followed Auric up a long stone stairwell that took them up to the highest floor.

Once at the top, they ducked under a partially collapsed beam and into a small circular chamber. Devoid of any furnishings, there was only a large ragged carpet and a few small candles present. Auric dropped to the floor with purpose, pulling aside the rug to expose a large wooden trapdoor.

In relatively good repair, the door opened soundlessly. Once open, Leoric peered into the cache and caught his breath. Stacks of parchments, many of them maps drawn in incredible detail, lay concealed beneath the floor.

"I found a lot of the maps in old basements where the parchments had fended off time far better than in the high towers of the city. Unfortunately little of what I found is written in a language I recognize." Auric answered the unspoken question. "The goblins, if they even searched some of the homes, did so quickly and without much interest. You assumed that I didn't try to escape, but I've spent time preparing," Auric explained.

Amazed by the extent of the materials that lay before him, Leoric stared dumbfounded at his companion. "How many years did it take to find so many?" he asked.

"Longer than I care to admit," Auric replied ruefully. "When I started, I was very careful, always watching my back. After a while though, well, the goblins didn't seem to notice us anymore. I've been here so long I don't think they could even fathom my escaping."

Carefully pouring over the detailed maps that lay scattered about under the trapdoor, Leoric still couldn't believe his eyes. *So many years spent dreaming of freedom. How does one stay sane?*

"When?" Leoric asked.

Auric shrugged his shoulders. "Soon. I've spent the last few years memorizing everything on those pages. I figured if I couldn't smuggle them into the camp, committing them to memory would be the next best thing."

"Why are you showing me?" Leoric asked suddenly. Auric had rarely been the friendly sort. That Leoric stood in this tower was dangerous and he was unsettled.

"I can't answer that for you, lad. At least not yet, I can't," the man responded with his usual evasiveness. "I just know that time is short, and that this knowledge should be shared."

"Time is short?" Leoric asked.

"Never mind that. One day you'll remember tonight," Auric answered, peering carefully out the window. Satisfied with what he saw, the prisoner turned back to crouch near one of the large stacks of papers he had pulled free.

"Why trust me?" Leoric pressed.

"I never said I trusted you, Leoric," Auric replied with a disarming look. "Now shush, I need some quiet while I study."

Frustrated by the old man's half-truths and prophetic quips, Leoric could see no other choice than to honour the man's request. They spent the next few hours perusing the parchments, deftly pouring over the maps and trying to glean any sort of understanding from the strange writings. Leoric spent the majority of his time carefully reading, as best he could, a large map that showed the Wilds as he had never before seen them depicted.

The wilderness stretched for miles in each direction, far further than he could ever have imagined while walking sentry duty on the battlements of Darkenedge. The woods still fell far short of rivalling the monstrous Aeldenwood, but it was impressive in its own right. The river that his small battered company of captives had crossed was marked and Leoric was excited by an indication that a large bridge lay to the north, spanning the body of water. Escape, for so long such a far-off and buried dream, quickly became a reality once more.

Auric's voice broke the silence. "I believe it's time to pack up."

"Now?" Leoric replied sadly. There was so much to study and he was positive that Joram wouldn't allow him to accompany the old prisoner again.

"It's getting late, lad, we should hurry. I haven't kept this place hidden for this long just to lose it when I need it most," Auric motioned towards the open window. "I'm also anxious to warm these old bones before bed," he said as he stowed away the remaining parchments.

Glancing out the high window, Leoric could already see that the night sky was much lighter. "The coals will be out by now, Auric. It will be a cold night for us, or a short one at that," Leoric answered.

"Nonsense, the coals will be fine, it's the growing light that worries me," he said, and without waiting for a reply, he ducked under the damaged doorframe and disappeared into the waiting darkness. Carefully following behind, Leoric almost ran into his companion once he reached the old stairwell.

"For the time being this room is our little secret," Auric said, staring intently at Leoric. "When the time comes, we'll speak more of it. I just need to know that you can find this place if need be."

"Aye, I can," Leoric nodded.

"And our secret?"

"Our secret," Leoric agreed. "For now."

"Fair enough," the man grunted in reply. "Fair enough."

Just as Auric had predicted, the coals of the fire were still burning brightly when they crept back into their modest lodgings. Dawn was not far off, and yet both men paused to bask in the little warmth that remained. Leoric deftly filled a wooden bowl from a metal pot he had left near the heat, settled down, and served up a large helping of soup. Laughing, Auric stretched and joined him. For long minutes, neither man concentrated on anything but refilling their famished stomachs. Auric soon finished and lay back, leaning wearily on one arm.

"Lad, I was wondering." Auric said as he poked a fire log with his foot.

"Yes?"

"As a soldier, you must be trained in all sorts of weaponry, no?" he asked.

Leoric finished a last spoonful before answering. "Our officers focused mainly on sword work even though I didn't take to it much. Our drill sergeant may be one of the few things I don't miss."

"That so, sword work?" Auric raised an eyebrow.

Leoric nodded. "I myself have always favoured the mace. I'm not really sure why, but a sword just felt wrong in my hands. It felt..." he paused as he struggled with his words.

"Violent, unmerciful, brutal?" Auric suggested.

"Yes! That's exactly what it felt like," Leoric agreed, giving the man a suspicious glance. Auric lay upon his pallet staring up at the smoke as it rose from the fire, curling out through the numerous holes in the ceiling. Not even Angvald had come so close to defining those feelings. Upon further reflection, he was not sure the big Kaleenian even believed his nonsense.

Shrugging, Leoric continued, "A blade never felt properly balanced in my hands. Strangely enough, I could never practice properly with the sword either, even though I knew the movements and had some skill. It was as if I could never finish a blow with such a horrible weapon. My instructors settled on my learning the mace, if only to keep me quiet."

"Ahh..." Auric replied knowingly.

"Why do you ask?"

"Oh, no reason really," the old man chuckled. "You know, I can barely remember what it feels like to hold a weapon in my hand; sword, axe or mace. It's been so long." he finished with a whisper.

"I didn't know you were a soldier," Leoric commented. No one knew about the man's origins, but he still hoped to glean something of the man's past this night. It was rare that the old man ever spoke this much.

"That's because I never said I was," Auric replied. "If I wanted you to know about my life, I'd have told you already."

"So you don't trust us then?" he replied angrily.

"Well, some of you I don't," Auric said. "Truthfully though, when the time is right, I might tell you something. But only when the time is right," He added playfully.

"What's that supposed to mean?"

Auric's answering chuckle hinted at something Leoric desperately wanted to understand. Try as he might, the old prisoner remained elusive about his apparent knowledge. Within moments the conversation was over, and only the man's loud snores remained. Puzzled, Leoric bedded down and fell fast asleep.

CB

The following evening he was back in camp watching the stars glittering brilliantly over the quiet fields. Leoric had found himself plagued by insomnia many times over the past few years. When the affliction hit hardest, he would lie awake for hours on end without reprieve. While stationed at Darkenedge, he grew accustomed to taking long walks along the high ramparts of the keep. The sentries often made light of his discomfort, and yet they were always buoyed in spirit by his arrival in their sector. Night duty, as Leoric knew far too well, passed slowly without conversation.

Since his arrival at the prisoner's camp, he hadn't slept well at all. His dreams were unsettled and his mind weary from the stress of captivity. On the long journey from the ambush site, he would collapse to the ground almost immediately asleep after each grueling day's march. That was not the case here in the shadow of the strange city.

This night, the first since returning from *Lok'Dal hie*, he found himself sitting peacefully on the back rail of one of the trade wagons. Puffing on his wooden pipe, one of the rare luxuries the goblins allowed, Leoric replayed the events of his recent expedition through his tired mind. The state of the buildings, the rows of empty houses, and even Auric's cryptic responses concerning his map collection. All of these thoughts only served to push sleep further away.

"Is there room on that seat?"

Surprised by the female voice, Leoric spun to greet the visitor. "P—p... pardon me?" he replied, stumbling over his words as he looked into a pair of dark eyes.

"I'm sorry, Leoric. I couldn't sleep and saw you here. I thought you might want some company," Kieri quickly dropped her gaze. "I shouldn't have come..."

"No, no." Leoric stammered. "Please do sit. I was surprised is all, Kieri. It's not often that I find others awake at this hour," he finished, hastily motioning at the open space to his left.

"Do you often come out here in the middle of the night?" the woman asked. She settled down at his side, carefully readjusting her long beige nightgown.

Shifting uncomfortably at the question, Leoric managed a wry grin. "I try to keep my clandestine meetings private, you know?"

Kieri laughed softly at the comment and playfully slapped his arm. He was acutely aware of how close they were sitting to each other. Even now, he could feel a slight stirring in his body and the quickening of his heart rate, leaving his cheeks flushed with colour. Avoiding Kieri's gaze while using the opportunity to lazily blow smoke from his mouth, Leoric tried valiantly to master his exhilaration.

"It's this place, isn't it?" Kieri asked after a momentary silence. "The city may be wondrous, even beautiful to look at, but it could never be home."

"I have to admit, the nights out here so far north can be stunning," Leoric replied with a nod. "But you're right, my home is Darkenedge."

"My family farm wasn't much, but I can still smell the lilies that my mother would place in the windows every spring. My father used to cook a fantastic rabbit stew; a recipe he swore had been handed down through the generations. A family treasure, as it were," Kieri replied. Her wistful expression was filled with sorrow.

"There isn't much in Darkenedge that anyone would grow fond of." Leoric pondered.

"Have you always lived there, Leoric, and been a soldier?"

"At Darkenedge? Oh no, I farmed out near Avery long before coming out to the Iron Shield," he replied.

"Angvald did mention something of that. You were married?"

"I had wife and child."

For the second time, Leoric found himself shifting uncomfortably. He rarely spoke about his past, and yet something in the way Kieri looked into his eyes gave him a measure of courage. "Alanna was twenty-eight when she died."

"And your daughter?" Kieri said quietly.

"I believe Maya is well, but I'd prefer not to speak of her," he answered, his eyes locked on the muddy ground at his feet.

The sudden soft touch of Kieri's hand along the contour of his cheek caused him to jerk away. It had been a long time since a woman had touched him so intimately. And yet, although pledged to another, Kieri did exactly that. Seeing his obvious discomfort, she looked away ashamedly.

"I'm sorry..." she said quietly.

"It's not your fault," Leoric replied apologetically. "It may sound strange to you, but no one has touched me like that since Alanna."

His senses were heightened and he could hear the soft rustle of the long grasses as the night wind blew briskly through the strands. He could feel the thin fabric that covered Kieri's leg as she sat so close. Without warning, she reached out and clasped his hand.

"What was she like? Your wife."

Amazed by the unabashed question, Leoric was equally surprised when he found he could answer. Speaking of Alanna had never been easy.

"She was my first love," he replied. "We met in the market and I asked right then if she would dance with me at the Winter Festival that evening. You know, I think she accepted because she was so surprised," he added with a sad smile. "But I did something right, and we rarely went a day without seeing one another. She was quiet and gentle, well-spoken, and so intelligent. How she ever fell for a country lad like me, I'll never know. She would laugh at the simplest things, and everyone was affected by her good nature. I loved her very much."

"I'm sorry for your loss," Kieri said. She gave his hand a light squeeze.

"She was a good woman. She also deserved a better fate," he added bitterly.

"Do you believe they watch over us, our loved ones who have passed? That they now live with the gods?" she asked.

Leoric shrugged. "I don't think it's for us to know the answer to that question, Kieri. Angvald would have you believe it, though," he smiled. "He reminds me every day that I will surely sit proudly at the table of my ancestors. There are times that I question his sanity. But, I guess I can only hope that Alanna smiles down on me, comforting me when needed. You know, she loved to dance, and maybe she's happy dancing up there in the stars," he spoke, his eyes scanning the night sky.

"With the gods." the woman added in a whisper.

"I have no trust in the providence of the gods," Leoric said sternly. "I will never forgive them for taking away my family. I would have gone in her place had I been offered the choice. In my mind, she dances alone, free from any gods."

"But who are we to question their reasoning, Leoric?"

"I would openly question anyone who dealt unwarranted pain upon another," he retorted. "I only have pain to remind me of my grief, an unfair punishment it seems that the gods deemed necessary," he continued. "I won't be party to that belief. Life is difficult, and tragedy strikes us all; it's as simple as that."

"I, for one, welcome the pain," Kieri whispered.

"Why?" he asked softly, wrapping his arm around her slim figure.

"It reminds me that I'm still alive."

Pulling her closer, he fought to stem the tears that threatened to spill forth. There was such agony and sadness in Kieri's words. He decided at that moment that she need only to ask for help and he would be there. As Kieri nestled deeper into his comforting embrace, Leoric hoped that Alanna would understand.

∛

In Raven's Dell, the wind blows cold,
Steps grow weary, bones grow old.
The sun bleeds red on ashen ground,
Wild whispers creep from barrow mound.
A war forgotten, a nation lost,
The price of freedom, a crushing cost.

Many a man in war here fell,
Their memory lost to Raven's Dell.

Leoric clapped loudly and whistled as Angvald finished his song. It had become something of a tradition for the Kaleenian to regale the men and women of the camp with tales of faraway places and peoples of Kal Maran.

During such performances, captivity was almost bearable. The songs reminded him of home, of the town tavern where he would sit among friends and share a pint while a minstrel sang. Surveying the room, Leoric realized that somehow they had found a measure of comfort despite their captivity.

"How can you all laugh?! Are you truly that happy?" called an angry voice from the crowd. "You toast to each other's health, and yet I wonder have you all forgotten where we are and what has befallen us?"

Merias stood on one of the few tables in the room, his eyes blazing and his body taut with fury. Everyone knew that he had been severely affected by Stephen's death. He had become irrational and openly defiant of their goblin captors ever since. His bruised face and bandaged ribs reminded those assembled of the price for such behaviour.

"You smile and pretend nothing's wrong even though we're here in the Wilds, fighting over the scraps that the goblins leave for us! Do any of you have the heart to hate them anymore?"

"He speaks truth," Drake agreed, standing at his friend's side. The border soldier, along with Leoric, had been one of the few who had spoken out vehemently against their captivity. As Leoric had paid a price, so too had Drake. "We have grown complacent."

Angry murmurs swept through the crowd, some heads nodding in assent, others downcast and wearing ashamed looks of sadness. As Leoric moved to voice his support, a grip like steel forced him back into his seat. Staring balefully at the assailant, Leoric struggled to break the hold.

"Sit down, lad, before you help those two buffoons get us all killed," warned Auric, the man's grip tightening in response to his struggles. "Ware the look on the bastard's face near the fire, Leoric, and tell me what you see," the old man inclined his head to the left.

Joram was watching the proceedings with feigned bemusement. Surrounded by his usual cronies and holding Kieri tightly around her waist, he failed miserably at hiding the dark glint in his eyes. Joram whispered something to one of his men, making it quite apparent that he wasn't pleased with Merias' passionate plea. After witnessing the reaction, Leoric calmed his attempt to break Auric's surprisingly strong grip.

"He's plotting something and will try to use this situation to further his own designs," Leoric said.

Joram often spoke adamantly about currying more favour with the guards. To work with their captors could only bring about good fortune, he would preach to the others in the camp. It was all Leoric could do not to throttle the man where he stood.

"His heart is dark and twisted. Little remains hidden from his eyes. He enjoys this." Auric agreed.

Accepting the strange comment, Leoric forced himself to finally look away from Joram. Angvald had pushed his way through the crowd and reached Merias' side by the time he had turned back to the impromptu proceedings. Whispering urgently in the man's ear, the big Kaleenian pulled the angry man from the table top, shoving him forcefully onto a bench.

"The Kaleenian saw the same," Auric nodded approvingly. "He is far more intelligent than he lets on. He sees truly into men's hearts, as do you, weighing them and judging accordingly. It would serve you well to keep such a man as your ally."

"What are you talking about, Auric?" Leoric frowned. Not for the first time since meeting the prisoner, Leoric was annoyed by the smatterings of advice the man felt compelled to share.

"One day you'll understand, Leoric. You'll see everything through these eyes and remember," Auric answered. And with that, the man winked and slipped off into the crowd.

Confused, Leoric barely spoke when Angvald and Cara joined him at the table. Understanding anything in this godforsaken land seemed impossible.

Thin winds whistle, the ghosts of arrows.
The fort of a handsome king laid low.
Guardian of the East, Great Watcher of the kingdom.
Fatuous, vain,
empty, and still.

And I, to whom the living things whispered,
could taste them nearing, foul in the air.
And when they shuddered,
the steel did sing.
When the stones crumbled, the men did shriek.
The Blood Moon rose, and I walked into the Wood.
—Unknown

CHAPTER XXII

The Watchtower of *Al'Taers,* Aeldenwood

The return trip to the winter encampment passed quickly. While less than a league from Dragon Mount's walls, Gavin did lose consciousness during the ride on account of his injuries. The journey was eerily devoid of any excitement. Even the men known to be boisterous at the worst of times kept to themselves. Many of the soldiers, Bider gathered, were coming to terms with their new allegiance to the Fey'Derin.

Bider, as well as the other veterans, were visibly concerned with certain revelations that had come to light regarding their commander. That Gavin Silveron had spent considerable time training with the Koriani unnerved most, but only Bider and Ethan Shade caught the distressed glance Gavin had given the tall woman in charge of the Koriani troops. Brynne Wolien's relationship with the captain brought up even more questions, and Gavin's self-imposed exile from the mage stronghold seemed a far more complicated story than Bider had first assumed.

ଓଃ

Gavin grew impatient once he had recovered at the Fey'Derin's winter camp. A stack of messages, many from friendly captains of northern companies wondering about the Fey's plan of action come spring, needed attending to. Penning his responses and dispatching them as quickly as possible, the young commander had still to meet with a representative of Duke Berry before his planned departure to the Aeldenwood. Business seemed unimportant in light of his deep concern that the world was on the brink of a momentous change.

The return of the Gorimm could signify any number of things, some far more treacherous than others, and he wanted to confirm his suspicions. The arrival of the lost tribe of the Aeldenwood could also force his hand, a position Gavin desperately wanted to avoid. Also, he had yet to make a decision regarding any revelations he would make concerning his own past.

Duke Berry had dispatched a familiar representative to the site. For the past decade, Herod Blackwain had captained his own company known as the *Delan Fere*, 'Shieldbreakers' in the old tongue. The stout, burly northerner sported a thickly braided beard that rivalled even Ossric's. Herod had fought in the southern Protectorate over the past two seasons and was responsible for defending several outposts that belonged to the famed Duke of Garchester. His company had also been instrumental in the defense of Matanis on the coast.

Gavin always enjoyed the man's company. Herod was an experienced soldier who discussed his tactics openly with the younger mercenary. Gavin had drawn upon this knowledge during many perilous situations over the previous busy summer seasons. His fellow captain had always been friendly, a rare trait among most of the coin-hungry mercenaries of the land.

Gavin gripped the man's thick muscled forearm in a welcoming gesture. "Damn fine seeing you again, Herod. But is that a few strands of grey I see in that mop of yours?"

"What a fine way to greet an old friend. Reminding him that he's older than the last time you met!" the mercenary soldier retorted.

"I'm sure the Captain is just confused, Herod," Ethan said from the entryway. The Eagle Runner was dressed in an immaculate long black coat and proffered a bottle of wine as he entered.

"How so, young Ethan?" the guest replied with a frown.

"The Captain may have thought you were Caolte," Ethan said with a smile. "When I squint you do look somewhat alike."

"Cursed Arne! I'm no grandfather!" Herod thundered. "A few stray greys are all I've got, not a full head of them!"

"I take it my wizened appearance is once again being brought to the fore. One of these days you'll all wish that you look like I do at my age," Caolte added as he approached the small gathering.

"Old?" Ethan asked curiously.

"Why, the perfect specimen of a man," Caolte deadpanned.

The men laughed as formal greetings were exchanged between the *Delan Fere* captain and the Fey officers. Ethan poured the wine, passing each man a goblet as the group settled down at the wooden table in Gavin's private quarters.

"How is Garchester faring these days? She took a decent pounding this past year," Caolte asked.

Herod's brow furrowed. "Well, we're still repairing the damage, but the citizens' spirits are quite high. Most of the damage was contained, but the battlements remain in a terrible state."

"The Duke left the walls breached?" Ethan asked.

"Duke Berry looked to his people first. With so many cities falling under the influence of the nobles from Imlaris, namely that bastard Yarr, he can ill afford to lose any of the support he now holds," Herod answered.

"A strategic move, but it could be costly should the walls remain open come summer," Caolte murmured.

"He'll get the work done," Herod avowed. "Matanis isn't in much better shape."

"We heard only rumours while in Garchester as to your defense," Gavin replied. "Your men came through well enough it seems."

"Aye, we took our fair share of casualties. Seeing as how we were responsible for the majority of the fighting in the mountain passes, we did quite well."

"How many short are you this year?" Ethan inquired. It was common knowledge that the devout northerner refused to hire men hailing from the south. Each summer of warfare cut deeply into the supply of Herod's remaining reserves. Most replacements sailed from the port city of K'oral in order to reinforce the company each winter.

"I sent a request for two score, but losing Henric was my biggest blow," Herod answered.

"He fell in the city? A fine officer and your longest serving, I believe?" Gavin said.

"I spent six years with him," Herod nodded. "The fool was sometimes too damn full of himself. He got caught in an ambush not far from the eastern edge of the Seracen Pass last summer. He tried to hold it against two companies. By the time we responded to the threat, it was too late. He fell in the rearguard trying to buy time for the rest of his squad."

"A terrible loss..." Caolte uttered under his breath.

"It's what we all sign up for," Herod stated. "You must put the anger and sadness behind you and move on. No sense agonizing over something you can't change."

"Now that is sound advice," Caolte raised an eyebrow and sent a withering look towards his captain.

"Not a word, Caolte," Gavin warned.

"Yes, sir," came the reply.

Three bottles of wine and many stories later, the men left behind tales of friends lost in order to discuss the present situation. Gavin was troubled by what seemed to be a lack of strength the allies of the Duke could muster in his defense. It was no secret in the cities of the south that few were willing to commit to the nobleman's cause.

"Where does the Duke believe the hammer will fall this coming campaign?" Gavin asked.

"Rumours keep swirling that Garchester will be hit again, but so much attention is being focused in that direction that some of us feel it could all be a diversion," Herod replied.

"How so?"

"Well, Duke Berry has defended the city time and time again. The support from the populace is almost completely in his favour; no one to be bought off, no company to play spoiler and betrayer. The belief in his abilities as a leader is absolute. If Gadian Yarr plays things differently, we may have too strong a contingent of contracted companies in Garchester. We would then be unable to respond adequately to a secondary threat."

"Sound points, but you're assuming the Duke's intelligence has been severely curtailed. It would be uncommon to have such little information concerning Gadian Yarr's movements," Ethan commented.

"Unfortunately, you have the right of it," Herod agreed, idly scratching his beard. "We can't get anything out of our usual informants."

"Any indication that their loyalties have been swayed?" Caolte asked.

"Not that we can discern. Only a dry well when it comes to information leaking from their camp."

"And Lord Dalemen?" Ethan pressed.

Herod shook his head. "Same thing, I'm afraid. The southernmost companies have been sending small numbers of men to his position near Avery for the past year. A squad here, a score there, and we have yet to pierce that mystery. Truth be told, every one of our agents sent to investigate has yet to return."

"Strange. There's nothing in that area of significance is there?" Gavin queried.

"Not that we're aware of. We've documented better than a thousand men crossing through that terrain, and we have no idea where they've ended up."

"A thousand men in the plains of the southwest wouldn't be that difficult to hide." Caolte mused.

"We'll keep an eye on things out east, but this summer might push us past our boundaries whether we agree or not," Herod stated.

"What's the Duke looking for from the Fey?" Gavin asked.

"Your continued support. Needless to say, without your men and my *Delan Fere*, he'd have no chance in holding off an attack. The *Ca'lenbam* is scheduled near Imlaris this year. The Duke will be attending for the first time in the hopes that his presence will sway a few undecided companies."

"His contracts better be well-laden with coin," Ethan declared. "The Duke will need to dip deeply into his stores if he wants to sway anyone."

"Even you?"

"Of course not," Gavin answered immediately. "I would be travelling north right now if my plans didn't involve supporting his policies. Caolte could be visiting his newest additions, and Ossric would be drunk in the Black Boar whispering sweet nothings to some pretty young lass, no doubt."

Chuckling at the comments, the visiting captain smiled. "I had to ask, Gavin."

"Understood."

An hour later, Gavin found himself escorting Herod back to the stables. The meeting had gone as expected, and the group unanimously agreed that Gadian Yarr was planning something unpredictable. His setbacks, both at Matanis and Garchester, were bound to have left a sour taste in his mouth.

"You're welcome to stay for the night."

"I can't, Gavin, although I do appreciate the offer. I have two more stops to make in this blasted weather before I can settle my affairs for the upcoming spring. I'd rather get everything done as quickly as possible."

"I understand," Gavin answered. "Anything else I can offer?"

"The food has been splendid and the spirits a welcome gift," Herod gestured to his newly laden saddlebags. "One thing though, what's with the mage?" he added quietly. "I saw him chatting with a few of your men this morning near the smithy."

"Tel'Andros is doing some work near the Aeldenwood border. Mage business I want no part of. I was asked to provide him a place of lodging, that is all," Gavin said dismissively.

"Ah," Herod said thoughtfully. "You won't mind me mentioning that to the Duke now will you?"

"Not at all," Gavin answered with a forced smile. "Safe journey to you always," he added.

The Duke would be none too pleased to hear of the mage's presence. Although quite progressive, the southern noble still carried many of the prejudices instilled by his forefathers. Distrust in the reclusive Silveryn Order was paramount among those beliefs.

Waving as the visiting captain rode out through the gates of the fort, Gavin hoped his suspicions would prove to be correct. He could ill afford to speak of such matters with Duke Berry unless absolutely sure that his assumptions were accurate.

C33

Gavin, Caolte, and Tel'Andros left early the next morning. Only a faint brightening of the eastern sky heralded the coming of dawn as the three men rode along the winding trail leading north into the fringes of the Aeldenwood.

Gavin had insisted they pack enough food to allow for an extended stay in the old watchtower. He couldn't predict how long it might be before the Aeldenwood would alert the Gorimm of their arrival. The ever-present danger of the Gath remained the biggest risk. With the new information gleaned at Dragon Mount concerning the Fallen, Gavin suspected that the coming days would be fraught with peril.

The Fallen had long been held as a mere unfortunate rumour by the mages of the Silveryn Order. Now, the Shield breach provided irrefutable proof of not only their existence, but also of distinct coordination between the defectors. The Council of mages had long avoided being used as pawns by the powerful clans of Old Caledun, but now they faced a new problem. How could a group so stubborn in their arrogance, come to realize that help would be needed in order to quell the threat of the Fallen?

Left unchallenged, the number of renegades would certainly swell. Surely they would perceive inaction by the Silveryn Order as a weakness and exploit it to its fullest. It also remained a glaring truth that one of the Fallen had been hired by the opportunist Gadian Yarr to help in the safe passage of the Lady Farraine. Gavin could feel the invisible chains of his past tightening as Yarr's political schemes gained momentum.

That evening, the trio camped on the edge of the forest. There, in the lengthening shadows of the Great Wood, Gavin dreamt once again...

He found himself walking through the ruins of a majestic city. Tall spires rose gracefully into the night, piercing even the tops of the ancient trees present within the boundaries. The trunks dotting the cityscape were enormous, easily larger than any he had ever seen. Here were the sentinels that had seen the passing of ages, each season but a brief flicker in their eternal existence. Gavin was drawn to the majestic trees, his hands sliding and probing along the coarse and knotted wood. A sudden sadness poured into him, enveloping his soul with a suffering wail.

Here, deep within the ancient forest, the call of that pain was so intense that he fell to his knees. He stared sadly at the towering trunks until it was no longer bearable, for the bark itself seemed to writhe in anguish. Defiant, he turned to survey the city that was itself a reminder of the generations that had already passed before his birth. In the constantly flowing river of time, he felt less significant than a single drop of water.

The stone buildings and incredible towers were in disrepair. Clear marks of a struggle still remained. Rusted armour and weapons, long left abandoned to the cruel elements, felt brittle to the touch. Crumbling skeletons told a story of loss as he walked deeper into the city. An unholy battle had been fought here, one that had seen thousands slaughtered in the streets. For how long had the bodies remained untouched, undisturbed by the arrival of any living creature?

The numerous shops and houses fared no better. Doors hung on broken hinges with many of the rooftops in a state of partial collapse. Evidence indicated that fires had ravaged whole city blocks. Black ash covered almost every street and structure in sight. Gavin passed through one section of an inner wall that had been bombarded into dust.

As he crossed a long bridge that spanned what was once a beautiful moat, he caught a momentary flicker of movement. Fighting back a sudden surge of fear, he turned to acknowledge the new arrival. A black wolf scampered quietly along the edge of the cobblestone road and paused to sniff idly at each and every doorway it passed. The creature's fur was matted and dirty, its breathing laboured in the silence of the night. Its nose was bloody, with long sweeping wounds crisscrossing the snout.

A putrid smell like that of a decomposing body in the sun, assaulted Gavin's senses. Gagging, he covered his mouth and nose in the hopes that it would minimize the odor. The wolf watched him with eyes as black as night, the pupils covered by a sheen of ebony darkness that emitted no light. With a shudder, Gavin realized the black wolf was blind. Worse, he knew why it had come...

Crossing the bridge, Gavin watched as the creature hounded his footsteps. Oddly, the beast refused to close the distance between them. Retching from the horrendous smell, he quickened his pace and passed under an archway that defined the foundations of a great castle. In the courtyard lay the dry bones of hundreds upon hundreds of soldiers. The battle fought here upon the very doorstep of the keep was a vehement last stand. Briefly caressing a discarded blade, Gavin eyed the area with a wondrous melancholy.

In the center of the blackened battlefield were the remains of five large tree stumps. Clutching his head in pain, Gavin tried to dismiss the feeling of despair that assaulted his mind. A sudden high-pitched cry brought him a moment of respite. The black wolf had reached the courtyard and was sitting back on its haunches near the center of the clearing. With blood dripping from its snout, the wolf threw its head back again and howled piercingly into the night.

For long minutes, Gavin dared not to move or even breathe. Finally trying to regain his balance, his foot brushed against a rusted breastplate. The creature's head spun immediately towards the noise, its black lifeless eyes holding his gaze captive. The horrible stare bore into his soul, and Gavin screamed as he tried to break the bond. His body trembled as the wolf began its approach...

With a start, Gavin opened his eyes, a scream ready to erupt from his lips. Clapping a hand quickly over his mouth, he tried to muffle the noise. Surveying the campsite, he looked for any signs of the scarred wolf. Only the covered forms of his companions and their three mounts were present.

It was only a dream...only a dream.

Gavin removed the soaked undergarment that clung coldly to his skin. Stoking the fire and adding a new log to the blaze did little to ward off the chill in his veins. Fully awake, it was now that he recognized the animal from his dreams. It was *Ordus*, the *Drayenmark* spirit of war and death that had stalked him during his dark vision. The blind wolf was a mythical idol among the descendants of the old blood. The seers gave rise to the belief that the beast followed the scent of blood, and that where *Ordus* trod, death would soon follow.

Sleep, Gavin knew, would not be forthcoming this night. Too many questions whirled about his troubled mind for rest to be truly considered. Sighing heavily, he gripped his shivering body with bare arms and sat hunched near the fire until the morning light crested the hills to the east.

CB

The three men approached the old fortification with trepidation. In the middle of a large grove, the Watchtower of *Al'Taers* loomed high overhead. Some of the building's worn stone blocks were cracked and split beyond repair. The structure reached a height not quite matching that of the surrounding trees, but impressive nonetheless. A solid black door of dense wood barred entry into the interior. Even the outer shutters of the tall windows were still intact, most thrown wide open. From their vantage point on the ground, the top floor appeared to be in good condition, and the peak of the roof looked sound. In the very center of it all rose the thick and healthy wood of an enormous tree, its highest branches creating a living roof over the entire structure.

Legends spoke of the tower as the home to a company of Gorimm hunters. The trackers were said to have roamed the wild expanse of the great forest while acting as a vanguard against any enemy movements to the southeast. Now, only the shadows of a time long forgotten survived within the stone walls.

Both Gavin and Caolte brandished their weapons as they approached the base. Gavin's blade glistened in his hand, while Caolte held his *Drayen* spear as he led the way forward. Tel'Andros was tense, yet his mind was clear as his eyes ceaselessly flickered about the underbrush. A soft blue luminescent glow surrounded the mage.

"Anything, Andros?" Gavin whispered, following his friend's lead and sliding noiselessly from the back of his mount.

"There is some latent sorcery present that I can't seem to identify. It's nothing that indicates trouble, though" the mage replied.

"Gath?" Caolte asked.

"None in the vicinity. How long that will last, I cannot predict."

The *Drayenmark* lieutenant passed the reins of his mount to the captain and dashed across the clearing. The sun was shining brightly that morning, creating a myriad of dancing shadows on the trails of the Aeldenwood. Caolte's figure appeared to flicker as he nimbly slid his crouched form skillfully along the edge of the walled stone.

Gavin watched the man disappear behind the tower and dropped to one knee. He often assumed a crouched position while covering his men on a sortie. Resting one hand lightly on the cold ground, he kept his sword at the ready. A brief tingle of energy crackled through his fingers as he touched the snow covered earth. Tense moments passed as the two men waited patiently for Caolte's return. The soldier eventually reappeared near the base of the building and motioned them forward.

The Fey'Derin officer was gently pushing on the ebony door as Gavin approached. Caolte appeared puzzled. "There's no discernable handle or trigger mechanism to open the door. Beautiful wood that *Aliendal*, and native only to the deep heart of this forest," he added.

"Nonsense, there must be a spell encased in the wood. Scholars have often referred to *Aliendal* as 'living wood'. A simple casting should reveal our next move," Andros said.

"As you will," Gavin implored and watched the mage with some interest. Andros had often attempted to explain the essence of Aer, but to no avail.

The two soldiers watched the robed mage murmur under his breath and complete a series of hand gestures that Gavin was unable to recall. This had always been his experience with the arcane, even when he was younger. As with seeing Aer, so too did the ungifted immediately forget the movements used to conjure a spell. Andros sulked and finally shook his head.

"Nothing..." he muttered.

Frustrated, Gavin circled the tower hoping to find a low window that could be reached with some creativity and effort. Seeing nothing, he returned to the south side and slumped wearily on the stoop.

"No luck I suppose?" Caolte joined his friend. "And here I was thinking you had a plan."

"Hmm, I guess going on instinct doesn't always work," Gavin answered sheepishly.

"In your case, this is one of those rare times," Caolte said, leaning back against the door.

Settling down, both men watched in amusement as Tel'Andros stubbornly continued his sending. By his reaction alone, it was obvious he was having no further luck with his incantation.

"It's a nice rest at least," Gavin said. Stretching his tired and cramped muscles, he yawned loudly and joined Caolte in leaning back against the doorway.

A barely audible click immediately grabbed their attention.

"What the —" Caolte yelled as he fell backwards alongside Gavin and in through the doorway. He looked towards his commander quizzically. "Any notion on how you managed that one?"

"I don't think I had anything to do with it" Gavin answered truthfully.

"Lieutenant, you are a fool. It's obvious that my last attempt opened the passageway," Tel'Andros broke in. "Don't tell me you believe that the credit should go to Gavin?"

Caolte cleared his throat uncomfortably, "Ware your tone, mage. Do not presume to know my thoughts. I was just curious is all."

Gavin was already examining the new surroundings. The main floor was a circular chamber comprised of one large area with two sets of stone stairs rising up to the next level. The stones near the center of the room had been cleared to allow for the earth to remain where the gnarled roots of the large tree were embedded. Staring directly upward, Gavin could see the spherical openings that allowed the tree freedom to penetrate all the way to the top floor. It was a stunning feat of natural construction.

"By the gods, the tree grows straight up the middle!" Caolte exclaimed, joining Gavin in staring upwards.

"Gorimm architecture was always based in the natural world, Lieutenant," Tel'Andros said. "The histories record that the elder folk focused much of their attention on the living earth and less upon what they considered 'the cold heart of mankind'."

"It's damned impressive is what it is," Caolte whistled appreciably.

As the men travelled through each of the levels, it was obvious that the tower had been long-abandoned. Only the crumbing remnants of some old broken furniture remained. If the Gorimm had once inhabited the place, no real evidence had survived the test of time. If the histories were correct, it was close to two hundred years since the last of the elder folk set foot within this edifice.

As they reached the top floor with an exit to a high open battlement, the trio entered a final room, one that could very well have been a study. The decaying shelves of what were once large oak bookcases cluttered the outside walls, their shape and form still recognizable after the passing of so many seasons. A large desk, also of oak, lay slumped near one of the two windows. Even a high-backed chair, the once plush cushions having disintegrated into little more than a grey tattered rags, remained in its place behind the desk. A hearth, cold and unused, was situated against the north wall, creating the only break in the smooth sides of the chamber.

The Aeldenwood tree, although much thinner near the height of its reach, still twisted its way through the study. The many tangled branches gave the chamber an unearthly look, and Gavin could sense an ethereal timelessness not present in the bare rooms of the previous floors.

"Incredible," Andros breathed as he entered the room. "There are still traces of old magic being used here. This was once a place of great power."

"Any danger with such dormant sorcery?" Gavin asked, carefully threading his way over to the old desk while deftly avoiding the outstretched arms of a few errant branches.

"Absolutely none, Gavin. Whatever spells were cast have only left a faint signature as to their origin. There is no real power remaining."

Peering out of the tall window, Caolte asked, "Well we're here, now what do we do?"

"We wait," Gavin replied.

In the year 3AE292, the first Silveryn mages to study the recent encroachment of the Aeldenwood through the land of Farraine found no correlation between the disappearance of the Gorimm and the subsequent forest growth.
—Lady Talia, *The Histories, Volume XI*

CHAPTER XXIII

Old Farraine, Aeldenwood

Alessan was hungry and terrified.

He had lost all feeling in his fingers and toes, and judging by the pale colour of his companion's face, Corian was faring no better. The two men were so tired that Alessan briefly wondered if death might be more welcoming than the aching pains and hunger they were being forced to endure on their trek.

They had been on the run for almost a full day and continued to stagger through the dark forest. Alessan had lost track of time, but faint light filtered through the leafy canopy above, and he believed that some daylight hours still remained.

How so much could have changed in such a short period of time was inconceivable. A new life, one that had only just begun, was being ruthlessly torn from his grasp, as was his hope for the future.

Although hearing no signs of pursuit, he refused to believe they were completely safe. The doomed expedition had ignored all warnings, and now a few hundred souls had gone to join the gods, their deaths terrible and cruel.

The fate of the brave men who had selflessly given them time to flee the attacking Gath remained unknown. Alessan could only hope that Sergeant Holt and the other Sylvani had found a way to fight free from the attackers.

With the slaughter at the Crossroads still fresh in his mind, Alessan was also plagued with a deep sense of guilt. How could he, of all those who had travelled south, have been spared? What of the numerous husbands, fathers, and mothers who had died? What of the young girl, whose name he would never learn? What cruel game did the gods play with the lives of the people of Caledun? Is not Arne supposed to be a forgiving god, one who watches over his people, one who protects, and one who guides? Shivering as much from his beleaguered thoughts than from the weather, Alessan chanced a look at Corian.

The big man lay slouched against a large oak tree, his ample body splayed out in a pose of sheer exhaustion. He had reacted far worse to the prolonged flight than Alessan, and his usual lively demeanor was now hidden behind a mask of agony and laboured breathing. Corian's silence was somewhat alarming, but at this point Alessan was glad for a period of quiet reflection. He was still recuperating from the shock of the event and trying to settle the rapid thoughts that continued to flicker like lightning through his mind.

Regardless of their discomfort, both men soon drifted off to sleep. Yet with every unknown sound they would jolt awake, their eyes fearfully scanning the surrounding foliage for any sign of the Gath. As they lay there in the dark, Corian finally broke his silence. With a heavy sigh the large man shifted and stretched his aching muscles.

"Well, Master Oakleaf, I've sat here trying to sort out my confused thoughts, knowing that had I only listened to your impassioned plea, we would surely not find ourselves in such a predicament. I can't even find the words to express my heartfelt sorrow."

"I'm not sure I'd have believed my tale had I been in your position, Master Praxxus. It hardly seems fair to put the blame on anyone but the Gath," added Alessan, a poor attempt at sympathy crossing his tired face.

"You know you could never be a businessman, Alessan," Corian said.

"How do you mean, sir?"

"You're too damn honest and too damn nice," Corian replied. "My business associates would have found every way to blame me for this catastrophe, and yet here you sit, cold and hungry, remaining a gentleman. There would be a knife in my back and foreign hands deep in my pockets before my contacts would have shown me such undeserved kindness."

"My mother would demand no less, Master Praxxus," Alessan shrugged, somewhat embarrassed by the kind words.

"Well you do her proud, lad, you do her proud."

"You know she doesn't hate you," Alessan added after a moment of reflection. "It's just that she changed so much after my father passed, and I think she's afraid to lose anyone else."

"Oh, I understand. Inigan is my daughter, and yet to her I was never really much of a father. I bought her things and kept her fed and sheltered, but I don't know anything about her. What she likes, what she dreams of, who she really is. It's a regret I've always had and have always said I would repair," Corian finished quietly.

"How old is she?" Alessan asked.

"Well, she would be nearing her twentieth summer I think, but finding her to wish her well is another problem in itself," Corian responded. "Was he a good man, your father?" the merchant asked boldly.

"That he was," Alessan smiled warmly. "You know, he never once acted like I was a *ba'caech*. He would take me out with him to cut wood, to show me the Lumber camps, and was always so proud to tell the men that I was his son. When I was with him, no one treated me like a disappointment."

"He was well respected then?"

"In Briar there are only a few traits that define a man's worth; strength and stamina. My father was a champion in both," Alessan answered proudly. "Every Festival of *Mach'nach* —"

"*Mach'nach*? Hmm, like the old seat of power for Caledun." Corian struggled with the unfamiliar word.

"The Festival of Midsummer's Eve," Alessan explained. "The Guild would hold various contests of strength, and Kayla and I would watch father win every year. He was proud, but never boastful of his accomplishments. I'm sure he learned that from my mother," Alessan added. "She was proud in her own way I guess, but didn't enjoy all the attention."

"Well it sounds like he was a good man and you're much the better to have spent time with him," Corian mused.

"Aye, he was the best," Alessan whispered. Awash with a sudden flood of poignant memories, Alessan and Corian sat quietly with only the sound of the Aeldenwood's many creatures breaking the stillness.

Cʒ

With the darkness still upon them, Corian struggled to his feet. Alessan followed suit, and after a brief discussion as to which direction they should head, the two exhausted men embarked on the next leg of their journey. The woods remained quiet as the two travelers headed in what they hoped was a southerly direction. Their earlier flight had taken them far from the familiarity of the King's Road. At least by heading south they knew that each step could only bring them closer to escaping the tangled undergrowth of the Aeldenwood.

For the better part of that long night, everything proceeded as planned. The two travelers even came across a much needed cache of wild mushrooms. Ignoring the thin layer of dirt that covered the stalks, Alessan devoured his portion with unmatched zeal. As he contently licked his fingers, he swore it was the best meal of his entire life. Corian also showed no hesitation even though the wealthy merchant was accustomed to far superior fare. At that moment, within the eerie splendour of the Great Wood, no better feast could have been offered.

It was after their meagre meal that an incredible realization struck the young man from Briar. Alessan had inexplicably become captivated by the strange forest. He was well aware of its horrors, but now it was its haunting beauty that had revealed itself. He found it a shame to have lived so close to such a mysterious place without ever having sought its hidden treasures. He found himself imagining a time when the forest trails were defended by the tree tenders of old, the long vanished Gorimm.

The Aeldenwood was said to have been a fantastical place of light, music, and beauty. For it to have fallen into such darkness pulled at Alessan's heart and his memories of those brief meetings with the stranger C'Aelis suddenly rushed to the fore. If they met again, he was determined to ask the Gorimm the many questions that riddled his mind.

As faint tendrils of light harkened the coming dawn, Alessan and Corian found themselves confronted by an interesting quandary. Somehow throughout the night, the two had wandered across an old trail. In front of them now lay two choices: a partially overgrown road branching off to their left and an equally unattractive path to the right. Still muddled after their harrowing escape, both men had little confidence in either of the two directions. With the heavy forest covering overhead blocking out the sky, determining where the sun rose was impossible. Their choice would be based on a whim and nothing more.

In the end Corian determined, in his mind at least, that the path to the left bore some signs of fresh passage and deemed it in their best interest to follow it. Alessan shrugged and followed as either choice was preferable to returning the way they had come. After a brief stop to harvest a small patch of edible roots, they trekked onward with their spirits higher than expected after all that had transpired.

It was midmorning when they came across the first corpse. With his heart pounding, Alessan bent down to examine the body of a young Sylvani soldier. The mercenary lay face down on the edge of the narrow road, his limbs bent in unnatural positions. Carefully rolling the body over, Alessan frowned at the lack of noticeable injury. A small amount of blood had splattered over the man's uniform, but only the twisted shape of his neck could explain his demise. With weapons missing, including his scabbard, Alessan wondered what might have befallen the man.

Corian cleared his throat and Alessan looked upward. The merchant was staring into the large branches bent over the woodland trail. There, high in the tree, were the dangling outlines of a bow and quiver. Upon further examination, a sword hilt could also be seen jutting above the side of the nearest branch.

"The man fell?" Alessan asked.

"Aye, and a shame at that," Corian nodded. "He must have scampered up to hide from any pursuers. To have survived the battle only to..." the last words were left carefully unspoken.

"Could the Gath be nearby?"

"A question we should do our best to leave unanswered. But look, he's of a size with you, albeit heavier." Corian motioned towards the soldier. "Where he is now, he can't possibly be in need."

"You're right," Alessan said reluctantly.

As Corian stripped the body bare, Alessan clambered nimbly into the overhead branches to reclaim the lost weaponry. He could still do little to shake the feeling that somehow he was stealing, an inappropriate act to be sure. Corian wouldn't hear of it, and knowing full well that the equipment would be useful, Alessan donned the armour. The leggings were somewhat long and the chest covering was a tad loose even after much tightening and fidgeting by both men, but an improvement it was.

Standing awkwardly in the trappings of the Sylvani, Alessan was surprised when Corian passed him his ornate gold dagger.

"I don't want to hear it, Alessan," the merchant cut off any objections. "You have an empty scabbard at your side. Just hold on to it until it's needed," he added.

Alessan slipped the weapon into his belt, the blade sliding in as if made for the scabbard. As his hand brushed the hilt a slight shiver traveled through his body, the sensation lifting the hairs on the back of his neck. He tried to shake the chill, and yet for long moments afterwards a curious feeling settled over him. Something hovered on the edge of his thoughts, yet he could not discern what.

The discovery of more corpses interrupted the strange moment. Only a few paces further lay the mangled bodies of two soldiers and a woman. The evidence suggested that the two mercenaries didn't die without a fight. Black blood lay pooling on the ground nearby, a sure sign that at least some Gath had been present. Although covered in blood, he recognized the face of Aliana, the woman he had visited not long after joining the merchant train. Gently brushing the dark hair away from her face, he closed her sightless eyes and wept.

With care, Corian and Alessan moved the bodies off the old path and into the denser underbrush, hoping that by doing so they would be left undisturbed. Little more could be done for the slain. Their weapons were broken, their armour shredded, and apart from a small sack of coins Corian pilfered from one of the men, nothing of value remained. With heavy hearts and ever more wary of the direction they had chosen to follow, the two companions trudged onward.

ʚ

Night fell once more and the two men found some measure of comfort on a make-shift bed of underbrush and leaves. Their stomachs were empty, but with the fore-boding darkness already upon them, they had little choice but to rest without food. Alessan closed his eyes and sleep overtook his tired body.

The oft comforting Aeldenwood of his dreams had been usurped. Instead of the expansive woods and familiar cottage, he stood in a large chamber with rough stone walls, wet and clammy to the touch. An ornate stone basin stood in the middle of the cavernous space. Carved into the outer lip was a mosaic of intertwined creatures, some common, others mythical. Even with the limited light of only a few torches fixed to the outer walls, he could see that the blue water was crystal clear.

Walking towards the low pool, Alessan drew a finger lightly across the liquid surface. The water was cool to the touch, and when peering downward he was rewarded with a curious reflection. It was him, of that there was no doubt, but the face of the man who stared back was different; it was hardened and tinged with a certain poignancy.

His hair was pulled tightly into a braid, and there was a slight shadow of a beard on his cheeks. A long scar ran along the edge of his chin, the prominent mark dark and red. His neck also showed signs of injury, with the mottled look of a recent burn like a fiery rash on his pale skin. Unconsciously raising his hand to gingerly trace the scar, Alessan was astonished by what he saw. His arm, lifeless and withered since birth, showed clear signs of healing and growth.

He spent a long moment staring at the limb, slowly turning it around and flexing it with a strength he had never felt before. His clothes, he also realized, were very different. He was dressed in peculiar hunting garb crafted from an unknown fabric. The outerwear seemed melded completely with his body, so fluidly did the fabric grip his skin. Fascinated by such a wondrous dream, Alessan was reluctant to turn away from the watery mirror.

Without warning, a sudden shift in the air threw him to the ground. Sprawled awkwardly on the floor, he looked back towards the basin. On the far side of the chamber stood a group of men, each clutching identical metal rods in their hands. There were other shapes hiding in the shadows behind the men who were in the midst of a heated argument. Alessan's gaze was fixed on a tall man standing on the edge of the small gathering.

He was nondescript in build, with a lean physique visible under his loose flowing black robe. The fabric was expensive and ceremonial, a design not common to any faction in Kal Maran, at least not one Alessan had ever seen before. He sported a long, oily mustache and his shoulder length black hair hung limply behind his ears. His eyes were bright blue and had an alarming air of pure haunting malice. The man suddenly cocked his head and turned to look directly where Alessan was struggling to his feet. With a shining glow surrounding him, the man snarled and lunged forward.

Struck by the fury written across the man's features, Alessan stumbled backward, his arms coming up in a vain effort to protect himself. In the back of his mind, a warning screamed that his attempt was useless as he knew there was little he could do against the attacker. Heeding the small voice, a wordless scream bubbled on the edge of his lips. As he scrambled backwards, he felt his grip on the dream slipping. His body was suddenly floating through the floor as a terrifying scream erupted from his throat...

Alessan awoke with a start. For the rest of the evening, sleep remained elusive.

ോ

Four days after their harrowing escape from the slaughter at the Crossroads, Alessan and Corian crossed an old stone bridge and noticed a definite widening of the road. Worn and cracked cobblestones covered the area, and a healthy growth of grass and weeds jutted out from in between a number of the weathered stones. It was obvious that the old road had seen little in the way of traffic for many years.

The two men had survived on good fortune and the ability to uncover edible mushrooms and herbs. With bodies nourished, their pace quickened and their steps were now more confident and purposeful. For the first time since the Crossroads, they spoke of things other than that sad event. Corian happily regaled Alessan with whimsical stories of his youth in the mountainous countryside of Innes Vale.

With slight trepidation, the two men pushed onward and as they topped a small rise they looked down on a wonderfully startling discovery - the ruins of what appeared to be an ancient city. Partially crumbling structures with rooftops that had succumbed to the elements, teetered precariously throughout the scene below. In what was once the city center sat the remnants of a large keep, its walls still solid and strong. Hundreds of trees grew in the middle of open plazas, their branches penetrating inside the buildings standing in their path. Many of the large fountains were empty of water and were instead overgrown with flowers and plants. Roads, houses, and walls sprawled over an immense area, the size of which astounded Alessan. To see so many buildings hidden within the depths of the Aeldenwood was incredible. From their vantage point on the hill, the ruins appeared to be deserted.

As they approached the gate, both men strained their eyes in the hopes of detecting any danger before it landed upon them. Alessan noticed that the walls and buildings showed no signs of damage other than the wear of time. Fire had not forced the people of the ruined city to flee, nor did any evidence point towards an invading army. The walls were cracked at their foundations by the growth of a number of huge trees, but were still in surprisingly good repair. As they carefully picked their way forward, Alessan could see some of the leafy boughs of the Aeldenwood growing directly through the rooftops of many buildings, most notably through the top of a tall tower. Fascinated, Corian and Alessan arrived at the bottom of the small rise with mouths agape.

At first, the unnatural stillness of the place was almost unbearable. The oppressive silence, so rare for a place that had once housed thousands of people, was distressing. As the travelers walked slowly up the widening path and under the cracked stone archway into the city, an intense feeling of loneliness filled their hearts.

Alessan craned his neck and stared upward as they passed under the wall, his eyes registering every detail. Large tarnished hinges, remnants of rotten timber that formed a decaying gate and colossal rusted chains dangling eerily in the wind, all lent the archway an air of somber sadness.

For the first time since passing under the shadowy boughs of the great forest, Alessan could finally look up and see the sky. Encouraged in spite of an ominous patch of blackened storm clouds, his spirits were lifted. A rumbling of thunder cut their exploration short and they were forced to seek shelter in a small house whose roof sagged deeply, but remained relatively intact.

Large drops of rain soon followed, and after a quick search of the deserted premises that successfully provided a battered and blackened iron pot, Corian set it outside in the hopes of collecting fresh rainwater. Although the two men had eaten relatively well, they had found little in the way of water besides a few stagnant pools. Although winter certainly raged outside the borders of the Aeldenwood, spring-like conditions dominated within. Alessan was aware that their survival had been quite dependent on the temperate climate, for without adequate supplies and shelter, the winter cold would surely have finished what the Gath had initiated.

The interior of the house had been picked completely bare. Outside of a few pieces of old furniture and shelving, there was little of value within the home. The prior occupants had taken most of their belongings with them. Corian did however find a battered tinderbox and flint that had both men eagerly anticipating a warm meal and fire to ward off the damp chill of the coming evening.

As the storm grew in intensity, Alessan climbed up to the partially collapsed upper floor and for a long time simply let his eyes wash over the incredible landscape before him. The hazy outline of the keep was still visible through the downpour, and he could barely contain his excitement to explore such a place. For the first time in days, his thoughts were not about danger and death, but of mystery and treasure.

Corian joined him and passed along a cup of rainwater that Alessan received with gratitude. Surrounded by the soothing pitter patter of the falling rain, both men sat quietly and said nothing. For another day, the unlikely pair had found a way to survive.

೮

"You know, lad, I think these ruins can be none other than those of Old Telmire," Corian pondered later that night as they lay huddled near the small fire they had succeeded in lighting.

"It's unbelievable," Alessan answered.

"I'm almost certain, but having never visited prior to its demise, I can't really be sure."

"We may be able to find proof tomorrow morning," Alessan said. "If the weather eases up, I'd like to continue our search and head to the keep."

"You could be right, but we can't lose sight of our goal. It is all well and good that we've found shelter and some small measure of comfort here, but I believe this place is no less dangerous than the rest of this damned wood. We should only loiter here briefly before continuing south."

Pausing to wipe a hand across his broad forehead, Corian looked pensive for a moment and said, "You know, Alessan, of all the places I've visited over the years, the small kingdom of Farraine was never one of them."

"Any particular reason?" Alessan asked curiously.

"Well, truth be told, the country was in a bad state. What with the trees growing in the farmers' fields and tales of disappearances in the woods. Farraine never struck the Vale as an important buyer of our luxury items when it was all it could do just to make ends meet," the big man answered.

"Isn't there always something that people want, or need, for that matter?" Alessan countered.

"My business is about profit, Alessan, not need. In my youth, the people of Farraine were preparing to leave their homes and livelihood. They made very poor buyers under such circumstances."

"So they had no money. Is that what you're implying?"

"Lad, you make it sound like I'm heartless," Corian shook his head emphatically. "It was business, that's all."

Sitting there by the fire, Alessan couldn't fight the momentary revulsion that he felt towards the rich merchant. For people to have had to abandon all that they knew, all that they owned, and all that they had built was such a tragedy. And that Corian Praxxus made no mention of their personal sorrows, but only saw fit to deem them unworthy of his business disgusted him. Alessan guessed that his family's plight in similar circumstances would be insignificant to the wealthy entrepreneur.

"Do you ever consider anything else besides business, or is that why your daughter won't speak to you?" Alessan shot back bitterly. "Or would it not be profitable to form a bond with her?"

A scarlet flush crept across Corian's face. Alessan wondered if he had not pushed the man too far, but the moment was fleeting.

Dropping his eyes in chagrin, Corian sighed heavily. "Alessan, I'm..." his words trailed off as he stood to his feet. Without another word Corian Praxxus, heedless of the drumming rain, quietly slipped out the broken door, his immense shadow flickering briefly upon the bare stone walls.

Sitting alone, Alessan fought the urge to follow the man. Although embarrassed by his outburst, his mother had often acted in much the same way, her reasons for doing so, her own. Knowing that being alone with his thoughts was as important to Corian as it had once been with Shani Oakleaf, Alessan kept still and stared quietly into the flames.

Blood washed away by tears of the gods.
Wounds cleansed, they will never heal.
Flashes of faces, memories of old,
they will never leave this cursed field.
We walk on and remember them.
—Rhaec, The Journals of Rhaec

CHAPTER XXIV

The Watchtower of *Al'Taers*, Aeldenwood

Sitting cross-legged on the ground and whittling away on a small piece of wood, Caolte sensed something in the air. "Feels like a storm's brewing," he said.

"It mightn't be more than a light dusting of snow. The forest covering does a good job at keeping us sheltered," Gavin looked up at the maze of branches covering most of the sky.

Caolte grunted and turned his attention back to his crafting. "Is that fool of a mage still playing with those strange markers we found?"

"They're warding pillars, not markers. If Tel'Andros' theory is correct, finding a way to activate them will enable us to set up a magic barrier around the area. I'm not sure about this magecraft, but with three nights behind us already, the Gath might be closer than we think," Gavin responded.

"Then why are we still here, Gavin?" Caolte stared darkly into the woods. "You have a feeling there may be enemies about, and you're seldom wrong. What's our visit proving?"

"By the absence of anything out of the ordinary, Caolte, it may very well be prov-ing much," Gavin answered cryptically. "In any case, we're not leaving, at least not for another day."

"No matter how hard you try to explain it, it makes no sense to this skeptic. That I've come to trust these strange feelings of yours is proof enough that maybe this old clansman is ready to settle down."

"You, settle down?" Gavin smiled. "You realize that you'd have to stay home with all of those children you're breeding. What excuse would you have to get out of the house then?"

"Bah! You sure know how to ruin a man's dreams, Captain..." Caolte chuckled.

Wary of the upcoming storm, Gavin decided it was time to track down Tel'An-dros. The mage was far too consumed with his findings in the Aeldenwood to pay proper attention to his surroundings. Struck by a familiar sense of foreboding, the safety of his childhood friend was now a priority. Gavin grabbed his scabbard and dagger, belted them into place, and walked swiftly across the clearing.

Three days had passed since they had gained access to the old watchtower, and the suffocating presence of the forest was wearing heavily on the three men. They had adequate supplies, warm clothing, and suitable quarters considering their sur-roundings, but finding an easy night's rest was difficult. Gavin's dreams had been a confused jumble of nightmarish visions, and Caolte had witnessed his friend's uneasiness grow over these last few days.

Tel'Andros, on the other hand, was practically childlike in his curiosity and en-thusiasm. The mage had spent his days eagerly examining the various Gorimm runes and wards put in place long ago. Truthfully, he did have some difficulty adapting to the unkind environment, what with his experience being relegated to the lush comforts of the Silveryn stronghold. He too, had slept poorly.

Although the search of the watchtower itself was interesting, without a doubt the *Aliendal* warding posts were the most significant find. Gavin could feel the considerable power residing within the strange markers even from a distance. There were four posts in all, each depicting one of the four cardinal points, and they all differed in size. Two were barely three feet in height, while the third one easily tow-ered eight or nine feet from top to bottom. The fourth was about Gavin's height, and yet was twice as thick as the other three. Strange runes and markings covered the wood, but Andros, a scholar of some renown among the Silveryn mages, had no success in deciphering any pattern or instruction.

Oddly, it was the older *Drayen* soldier who showed the greatest understanding of some of the symbols etched into the pillars. Caolte was quite adamant that some *Drayen* words from the old tongue, specifically those meaning 'shield,' 'arm,' 'shelter' and 'light' were present. Intrigued by the revelation, Tel'Andros returned to the four pillars for long periods of study following the discovery.

Caolte's comments did nothing to help create any bond of fellowship between the two very different men, as Gavin had at first hoped it might. Caolte's advice regarding the runes had instead driven a larger wedge between the two, and both men were far too headstrong to initiate any sort of reconciliation. With such bad blood and tension part of the history between both factions, Gavin was at a loss as to how to deal with their behaviour.

Gavin found Tel'Andros sitting near the northern pillar, large tome in hand and a pensive look on his face. The silver-trimmed robes of the Silveryn representative often evoked an inkling of rage in the young mercenary captain. Ir'Wolien and the manipulative members of the Council were to blame for that.

"Storm's rolling in, Andros. You might plan on returning to the tower before long," Gavin called out as he approached. Engrossed in deep thought, the mage merely mumbled his acknowledgement.

"If you really are interested in finding out what lies behind the meanings of these pillars, I don't understand why you won't speak to Caolte about it," Gavin commented, leaning against a nearby trunk.

Andros looked up in alarm. "The *Drayen* is only speculating about my findings. His people are not scholars just as mine are not bloodthirsty warriors."

This animosity between his two companions had done little to increase Gavin's enjoyment of the trip. Caolte and Andros had had nary a kind word to say to the other. The *Drayenmark* had long held a grudge against magekind and did not hide this fact. In general, the contention harkened back to the days immediately prior to the Shattering and the resulting aftermath. Countless lives had been lost after the Silveryn mages reneged on the pact they had struck with the High King. The mages were steadfast in their belief that with Darion Lordares' death, any existing treaty had died with him. Caolte was of another mind.

"You know, I expected more from you, Andros," Gavin said.

"What? In the matter of these pillars? It is no simple chore to work swiftly when a nearly forgotten language is involved. To experiment with the forces of Aer, even latent ones, can be dis —"

"I'm not speaking about the *Aliendal* markers," Gavin calmly interrupted.

Pausing for a moment with lips pursed, Andros looked away. "There's a history behind our two peoples, Gavin. You wouldn't understand."

"Understand? You're right, because I care nothing about that past! I'm far more concerned with the future, and having two intelligent men acting as children needs no explanation," Gavin fumed.

"How you can defend those uncivilized barbarians is a matter of concern," Andros muttered, meeting Gavin's scathing look.

"Is that the man in you speaking or the Silveryn Mage?" Gavin spat. "Or a combination of the two?"

"Listen to yourself, Silvares," Andros shot back. "You stand here in defense of a man who hails from a bloodline that was shunned by an entire kingdom, a bloodline that has shown itself corrupted by the taint of madness! Caolte Burnaise follows a maniac in Serian Rhone. You think he wouldn't put his *Drayen* spear in your back if asked to do so by his self-proclaimed king?"

Gavin's hand strayed towards his sword hilt. "You would do well to remember that you speak of my friend, magus. Caolte Burnaise has been a truer friend than any I've met in my life," Gavin glared defiantly. "Aye, that includes even you, Deowyn, and Brynne. And to speak of the *Drayen* taint seems doublespeak does it not, Andros? I would counsel you to curb your tongue, else I grow tired of your insults."

"My forefathers were advisors to the High Kings, mage!" a venom-laced voice came from behind the two arguing men.

"Caolte —" Gavin tried desperately to intercede.

Raising a hand to ward off his captain's attempt to interrupt, the veteran soldier stomped forward. "I'll remind you that my people, the *Drayenmark*, were betrayed en masse by greedy nobles that deemed it in their best interest to do away with a king and his entire bloodline. The Silveryn Order left us to die, as did the Gorimm, as did Alerond, and Farraine. In two hundred years of rebuilding our livelihood and our pride, only the Dwarves of Alerond have attempted to repair the damage done. Can you say the same, magus?" Caolte finished, his eyes ablaze.

Tel'Andros did not falter in the face of such fury. "The *Drayenmark* sealed their own fate. I will not stand here and debate the histories with you, Lieutenant, or you would be quite embarrassed."

"Enough!" Gavin roared, his voice reverberating through the small clearing. "This little game the two of you like to play is no more. If you cannot be civil to one another then I expect you to sit here in silence!"

Both men stared balefully at one another before backing away, their nods of agreement barely perceptible.

"I did come here for a reason, Captain," Caolte said. "The surrounding woods have grown deceptively quiet. I thought it would be best if we retreat into the tower until I can ascertain if any dangers lie in the area. If it is the Gath, we must be prepared."

"See to it, Caolte." Gavin ordered.

As the veteran officer started towards the tower, he turned back and spoke a final word. "I follow only one man, mage, and I would do so gladly should it mean even my death. Gavin Silveron is to whom I owe my loyalty. You would be well served to decide where *your* loyalties lie. And there's one more thing, Tel'Andros?"

"Yes?" The mage frowned.

"You were right about one thing. I wouldn't hesitate to use this spear on some-one's back, but it would be yours," Caolte said with a cold finality, briskly turning and heading back towards the tower, his tall form disappearing into the trees.

ପ୍ଥ

Waiting for Tel'Andros to join him on the ground level, Gavin paused to speak a word of safe fortune to his Fey'Derin lieutenant before firmly closing the black *Aliendal* door. Ignoring the mage, he swiftly climbed the tower stairs and re-moved the bow from his shoulder strap. Staring out of one of the high windows, he watched intently for any signs of danger as Caolte made his away across the clearing and into the surrounding brush. He was so focused on the nearest trees that he barely noticed Andros arrive at his side.

"Well, I hate to admit it, but your lieutenant was right about the weather. A storm is definitely on its way." A distant rumble of thunder accompanied Tel'Andros' words and a light rain began to fall.

As they waited, Gavin found himself preoccupied with his friend's safety. Of all officers in the company, Caolte was the least reckless. If anyone was to take their time carefully scouting the terrain, it would be the *Drayen* veteran. His cautious thoroughness was one of the reasons he was still alive after so many years employed as a mercenary.

As Gavin was pondering his faith in the man's abilities, a series of loud howls erupted from the northeast. With a white-knuckled grip on his longbow, Gavin realized that there was little he could do to help his comrade. As the tension mounted and the cries grew ever closer, Caolte suddenly burst from treeline, bloodied spear in hand.

"They're very close, Gavin!" he yelled, running towards the tower as the trees erupted with a cacophony of noise.

Without the slightest panic, Gavin reached over his shoulder and calmly notched a blue and grey fletched arrow. "Andros, I need you to shut the door behind Caolte when he arrives. Quickly now!" he ordered. The mage disappeared down the stairs and Gavin was confident that his command would be followed.

Caolte was less than thirty paces into the clearing when the first two Gath bounded out of the woods. With calm precision, Gavin sighted and let fly the first arrow. The second shaft was notched and ready as the first missile's steel tip pierced the chest of the nearest pursuer, stopping the creature instantly. The second Gath dodged to the side, but its effort was in vain. The second arrow penetrated its muscle bound right thigh. With a shriek of agony, the creature skidded and collapsed to ground in a heap.

Aghast, Gavin watched as the ebony denizens of the Aeldenwood poured forth, their slavering maws dripping saliva as they caught sight of their quarry. Letting two more arrows fly into the mob, Gavin chanced a quick look down the edge of the watchtower tree. He breathed a sigh of relief as he spied Caolte slumped wearily against the side of the great trunk, the soldier's eyes lit fiercely by the excitement of his escape.

Catching his captain's look of concern, the lieutenant smirked and called up. "Just need to catch my breath, sir. All that running has me wondering whether I should start training with the Eagle Runners again!" As he finished, Andros opened the door in a flash and pulled him inside. Moments later, the two men joined Gavin on the upper floor.

"By the gods, there's a lot of them," breathed Caolte in disbelief. Below them a veritable sea of black twisted flesh crashed against the ancient stone walls of the tower. Countless Gath boiled beneath the lower windows, their piercing cries of frustration agony to Gavin's ears.

"I guess this lends credence to the Lumber disappearances along the northern border of the wood," Gavin commented dryly. He had been one of the few outspoken men in the north who had warned the communities along the perimeter. The Lumbers of Briar had listened, but only briefly.

Turning to Tel'Andros, he asked, "Any forewarning of this in the studies of the Order?"

"Not that I'm aware of. How could this be?" The mage stammered. It was clear he was unsettled. "The Council has for years believed that the Gath numbers were increasing, but if this is any indication, even Ir'Wolien never predicted so many."

"With the absence of the Gorimm, it seems as though the Gath have taken full advantage," Gavin said, his voice filled with apprehension.

Always the pragmatist, Caolte's looked down on the horde. "Whether the two of you are surprised is of little importance as our predicament remains the same. The numbers below offer us little chance in close combat, regardless of our skill, and the defensive capabilities of this tower have waned. We need to decide on our next course of action."

"The warding pillars..." Andros offered.

"If only you'd asked for my input on the matter —" Caolte added with a frown.

Gavin ignored the comments and surveyed the scene. Little choice remained for the small group. By numbers alone, the Gath had effectively trapped them in the old watchtower. The door of *Aliendal* wood was strong enough to hold, but the integrity of the rest of the lower level was suspect. With the ease at which the smaller Gath bounded and leapt about, it was entirely possible that the creatures would find access to the tower.

Gavin promptly led his companions down below. Then, with dread, he watched helplessly as two of their enemies crawled through one of the lower, second story windows. Pure hatred gleamed in their shadowy eyes. He could also see the outstretched claws of another of the demonic beasts reaching through the very same opening.

With a determined set to his stance, Gavin tossed the bow aside and reached for his long sword. "Andros, get behind us. Caolte, to my left," he said resolutely.

With a confidence born from fighting alongside one another countless times before, Caolte took his position, *Drayen* spear balanced lightly in his hands. Andros scrambled backwards, his eyes still wide with fear.

The first of the small Gath launched themselves forward, and both Fey'Derin backed up with haste, the fury of the attack something they had rarely encountered. The creatures lusted for blood and were ferocious in their thirst for it.

Slashing to his side, Gavin found himself on the defensive, unsure of his swordplay for one of the few times in his life. The Gath fought so unlike anything human. He quelled a momentary flicker of doubt, timing his next attack perfectly. Running his opponent through, Gavin spun and watched as Caolte pinned his own attacker against the ceiling with his long spear. These were no mercenaries fighting for coin, and the berserker rage that so consumed the Gath terrified the Fey'Derin captain. With composed precision, the first wave of attackers was dispatched.

During the following moments, they had little time in which to speak or even think of anything but the battle at hand. With a renewed frenzy the newest attackers clogged the hallway, each creature raging to reach the slowly retreating trio. Trampling one another in their haste, the Gath pushed forward, but were contained by the cramped quarters.

As he continued to fight, Gavin wondered what the three of them would have done had they been forced to fight the creatures on open ground. He was certain that the powerfully swift beasts would have wreaked havoc on any large company, let alone against a minuscule group of three. Such a scenario would need serious contemplation were they to win free of their current predicament.

With nearly a score of the Gath slain, Caolte and Gavin reached the end of the hall and swiftly ran up the stairwell to the top floor. Refusing to cede more ground, the two soldiers prepared to make a stand with the higher ground in their favour.

"Gavin!" Tel'Andros called out without warning. "You need to see this now!"

Caolte stepped to the top of the stairs and waved him onwards. "Go! I can hold for a time, if need be."

With time running short before the next onslaught, Gavin sprinted down the hallway and joined Tel'Andros at the sentry window. As the mage lifted his arm to point at something in the distance, Gavin felt a sudden tightness in the air. With a startled cry, Andros was thrown violently backwards and slammed against the opposite wall of the hallway.

Gavin stared wordlessly at the mage's twisted body. Running towards him, he crouched down and gingerly cradled the fallen man's head. Tel'Andros was still breathing, but no matter what he tried Gavin could not find a way to revive his friend. The odds of surviving the encounter were now worrisome at best with an unconscious comrade to carry and only two defenders, he thought.

Gavin dragged Tel'Andros into an adjoining room. The small round chamber contained a relatively unscathed door. Before he could call out to Caolte, the grim veteran ran into the room, unhappily clutching a bleeding arm.

"One of the small bastards got past my guard," the *Drayenmark* yelled angrily. Catching sight of the unconscious mage, a puzzled look crossed Caolte's face. "And what happened to the mage?"

"That's a good question," Gavin replied as he slammed the chamber door shut, barricading the three men inside. "Whatever he wanted to show me may very well have struck him from afar. I had no time to investigate before pulling him inside."

"It's of no matter, Gavin," Caolte commented. "We have enough problems as it is. There are another score of those demons already inside the tower. We have two rooms to work with and little ground left to give."

"For the moment, tend to your wound. I'll see if I can come up with something." Gavin said hesitantly.

"Aye, sir," Caolte replied, carrying Andros into the small back alcove.

A sudden tingling in Gavin's neck caused him to pause. It was as if disembodied hands were running their fingers through his hair. The sensation was so unsettling that he froze.

You must prepare your companions, Silvares.

The words suddenly invaded his mind, but the thoughts were not his own. Gavin spun around, looking for the source of the strange voice. It had materialized so clearly, the whispering words so intimately invasive.

I am in the trees, Gavin, look for me not.

"But who are you? And how do you know my name?"

I am the one you came to find, as are you the very same to me, Gavin. Your name is but a small matter, yet now that I know it, my heart is gladdened and my spirit bolstered.

"Gorimm..." Gavin breathed.

"Gavin?" Caolte asked as he entered from the back room where Andros lay unconscious. He had already cleaned and bandaged the deep gash on his forearm.

"Nothing. I was just talking to myself is all," Gavin answered quickly.

You must be ready to depart ere I give you word. Your horses are tethered nearby, and I have calmed them sufficiently. The Silvaeri will be fine come morning, so you need not worry. The betrayer has been dispatched.

Silvaeri? Gavin asked silently.

The mage. Now listen, Greiyfois and I will be hard-pressed against this many Gath, and you will have scant time to move south.

Gavin's thoughts were alive with a sudden plethora of questions that he so desperately wanted answered.

The time will come for us to meet again, Silvares. At that time, the veil will be lifted and your path laid before you.

Throughout the course of his life, Gavin was never one to be uncertain. In the matter of this unusual voice, it was no different. He could sense something lurking behind each phrase that convinced him that the voice spoke the truth. Without any further doubts, he decided to trust his invisible aide.

Acknowledging Caolte's solid presence near the chamber entrance, Gavin spoke. "I need your trust now more than ever, my friend," he said.

"You need not ask, Gavin. You have it." Caolte replied solemnly.

Gripping his friend's shoulder tightly, he made his request. "I need you to bear Andros' weight upon those broad shoulders of yours. I will clear the way and you need only to follow."

Outside, the sudden call of dozens of wolves overwhelmed even the growls and shrieks of the nearest Gath. Almost simultaneously the Gorimm's voice resounded in his mind.

Go! And may your steps never falter.

"Now!" Gavin yelled and threw open the chamber door. The Gath horde came tumbling through the opening and into the hallway. Caolte was already sprinting back towards Tel'Andros, his spear now lying discarded on the cold stone floor. Like a man possessed, Gavin slashed at the first row of black fiends at a dizzying pace. The twisted beasts came at him from all sides. As he cleared the top floor, he glanced out the sentry window.

The scene in the clearing below was one of total chaos. A large pack of wolves had joined the fray, fangs and claws of their own clashing with those of the Gath. Standing alone inside the roiling mass of combatants, twin swords glowing in each hand, was a silver-haired warrior; their mysterious benefactor.

Gavin pulled his gaze away from the battle below and focused on his own difficult assignment. He met the next wave of attackers at the bottom of the stairwell and fought his way towards the second floor. Dodging the large sinewy forearm of the closest beast, he slid his sword deep into the Gath's chest. Black blood sprayed across his face as he tore the weapon free, barely sweeping aside a trio of smaller foes intent on knocking him down. As the third fell, Gavin's dagger lodged in its neck, a fiery pain lanced through his side.

Crouched among the various corpses, red blood now staining its claws, was a hidden Gath waiting to pounce. Cursing himself for missing the beast and knowing that he could very well be dead because of such a mistake, Gavin hammered his fist into its face. He followed up with a brutal kick to the stunned creature's head and spared it no further thought. Sliding under another with a wild stab to its chest, he finished the last enemy at hand and pressed onwards.

From the rare stolen glances out of the tower's lower windows, Gavin could see that the wolf pack charge was rapidly being countered. Their opportunity to escape was slipping through their grasp, and even the graceful heroics of the cloaked stranger were beginning to falter.

As despair threatened to overwhelm the exhausted mercenary, Gavin stumbled as his feet landed not upon stone but on soft earth instead. Somehow he had found his way back through the *Aliendal* door and into the clearing. Pausing momentarily to help Caolte with his burden, Gavin realized that the wolves had fallen back to the north, leaving a significant gap between his position and the last remaining Gath.

His rescuer had sacrificed ground in order to clear the area where Gavin had emerged. Stunned by the sheer scope of the carnage that lay about, bloodied wolves and Gath alike, Gavin locked eyes across the battlefield for one brief moment with the warrior.

"Thank you," he mouthed.

C'Aelis ... the voice finished his thought. *It is my name. Do not agonize over the deaths of my brothers of the wood. They would gladly do so again to win your freedom. Now go, Gavin Silvares, for time is short.*

Nodding in deference, Gavin moved swiftly and led Caolte forward as they both took turns carrying the limp body of the Silveryn mage. Soon the sounds of battle faded into the distance.

છ

Orn Surefoot had only been at the Fey'Derin encampment for a day before he found himself grumbling under his breath as he removed the heavy snow from blocking the gates. Although marked by Captain Silveron's scathing comments in Dragon Mount, Orn had never imagined he would find himself working alongside the newest recruits in the company, and as their equal no less. Unperturbed, Ethan Shade would deviate not one inch from the specific instructions left by the captain.

Orn was treated as a new member of the group; no exceptions, no liberties. Until he had proven himself properly fit to once again take up the mantle of the company, he had been assigned this miserable existence. Of course he had no one to blame but himself, but that made things little better.

By the gods I need a drink.

Bending his back against the bitter wind, the lanky scout got back to work. The latest storm had left plenty of snow, and it wouldn't be cleared on its own. Apart from the freezing weather, Sergeant Rockfar seemed determined to remind the scout of what it meant to be a recruit under his command. Orn obliged to every order as he would be damned before opening himself up to another opportunity for ridicule.

His return journey from the mountain fortress of the Silveryn mages had been difficult. With little more than the clothing on his back, he had made good time regardless. The events at Dragon Mount had opened his eyes somewhat to his foolishness. His injuries had slowed him, but he had persevered. Preferring to leave his past behind, as he had tried numerous times before, Orn Surefoot returned to his task.

Not long after, a ringing alarm rang out across the snow-covered compound. Leaning heavily on his shovel, Orn watched with some concern as a number of guards rushed atop the wall. Men soon called out for the gates to be opened, and Orn found a chance to slip unnoticed to a position up on the wall.

Looking down at the snow swept hills, his heart was suddenly filled with dread. Travelling with increased difficulty across the deep drifts left in the wake of the winter storm, were three riders. Even from that long distance, the men were recognizable, and all were slumped wearily in their saddles. From afar, it also seemed as though both Caolte and Gavin were favouring substantial wounds.

As the scout watched the slow procession, he fought the impulse to ride out and meet the men. Thankfully, others already had the same feelings and quickly acted upon them.

Ethan Shade, accompanied by a handful of his men, Bider included, galloped recklessly through the gates and across the snow. It was an exhilarating sight to see the Eagle Runners join the wounded travelers. Orn soon realized that his breach of conduct would not remain unnoticed for much longer. Grumbling to himself, he returned to the snowy courtyard, shovel in hand.

Spring, it seemed, could not arrive soon enough.

*"There is no honour among the savages, only treachery and murder.
It is what sets them apart from men."*
—General Liam Dresden *"Savages"*

CHAPTER XXV

Lok'Dal hie, The Wilds

The long days in the fields coupled with the late night spent in *Lok'Dal hie* with Auric had finally caught up with Leoric. A deep, dreamless slumber swept him away, carrying with it the cares and worries of a lifetime filled with tragedy.

Sharing a sleeping quarters with several of the other men, Leoric had learned to tune out the nighttime sounds that had interrupted his sleep so often during those first weeks in captivity. Angvald's snoring alone was enough to disturb even the women, who were lodged some distance away on the other side of the building.

Although dreamily aware of muffled whispers, loud creaks, and heavy footsteps, Leoric didn't wake from his slumber. It wasn't until he felt someone approach and lean in close that he finally reacted. By then, it was far too late. Leoric flashed opened his eyes in a panic as a grimy hand covered his mouth, muffling his cry of alarm.

"Hoy now, don't struggle, Leoric. Unless you'd rather be spitted like a hog here in your own bed," sputtered a voice. The speaker's hot breath in his ear made him shudder.

He felt the cold touch of a steel blade settle on his exposed neck as he struggled to make out the shadowy figure standing over him. It mattered little, he supposed, as it could only be one of Joram's henchmen. Leoric could do nothing as his wrists were forcefully bound behind his back and his mouth gagged with a dirty cloth. Only then was he marched out into the cool night.

Sure enough, Joram was there to lead the procession. The camp's resident tyrant couldn't mask his obvious enjoyment of the situation. He cackled loudly once they were out of earshot of the homestead and entered one of the storehouses.

Ealston, Joram's right hand man who rivalled even Angvald in size, toyed absently with a dagger as Leoric was dropped unceremoniously at his feet. The thug gave him a sadistic smile full of rotten teeth. The gruesome sight triggered a brief flicker of terror in Leoric's mind. It chilled him to think that this man lived for moments such as this, where he could dominate another without any fear of reprisal. The realization strangely gave Leoric some measure of courage, and the disgust he felt for Ealston strengthened his resolve.

I am not like these people. I am better than them and so I am a threat. He repeated this to himself in order to maintain his composure.

"I have a few questions that need answering," Joram sneered. "If I don't like the answers, you will be punished. And trust me, Ealston is anything but gentle."

The other men roared their approval. A dangerous glint of madness glowed in Joram's eyes as he stepped forward and tore the filthy cloth from Leoric's mouth. Snickering, Ealston leaned over, spat in Leoric's face, and gave his head a brutal yank forward.

"Give him the wrong answers, mate," the man whispered. "I want to enjoy playing with you in more ways than one"

"I'd rather die than have you touch me, you bastard." Leoric was defiant.

"Now, now, there's no need to worry. Ealston will treat you right," Joram laughed.

"Curse you!" Leoric retorted angrily.

Ealston lashed out with a vicious punch. Leoric cried out in pain, hoping he would call attention to his plight. As the first blows rained down, he rolled into a tight ball.

Joram motioned for the others to join in the beating. Fists and feet landed unmercifully against his body until finally the pummeling stopped and Leoric was left lying semi-conscious. Blood filled his mouth as he tried to regain his feet, but it was to no avail. In disgrace, he slumped back down to the floor.

"Now let's try this again," Joram chuckled. "And remember your answers will determine what I might let Ealston do with you."

A strangled cry caused everyone to look quickly to the entrance of the storehouse. In the dim light and through matted and bloody hair, Leoric watched two men enter the torchlit area.

Angvald swore under his breath as he moved into the light. He held the arm of the thug who had been guarding the entrance firmly behind the man's back.

"You touch another hair on his head and I'll snap this man's arm like a twig," Angvald threatened, maneuvering his way nearer to his fallen friend.

"There are four of us and one of you, foreigner," Joram mocked. "You're lying."

With an audible crack, Angvald wasted no time snapping his captive's arm. With a terrible scream, the crony fell forward clutching the break. Even Joram couldn't hide the momentary flicker of shock that crossed his swarthy face.

"A Kaleenian never lies. Now let's try this again," Angvald said. "Leave him alone."

"Are you mad?!" Joram shouted angrily. "You think I care about that fool? There are still enough of us to finish the two of you! You'll die for this!"

"I don't care about the other two, Joram," Angvald replied. "I'll take you out before I go down. My ancestors will look favourably upon such a sacrifice."

Silence reigned as Angvald held his stare. Joram twitched as he weighed his options. He would certainly know about the Kaleenian's military background and reputation as a soldier. Angvald felt he had risked much by issuing the challenge but he was depending on Joram's cowardly nature to work in his favour. It was imperative to save Leoric from his current situation. He would have to deal with the consequences of his perceived insolence another day. That hammer would fall sooner or later, but given some time and creativity, they might find some options. With Leoric's life at stake, Angvald decided to press the issue and took one step closer to Joram.

The confident gesture was all it took to break the stalemate. With a snarl, Joram motioned for his enforcer to gather up the now unconscious form of the fallen brute.

"You tell your friend that his infatuation with my woman is going to cost Kieri dearly. The next time I see him spending time with her, I won't hesitate to kill both of them. Understood, foreigner?" Joram said.

"You best be watching your own back, Joram, lest you find a knife stuck in it," Angvald replied with a dark smile.

"I'll remember that. You too, should be wary of the company you keep. Speaking out against our masters may bring unpleasant consequences," Joram threatened, walking off into the night with his small band of men.

Irked by the comments, Angvald lifted Leoric gently from the floor and ducked under his arm to better carry the weight.

"You can't keep taking these beatings, friend. Pretty soon there'll be nothing left of you to save."

"I didn't choose this battle," Leoric muttered, wincing in pain.

"Oh? You weren't speaking with Kieri the other night?" Angvald asked innocently.

"I just wish I knew how to save her," Leoric replied sullenly.

"That's the problem. A woman in that position needs to want saving before anyone can help her. She chooses to stay with him, whether it be out of fear or by choice, it matters little. She spends her evenings in his bed, and sadly she'll pay the price," Angvald paused. "You can't save everyone, Leoric."

അ

"You look awful," Auric commented, sitting down on the edge of Leoric's bed. "Eat this. Benoit sent it for you."

Smiling feebly despite the nagging pain in his ribs, Leoric accepted the bowl of soup. He thought about Benoit and how he always made certain that he ate well. Benoit was meticulous and selfless in his care for others at the camp.

"To be quite honest, Auric, I feel well enough to take on a nagging visitor if need be," Leoric quipped.

After spending many a day working alongside Auric, there was one thing Leoric knew for certain; Auric was anything but normal. Never had he seen the man break a sweat, even after what seemed like endless hours of carrying crates and moving supplies. While working in the city, he had neither complained nor acted as if his wiry body was inadequate for the strenuous tasks at hand.

Auric chatted incessantly about the places he had been and things he had seen. He avoided, as always, divulging any information about his capture long ago. Never did he show any weariness, and never did he convey the weight of hardship he most assuredly bore. Only his weather-beaten skin, like worn leather, marked him for what he was — a slave who had lived the better part of his life in the shadow of *Lok'Dal hie*.

Leoric was still fascinated by the collection of texts the old man had unearthed in the hidden parts the city. While it was clear that the goblins were only visitors, and recent ones at that, clues pertaining to the builders were scarce. No paintings or drawings had been found, and even Angvald, a gifted linguist in his own right, had been unable to decipher the symbols inscribed on the ancient parchments.

Cara and Drake both maintained that only an elder race could have created such an architectural wonder, and not without the use of magic. The Gorimm, forgotten except in children's stories and legends of old, seemed the only possible answer. Leoric kept his own suspicions private as he preferred to wait until more information was gathered before passing judgment. At the moment, the small group of friends could only speculate about the origin of the majestic city.

"How was your latest trip?" Leoric asked, taking a spoonful of the hot soup.

"Having Joram's goons along for the ride is like sleeping with scorpions," Auric grunted. "I got away late one night, but didn't find anything new."

"And the maps?"

"I still have them stowed away in the tower. It's too dangerous to keep them here in camp. One unlucky break with the guards and we'd be discovered." Auric replied.

"Any chance you could get Angvald or Ben to join you on your next visit?" Leoric asked.

Auric paused before answering. "I'm not so sure it's a good idea. Joram already knows we spend much of our free time together. It would be best to deflect his suspicions by inviting someone else."

The divisions in the camp had finally risen to the surface. Many silent witnesses to Leoric's abduction now realized the consequences of defying the ruffians who enjoyed intimidating others with their brutality. There were only two options: support the newcomers who questioned the unwritten laws of the camp, or stay quiet, do nothing, and suffer no harm. Leoric had seen it all before. Those faced with difficult choices, more often than not, succumbed to the path of least resistance.

And so, stalwart allies drifted away from the group and avoided them public-ly. Even Merias and Drake's fiery speeches had only really stirred the pot without bringing it to a boil. There was order to Joram's brutality, and with many a captive having lost so much, their grief led them astray.

"It makes sense, but either way you'll have to be careful," Leoric commented.

"Aye, it's getting harder every day to find people you can trust," Auric agreed.

"Any news about Kieri?" Leoric asked, doing his best to keep his voice low.

Auric sympathetically tapped Leoric's leg. "I'm sorry, but she hasn't been seen these last few days. I'm sure she's alright," he added unconvincingly.

Leoric knew what it was to feel the pangs of guilt and dealt with them as best he could. He had learned to live with the loss of his wife, and in some significant way, that made Kieri's unknown fate easier to handle.

"Warmer weather's on the way," Auric's comment broke the uncomfortable silence.

"How long?" Leoric asked.

"It's damnably hard to tell whether it's really summer or winter! This place has always been upside down when it comes to the weather. My best guess puts us close, maybe even two weeks away from springtime," Auric replied.

"We make our break for it then," Leoric decided.

"I didn't live this long just to see it all go to waste on the impertinence and impa-tience of youth, lad," Auric glared at his bedridden charge. "When the time is right we'll make our move, and not a moment before."

"I know you've been here a long time, Auric, but we must go. The north must be warned of *Lok'Dal hie*. If the Iron Shield is caught unaware by the goblins now marshalled and ready to flood to the border forts, the lands of the Northern Coun-cil will fall soon after."

"I'll be fine, Leoric," Auric answered. "I only need time to prepare myself."

Annoyed by the old man's response, Leoric studied his companion. The lined and wrinkled face betrayed nothing of his inner thoughts. Auric knew how to hide what he was thinking, and no scrutiny, however dedicated, was able to pierce his defenses.

Leoric desperately wanted to know what motivation Auric might have in return-ing to a world that had forgotten him, a world that fought itself as often as the goblins had warred among their own tribes.

And yet they are the savages...

The compound was rudely awakened by the trilling peal of a goblin horn. Every man, woman, and child knew instantly what the sound heralded — a muster. With muttered curses, the inhabitants of the camp straggled out towards the front of the central farmhouse.

Leoric helped corral a few of the smaller children towards the front of the lines. The goblins demanded each child remain seated while the adults were counted. As he helped young Rosa find her place, he could hear the whispered comments of the nearby prisoners. Glancing towards the clearing where the goblin guards were set up for the census, he frowned at what he saw.

A full squad of goblins had arrived, each one dressed in full armour and staring defiantly at the prisoners. Worried, Leoric hushed the children and took his place in line with Cara and Angvald at his side.

"Something's brewing," he whispered.

"Aye, this is no usual count," Cara agreed, her voice barely audible.

"I've got a fairly good grasp of their damned language by now. I'll try and make things out once that one starts talking," Angvald added.

The goblin in question was thick-bodied and bore several profuse scars crisscrossing his large chest and arms. This was no raw recruit, and it was apparent that he had seen many battles. His coarse hair, usually dirty silver for most goblins, had gone grey, denoting an age and experience unseen among the other captors.

Leoric frantically scanned the crowd for Kieri. It had been more than three days since he, or anyone for that matter, had seen any sign of her. Joram had used his influence to somehow keep her away from the fields and chores. Leoric was convinced that she could be hurt, or worse.

"There she is," Angvald noted, catching Leoric's anticipatory looks. "To the left, behind Joram."

Time slowed and the farm took on an otherworldly appearance as Leoric turned his head to follow the big Kaleenian's direction. The movement stretched on and his head moved at an agonizingly slow pace.

Kieri could do nothing to hide her bruised appearance. Trailing obediently behind Joram, she had an obvious limp. A sudden onset of rage flashed in Leoric's eyes, and only Angvald's iron clad grasp held him in check. She remained down-cast as she struggled across the yard, taking her place behind Ealston.

Joram walked forward and bowed to the goblin commander. As Leoric had seen others do in the city, he watched as the man dropped to his knees and subjugated himself, his forehead touching the ground.

"Why is Joram out there?" Benoit whispered from behind. "This doesn't bode well."

Wondering the same thing, Leoric understood that Kieri's plight could only be dealt with later, once his emotions had calmed and his thinking cleared. For the moment, he too was worried at the confident manner in which Joram approached the aged goblin.

"*Loriak shi na eden Portiak a fira orid ibn Gorann!*" the commander yelled, looking out over the assembly.

"Loriak, son of Lord Portiak, has come to visit the dogs of his people," Angvald did his best to translate. Joram remained prostrate as the imposing figure swept his hand over the congregation and continued in his native tongue.

"Dogs... bite the hand... provides for them. They can be leashed and controlled but still... they yearn for freedom! Show me the savage dogs!" Angvald continued to follow the speech with some difficulty.

Joram rose at that moment and pointed at two of the men standing in the front row. A loud gasp came from the assembled captives, one laced with shock and an-ger. Merias and Drake had both turned pale as the guards called for calm.

"By the all the gods, no!" Leoric cursed. "He wouldn't!"

"I think he has," Angvald replied woefully.

The goblin soldiers reacted quickly and dragged the two men forward, violently throwing their trembling bodies to the earth. Merias bent his head in sorrowful de-feat as he caught Joram's mocking smile. Drake rose defiantly to his feet and stood stoically in front of the goblin elder.

"*Riak na,*" the disfigured goblin said, meeting Drake's stern gaze.

In one smooth motion, one of the guard's stepped forward, drew a curved dag-ger from his belt, and slashed the prisoner's throat. Without a sound, Drake's knees gave out and he crumpled to the ground, blood pouring freely from his neck.

"Noooo!" Cara wailed. She tried to run forward, but was blocked by Leoric's outstretched arm. Many in the crowd cried out in dismay. Drake had been well respected and loved in the camp.

"If they mark you as one of his friends, you will die today, Cara. There'll be time to grieve and be with him once they are gone," Leoric said calmly. Joram was once again brazenly displaying the power he held.

They must laugh as they watch us kill each other while remaining broken and fractious, Leoric thought. *We do their work for them by hating one another.*

Merias, who had spoken so passionately in the common room about freedom and unity, was now on his knees before the row of guards. He turned back to look at his friends and then suddenly launched himself towards the goblin leader.

Surprised, Leoric watched the man actually wrap his hands, the hard, calloused hands of one who has toiled all of his life in the fields, around the creature's thick neck. The warrior reacted with incredible speed, chopping both hands away with a downward thrust and burying a dagger in the attacker's breast.

As Merias fell forward, he tried to clutch the weapon that lay buried up to the hilt next to his heart. Moments later he was dead, his blood already mingling with that of his fallen friend.

The commander calmly dusted himself off, readjusted his weapons, and spoke one last time before turning away from the prisoners. If he had been shaken by the ferocity of the sudden attack, he showed no weakness in front of his soldiers or the human prisoners.

"If you want to die, then I will grant your wish. If you want to live, be obedient dogs," Angvald interpreted, shaking his head slowly. "Oh no..."

"What is it?" Cara asked worriedly. It wasn't often that Angvald spoke in such a tone.

Ignoring her question, the big man started to usher the children back behind the front line. "Get the children away," he said urgently. "They don't need to see this."

"See what?" someone asked.

"By thee ancestors, just do as I say!" Angvald cursed.

It soon became clear why Angvald had reacted so harshly. The goblin soldiers descended upon the fallen bodies of Merias and Drake with a repulsive zeal. With children wailing and many in the crowd openly weeping, they hacked apart the flesh of two good men so as to leave nothing left to remember them by.

Orders were then given stating that the bloody pieces were to be left alone. To touch them was punishable by death.

Without a sound, the prisoners of the farm walked numbly back to their camp houses.

 os

Later that night, Leoric sat quietly with Cara. She had been close to Drake and had finally left the site of his death after much prodding from Benoit.

Nagging doubts about Kieri's safety crept into Leoric's troubled mind. He was still deep in thought when Angvald joined him after spending a while calming the children before they slept.

His friend sat down heavily at his side and remained quiet for what seemed like a long time. Finally, the bearded man spoke with words that carried honest conviction.

"Alright, Leoric, something must be done. But let's be smart about it," Angvald's dark stare was brimming with violence. "I want no one else to die because of that bastard."

A broken line, our dusty roads,
  'ere I see you once again.
Where once I placed my feet,
  My home, hearth, love, and life.
Lost to me, darkness evermore,
  came the march of the Wood.
—*Talos Weaver 'Telmire'*

CHAPTER XXVI

Old Telmire, Aeldenwood

With a hesitant hand, Alessan crouched down and brushed aside a small patch of dark earth covering a pattern etched in the stone courtyard of Telmire's old keep.

"Master Praxxus! Come look at this!" He waved excitedly.

With an exasperated smile, Corian joined him and looked down at the tiles. The faint outline of a broadsword clutched tightly in the paws of a lion was barely visible. Below the animal were three roses, a tint of red still noticeable in the worn design.

"The Black Lion of the House of Avagon," Corian nodded. "The crest of the founding house of Farraine and of the city itself. Without a doubt we stand in the courtyard of Rose Keep. It's said the gardens were made up of every type and colour of flower, and the beauty of the grounds were once rivalled by none in the whole of Kal Maran."

"What happened?" Alessan questioned.

"To the House of Avagon? Well that is a sad story, if it be true," Corian fretted. "The histories maintain that the last heir to that noble line died in the years after the Shattering of Kingdoms."

Alessan gave the merchant a puzzled look. "I thought the Shattering only concerned Caledun? Farraine was a separate kingdom, was it not?"

"Aye, you speak truth," Corian nodded. "But although Farraine was independent, its ties to the High King's throne, at least at that time, were very strong. Some scholars contend that the sons of Avagon paid with their lives for harbouring many of the noble fugitives and descendants of the High King's blood. But you can't always put stock in what those stuffy old scholars write."

Alessan's thoughts slipped back to that morning. After the heavy downpour had subsided to a light but steady drizzle, they had picked their way through the deserted streets of the ruined city. While passing numerous shops and homes, they had decided to venture into only a few of the dilapidated buildings. Sagging floors and weakened supports were far too common, and both men preferred to push on towards their real goal — the keep.

The two men had said little to one another after their heated conversation the previous evening. Still wracked by a sense of guilt over the biting comments he had launched towards his benefactor, Alessan left the door open several times for Corian in an effort to bridge the uncomfortable silence between them. It was to no avail. The powerful merchant from Innes Vale was in no mood for conversation. Speaking only in brief insipid sentences, the big man seemed preoccupied with his thoughts. So it was with great relief that Alessan listened to the man's recounting of the history of the place.

And so it was that they now found themselves entering Rose Keep. The entrance to the main hall was a sight to behold. Flanked by the imposing marble statues of the stately lions of the House, the gates had been completely removed. Even the mighty hinges that had at one time supported the massive wooden gateway were nowhere to be found.

Catching the bewildered look on Alessan's face, Corian offered an explanation. "The doors haven't been magicked, lad. The last ruling family had them ceremonially removed and placed at the site of the new castle built on the northern tip of Council lands. New Telmire was designed with its predecessor very much in mind."

Alessan felt like he was stepping back in time as he led the way through a large audience hall. Although the trappings of rank, power, and authority were long forgotten, the expansive chamber still invoked a noble reverence. Thick marble columns stretched to the very height of the tall ceiling, displaying part of the beauty that had once glowed throughout the hall.

With their feet echoing noisily in the cavernous chamber, they craned their necks in order to take everything in. Coughing as layers of dust, years in accumulation, rose into the air, Alessan brushed at a myriad of cobwebs dangling in various nooks around the hall.

Waving futilely at the cloying air, Alessan's eyes alit upon a strange discovery. Near the back entryway there was clear evidence that a number of feet had trampled across the surface. Alarmed, he signaled Corian over his way.

"Gath?" Alessan asked with concern.

"Can't be anything other than forest critters, young Oakleaf," the merchant said confidently. "You can see signs of small claw marks, so I don't think we need worry."

A brief search of the ground floor revealed nothing out of the ordinary. The kitchens were impressive, as were the large private dining chambers where the noble family would have certainly hosted many a formal ball for distinguished guests. Dust lay thick upon most of the floors, but further signs that something had passed through were in evidence. Corian refused to believe that they could be of Gath origin and silenced many of Alessan's queries with a stern look.

Their continued exploration soon brought them out a rear door and into a stunning courtyard and garden. The wild growth of the numerous flowers, roses especially, was beautiful to behold. Breathtaking vines crept up the walled enclosure and overgrown paths beckoned the young man, calling to his spirit. Alessan could only imagine how wondrous the place would have been when properly groomed.

With glee, he shouted for Corian to join him as he stumbled through some extravagant hedgerows and into the remains of a sheltered garden area. Inexplicably, as it was still later winter, there were numerous ripe red tomatoes on many of the plants.

Pulling a large fruit from the vine, Alessan bit into it and let the sweet, tangy taste flood his mouth. Wiping juice from his chin, he laughed as Corian's eyes opened wide with surprise and a beaming smile lit up his plump face. For the better part of the morning, the two men happily enjoyed Alessan's discovery, sating their ravenous appetites with the healthy fruits. Nearby, they also found a few beets and a batch of wild onions. They decided to stow the extra food in an old sack they had recovered along the way through the deserted city.

Far better provisioned than they had been in days and with spirits soaring, the travelers returned to the keep with a plan to explore the upper stories. Alessan was still hoping to find some hidden treasure, but the second floor consisted mainly of bare rooms, and the hunt left him disappointed.

As he entered a large circular room, Alessan could make out numerous old bookshelves circling the exterior walls. A reader himself, especially of the old legends and histories his father used to collect, Alessan whistled in appreciation. The sheer volume of books that could fit on the shelf space was impressive.

He brushed his fingers along the dark aging wood while slowly walking the circumference of the chamber. As he neared the far side of the room, he swore as a sharp pain suddenly shocked his finger. Muttering to himself, he carefully examined a sizeable sliver that was now jutting from his fingertip.

It was then that he noticed something strange about the nearest bookshelf. The light coming through a high open window illuminated a startling discovery. Suckling his bleeding finger, Alessan pulled a large piece of crumbling wood from the wall and exposed the steps of a hidden staircase. Clearing a large enough opening in which to slide through, he found himself staring upwards, and downwards for that matter, into a deep darkness that hid the remainder of the stairwell. Perched on the small landing, he realized that just as the wood had begun to rot from exposure in the main room, so too did a number of the stairs appear to be ill-suited for the weight of a man.

"Master Praxxus! Come look at what I've found!" he called.

With a careful step the big man inched his bulk partially onto the landing and stared into the darkness. "Well it's a stairwell, lad, and a dangerous one at that. Not too much else to see."

"You have no imagination, you know that, sir," Alessan scoffed. "This could have been a secret passage to a mistress' chamber, or even an escape route for the royal family of Farraine!"

Amused, Corian slid back out of the dark recess. "You're one of kind, young Master Oakleaf! You could be a storyteller with all of those fanciful thoughts bubbling around in that head of yours."

Alessan spent long moments wondering whether a descent into the darkness was worth the risk of a potential collapse. True heroes, he thought, would jump at the chance to explore the secret room regardless of the danger. As his left foot came to rest on the first step, the resulting groan from the old wood caused his mother's sensible and cautious voice to ring in his ears. With a look of longing, Alessan sighed and left the passage behind, preferring to follow Corian out of the library and into a new chamber.

◌

Daylight gave way to impending darkness, and the two men found themselves on the highest floor of the keep. The open battlements had proven far too unstable to attempt a visit. Alessan had a view from one of the tall windows and caught the crimson sunset through a thin layer of clouds. The rain continued to fall in a hazy mist.

Looking out across the eerily empty streets of Old Telmire, Alessan thought about his sister and the tales he wanted to tell her about his recent adventures. High above the ruins, it was easy to forget about the hardships of the previous days. The attack at the Crossroads faded like a distant memory once he had entered the deserted city. Biting into one of his tomatoes, he was hopeful that his fortune had finally taken a turn.

Suddenly, he realized with a pang of fear that the Aeldenwood wasn't ready to hand them their freedom so easily. "Gath!" Alessan hissed, desperately throwing himself flat against the wall, his eyes trained toward the distant treeline.

He motioned for silence as Corian moved slowly towards the other side of the high window, careful not to show his silhouette in the opening. Following

Alessan's whispered instructions, the merchant gasped as his eyes fell on the band of creatures moving far below.

The wiry Gath numbered a score. Nearby, another contingent of the twisted creatures crawled about with an uncontrollable energy and enthusiasm. The front-runners paused to sniff the ground as they wound their way through the main thoroughfare and towards the keep. But it was an upright figure that commanded Alessan's full attention.

In the middle of the pack walked a tall, robed man, his stride purposeful and swift. Alessan could not draw his gaze away from the hooded cowl. Corian seemed likewise stricken, and both men watched in paralyzed horror as the grisly procession crossed the very crest in the courtyard they had uncovered earlier that day. A darker feeling of despair and terror seized their hearts as the robed man paused and flicked his gaze momentarily over the cleared design.

He knows we're here!

Somehow dredging up the strength to tear his eyes from the creatures below, Alessan pulled Corian from the window as the robed man's head began tilting up towards their position. Leaning against the wall, gasping for breath, Alessan heard a harsh, guttural series of commands drift up from below.

"He's sending them up!" Alessan stressed. As he slumped breathlessly against the cold stone of the keep's wall, all hoped seemed lost to the young man from Briar. The peaceful search of the abandoned city and its hidden mysteries had been ruthlessly shattered.

"They've an idea we're here is all, Alessan. Let's head down that old back stairwell we came upon and see if we can't follow it out. If luck continues to shine our way, we might have a chance," Corian answered calmly, the faltering tone of his deep voice unable to hide his fear.

"But the staircase was awfully rotted," Alessan said with concern.

"Well you'll be going across first, lad," Corian failed miserably in his attempt to sound unconcerned.

Tracing their steps back through the haunting halls, the two men increased their pace as a long shriek tore through the musty corridors of Rose Keep. Echoing snarls travelled up from far below to the upper floors as Alessan led the way back to the old library.

Behind the tall, rotted bookcase, the partially eroded staircase beckoned the two runners. At Corian's urging, Alessan ducked through the opening and placed a foot down lightly on the top stair. The wood groaned in protest and he rapidly pulled it back.

"Our choices are somewhat limited, Alessan." Corian whispered. They both cocked their heads at the sound of the latest shriek, this one much louder and closer than before.

Taking a deep breath, much like he once did while swimming at the old pond outside of Briar, Alessan stepped forward. As quickly as possible, he stepped carefully and took the twisting steps of the old staircase down into the darkness, each stair bringing with it another creaking groan that set his teeth on edge. Corian followed directly behind, and even with the significant weight added to the weakened structure, the wooden planks managed to stubbornly hold.

Into the growing darkness they stepped. Reaching out with their fingertips to trace a path along the side wall, the men fled their pursuers. With two floors now descended, a series of loud howls caught their attention. Alessan guessed that the Gath were now above them and deemed it likely that they had reached the library.

It was while they were in between floors that a brilliant light flared from above. Without warning, the staircase as a whole, shuddered and began to come apart. With a cry of alarm, Alessan surged downward, the dim opening to a lower landing faintly visible from his vantage point. Behind him he could hear Corian's laboured breathing, the sound resonating loudly in his ears. All around them, the wood cracked.

Leaping over the last few steps, Alessan awkwardly tumbled to the ground, his knee smashing down painfully on a sharp fragment of stone. He turned back to urge on the big merchant and watched in horror as the staircase crumbled into pieces right beneath the man's feet. With a strangled cry of fear, Corian threw his arms up and tumbled down into the darkness.

"Noooooo! Corian!" Alessan screamed, scrambling to the edge of the stone stoop. He called out to his friend in the unseen blackness below but received no reply.

Acting quickly, Alessan rose to his feet and limped through the tunnel on his tender knee, vainly searching for another set of stairs that would bring him into the bowels of the keep. He wouldn't leave Corian alone with so many Gath hunting nearby. He had left companions behind once before, and once was enough.

With the sounds of pursuit far too close, as well as a nagging spike of pain rippling through his left knee, Alessan ran for all he was worth. Breathing a sigh of relief after finding his desperation rewarded for once with the discovery of a dimly lit stairwell that descended underground, Alessan barely paused as he leapt forward. Taking the steps in leaping bounds he continued to search for the fallen Corian Praxxus in the vain hope the man had survived the fall.

Heedless to direction and staggering blindly in the darkness, he frantically tried to orientate himself. In the silence of the gloom his desperate thoughts called out to his two-time benefactor. *C'Aelis, where are you? Why aren't you here to protect me?*

Whenever danger had struck, the mysterious elder had been there to intercede on his behalf. *How could this time be any different?* He wondered in frustration. That C'Aelis had frantically run off in obvious distress during their last conversation mattered little now. The warnings prior to the attacks at the Crossroads and the old Lumber homestead had, in fact, created a certain dependency. Here in the depths of the abandoned keep, Alessan could only wish fervently that help would arrive before it was too late.

For desperate moments, Alessan stumbled through the maze of hallways and rooms in the old keep. He called out urgently in a whispered tone for Corian. Terrified that the Gath were gaining ground on his position, fear threatened to overwhelm him as he found himself thrust vividly back to the memory of his harrowing escape from the Crossroads.

With his heart hammering in his chest, Alessan finally caught the sound of a faint cry for help. Turning sharply in the direction of the plea, he forced his tired muscles to fight on. In the faint grey light of the lower floor, his eyes finally began to adjust to the dimness. Navigating the passages with increased speed gave him a new boost of confidence. As another cry rang out, this one far louder and filled with panic, he ran forward with the chaotic howls of dozens of Gath filling the air.

Blindly rounding a corner and heedless to the danger that lay directly ahead, Alessan almost ran into one of the smaller Gath. A brief glance down the corridor also revealed the shadowy outline of a struggling Corian Praxxus. Steeling himself momentarily, he reached for the sword hilt at his side, and with some difficulty, pulled the blade free.

Gritting his teeth, he surged forward and plunged the steel blade deep into the back of the creature just as it turned to face him. Shrieking ferociously, it fell backwards with its claws reaching hopelessly for the sunken hilt. With black blood splattered across his Sylvani leathers, Alessan watched the Gath die.

"Alessan, why didn't you run?" Corian asked with a shortness in his breath. He was slumped against a back wall and covered with broken wooden pieces from the staircase. Pausing to reach back and claim his sword, Alessan assessed the merchant's condition and determined that the wounds were serious.

Corian lay propped up against the cold stone wall of the passageway, a bone in his leg protruded gruesomely from his torn trousers. Blood spilled from the wound and clotted thickly with the layers of dust caked upon the floor. Apart from the injured leg, a large piece of splintered wood had lodged itself deeply in his side. Judging by the man's laboured breathing and frequent grimaces of pain, Alessan knew that he was struggling to remain conscious.

"Sir... your wounds, they look..." he stammered.

A wearied look came over the merchant's face. "Aye, lad, they look bad, and trust me they feel even worse. But it's no matter to me, the gods have seen fit to call me home is all." Trying to remain positive, Corian even managed a weak smile.

"No, I can help support your weight and we can escape," Alessan vowed. With tears streaming down his dirt stained cheeks, he tried to shift his shoulder under one of Corian's arms.

"Alessan, it's no use," Corian murmured as another wave of pain swept over his battered form. "You have the opportunity to escape and need to take it."

"No. I won't leave you!"

Gripping Alessan's forearm tightly, Corian forced the young man to turn and meet his feverish gaze. "Listen to me, Alessan Oakleaf. Can you not hear the beasts closing in? You have scant time to worry about an old man like me. I led a good life, and I'll not have your death on my conscience as I go to join the gods." With tears of his own, Corian Praxxus let the grip on the arm fall free. "Now go...and don't you dare look back!"

"But..." Alessan said hopelessly. It was obvious that Corian was beyond his power to save.

"I need you to do one thing for me before you leave," Corian gasped.

"Ask of me what you will, sir. I'll do anything," Alessan said through his tears.

"Find Inigan for me, and make sure she is safe," Corian said. "You know I was searching for her, Alessan. You must let her know that I didn't want to grow old without her in my life. I've done many things over the years that I knew I would one day answer for, but Inigan, she deserved better. Please..." the merchant finished and lost consciousness.

Looking down sadly at the flamboyant master merchant from Innes Vale, Alessan wiped away a new flood of tears welling up in his eyes and replied to his friend one final time, "I will find her."

A series of growls, so close they sounded like they could be within a few paces, shocked Alessan from his state of grief. The immediate danger of his situation was all too clear, and he lurched to his feet with the bloodied sword clutched awkwardly in his hand.

Finding some untapped well of energy and courage, he ran through the dizzying dark corridors with a speed drawn from pure desperation. Sweat stung his eyes and black hair hung in wet ringlets about his face. Troubled, he listened to the searching shrieks of the Gath. It took a monumental effort to block his mind from thinking about Corian's ultimate fate. The merchant was lost, but the time for grieving would come another day.

Alessan had no idea how long he'd been running before entering a large chamber somewhere within the subterranean depths of Rose Keep. The close confines of the cramped passages gave way to the cavernous chamber with no forewarning. Startled by the change, Alessan froze and collapsed to his knees, his body finally giving way to the sheer exhaustion of the chase. As he fell, his heart sank and his newfound courage melted in the face of the numerous red eyes that glared at him from the blackness. Spinning fearfully, he realized that the fell creatures who called the Aeldenwood home, had led him into a trap.

With a snarling ring of twisted flesh slowly skulking all around him, Alessan felt something ripple in the recess of his mind. Confused by the sensation, he shook his head in effort to clear his thoughts while holding up his sword in a futile act of defense. Knowing death was so close, his thoughts turned dark. So much of his life had been without hope. A life spoiled by the circumstances of his birth — his curse. He had lived with so much pain and ridicule that only a few bright lights had ever managed to keep the darkness in his soul at bay.

Without warning, a blinding flash of light illuminated the gigantic room. The Gath, suddenly confused and afraid of the inexplicable glare, whimpered and shrank back towards the exterior walls. A sudden clap, like that of a ringing crack of thunder, echoed in the room and along the halls of the old keep. Staggering as if struck by a harsh wind, Alessan dropped his sword and frantically grabbed fistfuls of his hair, his eyes glazing over from the pain. The chamber began to swim in his vision as he watched the Gath succumb to an unseen force, their snout-like faces twisted in agony.

As the feeling intensified, darkness began to overwhelm him. Dizzy and confused, Alessan fell forward and knew no more.

SPRING

3AE338

*Listen to all proposals, but be wary. As much as you would like to be-
lieve that your services are indispensable to an employer; mercenaries
can be, and are, easily replaced.*
—*Captain Draven Shane*

CHAPTER XXVII

The Ca'lenbam, Protectorate

The Protectorate had selected a small valley north of Imlaris to hold this year's
Ca'lenbam, their Gathering.

A tall cliff to the north blocked the possibility of any passage by troops from that
direction. Only a small trail, large enough for perhaps two men walking abreast,
climbed up into the rock face, cutting a sharp path through the rugged terrain. To
the east and west, the valley walls sloped lazily upward, the boundaries on either
side obscured by the southernmost eaves of the Caeronwood.

The southern approach was packed with long columns of men and wagons
winding snake-like into the distance. The dust kicked up by feet and hooves was
enough to obscure the view for more than a league in the direction of the Protectorate's capital city. The mercenary companies approaching the meeting site were
easy to distinguish from the rest of the crowd. Standard bearers held their company
crests aloft on tall poles and the flags created a vibrant mosaic of colour as they
flapped in the wind.

Slowing his chestnut brown mare to a canter as he exited the western forest line, Gavin Silveron took in the majestic scene below. The sheer number of soldiers, tradesmen, wives, children and diplomats covering the valley floor would shock any inexperienced recruit. Although having attended many over the years, he could never look upon a Gathering without a great sense of awe.

Gavin turned to look at the many younger Fey'Derin riding in the vanguard and noticed various expressions of amazement on their faces.

"That all there is, Captain?" A booming voice called out from further down the line. "Small Gathering, I guess?" The hulking Ossric McConnal chuckled as he spoke.

"Careful now, Sergeant," Ethan Shade grinned broadly. "No need to scare the new recruits."

"You have a problem today, Sergeant Shade? If so, my boot to your arse might be of some service." Ossric called back, the enormous smile of his creasing his thickly bearded face.

"Enough," said Gavin, turning to stare at both soldiers. Both men nodded and whispered quick apologies. Gavin's voice had clearly been heard down the line and the other soldiers stopped their chuckling and stood at attention.

"Orn?"

"Yes, Captain?" replied the lanky veteran standing at Gavin's side.

Dressed in weather-beaten leathers, the disgraced scout's appearance was a stark contrast to the rest of the company. Most were armoured in various types of studded leather and chainmail with a smattering of heavier plate. All were adorned with a dark grey tabard complimented by a steel blue sash. Orn Surefoot wore only a decorative cloak in the same grey and blue company colours. The Fey'Derin symbol, a large crescent blade next to a smaller four pointed star, was sewn into the front piece of the mantle. That morning Gavin had designated the Eagle Runner as company herald for the *Ca'lenbam*.

"Find out who is in charge, make our presence known, and formally register the company. We'll set up camp near the north side and wait until we receive confirmation of our registry," ordered Gavin. "If you can confirm any rumours you might overhear, do so, but be warned," the captain added darkly, "I'll not have a repeat of last year's debacle. Understood?"

"Aye, Sir," Orn saluted. Pausing a moment to adjust his cloak, the huntsman headed down into the writhing mass of people gathered below. Within moments he was lost from sight.

Turning towards his men, Gavin waved over a small dark-cloaked rider. Clothed in black with only a small clasp at his throat displaying the Fey'Derin colours, the soldier's piercing eyes settled upon the captain.

"Coren, follow Orn and keep him out of trouble."

"Permission to remove the company crest, Captain?" asked Bider as he dismounted, his fingers fiddling with the clasp at his neck.

"Aye, but be careful. And try to find out if Khali's Reavers are in attendance," Gavin added.

At the mention of the Reavers, a collective breath of tension rippled through the men all along the line. More than a few fingered their weapons and grim faces replaced the awestruck expressions from moments earlier.

"I'll do some chopping if they're anywhere near, Captain," Ossric warned, brandishing his heavy axe with a look of murder in his eyes.

"They know well enough to stay away, Ossric," Gavin commented.

"Anything else, Sir?" Bider asked with a salute. Before leaving, the small man hesitated before adding, "Orn's on to you, Captain. He knows I'll be coming behind him."

"That's the point, Coren. It keeps him honest and afraid of the consequences. He may be an Eagle Runner once more, but I have by no means forgotten Dragon Mount," Gavin replied.

"Understood," grunted Bider as he handed the Fey'Derin clasp to his captain. Then, following Orn's lead, he entered the teeming crowd and immediately passed from view.

ભ

The Fey'Derin had weathered the last of the cold months in relative peace. The captain had spoken little about his harrowing adventure, although in a brief meeting with his senior officers he had disclosed some of the details. Caolte and Tel'Andros had kept silent about the journey as their captain had requested.

Gavin needed time to deal with everything he had seen, from the abundant Gath to the strange rescuer who could be none other than a member of the lost Gorimm. With the Earth Fiend's actions and Ir'Wolien's information and advice also fresh in his mind, he allowed his mind to slip back to a conversation that had taken place late one night after arriving back at the Fey'Derin encampment...

Caolte, with his arm heavily bandaged, and Tel'Andros still sporting an immense headache after waking, were sitting quietly in Gavin's quarters. The lieutenant was absently smoking his long pipe, his knife and usual block of wood absent for once.

"Are you sure of what you saw, Andros?" Gavin asked.

"For the third time, Gavin, it was a renegade, one of the Fallen. He was near the edge of the clearing, standing in the shadow of the trees and flanked by two enormous Gath armed with weapons. Highly irregular," Andros replied with a wince.

Puffing little circles of smoke from the side of his mouth, Caolte looked at both men. "Fallen or Silveryn, you can be sure I trust none of you," he commented.

"I fear it might be wise to change that attitude, Lieutenant," Andros answered somberly. "If the Fallen are in fact in league with the denizens of the Aeldenwood, the political troubles concerning the north and south will be as nothing compared to the terror that union might generate."

"Legends speaks differently. According to the histories, the Gath are little more than creatures that travel and hunt in small packs, much like wolves," Gavin shook his head. "If it was a Fallen that struck you down, then we must determine the extent of their control over the creatures."

"Those beasts could tear apart most mercenary companies by sheer force of numbers and a lack of tactics of any kind. They care little for their own lives and we are not accustomed to such savagery," Caolte interjected. "Unleashing an army of Gath upon the city states of Caledun would be disastrous."

"Would the Silveryn Council react to such a threat in time?" Gavin asked Andros directly.

Shrugging, a resigned look came across the mage's eyes. "I have to be honest, Gavin. The Council would debate and argue, then debate some more; but I wouldn't expect a swift decision."

"*Even with the Fallen confirmed as the puppet masters?*" The Fey'Derin captain asked in disbelief.

"*Ir'Wolien and the Council voted a long time ago to remain aloof from the greater world. Barring a clear threat to Dragon Mount itself, I can't see them bending one bit.*"

"*And the deaths of your young novices wasn't proof enough?*" Gavin questioned, his voice rising up in anger.

"*Easy, lad, he's not your enemy,*" Caolte cautioned. Gavin noticed that the man had come to the defense of the mage and found that reason enough to take heed of his retort.

"*There is no proof that a Fallen did indeed breach the Shield. Some believe that the magic inexplicably failed, as preposterous as that sounds,*" Andros explained.

"*I'm at a loss then as to what I should do, if anything,*" Gavin pondered. "*You should probably send a summons to Dragon Mount, Andros. Then we can only wait and see if the learned of the Order can shed some light on this situation.*"

"*And the mention of the Gorimm?*" Caolte asked quietly.

"*We keep that knowledge among us three. Until I know exactly what story lies behind that man's appearance I want it kept secret.*" Gavin turned his steady gaze from his officer to the young mage.

"*I am oathbound to report it,*" Andros hesitated.

"*But in truth you were not conscious at the time and therefore saw nothing,*" Gavin said with a deceptive look.

Shaking his head in resignation, the Silveryn mage slowly nodded. "*For the moment I'll omit your recollection of the rescue, but if pressed by the Council, I could lose everything.*"

"*Just keep it quiet for now, Andros. I have a feeling that events are coming to a head, events that will shape the land for years to come,*" Gavin replied with a faraway look in his eyes.

"*A feeling?*" Caolte broke the silence.

"*Aye, a feeling,*" the captain replied ominously.

The jingling harnesses on the horses of the column shook Gavin from his memory. He thought about Orn Surefoot and his new opportunity as spokesman for the company. The troubled man had made great strides in staying sober.

Although now cranky at the best of times, he had worked diligently as a recruit and had been reassigned to his old unit. The Eagle Runners had welcomed him back enthusiastically.

Gavin supposed that the veteran's biggest challenge would now reveal itself by the numerous temptations lying in wait at the Gathering. Makeshift taverns, each and every one teeming with drunken men and women trading stories, were far too numerous to count. A Gathering of this size provided enough ale and spirits to satisfy even the most devout of drinkers. If Orn, with the threat of expulsion now resting heavily on his mind, could deny his dark urges, Gavin would know that the man had finally turned a corner in his life; truly a breakthrough years in the making. Sending Coren as chaperon could only improve those odds.

Tel'Andros, on the other hand, was nowhere to be found. After sending his summons, the mage had then been summarily recalled to Dragon Mount to present a more detailed report of their findings in the Aeldenwood.

Although Gavin desperately needed advice, even from those he had spurned, he was already suspicious of any information that would be sent in return. Ir'Wolien's fingers were bound to have touched anything of note. Politics aside, ignoring the return of the Gorimm was not an option; contact had to be made again and questions answered.

Giving his word that he would return to *Galen'hide* before summer and handing everything of import to Eör and his recruits, Andros had taken leave of the company and headed north. Gavin couldn't help but wonder when next he would see his childhood friend. They had changed so much in the past few years, but he still believed in their friendship and saw the mage as a critical link to his past.

og

For over three hundred years, the mercenary companies of Caledun met yearly to discuss the terms of their new contracts. Spring was the time when employers set out to recruit soldiers for a myriad of reasons, ranging from simple patrolling and escort duties, to full on city sieges. All mercenaries would arrive at the annual *Ca'lenbam* and sign on to represent specific employers for the upcoming summer of warfare.

That there would be war between city states was a constant. The citizens of shattered Caledun warred; and they warred with all of their souls. Since the fall of the High King during the Shattering and the subsequent creation of the Mercenary Code of Conduct, the kingdom had never seen a summer without war. It was bred into the lifeblood of every citizen, be they a commoner or of noble birth. It was a rite of passage and a dream for many a young man to join a mercenary company and rise up the ranks while surviving year after year on the field of battle. With prowess in arms came social standing; with social standing came the opportunity for wealth and power.

Only small standing militias were allowed per city, and until now only the rebellious people of the *Drayenmark* and the Dwarven nation of Alerond were not subject to the binding Code of Conduct.

Orn slipped noiselessly through the packed crowds covering the valley floor. The bustling mass of citizens churned like a whirlpool, surging violently and heaving from every direction. With a thick layer of dust and human stench floating noxiously in the air, Orn decided to tie a wet cloth over his nose and mouth. Breathing without protection in such a claustrophobic environment was nearly impossible. More than once the nimble scout nearly lost his footing. To fall in such a crush of people could mean death, but Orn pushed on.

Glancing over his shoulder, he scanned the area for any sign of Bider. After last year's events at the Gathering, as well as his failure at Dragon Mount, Orn expected he'd be watched. His ongoing battle to stay out of the improvised taverns was made somewhat easier by the fact that there was company business to attend to. *At least that will give me a chance to shake Bider,* thought the Fey scout with a sly grin.

All manner of soldier was present at the Gathering. Veterans wore expressions of calm annoyance, yet they were also masterfully patient, an important skill in in battle as well as surviving amidst the organized chaos of another *Ca'lenbam*.

Newly promoted men, fresh from their officer's training camps, were barely able to contain their excitement and sheer astonishment at the scale of the proceedings.

Those unattached to a formal company, freelancers by trade, slouched against small tents containing their life's possessions. They displayed their smaller individual banners proudly and marked them for inspection by any potential employer.

No one could predict who would be hired by the nobles each spring. Chances were high that even most of the sell swords, an untrusted lot by reputation, would be bought by the Gathering's end.

The line for registration was painfully long. A series of plain wooden tables where scholars sat armed with parchment and ink were the only markers defining the recording area. As with the rest of the valley, men jostled for position near the front of the line. Very few companies had any influence based on their colours alone. It was their standing on the field of battle that had garnered respect and favour with the high ranking diplomats of the *Ca'lenbam*.

The reputation of Gavin Silveron's Fey'Derin was not lost among those assembled in the valley. Flourishing his cloak as best he could under the circumstances, Orn pressed forward and nodded slightly to those company heralds that moved aside for him. He made note of the colours and standards of those who showed respect, and pointedly, those who did not.

With the formation of the Fey'Derin five seasons prior, and having recently completed their third campaign in the south, significant rivalries had flared up with the other mercenary companies of Kal Maran. At each of the spring *Ca'lenbams* in the north and south, these rivalries often took center stage. Leaders paid close attention to those who were present as well as those who were conspicuously absent.

Over the years, Captain Silveron had forged strong bonds with only a select few. He had tried to remain aloof from the greater politics of the nobles who played at war. Many had called his stance a foolish one; others looked upon it as a testament to his courage and conviction. With the encroachment of Gadian Yarr's faction, even the determined Fey'Derin captain had been forced to pick sides. It was either that or return to the more comforting Northern Council territories of his early campaigns.

Although the company was paid with coin, even before fighting for Furnael Berry, Captain Silveron had never fought for the highest bidder. Only the Fey'Derin's exceptional skills in battle kept them among the top tier of the invisible mercenary pecking order and such respect, Orn noted with disdain, was in short supply among those gathered. *Not enough northern companies...* he pondered.

Orn was allowed to push his way forward close to the front of the line, but an unmistakable crimson and black standard ahead ruffled prominently in the light morning breeze. The dark red tabard, held aloft by a small contingent of well-armed men, owned the front rank of the registration. At the command of a young blond-haired guardsman, certain companies, regardless of their place in line, were pushed to the rear.

Cursing under his breath, Orn braced himself for the inevitable. Sliding both of his long knives from their sheaths, he stretched his taut neck muscles, adjusted the heavy cloak, and moved forward.

"Not today, Surefoot," came a soft voice. A hand tugged lightly at his elbow, the pressure slight yet unyielding.

Turning around to look at the speaker, Orn frowned when he saw the man who had been shadowing him. "They have no right to hold back companies, Bider. You know that as well as I."

"We are not in the north," Bider reminded his companion. "The Northern Council holds no sway here in the Protectorate. You know the Captain's orders."

Orn chuckled and slowly returned his weapons to their leather casings. Putting an arm around the smaller man, he headed towards one of the drink stalls. "Thirsty?"

"For water, you mean?" Bider deadpanned.

"Damn you," Orn replied with a sigh.

♋

The Fey'Derin mercenaries continued to push their way doggedly through the large crowds streaming towards the center of the valley and eventually found a clearing not far from the northeastern edge of the Caeronwood.

Gavin enjoyed the relative quiet on the fringes of the main assembly even though Ossric and Ethan both groaned at the distance that lay between themselves and the nearest tavern. Gavin had long ago lost his enthusiasm for the seedier side of the *Ca'lenbam*, but he smiled when thinking about how far the big sergeant would have to walk in order to find his bedroll that evening.

The camp went up with astonishing speed; it always did when a night of cavorting was on the horizon. As long as Gavin considered the work to have been completed adequately, the men were permitted their freedom. With the company very much on display over the next week, each and every soldier was held accountable not only for their behaviour, but also for the cleanliness of their squad's area.

The camp was divided into three sections: one for eating, one for sleeping, and one for training. The reputation of the Fey'Derin would surely bring about some excellent contests in the training yard once word spread that they had arrived. Freelancers often pitted themselves against his men in an effort to prove their skills. It was accepted by most that the Fey'Derin's prowess on the battlefield had been earned through hundreds of hours of diligent training. They were not wrong.

The first day had passed quickly. As the shadows lengthened, Gavin sat quietly with his senior officers while listening to Brock speak about what he had learned that afternoon. Upon arrival, the sergeant had been swiftly dispatched to make contact with a few of the companies known to be friendly with the Fey'Derin.

"The Sisters, Falconers, Helmsmen, and Iron Guard are all in attendance, but few other northern companies," Brock reported, his frosted breath clearly visible as the sun passed behind the valley wall to the west.

Only the Sisters of the Sword, a company of hardened women led by the tiny Dyana Fairwind, were considered true allies. The Sisters had made a name for themselves after arriving in the Protectorate the previous spring. They had aligned themselves with Duke Berry and successfully defended Matanis alongside the *Delan Fere*.

"Strange though, that so many of those are rumoured to have been hired out earlier than usual by the city of Delfwane," continued Ossric. "I'm sure Herod could shed some light on that subject. He, of anyone, would know the truth behind any of the rumblings."

"Aye, but the *Delan Fere* are nowhere to be seen. That in itself is cause for concern. It's no secret that Herod has been well paid for his services. Lord Berry has always been generous," Gavin nodded, "but without some sort of confirmation or preliminary report from either Orn or Coren, we can't assume that the Northern Council had its companies contracted earlier than usual."

Frustrated by the news, Gavin's eyes rested for a moment on each of his trusted men. "Well, nothing can be decided until the others return. I would like to speak with Duke Berry, though," raising an eyebrow, he turned to look at Brock.

"Aye, he's here, Sir. Near the center of camp where the nobles usually set up," the officer responded.

"Good," Gavin nodded. "And knowing Bider he'll be back by sun up, so we do have some time to prepare. Sergeant McConnal?" Gavin turned to the towering man who stood teasing the scraggly ends of his beard.

"Your orders, Captain?"

"Set up the watch rotation for the evening. Ethan will relieve you and your men come dawn. Keep an eye out for Herod's arrival as well. For this evening double the watch, standard sentries and perimeter. One can never be too safe." Pausing for a moment, he motioned to the other men. "Caolte and Ethan, I want you both with me. We have some time before we retire for the night to meet with the Duke and his men. He might be able to shed some light on the present situation."

Saluting, the Fey'Derin officers took their leave and got to work.

 જી

"Arne be damned!" hissed Bider. His body tingled uncomfortably, just as it had several times that day.

"Aye, I feel it as well. And it's much stronger this time," replied Orn.

The pair had spent the better part of their time at the Gathering in the makeshift taverns set up within the sea of tents that had sprung up around the enormous site. Their aim was to cover as much ground and speak to as many company soldiers as possible, all while hoping to separate fact from fiction. The *Ca'lenbam* was a breeding ground for tall tales and rumours and it took a special talent to discern the kernels of truth that could often be found in each conversation. The information gathered on their sortie would enable Captain Silveron and his officers to make more informed decisions in response to the usually plentiful contract offers that poured in.

The two Fey'Derin had found the time to return to the registration area and formally register the company. Afterwards, they had made short visits to two taverns and a brothel as they continued their search for useful information. Upon entering the current tent, their skin began prickling almost immediately, a sure sign that magic was being used in the vicinity.

Gavin Silveron had taken great pains to protect his men from the arcane arts. It was a company pastime on cold nights while huddled around the campfire, to wager on how much it cost the captain each year to visit the mages of the Silveryn Order. With the alarming increase in renegades that refused to follow the rules and practices of Dragon Mount, Captain Silveron had deemed it wise, no matter the cost, to guard his men against the usually undetectable attacks.

"Let's take a seat near the fire. We can observe from there," whispered Bider, pulling Orn through the crowd and closer to the fire ring.

Those in attendance were a diverse lot. Most were soldiers, and from the looks of their attire, men from companies down on their luck. Dirty tabards, rusted armour and ragged boots marked them as mercenaries down to their last few coins.

It didn't surprise Bider that so many soldiers could toss away what small fortune they had left in such a place. A demoralizing loss on the battlefield could scar a man. Years of death and destruction, torture and mayhem could darken a mercenary's outlook on life. Both Fey'Derin soldiers had been there at one point, and only through some strange twist of fate did they escape the downward spiral that had threatened to overwhelm them. Bider and Orn knew all too well the temptations that these men struggled with.

Seeing an open table nearby, Orn motioned to the other scout and surveyed the rest of the patrons in the tavern. Besides the men, the customary women of pleasure fawned over anyone who showed the slightest interest in their attentions or carried a heavy purse. The two Fey deftly fended off the advances of a few ladies who had pushed their way across the floor, immediately taking notice of their serviceable clothes and cleaner appearance.

Orn was delicate in his rejection of the advances, preferring to use his charm. Bider, on the other hand, had no time for such dalliances. Rude and somewhat hostile, the smaller man ignored the women as best he could and found a small table near the fire pit. Its copper chimney piped smoke out of the tent. When business needed tending to, there was little time for games. Pulling up a rickety wooden chair, he motioned to the closest barmaid to bring him an ale, two mugs and a pitcher of water.

"Two of them are sitting by the back entrance. I believe another is speaking with the bartender," Bider grunted as Orn arrived at the table, the two women dangling off his arms. They reminded Bider of leeches sucking on skin, ready to devour their host.

"Ladies, you'll have to excuse me, I have business to attend to," pleaded Orn, his arms held up in mock surrender as he sauntered to the table.

"We can both be your business. One for you and one for your friend," purred the closer of the two women. "He's a sweet one, isn't he?" she giggled.

"Stay any longer and I'll toss both of you out on your pretty little arses," Bider replied icily. Not sparing them another glance, he accepted the two mugs and tossed the barmaid a copper coin from his belt pouch.

"Arne's grace, Bider! Can you just try and be cordial for once in your life? I never thought I'd rather be entertaining with Ossric McConnal, barbarian that he is. When the Sergeant comes within spitting distance of a woman, it's like he's forgotten how to speak, let alone act," Orn chuckled as he took a long pull of his water, grimacing when he realized that it wasn't something stronger.

"Two of them by the back entrance, another by the bar," Bider repeated, remaining focused on the task at hand.

Adjusting his position, the older scout glanced nonchalantly in the direction of the rear tent flaps. Two figures, both dressed in nondescript clothing and light armament, slouched in the semidarkness. At first glance both men seemed no different than any other non-guilded mercenary in the tavern, except for their hands. Delicate and slender fingers, pale and unmarked, rested at their sides. The smooth ivory skin was in vivid contrast to their darkened roughshod uniforms. A typical warrior's hands, at any given time, were cracked, scarred, swollen and often bandaged.

"I see the two fools in the back," Orn nodded.

"The one at the bar isn't even hiding his nature. He's wearing a dark grey robe and attempting to blend in," added Bider.

"Gatherings don't necessarily frown upon mages, even renegades, but for a mage to be out in the open?"

"I know. Something's not right. Three establishments with mages... and that counts only the one's we've visited," Bider replied. "Renegades don't work together. Cursed Arne, they can't even coexist in the same city without some battle for power erupting."

"And now possibly three in the same tavern, at least one of them casting some sort of spell," growled Orn, scratching furiously at his chest in a vain attempt to stem the itch beneath his tunic. Bider glanced at the scout, knowing exactly how his friend felt. His own chest burned painfully as well.

The only downfall of having minor protection from magecraft was that the tattoos, in the vicinity of a spell, itched and burned as though a stray spark from a fire had landed upon the skin. The more powerful the spell, the more pronounced the sensation. It took time to get used to the feeling, but Bider and Orn had long since become adjusted to the sensation, and yet it was all he could do to stop himself from tearing at his tabard.

"Powerful magic for a tavern, don't you think, Orn?" Bider asked.

"Aye, haven't felt this bad since the Siege of Shand when that pack of renegades decided to tear each other, as well as the city's outer wall, down around our retreating vanguard."

"Let's wait for the robed one to leave," Bider smiled. "I think it's time we delve a little deeper into this mystery."

"You needn't ask twice, friend," answered Orn, the scout had already downed his first mug of water and poured himself another.

Bider had figured that one of the mages, preferably the one alone at the bar, would leave while the night was still young. Mages were notorious when it came to rest and relaxation. As the night progressed, none of the three suspicious characters showed any indication that their night was close to being over, and Bider began to feel uneasy about the whole situation. That three possible mages, undoubtedly renegades due to their lack of Silveryn robes, seemed oblivious of one another was a coincidence too impossible to ignore. If, with minor charms, the two company soldiers could detect the use of magic, then it was a certainty that three magicians would have felt the magecraft from across the camp.

Once again, Bider glowered at his friend, knowing the scout would not mind remaining in such an establishment, especially since the situation did warrant them blending in with their surroundings. Orn had taken the charade to heart even though his mug contained only water and he had downed the better part of eight mugs. Not surprisingly, he knew how to play the role of a drunk quite well.

"Take it easy, Orn, the last thing I need is a drunken lout on my hands," commented Bider with a sarcastic grin.

"Never you mind about me, I'll be fine," Orn stared balefully in return. "It seems I can hold my liquor tonight," the veteran's voice dripped with envy.

"You know the Captain's rule is your own fault. Charade or no charade, he'll strip you of rank like he did last year if you even think of touching any of my ale. You'd be a lieutenant by now if you could have controlled yourself."

Orn's demeanor changed drastically, as Bider knew it would. It was a risky plan to use against a man with a temper like the scout's, but the tactic was needed. Bider had seen the looks of longing the older scout had sent towards his mug and could see the man was slowly losing the battle amidst such revelry. Orn had few friends and he trusted only half of them. Bider had seen him at his worst and still accepted him, a reaction not lost on the company scout. Casting his friend a scathing glance, Orn stared into the bottom of his watery mug.

"I don't need lectures, lad," he finally said in return. Leaning back in his chair, the soldier became silent, seemingly lost in his thoughts.

Bider kept a close watch on his friend's response. With the situation still in doubt, he caught the anticipated movement out of the corner of his eye. "Time to go, Orn. Our quarry won't be waiting up for us. We still have work to do this evening."

The two Fey'Derin slipped out of the tent and made their way through the shadows, following closely behind the supposed disguised mages. Using company hand signals, the two men split off to either side of the well-trodden path. As far as Bider could tell, the mages had no idea they were being followed.

Still magic in the air, Orn signaled as they moved towards the command tents that belonged to the nobility and gentry at the Gathering.

I see no reason for either of them to be casting while walking about, Bider signed.

As if in response to his thoughts, the hairs on his neck began tingling, sending eerie chills up his spine. Spinning around, the Eagle Runner stared intently into the shadows that lay behind them. They had waited a few moments upon exiting the tavern, hoping to discern whether the third mage was connected to the pair they were tailing. No one had followed them as they had slinked off into the night, but something was not right.

We're heading towards the center of camp? Orn signed.

Once again, a feeling of unease crept over Bider. Pausing to scratch his scruffy chin, it dawned on him. *Cloaking! Another mage!* He signed frantically to Orn, but it was too late.

A wave of pressure hammered him backwards, throwing his body easily through the air as if he were no larger than a child. He came down hard and the breath exploded from his lungs. Pain ripped through his left side almost simultaneously. He knew at that moment that several ribs were broken.

Orn, to his credit, reacted quickly. Launching one of his long knives at the closer of the two armoured mages, he put up a fight. Coughing up blood and attempting to drag himself towards the shadows, Bider heard the sickening crunch as the blade penetrated the first mage's unprotected neck. The man began wailing in pain with a terrible cry that pierced the silence of the night.

A second wave of air rushed past Bider's broken body, this time hitting him squarely in the chest. Orn's second knife flew aimlessly past the robed mage as a half-dozen heavily armed soldiers converged on their location. As the first spear butts landed, he watched Orn's body crumple to the ground.

The warding pillars of the Aeldenwood hearken back to a time of
darkness and terror. Besieged on all sides by the forces of darkness, the
pillars were created by the Gorimm and their allies as a warning sys-
tem for those cities located near the borders of the realm.
—*D'aerias, Gorimm Keeper*

CHAPTER XXVIII

The Tower of *A'erinedor*, Aeldenwood

Alessan awoke to find himself alone in the middle of a barren plain.
The hot sun blazed overhead and the sky was devoid of any clouds. He
raised himself to a sitting position on the brown, brittle ground and took a moment to gather his bearings. There was a painful throbbing that hummed in the
back of his head as he struggled to his feet.

His memories were a chaotic jumble of fragmented images. He remembered
brief flashes of being chased through the caverns of Rose Keep. A faint feeling of
panic still lingered and although his memories were foggy, he did remember facing the terrible Gath in Old Telmire. He was surprised to find himself somewhere
other than the ruined city within the Aeldenwood. His final memory was of the
large chamber where he had been trapped by the Gath, their sadistic twisted faces
imprinted in his mind.

The sunbaked plain stretched as far as the eye could see, and not a creature stirred
in the empty wasteland. Only a small dark outline to the east showed any kind of

break in the flat landscape. Alessan could not tell what the silhouette was from such a great distance. He stood in a state of bewildered confusion with so many questions regarding his current predicament bouncing around in his mind. Forcibly, he refocused his unsettled mind and decided to head east towards the dark shape.

As Alessan trudged across the desolate plain, he took stock of his supplies and was happy to find that his sword was still sheathed at his side. The golden dagger he had been holding for Corian Praxxus was also present. His Sylvani uniform looked none the worse for wear. In fact, his outfit seemed far too pristine for one that had just survived a harrowing flight through dank and dusty old corridors.

Time passed slowly as Alessan forced his tired and weak body forward. Only the growing shadow in the east served as definitive proof that he was in fact travelling anywhere at all. The ground remained parched and flat in all directions.

Am I dreaming? He wondered as the sun paced itself far overhead. If this was a dream, it would reinforce his belief that the reoccurring Aeldenwood visions might be a thing of the past. Any pattern he had once perceived now seemed of no importance at all. *Am I going mad?*

Engrossed in his thoughts, Alessan failed to notice the ripple in the air directly behind him. Oblivious to the subtle disturbance, the now familiar touch of gently caressing fingers prompted his full attention. Turning to acknowledge his companion, Alessan breathed a sigh of relief.

"It's good to see you, C'Aelis," he gasped.

Likewise, Alessan, the Gorimm replied with a short bow. *I am also quite pleased to see you once again. I trust I did not startle you?*

The Gorimm looked far better than he had when last they had spoken. A day's travel from the Crossroads, C'Aelis had worn such a haggard look on his face that Alessan could remember his concern for the health of his strange friend.

Now, the clean and shimmering silver-haired Gorimm was pristinely groomed. He wore a beautiful green and grey robe with soft leather boots. Standing confidently on the hard earth, C'Aelis had regained the graceful stance that reminded Alessan of a poised hunting cat. Over both shoulders the Gorimm also bore his twin short swords, their bronze hilts gleaming with a polished shine.

"I wasn't startled," Alessan replied with a smile. "I may be a little on edge, but I believe I'm beginning to recognize your presence in my mind."

That is excellent to hear. I have not forgotten the pain I caused you when first we met.

"Oh that. It's of no matter," Alessan chuckled. "Unless you meant to cause me harm?"

Eriena strike me down, I wished no such thing! C'Aelis replied.

Alessan immediately experienced a profound feeling of remorse regarding his offhand comment. He realized that the Gorimm almost certainly had no ability to lie, so transparent were his feelings when speaking this way.

"I was just kidding, C'Aelis," Alessan laughed at his friend's obvious distress. The laughter itself felt cleansing to him, a release after so much pent up anxiety.

I believe there is much I have yet to learn about humankind, the man mused, his thoughts strongly conveying amusement. *And to think, it truly hasn't been that long since last I spoke with your race. But no matter, there will be time for that discussion after we deal with your present dilemma.*

"Dilemma? I would gladly take this one over my last," Alessan responded. "I'm not quite sure what has happened or where I am, but your presence makes me wonder whether I might be dreaming," he replied with a shake of his head. "The last thing I remember was being beneath Rose Keep. I'm a little confused…"

The stabbing pain that had been present when he first woke up suddenly returned with a heightened intensity. Alessan stifled a cry as the pain continued to swell in his stunted body.

A gentle but firm hand clasped his shoulder. *Alessan, you must listen to me. You are dreaming, but the pain you feel is real. You are in danger and need to control your emotions, control your thoughts. Believe not what you see or feel, lest they take true form.*

"True form?" Alessan gasped for breath, his fingers once more returning to massage his temples in a vain effort to abate the throbbing waves. His whole body was now shaking and through his pain filled gaze he suddenly caught sight of a fast moving cloud of darkness. The strange apparition was heading right towards them. In horror, he found himself helplessly captivated by the approaching gloom and unable to pull his eyes from the sight.

Alessan! You must listen! C'Aelis' voice suddenly roared through his mind, sending him reeling in pain but effectively breaking his frozen stare. *You must not fall prey to the dream. You must take my hand and follow where I lead. Alessan! Do you understand?*

It was the frantic tone in the man's thoughts that finally pierced Alessan's numbed senses. Never before had he felt such alarm from the Gorimm. With a cry of agony, Alessan thrust his hand into his companion's outstretched palm. C'Aelis' grip was like solid steel, unyielding and unbending.

Gritting his teeth, Alessan struggled to his feet. "Lead on..." he said and watched in wonder as the silver-haired Gorimm began to fade before his eyes. Glancing quickly at his own body, he shuddered fearfully as his own body also began to dissipate. In vain, he struggled to free himself from the Gorimm's grasp, but he was powerless against the supernatural grip. To his left, close enough now to distinguish the individual creatures, charged a twisted mass of Gath. Slavering mouths roared as they rapidly closed the distance. Screaming, Alessan braced himself as they overwhelmed him.

∞

Alessan slowly opened his eyes. The soft light from a nearby glass globe illuminated his surroundings. He was in a small well-kept chamber. Rows of shelves packed with old leather-bound books circled the room. Heavy velvet curtains covered both windows and a small oak desk was the only other piece of furniture of note other than the bed upon which he lay.

Sporting the same robes he had been wearing on the barren plain, C'Aelis turned from the window and smiled. In the dim light of the chamber the man's large green eyes glowed like exquisite pieces of jade.

You had me quite worried these past days, Alessan Oakleaf. To see your eyes open and your fever broken brings me much relief. For a time, I thought you were lost.

"I need a moment to collect myself," Alessan responded slowly. "Too much has happened in too short a time. I'm not quite sure what is real anymore."

When you are ready I will shed as much light on your recent adventures as is possible. Until then, take comfort in knowing that you are safe and have been for much of the last three weeks, C'Aelis replied.

"Three weeks..." Alessan breathed. "How?"

Now is not the time, Alessan, C'Aelis replied in a calm and patient voice. *You must take your own advice and rest your body and soul. I have an herbal tea prepared that should help you to relax. I trust you are interested?*

"Thank you, I am."

It took some time before Alessan downed the last of his tea. The warm drink had calmed his racing mind and a soothing wave washed over him. It also tasted wonderful. Even his mother's tea leaves lacked flavour when compared to the rich taste of the Gorimm beverage.

Stretching his arms about his head while wrapped in his thick bedding, Alessan glanced outside. Seeing a definitive change in the contour of the moon that peeked through the trees, he sighed and threw an expectant look toward his benefactor.

"How long?" Alessan asked heavily.

C'Aelis was sitting in a wooden rocking chair, his own cup of tea already empty and resting on a small end table. Greiyfois snored softly at his feet, the wolf's snout curled under the foot of his master. The smooth sheen of the animal's fur remained patchy in a few areas as old scars mingled with a newly healed gash that travelled the length of her left foreleg.

It has been seventeen days since I found you in the ruins of Old Telmire, twenty-one since last we spoke, C'Aelis answered. *Nearly a seven-day has passed since I pulled you from your True Dream.*

For the moment, Alessan preferred to ignore the strange term and asked instead. "How did you find me? And what of the Gath and Master Praxxus?"

You called to me, Alessan. Finding you was never a problem after your sending was received. The only obstacle to my arrival was time itself. My journeys had taken me far to the south. Greiyfois and I were somewhat hampered by a confrontation of our own with the Gath. As for those who had tracked you through the labyrinth beneath the castle, they were all slain by the time I arrived. Corian Praxxus —

"Wait!" Alessan interrupted. "Let's start at the beginning. Please explain this 'sending', as you call it."

Once again I am humbled. There is such a gap in our history that I forget how foreign some of my terms must sound. A sending is a silent call to one of my people when in need. Once a link has been established, we can communicate indirectly over longer distances. Although I knew you were far from my reach, I received your message of dire need, faint though it was.

"Can you send to me as well?"

C'Aelis nodded as he continued. *Yes, it is possible, but humankind tends to receive feelings as opposed to the words we wish to convey.*

"Like a breeze in my head?" Alessan asked, reminded of a brief moment in the catacombs.

Yes, that would be an apt description as to the sensation, C'Aelis agreed. *Very few of your race have had success in forming actual messages and Dwarvenkind can neither receive nor give a sending.*

"Any reason?" Alessan asked.

My forefathers all believed that their affinity with the stone of the earth blocks our ability, although even the most learned of our sages has yet to confirm this as an absolute.

Propping himself up among his numerous cushions, Alessan paused a moment to consider this new revelation. He caught the raised eyebrow of his companion and remarked, "I just realized that I have learned more about your people in the last minute than in our three previous meetings."

C'Aelis chuckled. *I don't believe there was ever time for tea on those occasions.*

Enjoying the lighthearted turn of the conversation, Alessan looked about the small chamber and suddenly opened his eyes wide. "You know, I think I've been here before. Or rather, it was a place in my dreams," he said with a certain amount of disbelief.

I am not surprised. We will talk more about all of your visions, Alessan, for you have shown yourself to be somewhat proficient in a talent my people thought long lost.

"Really?" Alessan exclaimed.

It is not yet the hour, young Oakleaf; let us deal with one set of questions at a time. There will be ample opportunity to bring to light other items of interest.

Alessan agreed with a tired smile. "In that case, you mentioned the slain Gath, but what about Master Praxxus? When I felt my mind almost shatter, he was lying wounded and those creatures had me surrounded," Alessan said with a deep sadness welling up inside.

I regret to inform you that I could find no trace of your employer, although I did see Gath tracks covering the ground where he had fallen. How the Gath were slain remains a mystery, but I do have a theory that I am not completely comfortable voicing at the moment.

Alessan's heart sank as he thought of the big jovial merchant. Without the trust of the businessman from Innes Vale, he would never have found the means to leave his previous life in Briar and strike out on his own. And yet this predicament, he realized, had come about because of that very same confidence. The world, it seemed, continued to play havoc with the rules when it concerned this young *ba'caech* from the North.

I am sorry, Alessan.

"Thank you," Alessan whispered and fell back into his thick blankets.

I believe the hour is late and it would be unseemly for any host to keep a recovering guest up for so long, C'Aelis said. *Our conversation can wait until the morning if you would so prefer?*

Catching the deep sorrow underlying the man's words, Alessan sent him a grateful glance and fought back a sudden onrush of tears. Blinking his eyes in frustration, he turned away and closed his eyes.

Thank you, he whispered in his mind.

You are most welcome, Alessan. Sleep well, the Gorimm replied.

In the darkness of the night, Alessan cried softly. At the doorway to the small bedchamber, C'Aelis pulled over a chair and sat as silent watchman for the remainder of the night. Slumbering comfortably at his feet, the young wolf shifted her body and snuggled closer to the Gorimm. Deep in thought, C'Aelis leaned back and watched the stars through the tall upper tower window.

og

A wonderful scent slowly brought Alessan back from a deep and restful sleep. Light was beginning to seep through the sides of the burgundy curtains, bathing the room in a gentle radiance. Yawning, Alessan stretched and made his first attempt at raising himself to a sitting position. His body ached and his muscles screamed loudly in protest. Wincing at the discomfort, he managed to slide his feet off the edge of the large bed and drop them onto the cold stone floor. Shivering, he prepared himself for the inevitable pain that would follow his attempt to stand.

With a gasp, he straightened his body and pushed himself to his feet.

It took a considerable effort to exit the room and reach the end of the hallway. Woefully, he eyed the stairwell now directly in front of him. Pausing to catch his breath, he leaned heavily on a nearby windowsill and looked outside.

He was surprised to find himself high above the forest floor. The tower gave a breathtaking view of the surrounding area as it peeked above even the towering trunks of the Aeldenwood. The bright light of the sun danced across the treetops like flames in a fire. The forest stretched far off into the distance, the green canopy broken only sporadically by similar towers, each of which looked like tiny poles on the horizon. It was at these times that the usually foreboding Great Wood enchanted Alessan. It seemed impossible that something so vast and beautiful could be home to something as evil as the Gath.

You have courage to be up and about, C'Aelis called in his mind. *Please wait where you are, I am happy to be of assistance if you wish to climb down for a midday meal.*

"Midday?" Alessan wondered.

I thought it best to let you sleep. Both your mind and your body needed rest, the Gorimm replied. *One can only push themselves so far before they fall off the edge. Even you, Alessan Oakleaf, must learn to control that stalwart spirit that resides within you. Temper the traces of rebuke and disgust that I can detect and replace them with feelings of hope. Your heart will rot if you do not take care.*

Alessan frowned. "I cannot change who I am," he answered tersely.

But you can always change who you become...

Alessan waited at the top of the stairwell until the nimble form of the Gorimm came into view. C'Aelis was dressed in his customary leathers. Twin swords were sheathed across his back in a crisscross pattern and a bow was slung over his shoulder. Alessan smiled and greeted him warmly, pushing aside any lingering objections to the Gorimm's lecture.

They made their way to a small nondescript kitchen on one of the lower floors. Compared to the serene beauty of the upper chamber, it was quite plain.

Do you enjoy mushrooms? C'Aelis asked as Alessan took a seat near the small cooking fire.

"Very much so."

Excellent. They will be ready presently. I also have another pot of water boiling for tea. You definitely consumed the last cup with vigor. A general feeling of amusement tickled at Alessan's thoughts.

From the open window, the air carried the unmistakable scent of new growth, a sure sign that the winter had finally loosed its icy grip from the land. Reminded of the abnormally temperate climes while journeying under the eaves of the great forest, he wondered if the Gorimm could really differentiate between the seasons.

"You've explained sending to me, but I have to admit my curiosity has been piqued. What exactly is a 'True Dream' and what on earth does it have to do with me?"

Setting his own cup down on the worn wooden table, C'Aelis locked eyes with Alessan. *If you truly wish an answer to your question, Alessan, it is imperative that you understand that your life, imparted with my knowledge, will never again be the same. I will be opening a door previously closed to you; a door you never even knew existed.*

"I've never been happy with who I am," he answered slowly, a sudden chill sweeping over him as he held the Gorimm's supernatural gaze.

Recent events, especially the fever that left you in bed for far too many days, have led me to believe that there is a reason that we have been united.

"Am I in danger?" he pressed.

Yes.

Breathing deeply, Alessan continued to hold the Gorimm's stare. "Then tell me."

I must first ask you one question, Alessan, C'Aelis cautioned.

"Go on," Alessan replied immediately.

Very well. How familiar are you with the greater world?

"Well, only a little I'm afraid," Alessan hesitated. "I know of Kaleen, the Shattered Kingdoms and the Free Cities. I'm afraid history wasn't a common topic of discussion in my family. My father loved the legends and stories of the North far more than anything else."

And of Valence or the Feradin? C'Aelis asked.

Alessan cleared his throat uncomfortably. "I know that Valence lies far to the east and I believe it has a Council of Lords, but I've never heard of the Feradin."

Then I believe you'll need to be patient while I explain something of the lands to the east, C'Aelis nodded. *Millennia ago, in the times of my forefathers, the forests of the Aeldenwood stretched across far larger tracts of land, land now empty and barren of trees. The borders of the Gorimm kingdom also reached far past the northern mountains and the southern plains of the Drayenmark. Peace still existed between the Gorimm factions and we had made contact with a number of races, the Kaleenians and humankind included. In the —*

"Wait a minute," Alessan suddenly exclaimed. "The Aeldenwood was larger than it is now and was then destroyed?"

Not exactly, Alessan. My people are caretakers of this wood, as the Feradin were caretakers of their own. When humankind began to expand their territories, the Gorimm Elders thought it in our best interest to pull back our borders. We hoped to avoid any future confrontations with other races. You see, it was never in our nature to be warlike or expansionist; we were simply the only ones here for a long time, C'Aelis explained.

"And so when the Gorimm disappeared..." Alessan shook his head in disbelief. "Without your guidance, the forest was simply returning to the size it once was!"

That is correct, Alessan. The Aeldenwood has suffered, in part, due to the arrogance of my people.

"You've mentioned this more than once. What do you mean by Gorimm arrogance?" Alessan probed.

Now is not the time, C'Aelis replied bitterly.

Alessan was suddenly struck by an intense feeling of anger and embarrassment. He could also detect a sadness enveloped by a sense of acceptance, as if the Gorimm who sat across from him had not been surprised by what he found upon his return to the Aeldenwood.

"I'm sorry, C'Aelis, I meant you no harm. Tell me then of my dreams," Alessan whispered.

C'Aelis gave Alessan a gentle smile and took a long sip of his tea before returning to their previous conversation. *In the northern expanse of the Kingdom of Valence we made contact with the Feradin, an elfin race who lived in the woods. Aside from their proficiency in warfare, there was much in common between our two peoples. They were long-lived, as are we, and for many years scholars from both races visited each another. It was the Kingdom of Valence that first introduced the Gorimm to the art of Dreaming.*

Dreamers, in the Feradin sense, were walkers of the mind; skilled sorcerers who could inhabit dreams and uncover a sleeper's fears and desires. Through the manipulation of Aer, our scholars brought back a slightly altered form of the strange power.

"How so?" Alessan asked curiously.

We did not agree with invading someone's secret thoughts. It was far too intrusive and lacking in honour. And so, over the years the magic of the Dream changed to become something reminiscent of soothsayers and seers of old.

"Predicting the future then?" Alessan guessed. "My mother always told me never to take stock in people who professed to know a man's future."

The Dreamers of my people see visions of the past, present and future, C'Aelis responded. *They cannot predict the future; only see a possible variation on what may indeed come to pass. A True Dream is one in which everything you experience is real.*

"But it's a dream, still?"

Yes, C'Aelis replied patiently. *But if wounded in such a dream, you would bear the mark upon awakening. If you die within a True Dream, so too does your life expire in the real world. True Dreams offer the deepest and most detailed interpretation at a vision.*

"But I was in a barren plain. It makes no sense," Alessan said doubtfully.

The meanings behind a vision are not always clear. Sometimes only after the fact does a dream make any sense, as with you here in this tower and the Gath pursuing you in the Aeldenwood. They were only nightmares until you experienced the actual events.

"And so these True Dreams usually last for three weeks?" Alessan asked.

Not unless the dreamer is lost, C'Aelis answered somberly. *And you, Alessan, were definitely lost. Granted, I can only assume that your fever hampered my efforts to seek you out, and your prolonged coma was worrisome. Had I not found you when I did, the Gath may very well have attacked. That they were expertly controlled speaks of another presence in your vision, one that showed a high degree of skill. That is what worries me the most.*

"And how did you find me? Are you a Dreamer as well?" Alessan pressed.

C'Aelis shook his head and smiled ruefully. *I have a certain affinity to Aer. It is, for the moment, the best explanation.*

Alessan chewed thoughtfully on his lower lip before responding. What he had been told was certainly strange and if he understood correctly, some level of magic coursed through his veins.

"So I have this power?"

In the simplest terms, yes, C'Aelis answered with no trace of humour. *You have the ability to manipulate your dreams as well as to search for those of people you know and care for. Gorimm Seers are something of a rarity and it is astounding that you possess the ability.*

"Is it really that uncommon?" Alessan looked up sharply. "The Silveryn Order have found many who possess magical abilities."

That is the quandary, Alessan. Never in the recorded history of your people has there ever been a human Dreamer. You possess a power never before seen in all of Caledun.

Alessan had no reply. Untouched on the table before him, his tea began to grow cold.

☙

Alessan and C'Aelis spent the remainder of the day relaxing in the front foyer of the old tower. Alessan contemplated the newest information his companion brought to light. That he had some sort of latent magic ability within him did not strike him as implausible. The possibility that some negative force was attempting to subvert that power however, was cause for a great deal of concern.

Throughout the course of the afternoon little was said, and for the most part a comfortable silence had settled between the two friends. Neither man seemed to mind, Alessan sipped slowly at another cup of delicious Gorimm tea while C'Aelis puffed serenely on his oddly curved pipe.

"Tell me about this place," Alessan said, surprising himself with the sudden flash of curiosity.

My people call it Natg A'erinedor; the Tower of A'erinedor in the tongue of your people, C'Aelis replied. He leaned back in his chair and exhaled a billowy cloud of smoke. *It was built in my youth and served as the northern watchtower for my people. I had already seen thirty turnings of the seasons before the Aliendal warning rods were added to bolster the tower's defenses. A'erinedor was a prominent figure in my people's history. She was the first general to successfully break the northern tribes of the Gorann, a feat that has never been duplicated.*

"Who are the Gorann?" Alessan asked.

Humankind refers to them by another name — Goblins.

"Goblins!" Alessan exclaimed. "The goblin tribes haven't been united in centuries."

Oh, I have no doubt of that, Alessan, but I am glad to hear they remain scattered all the same. They were once my people's greatest enemy and biggest regret.

"Regret?"

The Gorann are our cousins, C'Aelis replied quietly. *In the dark years at the end of the first age, before even Caledun had been founded as a kingdom, my forefathers threw them out of our ancestral home. It was a punishment that should have lasted only a century or so. We were wrong. The Gorann were filled with an uncontrollable bloodlust and sought revenge.*

The leaders of my people intended only to teach the Gorann a lesson in their banishment, but the exile only served to drive a final wedge between our races. The Gorann were bitter and jaded; their culture suffered and a realm of once great craftsmen became a warrior nation. A'erinedor brought them to their knees and shattered their rulers, but the victory was an empty one. The Gorann had grown arrogant, and yet it is my people in the end who committed the greater injustice.

C'Aelis grew serious and his words lingered in Alessan's mind like a cry echoing from a high cliff. "How old are you, C'Aelis?" Alessan asked after a short time had passed. It was the question that burned hottest in his mind and he could not ignore it any longer.

Counting the two centuries my people have been gone from the world of Kal Maran - three hundred and eighty-nine, he replied.

In stunned silence, Alessan took another sip of his tea.

Swift be steel, hard as stone. Tonight we watch, tomorrow atone.
—*Borderland saying*

CHAPTER XXIX

Lok'Dal hie, The Wilds

Leoric waited until the snoring sounds of the sleeping men in the room became regular before sliding soundlessly to the cold floor. With surprising agility, he deftly maneuvered between the long rows of bunks and headed directly for the back door. As he passed the final bed, a hulking shadow joined him and the two men carefully unlatched the rear exit.

Moving quietly between the converted farmhouse and the nearest warehouse, Leoric led the way into the closest field while keeping low to the ground. Pausing at the edge of the cornfield, he held his hand up as a warning to Angvald as they watched a trio of goblin guards patrolling the perimeter of the farm.

Timing their next move carefully, Leoric directed his companion to quickly breach the distance between their location and one of the many clear paths between the growing crops nearby. Months earlier, Auric had convinced their goblin captors that the corn should be planted closer to the farmhouse. By summer's end the stalks would reach high into the air, the perfect cover for a group of would-be escapees. For the moment, both men had to duck low in order to stay hidden from the sentries.

"Hsst! Angvald, you're going the wrong way," he whispered urgently. He could hear the shambling gait of the crouching Kaleenian in the next row.

The big man's orange-bearded face immediately poked through the growing cornstalks. "I always knew I could count on you, Leoric," he grinned and stepped to the borderman's side. "We're early anyway," Angvald whispered. "We both know Auric will be sitting there when we arrive. He's never late for a rendezvous."

It took the pair a short while to trek carefully out to a safe distance from the camp. Even from afar, they could make out the dark outline of a figure sitting cross-legged in the field. As they approached, Auric's deeply lined face broke into a mischievous grin. Greeting them quietly in the darkness, he motioned to the ground. Scattered all around the old man lay the treasure that they all deemed of greater value than a mountain of gold — maps.

Most of the charts showed detailed information of the lands the people of the Iron Shield had long thought unexplored. While some markings remained a mystery, they were far more concerned with learning the terrain than deciphering any goblin terms.

"Benoit and Cara?" Leoric asked as he took a seat on the cold ground. "Benoit will be here but I don't know if Cara got my signal at roll call this evening. She's been very preoccupied since Drake was..." Auric trailed off.

"She's carrying his child, is she not?" Angvald asked quietly.

"She is," Leoric replied with a nod. "It may be the only thing keeping her going right now. Ensuring that Drake's spirit lives on is of the utmost importance to her. Her love for that child will give her a reason to live."

All three men bent their heads to examine the various maps and charts of the wilderness while they waited for the rest of their clandestine group to arrive. They had been meeting regularly following the horrific slayings of Drake and Merias. The small community of captives had lived in perpetual fear since that day, and even one-time friends of the cruel Joram were on edge. Joram continued to rule by fear, but any trust he may once have earned was forever destroyed.

Leoric had kept a low a profile since the murders, but many in the camp still came to him for advice. Angvald had also become somewhat of a stalwart defender of the people. Although the big foreigner had warned Leoric of his own behaviour, it was Angvald's dominating appearance alone that kept some of Joram's ruffians in check. In due time though, both men knew that their luck was bound to run out. Joram's hold on the camp was still too strong and if the opportunity presented itself to exact vengeance upon them, Leoric was sure that the man would not hesitate to act.

Kieri was another matter altogether. She had remained steadfast in her loyalty to Joram, as inexplicable as that devotion was to Leoric. She had, however, continued to send him fleeting looks that conveyed far deeper feelings. That he was falling further in love with her couldn't be denied, and her painfully longing glances were almost too much to bear. It had been so long since they had spoken and he missed her terribly.

"Here they come," Angvald rumbled from his side.

Peering intently into the surrounding darkness, Leoric picked out the bent shapes of two more figures swiftly crossing through the short stalks of corn. Even from a distance he could easily distinguish the marked difference between the tall and slim scholar and the middle-aged headstrong woman.

Adjusting his spectacles as he dropped tiredly to the earth, Benoit made a brave attempt at a smile. Cara, on the other hand, looked like she hadn't slept well for days. Dark circles surrounded her blue eyes, and the once ready smile she had often flashed for friends had completely disappeared. Of the entire group, Leoric was most concerned for her.

"I apologize for my tardiness but it seems Joram and his goons are up and about this evening as well," Benoit said as he gratefully rested on the ground.

Auric raised his bushy eyebrows in alarm. "Are they aware of our plans, or just sneaking about?" he asked.

Benoit shook his head emphatically. "They aren't near the dorm rooms, like usual. They're at the grain warehouse making noise. I tried to get a quick look but I couldn't get near enough," he replied.

It was a well-known fact that just as Angvald tended to stand guard for Leoric, so too did Joram's cronies sniff around in the dark hoping to find another chance to strike. Thwarted once, they smelled blood and looked for every opportunity to corner their prey. *Like animals,* Leoric thought.

"We should kill them first, then deal with escaping," Cara muttered from her spot on the damp earth. "If we leave, who will stand up for those that are left behind?"

"Easy, lass," Auric raised a hand. "Joram's time will come, whether it be by our hands or that of another. Eventually evil minds turn on each other and Joram's group of thugs is no different. There will come a time when he feels the reins of power slipping and is forced to answer for his actions."

"But what's to stop another tyrant from taking his place?" she snapped back.

"If we have done our job well enough, supporting these people and keeping their hopes alive, we can only pray that someone with a good heart will fill the void," Auric answered patiently. "It is not for us to dictate that which the gods deem necessary."

"The gods have nothing to do with this, Auric," Leoric answered immediately. "No true god would sit idle and watch the pain we have all suffered. And if the gods *have* done so, then I hope to one day face them so that I can throw such suffering back in their faces."

"Friends, this is not why we have come here tonight," Angvald whispered sadly. "We must finish our plans and choose the time of our departure ere we tempt fate too many times and are caught."

The others nodded in agreement and Auric unrolled a large map that clearly showed the trails and waterways of the immediate area. On the other side of a large defensive wall lay freedom, but reaching the relative safety of the wilderness would be anything but easy.

"This is the last piece of the puzzle," Auric began. Pointing to a small stream that flowed through the valley and under the great wall, he continued. "If we can't get over the wall I believe that swimming under it may be possible. This is the new plan if the theft of the ropes fails."

Angvald shook his head. "But the stream lies much farther to the north then we wish to travel. If the ropes are obtained we should plan on hitting the nearest piece of that damned wall as possible. Time will not be on our side."

"I agree. If we travel too far north we'll lose much needed time to flee. The Wilds are too familiar to the goblins and we need every advantage possible," Leoric added.

"But if the ropes fail, Auric is right," Benoit chimed in. "This at least gives us a secondary objective. The last thing we want is to be caught atop the wall with no-where to run. We have no idea what we will encounter on top of that rampart. We need to be aware of where that stream lies."

"Fine, and if we obtain the ropes, where do we now stand?" Angvald asked.

"The collected food supplies have been incredibly difficult to hide, but if we are all in agreement that the trip should last close to a month, then we are ready to go," Cara replied after a moment's thought. "As long as we can hunt along the way, we should be fine."

"Excellent," Benoit agreed. "On my end I have managed to obtain three extra sets of clothing. The nights will remain cold and we'll need the extra layers I'm sure."

"And the torches and rope?" Auric inquired.

"The torches can be grabbed from the warehouse by the first runner so they are accounted for. The ropes are coiled neatly behind two large grain sacks and need only to be snatched the night of our escape. Obtaining a flint stone a concern but I believe Joram has one, it's just a matter of getting it from his home," Benoit finished.

"Kieri?" Leoric asked quietly. "She has access to the house..."

"Are you mad?!" Cara and Angvald hissed. "I'm damn sorry, Leoric but she's still in bed with the enemy and we cannot trust her," Angvald finished.

Watching the others as a whole nod in agreement, Leoric sighed. "It was just a thought."

Patting him lightly on the arm, Auric spoke in a gentle tone. "We know it's hard for you Leoric, but she'll be but a passing memory once we leave."

Leoric chose to ignore the comment. Turning instead towards the big man from Kaleen, he brought the conversation back on track. "Weapons, Angvald?"

"I think we have to assume we'll be going over the wall with nothing but our hands and feet," the man sighed heavily. "Everything in the mine is tightly guarded and my shift never works near the holding areas. Drake tried everything to get me posted near the armoury but with no luck. If I do obtain anything it will be on an impulse as I leave the mine that last day."

"That leaves the packs and maps. We currently have proper hiding spots," Leoric stated. "It seems that we have little excuse not to attempt this escape. I say we go the first night after the new moon; its light will guide us and the weather should be slightly warmer."

"Soon then?" Cara nodded.

"We have some extra time to prepare. Let's finish planning the route we'll take with these newest maps," Auric suggested. "With luck, we'll not need to risk meeting another time."

It was early morning before they slipped back across the fields and returned to the camp. As Leoric pulled the thin blankets over his shivering body, he knew that the gods had nothing to do with their escape plan. If it was to succeed, it would be due to their effort and careful preparation and not because of any supernatural favour.

○3

Two days later, Leoric witnessed the arrival of a new group of ragged prisoners. He had been working in a light rain for the better part of the morning when he spied a goblin patrol off in the distance. The field workers in the compound had often seen small chains of disheveled prisoners trudging off in the distance, but had received no new captives since Leoric and his band had staggered into the camp.

There were eight new arrivals, six men and two women. The men wore unkempt beards and moved with the subtle confidence of trained soldiers. Although they had inevitably endured hardships during their march to captivity, their bodies maintained the obvious strength and endurance that came with skilled training and combat.

The women had fared far worse. One of the two, an elderly woman with greyish white hair, was on the verge of collapse. Leoric nodded in approval as he watched two of the men gently carried her along the dirt path towards the camp's old farmhouse. The newest captives were ushered into the house, the goblin guards obviously impatient to put an end to their escort mission. With loud curses and a few heavy blows from the guards, the eight prisoners disappeared from view.

Leoric fought a rising red haze of rage, the very same feeling that always rose within him when witnessing such wanton cruelty towards others. Benoit's light touch to his elbow helped to dissipate the boiling anger that coursed through his veins.

As evening fell, the men and women of the camp returned home for supper and rest. The goblins had increased their working hours, as the days had lengthened with the arrival of spring and warmer weather.

The large common room was louder than usual as many spoke with the newest prisoners and sought news from the lands to the southwest. Leoric was pleased to see Angvald and Cara speaking quietly with one of the recent arrivals.

Their companion was tall and lean, standing almost shoulder to shoulder with Angvald. His arms bore the scars of war, and there was a smattering of aged grey hair sprinkled throughout his dark beard. The man's bright blue eyes scanned the crowd as he spoke with Angvald, and kept watch over all the activity in the room.

Leoric interrupted the conversation and reached across the table, taking the man's proffered hand in his own firm grip. "Well met, friend. My name is Leoric D'Athgaran," he said in a welcoming tone.

"Captain Finn Callum, Fortress Kelamyre," the man responded with a nod. "I understand you were stationed at Darkenedge?" he added.

"Aye, Angvald and I both," Leoric answered. "As far as I have seen, we are the only captive soldiers hailing from that border fort."

"Excluding Drake of course," Angvald grumbled.

"Drake?" Finn inquired with a raised eyebrow.

"He was a friend of ours, and a good man at that," Cara replied, her hand subconsciously moving to her stomach and gently rubbing the area. "He was murdered at winter's end by the bastards who keep us here and by one of our own," she finished with contempt.

"That Joram fellow you were mentioning, Angvald?" Finn asked, a dark flush briefly crossing his features.

"You would be well warned to keep any of your men from following suit with that spawn of evil," the big man replied with a frown.

"Are you all from the same company then?" Leoric asked.

"Aye," the soldier nodded. "I was just telling your friends that our scouting party was ambushed a little over two days out from the keep. Our Marshal had a feeling something wasn't right when dispatches were cut off between Darkenedge and our own fort."

"Sounds somewhat familiar to our own gaffe." Leoric mused. "Marshal Aram took offense to the new brashness the goblins were displaying. He sent our party out as a reminder that we still ruled the wilderness."

Finn shook his head dejectedly. "And it seems on both occasions it was the goblins who asserted their authority."

"How fare your men, Captain?" Cara asked.

"All things considered, they have held up rather well. There is a high level of trust between us," the borderman replied. "We lost four of our own on the journey, but our spirits are still high. Our goal was to survive, and now that we have, I aim to start planning our next move."

"Physically though, how are your soldiers?" Cara clarified.

"We're a good ways from any escape attempt, if that's what you're getting at," he replied hesitantly. "We're malnourished and beaten down. We won't be fully recovered before spring's end, at least not all of us."

No one said anything and an uncomfortable silence settled over the table. Leoric looked at both Angvald and Cara, the same unspoken question was on their minds. Could they trust a man they had just met? Granted, Finn Callum had said all the right things and had acted honourably, but a wrong move at this critical juncture and they could jeopardize their entire escape. *He's a stranger!* Leoric thought. Everything rested upon this one decision. Were he to gravitate towards Joram, regardless of his current apprehension towards the man, they would be killed.

As the silence lengthened, Leoric realized that Cara and Angvald were looking to him for guidance. How had he become the leader of their small band of rebels? *Well, gods be damned... let's try it*, he decided.

"Are you a light sleeper, Finn?" Leoric finally asked. Catching the confused expression on the new captive's face, he chuckled. "If not, you'll need one of us to come wake you this evening. We have much to speak about, and although I'm reluctant to sneak out once more, it might be our only chance."

The Kelamyre soldier responded with a beaming smile. "I sleep like a soldier, D'Athgaran, just tell me the time and place."

ᚳ

Having been caught unawares once since his arrival at the prisoner camp, Leoric had learned to sleep lightly. Even with Angvald's protection, he was determined to never be put in such a defenseless position again. His close brush with death at Joram's hands had initiated a now constant threat to his life.

Now, a dark figure loomed over him as he lay unmoving in his bed. He had detected the intruder's presence the moment they had crept into the room. It was the middle of the night and he had only just returned from his short meeting with Finn Callum. Tensing his muscles, he bolted upwards just as a hand was coming down across his mouth. A sharp gasp of surprise escaped from the intruder as he wrapped his arms tightly around the attacker's neck.

Shocked, Leoric realized immediately that he was holding a woman's slight frame in his rigid arms. Dropping the assailant to the floor, he caught a glimpse of Kieri's face peeking from beneath a dark hood. Casting about to see if anyone had been disturbed by the brief struggle, he grabbed her by the hand and quickly led her out of the dormitory and into the empty common room. Once safely away from the others, he turned to her with a bewildered expression.

"I'm sorry, Leoric," she stammered. "I... I... just needed to talk. I didn't mean to startle you, I swear."

"You shouldn't be here, Kieri! You know what could happen should you be caught," he whispered fiercely.

She clasped his hand and pulled him towards the outer door. Leoric fought to control his mounting suspicion that this was some sort of trap. If this was indeed a sick ploy by Joram to ambush him, with Kieri being nothing more than a pawn, then Leoric was determined to kill the man that very night with his bare hands.

Preparing himself for the worst, Leoric stepped outside and into the brisk, fresh air of the spring night. Glancing across the compound, he breathed a sigh of relief as it appeared to be empty. Smiling at Kieri, he continued to follow her into the nearest barn.

Tears glistened down her face as she stopped a few feet inside the barn. As Leoric reached to comfort her, he was startled; the woman's whole body shook uncontrollably. Pulling her into his strong arms, he held her tight.

"Kieri... shh... it's alright. I'm here," he murmured.

"I'm so scared, Leoric. I can't sleep, I can't eat. He threatens me daily and I don't know if I can take it any longer. I'm so scared!" she sobbed into his shoulder.

Her body continued to tremble violently and Leoric worried about her state of mind as she began to sob incoherently. Placing a steady hand under her soft chin, he guided her head up to meet his gaze. "Listen to me, Kieri, you need to focus. You're safe here in my arms, safe for the moment, so stay with me." The look of pure terror and pain that stared back at him shook him to the core. *Such terror...* he thought. Her behaviour set his teeth on edge and fueled the very same rage that he had, on more than one occasion, barely contained. Somehow, in some fashion, Joram would pay for what he had done to this woman.

"Kieri, stay with me," he pleaded as another series of tremors swept through her tiny frame.

"I'm so alone... I need help," she stammered as her body collapsed into his embrace. *Help.*

The word reverberated in his tired mind. Angvald had voiced the opinion that a person could only be saved if they truly wanted to be. To ask for help, the big man had said, was a crucial moment of defiance; and Kieri had now pleaded with him for help.

"I'm here. I'll help you, Kieri," he said with a conviction that would not be deterred.

He lost track of time as he held her, but it didn't matter to him. She was the first woman in such a long time that had found a way to captivate his wounded heart. His battered soul yearned for a connection. Leoric held Kieri tightly, whispering to her soothingly and calling her by name.

Finally the trembling subsided, and an exhausted calm settled over her body. Placing her gently in a patch of hay, he lay down quietly beside her. They breathed deeply in rhythm with eyes closed, and for a moment Leoric was sure she had fallen asleep. As he forced open his eyes in order to stave off a wave of fatigue, he found himself staring directly into her bright green eyes.

"How do you deal with your pain, Leoric?" she asked.

"I'm not so sure I know how to live without it," he replied.

"I was watching you, memorizing each line on that grizzled face of yours. And do you know what I think?"

"I know you'll tell me, so out with it," he smiled softly.

"I think you're a better man than I deserve, Leoric D'Athgaran. A far better man than a damaged soul like mine deserves," Kieri answered quietly and turned away from him.

"Kieri, there is no more battered a soul in this world than the one I carry. It's only when I am with you that I forget that fact. That's how I knew that there was something special in every look you sent, every glance you stole."

She wiped her hand across her eyes and defiantly shook her head. "How could you ever want someone who can't fight her own battles? Cara falls to her knees for no man, neither do others in the camp, and yet I do what that bastard tells me to do... because I can't help myself."

"If you are here to help soothe a man's aching soul then why can't I be here to fight your battles?" Leoric asked.

"You aren't just a handsome man, but one gifted with words," she said, and for a moment her voice was free of sorrow.

"I don't think this mug of mine has ever been called handsome, but you Kieri, are beautiful," he answered.

Blushing at the comment she ran her hand along the contour of his face and into his hair. "Well to me, you are fine-looking," she said, and for a long moment they stared at one another in peace.

"Joram will kill you," Kieri finally said.

Leoric nodded. "He'll not be happy. We have new friends that have arrived, and with Angvald at my side, he'll do nothing hasty."

"Then he'll kill me instead."

Sitting up quickly, Leoric took a deep breath. "No. From this moment onward if he so much as lays a hand on you, I will kill him, goblins be damned. You came to me for help, did you not?"

"Yes," Kieri whispered.

"I need to know right now whether you are willing to be with me. I can't protect you from afar." he said, taking her hands in his own, "I need to know if this is real..."

"Is it real to you?" she asked, looking deep into his eyes.

"Yes... yes it is," he answered.

"To me as well, Leoric, to me as well," she replied with a longing that conveyed far more than any number of words.

Catching the woman in a strong embrace he kissed her carefully on the lips. She kissed him back passionately.

Breathless, Leoric broke the kiss and remained solemn. "Then the first thing you'll do is never set foot in that bastard's house again."

"Where will I go?" Kieri asked.

"You'll take a bed in the woman's dorm. I'll arrange it with Cara." Leoric leaned forward and began to rise.

"No, tonight I will sleep beside you," Kieri said, determination in her voice.

"Kieri, we should be going," he answered, but he could barely hide the flush that had crept over his features. For the first time since Alanna's death, he was intensely aware of the contact of another woman's body, the soft curve of Kieri's hips and the delicate contour of her breasts. Without realizing it, their two bodies pressed together. His hands, gnarled and calloused from working the fields, slid along the length of her shapely legs.

In response, her arms curled lazily around his neck and pulled him downward into her embrace. They kissed slowly at first, both hesitant and self-conscious. But within minutes their actions grew more intense and a wave of passion rushed through Leoric's entire body. Shuddering with desire, he pulled back in an attempt to curb his sudden urges.

"I should be going... the risk is too great." he whispered in the darkness. He could do nothing to hide the desire that flowed within his body, and as he began to rise, Kieri's sudden grip stopped him in mid-motion.

"I need you Leoric. Please don't leave me, not yet," she whispered, her words barely audible over the pounding of his heart. In that moment the hardened borderman knew that this was no game. Too much emotion betrayed her feelings and he now knew that she yearned for him as he did for her. Leaning back towards her upturned face, Leoric kissed her fiercely.

"I won't ever leave you, Kieri, I promise," he declared. Sinking back into her arms, Leoric knew that he meant every word.

"Freelancers, by trade, are men without honour. They are not beholden to familial bonds and care for none but themselves. They are, in fact, the perfect killers."
—*Captain Gerald Armsmater*

CHAPTER XXX

Ca'lenbam, Protectorate

Duke Furnael Berry had arrived at the *Ca'lenbam* in style and with all the trappings of his wealth and power on display. As Gavin, Ethan and Caolte approached the leader of Garchester's large pavilions, the Fey'Derin captain realized that it was the first time he had seen the personable duke acting so much like a member of the gentry. Being that the yearly Gatherings were of such significance politically, Gavin wasn't surprised by the duke's motivations. Not only were hundreds of mercenary companies in attendance, but prospective employers as well.

With a brief nod to the final post of guards standing smartly at the doorway of the largest of the duke's tents, the three men were waved inside. Gavin was amazed by the sheer opulence of the place. Comfortable high-backed chairs surrounded an immense table with several scribes paging through stacks of documents. Several more clerks sat at smaller side tables, each working through their own piles of writing parchment. In the middle of the administrative chaos stood Duke Berry, his brow furrowed as he reviewed the contents of a manuscript held in his hand.

Turning briefly to acknowledge the newest arrivals, his eyes opened wide at the sight of the Fey'Derin officers.

"By the gods, if it isn't Gavin Silveron," the duke announced heartily and immediately discarded his work. He grabbed Gavin's forearm in greeting with his powerful grip. "You look well, Captain. Caolte, Ethan, welcome to you both."

Motioning towards an inner partition, the nobleman led the way into the rear of the large tent, his loud voice already requesting that food and drink be brought in for the guests.

Graciously accepting seats on soft cushioned chairs, Gavin spoke first. "It is good to see you, my lord. I trust you are enjoying this year's *Ca'lenbam*?"

"There's posturing like I've never seen," Furnael grimaced. "I've not seen the likes of it since I last attended council in Imlaris. There's enough money being thrown about to support all the refugees from last summer's warfare. And yet here we waste it on pompous displays of power."

"One's reputation *is* important at such an event, is it not?" Ethan offered, sipping at a glass of spiced wine handed to him by one of the servants.

"That it is, Lord Shade. I've never seen so many scoundrels fawning over my attentions as when I walk about the fairgrounds in this damned place. Like vultures looking for scraps of meat," the duke replied with disgust. "My presence here is necessary, but it doesn't mean I have to enjoy the spectacle."

Ethan's face briefly clouded over at the mention of his family title, but a nonchalant gesture from Gavin served as a reminder to keep his sentiments regarding the comment in check. Being called by a noble title in front of certain lower ranking mercenaries could, in the very least, be detrimental to company morale. Duke Berry saw it as a matter of etiquette by referring to Ethan's family line. He had never been made aware of the estranged relationship between the Fey'Derin sergeant and his father although the nobleman would have been aware of the rumours of a rift.

"I trust the winter months weren't too harsh for your citizens?" Gavin inquired.

"They suffered some, but we put much effort into the rebuilding process for those families who lost their homes. I believe were we able to provide adequate relief."

"And your defenses?" Caolte added with some concern.

The duke frowned at the question. "To be truthful, we have had to overcome a number of obstacles concerning the damaged walls. The first two companies I had working on them up and left mysteriously one night. Needless to say, we have fallen far behind in completing the repairs."

"Interference from a particular source, I would imagine?" Ethan guessed.

Duke Berry nodded. "My agents traced some rather large bribes back to some men connected with our 'friends' in Imlaris; but as usual, no tangible proof has allowed me to finger Yarr and Dalemen directly."

"Will the battlements be completed for the upcoming season of warfare? There can be little doubt that Garchester will be a prime target," Gavin added.

"I'm afraid I'm just not sure at this point, Captain. With some luck, and as long as this milder weather holds, we may have a chance. It is more than likely the walls will be incomplete come summer," the Duke replied, sounding quite defeated.

The four men were silent as they reflected on what this might mean for Garchester and the greater potential impact on the entirety of Caledun, should the city fall.

"By the way, have you heard anything from your informants to the south?" Caolte asked. "Captain Blackwain mentioned during his visit that nothing of value is filtering through. Not knowing why men are disappearing in the southern region makes me more than a little nervous."

Duke Berry shook his head in frustration and sighed heavily. "Whoever is in charge of their security is more than competent, I can tell you that. Three times we have received the heads of some of our best men and women, returned to us in leather sacks with their eyes, ears and tongues removed," he answered grimly. "Something is brewing, and in my estimation it involves the assembling of an army. For this to happen, it would indeed mean the breaking of the Code, something we never even dreamed could occur. The immediate problem remains that Gadian Yarr and some highly trained group or individuals are working in secret."

"An ex-soldier perhaps?" Ethan speculated.

"Or a member of the Thieves' Guild?" Gavin proposed. "That would explain their involvement in my assassination attempt this past winter."

"You may be correct, Captain," the nobleman said with pursed lips.

As the discussion drifted to possible nefarious plots, each one a little wilder than the next, Gavin found it difficult to dismiss the fearful tone in Furnael Berry's voice at the mention of Gadian Yarr's likely plans. Something dark loomed on the horizon, and the powerful councilor from Imlaris had dominated their conversations for far too long. The coincidence struck Gavin as too unlikely to ignore.

It was growing dark as the three Fey'Derin soldiers took their leave. Exiting the large pavilion with a promise to discuss contract terms on the morrow, Gavin sought desperately to find some relief from his brooding thoughts.

CB

For the first time since his return from the Aeldenwood, Gavin's dreams were beset by scenes of horror. His nightmares jumped radically from one terrifying vision to the next, each one involving either the vicious Gath or the mysterious Fallen.

As the creatures of the dark made their appearance, so too did the welcoming presence of the strange C'Aelis. A repeat of the Watchtower rescue was disturbingly absent. As Gavin fought through the dreams, C'Aelis only watched, the man's bright green eyes staring intently at the Fey'Derin captain... judging him, or so it seemed. With the insights gleaned from the annals of the Silveryn histories, Gavin's feelings of unease continued to mount.

Three times that night he woke with blankets drenched in sweat. Frustrated, Gavin felt no better rested once the faint light of the coming dawn crept through the cracks in his tent. Knowing that sleep would continue to elude him, the weary captain struggled out of his bedroll, cursing to himself as the crisp spring air stung his body.

At such an early an hour, the camp was devoid of activity. A few unlucky sentries on duty sat clustered around a small fire, and a cold morning frost covered the ground and supply crates stacked nearby. Enjoying the silence, Gavin reflected on the previous evening's interactions with the other mercenary companies friendly to the Fey...

He spent only a short time speaking with the other captains they had fought with in Garchester and had instead spent the better part of the evening partaking in drinks with Captain Dyana Fairwind of the Sisters.

The women of the northern company had fought together with the Fey'Derin during several campaigns in the north, and Gavin was glad that their bonds of fellowship had not suffered over the years. Dyana was also the abiding object of affection of the giant Ossric McConnal. Many of his Axemen reveled in reminding their sergeant of this, for it seemed that Dyana would have none of the man's attentions.

Curious news had also reached his ears shortly before retiring for the night. Herod Blackwain had arrived late in the day and sent his greetings along with an urgent invitation to confer at Gavin's earliest convenience. That the *Delan Fere* captain was so adamant about a meeting worried Gavin even more than the lack of information gleaned by Duke Berry's informants. Herod was not a man who acted rashly.

Caolte had made the rounds of the Gathering with some of his men, but had discovered no new information about the current state of affairs in the south. Lieutenant Burnaise could therefore shed no more light on the delicate political affairs of Caledun's fractures city-states and they were no nearer to confirming any suspicions or rumours than when Gavin had sent Bider and Orn off on their mission. Remembering with trepidation the past struggles of his best scout, Gavin rubbed his temples, trying in vain to stem the sudden throbbing pain in his head.

Brock and Caolte, both notorious early risers, waved as Gavin approached the campfire, this one on the far side of the camp near the food stores. Gratefully accepting a steaming mug of tea from the hardened lieutenant, Gavin sat down heavily.

"Bad night, lad?" Caolte suspected.

"Same old, same old..." Gavin muttered in reply while scanning the area for any sign of his wayward scouts.

Seeing the sharp look on his captain's features, Brock offered to check the sleeping quarters. Watching the warrior stride off purposefully, Gavin returned a gaze to his closest confidant in the company and spoke softly, "Coren's not around either, Caolte. Is there something I should know?"

"I guess that means my reputation has gone to *j'helak*," grinned the old veteran. "You hide the truth from your commanding officer one time and it seems to follow you around for a lifetime."

"Answer the question, Lieutenant."

"All right, all right, Gavin," Caolte implored, throwing both hands up in the air. "I have no idea as to the whereabouts of your two rogues. I haven't seen them since they left by your orders yesterday. Now stop looking at me like I'm hiding something from you and finish your tea. Gods know how you're always suffering from a chill when the spring months come upon us."

Grunting in reply, Gavin slowly sipped his beverage and savoured its warmth. All around him men began sliding out of their tents, faces still showing the bleary eyed signs of the previous night's revelry.

"If the contracts work out today, I think the men need some extra time off to enjoy the Gathering. What say you?" Gavin asked.

Caolte nodded as he continued to whittle away at a piece of wood that was taking shape as a small wolf, fangs bared in a snarl. "Aye, they need somewhere to spend their hard earned coin. With our winter camp being so far from any real settlements, more than a few might want the company of a woman, as well," he agreed.

"I'll wager you won't even go near one of those places now would you, old friend?" Gavin tested him.

"Hah! Karli would string me up by my toenails and that'd only be the start? It would be something far harsher than I've ever faced on the battlefield, to be sure."

More than half of the men had families that lived in regions beyond the closest town of Briar. Located far to the north, Briar had been home to the Fey'Derin winter camp for the past three seasons of campaigning. With their most recent battle near Garchester and with the safety of the forest trade routes in jeopardy, Gavin had opted to remain in the south this winter. As for Caolte's wife, a *Drayenmark* herself, Gavin knew that she would tolerate no excuse should she ever hear about her husband spending even a moment of his time with another woman.

"They haven't returned, Captain," interrupted Brock, a worried expression creasing his bearded face.

"Both of them? This could be a new tactic, staying away from the campsite until Orn is sober. What do you make of this, Caolte?" growled Gavin.

"Knowing those two ruffians, they may be hip deep in sheep's dung, but it could be important to let them work things out on their own. Let's give them some time to report in. I trust Bider has kept Orn safe and sober," Caolte replied as Gavin stared at him with a dark frown.

With his face pressed against the cold, damp ground, Bider tried to muster up enough strength to move. Each breath sent sharp jabs of pain through his chest. He could feel his broken ribs grinding painfully against one another as he tried desperately to shift positions in order to alleviate some of the pressure. His clothing was torn and his body bruised from the night's ordeal. As far as he could tell by his numbed extremities, he was also bound hand and foot.

In the dim light, Bider could see that Orn was bound only a few feet away. The other Fey scout was lying on his back, his top a bloody rag clinging tightly to his bruised body. A large gash was visible on the man's forehead and a slow trickle of blood traced a path down from his temple. So far every attempt to wake his friend had been futile, and Orn remained unconscious.

As best he could discern, they had been placed in a holding tent. What concerned Bider was the fact that they were alone. In a valley teeming with thousands of soldiers, it was safe to assume that more than a few should have earned a place in the drunken holding tent alongside them. Bider had made a career trusting his instincts, and at the moment, the situation did not sit well with the experienced campaigner.

He had already replayed the evening's debacle in his head countless times. He was embarrassed by their failure to adequately defend themselves, against the suspected the third enemy. They had been careless and were now paying the price.

"The Captain's not going to be happy," Orn spoke for the first time, his voice dry and parched.

"An understatement if I ever heard one," Bider replied, relieved that Orn was awake.

"If it's any consolation, I'm not hungover for once." The scout's attempted laugh turned into a coughing fit.

"I am not impressed."

Smiling with a painful wince, Orn chuckled. "For the first time in my life, I'd gladly take the pounding of spirits in my head over this unholy pain. How long have I been out?"

"Not long enough." Bider said sharply.

သ

By mid-afternoon Gavin's patience had worn thin. With two of his best men still missing, a dour mood had descended over the entire Fey'Derin camp. Every member of the company knew that if Orn had succumbed to spirits, the outcome would be terrible to witness and he would be expelled.

The combination of a restless night and the missing scouts did little to lighten Gavin's disposition. Even a vigorous contest in the training yard was unable to shake the captain's malaise. With their commander on edge, so too were the Fey'Derin; soldiers and officers alike stepped lightly.

Sergeant Fearan finally brought word. Approaching Captain Silveron, the thickset man cleared his throat and gave a sharp salute. He motioned towards three soldiers in dark purple tabards standing a few paces behind him.

"Captain, it seems we might have a problem. These three gentlemen would like a moment of your time to explain."

Brock Fearan was clearly displeased with the request. His jaw was rigid with tension and his stance was both stiff and unyielding. Judging by the formal introduction, Gavin gathered that his officer was upset and thought it best to engage in the strictest of *Ca'lenbam* decorum. His grey eyes registered the rank of the men standing before him.

"Lieutenant, how may I help you?" Gavin addressed the senior officer.

"There are two matters we need to —"

"A soldier respects his superiors, especially a commanding officer. While in our camp you will show the Captain the respect due his station," Brock interrupted, his face red with anger. Caolte nodded in agreement while gripping his spear tightly, his knuckles bone white.

The soldier paused and finally gestured to his two companions, both of lower rank. All three saluted before the guard continued, "I apologize, Captain. I'm afraid it has been a long morning," he tried a second time.

"You have my attention, Lieutenant," Gavin spoke evenly.

The man nodded crisply. "As I was saying, I have two matters that I need to discuss with you. If we could retire to a more suitable location in which to do business, I would be happy to deal with these pressing issues as quickly as possible."

It took some time for the Fey'Derin officers to assemble for the meeting. Ossric looked somewhat haggard as he had only just been awakened by Gavin's summons.

Only the visiting lieutenant was permitted entry into the command tent. Both guardsmen remained under surveillance at the entrance.

"Go ahead, Lieutenant, we're listening," Gavin said without a trace of warmth.

Shuffling through a stack of papers pulled from the leather pouch he carried, the officer passed over a single sheet of parchment.

"And this is?" Gavin asked patiently.

"Your contract offer for this summer, Captain," the soldier replied.

Gavin glowered at the man. "You must be new, Lieutenant. The Fey'Derin have never dealt with contract matters through an intermediary. If your employer is interested in our services, they are free to schedule a time with any of my officers."

"I respectfully beg your pardon, Sir, but this will be the only offer you receive at this Gathering. I'm afraid the rules have changed. My Lord Gadian Yarr will be making the same offer across the board. If you do decline, it will be reported to the nobility pavilions where a scribe will record your reason for displeasing Lord Yarr."

"Are you daft, man?! Gadian Yarr does not dictate the happenings of an entire Gathering! You can tell that sniveling, pomp —" yelled Caolte. Ethan Shade quickly placed his body in between the clansman and the soldier.

"I'm afraid you'll have to excuse my Lieutenant," said Gavin as he crumpled the parchment in his hands. "It really has been a long morning."

Sneering, the foreign officer rummaged through his papers once again, this time pulling free two thick documents covered with the official *Ca'lenbam* insignia.

With a gloating countenance, the man handed over the papers, "I'll leave these with you, Captain. The magistrate won't take kindly to any tardiness."

"And these are?"

"The arrest and detention reports of Orn Surefoot and Coren D'Elmark," he replied.

ෆ

Bider was frustrated. In the dim light of the tent it was hard to tell how much time had passed since he had come to, and he had no idea how long he may have been incapacitated. He could hear enough muffled sounds of activity from outside to warrant the belief that it was morning. Morning of which day was an altogether different matter.

With his pride still stinging from the initial shock of being outwitted, he had managed to fight off numerous waves of nausea and pain as he valiantly tried to free his hands from the coarse rope that bound them. All of his efforts to that point had been futile, granting him not the freedom he so desperately craved, but only chaffed wrists and bloodied hands.

He had managed to shift his bruised body enough to allow some weight to be taken off his injured ribs. The relief was minimal but a step in the right direction. Glancing at his companion, Bider wondered how extensive Orn's injuries truly were. The scout had been drifting in and out of consciousness, all the while vehemently denying anything more serious than a throbbing headache.

Orn had spent the better part of his life fighting for companies in Caledun. He had once captained his own company; eventually losing the position when his intoxication on the field of battle resulted in tactical errors and an unexpected defeat. Lately, the old soldier had been complaining of terrible aches in both of his knees. Stripped of his rank and wounded on many occasions, Bider worried if Orn's current injuries might not push him back over the edge.

Silently vowing to remain steadfast at his friend's side, Bider tried again to get himself into a sitting position in hopes that by further elevating his body, the pain would lessen and he could seriously entertain the possibility of escape. He was less concerned about being bound than by his injuries. If completely healthy, the bonds that held him would be no match for his ability to contort himself and defy the physical limitations of his body. Unfortunately, the agony was simply too intense to try anything drastic.

Long moments passed before he mustered enough strength to make another attempt. Gritting his teeth against the oncoming pain, the small man twisted his body, pulling his arms underneath his legs as he did so. For most men, the maneuver would appear excruciatingly painful, if not entirely impossible. Despite his best effort, a sharp cry escaped his lips. Breathing heavily after the ordeal, but resting far more comfortably, Bider cocked an ear towards the tent flap, straining to detect any change in the sounds coming from the camp.

"I guess it's my turn next," Orn said in a tired, raspy voice.

Glancing to his side, Bider could not help but smile weakly at the comment. Despite their predicament, the wily old veteran had found a way to diffuse the tension in the air.

Shaking his head, Bider replied, "Sorry, old man, no grey hairs allowed during this escape. I'm afraid you're finally out of luck."

Spitting up blood as he laughed, Orn did manage to right himself with Bider's assistance. With the scout's hands bound in front of his stomach, he was able to move about relatively freely. Regardless of their recent success, they both knew it would take some time before they could entertain any thoughts of making a run for freedom; both of them suffered from serious leg cramps from lying in such awkward positions.

"Any ideas on who took us out?" Bider said.

"The mages were definitely renegades, but the guardsmen wore tabards I didn't recognize."

"Black on purple, no?"

Orn agreed, closing his eyes as he fought back another wave of nausea.

"Haven't the Regulators been known to use that colour?" Bider asked.

"They're purple on black, a big difference," Orn replied.

Both men sifted through their memories, trying in vain to identify the uniforms of the men who had accosted them. "I'm at a loss," Bider said, his frustration once again barely held in check. "Any ideas?"

When Orn didn't reply, Bider leaned over to check on his friend. Sighing, he realized that no reply would be forthcoming any time soon; Orn Surefoot had fallen unconscious once again.

∝

"Caolte, you're in command. I want the men to be ready for a quick departure," ordered Gavin as he donned the remaining pieces of his armour. Throwing his tabard over his head, he exchanged leather gloves for mailed gauntlets. "I don't have to warn you to be careful and extremely discreet while you go about your preparations. We are sure to be under surveillance."

"Anyone familiar with the Fey'Derin would have known that such a contract offer would be immediately refused," Caolte agreed.

"I know. That is what has me worried. Apart from Khali and his band of butchers, we've made no enemies that I am aware of," Gavin frowned.

"Gadian Yarr has fielded armies against our employers these last three years though," Caolte added.

"And you believe that is reason enough to insult and alienate a company? Most captains here won't look kindly upon such an uncompromising offer."

"It really makes no sense, Gavin," Caolte said, shaking his head in disbelief.

"Gadian Yarr is a cunning politician. Making such a drastic proposal wouldn't have come without substantial consideration of the consequences. If he has unified the southern city states into a binding nation then he has betrayed the Mercenary Code of Conduct and will be judged harshly by the North, the *Drayenmark*, Innes Vale and the Shield."

"Agreed Gavin, but could this be nothing more than backlash, if indeed Bider and Orn were causing a ruckus last night? It wouldn't be the first time those two have ended up in chains."

"Not this time, Caolte. Like you said yesterday, we've discussed this scenario over the past two seasons. It has coloured our contract choices these last two campaigns and now, with battle lines finally being drawn, we need to stay the course. All of the planning we've made with our allies will now, hopefully, pay dividends. I need you to send word to Duke Berry and have him immediately join you. He is not adequately protected at the moment, and the Fey'Derin can escort him north, if not to Garchester." Gavin's orders were concise and crisply delivered.

"He'll not be pleased, Gavin."

"I don't care. Caolte, we need him alive. It is your decision on how you manage it, but he needs to escape the Gathering in one piece. If Gadian Yarr has decreed his contract offer as the only one, the Duke is in great danger."

"Agreed," the veteran nodded.

Reaching for his sword and strapping it to his back, Gavin paused momentarily before adding another command. "I also want every soldier carrying foodstuffs in their saddlebags. Nothing is to be left in the wagon, within reason of course."

"And the wagon?" queried the lieutenant.

"Not a factor," he replied immediately. "It's more important we have enough supplies on the men. If anything ever happened to that wagon we'd be hamstrung."

The clansman nodded and barked for someone to find Era Colwyn, the company quartermaster, before asking another question. "And yourself, Gavin? How long do I wait?"

"If you have no word from me by noon, don't look back and ride into the woods. Strike for the camp and round up any of our recruits still in training with Eör. He has them well-trained and they'll be ready if it comes down to battle. Don't tarry though, make haste for Dragon Mount. I will meet you there."

"Will the Order allow us entry?" Caolte asked hesitantly.

"Tell them I'm coming and Ir'Wolien won't think twice about the full company passing through the Shield. Speak with Tel'Andros and inform him of what has transpired. With luck, he can act as our intermediary with the Council until I arrive."

"Can we trust the mage?" the *Drayenmark* asked quietly.

Staring balefully at his friend, Gavin tried only a little to hide the anger in his voice. "Put your feud aside, Lieutenant. Our list of allies grows short and I'll not have the Fey'Derin's safety jeopardized. Understood?"

"Aye, Sir!" saluted the old veteran. "And, Gavin..."

"Yes?"

"Safe journey to you always."

With that, the clansman threw aside the tent flaps and was gone. Taking a deep breath, Gavin Silveron clasped the formal cloak around his shoulders, glanced for a final time around the command tent, and made his exit.

The first documented finding of the rare Aliendal wood dates back to the First Age. It was discovered by the renowned seer, R'hiale, while roaming the foothills of the E'rienn mountain range. The wood was used for the first time in the construction of the doors at the royal family's palace in C'aisil Chro.
—D'Elias, Gorimm Keeper

CHAPTER XXXI

The Tower of *A'erinedor*, Aeldenwood

It would be three days before Alessan felt strong enough to make his way about the tower on his own. Strangely, although still exhausted from his experience in the ruined city of Telmire, his body had recovered quickly, and his withered arm felt stronger than ever before. Under the watchful eye of C'Aelis, he had started rigorously exercising the limb, and unbelievably, the arm had responded to the training. The rapid healing was a mystery to Alessan, but C'Aelis remained tight-lipped about the subject.

During their time at the tower, Alessan told stories of his life growing up in Briar. He preferred to avoid some of the more pressing topics on his mind and found comfort in discussing his childhood. C'Aelis remained aloof, and no matter how many probing questions Alessan asked, the secretive Gorimm refused to elaborate on the details of his past.

One interesting bit of information that he did divulge concerned the members of the Fey'Derin. Alessan was well aware of the elite mercenary company as they usually set up camp not far from Briar and had often visited the Black Boar. C'Aelis revealed that he had recently been in contact with Captain Silveron; a meeting that also entailed a deadly altercation with the Gath. Although he remained vague about the reason behind the encounter, C'Aelis confirmed that the Fey'Derin soldiers had escaped relatively unscathed. What the mercenary captain was doing in the Aeldenwood was yet another question that piqued Alessan's curiosity.

Now he stood uneasily at the edge of a swiftly moving stream. Located only a short distance from the Tower of *A'erinedor*, C'Aelis had led him to the stream when he had asked if there was somewhere he could bathe. The dirt and grime from his recent escapades were now caked in thick layers upon his skin. Growing up in the meticulously clean Black Boar, Alessan could no longer stand the filth or the stench.

Standing at the edge of the water, he carefully dipped his foot into the cool water. The shock of the frigid temperature made him second guess the entire idea of washing. Before he could change his mind, he peeled off his clothing and threw each piece off to the side. Then, taking a deep breath, he plunged in. The cold was invigorating and an icy numbness ran up his spine. Wasting no time, Alessan started to scrub furiously at the dirt covering his pale skin.

Finding a small rocky overhang a little ways upstream, Alessan lay back and let the rushing water run over his head and shoulders. Enjoying the sensation, it took some time before he had the strange feeling that someone was watching him. Quickly dunking his head and pushing the hair away from his eyes, he smiled as he recognized the visitor. Greiyfois, tongue lolling about happily from her fanged mouth, was perched on the edge of the stream, her dark eyes staring intently at him.

"Hey, girl!" he called out happily.

The last few days had given Alessan the opportunity to spend some time with the young wolf. In many ways, it seemed as though she was watching over him just as closely as C'Aelis did. Whenever the Gorimm was absent, it was now routine to see Greiyfois at his side instead. He had never seen a wolf act so tame and it did take him a while to come to trust her. Now he greeted the animal warmly, and in response to his laughter, she let loose a short howl and launched herself into the stream, her legs churning furiously as she paddled towards him.

They played together for a long while until finally the cold water began to numb Alessan's entire body. Chilled, and yet content, he scrambled ashore and dried himself with a blanket he had found in the tower. Greiyfois shook herself vigorously, showering him with a fresh barrage of cold water. Laughing, he patted her on the head, his hand coming to rest near the long scar that marred her shiny coat.

"Was it the Gath who did this to you, Greiyfois?"

Immediately, a set of images flashed through his mind, vividly depicting the events that resulted in the wound. The first showed a dizzying chase through the forest, the trees flying by at great speed. At Greiyfois' side, never once slowing the pace, ran C'Aelis. He sported a look of extreme determination and concern. All around the forest Alessan could see other fast moving shapes keeping pace with the fleet Gorimm.

The second flash of images showed a chaotic fight at the base of an old tower, this one with an immense tree reaching up into the sky from the middle of the structure. C'Aelis and a pack of wolves were surrounded by the churning, twisted bodies of numerous Gath. Alessan could tell that he was watching the scene from Greiyfois' viewpoint, but the chaos and terror of the battle felt very real.

It was the last vision that struck Alessan with the greatest intensity. There, during a momentary lull in the fighting, a strange trio of figures crossed through Greiyfois' vision. He recognized Captain Silveron and Lieutenant Burnaise immediately, but in their arms lay an unconscious man, one who wore the unmistakable robes of a Silveryn Mage.

Giving the wolf a final pat on the flank, Alessan donned a new set of clean clothes that C'Aelis had provided him. His tattered old Sylvani uniform was so filthy that no one, not even his mother, could scrub away the sweat and dirt that clung to those rags.

Feeling more like himself than he had in days, Alessan flexed his weak arm. Encouraged by the strength he found in the limb, he headed in the direction of the tower with Greiyfois padding silently at his side.

ଔ

"I've been thinking about something, C'Aelis," Alessan commented. It had been some time since his return from the stream with Greiyfois.

Yes?

"Well, along with Captain Silveron and Lieutenant Burnaise, you curiously omitted the third member of the party in the Aeldenwood that night," Alessan stated, knowing that the unexpected revelation would likely catch the Gorimm off guard.

C'Aelis sent a dark look towards Greiyfois as she lounged comfortably near the fire. The wolf looked chagrined and followed up the piercing stare with a whimper.

Alessan continued, "Strange how you could have missed two men carrying another, and wearing the robes of the Silveryn Order, as well?"

It can be awfully hard to find a stalwart companion these days, and you, Alessan, may be far more trouble than you are worth, the Gorimm replied ruefully.

"Are you a supporter of the Order, C'Aelis?" Alessan inquired cautiously.

The Silveryn Mages were ever at odds with my people, but we respected their scholars as they did ours. The Order tended to... meddle... far more in the political affairs of humankind than did the Gorimm.

Alessan frowned. "But you also had an advisor to the High King, did you not?"

A flitter of amusement tickled Alessan's thoughts as C'Aelis answered. *You are well versed in certain matters of history, Alessan. You are correct; both factions had a designated advisor to the High King of Caledun. Regrettably, as the Shattering neared, my people failed in that capacity."*

"How so?"

The Gorimm elders, sensing that the fate of Caledun was at hand, opted to leave your kingdom bereft of Gorimm guidance, stating that it would be unwise to offer undue advice in such politically volatile conditions created by man. The move was strongly opposed by many of our leaders, myself included.

"And the Order?" Alessan asked.

The Silveryn Order was embroiled in dangerous liaisons with several powerful members of the Gorimm's most esteemed Houses. They would fall as well. The lack of guidance from both parties may very well have influenced the terrible events leading to their demise...

"Wait a minute, here you go making no sense again," Alessan said, with a look of confusion on his face. "What were the mages and the Gorimm plotting and how could you have delayed the assassination of the High King without prior knowledge?"

The silence that greeted his inquiry was answer enough. Alessan looked at C'Aelis with a raised eyebrow. "By the gods, you knew! You knew the king would die and yet you did nothing!" he said angrily.

It is not so easy to explain, C'Aelis replied defensively, a touch of irritation lacing his sent thoughts. *It was a tumultuous time for the Gorimm and we were divided as never before. We ignored the threat to Darion Lordares in an effort to heal the divisions between our disparate factions.*

"C'Aelis, you speak in riddles when I ask about your people. You speak of arrogance and sorrow, yet you answer nothing and expect me to understand everything as though a Gorimm myself. You abandoned humankind, watched Caledun fall, and condemned an innocent man to death!"

It was not our place to alter the destiny of one man.

"One man?!" Alessan raised his voice. "I know that you only recently returned to this land, C'Aelis, but is that what you tell yourself? That it was the life of only one human?! Thousands upon thousands were slaughtered during the Shattering. The *Drayenmark* were nearly destroyed and hundreds were enslaved and forced to work for the nobles who took power. Until the advent of the Mercenary Code, Caledun was in a state of chaos and despair."

We had no idea... C'Aelis whispered in his mind. Once again the feelings of shame, revulsion and regret crested a wave of utter frustration. *You must understand, Alessan, those repercussions are not what we planned. Nothing happened as it should have. We were fooled by those the Elders trusted, one who exploited our growing vanity and greed, and sent this land into a dark age...*

"Cursed Arne, you make no sense!" Alessan spat and turned to leave. "Couldn't you have done something? Couldn't you have at least warned him?!"

Some of us did try to help. Some of us saw the folly in the ways our Elders were leading our people, but we were so few. A warning was sent, and I always wondered whether the message was ever received. Recent events indicate that it may have been.

Alessan threw his hands up in air and made his way briskly across the clearing and stormed into the woods. He called back to C'Aelis, "I give up! I can't decide whether to hate you or pity you."

ᘓ

After the heated argument, Alessan returned to the bank of the small stream where he had bathed earlier that day. Sitting on the grassy slope, he removed his boots and dangled his feet in the cold water. A sudden feeling of homesickness gripped his heart and he valiantly fought back tears.

He realized that he missed the day to day drudgery of the Black Boar. Each day in Briar, albeit relatively boring, had at least some order to it. He knew upon waking what was required of him and which chores had been assigned. Breakfast was always provided with a smile, even on the grimmest of days. He missed the old, practical Varis, always ready with a story. He even missed the man's lectures on virtue and discipline. Above all, he would trade so much for the chance to hear his sister sing once again.

Here in the expanse of the unfamiliar forest, nothing seemed to make sense anymore. The revelations of the past few days were still spinning in his head; some form of magic was in his family line, of which he did not know the capacity or limit, goblin-kind was kin to Gorimm-kind, and the Gorimm were party to the darkest period in the history of Kal Maran. It was all too much for Alessan to take in.

He lost track of time as he sat upon the bank, brooding and tired. The shadows had lengthened by the time he started to pay attention to his surroundings again. The grand adventure he had once sought so desperately had not turned out as anticipated. Corian Praxxus, he thought, would have found a way to enjoy the journey all the same. He smiled sadly when thinking about the big merchant.

I thought you might be hungry, so I took the liberty of preparing some food and tea. I hope not to have been mistaken in my assumption?

How does he do that? Alessan wondered. He had been completely unaware of C'Aelis' approach.

I really don't try to startle you.

Ignoring the answered question, Alessan looked over his shoulder at the Gorimm. "I take it this is a peace offering of sorts?"

Of sorts, C'Aelis nodded. *I know I haven't been overly forthcoming with information, Alessan, but I assure you that hurting you was not my intent. I too, find our circumstances quite difficult to manage. It is not every day that you arrive alone in a place you once called home, and yet feel as though you are now a stranger.*

Alessan sighed and motioned for C'Aelis to sit at his side. "You know, that may very well be the first thing you've said that I actually understand. I guess we are both lost and lonely."

C'Aelis remained silent as he passed the warm bowl to Alessan and pulled off his own boots. Dipping a toe tentatively into the water, he watched with satisfaction as Alessan took a large mouthful of cooked mushrooms.

His anger finally dissipating, Alessan glanced sideways at his friend and asked, "How does one pass the time when you live forever?"

C'Aelis smiled. *We don't live forever, Alessan, although yes, we are long-lived.*

"How long?"

"For some, it can be up to a thousand years. Many of our current Elders have seen at least six hundred summers.

"Are you an Elder?"

My family's longstanding heritage and prestige will undoubtedly bring about at least an offer to sit on the Council, but whether or not I choose to accept is undecided for now.

"Why is that?"

My personal feelings regarding a number of important issues have caused numerous rifts within the Council. Unless my views are treated fairly and with respect, I will regretfully choose to decline.

"So the Gorimm don't differ as much from humankind as I first believed," Alessan commented with a note of humour in his voice. "Squabbling nobles have resulted in the deaths of countless mercenary soldiers since the founding of the Code. Even when the High King reigned, I'm sure the nobles fought over who sat closest."

I'm afraid my absence has left me somewhat deficient when it comes to terms associated with both your history and humour. Although I have done some research since my return to the Aeldenwood, I wonder how easily some of the less free thinking of my kind will adapt to such radical changes.

"Could you really expect anything different with the passing of two centuries?" Alessan asked in disbelief. "Things change, even for you and the Gorimm, C'Aelis. You must have foreseen the great changes to come in Kal Maran."

That may be true in the case of humans, but with the Gorimm that is where you are wrong, C'Aelis nodded, his silver hair bouncing lightly. *My people, because of their long lifespans, are extremely hesitant to any type of change. The smallest decision made by our Council might involve years of debate, a luxury the people of Kal Maran do not have. You would be surprised, Alessan, at how little my culture has changed over the last millennia.*

"That's incredible," Alessan answered. "It's like you're stuck in time."

C'Aelis smiled. *That is one way to look at it.*

ଓ

You must learn to anticipate the thoughts of your enemy, Alessan. A momentary advantage in a fight could easily turn the tide of any battle.

Gasping for air, Alessan leaned heavily on his short sword. "That's easy enough for someone who reads minds."

I cannot read minds, C'Aelis replied with his usual patience. *There is no time in a sword fight to focus on another's thoughts. It is a matter of practice and intuition.*

"If you haven't already noticed, I don't exactly have the proper physique for this type of work," Alessan replied sarcastically.

Your physicality is no excuse. In fact, many opponents will surely underestimate your abilities, granting you an immediate advantage you must look to exploit, the Gorimm replied.

Nodding slightly, Alessan hefted his blade and moved forward. "I can respect that approach. But at the moment, simply surviving a fight would be a miracle."

C'Aelis lifted his own weapon. *You are always interesting, Alessan Oakleaf. I can honestly say, I never know how you might react.*

They spent the remainder of the day sparring in the small grove surrounding the high tower. Alessan had reluctantly agreed to attempt to learn the basics of sword fighting. Thinking about the sheathed sword at his side, it made no sense to Alessan to avoid learning how to wield it skillfully.

The sky peeking out from in between the thick leaves of the overhanging branches soon warned of an impending storm. The wind had picked up since the training session and even now the smaller trees swayed dangerously. As the two men moved about the small clearing, the rumble of thunder sounded ominously in the distance.

Seemingly oblivious to the coming deluge, C'Aelis spared no upward glance to the surrounding trees. Instead, the agile Gorimm continued to instruct Alessan on the use of his weapon and also the proper manner to care for the sword. For someone who professed to be the descendant of a relatively peaceful race, C'Aelis was an obvious master at wielding twin blades. Alessan watched with rapt attention as he remembered daydreaming about experiencing this type of training while completing his chores at the Black Boar.

Alessan continued to sport the Sylvani leather armour he had obtained in his flight through the wood. It fit far more snugly than it once had. C'Aelis had been busy while he had been recovering, mending the tears in the armour as well as altering the fit to properly protect someone of Alessan's size. His weapon had also been sharpened, and he could find no trace of the thick black blood of the Gath that had once stained the steel.

Breathing heavily after running through a variety of exercises, it soon became obvious that he would never amount to much of a fighter, a fact even C'Aelis could not deny. His body had neither the stamina, nor the strength, to sustain a prolonged series of combat moves. Even with the growing strength in his weakest limb, he simply did not have the endurance of a true warrior. Oddly, the discovery pained him far less than expected. Accustomed to the bitter life lessons of his past, in this instance Alessan merely shrugged off the setback. He chose instead to focus on the magic that only he possessed.

Well aware of the lurking danger in the great forest in which he now took refuge, it only seemed prudent to learn something of defense in the event of another ambush by the Gath.

"Why exactly do I have to practice so much?" he asked in between deep breaths. "With what I've learned I think I can defend myself long enough to stay alive until help arrives. I can't possibly learn everything right now."

You have been long in your recovery and we must prepare for a journey. Many dangers will present themselves throughout our travels. We will continue with these lessons daily, even while we travel, C'Aelis replied assuredly.

"And when exactly was I going to be informed of our destination, or the actual journey for that matter?" Alessan asked, somewhat annoyed.

You asked me to provide you with answers after saying that your trust in me had waned. My reluctance to speak of my past is to blame. This journey, I hope, will explain much.

Alright, you have my attention. When can we expect to be travelling?"

If the weather continues to hold, we will be leaving at first light and heading northeast. We have far to travel if we are to arrive in Scholaris before spring's end, C'Aelis replied.

"Scholaris..." Alessan mouthed in wonder. "But the historians of that strange temple are said to frown upon visitors."

I believe in our case they will make an exception, C'Aelis replied with some amusement.

"Why there?" Alessan inquired.

It has long been known as the greatest store of knowledge in all of Kal Maran. I believe it is the only place where I might find what I am searching for.

"And what are you searching for?"

A way to free my people.

Private armies are strictly forbidden. Any deviation from this law will result in the immediate dismantling of said army, as well as prison time for any offending officers. The captain will appear before a military tribunal as selected by administrators of the Ca'lenbam. The tribunal's judgment is final.
—*Mercenary Code of Conduct*

CHAPTER XXXII

Ca'lenbam, Protectorate

The members of the nobility and their representatives were always assigned space near the center of the encampment. Personal retinues were comprised of the only common soldiers allowed anywhere close to the gaudy pavilions. A Gathering was really an excuse for rich and powerful men to showcase their wares. Although a forum for war, the *Ca'lenbam* was no different than any other facet of life for the nobility, and Furnael Berry's disdain for the proceedings was a rarity among his peers.

On occasion, the respective captains of the attending mercenary companies were allowed entry to the centermost part of the camp. New rates or minor ratifications to the Mercenary Code of Conduct usually constituted reason enough for these meetings. Most nobles objected to the lowly born captains being given access to their exalted compounds. Once again, as evidenced by the previous evening's conversation, Duke Berry was an exception to the rule.

On this morning, warm for so early in spring, Gavin could sense something was afoot. He couldn't shake the uneasy feeling in his gut, no matter how hard he tried. If Coren had been there, the scout would most assuredly have agreed with Gavin's instincts.

Thinking about the diminutive Fey'Derin brought a second wave of uncertainty. Gavin had replayed the conversation in his mind again and again. It made no sense to him that both Orn and Coren were under arrest and in confinement. Had they been intoxicated, they would have simply been tossed into a holding tent for the evening and released the next morning. If they had been a part of something more serious, they would have been sober; of that he was certain. He assumed that the two Fey'Derin had uncovered something sinister and were now paying the price for their discovery. At the moment, he preferred not to fret. Worrying was a waste of energy. Once any available options were presented, he first needed to face a magistrate.

Gavin adjusted his uniform and entered a large pavilion adorned with purple and black banners. He had been told that it was here that any who held grievances against the season's sole contract offer could state their cases. As expected, Gavin found more than two dozen company captains inside, all in formal regalia. They stood in small groups, whispering in hushed tones so as not to be heard.

The mercenaries across Caledun often fought alongside likeminded companies, usually those that agreed with their choice of contract, although some did fight only for coin. Gavin had long ago lost patience with the politics of warfare, but had no choice but to remain involved for fear of the consequences. Nodding to a few men he recognized, he made his way towards Herod Blackwain and Dyana Fairwind.

"An interesting gathering of captains," he commented, accepting a glass of wine from Herod and nodding to Dyana. Her hazel eyes flashed at the mention of the assembled leaders, and her short hair bobbed up and down as she shook her head angrily.

"It's an atrocity! Just give me one moment alone with Gadian Yarr..." she hissed.

"Dyana's right, but this seems far less crowded than I would have expected. There are well over three hundred companies camped outside, and yet a mere twenty present themselves for a formal grievance?" Herod replied.

"Have you found out the employer's name yet? I was given little information when the messenger arrived this morning; only that the offer was being funded by Gadian Yarr and his associates." Gavin said, clearly frustrated.

"Then I know little more than you. I don't like surprises, Gavin, and I fear we are about to receive another," Herod looked towards the back entrance with concern.

Flanked by an honour guard, a fully armoured warrior entered the room. He wore the customary short, close-cropped hair and scarred face of a seasoned veteran. Although older than most, he was tall and physically imposing, with an intimidating gaze that commanded the attention of everyone in the room.

"By the gods, it's Gerald Armsmater," whispered Herod.

"The mercenary leader? I thought he retired years ago." Dyana said, a confused look crossing her face.

"So we were led to believe," Gavin replied darkly. "If he is the hidden hand behind the occurrences in the south, we may have underestimated our adversaries..."

Gerald Armsmater was one of the few commanders who had achieved legendary status since the fall of the old kingdom of Caledun. He was considered to be the embodiment of everything that was good in the profession: honourable, cunning, intelligent, and skilled. The aged captain of the Golden Griffins had dominated battlefields for the better part of three decades. His story gave hope to all soldiers who aspired to greatness and to those commoners of low birth; for Gerald himself was the son of a simple farmer.

He had garnered such renown that most of the nobility could no longer afford to pay him. With his supremacy over the battlefield, victory was almost always assured. The man's career was marked by countless triumphs, as well as the heartbreak of losing many men to violent deaths. He was mentioned in the same breath as some of the great leaders of the past: Tomas Greydawn, Ellis Bek, and the depraved Duke Roland Caldwell. By all accounts, Armsmater had retired four years prior, choosing to leave the life of ceaseless combat and disappearing into obscurity.

"Please be seated, gentlemen," called out an accompanying herald. "The General is prepared to address your concerns and answer any questions you may have concerning your contract offer."

Slowly, the mercenary captains found room at a large oak table carried in directly behind General Armsmater's guardsmen. As with every administrative meeting at the Gathering, where each captain sat denoted a hierarchy of sorts among those assembled. Gavin remained standing, Herod and Dyana at his side. The blood soaked fields of Caledun had not seen such a title used since the time of the Shattering.

"Captains, I greet you all warmly. I have had the honour of fighting with some of you in the past, and I must admit that I find it troublesome that you are seated here before me. Others I knew once as enemies, combatants who fought bravely and handled themselves splendidly when faced with adversity," Armsmater began. "But in truth, I am not here before you to listen to your numerous queries and objections. I am also not here to give you one last chance to change your minds or to put an end to your ill-counselled actions."

"Pardon me, sir," the room fell silent as Gavin interrupted. "Few here would ever dream of disputing your reputation, but there has been no general in Caledun since the Shattering. The Code prohibits such a declaration, or the requisite formation of any army larger than two hundred and fifty men under one commander. Only the Chatter Folk of Delfwane have ever received leniency on that matter."

Gerald Armsmater's steely-eyed gaze narrowed slightly, almost imperceptibly, but the gesture was not lost on the Fey'Derin captain.

"Silveron, isn't it?" the general pronounced for all to hear. "You run a good company: disciplined, skilled, obedient, and yet with men of questionable reputations. But you are a man to be respected on the field of battle, or so I have been told."

"I appreciate the compliment, sir," Gavin replied.

"You've made some interesting decisions regarding your allegiances... I am disappointed, but can't say that I'm surprised to see you in such company as this," he swept his arm over the men seated before him.

"Again, with all due respect, sir, Captain Silveron asked you a question," a black-garbed soldier positioned at the doorway called out. Gavin noticed something familiar about the man, but could not place him.

"Young Silveron speaks the truth; the Code does forbid such an assignment," Gerald nodded, drumming his fingers on the edge of the table. "Fortunately for me, the Code no longer holds sway in the Protectorate. My army, and those I have hired at this rabble of a Gathering, now dictate all terms of the Code."

Glancing sideways at his companions, Gavin tried to remain calm during the uproar the man's bold statement had elicited from those gathered.

"I have nothing but respect for you, Gerald. Cursed Arne, we fought at each other's sides many a time, but you go too far!" announced Tarben Eld, one of the more veteran captains near the front of the table.

"I remember fondly those times, Tarben. I do." Gerald smiled and for a moment his features softened.

"Spare me the pleasantries, Gerald. I want an answer."

Holding up a heavy gauntlet, the general calmly waited for silence. He then continued in a very businesslike tone. "I will repeat this only once, so you would all do well to remain attentive. My army, the Protectorate Army, is camped less than a league to the south. I have the freedom to do what I will with those who have deemed themselves not worthy to follow our march north. Garchester has already fallen, and Matanis is already on the brink."

Gavin reeled in shock. *Lord Berry had lost his city*? Little doubt remained that the nobleman's life was also in danger. Gavin tried desperately to collect his thoughts.

"You've launched an attack before the summer season?" cried Herod in disbelief. "Have you gone mad?!"

General Armsmater gave Herod a sly grin. "I can assure you that I am perfectly sane, Captain Blackwain, but let us return to the matter at hand. All of you, your rank as captain with your current company is hereby revoked, and your status as officers is under review."

The table erupted in chaos as the captains rose furiously and howled their objections. General Armsmater continued to speak over the din.

"Your men will be incorporated into the Protectorate Army in order to quell any heroic notions of rebellion you may be entertaining. I will personally meet with all of you to determine your new status and assignments. Your men will be paid well, but their loyalty is now to the Protectorate. It is time we forged a new nation out of the ruins of the old."

"And Gadian Yarr is the one to lead us to this promised land, *General*?" Gavin fought to maintain his poise.

"The matters of the Protectorate are for those of the inner council to decide and not the concerns of the common soldier. You would do well to stay silent, Silveron, lest I grow weary of your tongue." The general's voice was like iron. "You have until tomorrow to notify your men. By mid-morning, you are all to report to my command area. At the appointed hour, my officers will have further instructions for each of you."

And with that, Gerald Armsmater, legendary soldier of fortune, broke the very foundations of the Mercenary Code, and left the pavilion.

"Has the man gone daft?!" asked Herod, amidst the uproar that continued following the general's declaration. "He must know that all other political factions won't stand for such behaviour. Gadian Yarr has just declared war!"

"Come, let us leave this place. I need to speak with the magistrate before rejoining my men," Gavin said, leading both Herod and Dyana outside in order to escape the angry, raised voices coming from within. Arguing at this point, Gavin thought, was nothing but a waste of time. It was obvious there would be no talking sense to the newly declared general. Armsmater had made his choice; soon Gavin would have to make his own.

"It's certain that our companies have been under watch since this morning," Herod stated as they pushed through the crowd.

"I took precautions before coming here today. We've known for some time now that something was amiss, and I wasn't going to chance the lives of my men," Gavin replied. He suddenly pulled both Herod and Dyana into a space between two large tents.

He gripped their arms and whispered, "Listen to me, both of you. Get your soldiers moving the minute you arrive back at your camps. My men will be drawing enough attention as it is, so use my Fey'Derin to cover your own escape."

"Gavin I wo —" Dyana tried to express her concern.

"We don't have time!" Gavin hissed. "Promise me you will get your soldiers out and head north towards Dragon Mount. Tell them Silvares sent you, and you'll be granted entrance. There's no time for explanations."

To his credit, Herod Blackwain paused only briefly before nodding in assent. Dyana took a moment longer to weigh her options. Then, with a fiery determination in her eyes, she also agreed.

Satisfied, Gavin turned away from his companions and disappeared into the crowd. He had little time before the Fey'Derin made their move. It was essential that Orn and Coren were back in his custody as soon as possible. If not, there was no guarantee they wouldn't be slaughtered the very moment the Fey'Derin treachery was revealed. Gavin had never left a man behind – ever; and he had resolved not to break that rule on this occasion.

Thankfully, the offices of the magistrate were within close proximity of the central pavilions, allowing for a short walk through a far less crowded thoroughfare. Spotting the sign on a large tent, he rushed inside, avoiding two drunken louts loitering by the entrance. Gavin was surprised to find a dozen of the general's guards already stationed in the interior. It was now apparent that Armsmater had every key sector garrisoned with his own men; all loyal to the core, no doubt.

The magistrate's tent was sparsely decorated with only a few wooden tables and several chests full of documents on the ground. Two elderly gentlemen, dressed in costly aristocratic livery, sat patiently behind one of the tables, quills in hand. Pushing past the two of the general's guards, Gavin approached.

"State your name, rank, company, and request," droned one of the scribes with disinterest.

"Gavin Silveron, Captain of the Fey'Derin, here upon summons for the release of Orn Surefoot and Coren D'Elmark."

Shifting through a large stack of paper at his side, the scribe pursed his lips thoughtfully as he retrieved a series of documents. "Both men were arrested for assaulting the General's soldiers. Surefoot is also being held in connection with the resulting death of one of those same men. It does appear that both your soldiers were intoxicated at the time of their arrest."

Cursing silently, Gavin knew that the damning report had to be a lie. That Armsmater's soldiers were involved could only mean one thing; the two scouts had sifted through the rumours and had gleaned enough information to warrant an attack. For the moment, this was the scenario Gavin chose to believe. He preferred to trust his men and give them every benefit of the doubt. If, in fact, they were to blame, Gavin swore they would come to rue this day.

"I would like to speak with my men, please. As well, I would request that they be released into my custody pending a formal review of the incident. If you look at my record, you will see that it is impeccable; both men will not be leaving my sight," Gavin stated.

"I'm sorry, Captain Silveron," the scribe replied, shaking his head. "General Armsmater has declared that all serious cases pending review are to be dealt with by the General exclusively."

Gavin nearly choked. Struggling to compose himself and control his mounting frustration, he probed further. "And how many other cases would that include?"

Shifting through the papers once more, the man finally replied. "Why, it appears to be only yours, Captain. My sincerest apologies that I could not be of better service to you, sir, but you may inquire regarding the fate of your men at General Armsmater's pavilion."

Cʒ

Ethan Shade, wearing his long, black leather coat, stood inside the tent entrance, impatiently fingering his rapier. "Nearly time, Lieutenant," he said, peeking outside for what seemed like the tenth time in the last few minutes.

"Damn you, Sergeant! If I hear another word out of those lips of yours, I'll have you castrated," Caolte Burnaise growled.

"Understood, sir," Ethan replied quietly. "We're all worried, Lieutenant, I'm sure Gavin is fine," he added after a moment's hesitation.

"Gods above!" Caolte fumed, throwing a dark look towards Ethan. The Fey'Derin's second-in-command added, "Ossric, please tear this man's tongue out. That's an order."

Tension filled the air at the Fey'Derin camp. With their captain now absent for the better part of the morning, his whereabouts unknown, the company officers realized that their plan might commence without the one man they all trusted. With preparations for their escape now complete, there was nothing any of the officers could do but wait.

"Caolte, I know the Captain said he would be here, but we need to be realistic. He gave us an order, and if it were to be his last, then I plan on executing it," Ossric said, rising from his seat and pacing about the tent.

The veteran lieutenant sighed deeply. "I know, I know..." he muttered to himself.

Caolte Burnaise had known Gavin far longer than any of the other men in the company. There was no secret that the *Drayenmark* warrior also knew much about Gavin's shrouded past. He had even trained him for a short while during his rapid rise through the mercenary ranks, and it was wearing on him that no word had been sent by his friend.

Placing a hand on Caolte's shoulder, Brock mustered a weak smile. "He'll be fine, Lieutenant. Let's worry about the rest of the men."

"I trust that all preparations have been made?" Caolte asked, looking to the Eagle Runner sergeant.

"Aye, sir," Ethan answered. "All saddlebags are packed and ready. The men have placed them just inside their tents, easily within reach once we give the word."

"Estimated time for a full departure?" Caolte inquired.

"As fast as a watch change, quicker if the newer recruits keep their nerves under control," Brock answered.

"I placed all recruits in my squad with a trusted veteran. If there's a breakdown, they will be guided through any difficulties," Ethan added.

"Good. I trust the others have done the same?"

"Aye, sir," the others responded in unison.

"Has Duke Berry arrived?" the *Drayen* lieutenant finally asked.

"I have six of my best Axemen escorting him even as we speak," Ossric replied confidently. "It would have looked too suspicious if I had met the Duke, so Kevan is leading the squad."

"Excellent. He's a competent soldier and will keep the man safe," Caolte commented. "Sergeant Shade, pass the word that we'll be leaving immediately upon Duke Berry's arrival."

"Yes, Lieutenant," Ethan confirmed the order with a salute.

Caolte looked over the assembled officers. "Alert all sentries that their partners should have mounts ready and tied to their own. Also, check with Garett and see who's on point. He'll know by now what sort of opposition we'll face in the woods to the west. The Eagle Runners will form the rearguard, Ethan. Choose your best for that assignment," Caolte ordered.

Ethan nodded curtly and ducked under the tent flap. Lieutenant Burnaise turned to the rest of the officers. "Alright then, gather your belongings if you haven't already done so. Don your armour and wait with your squads, I'll pass word through Ethan's runners once I'm ready. Gods be with us."

༄

"Please be seated, Captain Silveron, and make yourself comfortable," General Armsmater said.

"I prefer to stand, thank you," Gavin retorted cautiously.

"Come now, sit and relax," the famous general replied. "I merely want to speak with you; nothing more, nothing less."

Gavin took a seat across from the aged mercenary commander and sat in silence. His visit had been expected. The soldiers guarding Gerald Armsmater had been briefed, and they let Gavin through with no questions asked. He had been forced through three separate checkpoints, bypassing numerous diplomats waiting for an audience with the new commanding officer of the Protectorate Army. News of the general's appointment and subsequent declarations had swept through the *Ca'lenbam* like a bristling fire over grasslands. Gavin was disgusted by the thought of the political maneuverings that were likely to be in full swing, with members of the nobility trying in vain to cement their highborn status with the new regime. Gavin likened the response to a pack of wild dogs devouring their prey, each one tearing at the corpse in the hopes of receiving even a tiny scrap of anything that remained.

Gavin had been ushered, without pomp or ceremony, to the main administrative quarters of the nobility, where the once retired general was busy setting up his command post. Heavy, military-style tents were being rapidly placed where gaudy pavilions had once stood. It seemed to him that the new General of the Protectorate had little patience for the comforts enjoyed by those of noble birth.

Lords and ladies, wearing their finest clothing, were making unsuccessful attempts to countermand General Armsmater's orders. Their complaints fell on deaf ears, as stoic, hardened soldiers refused to entertain the spoiled prattling of the upper classes. Despite the circumstances, Gavin couldn't help but be somewhat amused. If anyone in all of Kal Maran could use a little humbling, it was the nobility.

"Feran will be arriving shortly with some refreshments. And don't worry, Captain, we will be dealing with the unfortunate criminal charges against two of your men. Until then, we have some time to discuss some matters of great importance," Armsmater said with some embellishment. "To begin, I would like to commend you once again on your Fey'Derin company. They are excellent soldiers, well-trained and quite an interesting lot, no?"

"My men are no concern of yours, General," Gavin answered firmly.

"Ah but they are, Captain. You see, we have been watching you very closely these past few years..."

"We?" Gavin interjected.

"My associates and I," Armsmater smiled cunningly. "Now, as I was saying, your company has proven quite effective on the battlefield regardless of the checkered histories of your men. It is an accomplishment that I deem impossible to overlook. So much so, that we have decided that you would be a worthy ally."

"You treat your allies strangely, General; taking away their company, and yet praising their ability to lead," Gavin retorted.

"Point well taken, Captain Silveron, but let me explain," Armsmater implored, waving in a guard carrying a silver tray containing goblets of red wine and a thick loaf of fresh bread.

"Please go on," Gavin said politely.

"I don't negotiate. My reputation over the years will attest to that. I make an offer, and it is either accepted or refused. And yet," he continued, "here I am, breaking bread with you, in an effort to change your mind. Many would say you have been granted an exceptional honour."

"I'm listening," Gavin replied.

"Excellent! That, at least, is a beginning," Armsmater laughed. "Now then, may I ask you something, Captain?"

"As you would say, General Armsmater, for the moment you hold all of the cards, and therefore I would be remiss in declining."

The general sipped his wine. "For a man who shies away from political opportunities, you seem well versed in the intricacies of negotiation, young Silveron."

"This is a business negotiation, is it not?"

"Well said, once again," Gerald chuckled. "And so, on to my question. I was wondering where you hail from, Captain? I will admit that despite my best efforts, your past continues to elude me. From what I can gather, it seems as though you did not exist before walking into the training yards of Black Company seven years ago."

"What importance does my past have with your offer? I fail to see the significance as part of this negotiation," Gavin said, with a tinge of impatience.

"When one seeks to form an alliance, Captain, one should know everything possible about the other party; even more so, if the man were to become an enemy," he added pointedly. "Do you really have a problem with the way our world is fashioned?" he continued. "This shattered kingdom has provided for you and given you a purpose in life. Men with our skills have been given the rare opportunity to make something of ourselves, attaining both wealth and power."

Gavin took a moment to contemplate before responding. "There are many problems with our world, General, but I do believe it should remain governed by the Code if the only other option is open war."

"The Code is outdated!" Armsmater's voice rose up in anger. "It was created to control the anarchy that erupted over the death —"

"Assassination," Gavin corrected.

"— assassination... of a king," he conceded. "In the aftermath of the Shattering, the populace needed guidance and protection, hence the reasoning behind the Mercenary Code of Conduct. Its time has come and gone, Captain Silveron. Is it so wrong to hope for unification?" Armsmater asked.

"I have no problem with a unified kingdom, but I do not believe its leader should be Gadian Yarr," Gavin answered truthfully. "Nor do I believe in the cost in lives it would take for peace to be forged from such bloodshed. It isn't worth the end result."

"Men die every summer, Captain," Armsmater countered. "It has become a way of life. And who would you place in Gadian Yarr's stead? The mad, true heir, Serian Rhone? He would drive the world further into shambles."

"And his son, Kaimon?" Gavin suggested. "By all accounts, he is a good man, in no way tainted with the curse of madness beset on his forefathers."

"He is precisely no different than his father! Can you be so blind, Captain Silveron? I offer you a chance to fight at my side, with the power of a unified nation behind us. I am offering you a post in my command, a valued member of my war council," Gerald Armsmater paced impatiently around the room as he spoke, his eyes displaying a fervor that Gavin found disconcerting. The legendary commander exuded a powerful aura; one that even Gavin could see was incredibly alluring.

"I am not interested," Gavin answered flatly.

"If money is your concern, I can pay you handsomely. Our coffers are deep, and one officer's pay is of no concern. Think on it, Silveron, and don't try to tell me you aren't sorely tempted by my offer."

Gavin nodded. "I can admit I am not immune to praise, General, but I am still not interested. Flattered, yes. My company will travel north after this year, as it has been too long since we have been home. I do have one contract yet to fulfill before we do so."

"Signed with that fool, Furnael Berry?" Armsmater asked menacingly.

"He is my employer, and more than a fair one at that. After this summer, I think I will leave you to your war."

"You are a fool, boy," Armsmater hissed.

"Perhaps, but you realize that your proclamation will bring about the combined wrath of the other leading factions of the land. Glenvale, the Northern Council, and especially the *Drayenmark,* will not be pleased," Gavin responded calmly.

"You forget, Captain, that the merchants of Innes Vale will support the highest bidder, and the Iron Shield has been hard-pressed on all fronts this past year. They will have scant little to offer the north. Even the Dwarves of Alerond refuse to embroil themselves in the affairs of men," Armsmater replied knowingly. "Were Furnael Berry to mobilize, there would be no help coming from Glenvale this season. By next year, the south will be firmly in Gadian Yarr's control; a new nation set to increase its borders come spring."

"I don't deny that possibility, General."

Gavin realized that he was in uncharted territory now that he had refused the renowned commander's offer. Glancing at the entryway, he tried his best to discern the time. Judging by the shadows near the open doorway, he knew he had scant time remaining before his men rode out. He would never see the light of day again were they to move out while he remained with the general. And there was still the matter of Orn and Coren.

"Please excuse me, General, but I really must be going. My men will be wondering what is keeping me, and as per your instructions, there is much to discuss with them. I have only need of the two men you currently hold."

"Your men will remain in my custody," Armsmater replied distractedly.

"Then I wish to speak with them. It is within my right to do so as their commanding officer," Gavin replied, having no other choice or angle to work.

He realized then, that Gerald Armsmater was not of sound mind. Something inside of him, be it a result of age or something else, had snapped. He could not even comprehend that someone would dare defy him. It was clear to Gavin that Gadian Yarr had corrupted the legendary warrior with promises of unprecedented power. Long ago, Gavin had been taught that unchecked power easily corrupts, and before him now stood a man who proved such a proverb to be true.

Armsmater glared at Gavin, his eyes full of anger. "Guards! Bring the two prisoners here. I have need of them!" he barked at the two men standing at attention near the entryway.

Gavin watched in despair as the two Fey'Derin scouts were brought out before him. Coren managed a weak smile, although his face was etched with pain. He was thrown forward and crumpled to the hard ground. Coren was badly bruised, and his clothes hung from his body in bloody tatters. He looked to have been beaten by a mob, but he was still breathing.

Looking at the other scout, Gavin wasn't even sure if Orn Surefoot was still alive. He was bleeding from a deep head wound, and had a gruesome broken bone protruding from his lower left leg. Blood had soaked through his clothing at the knees, clotting where Gavin assumed there was another terrible wound. Orn's eyes were glazed over, but he recognized Gavin immediately. It must have taken a monumental effort for the man to croak out one simple sentence. "I was sober, Captain."

"Silence!" roared the general, backhanding Orn across the mouth.

"By the gods, what have you done?!" Gavin sputtered, barely able to control his mounting fury. Few were the times he could remember being so close to losing all control.

"I have done nothing! These men attacked my soldiers and were dealt with harshly, as we do with all transgressors!" Armsmater shouted in return. "And I will ask you once again to change your mind, Captain, and accept my offer of alliance. Will you join the Protectorate?"

"I have already answered your question! Now release these men into my custody, and let me be gone. I have no quarrel with you and only wish to leave, but your treatment of my men is an offense," Gavin treaded carefully.

The next few moments would forever be etched in Gavin Silveron's memory. Time slowed almost to a standstill, and even the scream that echoed from his own throat was drawn out and slurred. Gavin watched in horror as Gerald Armsmater drew his long belt knife while ruthlessly yanking Orn's head back by the hair. Gavin made eye contact with Orn, and for a brief moment, there was complete silence.

Then, with savage glee, the general drew his knife across Orn's throat. Blood gushed forth from the wound as the scout fell face forward and buckled to the earth, his lifeblood pouring out beneath him. As he lay there motionless, it pooled under his cheeks, soaking slowly into the hard, dry ground.

"NOOOOOOOOOOOO!" Gavin screamed, his cry echoed by Coren. Running to the fallen man's side, Gavin cradled Orn's lifeless head in his arms, blood soaking through his company tabard and drenching his hands.

"I will ask you one last time tomorrow, Captain Silveron," said a voice. The words were muted, spoken as if from a great distance. Lifting his head, Gavin locked gazes with the man who had murdered Orn.

"You are a dead man," he swore.

"I think not, Captain," Armsmater replied. "Your other soldier dies in the morning if your answer is not to my liking. Remember, *I* am now the law of this land," he finished and left the room. His guards followed, with Coren being pulled roughly behind.

Sitting there, alone with the still warm body of Orn Surefoot, Gavin wept.

In times of old, protected by the ever-present An'Dari, the High Kings of Caledun hunted in the untamed wilderness of the Iron Shield, heedless of any danger.
—*Valen Col, The Uncharted Wilds*

CHAPTER XXXIII

Lok'Dal hie, The Wilds

The column stretched out far off into the distance. Long rows of goblin fighters strode purposefully along the dirt road. It was difficult to see more than the top half of each warrior, so thick was the cloud of dust that billowed up from their marching feet. Tall, fluttering banners were held high by standard bearers, and the snap of the pennants could be heard even from a distance. Accompanying the jangle of metal armour and weapons, came the pounding of war drums; the deep, booming reverberations causing the very ground to rumble.

The goblin soldiers kept their eyes fixed on the road before them, their gazes unflinching even while faced with the brilliant rays of the rising sun. A veritable train of wagons and pack mules brought up the rear of the long column. The goblins were well armed, with each warrior carrying some type of sword, heavy maul, or hammer. Those marching beneath certain standards also carried crossbows, steel-tipped spears, and barbed pikes. The formations wore dyed tabards in an assortment of dark colours overtop of studded leather armour reinforced with metal plates. They marched as a unified whole, at once both confident and with resolute purpose.

"How many do you count?" Leoric asked. He leaned against the handle of his shovel, staring at the passing column with genuine concern. He had been watching the early morning procession for quite some time before Finn Callum had sauntered up to join him.

"With the dust those bastards are kicking up, it's hard to tell. At least four thousand," Finn replied, anxiously biting his lower lip. "But I'd wager there are more than a dozen unique standards assembled down there. Why they aren't all tearing each other apart is my greatest concern."

"Even over their numbers?" Leoric asked with some surprise.

"Aye, even over their numbers," Finn replied sternly. "Someone, or something, must have had a hand in this unification of the tribes. The goblins' bloody civil wars have kept our lands relatively safe from any military campaigns for ages. The savages have always done much of the nasty work of the Shield themselves. Something has changed the order of things here in the Wilds, and I believe it is just as important to uncover that secret as it is for you and the others to escape and warn the borderland keeps."

"Gods... there are a lot of them. It looks like the *Derlak, Sunfo'ol, She'rian,* and *Trafa'l* are leading the whole procession, but I don't recognize that black banner in the vanguard," Leoric commented.

Finn squinted into the morning light before answering. "There's a serpent on the banner, so that would be the *Mori'el.* They live near the southern edge of the Wilds, closer to Kelamyre than Darkenedge. Our patrols have engaged with them often, and they were part of the ambush that tore my company apart. I'm surprised you haven't heard of them."

"The Marshal always believed that the tribes were hiding their true strength, and the difficult terrain in the Wilds always did hamper our attempts at determining even approximate troop numbers. Before we were ambushed, I don't think any of the veterans of Darkenedge had seen a raiding party number much more than six score, all from the same tribe, of course," Leoric said, continuing to marvel at the terrifying sight.

"Any of the keeps, Hilltop included, would be hard-pressed to hold off a siege against an army of this size," Finn stated.

"I think you may be right."

"I doubt this army represents one of the lead elements of our enemy," Finn explained patiently. "If the outlying patrols of our forts have already been hit by sizable forces, it is fair to assume that large companies of goblins already lay claim to much of the land we once patrolled with relative impunity. Did you note the way they marched, Leoric?" he asked.

"Like they've been training for a lengthy period of time," Leoric answered gravely.

"Exactly," Finn nodded. "And that can only mean that this invasion has been a long time coming."

"The Shield must be warned," Leoric declared, a determined tone to his voice. "I have been waiting for a sign, something that would prompt me to act, but I still wonder why the others would follow me."

"You have an element of trust in those eyes of yours, Leoric; that in itself brings confidence and a calm assurance to any who call you friend. Unlike Joram, you don't strive for power and influence; it is instead part of your nature. Strangely, Auric possesses a similar aura."

"Auric?" Leoric questioned, raising an eyebrow.

"There is much that man hides, always speaking with that evasive tongue of his. Look past his strange demeanor, and I guarantee you'll find something deeper. When he was younger, he would have been a formidable presence. I suspect that after a lifetime of slavery that he is tired and knows that the better part of his life is now behind him. It is easier to let a younger man take up the burden."

"Burden?" Leoric asked, confused by the soldier's choice of words.

"The burden of leadership, Leoric," Finn answered simply.

"The leadership of our community is not in question, Finn. You are the highest ranking officer among us; that mantle is yours," Leoric replied.

"My rank means nothing to these people, least of all to those who have watched you defend the weak and support the greater good," Finn added.

Falling silent, Leoric frowned and turned back towards the procession. Hearing such compliments from Finn Callum made him uncomfortable. He was a simple retired farmer, thrust into the role of soldier after circumstances had left him bereft of wife and child. He was no leader of men, no champion of the poor; only a man hoping to do some good in a world filled with despair.

"What kind of leader leaves his friends?" Leoric asked.

A rueful smile appeared on Finn's lips. "The kind that ensures those left behind have the confidence to weather their own storm. You'd be surprised by the result of a little inspiration."

"You know, for a borderland captain, you have quite a way with words." Leoric chuckled. "In all seriousness, I'd like your honest assessment of that army," he motioned towards the slowly disappearing dust cloud.

"Well for one thing, they are slow. Without any mounted troops, I think that even in unknown territory, your band would travel faster. The wagon train will be slowed by the mud when it rains and, in general, by the tangled trails of the Wilds. Granted their outriders are most assuredly swift, but I would say the lot of you have a chance," Finn finished.

"I agree with your assessment, Captain Callum. We leave soon," Leoric declared. "When?"

"Tomorrow night."

ɔ

With the difficult decision now behind him, Leoric was now focused on the countless small details that needed his attention. If the escape attempt was to have any real chance of success they needed to be prepared. He quietly passed confirmation to the others in the small group, each member's reaction revealing an overwhelming sense of relief. Cara's eyes had immediately welled up with tears; of joy or sadness, Leoric could not tell. Benoit and Angvald had gripped him tightly in a communal embrace. Lastly, Auric had merely given a slight nod, with what seemed like a look of approval dancing behind his cagey eyes. Recalling Finn's earlier comments, Leoric could not help but pause and wonder what the old man might be hiding behind that gaze.

Leoric turned his thoughts back to the business at hand. It would not pay to make a mistake now, not after the great risks they had all taken in preparing for the journey. Yet he could not get Kieri out of his mind. She was completely unaware of the plans, and had no idea what was soon to occur. She would go to sleep tomorrow evening under his protection, but would wake to find him gone... vanished... and soon to be nothing more than a memory.

I promised her I would protect her...

Disheartened, Leoric silently cursed his luck. It felt like a cruel twist of fate and tragically poetic, that after such a long period of struggle and frustration, that they would be blessed with only one short week together. For Leoric, it was a time like few he could remember.

After moving out from under the brutal hand of the sadist Joram, Kieri had quickly rediscovered her love for life; a love that she communicated flawlessly with every word, gesture, and smile. Leoric had known her to forever be wearing a look of sadness, but that had disappeared. The weight that she had carried while with with Joram had dissipated, almost as if it had never existed.

She had moved into the dorm with the other women without much notice. Joram had attempted to persuade her otherwise, but with Leoric's powerful presence looming at her shoulder, she had refused the man. Joram had reacted by sending a dark stare of hatred in their direction as he stalked back across the compound towards his private home.

Leoric had remained on guard with Angvald that night, certain that the once dominant bully would undoubtedly strike out in revenge. Leoric believed that it was not in Joram's nature to do otherwise.

But nothing untoward had occurred; at least not as of yet, Leoric reminded himself. The camp itself remained on high alert for the better part of the following days, with most captives anticipating a final showdown between the camp's two divided factions. Seven days after Kieri left Joram for Leoric, most were still waiting for the moment of retribution.

Leoric soon found himself among the press of people jostling to find a spot within the common room. Surrounded by a bevy of friends, Cara and Angvald included, Kieri caught his eye from across the crowded floor. She waved at him, and Leoric could barely suppress the urge to throw aside all his carefully laid plans and remain here in the camp with her. How she had managed to capture his heart remained a mystery, one that he had little compulsion to solve. He preferred to simply enjoy every moment that remained.

"What's with the sad look?" Kieri frowned, hugging him tightly.

Feigning surprise, Leoric gave a weak attempt at a smile. "I was just thinking is all. Can't a man do that without being questioned?"

"Sometimes you are so odd," she smiled, kissing him lightly on the cheek. It was a small public gesture that had become quite frequent. It reminded Leoric that Kieri had truly chosen him, and that she was unafraid of hiding that attraction.

"I saw you talking with Angvald and Cara. What lies were those two telling about me?" he asked mockingly.

"Now look who's asking all the questions," Kieri pouted, wrapping her fingers around his hand. "And I'll have you know that Angvald warned me that you'd ask just such a question, so I can only wonder if his tales aren't really true."

Leoric gently led her through the crowd, his heart pounding as he struggled to deal with his present dilemma. Leading her towards the back entrance, he gamely avoided her curious stare as she realized where he was leading them.

Once outside, they walked silently towards one of the large wagons that Auric lovingly maintained for his journeys into *Lok'Dal hie*. Holding Kieri's hand tightly, he continued to avoid her eyes, even as he gently lifted her into the front seat. Sliding into the spot beside her, he looked up and stared off into the night sky.

"Leoric, what's wrong?" Kieri asked. "You don't seem yourself."

Ignoring the question, Leoric continued to watch the stars. "Do you ever wonder whether or not people in whose lives we've spent time remember us? Do we ever enter their thoughts on occasion?" he asked quietly.

Kieri firmly grasped his chin, turning his head in her direction. "Look at me," she said, a touch of sorrow in her voice. "Tell me what's going on. Is this about your daughter?"

Leoric glanced downward at the mention of Maya. Everything led back to her, whether he wanted to admit it or not. Just as he had abandoned her, so too was he now planning to abandon the woman he loved.

"This isn't about Maya," he finally said. "Kieri, would you miss me? Would you forget me if I was gone?" he asked abruptly.

She looked deep into his eyes. "Leo, you know I would. I would miss you every day and would always wonder about your well-being. But why ask such a terrible thing?" she whispered.

In that moment, broken by her sheer anguish and confusion, Leoric made one of the most painful decisions of his life. Reaching out and grasping Kieri's outstretched hands, he pulled her close.

His body trembled as he whispered in her ear, "Kieri, I have to leave you."

"W... what are you talking about?" she cried, devastated by his words. Tears ran down her cheeks as she tried to pull away from him, but he would not let her go. Unwilling to prolong the hurt for any longer, Leoric looked at her earnestly and told her everything.

◌ℨ

On the appointed night, sleep, as Leoric knew it most assuredly would be, remained elusive. Hours after he had finally settled down upon his old cot, he could barely contain a rising tide of nervous excitement. From the moment his head had touched the uncomfortable pallet, his heart had started pounding. It took some time before the feeling passed, and although he had found a way to keep his nerves under control, he was by no means calm.

To pass the time as he waited, Leoric continued to go over each item that was needed, each movement that would be made, each part that they would all have to play if the escape attempt was to be successful. The food had been well secreted, and the ropes, torches and extra clothing carefully hidden within bales of hay. The crucial maps were safely held by Auric, but Leoric's mind mulled constantly over each and every detail.

Only the tinder and flint remained absent from the list of items they had painstakingly hoarded and secreted away. That it remained in Joram's house only further aggravated the situation. It was not so much that Joram had access to an essential tool that infuriated Leoric, but rather that the man continued to fawn over their goblin overseers.

After Leoric's heartfelt confession, Kieri had bravely offered to steal the tinder and flint, but he was adamant that she remain uninvolved. The last thing he wanted was to put her in any danger, and a return to that dark house could only end in tragedy.

They spent the rest of the night together, speaking about life and all of their possible futures. Leoric would remember the evening for the rest of his life; so perfect were the stars, the warm breeze, and her company. They had slept outside, risking the wrath of their goblin captors, and found comfort in holding one another. Leoric had vowed to return and rescue her once his mission in the Iron Shield was over.

Kieri insisted that he not change his plans for her sake. She trusted him, and believed him when he said he would return for her. Leoric could do little but fret over her future. He had entrusted Finn Callum with her continued protection, but he was still worried.

Lying there in the deepening gloom, Leoric was struck by how much he was going to miss her. Somehow Kieri had penetrated the walls he had so painstaking built around his heart, bringing him so much joy in so little time that he wondered if it was all just a dream. *Alanna would have really liked her*, he thought sadly. *And Maya too...*

In full darkness, and with the exhausted snores of the other men surrounding him, Leoric quietly slipped from his bed and crouched patiently on the floor. He listened to the heavy breathing and waited until he was completely sure that the others were sound asleep. Passing the cot that held the large sleeping shadow of his good friend Angvald, Leoric paused and reached out a hand. Immediately it was clutched by the iron grip of the big Kaleenian.

As they had practiced numerous times before, the two men swiftly crossed the open compound, careful to avoid any of the patrolling guards. They staggered their departures from the homestead in order to keep activity to a minimum. Leoric had ordered everyone to keep to the routine. It had worked up until that point and to alter it in any way seemed foolish.

The plan was simple. Auric would meet them in the field with the maps. Cara and Benoit would collect the stolen food supplies, meet up with Auric, and wait until Angvald and Leoric arrived with the ropes, torches, and clothing. Once together in the field, they would do a final check of their supplies and immediately head west, hoping to reach the defensive battlements before dawn. At the base of the wall, they would quickly decide whether a roped descent was possible. If not, the group would swim the river located two leagues to the north.

By morning they expected to have put enough distance between themselves and their captors to allow for a chance at freedom. Leoric felt that if they could shirk pursuit long enough to reach the large river crossing, the group would have a fighting chance.

The warehouse door creaked noisily as Leoric and Angvald slipped in through the entrance. The darkness was so complete that Leoric needed a moment to fight off a bout of disorientation. Walking briskly through the pitch black area, he barely contained a curse as he tripped over a soft bundle on the ground. Curiously reaching down to see what was in his path, a muffled sound from further ahead caught his attention. As his hand came to rest on the object at his feet, he knew instantly that it was a body.

The hiss and sputter of torches being lit immediately followed his discovery. Backing up and away from the body, Leoric watched in horror as the light slowly illuminated the garish countenance of Joram and his goons. The borderman's heart sunk even further when he realized that a half dozen goblin guards stood stoically in the shadows. A quick glance at his feet confirmed his belief. On the ground lay the motionless forms of both Cara and Benoit.

"So good of you to join us, D'Athgaran," Joram gloated, his eyes flitting across the fallen bodies. "Your friends have already arrived, although I'm not sure they intended to arrive like this." Without faltering, he casually motioned towards the rear of the group.

In horror, Leoric watched as Kieri was carried forward, her mouth gagged and her arms bound tightly behind her back. Her face was pale with several large bruises visible. Fighting a murderous rage, Leoric was calmed by Angvald's firm grip upon his arm.

"Control yourself, Leoric, or she'll be dead before you know it," Angvald whispered.

Joram walked over to Kieri, removed her gag, and kissed her roughly on the lips. Revolted, she valiantly struggled to escape.

"If you needed tinder and flint why couldn't you just have asked?" he said with a devilish grin. "For the right price I might have even conceded to the request."

"Leoric, I'm sorry!" Kieri wailed. Apart from the bruises, the stricken look on her face told the tale. "He made me tell him. I just wanted to help!"

"I know Kieri, I know," Leoric shouted.

"I love you, Leoric. Know that I love you!" she called out.

Hearing the exchange, an angry flush darkened Joram's features. With a cry of rage, he turned and backhanded the defenseless woman. Shocked by the blow, she cried out in pain.

"Shut up, woman! You're mine now, and you will love me!" Joram shrieked.

A wave of outrage overcame Leoric, and he lost all control. "You bastard, I'll kill you!" he roared while unfurling a cocked fist. He caught Joram standing flat footed and sent him sprawling backwards.

Even as the blow landed, two goblin guards attacked, their axe shafts striking his ribs and dropping Leoric to the floor. The blows continued to fall, each one sending ripples of pain through his battered frame. Dimly, through the agony, he could see Angvald valiantly struggling against his own guards and paying a severe price for his courage.

With his senses reeling, Leoric was eventually dragged to his feet. Unable to support his own weight, he hung limply between the two goblin guards, their expressions a mix of disgust and hatred.

"You would do well to know your betters, Leoric," Joram sneered as he threw a hard right.

Leoric spat and locked eyes with the leech. "It looks as though you've been in a fight Joram, one that wasn't going too well either."

Sputtering with fury, the man rained down a series of blows, but Leoric barely felt them. His body hurt enough without the added attack. Instead, he focused his gaze upon the sobbing form of Kieri. She had once again paid the price because of his actions. Had he just been able to keep the secret of his impending departure she would never have attempted to retrieve the insignificant item. She had only tried to help and now she would be tied to the bastard once more, for Leoric had no doubt of his own fate.

"Do what you will with me, Joram. If you plan on killing me then get it over with. I've had enough of you and will welcome a break from that ugly mug of yours," Leoric said wearily.

Joram laughed. "Oh, death would be too easy a fate for you and your friends, Leoric. Killing you would end your pain, and I want you to be tormented for the rest of your long, hard life. I want you to remember that from this day forth, Kieri will be spending her nights in my bed. I want you to know she will be pleasing me, and my men, and there is nothing you can do about it."

Stunned by the outburst, Leoric said nothing.

"That's right you fool, it's off to the *Shalo'k* Mine for all of you. Goodbye, Leoric, I hope I haunt your dreams," he finished in a quiet whisper meant only for Leoric's ears.

As he was led away, Leoric felt an overwhelming sense of failure grip his spirit. Sending a final stoic glance towards Kieri, he could do little to hide his dread. And yet, through the pain, one small thing kept his spirit alive; pushing aside the despair, he clung to it as a doomed swimmer might to a piece of flotsam.

They had not captured Auric.

Pay your soldiers on time. It's the most important advice I can give. If you don't, they will seek their just retribution. I speak, of course, from experience.

—Duke Roland Caldwell

CHAPTER XXXIV

The Caeronwood, Protectorate

Caolte was speaking with some of the Eagle Runners from the rearguard when the news that Gavin had returned reached his ears. Breathing a deep sigh of relief, the clansman ignored the courier's worried tone of voice. He was so relieved that the Fey'Derin captain had returned to them unharmed that all other concerns were secondary.

Walking briskly to the far end of the encampment, Caolte was curious as to the behaviour displayed by some of the men. Seasoned veterans, he noticed, wore masks of pain and sadness. There were too many men near the east side of the camp to warrant the return of only Gavin. Only the officers had been briefed about the currently volatile situation in which the company found itself.

Something was amiss.

Worried about the captain's safety, Caolte pushed his way through the growing throng of soldiers.

Gavin was kneeling down at the edge of the camp. Ethan, and Ossric stood quietly at his side, their hands resting gently on the man's shoulder. A half-dozen steps to their left stood the grim-faced Furnael Berry, with Ossric's Axemen surrounding him protectively.

From the waist down, Gavin was covered in blood.

It had soaked through his company tabard, deepening the sharp colours and staining his hands. Dried flecks covered his forearms, face and boots. At his knees lay the lifeless corpse of Orn Surefoot.

"Gods no, what happened?!" Caolte cried, running forward and kneeling beside his friend. Turning to the nearest soldier he yelled, "Get some water and blankets, and hurry!"

Gavin's face was devoid of all expression. His eyes were languid and dull, and his entire body trembled slightly. Oblivious to the questions thrown at him, Gavin slowly raised himself to his feet and shambled off in the direction of his command tent.

With deep concern for his stricken commander, Caolte took action. "Ethan, take your squad and tend to Orn's body. The rest of you get back to your posts. This changes nothing, and I need you all, however hard it may be, to return to your stations and stand ready," the clansman ordered. "We'll honour him when, or if, time permits."

Aware of the anguished expressions on the men's faces, Caolte continued, "Orn would understand. He would be more concerned with our safety than with a solemn ceremony. That old scoundrel would wish us all drunk right now; sadly, we can ill afford such a luxury."

Ethan and Ossric both nodded while some of the men smiled sadly at the comment. The fallen scout's love of spirits had never been a secret. Calling out to some of his soldiers, the noble born Sergeant Shade ushered his men to Caolte's side. One of the scouts immediately covered the body with his company cloak. Caolte approved of the soldier's gesture and motioned for Ossric and the newly arrived Sergeant Brock to follow after Gavin's retreating form.

They found Gavin peeling off his garments, the damp clothing becoming a bloody pile at his feet. His movements were slow and measured, those of a man lost in thought and sorrow.

"Gavin, we need to know what happened," the *Drayen* asked gently.

In a quiet voice, Gavin recounted the events of the morning, glossing over none of the brutality when describing Orn's execution.

"Gerald Armsmater? Are you sure, Gavin?" Ossric muttered in the stunned silence that followed the account. The big man was shaking his head and leaning on the back of a wooden chair for support. Ossric had once served with Armsmater, and had even risen to sergeant before an unfortunate series of events had led to his expulsion. Ossric had often recounted stories to his squad about the man who now stood accused of Orn's murder.

"I'm sure Ossric... I'm sure," Gavin replied.

"Has he gone insane?" wondered Caolte aloud.

"What do we do, Captain? It doesn't sit well with my heart abandoning Bider — but my common sense says that it remains our only course of action. We must leave, and leave now," Brock insisted, a flash of guilt crossing his scarred face.

"We will proceed as planned, gentlemen. Caolte will lead the vanguard, hitting any sentries hard and fast before they have a chance to sound the alarm. I trust you already know their whereabouts. Every second will be crucial, and one wasted minute could very well mean the lives of many," Gavin declared, donning what appeared to be regular tradesman garb.

Reaching into the saddlebag he had packed, Gavin pulled out a strange black cloak. At first glance, it seemed quite nondescript and plain, but when Gavin pulled it around his body, the very nature of the article seemed to shift. The three Fey'Derin officers gasped, and Ossric rubbed his eyes in disbelief. Instantly, the cloak had transformed, chameleon-like, and matched the tent's drab colourings. It was difficult for the men to follow Gavin's movements as he strapped a sword to his back, hiding it well beneath the strange cloak.

"A *C'Avenlok*," Ossric exclaimed in awe. "How did you ever come by such a prize?"

"Don't do this, Gavin," Caolte pleaded, ignoring Ossric's comment. It now dawned on the men what Gavin intended to do. He was not going to leave Bider in Gerald Armsmater's hands to die.

"Coren won't die tomorrow, nor will the company be involved in his rescue. I'll —"

"He'll understand, Gavin," Caolte interrupted. "You have to let this go. Vengeance and hate are poisons to your soul; they will consume you."

"I do not seek vengeance, Lieutenant; I seek to save Coren D'Elmark," Gavin announced.

"Gavin, I can see it on your face. The last time you had such darkness in your heart was the morning we buried the dead at Parksya Ridge. I'll not have you go through that again," Caolte implored. "The *Drayenmark* have a saying, *E'lie na hero'n mach, e'lie an ga'en* — 'A heart consumed by darkness, is a heart no longer'."

Ossric and Brock watched the exchange with interest. Neither Caolte nor Gavin ever spoke of the infamous battle in which the young captain, a mere squad leader at the time, had gained his fame and Black Company was all but annihilated. For the first time in five years, both officers wondered at the 'darkness' of which their lieutenant spoke. A deeper story lay at the root of that ill-fated battle and both men, for once, looked at their commander with trepidation.

"I will go to Coren," Gavin continued, a fire smoldering behind his eyes. "You are to win free with the Fey'Derin, Lieutenant. We will regroup at *Galen'hide* and then travel to Dragon Mount. I need to seek counsel with Ir'Wolien. He may know more of these recent events."

"Gavin..." Caolte tailed off.

Gavin unclasped the cloak, folding it quickly and placing it in a small black backpack. Slinging the bag over his shoulder, he turned and faced Caolte one last time.

"That's an order, Caolte. I'll brook no further argument from you or anyone else. Safe journey to you always," Gavin finished, sending a sharp look at his remaining officers. Without looking back, the Fey'Derin captain left the tent and was gone.

Safe journey to you as well, Caolte thought.

ભ

Less than a quarter hour later, Lieutenant Caolte Burnaise, acting commander of the Fey'Derin, crouched beside two of Ethan's soldiers. They were lying hidden in a dense growth of shrubbery, knee deep in cold, clammy mud, and desperately trying to track the three sentries Garett had spied earlier in the day.

The young scout had done well, ferreting out three hiding places that housed enemy soldiers spying for General Armsmater. If everything was going to plan, thought Caolte, Ossric should already be engaged with the enemy at a hidden site, a series of watchtowers discovered less than a league away, and Brock at a second encampment further to the north. Both watchtowers were thought to have ten soldiers stationed inside, the standard squad size of most mercenary companies.

The Fey'Derin had managed to slip into the Caeronwood, the wide expanse of trees located in the southland of old Caledun, without being noticed. Minuscule when compared to the mammoth Aeldenwood, the smaller forest did not hold the same reputation of being home to creatures of darkness. The Gath were not known to stalk under the eaves of the Caeronwood.

Reminded of his childhood, Caolte relished the smells and sounds of the wood. An earthy aroma, heavy and intoxicating, filled his nostrils. Breathing in deeply, he plunged into the woods with an elation that belied the gravity of the situation. Unlike the Aeldenwood, the intimate closeness of the trees did not feel suffocating.

With enemies stationed to the north, east, and west, Gavin had hoped to create difficulties for their pursuers by striking a trail northwest through the forest. Caolte had agreed that the company's ability to travel both quickly and stealthily would enable them to gain enough ground to escape once they broke the forest line; still a long few days away.

Only time would tell what countermeasures General Armsmater had put in place for just such a defection. Caolte expected the general would have known that some companies would take the breaching of the Code, and his new title, as an insult. The *Drayen* veteran prayed that Gavin had not underestimated the more experienced commander.

"Hie! 'Ware!" hissed the scout under his breath. "Here they come."

Caolte followed the man's gaze, spying their targets about fifty paces away. The three soldiers wore the same purple and black tabards that had appeared in alarming numbers at the *Ca'lenbam*. For men trained by the best field commander of their generation, they were paying little attention to their surroundings. With hand gestures, Garett had been able to guide the Fey'Derin lieutenant to within an unobstructed bow range. Pulling a grey, fletched arrow from his quiver, Caolte carefully raised his bow.

"Garett, I'll take the one on the left, the one not wearing his helm. Take the officer, and I should have enough time to finish the third one off before he can escape."

"Yes, Lieutenant," responded the archer, bow already nocked and ready to fire.

Holding steady, Caolte sighted his target along the shaft. Although he may have mirrored the same move more than a thousand times throughout his lifetime, the *Drayenmark* officer could only marvel at the calmness that swept through his mind and body as he held his bow up high. Pausing only for a moment longer, Caolte let fly the first arrow.

The first adversary was struck through the neck, the soldier stunned as he tried in vain to take a breath. Blood poured down over his chest, and he sagged to the earth while desperately struggling to withdraw the arrow.

Before the second soldier could turn towards his fallen comrade, a shaft penetrated the area above his heart. Crying out in pain, he too, fell to ground. The third sentry took but four running steps before Caolte released his second shot, striking the man in the back near his lower spine.

"Move, now!" Caolte ordered, reacting before the third soldier even fell to the forest floor.

Garett whistled and ran silently ahead as the woods behind the two men erupted in a commotion of sound and movement. Suddenly, a full score of Fey'Derin soldiers appeared, confidently leading their mounts.

"How far do we travel, Lieutenant?" a mercenary asked, walking up to Caolte and gripping his forearm.

"Well met, Cail," Caolte answered, greeting a second squad leader as he approached. "Aren, take your men on a small sweep to the west. Make sure we haven't missed any sentries. Cail, your men will continue pushing northwest, but be wary, Garett believes there may be a larger encampment towards the High Road. I'll be following behind you with my own command, but I need to speak with Sergeant McConnal before I head out. Understood?"

"Aye, sir," the men replied.

It wasn't long before Ossric McConnal came striding confidently into the small clearing where Caolte and his men were waiting. Ossric beamed with a huge grin and made his way over. "I see you have matters in hand here, Lieutenant."

"It went as planned," Caolte agreed. "And you, Sergeant, how did you fare?"

"Well, aside from a nasty cut to Dorne's arm, we came out relatively unscathed. I know Brock met with more resistance than we anticipated. He sent word that they attacked only seconds before a shift change. We slew a score."

"Casualties?"

"Two dead, both in their first season, and maybe a half-dozen wounded. Hitting the first watch by surprise made a difference. Brock said they are well trained, far better than most we face in the field," Ossric replied.

"Any word from the Eagle Runners?"

"Not yet. They'll still be within sight of the Gathering," Ossric shook his head, "Ethan wanted to stay as far back as possible, just in case we missed a forward sentry and they sent runners. Of course he's also hoping Gavin heads into the trees somewhere near our position."

"He may try in Herod's direction or even towards the Sisters. It might be safer," Caolte replied.

"Have you heard from Captain Blackwain since this afternoon? Last Brock heard, Herod was prepared to strike out northeasterly with the setting of the sun. By then, Armsmater will no doubt be focused on our escape to the west."

"Makes sense, but I'm still worried about the general. If memory serves me well, Armsmater was rarely on the losing side of an engagement. We are treading in deep waters right now, friend."

Ossric managed a weak smile. "I know Gerald, and trust me, this won't sit well with him. We've made a dangerous enemy today."

"He made a dangerous enemy of us when he murdered Orn. What that man did to an unarmed prisoner is sickening. A warrior deserves to die with honour, a weapon in hand, and with battle lust flowing through his veins. If it's sympathy you're looking for because you once followed such a man, you'll find none here, Sergeant," Caolte spat.

The *Drayenmark* were notorious in matters of honour and decorum. Ossric knew that any clansmen would proudly sacrifice themselves to avenge a fallen comrade. Years fighting abroad had changed Caolte, although he would refuse to admit it. Beneath his well-spoken, calm exterior, lurked the Caolte Burnaise raised as a true clansman; volatile, passionate, and proud. The lieutenant's sudden outbursts, often blunt and passionate, were well known by the company. Although it pained the Fey'Derin sergeant dearly, Caolte had spoken the truth. Ossric had once called

Gerald Armsmater friend — and now the bloody corpse of Orn Surefoot clouded the memories he had once cherished.

"Give your men a quick rest, no more than a few minutes, and follow my trail. With luck, we'll both meet up with Brock near the riverbank,"

Caolte dictated the newest set of orders to a distracted Ossric.

"Stay safe, Sergeant," Caolte called out.

"And you, Lieutenant."

ᚶ

Dodging a weak thrust, Ethan Shade spun by his opponent, burying his rapier in the man's back. Slumping to the ground, the man cried out. Without emotion, Ethan drew his knife and silenced the enemy soldier. Assessing the empty clearing, he whistled. If any of his men were still alive, they would surely head in his direction. Catching sight of one of his squad leaders, Ethan waved him over.

"Warren, gather who you can find from your command, any stragglers as well. We've worn out our welcome here, and must move on," he said, wiping his blade down with the edge of the dead man's tabard.

"Yes, sir. We head to the riverbank, correct? And has there been any news from the others?" Warren replied.

"I know Pieran's squad was hit hard, at least three down, and even more wounded. As for the rest of the company, the last runner I spoke to reported success on all fronts, although resistance was heavy on Sergeant Fearan's side. Casualties have been minimal." Ethan shook his head, "I have to admit, Armsmater isn't overrated in the least. He had men pouring through this area as soon as that first runner got past us."

"We lost Devan and Syre before we knew what was upon us," the Fey soldier replied.

Ethan still could not believe the speed at which the Protectorate guards had responded to their departure. Granted, the advance elements of the company, that is everyone but his twenty men, were well ahead of the pursuers, but Ethan had never thought it possible that he would be retreating so quickly. He had hoped to create confusion on the perimeter as his friends escaped deeper into the forest.

Instead, he had found himself on the defensive, struggling to contain the three rushes that Armsmater had sent to overwhelm the rearguard. Thankfully, Gavin had ordered two squads to remain behind, a decision that may very well have saved their lives.

As the rest of the soldiers gathered, he quickly took stock of his men; fifteen alive, four wounded. Ethan estimated nearly two score of the enemy dead, a decent showing for two consecutive gambits, and a surprising ambush.

His men had moved quickly once the first engagement had commenced, warned by a runner that more of the enemy had been scouted than first believed. With practiced ease, the first few opponents had been slain, few of them aware of what was transpiring until far too late. But from that moment on, it had become a running, perilous battle under the budding leaves of the Caeronwood.

"We still hold a slim advantage. They can only be guessing at our numbers. We must use that edge in order to further confuse their efforts in tracking down the rest of the company," Ethan said.

"A skirmish line to the west might work," Pieran offered.

Ethan nodded in agreement. "Yes, if we lend the impression that we're moving westward it may gain Lieutenant Burnaise more time."

"My squad is still relatively unscathed, sir, I'll take front line," Warren added as he bandaged one of his men's bleeding arms. "With luck, Pier can get the wounded out ahead, and we can follow."

"Agreed, but we take no more chances. The enemy has too much of a presence in these trees now for us to match him attack for attack. No heroics from any of you, understood?" He stared assuredly at the fifteen veterans who had formed a semi-circle around him. "We want to be warming ourselves by the fire near the Rillsong tonight men, so keep your eyes open and your wits about you."

Melting back into the trees, the Fey'Derin began their slow trek towards the river. The Caeronwood was divided into two parts by the large waterway that was home to the region's best fishing grounds. Fishermen and their families had long ago established trade routes along the length of the river, building numerous way-stations where they could sell their stocks. The Fey'Derin were to regroup a league south from one of these trading posts.

The Rillsong was little more than a collection of wooden warehouses and a small building that doubled as the area's tavern and inn. Although solidly built, the buildings were old, and their proximity to the wet shoreline resulted in much damp moss growing on the exteriors. At the busiest of times the tavern was only half full. With the arrival of the spring months and the onset of warmer temperatures, the captain had directed his men to camp downstream in the hopes that their presence would remain undetected.

Pausing behind a tall oak tree, Ethan drank deeply from his water skin. At their current pace, his command should reach the perimeter sentries by early morning. The onset of darkness had played havoc with their sense of direction. Although adding an hour or two to their travel time, they may have inadvertently avoided another confrontation with Protectorate forces.

A sharp whistle pulled Ethan's attention to one of the soldiers crouched nearby. *Patrol sighted; east; two score; infantry and support archers.*

Reacting quickly he replied with his orders. *Five with me, rear attack, soft line for defense and retreat.*

The orders were passed quickly along the line. Ethan planned to strike hard after flanking the front line of oncoming soldiers. Two score of these highly trained men were far too many for his battered and exhausted company to handle. With luck, enough confusion would be caused by his maneuver, effectively forcing the guardsmen to slow their progress. With full darkness almost upon them, Ethan predicted his opponents would be bedding down for the night before long, and this attack may force their hand. One lightning strike was the only chance they would have before a stealthy retreat.

Warren and four of his men gathered near Ethan's position, all signaling that they were ready to proceed. Moving well, albeit slowly in the darkness, the small complement of Fey'Derin travelled south and found good cover in which to conceal themselves. Before long, the unmistakable sounds of troop movement carried through the air. Trying desperately to silence the pounding of his hammering heart, the Fey'Derin officer put a steadying hand on the shoulder of one of his younger recruits. The waiting was unbearable.

Finally, after allowing the enemy soldiers to trudge carefully past their position, Ethan made his move. As one, the Fey'Derin raised themselves from their covering and slid forward, still wary of the need to remain silent. With their eyes now adjusted to the descending darkness, Ethan struck first, burying one of his daggers deep into the nearest man's back, while covering the subsequent gasp of pain with a gloved hand.

To his flanks, more Protectorate soldiers fell to the ambush, silently borne to the earth by the stealthy Fey'Derin. Ethan had estimated that his squad could wound or kill at least ten men before there would be an organized counterattack. Unfortunately, he had been wrong; it took only seconds before a cry of alarm sounded to their left.

Disarming his closest opponent, Ethan's second dagger took the man above his stomach. Cursing, he realized that his weapon had struck bone and was lodged between two of the man's ribs. Releasing the hilt, Ethan pushed the dying man to the ground, immediately dismissing him from the encounter.

Chaos had erupted all around him. To the best of his knowledge, only one of his men looked to have fallen. Spinning aside from an axe smash, he fended off the attacker with swift stabs of his thin blade. He had whisked his rapier out, slicing a thin gash along the soldier's exposed forearm. Ignoring the man's grunt of pain, Ethan followed up with a crushing blow to the soldier's face with the hilt of his weapon. Blood poured from the warrior's shattered nose as Ethan desperately avoided another swing. He knew with certainty that they would soon be overwhelmed.

"Fall back! Disengage!" he shouted, trusting in fate that all of his men would hear and obey the order. Cut twice on his left arm, Ethan finished off a third attacker and dove to his left, plunging into some deep brush that sloped down into a small gulley they had scouted earlier that evening. The small stream at the base ran westward, easily the best point of reference to follow in the deepening gloom. Ethan could still hear the faint sounds of steel clashing, the sound reverberating in the otherwise silent forest.

Sheathing his remaining dagger after quickly slicing a long strip of his cloak to use as a bandage for his bleeding arm, Ethan prepared to set out towards the rendezvous point. As he took his first steps, a solid mass of shadows and noise came crashing through the foliage. Diving instinctively out of the way, he strained to make out how many men had fallen down into the gulley. As one man lay in the water, stunned by the fall, the attackers regained their balance and pulled daggers from their belts. Illuminated for a brief moment by moonlight filtering through the treetops, Ethan's gaze registered the grey cloak of the man floundering in the stream. He was a Fey'Derin.

Throwing his dagger even as he dove to intercept the second guardsman's downward slash, Ethan thought that he may have been better off escaping during the confusion. The dagger struck true, embedding itself deep in the closer adversary's back. Ethan's leap had been hampered by the slick rocks lying under the water at the base of the shallow stream. Misjudging the unstable ground proved costly. The soldier's dagger bit deeply into his side, a hot burst of pain stunning his senses. Swallowing a mouthful of water as he strained to regain his balance, Ethan was relieved to see his companion strike hard with his own blade.

"No heroics eh, Sergeant Shade?" Warren grinned darkly as he pulled Ethan out of the water, throwing an arm around him for support. Smiling exhaustedly, Ethan could only shake his head at the man's remarks.

He dressed his wound quickly, still chuckling from the barb. Then, Ethan and Warren set out, striking westward along the muddy banks of the small stream. Soon, all sounds of the struggle were lost.

CB

"They are a well-trained command, Lieutenant," Sergeant Fearan commented. "They responded well after our initial strike, falling into a defensive shell, pulling their wounded into the middle. Kept a few of them alive, that's for sure."

"Gerald Armsmater didn't earn his weighty reputation for being an inadequate commander," Caolte replied.

The company, minus the sentries and the two officers, had bedded down for the night. The small campsite could barely contain the entire complement of soldiers. With only light shelters packed for the trip, what with the larger tents still pitched at the Gathering, most of the men huddled together for warmth. No fires would be lit for the next few days, and the men grumbled while grudgingly accepting the cold supper that Era Colwyn had prepared for them — hard biscuits and water, hardly appetizing.

All of the Fey'Derin were accounted for, save the two squads Caolte had dispatched under Sergeant Shade's command. They were expected to arrive later that night. With luck, the rearguard would gain a few precious hours of sleep before moving out in the morning. Ossric would replace them with a squad of his own, followed by Brock's men the next day. Duke Berry was in the lead group. The flamboyant nobleman defiantly insisted that he be allowed to fight alongside the men who were risking their lives in his defense. Caolte, of course, refused the request.

Casualties had been expected and yet, far from any usual fields of battle, it seemed as though the loss of those men slain throughout the day's skirmishes hurt Caolte far more than usual. Brock's men had encountered a strong counterattack, and the recruit-heavy squads under his command had taken losses. All told, eight men had died. It pained Caolte that their bodies had been left behind; yet another sign of the changes that had come to the fractured kingdom. Under the Code, a company's slain soldiers were treated with respect, and burials were an important aspect of each summer of warfare.

"How are your youngest men faring?" Caolte asked.

"They're holding their heads high. Not a small feat considering they lost friends, eight of them, this afternoon. They accounted themselves well in battle. This was their first, and the experience will serve them well in the end," Brock replied.

"And Auran's squad, have you decided what you'll do with them?"

"Dividing them up into other squads will hurt their confidence. They will bond together strongly in their grief, and I think they'll be the better for it." Brock answered solemnly.

"And as squad leader?"

Brock took a thoughtful pause before answering. "With Auran dead, they have no veteran presence. I believe I'll move Avery over from Tam's command. He's been with us for three years and has a sensible head on his shoulders. He'll keep them focused and well prepared."

"A good man and solid soldier," Caolte nodded in agreement.

The two men slipped into a comfortable silence, Brock busying himself with cleaning and bandaging a minor cut on his thigh, and Caolte, as always, whittling a fresh stick of wood in to some new creation. The gentle sound of the river current lapping at the banks filled the air. Caolte found it hard to believe that only a single day had passed.

"Can I ask you something, sir?" Brock asked hesitantly.

"That all depends on what you are asking, Sergeant," Caolte replied in a coy manner.

"Well, Ossric and I were discussing something you mentioned earlier today, about Parksya Ridge and Captain Silveron."

"And?" the clansman locked eyes with Brock.

"It seems there's more to that story. I — we believe, that maybe it's time we knew the truth about that battle. If you have concerns about the captain then we, as officers, have a right to know what took place on that field of battle."

"What happened there is not for me to tell, Brock. It's Gavin who must put those demons to rest on his own terms. He will speak of it when he is ready," Caolte answered. "And I don't doubt the man who leads us either; I willingly follow him. He is already a brilliant commander, but with much potential still untapped. There is something grander about him than the words he uses, the way he carries himself, or the skills he possesses. He is also a friend, and may be our only hope in facing Armsmater. You would do well to remember that he gave you a second chance at life."

"I didn't mean any disrespect, Lieutenant," the officer protested.

"I know you didn't, Brock, but look to yourself. It's far too easy to find fault with our peers, but rare is the man who can find the courage to face his own weaknesses. Gavin has yet to face that darkness, but to doubt him is to ignore the strength of his character. Have you faced your own darkness, Sergeant?"

"What darkness, sir?"

"*T'aheris ein, t'aheris r'aena, t'aheris e'lie,*" Caolte whispered carefully.

"Strength of mind, strength of body, strength of heart," Brock translated.

Caolte nodded approvingly. "The *Drayenmark's* warrior creed. Words of wisdom we might all learn from, Sergeant Fearan."

CB

The rearguard stumbled into camp two hours later. Ethan, supported by his young squad leader, managed to give a tired greeting as he was tended to by the company healer. As he smoked his long pipe, small tendrils of smoke drifted lazily through the clearing.

Of the twenty soldiers that had set out with him, only ten had returned alive. The fighting had continued well into the night, and it had taken a concerted effort to break the pursuers' line. Ethan expressed concern that some of his men might be still alive, lost in the tangled undergrowth of the forest. Scouts were quickly dispatched in the hopes of finding some of the missing men. Ethan had lost three of his five flankers, and he silently cursed himself for attempting such a daring plan.

Caolte walked among the survivors, complementing their bravery and praising their courage. Many of the stationed soldiers also passed by, offering words of encouragement or sending a wave of greeting to a friend. Each soldier bedding down in relative comfort, safe from attack, knew they owed that moment of peace to the returning Fey'Derin under Sergeant Shade's command. They also expected to be called upon to perform the same duty in the coming days.

"How does it feel, Sergeant?" Caolte asked, joining his officers for a brief council before the exhausted Ethan was dismissed to seize what sleep he could with what little remained of the night.

The officer grimaced as he shifted position, his left arm cradled tightly against his body. "It's not so bad if I'm not moving."

"Not a promising prognosis with a lengthy trek planned for the morning," Ossric stated. "Ride when able, Ethan, it might keep the pain at bay."

Ethan nodded. "Aye, it might be the only way I can get by without help. How many did we lose? I saw a few familiar faces missing around camp."

"With your losses, we're at twenty-one slain. Not exactly the best way to begin a long journey, but acceptable losses considering the unexpectedly tenacious response. I lost too many of my youngest after a stubborn defense held us at bay, but we made it," Brock winced, still pained by the loss of his newest soldiers.

"Is anyone else wondering whether Herod's men have any chance of breaking free? They have less than half of our cavalry —" queried Ossric.

"In these woods, the horses don't matter. I am far more concerned about their far less experienced command group," Ethan added.

"Even though we fulfilled our part of the bargain by keeping the Protectorate occupied, I can't imagine how his men will sustain a prolonged march without better preparation," Caolte replied.

"How do you mean?"

"Herod is a good man, but an uncreative soldier," Caolte said, giving his honest opinion. "He had no forewarning this would ever happen. He can in no way be as prepared as the Fey, and if he runs into serious resistance, he may very well break through, but he'll lose half a company doing so."

"How are we in any better a position?" Brock interjected.

"Gavin had the area scouted a week before we arrived," Caolte explained. "He knew what to expect. You remember when Orn left to hunt game? Well, he was working for Gavin, spending some time on these riverbanks and forest trails, preparing a route for the company should events go ill during the Gathering. Without that advantage, I don't believe Herod, although I wish him luck, will fare as well."

"Seems Captain Silveron knew something we didn't..." Ossric's deep voice rumbled.

Caolte shrugged, "You all know Gavin's been sensitive to such things, strangely so, always trusting his natural instincts. I used to find it eerie and a little disconcerting, but that man has kept us alive with those same instincts for the better part of five years, and so I just grew to accept it."

"Was he like that in Black Company?"

"Yes, but far less confident, Brock. He was tentative about voicing his opinions, but even then Captain Holdam paid attention to Gavin's inclinations. It was Parksya that changed him. He became more like the man we know now; confident, steadfast, and trustworthy," Caolte finished, "but darker... sad and melancholy."

"Still no chance on shedding some light on that subject, sir?" Brock made the futile request.

"None," the old warrior answered.

"Tell us something else about Gavin, then," Ethan insisted.

"I'll tell you about his first battle," Caolte began, the officers listening with rapt attention. "You have to remember, Gavin came to Black Company fully trained, or at least very familiar with both a blade and a bow."

"It was the Koriani, no?" It was Ethan who spoke.

Caolte shrugged. "Possibly. He was definitely no green recruit out there in the practice yard. Far from it, although he'd tell you different."

"Interesting. I wonder how he was able to be trained by those black garbed warriors," Brock questioned. "They make me uneasy."

"I myself, and not a few other veterans, have always maintained that young Gavin held back in the training yard in hopes his skills wouldn't be noticed. Well, no matter how hard he tried to throw a contest in the yard, his pride forever gave him away," Caolte laughed.

"I can't imagine the captain ever lying down with a sword in his hand," added Ossric in disbelief.

"I can't even count the number of bruised egos Gavin dealt out to the veterans of our company in that first summer," Caolte nodded in reply. "It did cause some jealousy, but most of the men took to Gavin's good nature, and he was well respected for his swordsmanship. And yet, no one could ever get him reveal anything about where he had developed his abilities."

"In any case, Captain Holdam signed an escort contract that summer. Half the company wasn't needed, and a lot of the men were happy to stay home with their families for an extra year. We had campaigned in the east the previous season, fighting against nobles alongside the Rhone brothers near Donegal's Stone, and were late in returning that winter. Well, Gavin and the recruits of his squad jumped at the chance to go on escort, and being in my command, I went along; although truthfully, I would have rather been at home with Karli."

"While escorting a fat merchant from Copenrun, we ran into a rogue group of brigands. Obviously weak and undernourished, they were many; and numbers often breed courage and boldness. I can still hear Gavin's voice rising above the panic of that afternoon. 'Shields up, pull in those ranks, steady on the left.' He took command with nary a thought."

"I agreed with his choice of tactics and let the boy lead," Caolte chuckled. "The defensive strategy kept us and the rich fool alive, and by the gods, his swordplay was dazzling. For the first time, unrestrained by the practice yard, Gavin cut such a swath through those fools that half the company merely watched the display with mouths agape. He was so fast that I could barely keep my eyes on his blade."

"But strangely enough, once the enemy had been routed, he called off those who were giving chase. 'They are starving,' he said, 'and they are desperate. Leave them be.' And with that, Gavin left a good portion of our foodstuffs on the ground, and one of the merchant's pack mules to boot," Caolte laughed.

"If I know the merchants of Innes Vale, that man could not have been pleased," whistled Ethan with a smile.

"He was furious, and I had to answer for Gavin's behaviour, being the commanding officer. Needless to say, Gavin spent a lot of time cleaning the camp for the remainder of the trip, but was eventually promoted to squad leader. He also spent his earnings that year repaying the debt he owed me for the loss of that mule. Ask him sometime about mushroom and potato soup. It's all he could afford to eat that winter!" Caolte bellowed.

"He hates mushrooms!" Ethan roared.

"Oh, I know," Caolte winked in return.

"He's a good man, our captain" said Brock after the laughter had subsided.

"The best," Caolte Burnaise replied.

A few minutes passed before Ethan finally struggled to his feet.

"Well then, if there aren't changes in the plan for tomorrow, I'd best be heading off," Ethan looked towards the lieutenant. "But thank you for the story."

"Everything will proceed as planned. Brock has point, Ossric the rear. I'll travel with Era for the morning and issue any further orders after our midday meal."

"Snack, you mean," Ossric interjected.

"It's better than nothing, isn't it, Sergeant?" Caolte retorted.

"If anyone could do without a meal or two, it would have to be you, McConnal!" Brock added, and a second wave of laughter broke out.

Surveying the men Gavin had entrusted with the safety and training of his soldiers, Caolte believed the young captain had made strong choices; the steady Ethan Shade, the dependable Brock Fearan, and the giant Ossric McConnal, had all performed admirably, just as Gavin had predicted they would.

The Fey'Derin, the clansman sighed, would survive; and although pained by the losses of the day, Caolte knew that if they could reach the northern edge of the

Caeronwood in such spirits, they would be fine. Watching the three men leave and wishing them all a good night, he only wished Gavin could have been there to share in the moment.

Fighting amidst the chaos of the battlefield takes some nerve, but it is the mastering of oneself within that chaos that takes true courage.
—Captain Druan Warder, An'Darim

CHAPTER XXXV

Shalo'k Mine, Lok'Dal hie

Angvald and Leoric were led out of the warehouse and tied securely to the back of a small wooden wagon. With their wrists lashed painfully together, escape was an impossibility. The still unconscious Benoit was tossed into the back of the wagon, and it was soon flanked by two merciless goblin guards. There was still no sign of Cara as a shouted command spurred the horses into motion.

Awkwardly attempting to crane his neck in order to catch a final glance of Kieri, Leoric was rewarded with the sharp crack of a whip across his neck. Stifling a cry, he sent a baleful glance towards the goblin jailor sitting smugly atop the wagon. Ignoring the sharp pain, Leoric continued his bold stare even as a second series of lashes landed across his arms. *I will hold my head high*, he vowed silently.

They travelled north past the city of *Lok'Dal hie* and into the small mountains that lay beyond. Earlier, they had passed the small hillside where Angvald and Drake had worked each morning. Not a soul could be seen, and the moonlit landscape was devoid of any movement. The silence was unsettling.

The trail continued through the rugged countryside and eventually brought them to a dark opening near the base of one of the smaller peaks. No sign or activity was in evidence, and no guards patrolled the area. There was absolutely no indication that below the surface of this nondescript opening lay the mine of *Shalo'k*. It was the perfect location for such a place to exist.

No way to find you once you went below, Leoric thought to himself.

Leoric, Angvald, and Benoit, who was now awake and completely bewildered, were led into the gaping maw of blackness. Their captors said little, pushing and prodding the prisoners when needed, but rarely speaking aside from a rare grunt or command. From the nervous behaviour some of the goblins exhibited, Leoric deduced that even those who called *Lok'Dal hie* home were wary of this place. That, in itself, was enough to turn his blood cold.

Beneath the earth, all sense of time was soon displaced. Leoric could only guess at how long they had travelled through the winding corridors of the mine. The cold passageways were only dimly lit by sporadically placed torches, and eerie shadows danced across the roughhewn walls. Leoric was still numb and confused by their shocking apprehension.

Only the fact that the enigmatic Auric was still free kept his spirit somewhat hopeful, but as they wound their way into the depths of their new prison, Leoric was filled with despair. There was little chance anyone would find them in this place. He did, however, fervently hope that Auric might still win his way back to the holdings of the Iron Shield and warn the people of Kal Maran of the goblin hordes ready to march. If the old man failed, things looked grim for the unprepared men of the borderlands.

They had never expected the savages of the Wilds to show such cunning and military savvy. It now seemed as though the peoples of the north might sadly pay for this ignorance with their lives.

The tunnel eventually led to a small barred doorway that sealed off the shaft, blocking any further descent. The door was rusted and partially bent at the base, as if someone, or something, had spent time futilely clawing at it to escape. One of the guards fished through a sack and drew out a small, copper key. Fitting it in the lock, the goblin pushed the door open, giving the three prisoners their first glimpse of the mine.

The enormous cavern was bathed in the ruddy glow of torchlight. Shadows flickered along the rough stone walls and a wave of heat washed over Leoric. The tunnel opened up into a large circular chamber with tall metal spikes jutting from the rock. Leoric could barely contain his revulsion at the sight, and his stomach reacted angrily. On each long and rusted pike, were the pierced and decomposing heads of men, their mouths agape in horror. Each severed head showed the emaciated visage of a man who had died what must have been a horrible death.

Shuddering at the grisly sight, Leoric could barely suppress his loathing. The goblins, he had come to believe, were far more civilized than his initial impressions, yet the horrible foyer of the *Shalo'k* Mine proved the contrary. A civilized race would not stoop to such a level of barbarism; a civilized race could not possibly be this cruel.

In silence, the goblin guards ushered them through the macabre entryway and deeper into the mine itself. The floor of the main room, one with large barrels and wagons placed in neat rows, was empty of life. The deserted space did not help quell the fear in the pit of Leoric's stomach. From two metal wires hung the flayed bodies of two prisoners, their skin lying in dried tatters beneath their listless forms and darkened red splotches of old blood stained the floor. As they marched by, Leoric could not tear his eyes from the grim spectacle.

The room itself had five separate openings cut into the rock, each one leading into darkness. All of Leoric's senses screamed for him to flee, to put up a mad struggle against his captors in the hopes that he could evade the suffocating depression of the place. Regrettably, the ropes that bound him were far too tight, and his hands were already purple and numb from the loss of circulation.

The goblins shoved the three men down the leftmost corridor, one where the torchlight seemed even dimmer than in the previous chambers. Almost immediately the stench of unwashed bodies, feces, and decay assaulted Leoric's nostrils. With mounting apprehension, the borderman silently trudged down the tunnel, his nose burning from the heavy scent. *People have died down here ...* he thought to himself. *Will I now join them?*

After a brief walk in which the ground continued to slant sharply downward the further they progressed, the goblin guards brought the small procession to a halt. They had reached a small square chamber that was obviously being used as a guard station for this particular area. Four goblins stood conversing off to the side. Leoric recognized one from his own retinue.

The *Shalo'k* guards had a cruel look in their eyes that worried him. He could tell that these were creatures who relished the opportunity to dominate and destroy a human being. In the goblins' stares he saw nothing but disgust and disdain for him and his comrades; a sure sign of things to come.

Shaken, Leoric barely registered the short trek through the guard station and down the dark corridor where the cells were located. The hinges of the cage doors shrieked in protest as the rusted metal was pulled away. The cells reeked of more death and decay. They were small, barely four feet by four feet, and held no cots or other furniture.

Benoit voided the contents of his stomach on the floor as he was thrown nearly over top of a half-eaten corpse. Rats scuttled away from the body and into the darker corners of the room. One of the new guards brandished a short wooden rod and brought it down heavily across Benoit's shoulders. Slumping in pain, the man cried out and fell to the ground.

Both Leoric and Angvald immediately attempted to come to their friend's aid, but the guards dealt with them in much the same fashion. Each blow landed with a precision that bespoke of practiced cruelty. Leoric shielded Benoit as a large coarse sack was thrown into the room. Barking a series of unintelligible commands, the guards stood in the doorway and waited expectantly.

Angvald immediately opened the sack and motioned for Leoric to begin lifting the corpse. Shaking his head in disbelief, the borderman dropped back to his knees and began pulling at the decomposing body.

"We do this with honour, Leoric, as we would all want for ourselves," the big man said quietly. "I fear for this man's fate in the afterlife if his body lies here discarded on the floor, forgotten. This man's spirit deserves better."

Leoric nodded solemnly. "To do anything less, Angvald, would be to become like them," he nodded, casting a quick glance towards the waiting jailors. "I only wonder at how many souls we've missed."

"The gods will look to their wayward spirits. It's all we can truly hope for, Leoric. The tortured souls of *Shalo'k* are beyond our reach now," Angvald answered.

"The gods left us long ago, Angvald."

Turning from his friend, Leoric carefully lifted the body, his fears momentarily forgotten.

CB

The next day brought with it a new series of horrors. Leoric, Benoit and An-gvald were roused from an exhausted slumber and given a small portion of food and water. The food consisted of a piece of moldy bread with a bowl of gruel so revolting that none of the men could stomach it. The water, brackish and foul smelling, was no better. Aware that he needed to drink something, Leoric forced down a few mouthfuls of the liquid and then passed the jug to Angvald. Only Benoit refused the water, even after much pestering. Not long after, the door was thrown open, the plate and jug collected, and all three prisoners firmly pushed into the corridor. They joined a small contingent of other prisoners shambling towards the main chamber

The other miners were extremely emaciated and many suffered from a deep cough that wracked their fragile frames. Their skin was covered in a thick film of dark soot and grime, the layers giving each man a ghastly appearance that Leoric found disconcerting. Most wore little more than fouled rags, the strips of cloth barely covering even half of their bodies. Each and every man also sported the ugly scars of torture; some of the wounds had long healed over, while some were infect-ed, and others still were relatively new. Some men were even missing fingers or toes, while others showed clear signs of burn marks.

But it was the dead look in their eyes that gave Leoric pause. They were devoid of all expression. There was such an emotionless despair conveyed in each lifeless stare, that it seemed as though they waited only for death.

No one spoke as Leoric was pushed down one of the many tunnels branching from the large central chamber. Separated from Angvald, Leoric held tightly to Benoit's arm, guiding him along. The scholarly man had yet to recover from the shock of the previous day, and Leoric was unsure of his friend's state of mind.

The two companions spent the next hours, each one drearier than the last, hauling chunks of raw iron ore from the depths of one of the numerous tunnels that crisscrossed the mine. Leoric found himself in a veritable maze of twisting turns, sharp inclines, and intermittent chasms. There existed, as far as he could determine, no real organization or pattern to their placement.

In a moment of clarity, Leoric realized that the tunnels were more haphazard than planned. *The goblins didn't know what they were doing, and still might not! How was this even possible?*

For the remainder of the day, this thought was the thin thread of sanity that kept his mind focused and away from the pull of anguish and despair. It waned by the end of that same shift, but he was well aware that he had fought off the very same fears to which he was certain the long-time dwellers had tragically succumbed. Of course, it was foolish not to expect prolonged exposure to such drudgery would eventually compromise even the strongest of minds.

Suddenly, a horn sounded, the loud pealing note echoing off the tunnel walls. The other miners, men who had said nothing throughout the entire day, the same men who did their jobs with little emotion, slowly turned and began the long shamble back towards their cells. It was what they had been conditioned to do, what their broken spirits had now resigned themselves to.

Angvald was sitting with his back to the wall when Leoric and Benoit returned to the cell. The big man sat with his eyes closed, his dark red locks already sporting a thin layer of dust. He smiled wearily as they joined him, Benoit cringing at the sound of the door being slammed shut.

"It's good to see you both," he said quietly.

"And you," Leoric replied.

Angvald took a sip from a new jug of foul water and passed it along. "This place may be the end of us, Leoric," he said.

"They are alive, Angvald, just very close to death," Benoit said from the shadows. They were the first words Leoric could recall the man uttering since their arrival at the mine.

Angvald shook his head angrily. "Any spirit that ever existed within these poor souls has been so terribly crushed that to consider them among the living is a farce. They are mere shells of their former selves... shells of humanity."

"We can't change what happened to them, but maybe we can alter their futures," Leoric replied.

"They are lost," the Kaleenian said.

"Stop it!" Benoit screamed. "I can't become what they are, I can't... Please!"

"I have only faith in my gods, and after what I have witnessed here... I struggle," Angvald replied. "I can see no other end to our story, Benoit."

"Then what can we do?" the man shuddered.

"We keep each other alive," Leoric responded.

"Why bother? We will die here regardless. Would it not be better to forget how to feel, to forget who and what we once were? To become like the others..." Benoit trailed off.

"No. We hold out hope for those who are here, because if they can't be saved then how can we have faith in ourselves?" Leoric stated with conviction.

They fell silent, each man lost in thought. Leoric could think only of Kieri. At his side, Benoit wept. Leoric wrapped an arm around his thin shoulders. Time held little meaning any longer, but Leoric judged that long hours passed before the quiet, soft-spoken Benoit drifted off to sleep.

Extricating himself carefully from his slumbering friend, Leoric slipped off into his own dark corner. As he crawled past Angvald, a hand shot out from the darkness, gripping him tightly on the wrist.

"You are right, Leoric D'Athgaran," Angvald said. "We must fight on, if only so that those who are here can be remembered."

Leoric slipped his wrist from Angvald's grasp and offered him his outstretched hand. The big man smiled and accepted the gesture of solidarity.

Then, with a final nod, Leoric curled up into his corner and wrapped   his arms around himself. Huddled on the damp floor, he attempted once more to abandon his painful thoughts of Kieri. Try as he might, he would not sleep that night.

&#x03;

She has been with that monster for three full days...

The thought consumed his every waking moment; allowing him no comfort, no solace, especially in the darkest of night when sleep eluded his tired and weary mind. His failure to keep the woman safe gnawed at him, battering his already deflated spirit. Had it not been for Benoit's desperate need for support, Leoric wondered if after three grueling days spent beneath the earth, whether he would not have already succumbed to his own deep sorrow.

Drinking his small portion of brackish water from the cup they all shared, he vainly tried to loosen his knotted muscles and painful aches. The thick layers of dark soot and grime that covered the other slaves in the mine had now started to settle upon the three of them. Angvald looked even fiercer with his tangled beard coated with the dark dust. Long familiar with the man's usually jovial nature, Leoric was steadily becoming concerned with the Kaleenian's prolonged silence.

Benoit, after his original outburst, had become quiet and brooding. He barely spoke beyond a grunt or two, acknowledging questions only when they were repeated multiple times. For such a gentle man, the rigors of the mine continued to wear away at his strength, and the resigned look of sadness that lurked behind his every stare warned of something worse. Sadly, without the will to live, Leoric knew the man would not last long.

Scratching idly at the rough growth of his beard, the borderman stretched one last time as the jingle of keys rattled from further down the dark hallway. Gently rousing the others, he awaited the opening of the cell, content at least to be some place other than the small, claustrophobic room in which they were quartered.

The slaves worked tirelessly. Their fear of torture spurred on even the most exhausted of men, forcing each and every one of them past the point of breaking. Twice during that morning, Leoric tragically watched some men die at their posts. The first to fall, a man thin and emaciated beyond compare, simply lifted his head to the heavens and sank to his knees, his load of ore falling from his hands. He had uttered no sound.

Even before the goblin jailers arrived with whips in hand and lips bared in evil grins, Leoric knew the man was dead. That he had already gone to the heavens mattered little to the goblins. They flayed the man's corpse with a zeal that quenched even Angvald's robust spirit.

The second casualty quietly dropped his load and simply decided it was time to die. Much like the first, the slave said nothing, acknowledged no one, and sat with his back to the wall of the tunnel where he was working. Closing his eyes and letting loose a deep sigh of relief, he had merely slumped to the side and died. The action had seemed so peaceful and tragic that Leoric fervently wished that if he were to die here, that it be much in the same way.

He had seen enough now to know that he would surely perish within this mine. Locked in a cramped cell, overworked and terribly malnourished, he harboured no real hope that he and his friends would ever escape.

The remainder of the day passed by in a mottled blur, his constant musings about Kieri's fate further sapping his already dwindling strength. With no idea as to the passing of time, what with the sky far above them, Leoric was surprised when the loud horn that signaled a welcome end to a dreary day sounded. Once more accepting the meagre offerings that passed for nourishment, Leoric gratefully sank to the damp rock floor of his cell.

At his side Benoit retched as he tried to stomach the disgusting mush. Concerned that his companion had not been able to keep anything down for the last few days, Leoric began to worry about the fate of his friend. Without the small portions of food to help sustain their flagging energy, a bout of dehydration could only speed up the inevitable.

How much time had passed before Leoric suddenly bolted awake, he did not know, but something had stirred him from his restless slumber. It was obvious by the slumped forms of his two companions that it was not the arrival of the jailors, for they too would surely be awake.

Shivering, Leoric cocked an ear to the cell door and strained his ears, hoping to detect that which had woken him. Try as he might, nothing to his knowledge seemed to have broken the heavy silence.

Shaking his head to clear his thoughts, Leoric suddenly worried about his own health. He had been so preoccupied watching the struggles of his two friends that he wondered if he was deteriorating quicker than he had first believed. *Could I be losing my mind? Could I be jumping at shadows and hearing things because of my own fatigue?*

Gripped by a sudden shiver of fear, he almost missed the scuff of sound from beyond the doorway. Leaping immediately to his feet, he pressed an ear to the door, desperate to confirm the sound he was positive he had just detected. His sanity depended upon it.

He heard it again; a slight scuffing sound, reminiscent of a boot hitting the ground, on the other side of the door. It was close, maybe a few cells down from his own, but without even a small opening from which to observe, Leoric cursed under his breath. Dropping to his stomach in frustration, he lay prone upon the filthy floor and tried his best to scan underneath the wooden door. With the darkness deep and profound, there was scant hope that anything could be observed, but he strained his eyes intently.

As the sound faded and reappeared, he wondered whether it simply belonged to a small rodent scuttling about in the hopes of finding some midnight snack. And then, Leoric spotted the faintest movement scant inches from his face. Backing up in alarm, he stared at the doorway with a mix of fear and apprehension. *What creatures lurk in the depths of this damned place?*

The quiet scraping of metal upon metal continued and Leoric tensed. Reaching back with one arm, he fearfully yanked on Angvald's sleeve. As the big man groaned and struggled to rise, the door creaked and swung inward. Fearing the arrival of some new monster from the depths of the mine, Leoric cringed.

Two figures lurked in the entryway, both paused a moment and glanced down the corridor before slowly stepping closer. Speechless, Leoric made out their dim features and shook his head in disbelief.

"Time is short, lad," Auric whispered urgently. The old man gripped him solidly around the shoulders and lifted him to his feet.

"My god, I must be dreaming! But how ...?" Angvald breathed from behind Leoric, the Kaleenian's eyes opened wide in disbelief.

"Auric speaks the truth, Angvald; there will be time for the telling of this tale once we have won free of this cursed place. For now we must make haste," Finn Callum added, a naked blade held comfortably in his hand. Even in the darkness, Leoric could see the dark stain on the steel, a sure sign that goblin blood had been spilled.

Overwhelmed, the three prisoners staggered out of their cell and into the corridor. Pausing a moment before following his companions, Leoric was overcome by a sudden wave of emotion. In the fetid, stale air of the *Shalo'k* Mine, hope remained, and he was determined never to let that hope fade again.

Haunted by restless spirits of old, the Vale houses the burial chambers of the most venerated Gorimm of our past. Wards have been placed to safeguard these honoured tombs. Our history must always be protected.

—*S'Aelian, Gorimm Keeper*

CHAPTER XXXVI

P'haerin **Vale, Aeldenwood**

As the days passed, Alessan's body continued to gain in strength. He could find no suitable explanation for his increased endurance. Other than continuing to drink the strong herbal tea that C'Aelis brewed, he did little of note. The daily workouts with the Gorimm were now routine, as were his cold baths in the small stream. His appetite remained quite ordinary, and yet something had definitely changed...

I apologize for disturbing your thoughts, Alessan, but I believe it is time to begin our journey. The packs are ready, and the tower is sealed, the voice sounded in his mind. *Greiyfois, it seems, is more excited than we are,* C'Aelis smiled.

Looking towards the edge of the clearing, Alessan was amused as he watched the young wolf run and bark in obvious excitement, her tongue hanging comically from her mouth.

"I wasn't really thinking about anything important," Alessan said aloud, stretching as he rose to his feet. Staring back at the large tower, he felt an unexpected tinge of sadness. "You know, I'm really going to miss this place."

It has served us well, has it not?

"It really has," Alessan replied. "But who's to say we won't sip tea together here once again?"

You have a way about you, Alessan. You think not unlike some of the men I once knew; you are filled with hope. It is a refreshing outlook, for my people think much differently.

"I think I'll take that as a compliment," Alessan laughed.

As you should! C'Aelis replied.

The two men travelled light, each carrying a small backpack as well as their cloaks and blades. Alessan had fashioned a walking stick for himself that morning, and C'Aelis carried a full quiver of arrows with his beautifully crafted longbow. They were headed northeast to a place known as *P'haerin* Vale. C'Aelis had explained that this small valley contained magical wards that the Gorimm had fashioned long years before. When activated, the wards were a form of protection over the forest, or so the C'Aelis had inferred.

After a short rest, the pair left the thicker underbrush and started to follow a weathered dirt path. Eventually, smooth cobblestones appeared underfoot, and the path widened into an ancient road. Parts of the roadway were cracked, the old stones having succumbed to both weather and weeds.

It was late afternoon by the time Alessan found himself standing in front of an ancient archway, the structure no less weathered by time than the road that passed beneath it. At the edge of the old flagstone path, Greiyfois suddenly whimpered and let loose a plaintive whine. Bending down on one knee, C'Aelis gave the wolf a warm embrace while ruffling the fur of her head and whispering soothing words in her ear.

Intrigued by the wolf's behaviour, Alessan watched as she flopped down on her belly and settled her head timidly on her front paws. "Is she afraid?" he asked with some disbelief. Greiyfois had battled the Gath without ever once showing signs of fear, and yet here she was in obvious discomfort.

Greiyfois and her descendants have never felt comfortable in P'haerin Vale. I believe her acute senses make her far more attuned to the spirits present in the valley. She will remain our rearguard, but not one step further will she venture towards our destination.

"Is it that bad in there?" Alessan pointed to the partially collapsed archway. "And what exactly do you mean by spirits...?" he asked nervously.

The restless spirits of my ancestors have been known to walk the ruins of this place. They hold no sway over the lives of the living, but still do they wander, still do they seek out visitors to P'haerin Vale.

"Are you speaking of ghosts?" Alessan frowned.

They could be called such, yes, but the spirits you see here in the Vale can often take on their true forms, so much more than the discorporate phantoms of which you speak.

"But they aren't... real?" Alessan replied with obvious hesitation.

No harm will come to you, Alessan, C'Aelis touched him lightly on the shoulder. *But it is for you to decide whether you would feel more comfortable awaiting my return here at the entrance.*

Shaking his head, Alessan braced himself. "I'll be fine, C'Aelis."

Even after speaking, he was unsure whether the words had been spoken for the Gorimm's benefit, or his own.

The sure-footed Gorimm led the way beneath the crumbling arch, picking his way carefully through the jumbled boulders and cracked flagstones. The mist swirling around the base of the entrance into the Vale thickened as they proceeded downward towards the valley floor. From wispy tendrils blown about by the light breeze, to heavy clouds of fog that seemed to weigh down the very air itself, Alessan fought to keep his breathing under control. The mist was anything but natural, of that he was sure.

It is one of the defense mechanisms of this hallowed ground, Alessan. The mist does contain some degree of sentience, but it is only concerned with those who harbor ill intent when entering the Vale.

The revelation that the strange fog had some level of consciousness only increased Alessan's nervousness. The mist refused to dissipate, even as they reached the lower valley.

Standing where few humans had ventured before, Alessan's wide-eyed gaze lingered on the rows of ornate marble tombs that lay before him. They were each protected by a shelter made of black wood that appeared to glow in the faint morning light, weakly penetrating the deepening fog. The wood itself was decorated with arcane glyphs and symbols. Open on all four sides, it was a wonder that the shelters had not yet succumbed to the elements.

The sorcerers of my people have long protected P'haerin Vale from the harsh climate of the seasons. C'Aelis' voice suddenly sounded in Alessan's mind. *The weather never changes here, nor does the rain or snow fall and damage the resting place of my ancestors.*

"I understand," Alessan answered. He cringed as he was struck by how loud his voice sounded among the tombs of the dead. "Is this where your Elders lie?" he asked in hushed tone.

C'Aelis nodded. *Yes, our Elders lie here in honour, as do the members of the royal line and other celebrated Gorimm.*

"A royal line? So the Gorimm once had a king?"

There was a time when my people were ruled solely by a king and queen, although those were not exactly the titles our leaders used, C'Aelis answered, continuing to lead the way through the rows of carefully preserved tombs. *Now, the descendants of that great line act as advisors on our Council; their voices carry more weight than most, but no longer wield absolute power.*

C'Aelis made his way unerringly through the maze of sarcophagi and to the middle of a small grove of trees still shrouded in mist. How the trees could grow so strong in the gloom of the Vale was difficult to comprehend, but Alessan had already accepted such oddities about the otherworldly place.

In the center of the clearing was a small raised dais with four black columns of varying sizes. Two were tall, thin, and sat upon a thick bases of stone. The second pair were short and squat, standing barely above three feet. Alessan noted that their positioning matched the four cardinal directions.

The warding columns, as C'Aelis called them, were not carved out of stone as Alessan had expected them to be. The pillars were crafted out of the same strange black wood used in the construction of the ancient tomb coverings they had just passed.

Intrigued, Alessan curiously inspected each ward pillar. The smooth black surface felt as if a heat source lay hidden beneath the outer layer. Gingerly running his hand along the length of the tallest of the four posts, Alessan traced the intricately carved runes. He tried to discern some sort of pattern in the numerous whirls and curved lines, but found none.

C'Aelis joined him beside the smallest of the four columns. Tracing the contours of the runes almost lovingly, the Gorimm's eyes took on a faraway look, as if lost in some poignant memory.

"Is there any reason why they aren't all identical?" Alessan asked after some time had passed. Crouched upon one knee, he was still carefully inspecting the column.

The mages who helped in the creation of these artefacts claimed that each direction — north, south, east and west — contained a different set of magical energies that could properly align the forces of the earth, and in so doing, channel the Aer to warn of incoming danger, the Gorimm replied.

"And there are always four, then?"

That's correct, C'Aelis nodded. *If one of the four columns were ever to fail, the magic would be dispersed into the surrounding forest. Long did our scholars study the effects of the* Aliendal *wood before the proper alignment was perfected.*

"*Aliendal* wood?" Alessan asked, running his hand lightly across the heated surface of the nearest pillar.

The black wood is said to be imperishable. The Aliendal trees are very rare, and found only in the deepest regions of the Aeldenwood. There are places that remain closed even to the Gorimm; where the Aliendal trees grow is one of them. Few have been the times we've been granted leave to cultivate the wood. Many have ventured to find the rare Aliendal wood, only to never be heard from again. C'Aelis replied, the thoughts carrying a serious note of warning.

"Fascinating..." Alessan murmured.

I must apologize, Alessan, but I will need some space to perform the rites of activation, C'Aelis said, moving to the largest of the pillars. *I am oath bound by my heritage to complete the ward activation in the manner I have been taught. To do so I will need to remain alone upon the dais. You are welcome to watch, or if you prefer, to walk the grounds on your own. Be at ease here in the Vale as no harm will come to you.*

"All right," Alessan shrugged. "Will it take long?"

It is not a long incantation, although I am somewhat out of practice.

"How many are there beyond this one?" Alessan asked, stepping down off the dais.

There are sixteen in total, C'Aelis replied. *Of those, I have activated only six. It was my intention to visit those that lay near the remains of the Gorimm capital city first, but the Gath were simply too alert and too numerous. I cannot face those infernal creatures too often, or I will eventually be overwhelmed.*

"I could always go with you," Alessan offered, surprising himself.

The Gorimm's face glowed at the comment. *You continue to surprise me, Alessan Oakleaf. For someone who often speaks of his shortcomings, you possess more courage than many more accomplished men.*

Unable to find the right words to express his gratitude, Alessan was content to lean against the nearest tomb and watch C'Aelis begin his incantations.

Stretching his arms high above his head, C'Aelis closed his eyes and began to sing. It was the first time Alessan heard the Gorimm's voice. The notes carried beautifully in the tranquil clearing, and he was instantly captivated. With eyes firmly closed, C'Aelis began to sway as he turned east to face the smallest pillar.

In response to his quiet chant, the top of the pillar slowly opened, not unlike a flower coming to bloom. Eight triangular petals blossomed, and a number of glowing beads, each the size of a pearl, hung suspended in the air directly above the point. With one arm outstretched, C'Aelis placed a hand over one of the runes, this one a bright sun carved into the *Aliendal* wood, and sang a new string of arcane words.

A bright light erupted from the center of the pillar, and one of the smaller glowing pearls spinning around the greenish glow flew upwards into the sky. Smiling briefly, yet keeping his eyes closed, C'Aelis breathed a deep sigh of relief and began to chant once again, this time slowly turning to face the western column.

The next ward pillar reacted in much the same way, and Alessan remained transfixed by the ceremony. *No one will ever believe the things I've seen,* he thought to himself.

As the Gorimm moved on to the third portion of the incantation, Alessan caught a whisper of sound, like the murmur of voices, coming from somewhere behind him. Apprehensively tearing his gaze from the spectacle, he turned and scanned the shrouded Vale, straining to catch a glimpse of what he had heard. Nothing appeared in the mist, and yet as he was about to blame the sound on his imagination, there again came the quiet murmur. Spinning around, he was sure the voices had come from directly behind him and on the other side of the large trees that encircled the clearing.

Careful not to interrupt C'Aelis, Alessan walked slowly into the mist, intent on determining the source of the sound. The fog parted as he walked past a series of sarcophagi, the mist enclosing his small form immediately as he made his way forward. For a brief moment, an inexplicable fear alerted his senses, but remembering his companion's words, he trusted that no harm would come to him. Finally, with the sheer walls of the northern edge of the valley slowly materializing through the mist, Alessan's breath was suddenly caught in his throat.

Not ten paces from where he stood, the solid forms of two Gorimm sat quietly between two of the tombs. Blinking his eyes in disbelief, Alessan stared at the two figures, positive that they could be nothing more than a trick his mind was playing on him. The two figures, one a woman with silvery long hair, fiddled absently with a pair of wickedly curved long knives, while the second, a Gorimm male, quietly read from a thick tome held reverently in his long, slender fingers. In sharp contrast to the woman's military garb, the male wore a red robe decorated with gold symbols along the sleeves and hood.

The two Gorimm were holding a conversation, neither particularly focused on the other. The scene was so lifelike, so intimate, that Alessan believed it must be real. *Were these a pair of the restless spirits that C'Aelis had mentioned?*

Deciding to circle the pair and seek refuge behind the nearest sarcophagus, Alessan carefully picked his way through a jumble of cracked stones and fallen boulders. As he passed behind what he believed to be ghostly apparitions, he caught a smattering of the conversation as it drifted through the air.

"If you had charged D'Arios with protecting your flank, the Gorann would never have reached the Hinforth Heights and caught you unawares," the robed man was saying.

"How was I to know that M'Erian would be slain that morning, and his company fall so swiftly into disarray?" The woman was angry. Her response had been curt and bereft of any kindness.

It took a moment before Alessan realized that the two Gorimm had spoken aloud. Once again he was captivated by the speech of C'Aelis' people. Puzzled, he continued to watch the two with interest. Edging a little closer in the hopes of overhearing more of their conversation, he stumbled as his foot caught a piece of stone jutting out crookedly from the ground. Falling against the nearest coffin, he stifled a curse.

Alessan immediately felt a chill settle over his shoulders. Hurriedly glancing up, his eyes looked directly into a large pair of luminous green orbs. The female Gorimm was staring intently at him; her large emerald eyes seemed to bore into his very soul. With trepidation he realized the warrior woman had risen swiftly whilst her companion was just now rising to his feet and also turned to stare in his direction.

Who are you!? Her threatening voice ripping into his mind.

"I... I..." Alessan could do little but stutter. Backing away with haste, his left heel caught the very same stone. With a cry of alarm, he lost his balance and fell backwards. Alessan flailed his arms and fell much further than he had anticipated.

The air burst from his lungs as he hit the bottom of a shallow pit. Somehow, as he slipped around the two spirits, he had failed to see the gaping hole. With some embarrassment, he realized he must have been standing at the lip of the pit as he observed the two Gorimm. Alessan reached back to push himself to his feet, all the while keeping his eyes trained up at the opening of the small pit.

As his left hand reached to brace himself, his fingers closed around what felt like polished wood. Risking a quick glance at what he had found, Alessan's eyes opened wide in disbelief, all concerns about the Gorimm spirits instantly disappearing from his mind.

His hand gripped the shaft of a gleaming silver axe.

How long he remained transfixed upon his discovery, Alessan had no idea. But it took numerous sendings by C'Aelis to break his shock and remind him of where he was. Within a few moments of replying to the urgent summons, the Gorimm's head leaned over the edge of the pit.

 os

"Incredible!" Alessan breathed, holding up the axe. "It's a Lumber's weapon, that's for sure, just look at the carvings along the hilt," he said.

C'Aelis recoiled from axe as it was held out in front of him, and Alessan could see that the Gorimm was uncomfortable being so close to the glittering blade.

The hilt was decorated with a series of etched runes, all familiar to Alessan. The words 'hearth' and 'home' figured prominently along the length of the long wooden shaft, while a symbol reminiscent of a coat of arms decorated the base of the handle. A carved pair of matching vines finished the display, the leafy coils curling up and around the whole length of the wooden handle and disappearing into the bright steel of the double blade. But beneath the carvings something appeared amiss. Unsure of an uneasy feeling that tickled the back of his mind, Alessan stared intensely at the axe haft. He was convinced that something lay beneath the symbols. Shaking off a sudden chill, he tried to calm his racing heart. Regardless, it was without a doubt, the legacy of a Lumber. *But how had it come to be lost here in the hallowed grounds of a Gorimm ancestral burial vale?*

Alessan and C'Aelis had returned to the clearing next the warding pillars. In a jumble of confused words and unorganized thoughts, Alessan recounted what had just transpired. C'Aelis followed as best he could, asking questions when needed, but after each response, the frown on his face seemed to only deepen.

You are positive that female Gorimm actually acknowledged your presence? C'Aelis asked again.

"Are you even listening to me?" Alessan exasperated. "She turned and looked right at me, and then spoke directly in my direction."

The spirits have often been seen, but never have they conversed with a visitor to the Vale... and to be speaking aloud?

"But how often have men visited *P'haerin* Vale?" Alessan responded.

You speak truthfully on that note, Alessan, but that only means more questions. I wonder if your burgeoning power is connected to all of this? C'Aelis suggested.

Alessan shrugged and continued to finger the sharp edge of the axe. "I have no idea, but I know one thing, this axe shouldn't be here, not without a body, at least. A Lumber never parts with his axe - never."

Within these woods, the presence of that weapon of evil is a travesty all its own, C'Aelis said bitterly.

"Now wait a minute, the Lumbers were only protecting themselves and their homes in the only way they knew how. If you want to lay blame on the doorstep of another, look to your own people first, C'Aelis. The Lumbers simply do a job, a dangerous one at that, and without the Gorimm's disappearance they wouldn't have needed to," Alessan retorted angrily.

C'Aelis sighed heavily. *I apologize, Alessan. Sometimes it is difficult to confront the fact that my people have failed those we once cared for. The fault is our own, but it is nonetheless a bitter failure to accept.*

The pair sat quietly for a few moments. As Alessan continued to trace the carved vines with his fingertip, C'Aelis suddenly reached out a hand.

Could I see it, just for a moment? He asked politely.

Alessan shrugged in return, passing the weapon over with one hand. As the Gorimm grasped the outstretched handle, he cried out as it pulled his arm down and fell to the ground, the metal clanging loudly off the flagstones.

By the gods that's heavy! How do you manage to hold it like that?

"Heavy?" Alessan looked up in surprise. "It weighs almost nothing".

Well, if we thought our day could get no stranger, we were mistaken. That weapon would take both my hands to wield...

Not quite convinced by what C'Aelis was saying about the weight of the axe, Alessan reached down and grasped the weapon with both hands. It came off the ground with ease. Startled, Alessan grinned. "It's like it was made for me..." he said nervously. Again, that tickle shivered in the recesses of his mind.

Suddenly, a loud howl of alarm echoed off the valley walls. C'Aelis leapt to his feet, his twin swords already withdrawn and in hand. Alessan, to his credit, was only a moment behind the extremely nimble Gorimm.

Greiyfois is in trouble. I must go ahead, Alessan. Don't tarry, we may have a long chase ahead of us this morning!

Alessan ran after the fast disappearing form of his companion. Even on the best of days, the young man from Briar would have found it impossible to keep up with the fleet-footed C'Aelis. Nevertheless, he clenched his teeth in concentration and forced his aching muscles to push harder. A second plaintive howl added to his frantic pace as he left the eerie burial vale behind and raced upwards along the sloping path.

Reaching the archway only a few minutes later, he braced himself for what he feared was yet another confrontation with the Gath. Instead, he pulled up as he saw C'Aelis down on one knee carefully inspecting the young wolf's left flank. Alessan breathed a sigh of relief when he noticed the twisted bodies of two Gath crumpled on the earth only a few short paces from his friends. Fascinated, he watched as one of the corpses twitched, its throat torn out and one of the creature's arms nearly torn off. Greiyfois had not been kind.

She is a warrior, our Greiyfois. C'Aelis sent in response to Alessan's silent thought. That the strange Gorimm could seemingly read his mind at will was still somewhat disconcerting. *She slew both forward scouts, but you can be sure that a war pack hunts nearby.*

"Where shall we go?" Alessan gasped.

The Vale would mask our presence, and with the wards now activated, we have two choices; hide or run. Motioning towards the mangled corpses C'Aelis frowned. *I don't believe the creatures would suspect anything other than a wolf attack, but we can't be sure...*

"The thought of being trapped in the Vale doesn't exactly warm my bones. I feel better than I ever have, so I'm ready for a run," Alessan replied, flexing his right arm and realizing that the Lumber Axe was still clutched tightly in his left hand.

C'Aelis' frown only deepened. *I see you have already grown attached to the weapon.*

"Don't you find it the least bit curious that it is feather light to me?" Alessan reacted. "You yourself have often said that the gods work in mysterious ways. This could be such an event!"

You are more stubborn now than you were when healing, Alessan, the Gorimm nodded his head. *The blade has shown an affinity to you, and you alone, so I can't disagree. It does not mean that I need enjoy its presence.*

"Agreed," Alessan replied with a curt nod of his own.

Then we head north. There is an old tower six leagues ahead where we can rest. After that we will strike east and into the foothills of the Druine Mountains. Scholaris lies in that direction, although it is still a long ways off, C'Aelis said, petting Greiyfois on the head. *Are you ready, Alessan?*

"I'm ready," Alessan replied.

C'Aelis grudgingly helped Alessan attach the weapon to his back using makeshift straps of leather. Setting a slow but steady pace, C'Aelis loped off into the forest, Greiyfois fast on his heels. Alessan broke into a shambling jog that kept him within sight of his two companions.

And so, the strange burial vale of the Gorimm was now behind them, the crumbling stone archway once more forgotten amidst the veritable sea of trees surrounding it.

The summer campaigns shall begin no less than twenty-one days after the conclusion of the spring Gathering. Companies must report to their designated posts as determined by their employer within that period or risk a breach of their contractual agreements.
—*Mercenary Code of Conduct*

CHAPTER XXXVII

Ca'lenbam, Protectorate

G avin walked nonchalantly through the teeming makeshift arteries of the *Ca'lenbam*. He was still boiling with anger over his encounter with Gerald Armsmater, but somehow managed to maintain a calm outward appearance as he made his way through the crowd. The ability to harness his emotions was one of the critical skills he had learned while serving with the Silveryn Koriani. Failure in this regard could result in rash decisions that might very well end one's life.

Gavin had no intention of dying without first taking revenge for Orn's death. Caolte had often warned him about the seduction of vengeance, but there was no denying the burning coal of anger that had settled in his breast. Gerald Armsmater had broken the Mercenary Code. It was a serious offense that revealed how arrogant Gadian Yarr had truly become, but the meaningless death of Orn Surefoot belied any explanation.

I was sober, Captain...

The words echoed in Gavin's mind as he moved closer to the center of the large Gathering. He preferred not to fret over how long those words might haunt him. Instead, his priority was the safety of Coren D'Elmark.

Out of uniform, Gavin looked no different than hundreds of other freelance mercenaries milling about the various taverns and company pavilions. The Fey'Derin tabard was well-known, and it was only through discretion that he would stand a chance of reaching an area relatively close to the new general's purple and black command tents. It was impossible to know how long Coren would be left alive once word of the Fey'Derin's flight to the Caeronwood was reported. Gavin refused to leave anything to chance; if a daring late afternoon rescue was the only option, then so be it. He would not leave Coren behind to die like a defenseless animal.

Choosing an alley adjacent to the heavily guarded pavilions of the Protectorate's upper class, Gavin set to work. He had already purchased everything he needed to cover his retreat. Shouldering his way to a spot between two smaller tents, he unfurled his new purchase and quickly set up a tent of his own. He placed bandages and two bedrolls, among other supplies, within the small space. To any who now passed by the location, his living space looked akin to any of the other freelancer tents assembled amidst the general chaos of the Gathering. Curious onlookers would see nothing of interest.

Pleased with his progress, Gavin ducked into the tent and unbuckled his long sword, tossing the blade on the nearest bedroll. Pulling a blanket over the weapon, he took three thick bandages and packed them in his backpack along with the *C'Avenlok* cloak. Slipping a small, thin blade underneath the left bracer on his wrist, Gavin rechecked his equipment one last time before exiting back out into the busy alleyway. Immediately swallowed up by the crowd, to any observer, he was now merely one mercenary among many.

ॐ

Time had lost all meaning to Bider. He felt as if many days had passed since Orn's death, but he would have most certainly been killed if this were true. He could feel a constant throbbing pain in his ribs and legs, and there was a distinct numbness in his hands due to his tightly bound wrists. There was a steady dripping of blood coming from his mouth and Bider was surprised he was still breathing at all. Gerald Armsmater may not even have to slit his throat to finish the job; a bit more time may very well accomplish the same result.

He lay with his head against the cool earthen floor of the tent, his face turned sideways and his body contorted uncomfortably. There was little chance that his muscles would respond to his attempts at movement. They had already decided that the searing pain was unavoidable, and any kind of struggle would only increase his discomfort.

A small breeze rippled across his exposed back, the cool air igniting a fresh round of biting sensitivity. Moaning in displeasure, Bider tried to turn in order to see who it was that had entered the tent. His ears, although partially blocked by blood and dirt, were still sharp enough to catch the quiet swish of a cloaked individual. Seized with a terrible premonition that his end was near, Bider valiantly struggled to escape his bonds.

The gentle touch of a hand landing near his wrists almost caused his heart to stop. Moaning loudly, Bider somehow found the strength to shift his body away from the searching hands. *Please help!* His mind screamed in terror.

"Shh... Coren I need you to relax. It's me, Gavin," whispered a calm voice in his ear.

Bider was speechless, once again the hands returned to his bound wrists, this time the action accompanied by the unmistakable ring of a weapon being drawn. Bider could see no one at his side and he watched as a floating pair of hands carrying a small dagger entered his vision. Flinching at the strange sight, he shrank away.

"Coren you must focus for me," Gavin's voice whispered once more. As the blade severed the bonds that had held him, Bider tried in vain to flex his tingling fingers. As the blood returned to his extremities, so too did the pain. With his fingers twisted in agony, Bider blinked in surprise as the floating hands placed the dagger on the ground, reached upward, and made a motion as if to remove a hood.

There before him was the grim, determined face of Gavin Silveron. For a moment, Bider wondered if he was delirious and only imagining the ghostly appearance of the man he had prayed would save him. "Captain ... is it really you?" he managed to stutter.

Gavin nodded. "I apologize for the sudden appearance, but explanations will have to wait. Let's get the rest of your bindings cut and ready ourselves to move."

Bider winced as his legs were freed. "That's the problem, Captain," he replied dejectedly. "I don't think I'll be able to walk."

Gavin looked up in alarm. "How bad?"

"I won't lie, Captain. I have broken ribs for sure, I've lost some teeth and my nose is definitely broken. Also ..." his eyes trailed down to his ragged pant leg and Gavin cursed under his breath as he pulled aside the clothing. Coren's left ankle was terribly disfigured, swollen and obviously broken. There was little hope the limb would be able to hold any weight whatsoever.

Gavin remained in a silent crouch for a long moment, his stare determined and searching. A momentary flutter of despair swept through Bider and he wondered whether Gavin would be forced to abandon him there. *I won't be the cause of his death!* Bider vowed.

"Stop looking so worried," Gavin said. "This somewhat complicates matters, but I don't believe it's anything we can't handle."

"You should leave, sir. I'm just going to be in the way."

Gavin turned and unclasped the strange cloak that kept most of his body concealed. "Nonsense. I didn't send the company out under Caolte without reason. I'll be damned if get this far and not manage a path out of this cursed place."

With some feeling returning slowly to his hands and feet, Bider rubbed his legs in the hopes of stimulating the circulation. He was determined to escape, even if it meant hobbling his way out of the tent. Accepting a bandage from Gavin, he gently dabbed at the wounds on his face, clearing away much of the congealed blood and cleaning up his features somewhat.

Shouts of alarm suddenly reached their ears. Reacting with astonishing speed, Gavin tossed the cloak towards Bider and slid to one side of the tent entrance. As the flap was thrown open, Bider scrambled to cover himself with the strange article of clothing. Two purple and black-garbed soldiers entered the tent with weapons drawn. They instantly spotted Bider's struggling form, his body only partially covered by the *C'Avenlok*.

Gavin attacked before they had time to register his presence. With practiced calm, he stepped forward and eliminated both men; the first with a dagger pulled across the throat, the second with a vicious twist to the neck. All told, the killings had taken barely a heartbeat. Silencing the choking man with a merciful stroke, Gavin cocked an ear towards the tent flap.

Reclaiming his blade, Gavin motioned towards the back of the tent. "We'll go out the rear. It's not far. We will be staying nearby tonight."

"Nearby?! And how will you hide an injured man?" Bider watched Gavin cut a large slit in the heavy canvas. Pulling open the ragged slash, the captain peered cautiously outside.

"Have you ever noticed how people generally notice odd behaviour?" Gavin asked. "A skulking man in the shadows, a hooded stranger, someone walking too swiftly, or too slowly for that matter. What better way to remain unseen, than to simply act like we belong."

"Cursed Arne, we're just going to walk out of here?" Bider exclaimed.

"In a manner of speaking, yes. I'll support you, and we'll make our way to the freelancer's area just a short walk from here. No one knows you're missing; for the moment, that remains our greatest advantage."

Agreeing to the plan, Bider slung his arm around Gavin's shoulders and grimaced in pain with each step. The two men exited the ripped opening in the rear of the tent and casually made their way through the laneways between the pavilions. Bider could feel the grind of bone on bone, his broken ribs rubbing painfully against one another. They managed to pass through the area with few glances in their direction.

As they walked through the throng of people present on one of the larger thoroughfares, Bider couldn't help but wonder if it was all but a dream. Was his ordeal truly over, or was he still lying unconscious in captivity? Shaken by the thought, he relaxed as they were swallowed by the crowd. They were now just another pair, albeit an odd one with his numerous injuries, amongst the soldiers and craftsmen attending the *Ca'lenbam*.

Limping along and bravely fighting the pain, Bider felt his hold on consciousness slipping away. Catching the pale look on the scout's face, Gavin shouldered more weight and continued to speak words of encouragement. That Coren D'Elmark was alive and had mustered the strength to travel even the short distance from his prison tent, demonstrated extraordinary courage and resiliency.

With black spots dancing in his vision, Bider sighed gratefully as the captain pulled aside the flap of a nondescript tent and slipped inside. A sudden weariness, heavy and unforgiving, settled over his small frame. His knees buckled as he fought to keep his eyelids open. Sinking down on to the nearest bedroll, Bider closed his eyes and succumbed to his exhaustion.

 catch

Gavin looked across at the sleeping form of his companion with relief. As he had hoped, the Fey'Derin push to escape into the Caeronwood had curtailed Armsmater's efforts to use Coren as a pawn. It was unlikely that the general could ever have predicted that Gavin would attempt to rescue his captured man. By his lofty reputation alone, Gavin knew that Armsmater would never hesitate in sacrificing one man for the good of a company. The potential risks would have been assessed and the attempt steadfastly refused by the general.

The retired mercenary's hard and unforgiving nature had unwittingly created an opportunity for Gavin. With relative ease, he had extracted the wounded man from an armed camp. As Coren slept soundly, Gavin checked the scout for any other troubling wounds. He detected a number of minor wounds, but only a thorough examination by a proper healer could discount any number of other possibilities. The general's soldiers had not gone lightly on the man. In silence, he gently poked and prodded Coren's exhausted body.

Finally content that the broken ankle and ribs remained the most serious injuries, Gavin carefully cleaned each gash, and with little resistance, managed to rouse the scout in order to properly bind his ribs and splint the broken limb. Satisfied with his work, Gavin leaned back on his own bedroll and closed his eyes. It would be a long few days, and he would need as much rest as possible. He also had a nighttime rendezvous to attend to...

"The cloak, is that how you killed the man who hired Khali's Reavers?" Bider asked.

He had slept soundly for the entirety the day and well into the next. Now, propped up with against the wall of the tent, he carefully sipped from a large bowl of soup that Gavin had secured that afternoon. With a long night's sleep behind him, his appetite had returned. He had regained something of his colour as well, and a healthy flush had returned to his cheeks.

"Lord Avery," Gavin nodded, tearing a large piece of bread in half. "The cloak did play a role, yes."

Bider accepted the bread and took a large bite. "Where did you get it?"

"The *C'Avenlok* was a gift," Gavin replied.

"A gift?" Bider said, surprised by Gavin's answer.

"Aye, a gift."

C'Avenlok cloaks were something of a legend among the thieves of Kal Maran. Having once belonged to one of these loosely organized guilds, Bider had heard rumours about such magical cloaks of concealment. They were said to have been created by renegade mages during the early years of Caledun's existence. The Silveryn Order had been recently founded and their near-absolute control over all things arcane and magical had only just begun.

The cloaks had been gifted to the best assassins in the realm, often members of the High King's An'Darim, the personal company of the king. After the annihilation of that very same command during the chaos caused by the Shattering, it was assumed that the artifacts had been lost.

Over the years, it had become something of a custom for thieves and assassins of great skill to be questioned about the use of a *C'Avenlok*. It was considered a mark of honour and respect to be so questioned, for it assumed their skill so high, and their successes so improbable, that only the aid of a *C'Avenlok* could explain it. The Thieves' Guild claimed that they had two cloaks in their possession, but since no one knew how many, or even if any, had ever existed, the claim was considered to be false.

Sensing little more information would be forthcoming about the gift, Bider abandoned the train of questioning and pursued another. "How will we know if the company has won free? It will be hard to pick a place to rendezvous with them if Armsmater's men get out ahead of them," Bider asked.

"Lieutenant Burnaise will lead the company to where he believes they can more easily break through. Plans had been set in motion long before this day, Coren," Gavin answered. "The Fey were given direct orders not to wait for us. I have a much different route planned," Gavin replied with a smile.

"We're not to rejoin the others then?"

"We'll see them once we reach Dragon Mount. I'd like to give you another day to restore your strength before we head out. Armsmater won't expect us to remain here at the *Ca'lenbam,* so I'm fairly certain we'll be safe for another day or two."

"And after that?" Bider asked.

Gavin shrugged. "The General will need to assert his authority after the loss of the Fey, as well as the *Delan Fere,* and the Sisters. He'll curtail movement in and out of the Gathering and effectively silence any remaining dissenters among those captains still camped here. We need to be gone before that happens."

"Alright then," Bider nodded his approval. "What's our route?"

"We head east towards the trading town of Wickam," Gavin responded. "It lies on the eastern edge of the Caeronwood. The town is larger than most, as it lies on the busy trade route from Matanis on the coast. Once there, we'll replenish supplies and head north along the edge of the wood. I doubt we'll meet many travelers, and with horses the journey will be relatively easy on you."

Bider watched as Gavin grabbed the backpack containing the *C'Avenlok* and slung it over his shoulder. "Is it safe to go out?" he asked as the Fey'Derin commander prepared to leave.

"Get some rest, Coren. Come tomorrow, we depart from this place," Gavin replied darkly.

"Captain, you're risking too much."

"I have an urgent message that needs to be delivered," Gavin replied, swiftly pulled the tent flap aside. Without another word, he was gone.

ᛒ

The pavilions were abuzz with activity as Gavin pushed his way through the crowds. The setting sun brought welcome relief from the surprising heat of the afternoon. During his last foray into some of the taverns earlier that day, the warmer temperatures had almost been unbearable. The mass of people packed into the valley did little to add to the charm of the event. It was a wonder anyone felt the need to leave their private encampments for the chaos of the *Ca'lenbam* markets.

He had learned something of the fate of his friends and his company while drinking with two hard looking men from a southern company who had little chance of recognizing his face. They had divulged what little they knew of the Fey'Derin's escape; the company had fought hard, there had been casualties, and the battle continued to rage in the forest.

For a man who had always taken great pride in how informed he had always been in matters concerning his men, it galled Gavin to have to rely on second-hand information. To appear overly interested or supportive of either the Fey'Derin, or the Captains Fairwind or Blackwain, would be dangerous, so Gavin could learn little more about the fate of the companies.

As he neared the center marketplace of the Gathering, he noticed that an unusual number of people were streaming into the area. Stumbling over a man's foot, he muttered a quick apology. Following the steady flow of onlookers, he was herded towards a large open space that had been cleared by a significant number of men wearing the purple tunics of the New Protectorate. Curiously, he watched as workmen arrived with large bundles of wood, while others busied themselves with the construction of what appeared to be a large platform.

Tapping a young woman standing nearby on the shoulder, he leaned down and shouted above the considerable din. "Pardon me, but what's going on here?"

"Where've you been the past few days?" she exclaimed. "One of General Armsmater's new captains is holding a public execution for those captured yesterday. The traitors are to be hanged as a warning to those who might rebel."

Gavin's world began to swim. He knew that to betray his allegiances now would mean his end. It was apparent that many were content to throw their lot in with the new order. The whole affair made him sick.

Struggling to remain indifferent, he pursued the questioning. "Who's going to hang?"

"Not sure, really," she replied. "They're all Northern company men, though. Some of those funny sounding names, as well as the Sisters."

Gavin nodded amiably, even as he fought to quell a rising fury at the news. He was certain he would see some of his men paraded out in front of the crowd to die. And this time, there was nothing he could do about it.

You can't save everyone, Gavin ... Caolte's gruff voice came to him as he watched the final boards of the gallows being hammered in place.

Time slowed to a crawl as nooses were tied to the scaffolding. An expectant hush settled over the crowd and more Protectorate soldiers arrived to help support those that barely contained the heaving swell of spectators.

Gavin watched a small company of mounted guardsmen clear a path through the people, each mount pulling or dragging a man in its wake. In horror, he registered the defeated looks upon the features of those who yet struggled proudly to stand. The first dozen wore the torn and disheveled tabards of Herod's *Delan Fere*. The next five were women; most of them staring stonily forward even with their uniforms in tatters, many of them exposed cruelly to the leering stares of ogling men. And last, one of the men helping another, came three soldiers who Gavin immediately recognized.

Gryn Stormeld, an Axemen, Robyn Squires and Liam Garivald, both Eagle Runners, wore expressions of quiet dignity as the crowd roared their approval when one of the women staggered and fell to the ground. All three men had been long-serving members of the Fey, and their loyalty had never been questioned while they served.

By the gods, Gryn has three children back home. Gavin agonized as they were pushed roughly up on the platform. The big Axemen was from Briar, his Lumber blood clearly visible by the nature of his towering frame. The two Eagle Runner scouts held their heads high and directed their eyes forward, impervious to the insults that were being hurled in their direction.

The lead rider, a powerfully built middle-aged man, dropped to the ground and held his hand up for silence. For long moments the crowd showed no signs of acknowledging his presence, perfectly content to continue screaming at the captives.

A quiet hush of anticipation settled over those assembled and little time remained if he was going to try something, but he knew it would be in vain. Only with the combined might of an army could he ever have hoped to free the twenty odd captives that faced death. For one of the few times in his life, Gavin felt powerless.

"There will be no quarter shown those who would defy the laws of the New Protectorate!" the man roared. "In the General's absence, I have been given the power to grant life or death. Here before you stand men and women who have denounced Lord Gadian Yarr. Here before you stand traitors to order, soldiers who seek to plunge this land back into chaos and anarchy. They are traitors and their lives are now forfeit." Pausing, the officer surveyed the crowd before continuing. "But it is you, the people of the south, who we protect, and so I ask of you, do you wish to spare the lives of those who stand accused before you?"

The resounding roar made Gavin's heart sink and his stomach clench violently. Gavin watched a triumphant grin spread across the man's face. Then, with a satisfied nod towards the crowd, he raised his hand and turned towards the men who stood poised near each of the condemned. With a loud cry, the Protectorate captain dropped his arm.

Averting his gaze, Gavin heard the strangled cries of the fallen. Closing his eyes, the Fey'Derin captain hung his head in shame. "I'm sorry ..." he whispered.

଼ଃ

It's too godforsaking hot to be out here. Knight-Captain Goran Perras thought to himself, trudging back through yet another deep thicket on the edge of the Caeronwood. Using his sword to push aside a low hanging branch, he fervently wished he was back in the wide open fields of the southern Protectorate. It was there, along with two thousand other men, that he had trained under the strict tutelage of the famed Gerald Armsmater.

Goran was a solid mercenary man, having served well in three companies prior to his invitation south to work as one of Gerald Armsmater's officers. He had risen through the ranks, somehow impressing the general with his adherence to the man's expectations and a brutality and cruelness Armsmater found likable. Now, as second-in- command of the entire army, respected and feared by his men, Goran found himself frustrated after the day's running battle with the fleeing companies of the Gathering.

The general had warned of this possibility, and with only one real exception, the coup had been bloodless. In Goran's mind, this boded well; what with an unavoidable clash expected between the supporters of that fool Berry and the esteemed Lord Yarr. How anyone could side with the foppish noble of Garchester mystified

Goran. Berry's city was in shambles, falling with little resistance only a week ago. The duke's armies were defeated, his allies few, and his chances for survival slim. Goran had learned long ago to side with power, and Gadian Yarr held all of the power in the south.

Finally breaking free of the tangled brush, the veteran officer waved at some of his men and explained that he was heading in for the night. With the general personally leading the push against the troublesome Fey'Derin, he had been left in charge of the *Ca'lenbam* security.

His men had been thorough in searching out those who disagreed with the new order. Even now, more than a dozen members of various companies lay bound and awaiting execution. That evening had already seen the public hangings of several *Delan Fere*, a few Sisters of the Sword, and three Fey'Derin.

Altogether pleased at the ground gained after only a day, the Knight- Captain walked briskly towards his command tent. A nice steaming tub would do wonders, he thought, as he pulled aside the purple flap of his pavilion.

Cursing silently as he stumbled into complete darkness, he wondered at his two young pages' dereliction of duty. *How do you forget to light your officer's candles at night?* Goran shook his head in disbelief. In a slow shamble, the man crossed through the main room and slipped into his private bedchamber. With a little luck, he would have some time to entertain a lady or two after his bath. Expecting the general would be very late in arriving, Goran planned to take full advantage of his commander's absence. The old general did frown upon his nighttime dalliances.

Unbuckling his sword belt, Goran reached towards his small bureau, anxiously searching for his tinder and flint. As his hands came to rest atop the furniture, he suddenly had the strange feeling that he was being watched.

Squinting in the darkness, he called out, "Werran, if that's you, you'd best be bringing a light and a woman or I'll take out my frustrations on your hide! Werran?!"

"I'm afraid I might not be who you were expecting..." a voice answered from the darkness.

Infuriated by the intrusion, and yet inexplicably terrified by the tone of the speaker, Goran Perras spun towards the voice. It was then that he realized his sword already lay discarded. As he frantically reached into his boot top for his dagger, the sudden flare of a torch filled the room.

"You!" he breathed in surprise.

It was the last word Goran Perras would ever breathe, and the intruder's face, the last he would ever see.

ଔ

"Cursed Arne, they fight well," Gerald muttered as he leaned with his back against the nearest tree. Twice now his squad had been hard pressed to hold back a determined charge from the Fey'Derin rearguard.

"They are brave, General," panted the soldier at his side.

Few men over his long heralded career had impressed him as much as this upstart captain from the north. The Fey'Derin fought cohesively and were extremely well trained. It galled the general even further now that the brash young commander had opted to defy his decree and flee.

The young Silveron was ruled by his emotions, a trait that would surely cripple any real commander. Soldiers signed up to fight for their officers, it was their duty and not one to lament over. Men and women had died in battle since the beginning of time. One captain could do little to change that fact. The sooner Gavin Silveron realized the truth about his profession, the better. Until then, his men may fight passionately in his name, but his self-doubt will eventually prove to be their undoing.

The stubborn defense by this one company had resulted in some defeats in the area. Both the Sisters of the Sword and the *Delan Fere* had passed through much lighter defenses on account of the respect warranted by the Fey. Armsmater was furious about this development.

Glancing towards the darkening sky, the old man shook his head and turned to the soldier at his side. "Private, I believe it is time this old soldier returns to rest his creaking bones."

"Aye, sir!" the man replied smartly. "I will send for an escort."

"No need, no need," Gerald shook his head. "I can find my way back."

The trek back through the shadowy woods gave Gerald time to evaluate all that had transpired that day. Although pleased by the effort his new soldiers demonstrated, the escape of Silveron's Fey'Derin was unfortunate.

Running through each and every order, engagement, ambush, and counterattack, Gerald Armsmater soon found himself closing in on his large tent. Saluting the alert guard standing at the entrance, the Protectorate commander ducked inside and headed towards his bedchamber. A quick change of clothes accompanied by a meal would still allow him a few hours to pour over the maps of the region. If there still remained an opportunity to catch the fleeing mercenary companies, a plan needed to be devised that very evening.

As he crossed the main chamber of the large pavilion and moved into his personal quarters, the general tensed, his senses screaming in alarm. Brandishing his sword, the veteran campaigner knew something was amiss. In the darkness he could smell something tainting the air, the faint trace of iron in the odor. Calmly lighting the candelabra that stood near the entrance, he gazed about the room.

On the bed, sightless eyes staring forward, lay the severed head of Goran Perras. In stunned silence, Gerald Armsmater unfolded a small piece of parchment that had been crammed into the dead man's mouth. With a muttered curse, he read the carefully scrawled words:

> *Your Knight-Captain is the second unfair casualty of this war; Orn*
> *Surefoot was the first. I missed you in your tent this evening, but I can*
> *assure you, we will most certainly meet again.*
> *I warned you not to make an enemy of me.*
> *Silveron*

Crumpling the note in his hand, the General of the new Protectorate looked over his shoulder and called for one of his servants. "Derius, fetch me Oriel! I have need of a mage. This man can only push me so far!"

With the presence of a far more organized resistance than anticipated near the southeastern reaches of the Wilds, the goblin savages have hampered our attempts at discovering a safe passage along that route. The reason for the increased goblin presence is not known, but remains a serious concern.

—Lord Crispin, 'The Explorers,' Volume II

CHAPTER XXXVIII

Lok'Dal hie, The Wilds

Leoric's flight through the dark, twisted tunnels of the *Shalo'k* Mine was akin to something out of a nightmare. As he stumbled behind the steadfast Finn Callum, Leoric couldn't help but wonder if the escape was some trick of his mind. Could it be only a vivid dream, a hallucination perhaps? Did it feel so real because it was what he had so desperately hoped for?

As they passed through a small guardroom at the end of the dark corridor just beyond their cells, Leoric gasped and came to a halt. The slain bodies of four goblin guards were strewn about the room, confirming Leoric's hopes when he had first spied the black blood dripping down the length of Finn's sword; goblin blood had been spilled this night.

Only a scant few feet behind him, Benoit rushed into the room, nearly crashing into Leoric's back. Looking about the chamber, the scholar's eyes opened wide as he wretched what little contents remained in his stomach onto the floor. Benoit then fell to his knees, sour bile burning his parched throat.

"We don't have time to stop," Auric gasped, pulling Benoit to his feet. "If we don't flee this place before an alarm is sounded, we'll all be dead. We'll speak once we reach the surface, but until then we must press on!" Without another word, the old man uncorked a flask of water and passed it around to the three escapees. "Careful now, lads, drink deeply but slowly. Not too much," he cautioned.

Benoit was immediately bolstered by the fresh water, the first taste in so long, and drank greedily from the canteen before passing it to Leoric. Lifting the container to his lips, Leoric was refreshed as the cool water quenched his thirst. Water poured down his chin, but he cared little. All he could do now was to focus on keeping his feet moving. Angvald grinned mightily as he received the proffered flask, his dust laden beard shaking with anticipation. With a hearty breath, he tipped the container and drank deeply.

The large circular chamber acting as the central hub for the discrete sections of the mine was deserted, and the five men slid along the edge of the nearest wall. Although it seemed as though no one was in the vicinity, Auric was taking no chances. They walked carefully in the shadows, progressing in a single file as they slowly traversed the cavernous room.

That only so few could guard so many... Leoric was horrified. Such was the despair of this mine.

Leoric had no idea which passageway they had been ushered through when they had first arrived. He was embarrassed to think that even if they had devised some miraculous escape from their cells, it was likely they would never have found their way through the maze-like tunnels of the numerous shafts.

Thankfully, Auric showed no hesitation as he led them around more than half the circumference of the chamber and directly into a tunnel opening that appeared no different than any other.

The tunnel ran in a straight line for a hundred paces or more before sloping sharply upwards. It was not until the small party of fugitives had made what felt like considerable progress closer to the exit that Leoric allowed himself to breathe a small sigh of relief. With his memory still hazy, he could do little to shake his feeling of helpless confusion as their path began to curve sharply. The surface lay above them, and he was determined to see daylight once again.

Auric never looked back while leading the small procession. The enigmatic old man possessed a level of endurance that astonished Leoric. Whereas the rest of the men staggered through the tunnels short of breath and gasping for air, Auric never once faltered. Leoric couldn't truthfully say that he understood the strange man, but he had never once doubted him. Leoric had trusted Auric with the original escape plan, and he trusted him now here in the depths of the mine.

Eventually, they reached a crack in the rock wall that opened up to the fresh outdoor air of that spring night. The incredible sense of freedom they felt as they broke the surface was overwhelming.

"How did you manage to find us?" Leoric asked. "No one finds *Shalo'k*."

"I tracked them on the night you were all captured. I don't believe they would ever consider the notion within the realm of possibility," Auric said, quite befuddled. "The goblins never really made a secret of where they were taking you. I knew the direction and headed your way," Auric finished with a shrug. Digging into his backpack, he pulled out a large loaf of bread.

"Compliments of Cara," he grinned.

"How is she?" Angvald inquired.

Finn sulked as he answered. "Her leg's broken and her ribs are definitely bruised..."

"The baby?" Benoit croaked, the question lingering almost too long before anyone spoke.

"We don't know just yet," Auric replied sadly. "She's a strong woman, and the baby is Drake's. That in itself may give her the strength to recover, but we cannot assume the will of the gods."

Biting his tongue, Leoric kept silent at the mention of such superstitions. *Now is not the time*, he thought. Guiding the conversation back to Auric, he asked. "So, it has been three days then?"

"Yes. I noted your location and immediately returned to the camp. After speaking with Cara, Finn, and Kieri, we made the decision to return and attempt a rescue. Captain Callum made it all possible," Auric explained.

"Don't listen to Auric's ramblings," Finn acknowledged with a slight grin. "He gives himself too little credit. I've seen a lot of men fight, but Auric dismantled the first two guards with remarkable skill."

"I think our Captain exaggerates," Auric said, attempting to deflect the praise.

The officer from Kelamyre shook his head. "Nonsense, Auric, I know what I saw. I carry the blade of one of those bastards only because Auric didn't shatter it."

"And the guardroom?" Leoric questioned further, amazed by the story so far.

"That one I did have had a hand in," Finn replied with pride. "They had no idea we were there, let alone would they ever have expected us. We killed two before the others could react and... well, you've seen the outcome," the soldier finished.

"There were only six guards?" Angvald said incredulously.

"Aye, six of the savages guarding over fifty," Auric nodded. "What need is there to guard those unable to run, even if they tried? We saw some of the other men being held below. Many have lost the will to live, but we opened their cells nonetheless."

Recalling the horrific dead eyes of the miners consumed by despair, Leoric shuddered.

൙

The mine wasn't as far away from the prisoner camp as Leoric remembered. The night of his capture, with all the worry of his impending fate, had clouded his mind, and he had been unable to judge the distance accurately. In less time than he expected, they came jogging into the open courtyard near the homestead. They approached without the need for stealth, as Finn had already informed them that the usual trio of guards had already been overpowered by the men under his command.

Cara stood stoically in the courtyard with one leg splinted. Leoric wasted no time in discovering the whereabouts of the woman he loved. After a quick embrace, Auric disappeared to retrieve their supplies and equipment while Finn slipped into the old farm house. Benoit accepted another large mug of water, his chest heaving as his short breaths came in ragged gasps.

Leoric drank quietly and then turned to face Cara. The look of sadness she wore was confirmation that she knew what he was about to ask.

"Where is she?" he asked apprehensively.

Cara averted her eyes. "Joram took her. We tried to protect her, and she fought him off for days, but he would hear none of it last night. The murderous look on his face was terrible... Leoric, he's gone completely mad."

"I asked where she was," Leoric repeated, this time with an edge to the words.

Cara stammered, "Last night, they took her by force. We heard screams from his house, but haven't seen her since," she trembled as she spoke. "I'm sorry, Leo, we tried to help her."

Leoric moved forward and held the shaking woman. "It's not your fault, Cara. This is that bastard Joram's doing and it's time I set things right."

"No! You must leave now before you lose any more time. The goblins won't be kept in the dark about your escape for much longer!" Cara pleaded.

"I must see Kieri first," Leoric replied defiantly as he started across the compound, his determined strides taking him towards the small house belonging to the traitor.

As he closed the distance, the rage that had built up over the past few months threatened to erupt from his very being. Any nervousness and fear he may have previously felt regarding the long awaited confrontation with Joram had evaporated. Shaking with fury, Leoric tightened his fingers into rigid fists and approached the wooden door.

He did not bother to knock.

Throwing open the door, he charged inside without any hesitation. He couldn't believe the scene there before him. Kieri's bound and gagged figure was securely fastened to a beam in the front room. Her head slumped forward, and even in the low light, he could see dark bruises adorning her body.

His blood boiled as he spotted the reason for his outrage, Joram, sitting in a chair by the crackling fire. The man held a haunch of meat in one hand, a flagon of ale in the other. As Leoric stepped inside, a look of dread crossed the man's features. Joram cried out for help, his eyes white with fear.

"D'Athgaran, you'll die for this outrage!" Joram shouted, surging to his feet and spilling food and drink in the hopes of escaping Leoric's charge.

With a satisfying crunch, Leoric connected with a heavy forearm to the man's chest. Joram staggered backwards and fell over the chair near the fire. "I warned you, Joram, you were not to touch her again!" Leoric uttered coldly while stalking his adversary. He gave no thought to the consequences of his actions, feeling no remorse and no pity. He had only one goal in mind, and nothing short of his own death was going to stop him.

Joram scampered backwards along the floor, blood already seeping from his mouth. As Leoric bore down on him, the bully's gaze darted momentarily to something beyond Leoric's left shoulder. Realizing the error in allowing his rage to consume him, Leoric threw himself desperately to one side. Despite his efforts, a heavy blow landed on his back, pain lancing immediately through the area.

Hitting the ground rolling, Leoric quickly regained his feet and turned to face Ealston. Joram's imposing henchman stood there grinning wickedly. Tossing aside the broken remnants of the chair he had used to attack the borderman, he slipped a long, bone-handled knife out from under his tunic.

"I've waited long enough to kill you, Leoric!" Joram barked.

Warily attempting to keep an eye on both men, Leoric watched with apprehension as Joram toyed absently with a dagger. Unarmed, Leoric knew he was in trouble.

A voice from across the room brought them all to a standstill.

"Leoric! Don't do this! Run. Run while you can!" Kieri's eyes blazed with defiance, and she screamed in Joram's direction. "You got nothing from me last night, nor will you ever, you bastard. You will go to the depths for your actions here among us!"

There was a conviction behind the words, so much so that Joram visibly paled as he stared wide-eyed at Kieri. With an agonizing cry, he hurtled towards her with his blade upraised. "You twisted whore! I'll kill you!"

Leoric caught him in mid-stride, his powerful frame colliding heavily with Joram's shoulder, bearing them both through a wooden table and crashing to the floor. With satisfaction, Leoric watched the blade skitter across the floor and out of reach. Expecting that Ealston would already be coming to the aid of his master, Leoric struggled to his feet. Once standing, he pushed Joram back to the floor in an attempt to create some space in which he could maneuver.

Ealston failed to anticipate the sudden attack from behind. Just as Leoric had been preoccupied with Joram, so too did the big henchman forget to guard his own back. With a deep growl, Angvald wrapped his arms around the man, knocking the weapon from his grasp and launching him towards the wall. There was an audible crack as the man fell heavily to the floor. In two short strides, the Kaleenian was standing over the fallen henchman. With a mighty twist of his powerful arms, Angvald snapped the man's neck. Sinking to the floor, Ealston died without a sound.

Seeing his man fall, Joram dove forward and jumped on Leoric's back. Momentarily stunned, Leoric fell to his knees under the man's subsantial weight. With surprising strength, Joram wrapped his arms around Leoric's neck and started to crush the air from his windpipe. The shoulder weakened by Ealston's attack denied Leoric any leverage as they fell backwards, Joram's grip tightening. A stab of panic entered Leoric's heart, realizing that he now lay helpless. In a daze, he could see Angvald slowly regaining his feet and heading his way, but already his vision swam dizzily.

Struggling to draw breath, Leoric's outstretched hands clawed at the floor. With patches of light blinking across his vision, his hand suddenly came down on a cold metal object; it was Joram's discarded dagger. With a rugged determination born out of fear, he closed his hand tightly around the weapon.

With a combined cry of rage and pain, Leoric thrust downwards, the dagger sinking deep into Joram's flesh. A gush of warm blood washed over his hands and he tried desperately to roll away. As he did, one of Joram's flailing arms caught him with a glancing blow across his temple. A bright flash of pain shattered Leoric's thoughts as he rolled aside, his vision now blurry and muted. It took him a few moments to clear his mind of the ringing pain caused by the blow. As every second passed, he was sure that his defenseless position would mean his death. Leoric shook his head futilely and waited for the inevitable final blow; but it never came.

As his spotty vision finally cleared, he scanned for his enemy. It took only a second to find the man. Joram was dead, his sightless eyes staring up at the ceiling of his cursed home, blood still pouring from a ghastly wound. Embedded in the man's neck was the dagger. Leoric had driven it through with his last ounce of strength and buried it up to the hilt.

As the red film slowly faded from Leoric's eyes, he looked at the gruesome scene in dismay. Angvald stood in the doorway, his large frame outlined in the early morning light. The Kaleenian's face look distressed as he crossed the floor in three purposeful steps and helped Leoric to his feet.

"Leoric, are you hurt?" he asked with concern.

Pausing a moment to compose himself, Leoric simply shook his head. He took one last glance at the carnage in the room, the corpses near his feet, and the still form of Kieri, and collapsed. "Check Kieri," he managed to gasp.

Sometime during the violent struggle, one of the broken pieces of furniture must have been thrown in her direction. A large lump had already formed on her temple.

Angvald darted to her side. Bending down, he calmly checked her breathing and lightly touched the wound. In response, the woman's eyes flickered open. With a weak smile, the bearded Kaleenian held her close. "She's fine, Leoric... she's just fine," he said, his voice filled with relief.

The trio staggered out to the courtyard. There, mustered near the back of the nearest warehouse, was a small group of people. A whispered cry of joy rose up from those assembled as Leoric, Kieri, and Angvald joined them. Cara smiled broadly as she embraced Leoric.

"There will be repercussions after the events of this night," Auric said. In his hands he held bags of supplies. Coiled around his shoulder was a healthy length of rope and a rounded leather map case poked out from one of the bags. "The bodies must be buried and any trace of their existence hidden. Some of us need to be departing," he added, looking anxiously to the west.

Cara nodded in agreement. "Benoit, Angvald and Leoric must leave before the opportunity to escape grows any shorter." Glancing at the sky, she frowned. "Judging by the light, you're already far behind the proposed schedule."

Wasting no further time, goodbyes were quickly exchanged. Standing apart from the others, Kieri and Leoric held each other in a tight embrace. Brushing aside a stray lock of her golden brown hair, he gently lifted her chin. Kieri's eyes filled with tears as she pressed herself against him. Oblivious to their surroundings, they kissed each other passionately.

"If you ask it of me, I will stay," he whispered.

"I love you, Leoric D'Athgaran. Nothing can change that. You hold my heart now and always," Kieri wept. "But you cannot remain here with me. We both know that your path has already been chosen."

"I cannot bear to lose you again..." Leoric trailed off.

"You once asked me if you would be remembered. I will never forget your courage, your generosity, and your understanding. Although apart for now, you will be in my memories each and every day," she declared.

"One day, I will return for you," Leoric vowed. "I swear to you, Kieri, you will not die a prisoner in this place."

Putting a finger to his lips, she whispered, "Shh. Let's not speak of the future. I know that I will be in your heart. For now, that is enough."

"But —"

"Leo... just hold me one last time," she asked of him.

Their tears mingled as they stood frozen in each other's arms.

"Go... please. Be safe," Kieri whispered.

With a nod, Leoric hefted his backpack and slung it over his good shoulder. He hugged Cara, uttering some parting words, and then joined Angvald near the edge of the field. Beside Angvald stood Finn Callum, the Iron Shield captain greeting Leoric with a warm smile.

"May the gods watch over you both," Finn said as they embraced. Offering his blade hilt to Leoric, the officer added. "Take the blade, you'll be needing it more than I."

Leoric pushed it away. "Bury it here in a secret place. Use it if ever the need arises. The people here will look to you and Cara now, Captain, and you'll need to keep them safe."

"Leoric, I cannot acc —"

"Nonsense," Angvald interrupted. "You have given us a chance to warn those who are in need. You have risked your life for strangers and for that we can never repay you." Placing a large hand on the soldier's shoulder, he continued. "I also know that the gods will look favourably upon you because of your actions. You are an honourable man, Finn Callum, and I am proud to call you a friend."

With a serious nod, Leoric gripped the man's arm firmly. "And besides, Angvald prefers the axe, and I prefer the mace. You have the skill to wield the sword. Keep them safe friend," he finished with a wink.

With a final look at Kieri, the woman standing proudly at Cara's side, he headed into the field and began to run. With his brawny arms raised in triumph, Angvald leapt after him, and in short order they had put the homestead well behind them.

&

The great wall built to guard the fields of *Lok'Dal hie* loomed above the four small figures. Leoric had forgotten how immense the structure truly was. It seemed like ages had passed since he had last travelled so near. In fact, it had been close to eight months since he had been so close to the great battlement.

"It's bigger than I remember..." Auric breathed in awe.

Shocked by the sudden realization that the old prisoner had not been at the wall in well over two decades, Leoric placed a comforting hand on the man's wiry shoulder. "You'll never have to see it again after tonight, Auric," he said.

"I know," Auric replied.

Apart from three daggers, one long knife, and their new sets of clothes, the escapees carried little else. Their first failed escape attempt had resulted in the confiscation of most of their secretly hoarded supplies, including the majority of the food they had collected. Apart from the maps and rope, both of which Auric had been able to conceal while avoiding detection, the four men were going to have to rely heavily on the land to bolster their energy. If they could scale the wall without trouble, freedom lay on the other side.

Leoric was certain they wouldn't need to trek further north to swim beneath the small channel that directed water into the fields. Auric swiftly threw one end of their rope, catching it on one of the high stone crenels. Soon they stood together atop the wall.

"Auric, you have been here the longest. The first descent is yours." Leoric said unflinchingly.

"Thank you, lad," Auric said, his eyes glistening and a tear sliding down one of his weathered cheeks.

Benoit followed next and Angvald third. As each man reached the ground, Leoric breathed a sigh of relief. No matter what happened during his own descent, the others would be able to carry on. Waving at his three companions, Leoric found himself almost reluctant to step over the edge of the battlement.

His time at *Lok'Dal hie* had changed him for the better, even though so much heartache had come with that change. For the first time in many years, Leoric felt alive like he had rarely felt before. His hardened soul, closed to the outside world for so long, had begun to heal because of the touch of a woman and the strength of his friends. He was looked to as a leader and vowed never again to seek refuge behind the walls of his fears.

Most satisfying of all was his belief that he had forged his own fate and his own luck. He now walked a path that no god had decreed for him. He was free because of the sacrifice of others, not because of the whim of some god.

I am my own man and I will do as I please.

Standing alone atop the wall, Leoric gazed back across the wide open fields of *Lok'Dal hie*. He imagined Kieri standing in the compound, that disarming smile upon her face. Making a silent promise to return and save the woman he loved, Leoric grasped the rope and turned away.

"Goodbye..." he muttered, stepping over the edge of the wall.

ೞ

Kieri stood quietly beside Cara in the same spot where they had watched the fleeing figures cross the nearest field and head off to the west. Both women had remained standing there staring into the darkness even after the shady outlines of their friends had long disappeared from view. She had valiantly held back her tears as Leoric left the compound, but in the end, the emotion of their parting was far too painful to hide. Now that the men had vanished into the night, a heartfelt sob wracked her small frame.

Leaning on her healthy leg, Cara put a comforting hand on Kieri's shoulder. "It's all right, Kieri, it's all right..."

"I miss him already," she replied between ragged breaths.

"You know he would have stayed for you," Cara said quietly.

Wiping a fresh set of tears from her cheeks Kieri turned towards the other woman. "Like Drake would have done for you, had he lived to see this night?"

"Yes, he would have stayed, the brave fool," Cara eyes brimmed with her own sorrow. "And I would have sent him away, just as you did Leoric."

"I had no choice," Kieri shook her head in frustration. "I had no choice," she repeated.

Subconsciously she let her hands slide over her belly, caressing the area with loving care.

Glancing at Kieri, Cara's eyes widened. "Does he know?"

"He wouldn't have left had he known," Kieri replied.

"And it is his?"

A tremor of fear rippled through Kieri's body, but her eyes blazed with passion as she proudly met her friend's intent stare. "After Leoric and I were together, I never let Joram touch me. Even when Leoric was gone, I fought him off."

"Good," Cara nodded.

Putting her hands tenderly over her stomach, Kieri closed her eyes and whispered. "The child I carry is Leoric's."

Come all ye children, look what I've found,
Come find a seat, come gather 'round.
For here is a tale of magic and might,
A tale of courage, a tale of fright.
—*Author Unknown*

CHAPTER XXXIX

Wickam, Protectorate

The town of Wickam materialized unexpectedly in the early morning mist. A lengthy drizzle brought with it a thick fog that greatly hampered Bider's vision. Constantly adjusting his position on the mount, the young scout tried to find some semblance of comfort in the saddle. He had never been a strong rider, and his natural lack of skill, compounded by his various injuries, only hindered him further.

Four hard days of riding could take a toll on a healthy man, let alone one in his condition. Gavin had insisted they push onwards, promising a rest once they reached the town that could now be seen through the dissipating fog. The tall spire of Wickam's Church of Arne stabbed upward, the steeple seeming to float while the base of the structure remained hidden. As with most towns, the church towered high above the earth. The place of worship and piousness reached up to the heavens and the high realms of the gods.

Reflecting on the harrowing flight from the *Ca'lenbam*, Bider was anxious to finally arrive at their destination. The night of their escape Gavin had returned to their tent and hurriedly gathered up what little supplies he had collected. Bider was shocked by the stern look etched on his captain's features. Gavin Silveron had looked grim and dejected; older suddenly than his years, with deeply creased lines of worry now fixed near the corners of his eyes. Bider knew better than to broach the subject with the notoriously private man, preferring instead to busy himself with struggling to stand, a feat that had taken considerable effort in his state. The horses were tied just beyond the tent, the two animals saddled and ready for a quick departure.

The next four days had passed in a harrowing blur. Bider had only sporadic memories of the first day of travel. In a cloudy haze, he did remember a nighttime ride and foray into the Caeronwood, the forest the two riders had shadowed since their departure from the *Ca'lenbam*. They had slept in their saddles, stopping only briefly to rest and water the horses. Gavin had remained aloof.

Bider grimaced as he shifted once more in his saddle. Although healing rapidly, his broken ribs still ached. Sleeping with the injury was almost impossible, as every shift while slumbering brought with it stabs of sharp discomfort. His ankle was another matter altogether. Even with Gavin's promise to have the learned healers of Dragon Mount examine the break, the young scout wondered if he would ever fully recover from the serious wound. The new guards of the Protectorate had been quite thorough while beating him.

"How long do you estimate, Captain?" he turned in the saddle.

"We'll be there soon enough, Coren," Gavin said, a flicker of relief dancing in his eyes for the first time on the journey. "I'll even buy the first round if you manage to not ask me the same question again," he quipped.

Amused by the response, Bider willed himself ever closer to Wickam.

Gavin was grateful for Coren's excitement. The last few days had been grueling for the injured man, but Gavin knew that any delay in reaching the town would have spelled their doom. No doubt his clear message had been received, and if Gerald Armsmater's reputation was even partially accurate, the man would soon be seeking retribution. And so, Gavin had planned on being nowhere near the *Ca'lenbam* when the search for his whereabouts began.

Although Coren's body was healing rapidly, he was still concerned about the young scout's psyche. The Eagle Runner had been very close to Orn and he had yet to broach the subject of the man's unjust death. Gavin had also chosen to remain silent, at least for the time being, regarding the hangings he had witnessed at the Gathering. The reaction of the crowd, so bloodthirsty and frenzied at the event, had rattled him more than he wanted to admit. That so many people saw nothing wrong with the coup that had left so many men dead, was unsettling in and of itself.

Did no one truly realize that Gadian Yarr's play for power in the south was only the beginning? The powerful councillor from Imlaris would not be content with the cities comprising the Protectorate. His nomination of a general and subsequent fielding of an army only promised more bloodshed.

Shrugging off the troubling thoughts, Gavin attempted to focus on the present. Although everything had progressed as planned these last four days, an unsettling event that had transpired while camped beneath the protective cover of the Caeronwood had left him uneasy.

Taking shelter in the forest after the overcast sky threatened a heavy downpour, Gavin set up camp and left Coren to rest as he went searching for a source of fresh water. Discovering a stream only a few hundred paces into the woods, he bent down to fill their canteens, his hand coming to rest on the forest floor. A sudden shudder spread through his fingers, and he was inexplicably drawn towards a small clearing.

He walked quietly among the trees in the small grove, marveling at its beauty. A small pond in the center of the clearing caught his attention. Lightly brushing the surrounding trees with his fingertips, he meandered through the copse. As he neared the water, his hand brushed up against an immense oak tree towering hundreds of feet in the air, its branches thick and strong, the leaves lush and green.

Abruptly, a bright flash blinded him and he stumbled to the ground with a sharp cry. A terrible vision suddenly filled his mind. It was as if he was seeing through the eyes of some creature; the beast moving with great speed through the trunks of a forest. The heavy pounding tread of the creature's gait sent shivers through Gavin's spine. Ragged breathing accompanied the vision, the sound inhuman and terrifying. Suddenly, the scene faded from view and he found himself lying on his back along the water's edge.

Instinctively, Gavin knew he had been warned. Something followed them; something with an undeniably sinister intent tracked the two Fey'Derin. Without pause

and without a word of explanation, he had packed up the camp and helped a groggy
Coren back into his saddle.

This wasn't the first time that he had been warned by a dream. After leaving the
confining borders of Dragon Mount some years earlier, Gavin had periodically
experienced the same phenomenon. He believed it must be something inherited
at birth, a characteristic that revealed some sort of bond with the land of Kal
Maran. He also suspected that two other men were also unwilling recipients of
the same trait.

With the first destination of their journey north in sight, Gavin was relieved. His
earlier apprehension dissipated as the number of leagues they travelled increased.
He was satisfied with their progress as they soon passed from the outlying farmers'
fields on to the rough cobblestone streets of the trading town.

Situated along one of the major trading routes in the south, as well as being a natural hub for the northernmost villages and towns in the Protectorate, the town of
Wickam had shown continued growth over the years. The two men rode nonchalantly down the main thoroughfare, and after passing a number of smaller taverns,
settled on a large three-floored inn named The Brimming Tankard. Tethering their
steeds out front, Bider waited patiently as Gavin entered the establishment in order
to make arrangements for their stay.

A short while later, both men sat across from one another smiling contentedly as
they enjoyed long pulls from nearly overflowing mugs of ale.

"You know, at this very moment, sir, I can almost pretend that I don't look and
feel quite terrible," Bider laughed.

Downing the last of his first mug in one long swallow, Gavin grinned. "That
might be true about the feeling, Coren, but Sergeant Shade has always said you
look terrible, even in the best of circumstances."

"If you weren't buying, Captain, I'd take affront to that!"

୦ଓ

That evening, after a long and very restful sleep, Bider found himself sitting
quietly near the common room fireplace with long pipe in hand. Blowing

lazy circles of smoke across the room, he sipped at another large mug of the dark homemade brew the owners of the Tankard boasted was the best in the region.

Gavin had disappeared sometime during the afternoon, leaving a hastily scrawled note stating that their funds were low and needed to be replenished. Knowing the captain to be resourceful, Bider still couldn't imagine what the man might have in store to remedy that predicament. With Captain Silveron, it was best not to imagine too little, lest you be surprised.

Time alone gave Bider the opportunity to organize his own thoughts. The town of Wickam had struck a melancholy chord within him, and dealing with the flush of memories was something he preferred to do on his own. While travelling with the Fey'Derin, he had passed through many villages, towns, and cities, but only a few reminded him of his shameful past.

Raised in the streets of Green Bend, a fair sized town situated a short ride from the northern port city of K'oral, Bider had never known his parents. He was an orphan and had lived with various families and in some orphanages. Each home blurred together to form muddled memories of hungry nights, cruel bullies, and feelings of intense loneliness.

He had started thieving for no other reason than to feed himself. At least that was how he had justified his actions... at first. Working on the docks at the local wharf, he led a punishing double life that had connected him with far too many of the wrong type of person. It was his mounting greed that had cost him his employment at the docks, although truthfully he had been paid very little. It was his also his greed that had led to him being found by Captain Silveron and Orn Surefoot one fateful autumn evening.

He was extraordinarily lucky to have been found alive. Refusing to concede to the demands of the insular thieving guild, he had avoided the vindictive thugs for days before an unfortunate encounter in an alleyway brought about a vicious beating. They warned him that if he deviated any further from the strict order of the association, he would eliminated. That meant nothing more than a slit throat and a never-ending sleep at the bottom of the river.

Yet for some reason, Gavin Silveron had perceived something in the small thief that even Bider himself could not understand. And so, he had been spared, and had vowed to spend the rest of his days standing dutifully at the side of the man who had seen fit to grant him a new life.

With the memory of that difficult time, came the flood of emotions associated with the unjust passing of Orn Surefoot. It was the old scout who had been his constant strength, helping him adjust to life with the Fey'Derin. Throughout his somewhat tumultuous training, it was Orn who stood up to defend the young recruit thrown into their midst. Bider found it impossible to believe the grumpy veteran scout, a master at his chosen skill, was truly gone. That the man had seemingly banished his demons, walking sober in his last few months, made it all the more difficult to accept.

Wiping a hand across his teary eyes, Bider glanced about the room. It was rare that he showed such emotion, and yet Orn had been his greatest ally and would be sorely missed. Bider decided that if ever a chance were to arise where the newly proclaimed General of the Protectorate was within reach, nothing short of a miracle would stop him exacting revenge. Orn Surefoot deserved a better fate, and Bider would be damned if Gerald Armsmater was never held accountable for the murder of his friend.

A smattering of applause eventually commanded Bider's attention. With a heavy sigh, he tried his best to push aside the painful memories and focus on the present. As the mild applause faded, he squinted in the smoky lantern light of the Tankard's common room and could barely contain his surprise when he recognized the man sitting comfortably on stage, black lute in hand.

By all the gods ... do we know nothing about this man? Shaking his head in disbelief, he listened to the haunting melody.

> *In whispered words and shadowy voices,*
> *the wind speaks of a tale, long in the telling.*

> *Of a fallen place, wondrous to see,*
> *so beautiful to behold.*
> *Of a land now forgotten, a history never known,*
> *An elder race, the true people of old.*

In darkening light, she stands alone,
the broken heart of a land far gone.
Towers crumble, only shattered stone,
She remains my one true home.

Entranced by Gavin's performance, Bider caught himself holding his breath. He realized how little was actually known by the soldiers of the Fey'Derin of matters concerning their captain. *To have hidden such talent...*

His parentage had never been spoken of, his previous life among the Silveryn Mages only recently revealed, and yet Bider knew that he would die for the man without a second thought. Something in the way he looked at you, that confident gaze that conveyed a genuine respect and belief in your abilities. Granted, for many of the men of the company, Gavin had saved them from a life of shame, but that wasn't the only reason the Fey'Derin followed the grey-eyed man.

In silence, Bider watched his captain perform for most of the evening, the crowd encouraging the visiting musician. Gavin possessed obvious talent and proceeded to show it. Although apparent that he was out of practice, with a few songs behind him, Gavin confidently hit his stride. From brooding melodies, many unfamiliar to the patrons, to fast moving jigs, the songs had the Brimming Tankard jostling with delight.

CR

"If you don't mind me asking, sir, where did you come across that bit of skill?" Bider ventured, the two men sitting quietly at a small table near the fire. The inn had wound down for the night, and the two Fey'Derin mercenaries were among only a handful of patrons still awake.

Gavin shrugged. "You've heard much about the Koriani?"

"I guess I have," he answered. "They're the soldiers of the Silveryn Order, men and women who excel in the art of combat. I was there when you fought your duels, sir."

"And that is where you're wrong, Coren," Gavin replied with a knowing glance. "The Silveryn Mages don't simply have elite soldiers in their employ. Rather, for the most part, my childhood was spent studying the natural world and learning to read and write. We were introduced to various disciplines, one of those being music. I took to the lute quite quickly," he said with a wistful smile. "Back in those days, life was much simpler."

"And the military training?" Bider asked.

"Oh, we trained every day, be it sparring or conditioning, but it wasn't given any more focus than the arts. We were expected to excel in all disciplines, and failure was not an option. Once older, some of the more intelligent students became scholars, whereas the majority joined the ranks of the Koriani."

"At what age?"

"I had seen thirteen summers when I won my first bout in the Order. I beat a man by the name of Kilian Sanford. He'd been a proud member of the Koriani for over thirty-five years when I defeated him. He'd once been ranked as a Koriani Eighth. It was unfortunate that he fell so low, as he did possess adequate skill."

"Incredible...and you were ranked?" Bider pressed, happy to have caught his commander in a very forthcoming mood.

"I left Dragon Mount the eve of my friend Brynne's bout to achieve Koriani Second. At the time I had already broken my ties to the Order, much to the chagrin of many," he replied with a frown. "They couldn't understand why I would give up my so-called position of honour. I was Koriani Third when I departed, and I've never regretted leaving."

"And why did you leave?" Bider asked cautiously.

Staring intently at Bider with eyes twinkling, Gavin smiled. "That, my friend, is not your concern."

☙

Bider was looking forward to another restful sleep and the renewed energy it would surely bring. Their long journey would continue in the morning. Gavin had made a tidy little profit playing the part of minstrel, and although they were thoroughly enjoying their stay at the Tankard, there were more pressing matters at hand.

Tumbling into one of the room's small beds, Bider could barely contain a feeling of pure contentment. As the days had passed, and the slow process of healing had continued, he kept up his belief that events would continue to improve. With distant rumblings of thunder forewarning a wet evening and an even wetter morning, Bider closed his eyes. Lying there surrounded by thick pillows and warm blankets, he suspected that Gavin was standing guard. A last glance before falling into a deep slumber confirmed that belief. At the window, arms crossed over his chest and with a familiar determined look on his face, stood Gavin Silveron. Sleep came swiftly for Bider.

An incredibly loud crack of thunder jolted Bider from his sleep. Grunting as the pain caused by the sudden movement jarred him, he looked towards the room's window. A momentary flash of lightning illuminated the pensive face of the Fey'Derin captain, the man staring intently out into the storm.

"What is it, sir?" Bider asked, noting a subtle change in Gavin's stance.

Gavin spoke without moving his eyes from the window. "I believe that our visitor will arrive soon. Whatever has been hunting us possesses far more endurance than I expected. I think it has travelled a long distance to find us. Do you feel it?"

Confused, Bider pushed aside his blankets and began searching for his discarded clothing.

"Your tattoo, Coren," Gavin indicated by touching his chest. "Do you feel it?" He reached for the crossbow purchased earlier that day. In one swift motion, Gavin pulled the drawstring taut and notched a steel bolt. "We'll soon have company."

Once mentioned, Bider immediately detected a faint itch over his heart. How Gavin had so easily detected the slight sensation was impressive. As he donned his leathers, Bider could sense that whatever magic was involved was rapidly drawing closer.

"Where do you need me, sir?" he asked hesitantly, his quivering voice revealing how afraid he truly was.

Gavin marched across the room and gripped him hard by the shoulders, "What hunts us is a creature of dark magic, Coren. It's not something we can face together, not with your injuries. I ask of you only two things —"

"No, Captain! I may not be mobile, but I still have my daggers and my mind. I can be of some use," Bider interrupted.

Gavin shook his head. "Coren, I will order you if I have to."

"Fine," Bider conceded reluctantly.

After the scout's reluctant nod, the Fey'Derin captain continued. "Good. First, prepare the horses for departure, and leave a bag of coin with the innkeeper. There's no reason for us ignore our responsibility to our host."

"Secondly, take the crossbow and wait for an opening. You'll have one shot to slow this beast down, and if I'm in need, you'll be the only one able to buy me enough time to stay alive. Understood?"

"Yes, sir ..." Bider managed to whimper. Talking had suddenly become difficult and his breathing shallow.

Then came the steady tread of a large creature. Even over the rain and thunder, the booming steps could be heard. Whatever pursued them was massive, and the Fey'Derin mark began to burn painfully. Fighting a terrible urge to scratch the tattoo, Bider stumbled out through the doorway and cast one last glance at his commander. Still at the window, Gavin Silveron was steadily checking his weapons, the straps on his boots and gauntlets, the position of his daggers, and the tightness of all bindings.

As Bider pushed through the confused and worried patrons downstairs, concern for his captain weighed heavily on his mind. Trusting Gavin, he exited the inn and hurried towards the stables, crossbow clutched tightly in hand.

03

A *Sciloc*.

It was a demon. It hailed from *Lok'Mor*, a plane of existence forbidden to humankind. A place where it is said the first Gath-like creatures called home, if such a barren landscape could be called such. It had been more than a century since the last of its kind had terrorized Kal Maran, and at that time it had been the machinations of a madman that had brought forth the demon.

Gavin knew of only one way to summon the creature that approached the inn: magecraft. That the renegade Fallen were in league with the leaders of the new Protectorate was now undeniable. This could only mean that his plea for support from the Silveryn mages desperately needed to succeed. Without arcane help there would be little courageous men or the strength of arms could do in the coming battles. The Council needed to send aid.

Finally satisfied with his armaments, Gavin calmly made his way down to the main entrance of the inn, unable to decide whether the demon posed a greater threat than the Fallen. Breathing deeply to calm himself, Gavin made his way methodically through the awakened customers of the inn. It took him long minutes before he reached the other side of the common room. Pulling his cloak over his head, he ducked out into the storm, pausing only a moment to adjust the dagger in his boot top.

Bravely taking his stance in the middle of the drenched road, Gavin waited. The rain poured down, and if not for the frequent slashes of bright lightning, the road would have been covered by darkness. Pelted by the biting cold of each drop of frigid spring rain, Gavin ignored the rampant screams from the Tankard and neighbouring buildings, focusing solely on the road before him.

The steady tread of rumbling footsteps signaled the creature's presence. Gavin found himself fighting off a tightening grip of dread that threatened to sink his courage. Conjuring up long years of strict mental training under the tutelage of the Koriani masters, Gavin flexed his fingers and continued to wait.

It advanced on his position in such a flurry that to have blinked may have cost him his life. The creature never slowed, suddenly appearing in the midst of the heavy rain. Charging with claws upraised, the *Sciloc* shrieked, the cry so inhuman it was impossible to describe.

The demon stood at least twelve feet tall. Its skin was a reddish brown, the colour of the wet sands of Kaleen, but it was also covered in patches of thick, dripping ebony fur. The Sciloc's sloped forehead and ridged brows concealed a blank, dead stare. One glance at those eyes almost broke Gavin's confidence, already under heavy siege. Solid legs the size of tree trunks covered the distance between the two combatants, and long sinewy arms thrust outward with edged claws.

Throwing himself clear, Gavin was almost skewered by the initial lunge. He tossed his sodden cloak aside, knowing that anything impeding his agility would mean certain death, and drew his sword. Men were never meant to do battle with a *Sciloc*; at least not those that hoped to live and tell the tale. Fighting defensively was his only option, he thought, dodging two more deceptively quick swipes by the glinting claws.

As the battle raged across the yard, Gavin studied his foe. The Koriani, if they had taught him anything, had instructed him in the ways of the duel. With adept skill, as he had that winter dueling in the courtyard of Dragon Mount, he slipped back into old habits. Every opponent possessed a weakness, and it was the exploitation of that flaw that would grant him the advantage he so desperately sought. The demon out-reached, out-muscled, and potentially out-maneuvered him. Any attempt Coren might make to aid him would involve waiting for the right moment — the perfect opening. There would be no need were he to fall in the opening exchanges of the battle.

What Gavin did ascertain from the *Sciloc's* initial charge was that it was already lost in a berserker frenzy. As with the Gath, here was an enemy that cared little for its own safety. It was mindless, a being whose sole purpose was to hunt a target and slay them.

Unaware that the bout was now being witnessed by the majority of the customers at both The Brimming Tankard and the surrounding establishments, the man and demon spun, circled, lunged, and attacked one another across the breadth of the road.

Gavin fought in silence, his eyes locked on his opponent. The *Sciloc* was much the opposite, shrieking in fury and howling in frustration, forcing many onlookers to cower in fear. Ducking an incoming strike, Gavin leapt forward and scored a blow to the beast's arm, black blood flying wide.

Ignoring the stab, the *Sciloc* nearly decapitated the mercenary captain with a return swing, the sharp claws whisking mere inches from Gavin's face. To have risked so much for a wound that seemed to have accomplished so little caused Gavin some concern; staying alive had suddenly become a much more difficult proposition. Again the tireless demon launched itself forward, and Gavin fought hard for the next few moments just trying to keep his balance.

But amidst all the frantic movements, the beginnings of a plan started to form as Gavin watched the demon shift quickly from position to position, always ready to strike, always on the attack. If Coren could glean even a small portion of his idea, Gavin knew he might have a chance. As it stood, even though he had scored a number of minor wounds to the beast's forearms and chest, his opponent's huge advantage in height and reach prevented the possibility of a critical strike.

Clearly frustrated, Gavin focused on keeping his footing on the increasingly treacherous ground. Even now, he could feel the mud giving way as the rain continued to pour down. Fighting the creature in much deeper mud would be disastrous. Warily confronting the *Sciloc*, Gavin dove to the right, barely avoiding another brief flurry launched his way. There was no time for a hurried word of warning, and Gavin knew that only one option remained; he would have to trust in the Eagle Runner's abilities. Coren was intelligent enough to identify the ploy, he was sure of it.

Bider watched the two combatants with increasing worry. The demon creature was obviously bigger and stronger, but Gavin possessed the uncanny ability to narrowly avoid each and every attack directed his way.

From the onset of the battle Bider had searched for an opening that could aid his commander, but a clear shot at the beast's head seemed far too risky. It tended to bounce its head back and forth, weaving erratically, and he feared a missed shot would be the end of the captain. With his considerable injuries, resetting the crossbow for a second shot seemed unlikely. He would have one chance, and one chance only, to make his attack count. Try as he might, Bider could not fathom why in Arne's name Gavin kept diving to the right, never quite able to get the demon to expose its neck.

In the distance a ringing alarm sounded, and the hurried tread of the town's militia could be heard approaching from the north end of Wickam. Even with a squad of soldiers, Bider feared the demon could easily tear apart any mass attack. A few lucky blows might land, but Gavin's efforts had already demonstrated that the creature's hide was thick beyond compare.

As a dozen or so figures emerged near the top of the street, the young scout could tell that these men were poorly trained and completely inadequate in the face of such danger. Panic stricken looks were etched on each of their faces, their weapons falling from listless hands. The demon allowed his gaze to sweep over the small company of militia for only the briefest moment, and yet they had all been unmanned. Cowering in fear, they could barely stand as they watched the combatants fight across the treacherous ground.

Once again, Bider winced as he watched Gavin evade yet another frantic bout of attacks, dodging to the side with less ease than he had at the onset of the battle. Bider was worried that the man's endurance was flagging. He was already attacking with far less frequency and fervor. Every moment of respite that Gavin gained was used to conserve his fading stamina.

"Why do you keep going to the right side?" Bider agonized, calling out to no one. Behind him, the horses threatened to break his concentration as they struggled to break free from their tethers.

The demon strikes and Gavin moves right...not left...right...but why? Studying the opponent, as he had once been taught by Orn, it finally made sense. Gavin wanted him to focus not on the thick-skulled head of the terrible demon, but instead on something entirely different. Gavin was fighting in a manner that accentuated the creature's mobility. Taking this into consideration clarified everything; the demon planted his clawed feet in the same manner each and every time Gavin evaded to the right. The mercenary captain had done so in such an inauspicious manner that Bider doubted the *Sciloc* had detected the ploy.

Bider could now see the opening form as the demon's powerful leg locked for those precious seconds it would need to turn its girth to the side in an attempt to track the wily human. Raising the crossbow to take aim, Bider watched in dismay as Gavin's boot suddenly slipped in the mud. Immediately, the creature recognized the advantage and closed in. Forcing himself to watch, Bider could barely breathe.

Gavin knew it was bound to have happened sooner or later. With the rain continuing to pour down in sheets, his footing was only going to deteriorate further. The second he felt his boot sink into the thick mud, he knew that his foot had found no real purchase on the solid ground underneath. The *Sciloc* would be faster this time, and there was little he could do but brace himself for the charge.

He managed to avoid the demon's claws, but the thick forearm of his foe caught him across his midsection. He was thrown through the air like a child's doll. However, the torrential rain turned out to be somewhat of a blessing. The softened earth yielded to his body, allowing a measure of cushioning as he landed, his breath crushed violently from his lungs. The unmistakable crack of several ribs, minor injuries considering the distance travelled, also greeted him upon impact.

Now I can only hope that Coren understood...

In response, an ear shattering shriek assaulted his senses. Scrambling to his feet, Gavin pushed aside the pain and exhaustion. Reclaiming his sword, he ran back at the *Sciloc*, the creature clutching at the long steel bolt from Coren's crossbow. It had driven straight through the demon's left leg, right near the knee, just as Gavin had fervently hoped. Unable to support its own massive weight, the creature had collapsed.

In four powerful strides, Gavin reached the *Sciloc*. Using the creature's body as leverage, he pushed off its wounded limb and drove his sword directly up under the monster's chin. The blade slid soundlessly through the flesh, piercing the demon's brain. The stunned beast died with nary a sound.

Only the continued sound of falling raindrops broke the silence. At some point during the battle, the lightning and thunder had abated. The hushed cries of children drifted sporadically through the night air. No one it seemed, from the customers of the inns to the slack-jawed militia standing in the street, dared to utter a sound. They were all speechless after what they had just witnessed. Bider was as silent as the next person. Even with the demon creature felled, he was still clutching the crossbow in a rigid grip.

Gavin stood in the middle of the road, head down, and shoulders shivering in the rain. The mercenary captain appeared to be cut from marble, so still did he stand. Bider limped to his side and passed him his sodden cloak, collected from the wet ground.

"We can't keep this up, sir," he commented. "We'll never make it to meet the company if neither of us can stand."

"I know, Coren," Gavin replied, his eyes on slain demon. "I know ..."

"What was it?"

"A *Sciloc*. A demon that doesn't belong in our world."

"The renegade mages?" Bider offered, wiping wet hair from his eyes.

"Yes," Gavin nodded.

The two men stood silently side by side for long minutes, neither possessing enough strength to speak further. Come morning they would be on the road once again, but for the moment Dragon Mount was still leagues away. With a new partner in the Protectorate coalition now unmasked, any earlier optimism had quickly soured.

One of the militia finally crossed the street and approached the pair. "That was incredible, my lord. You're a man of exceptional skill," the soldier gushed.

Gavin still refused to look up from his slain enemy. "I am no lord, and I had help," he replied grimly, pointing in Coren's direction.

Confused by the response, the militia soldier shuffled from foot to foot, desperately trying to avoid staring at the large carcass laying only a few scant paces away.

"Umm...well, what do we do with it?" he asked hesitantly.

Gavin lifted his gaze and raised an eyebrow as he looked at Bider.

"Burn it," the scout replied.

"We live to serve. It is all we know."
—Scholaris Monk

CHAPTER XL

Scholaris, Druine Mountain Range

Alessan and C'Aelis sat quietly around the small fire, sipping water from a flask and eating lunch under the trees. The hot sun pierced the thick canopy of leaves above and danced as a multitude of spots upon the ground. Head nestled on one of her paws, Greiyfois dozed quietly in one of the sunbeams, oblivious to the chatter of the men.

"I've always wondered what it would have been like to have more siblings. Two sisters and a brother must have been amazing, I bet." Alessan exclaimed.

Don't be so quick to believe that! C'Aelis commented, the amused tone reaching Alessan's thoughts. *Oh, there are some advantages to growing up with an older brother, but it is by no means the easiest bond. I can't count the number of times F'Eran and I found ourselves in trouble, with me being the recipient of much of the blame, no less!*

"But they're good memories all the same?" Alessan asked, hopeful that he was correct.

I guess they are, but still do I sometimes wish things had been different.

"Are you still close now that you're older?"

An unhappy expression clouded the Gorimm's features. *My brother and I no longer see things in the same light. Our views are very different when matters concerning our people are discussed.*

"Hmm, did he support those that wanted to leave the High King to die?"

Yes, although your wording isn't completely accurate. My brother felt as my father did, that the Gorimm had outgrown the uncivilized peoples of Kal Maran. Instead they made a pact with those who couldn't be trusted.

"And will I ever be told who 'they' were?" Alessan pressed on with his inquiry.

The people to whom I refer were masters of the arcane, more than that I cannot say, for I know far too little myself.

"Hmm, the Silveryn Order then? There are no other groups of people who practice magic," Alessan suggested, confident he had unmasked some of the mystery surrounding the Gorimm.

Not everyone who practices the manipulation of Aer does so openly, Alessan. It is there that your hypothesis makes an incorrect assumption. In a way, the Order played a role in our downfall by poorly guiding those magicians we dealt with.

"But I thought the Silveryn Order controlled everything having to do with the magical arts across Kal Maran?"

C'Aelis smiled ruefully. *Once more you have assumed incorrectly. The Silveryn Order definitely seeks to control all those who show talent, but that in itself is a nearly impossible task. Kal Maran is a very large place as well. The Order is not the only organized users of magic. There are many wilders —*

"Wilders?" Alessan interrupted.

Those who show no spark at a young age, but manifest a wilder affinity to the earth later in life. The change is usually attributed to grief, fear, or a significant emotional shock. They are named wilders by my people because the event that triggers this latent power often leaves the person scarred in some way, making them difficult to harness. Many soothsayers and village seers fall into this category.

"I never knew..." Alessan said. "We've always been told that the Silveryn Order controls all things magical."

The Order continues to visit your village? C'Aelis asked.

"Oh no, the merchant caravans are our best source of information," he replied. "My grandfather sometimes spoke of a mage that visited the town once in his youth. The man lined up everyone under the age of nine and tested them for magical talent. Only one girl was taken that day."

Taken?

"Well, the family was paid an enormous sum of money to allow the child to go. My grandfather said that soon after, the family left Briar for Glenvale. Why stay in a small town when you can live with all the luxuries a city can offer?" Alessan shrugged.

The two men sat quietly as they finished their lunch. Alessan poked at the fire with a stick as he grappled with the revelation. The existence of these wilders fascinated him, but he was somewhat unsettled after the conversation. His own power had appeared without warning. The Gath attack deep inside Rose Keep had been such a terrifying moment. *Could it have triggered something? Could I be a wilder?* Alessan pondered.

"What exactly is Aer?" Alessan asked, a cold shiver accompanying his query. The prospect of magical abilities still frightened him.

The large, bright eyes of the Gorimm stared mindfully back at him. *In the simplest of terms, Aer is the life force of our natural world: the earth, the trees, the wind, the water, and the stars — everything. Those who can manipulate it draw their power from the world around them.*

"Because of my dreaming power, can I do the same?" Alessan asked with some apprehension.

I'm curious, Alessan. Do you sense anything strange about me? C'Aelis prompted.

"There are plenty of things I find strange about you, C'Aelis, but it wouldn't be polite to comment on such matters," Alessan chuckled.

I meant at this moment, C'Aelis' response tickled his mind. Then the Gorimm reached for his twin blades, holding them firmly at arm's length.

Alessan watched as his companion held out the blades and murmured quietly under his breath. It was one of the rare times that C'Aelis had ever spoken aloud. The words were completely unintelligible, and yet they carried a melodic tone that soared through the air of the forest.

A soft green glow appeared around the sword blades. The radiant light crept up from the hilt, travelling steadily to the point of both weapons. More confounding than the glowing blades, was the white shimmering light emanating from C'Aelis himself. It was faint, but it encircled the Gorimm from head to toe.

What do you see? C'Aelis whispered in his mind.

"You're...shining. Not like the swords, but there's a light..." Alessan answered.

Then you do have an affinity to Aer, although its origin still eludes me.

"How do you mean? Could my battle below Farraine have woken it?" Alessan proposed.

Never has a wilder become a dreamer, just as humankind has never produced one. There was a guarded tone in C'Aelis' sending.

"You've said it yourself that history doesn't always represent the truth. Could it be that I am the first?"

Perhaps, Alessan, but there must have been some catalyst, something that changed you or an ancestor enough to allow the power to be transferred to you.

"But I'm a *ba'caech*," Alessan said, shifting uncomfortably. The movement caused the Lumber axe strapped on his back to budge. Reaching behind, he pulled the weapon free from its bindings and thumbed the blade.

It would not be a physical trait, C'Aelis responded, glancing sympathetically at the young man. His eyes suddenly widened as he watched Alessan handle the blade.

The people of Briar, they are all Lumbers? the Gorimm asked anxiously.

"Well, of the men, I'd say every household includes at least one or two members of the Guild."

And every one of the Lumbers carries an axe of their own?

"Of course! The Lumbers' Guild doesn't allow full membership status to any-one who hasn't finished crafting his weapon. To my knowledge, no one has ever failed the final ceremony in the Great Wood," Alessan replied, a confused look on his face.

What exactly is this ceremony? C'Aelis pressed.

"The apprentice, after spending many hours at the forge working with a master smith, must remain one night in the Aeldenwood. When the full moon rises, the man fells one tree; a final act proving that he has no fear in the face of our great-est foe. He then asks a blessing from *Fwaera*, the Elder Goddess, and remains on guard, alert, and ready to defend himself should evil seek to destroy him. In the morning, carrying the freshly cut stump of the fallen tree, the apprentice is welcomed into the Guild. There is a festival that evening to celebrate those men who have recently joined the ranks of the Lumbers," Alessan said.

Fwaera... I wonder...

"What is it? You're hiding something, C'Aelis," Alessan looked on in frustration.

Can I see the weapon? C'Aelis asked politely.

Alessan passed it to him and the Gorimm accepted the axe with an obvious look of disdain and disgust. He whispered once again under his breath, chanting as he had over his own blades.

Alessan sucked in his breath as a white glow emanated from the hilt and blade. "Blessed Arne, is it magical?!" he exclaimed.

There is power within this axe. I wonder whether the Elder Gods are not as dormant as we have been led to believe, C'Aelis wondered. Hastily passing the weapon back, his forehead was creased with worry. *The magic of your weapon, Alessan, could mean that the Lumbers and their families could carry the talent within themselves. Your affinity with Aer could very well have come from your father. The possibilities of so many people attuned to the natural world may explain the Guild itself...*

"How do you mean?"

By being attuned to the restlessness of the forest combined with the natural world in chaos after the disappearance of my people, it could be that your ancestors were only trying to correct the delicate balance we shattered.

"With divine guidance from the gods?" Alessan ventured.

C'Aelis rose from his seat and shouldered his backpack. Grabbing his black bow, he helped Alessan to his feet. *It is very possible, but I need time to think. In any case, we must be off. Hopefully we can also find answers to some of your questions, Alessan. There is magic in the Guild of Lumbers. How exactly it came about is still unclear, but there is no doubt it exists and has possibly bled into the bloodlines of those border towns along the Aeldenwood. The Silveryn Order must have no idea... If the monks of Scholaris can't help explain, then I'm afraid your powers may remain a mystery.*

Rushing to follow his companion, Alessan called for Greiyfois to follow. They continued their trek in silence, both men consumed by their own thoughts. As the ground passed swiftly beneath their feet, Alessan held the axe in his hand. C'Aelis' argument made sense, too much so in fact, and Alessan couldn't take his eyes from the weapon.

Magic in my veins... magic in Briar... divine guidance... destiny, he contemplated.

೦ვ

The journey through the northern expanse of the Aeldenwood passed swiftly and with little commotion. If any more Gath were roaming near P'haerin Vale, they had missed C'Aelis and Alessan's frantic escape.

The effort to elude the creatures had taken its toll on the young man from Briar. The steady pace his Gorimm companion set that first day had left him sore all over. His throat burned, his legs ached, and yet he voiced no complaints. The mere thought of facing the mindless fury of the demonic Gath was reason enough to push onwards.

Greiyfois remained with the two travellers, the wolf's wounds having finally healed. Although she would likely retain the scars of her battles with the Gath, she showed no signs of any prolonged damage. The animal was a welcome addition to the quiet procession. Alessan remained somewhat uncomfortable with the long stretches of silence that dominated large portions of the day; for if he did not speak aloud, no sound was ever heard. The fact that C'Aelis spoke in his mind was becoming less intrusive, but Alessan missed the simple sound of a voice other than his own. With Greiyfois, he had a companion whose barks and howls helped break the monotony of each day.

Alessan persisted with his sword training. Although continuing to struggle, he had shown improvement. The techniques involved highlighted his physical condition, but as the days passed and their destination grew closer, he knew that were trouble to arise, he would be far more prepared than ever before. His arm had continued to strengthen mysteriously, showing definite signs of growth. The once shrunken limb had thickened noticeably, but why, neither man could guess.

The pair finally reached the southernmost edge of the Druine Mountains as warmer nights and stifling days were ushered in by the late season. The temperature changed far less under the strangely warm cover of the Aeldenwood trees. Looking through the breaks in the foliage, Alessan stared in amazement at the rocky walls of the mountains towering thousands of feet above the forest. Growing up in Briar, he had never seen any mountains from such a close distance. An ecstatic feeling of awe swept through his body every time the trees thinned and he was able to catch a glimpse of the majestic formations.

"I never imagined they would be so beautiful!" Alessan stared.

At his side, C'Aelis nodded. *Although I desperately love the woodland, the mountains of Kal Maran are magnificent. There is something so impressive about those lone peaks rising high into the sky.*

"And Scholaris is atop one of those peaks?" Alessan marveled.

No, no. The temple lies only a thousand feet up the north side of that peak, the one my people call Gor' A'gane, C'Aelis corrected, pointing a long slender finger up towards the flat-topped mountain behind the nearest peak.

"The *Gor' A'gane*?" Alessan twisted his tongue around the unfamiliar word. "Does the name mean anything in particular?"

It translates to... 'mind of the giant', or something akin to that.

They hoped to skirt around the base of the approaching peak and reach *Gor' A'gane* by nightfall. They would camp at the base and begin their ascent the following morning.

"You know, many of the people of Briar wouldn't believe that I'm visiting Scholaris. The tale of the historian monks always sounded more fantastical than true," Alessan said with a nervous laugh. "Come to think of it, I sometimes think I'm dreaming this whole adventure. One day I might go to sleep here and wake up back in my soft warm bed at the Black Boar."

And why wouldn't they believe you, Alessan?

"Scholaris is more of a legend than anything else in Briar. If it hasn't anything to do with the Lumbers, you can assume the townsfolk won't take it for truth," he replied.

Even though the story comes from one of their own? C'Aelis' question was accompanied by feelings of surprise and confusion.

"Me? One of their own?! Ha!" Alessan laughed, his sarcastic tone not lost upon the Gorimm. "I was an embarrassment, a defect not to be acknowledged or seen."

Your father didn't agree...

"My father commanded respect," Alessan declared. "Had he lived, maybe things would have been different. My mother may have continued to smile, and I would have left Briar with the blessings of my family instead of their disappointment."

My father always reminded me that all things happen for a reason, Alessan. Could it not be that without your father's passing you would never have found the courage and resolve to leave behind that which you loved?

"If my mother's pain exists only to further my own path, then the gods are less merciful than I once believed," Alessan replied angrily.

Alessan...

With his head down, Alessan stalked angrily off into the woods. "I need to be alone. That means staying out of my thoughts as well," he fired over his shoulder.

Standing alone, the Gorimm watched his young charge disappear down the small overgrown path. At his heels, as she had been more often than not these past weeks, Greiyfois padded lightly after him, the young wolf nuzzling her furry head into the young man's hand.

Watch him, Greiyfois, C'Aelis sent.

The following day found the trio beginning their ascent up the immense rock face of the *Gor'A'gane*. The treeline eventually thinned as they trekked further up the north face with only a sparse crowd of stubborn trees defying the hard earth. The original trail C'Aelis had followed was now far behind them, and they continued to tread over a much larger path that held the ancient ruts of passing wagons.

There was a time, C'Aelis reflected, where the Temple caretakers had welcomed all to their small compound, offering to spread the glory of all the knowledge their vaults contained. In the dark years following the Shattering of Kingdoms, the political chaos that resulted saw Scholaris pillaged and their treasures assumed stolen or destroyed. C'Aelis warned Alessan that there was the possibility that the legendary store of knowledge no longer existed.

Cresting a particularly steep rise, Alessan looked ahead in astonishment. Below them, less than a thousand paces from where they stood, the sheer walls of the mountain sloped downwards into a verdant valley. It was as though one of the gods had carved out a few acres of pristine countryside in this spot on the mountain.

The rolling terrain was lush and vibrant, small herds of cattle grazed lazily within a large fenced enclosure surrounding the southern point of the valley. A small river wended its way through the center of the terrain, and a wooden mill of a modest size, its water wheel turning steadily, stood beside the most dominant structure in the area.

The Temple of Scholaris showed absolutely no signs of damage from the Shattering. It was built of immense stones and comprised of wondrous arches and a grand concourse. The architecture was impressive, even from a distance. The elaborate windows were made of multi-coloured glass, dark reds and blues glinting beautifully in the bright sunshine.

Only two outbuildings were close to the large structure; one obviously a barn, while the other appeared to be a small chicken coop. From their high vantage point, Alessan spied a few robed figures walking about the grounds, their movements relaxed, yet purposeful.

"It's incredible!" Alessan proclaimed. "I wonder how many monks live here?"

Unless things have changed since I left, there are seventeen monks who call the temple home, C'Aelis replied.

"An odd number," Alessan uttered.

The number is representative of the seventeen Elder Gods; those that have been in existence since the beginning of recorded time, C'Aelis responded.

"You're mistaken, C'Aelis. There are only thirteen Elder Gods, not seventeen."

Trust me, young Oakleaf, there are seventeen. Not every Elder God maintains worshippers. Although it does significantly lower the power and influence the deity might have in this world. The Elder Gods did not simply disappear because of the emergence of new deities like Arne or Fengar.

"Fengar?"

An eastern god, my friend, C'Aelis chuckled.

Digesting the information, Alessan remained silent and walked on. Every day it seemed, brought with it new revelations. He realized now how truly naive he was before coming into contact with the mystical Gorimm.

As the three companions began the long trek down into the valley, Greiyfois paused and whimpered. No amount of coaxing could alter the animal's resolute stance.

She is uncomfortable in such an unfamiliar place. Her home is the Aeldenwood, and here high upon the mountainside she feels farther from home than she really is. C'Aelis smiled sadly, brushing her affectionately. *I should have expected as much. I believe she'll wait in the nearby woods for us to return.*

Stooping down to meet her, Alessan embraced the wolf, nuzzling his face in her soft fur. "I'll see you soon, Greiyfois," he promised.

Alessan and C'Aelis continued down the rough mountain trail. The path had scarcely been used in some time and was in serious need of repair. Carefully picking their way through the loose rocks, the sun descended behind the nearby peaks as they reached the inner courtyard.

On the large stone steps of the temple stood a tall man dressed in an immaculate white robe. His head was shaved, and he stood with his arms folded carefully over his chest. While the stance wasn't hostile, it certainly wasn't welcoming.

C'Aelis never faltered as they approached the man. Bowing expertly, he stopped at the bottom step and focused his gaze on the monk. Time passed, and a continuous silence prevailed over the courtyard. Alessan realized that the two men were probably conversing in the same way that C'Aelis sent his thoughts to him.

"Your arrival is highly unusual and yet not as unexpected as you might think," the white-robed monk finally broke the silence, bowing in the direction of the Gorimm with deference. "You are both welcome to Scholaris. Our knowledge is your knowledge, your knowledge is ours," the man intoned.

Fidgeting uncomfortably, Alessan bowed awkwardly and smiled. "Thank you for opening your home to us. I am honoured."

With an approving smile, the monk looked to C'Aelis. "You did not mention that your companion was so well spoken. You do your family proud."

Alessan beamed.

They were led through the large double doors of the temple. Every room they passed was bare and austere. The materialistic comforts of the greater world were not missed within the walls of Scholaris. Only what was necessary could be found in each chamber, be it a plain wooden bed or the simple utensils found in the kitchen.

Catching Alessan's thoughts, C'Aelis interjected. *The monks of this place don't believe in frivolities. They are a very simple people, focused solely upon their task of gathering knowledge and compiling the histories of Kal Maran. They consider even our accoutrements wasteful and impractical. Our clothes and supplies only serve to distract us from the true meaning of our lives, or so they believe.*

Alessan studied everything in sight. Of the other residents of Scholaris, they saw only two. One, a short thin woman wearing a light blue robe passed them without even a glance; the second, a man wearing a charcoal grey robe smiled as they passed him a hallway, the man's eyes glinting mischievously in the torchlight.

Be wary of him, C'Aelis warned. *He represents Declavis, the God of Thieves. Don't ever forget that each of these monks has taken on some of the characteristics of the gods that they worship.*

They were led upstairs and into a small bedchamber containing two small wooden beds, each with one thin wool blanket. The rest of the room was devoid of any furnishings, with the exception of a small chamber pot.

"The vault will not be accessible until the morning. Until then I urge you to spend time meditating in silence before retiring for the evening. I will have Brother Tarius bring up a small repast for you, but I do insist that the bowl and spoon be returned to the kitchen before the evening is done." The monk spoke with complete seriousness.

"Thank you," Alessan smiled, afraid that he might insult their strange hosts. Nodding, the man bowed slightly and backed out of the small chamber, closing the door firmly behind him.

It is quite astonishing that Scholaris has not changed since I last visited. With the upheaval that rampaged across this land over the last two hundred years, these monks remain frozen in time. They have neither aged, nor changed in any discernible way, C'Aelis said, the footsteps of their host receding.

"How many times have you visited? And what exactly did you say to gain us admittance?" Alessan asked curiously.

Unbuckling his backpack and carefully folding his cloak, C'Aelis smiled warmly. *If I told you all of my secrets, Alessan, how would I get you to stay with me? Tomorrow you may learn far more than you ever could have imagined. Within the vaults of Scholaris lie the answers to all the questions ever asked. Figuring out where to look is the difficult part.*

"Is it really as wondrous as you've led me to believe?" Alessan flopped down on to his hard bed and stared up at the ceiling.

Better, C'Aelis replied, and somehow Alessan knew from the man's tone that he spoke the truth. *But for now, we need to rest our weary bodies and replenish our strength. After supper we would do well to take our host's advice and sleep. Tomorrow will be a long day.*

Although he took his companion's advice to heart, it would be a long while before sleep finally consumed him. And even then, Alessan's dreams were dominated by visions of thousands of books and a never-ending chamber of knowledge.

The means of forging the famous Drayen Spear is a closely guarded
secret. It is held by the Dwarven smiths who were commissioned to fash-
ion the weapon long ago.
—Lord Devonshire, 'The First Book of the Old Blood'

CHAPTER XLI

The *Drayen* Plains, Protectorate

Gavin and Bider's short trek through the foothills of the *Karipaal* mountain range brought back a flood of memories to the young Fey'Derin scout. It hardly seemed possible that less than a year earlier, the Fey had ridden through this very same countryside. That trip had been a celebratory one after the recent successful defense of Garchester.

That so much had changed since that time seemed incomprehensible.

Now, with the Code broken and Garchester in the hands of the enemy, Bider's world was suddenly fraught with peril. The Fey'Derin and their skilled captain were now marked men, fugitives in a world that had once been orderly, if not always fair. The Mercenary Code of Conduct had been created and amended over the years so that no one man could easily take control of large portions of old Caledun. For over two hundred years it had served its purpose, but now things had gone terribly awry.

"How did we not see this coming?" Bider asked, the two men guiding their mounts through a tangled mass of broken boulders.

"I spoke with the officers of this very possibility," Gavin frowned. "But as much as we discussed the prospects of a coup, we were far too complacent. Even Duke Berry, a man who I would never wish to confront on the political scene, didn't believe such a feat was possible."

"Because of the money involved?" Bider asked.

Gavin shook his head. "It had nothing to do with money, Coren; it had to do with the army."

Bider considered the statement. "I'm afraid I don't follow."

"Gadian and his followers always possessed the means to fund a large summer campaign. They did it often enough in the last decade as proof, but it's an entirely different logistical endeavor to supply an army," Gavin answered. "Unlike a brief summer or fall contract, to field an army means feeding them all year round."

"But why doesn't he just hire out the mercenary companies he needs each year?"

"A paid army brings with it loyalty, or at least a sense of loyalty through its stability. Garchester, for instance, won't become a settled city for a long period of time. Duke Berry was extremely popular among the common folk, and they won't soon forget this coup. To quell an unruly city takes soldiers, and it's a task the regular mercenary companies are ill-suited for. With his new Protectorate Army, he will have enough loyal soldiers to garrison his new acquisitions," Gavin finished.

"Then what real hope do we have?" Bider asked worriedly.

"Well, the one thing that most disturbed me at the Gathering was the apathy shown by far too many of the other companies. I fully expected a far greater number of captains to take offence at the newly dictated mandate for the South, and yet apart from a half-dozen leaders, most companies signed on without a fuss. Instead of a long list of allies to contact, our friends are few."

"So we'll head north then, to warn the Northern Council," Bider nodded.

Gavin thought differently. "Heading north wouldn't be my first choice of action. I would prefer not to leave my allies alone if Gadian Yarr does choose another target for the summer. We have longstanding friendships with both the Sisters of the Sword and the *Delan Fere*; alliances I'm loath to break. Duke Berry has also treated us well, and he'll be in sore need of help after losing his city." An ominous look crossed his face as he added a final thought. "There is also the matter of Gerald Armsmater ..."

* * *

They rode silently for the next league or so, Bider taking the time to properly digest the information received from the usually tight-lipped captain. The two men continued to wind their way through the rugged countryside, travelling in a northerly direction along the eastern edge of the Caeronwood.

Where the Protectorate would strike next couldn't be predicted. Bider knew that as forthcoming as Gavin had been, the captain wouldn't speculate further without first consulting with his Fey'Derin officers.

How the company fared was another matter altogether. Gavin remained hopeful that Lieutenant Burnaise was still leading the men through the forest, striking for the northern base camp and then Dragon Mount.

Two days out of Wickam had unfortunately brought little reprieve in the matter of his injuries. Although his ribs were far less tender than a week earlier, the nagging aches and stabbing pains continued. His broken ankle remained his greatest concern. The pain from that wound was ceaseless.

Having spent the last two years of his life training in the art of tracking and scouting, Bider was extremely nervous about the condition of the wound. A scout with a limp was far less useful, and could even be a liability in a tight situation. He hoped that Gavin's promised healing by the Silveryn mages would be helpful.

Riding for the better part of each day was by no means helping the matter. A man in his condition should have remained in bed for weeks. That Gavin, still battered himself after his battle with the *Sciloc*, saw fit to keep them moving northward, spoke to the seriousness of their situation.

Since leaving the town, the spring rains had finally eased their assault upon the land, and the bright sunshine had greeted them throughout most of their journey. Warmed by the rays of the sun, it was easy to forget the ordeal that they had only just left behind. Despite the unwelcome mud, Gavin and Bider had made good time, crossing some distance into the *Karipaal* foothills by the end of the first day.

Although Gavin sensed no immediate danger in the vicinity, he refused to tempt fate a second time. The captain was relieved that no harm had come to any of the innocent townsfolk in Wickam. Bider suspected that the man wanted no further deaths weighing on his already burdened conscience.

* * *

The pair passed the northern edge of the Caeronwood a few short days later. Angling a little northwest, Gavin led them out into the *Drayen* Plains — a place sheathed in blood and betrayal. It was on these plains that the future of a kingdom had been decided. Here the armies of the High King Darion Lordares met their defeat through treachery, and the fate of Old Caledun had been sealed.

It had been mid-autumn when the news reached the ears of King Lordares that a large force of disgruntled peasants had started to revolt. Over the years, the prolonged wars in the Iron Shield had drained the economy and many in the land also feared an invasion from the Wilds. With the north in a panic, sudden raids from rebel groups left the southern cities cowering in fear. Faced with enemies attacking the country from within, as well as the prospect of a goblin invasion, the king was left with few choices.

A week before the Festival of Solstice, the majority of the king's forces were ordered from the capital city of Magnach. The monarch traveled with them, hoping to quell the dissidents in the realm by meeting with them. He feared there would be great bloodshed if he himself did not arrive to hear the people's grievances.

The discussions held between both sides were promising, and the thousands of disgruntled peasants, all of them descendants of the Old Blood, were surprised by the honesty of their king. They came to the realization that they had been intentionally fed lies, leading ultimately to their rebellion under false pretenses. It was then that the undercurrent of a dark plot was exposed; but by then it was far too late.

With most of the An'Darim guarding the young heir, the king and the *Drayenmark* were ambushed on the *Drayen* Plains. Betrayed by those councillors he had once trusted, the king's small force had nowhere to run. These plains saw the Queen fall prey to the murderous blades of their enemies and the near destruction of the king's entourage. The peasants were shown no mercy; slaughtered to almost every man, woman, and child, an entire generation of *Drayen* folk were annihilated.

Protected by a few elite An'Darim, the king won free, retreating quickly to the safety of his walled city, but little hope remained. In four short days, the city of Magnach was overrun, the king assassinated and the land of Caledun sundered into dozens of city states, all vying for power and influence. The time of Kings had passed.

The Plains themselves looked no different than any other. Wide open grasslands stretched from horizon to horizon, the only break to the flatness coming from the hills to the east where the old cities of the Silveryn Order lay nestled. Large herds of *Drayen* elk ranged across the prairie land, the animals grazing on the countryside even throughout the winter months. The temperate climate of the south allowed them to dig and graze even during the harshest times of the year.

For six days Bider and Gavin travelled steadily north, seeing no living thing on the Plains apart from these animals. With supplies running low, Bider now scanned the horizon line with anticipation. Although far from mobile, the scout was sure that given the opportunity, his protesting stomach would spur his weakened body into action. With his hand on his forehead, shielding his vision from the bright sun, Bider waited. If he had learned one thing as a Fey'Derin, it was patience.

ᛣ

"Definitely riders," Bider pointed to the northeast. "Easily more than a company, maybe even two."

Gavin nodded and studied the long column that lay off in the distance.

"Any chance you can make out those banners?" he inquired. "The last thing we need is to cross paths with men who owe their loyalty to the new Protectorate."

The column was still far off, but if the two Fey'Derin travellers had spotted them in the open spaces of the *Drayen* Plains, it was a sure bet that the column's scouts had done the very same with their position. Another day had passed and still little was seen roaming the land. Bider had spotted the riders though, the scout spying a small smudge on the horizon. He had rapidly assessed that it was the dust stirred up by a swift moving group of mounted troops.

As they breached the distance, Bider realized he had been only partially correct. Even from this distance it had become clear that among the horses also trotted the smaller stout mountain *Sheves* or ponies.

The sturdy animals were notoriously stubborn, shaggy, and with voracious appetites. They were also not native to the mainland of Kal Maran. The Dwarves of Alerond, upon fleeing their ancestral home far across the ocean to the west, brought the animals with them. The *Sheves* were used exclusively by the Dwarves of Alerond and their presence in that convoy was no longer a question.

As they waited, Bider breathed a sigh of relief as the bothersome winds relaxed and allowed the numerous standards to be displayed. "That's clearly the *Drayenmark* hawk and the black mountain tower of Alerond." He sent Gavin a questioning look. "We're short on supplies, sir, they may be able to provide help," he offered.

"Is that hawk gold or silver, Coren?" Gavin squinted into the sun. "Gold, sir," Bider answered after a momentary glance.

"Any particular reason why you'd ask that, Captain?"

Gavin pursed his lips before replying. "The gold standard is reserved only for members of the royal family. If Serian Rhone, or even his sons, are travelling about the northern countryside of the Protectorate, they'll soon be dead men. Once word reaches anyone connected with Gadian Yarr..." the Fey'Derin captain left the ending unspoken.

"Then our choice is simple, is it not?" Bider said, spurring his mount into action.

"As long as it isn't Serian Rhone, we should be fine," Gavin replied quietly.

Pulling up, Bider turned painfully in the saddle. "Why?"

Gavin waved his hands in defense. "Serian Rhone and I aren't exactly friends..." he grinned mischievously, spurring his mount ahead and angling towards the large column.

Shaking his head with some frustration, Bider could do little but follow.

As they remained somewhat removed from the campaigns of the summer, Bider had never seen a *Drayenmark* war party. The Old Blood refused to follow the dictates of the Mercenary Code, operating in a far different fashion than Bider was used to. For starters, the *Drayen* soldiers numbered well over four hundred, almost double that of most companies. Serian Rhone had, on occasion, sent smaller armies to assist in certain battles, namely those that involved city states that refused to show loyalty to the ruling councils of each area. In the Protectorate, very few of those cities remained under their own rule, the most prominent being the southern free city of Delfwane.

The men were dressed in simple brown leather armour with no visible signs of their allegiance displayed besides the numerous standards that snapped in the wind. They were all mounted, and each man looked at ease in the saddle. These were all men who knew how to ride. Their hair was adorned with a variety of feathers and ties, creating a mosaic of colour Bider found somewhat difficult to follow. It strained one's eyes to have your senses assaulted by so much vibrant colour. Many of the men were tall and lean and their faces were clean-shaven.

But despite physical differences, they all appeared to be kin, or they at least displayed a unity in both movement and overall appearance, including the weapon each man carried. The *Drayen* Spear had a famous reputation in Caledun. There was a familiarity in their features that reminded Bider of Caolte Burnaise. The resemblance was striking.

Forged by the Dwarven smiths, the crafting of its polished black wood and steel tip was a technique that few had knowledge of. It was the most guarded secret of the descendants of the noble families of Old Caledun. Little was known about the weapon, other than its famed resilience and distinct ability to maintain its sharpened edge at all times. The spears were easily distinguishable, even from afar. The glossy black shafts could be seen twirling lazily in the grasp of some of the soldiers, while others had the weapon prominently displayed in uniquely woven slings attached to their saddles.

The Dwarves of Alerond, far less in attendance, maybe two score, were also easily identified from a distance. The thickly bearded men of Alerond rode clustered together near the middle of the column, the shaggy coated *Sheves* grunting in constant complaint. In sharp contrast to the light armour of their companions, the smaller, barrel-chested men wore their heavier metal armour with ease. Bider was reminded of the Fey'Derin Sergeant, Eör Rockfar. The officer had always been the first to quell any one boasting about their strength. The veteran Dwarf was easily the strongest man in the company, except perhaps the massive Ossric McConnal.

As Gavin and Bider gained ground on the war party, a small contingent of men broke formation and galloped in their direction. Their intent unknown, Bider carefully loosened the straps binding his crossbow into place. One could never be too careful.

It took only a few minutes before the *Drayenmark* vanguard had crossed the empty plain, pulling up their mounts mere paces from the two Fey'Derin. They silently gave way to one man in particular, a mounted soldier who calmly surveyed the two travellers before waving away two large men who rode nearly at his elbow.

Surprisingly, it was Gavin who spoke first. Gracefully dismounting, the Fey'Derin commander briefly inclined his head towards the lead rider. "It has been many years since I've seen you Prince of Caledun," he said solemnly.

"I'm not sure my father would have taken kindly to a visit from one of the few men to have ever lectured him on policy and lived to tell the tale," the young man answered grimly.

"Caolte and I were merely answering the question your father had put forth, my lord. I trust, then, that your sire is well?" Gavin replied.

A brief flicker of sadness crossed the man's face at the question. "He is well, although with each passing year the fevers come with greater frequency. I trust Lord Burnaise remains as spry as always? I can't imagine that able man not being at your side..." the prince replied with a smile.

Lord Burnaise...? Bider wondered.

"Much has transpired these last months, my lord. If you would put aside your father's decree on my presence here, my companion and I could benefit greatly from some assistance. I have much to speak of," Gavin said quietly, the words obviously meant for as few ears as possible.

Frowning, Kaimon Rhone studied Gavin for a moment before nodding and dropping lightly to the ground.

The *Drayenmark* prince made an immediate impression. The youthful heir to the long abandoned High King's throne was taller than most men, his brown hair tied back in the usual fashion of his people. As he dropped to the ground from his grey stallion, Bider was struck by the grace of his movements. His stride was purposeful and efficient; Kaimon Rhone wasted nothing in each step. For a moment, Bider was reminded of his own companion. Gavin often walked in the same manner, but the Fey'Derin captain did so with far less confidence, if that was even possible.

Here was a man who would have been a great thief, the scout thought to himself, amused by the idea. *The heir to a broken kingdom... a thief.*

Kaimon wore leather armour dyed black, and unlike the men in his retinue, he carried a sword strapped across his back rather than a *Drayen* Spear. Casting a swift glance towards the man's mount, Bider did recognize the feathered tip of the *Drayenmark* weapon poking out from one of his horse's saddlebags. The only trappings of rank and lineage were simple and humble. A small patch, identical to the standards that fluttered in the wind, had been sewn onto his armour, and a golden chain glinted in the afternoon sun, the light sparkling as it caught the small figure of a hawk in flight.

As Kaimon approached, his hand unconsciously rose to the necklace, his fingers nonchalantly twirling the crafted bird. Once close, Bider was also struck by the prince's striking grey eyes, very much like the hawk painted on the Rhone family banners.

Grasping Gavin's outstretched arm in a traditional *Drayen* grip, Kaimon turned and waved forward another member of the small squad. "Kalen, come here," he called and then turned back to Gavin. "My father's sentence only makes your life forfeit in his lands. Here upon the Plains you may speak freely. I, for one, never agreed with him on matters concerning you and Lord Caolte."

"Caolte managed to dig his own grave far before that day, but I offer my thanks to you and your borther." Gavin answered. He gripped the newcomer's arm in similar fashion. "You have grown, Prince Kalen," he added with a smile.

The family resemblance between the two brothers was uncanny. One seemed to be nothing more than a second version of the other. Bider knew the two princes were almost five years apart in age, but they could be nothing other than brothers when placed side by side. The younger Kalen, already tall despite having a few years still to grow, carried himself in much the same manner as his older brother, if somewhat less assured.

"And you, Gavin, there is pain hidden behind those eyes," the *Drayen* prince said. The familiar manner in which all three men spoke to one another brought up further questions for Bider concerning the captain's background and history. Already a Koriani weapons master, here lay evidence that the young commander had also spent time in the *Drayenmark* holdings to the east, a territory heavily guarded by its troubled ruler.

"What brings the two of you this far west?" Gavin asked. "Now is not a good time to be travelling the Protectorate," he added.

"Lord Blackhelm is long overdue, and Lord Där, Alerond's present emissary, is troubled by his absence. No word has been sent or received ere last summer from the west, and even my father begins to wonder at the state of affairs here in the south. My brother and I were anxious to leave the often suffocating world of a prince and decided to use this opportunity to travel with our war bands. By your vague comments though, I fear events have occurred that place us all in danger," Kaimon replied.

"I'm not surprised that word hasn't been received from Alerond, but from as far back as the summer? That is definitely not welcome news," Gavin frowned.

"Come then, we'll make camp here this evening," the young prince interrupted. "We can meet with Lord Där immediately as the men prepare the evening meal. I have a feeling you have much to tell."

"That I do..." Gavin whispered.

ᴄ℘

That night, camped under an incredible display of stars, Bider found himself blissfully ignoring the ordeal of the past week. The *Drayenmark* were an incredibly generous people once you had been accepted within their fold. Gavin and Bider were welcomed with open arms once they had received the approval of Kaimon and his younger brother, Kalen.

Captain Silveron retired to a secluded spot immediately upon his arrival. Accompanied by the two princes and a grey-bearded dwarf, the four men conversed for hours, all four deeply concerned by the present state of affairs.

For his part, Bider had insisted on helping with something, even in his present condition. He spent some time preparing the cooking fires alongside a few friendly men. With the sun setting and the soft light of dusk waning, Gavin and the others rejoined the rest of the column. Kaimon had asked the captain to repeat his telling of the terrible events of the *Ca'lenbam*. Both parties listened in shocked silence.

Now, hours later, Kaimon and the *Drayenmark* soldiers lit an immense bonfire and began to dance the night away in revelry. Bider thought they were an odd people, the *Drayenmark*, to so easily put aside the unsettling news of that evening. But as Gavin quietly explained, to dwell upon that which could not be affected this night was to waste an otherwise glorious evening. Bider begrudgingly succumbed to the idea, although it wasn't easy.

Large slabs of elk meat roasted on large metal spits near the flames, carefully monitored by a small group of proud cooks. The men took turns singing songs, their deep voices carrying far into the cool nighttime air. Even the far more reserved Dwarves seemed to relax and enjoy themselves.

Taking a large bite from a piece of the tender meat, Bider was content to let the savoury meal settle his rumbling stomach. Accepting a large jug of spirits, he washed the meat down with a mouthful of the scorching liquid the Dwarves had provided. The dark spirits burned all the way down his throat, but also warmed his stomach. Spying Gavin across the camp through the flames, the scout watched him as he carried on a conversation with Där, the Dwarven diplomat. The small man's thick chest heaved in response to whatever the captain was recounting, his beard bouncing as a roar of laughter tumbled from his mouth.

The Dwarves, he found, were an interesting lot. Far more reserved than Eör Rock-far, they did, however, laugh heartily at almost everything, even the most mundane of events. When one of the *Drayen* soldiers had fallen over dead drunk and lit his leggings afire, it took long moments before the powerful men from Alerond could stop howling with laughter. Granted, the fire was small and easily smothered, but still did those men laugh. Bider found their good humour infectious, and so did many others present.

Even Prince Kalen was untroubled, much to the approval of his mild- mannered older brother. The boy, for Bider knew he could nary have seen more than sixteen summers, seemed more embarrassed than anything by his brother's gentle barbs, but remained good natured. Gavin had mentioned privately to Bider that the youngest prince was known to possess a temper akin to his father's.

After finishing his meal, Gavin stood up and walked into the bright glow of the firelight. There was something about his stern gaze and upright bearing that tugged at the Fey'Derin scout. Bider had seen the pose often, especially when the captain was about to address the company. Here at this time, in such a perfect setting, it was as if Gavin Silveron held more power and authority than even the Rhone Princes.

Raising his hand for silence, Gavin deflected the numerous barbs and crude comments thrown his way by the boisterous group. Finally, as the heckling subsided, he walked around the fire and approached both royal siblings. It was in perfect silence that the Fey'Derin captain approached the two men.

With a respectful bow, Gavin addressed them. "My lords, I feel that under these unfortunate circumstances, Coren and I can offer you little in repayment for the generosity you have shown us this evening. I ask of you instead for permission to sing for the two of you. It is a gift that pales in comparison to the great service you have done to bolster the spirits of two tired travellers."

"Have you forgotten that I have heard you sing, Gavin Silveron? How long ago has it been since you played in my father's hall?" Kaimon asked with a knowing smile.

"I've lost track of the years," Gavin replied sadly.

"Well, what you offer is more than enough. But sing not for us, Captain Silveron, sing for all who gather around the fire this evening," the clansman replied. "We would be honoured."

Nodding graciously, Gavin retrieved his lute and rolled over a larger piece of firewood to use as a stool. Perched on the stump, he ran his fingers lightly across the instrument. The resulting series of notes rang clearly out into the night air and an expectant hush settled over the assembly. Leaning back while enjoying another hearty mouthful of strong spirits, Bider listened with rapt attention.

"The Long Way Home," Gavin announced, the words bringing a holler of approval from the *Drayenmark*.

> *Long have we wandered, two souls on their own,*
> *In a world of darkness, of nightmares, of dreams.*
> *We once walked, the stars were our guide,*
> *How long has it been, since we've been home?*
>
> *For the long way is often alone,*
> *but if I gave you my life, would it take you home?*
> *For the long way has passed you by,*
> *but if I gave you a smile, would it take you home?*

In days gone by, the world gave us her strength,
The grass, the trees, the wind, and the air.
We gave her love, she showed us her soul,
How long has it been, since we've gone home?

For the long way is often alone,
but if I gave you my life, would it take you home?
For the long way has passed you by,
but if I gave you my love, would it take you home?

As his fingers played across the strings of his lute, Gavin sighed happily. Over the years, he had never lost his passion to play music, only the time and privacy that were often required. He wasn't lying when he told Coren about the source of his teachings in the halls of Dragon Mount. It was one of his few fond memories; Brynne had played the flute back then, and they had often found themselves in the gardens of the fortress whiling away their days with song.

While he played, the world seemed to recede from his vision and every distracting thought ceased. His teachers had often commented on his connection to the songs he played, impressed by the emotion his voice evoked. It had never matched Brynne's crystalline sound, but together they blended as one.

Guilty thoughts about the Koriani woman he had left behind haunted him. Danys Ford held the key to his troubled heart, but there were still times that Gavin wondered whether Brynne still held sway over his soul. To think about both women was too painful to endure. Banishing these burdensome thoughts, Gavin returned to the solace and security of the music.

With a renewed intensity, he let the emotions of the song flow through his hands. With his eyes closed, he sang the last chorus line, his quivering voice adequately holding the final few notes with confidence.

"For the long way is often alone,
but if I gave you my life, would it take you home?
For the long way has passed you by,
but if I gave you my soul, would it take you home?"

The song was incredibly sad and yet tinged with a note of hope. It would be the first of many songs that evening. Having recently seen Gavin perform, Bider was still no less excited and awed than anyone else in attendance. It remained such an oddity to see the graceful sword master play the lute so skillfully and with such passion. That the man had kept his talent so well hidden these last few years was almost the greater surprise.

The revelry lasted long into the night, with more food and plenty of spirits passed around the blazing fire. Dawn had already begun to lighten the darkness by the time Bider limped and staggered towards the small tent he and Gavin were sharing. The captain was slumbering near the warmth of the fire, and Bider could barely recall the last hour or so.

With the world spinning from the excess of spirits consumed, the young scout collapsed in a heap. Although he was bound to feel the ill effects of the potent Dwarven liquor the next day, for the time being he could barely move, let alone be bothered by such consequences. With the sun nearly peeking out over the edge of the horizon, Bider slept.

Oblivious to everything, the camp slumbered.

Winter howls, the Wilds uncharted.
Of hurried step, and fleet of foot, Eyes watch, they wait,
As hunters stalk by night.
—Unknown

CHAPTER XLII

Goblin Territories, The Wilds

Leoric leaned against the rough bark of the oak tree, his muscular shoulders slumping wearily despite his valiant effort to conceal his fatigue. The others needed their rest more than he did, and so he bore the burden of the first watch.

Looking at his slumbering companions, he could see the lines of exhaustion on Benoit's face even as the man slept, albeit fitfully. Of the four men, it was the scholar who had suffered the most. The harried pace of the previous two weeks had left the naturally quiet man even more morose, but this was also true of the other men. They had all retreated within themselves as they journeyed through the merciless terrain of the Wilds.

Even Angvald, the towering Kaleenian with his steadfast strength and endurance, had struggled these last few days. The lack of food played a role in their recent lethargy, as the game had been scarce and their means far less sophisticated than any of the men would have liked. Fortunately, they had been able to scavenge wild berries and cayan roots, both meagre but sustaining sources of nourishment.

Leoric allowed his thoughts to wander. As always, his musings were dominated by visions of Kieri. His memories of her every smell, every sound, and every movement were unable to alleviate the horrible ache in his heart. His mind was still under assault by the experience of his captivity, and with that came the recollection of Joram's savagery and of the Shalo'k Mines...

Those scars ran so deep that Benoit had recurring nightmares of the place. Auric, Angvald, and Leoric would take turns rousing the man once he started whimpering. Benoit was haunted by the eyes; the dead eyes of those still trapped in that infernal place. Leoric couldn't blame him. Those very eyes haunted his own dreams.

Rubbing the numerous aches in his neck, the borderman sank to the ground. With no fire lit, he grudgingly pulled on an extra tunic in an effort to ward off the chill of the wet and unseasonably cool day. Refraining from closing his eyes, even for the briefest of seconds for fear of succumbing to his fatigue, Leoric reflected on the events since the night of their escape.

After landing on the ground below the great wall, Auric didn't allow anyone the opportunity to revel in their accomplishment. Having tied a Highwayman's hitch, they were able to reclaim the rope, and Leoric was confident that little evidence remained of their descent. With their escape occurring far later then they had originally planned, the fleeing fugitives shouldered their scarce supplies and ran into the woods.

The next week passed in a blur of constant movement. The small group scavenged, hunted, and slept sporadically, their routine far from normal. More than once they had been roused from a restless slumber by the sounds of pursuit. Those nights, as the four men crashed blindly through the brush, had been the most terrifying. Running scared through the daylight hours was unsettling enough, but in the heady darkness of the Wilds at night, it was nearly unbearable.

Leoric had no doubt that their luck had been inconceivable. Angvald, of course, was determined to claim it as divine intervention, but Leoric would hear nothing of it. Auric watched the proceedings with his astute grin that the borderman had grown quite fond of.

Although they remained one step ahead of their goblin pursuers, the true test would come when they reached the river crossing. Both Angvald and Leoric had recognized the large tributary on Auric's stolen maps as the one they had crossed the previous winter. It was there that the fiery Halas had succumbed to his injuries. The river posed the greatest threat to their freedom. How long they might be delayed at the water's edge may very well determine their fate.

Each member of the group had offered opinions on how best to approach the situation: a raft, swimming, finding an appropriate place in which to safely ford the waters, and Leoric's own; that they use the goblins own contraption to facilitate their escape. Each idea had merit, but no decision could be made until the river was reached. Until then, the good-natured banter over their separate plans provided some rare moments of camaraderie and normalcy between the escapees.

"You look like you've seen a ghost, lad," a familiar voice whispered in the night.

"Curses! You gave me a fright!" Leoric swore, scrambling to his feet. Even at well over fifty summers, Auric could be stealthier than a mouse.

"I didn't mean to disturb your thoughts, but as much as you believe the contrary, you do need sleep like the rest of us," Auric stated.

Leoric cast a glance up at the night and squinted. "Time passed quickly tonight," he muttered. "Either I'm falling asleep, or time is skewed in these damned woods."

"I think this land is beautiful," Auric replied with a surprised look. "Can you find another place in this world so carefree and wild, so full of life and untainted by the hands of mankind?"

"I find this place terrifying..." Leoric shook his head and smiled. "I guess I'll see you in the morning." Turning to leave, he was held back by one of Auric's gnarled brown hands.

For the first time since meeting the enigmatic man, Leoric watched a spasm of doubt cross Auric's wrinkled face. It pierced his heart to see a look of such sadness, and he reached out to grip the venerable man's hand. "Auric?" he whispered fearfully. "What is it? What's wrong?"

At Leoric's words, the old man merely smiled sadly and held his hand. "I have need of a favour, and I find myself troubled asking it of you, even though I know I must."

"Tell me..." Leoric said uneasily.

"You see, I've agonized over a moment such as this for more than half my life, Leoric," he said. "I've lived a relatively simple life despite its hardships, but I have always regretted one thing; my lack of family. There were times when I so desperately wanted to settle down, but I allowed my burdens to consume my life…"

Unsure of where the conversation was heading, Leoric remained silent and patiently waited for his friend to collect his thoughts.

"I need you to make me a promise, Leoric D'Athgaran."

"A promise?" Leoric was more than a little confused by the request.

"Yes," Auric nodded.

"I cannot agree to anything until I hear you out, Auric," Leoric responded. "But I will listen to what you have to say."

Auric continued, "When the time comes, Leoric, I need you to promise not to put your own life on hold for duty or for your responsibility to the destiny the gods have chosen for you. Walk your own path, and refuse to sacrifice happiness," he said, meeting Leoric's confused stare.

"I'll never again show faith in the gods above. You know that," the borderman replied darkly. "I'll do as you ask, but I never thought you were a pious man? This is the first I've heard of this matter with you. I don't understand…"

Auric smiled sympathetically, "For the moment, understanding may elude you, but don't doubt my belief in the gods that protect us and guide our lives."

"Then why?" Leoric pressed.

"I believe the gods set us on our paths with a goal in mind. The difference lies in how we arrive at the end. Why must one man walk a life of loneliness in order to complete his destiny? Let your own heart guide your steps, Leoric, that you arrive at the end of the road in a different fashion should matter little; you'll arrive there all the same."

"But —"

Auric released the borderman's big hands and turned away. "When we arrive at the river, time will be short. I will be ready then," he added wistfully.

Agitated by the conversation, Leoric stared at the forest for long minutes after Auric disappeared into its impenetrable shadows. That evening in the Wilds, Leoric D'Athgaran eventually drifted off, but he couldn't help but wonder about what he had promised. A peculiar doubt had been aroused in his mind by Auric's request. It had all seemed far too simple…

* * *

Two days after the nighttime discussion, Leoric found himself crouched in a dense thicket with Angvald, both men up to their ankles in mud. The overcast skies had not let up, and they were soaked, shivering, and miserable.

"I count six," Angvald said in a hushed tone.

Following the Kaleenian's line of vision, Leoric caught sight of some trailing soldiers of what appeared to be a small goblin patrol. "Scouts attached to a larger company perhaps?" he ventured.

☙

Angvald shook his head. "Not many scouts travel so closely together when on duty. I'd guess they don't know we're in the vicinity."

"Good point. They are travelling east, something we haven't seen as of yet."

"A welcome change if you ask me," the big man said with relief.

The members of the patrol were clothed like the goblins from the prisoner camp; hard looking warriors wearing a combination of studded leather and chain armour. Long plumes adorned their dirty white hair, denoting their clan affinity; but to both Leoric and Angvald, the red and white band with a black slash was unfamiliar. The half dozen goblins chatted amongst themselves, oblivious to the two men crouched on the small rise north of the game trail the soldiers were evidently following.

Even more interesting than the presence of the patrol, was the prize carried by two of the goblins on a long wooden pole held between them. An enormous stag swayed ponderously, the legs of the animal bound securely to the wooden shaft. Leoric's mouth watered at the sight of the slain beast, his stomach rumbling in distress, reminding him of how long it had been since they had eaten meat of any kind. Had the stag not been a part of the procession below, he was sure that he and Angvald would have fled long ago to warn the others. As it stood, both men were unwilling to let the badly needed food slip away so easily.

"They have no idea we're here," Leoric whispered. "We might be able to track them... and that stag looks like it would make quite a feast."

"We're not exactly the smallest two scouts you'd find," Angvald quipped. "But I bet Auric would take to this task like a fish to water, no?"

"I think you're right," Leoric responded and sidled backwards, careful not to make a noise as he crept deeper into the concealing foliage. "I'll get the old man, you keep an eye on which way they travel."

Less than an hour later, Auric returned to report his findings. As expected, he had been just as interested in the prospect of a real meal as the rest of them and had accepted the task without complaint.

"They're in a small clearing a few leagues from here. It's really nothing more than a small campfire in front of a large dark hole in the ground. It could be the entrance to a cache of supplies — maybe weapons and the like."

"Defences?" Leoric asked.

"None really. The clearing is in a patch of dense wood, covered on all sides with a bit of a rocky slope to the west. That's where they've dug into the earth. I expect those soldiers are merely stockpiling in case of an emergency," Auric speculated.

"Or stockpiling for new arrivals from Lok'Dal hie?" Benoit added.

The old man nodded. "Aye, could be that as well. In any case, we have to make a decision. Either we delay and plan a nighttime ambush with the risk of being over-taken, or we press onward towards the river."

"Truthfully, I need to eat a good meal. If we're overtaken without regaining something of our former energy, we'll go down without a whimper," Angvald spoke. It was apparent to the others that the large warrior had lost weight.

Leoric settled his gaze on Benoit. With an embarrassed look, the man seemed indecisive. "Speak freely, Ben, we make this decision together," Leoric said.

"I'm hungry and I'm tired, Leoric, but I'm no fighter." Brandishing his belted dagger, he swore, "Cursed Arne, I don't know the first thing about defending my-self, let alone attacking trained guards. But we aren't going to reach Darkenedge in our current condition. If we can attack safely then I believe we have no choice... we need to eat."

"Auric?" Leoric said.

"I agree with, Benoit. If beset by our pursuers now, we don't stand a chance." He spoke with confidence. "What say you, Leoric?"

Once again Leoric was struck by the realization that these three men were look-ing to him for guidance, looking to him to make the final decision. Seizing the responsibility, the borderman shook off any misgivings and met each man's eyes with an unyielding look of his own.

"We have a few hours until dark. Let's rest up and plan the attack. Angvald, you're the most experienced warrior among us, so I'll defer to you for the final approval of any ambush. Auric, I'll need your input as well." Turning to Benoit, he wrapped an arm around the thin man's shoulders. "Benoit, I need your courage. You're the smartest man here and you'll advise where you feel most comfortable."

With all three companions nodding their approval, the escapees set to work.

Auric's description of the small glade had been accurate. Surrounded by the dense woods, the fire pit and black hole cut into the earth were situated in the center of the clearing. Three of the goblins were sleeping while two sat quietly by the fire. The sixth was last seen disappearing inside the opening in the ground.

ങ

Hidden by the thick trees to the east of the clearing, Leoric crouched, his body taut and ready to react. A long knife in his hand, carefully keeping the cold steel from glinting in the sparse moonlight, he was to be the third man to join the fray. Auric and Angvald had carefully circled the area, positioning themselves on either side of the oblivious guards. So far into the uncharted Wilds, it was almost certain the goblins wouldn't be expecting any late night arrivals.

Benoit was positioned opposite Leoric, a little deeper into the woods for his own safety. The scholarly man was acting as a rearguard defense, in position to warn the others should unexpected reinforcements come from the direction of *Lok'Dal hie*. The last thing their battered company needed was unwanted visitors.

The element of surprise was their biggest advantage, perhaps even the only one, and Leoric was counting on it working in their favour. He was starting to fret as the minutes slipped by, when a sudden slight movement along the treeline next to the closest guard drew his attention. Angvald, despite his great bulk, was nothing more than a shadow as he emerged from the edge of the dense cover.

The recent poor weather, cursed by all four men, was now a welcome boon for the ambush. Auric and the Kaleenian had smeared mud from the wet forest floor all over their bodies. Only the whites of their eyes would be visible to their foes. By the time Leoric picked up Auric's movements, his shadowy outline was nearly upon his target.

Gripping the long knife firmly in his hand, Leoric did his best to quell the now familiar trace of reluctance that came over him whenever he wielded a blade. Clenching his fist arduously around the leather wrapped hilt, he rushed forward, crashing through the woods with a complete disregard to stealth.

Both guards leapt to their feet, alerted by the loud disturbance outside the camp. In two short steps, Angvald and Auric were upon them. Soundlessly, the goblin soldiers collapsed to the ground with throats slit, their gasping attempts to draw breath smothered by their attackers' hands.

As Leoric broke free from cover, Angvald waited by the side of the underground entrance, bloodied blade at the ready. Leoric ignored his friend, focusing instead on the nearest goblin struggling groggily to his feet. Mere seconds had passed since his charge, and yet already the three previously sleeping warriors were close to regaining their senses.

Auric buried his blade deep in the chest of the nearest guard and moved deftly on to the next opponent. Leoric blocked a feeble punch from his attacker, batting aside the weak swing and never slowing his progress. Dropping a shoulder, he launched himself at his unbalanced adversary. He sent the guard flying backwards. Without pause, Leoric stabbed downward and yanked back on the blade. As black blood spurted up from the wound, he silenced the goblin with a second strike.

Angvald thundered forward as a goblin exited the tunnel in a run. Surprised by the towering Kaleenian, Angvald easily overwhelmed the smaller foe, driving his dagger into the soldier's abdomen, spinning behind him, and breaking his neck with one sharp twist.

To Leoric's left, the last slumbering guard fell with a piercing wail. Without a word, Auric dispatched the man. For long minutes all three men stood outlined in the firelight, their heavy breathing the only sound in the clearing besides the crackling of the fire. Surveying the carnage, Leoric found it unsatisfying to have slaughtered the unarmed soldiers — goblins or not.

As if in answer to his thoughts, Auric spoke. "It had to be done. Warriors live to die in battle. They did so, if not exactly on their own terms," he commented impassively.

"They would have shown us no mercy," Angvald spat on the corpse at his feet. "May their souls never find rest with their ancestors."

Nodding grimly, Leoric knew that both men were right. Long past was the time for mercy. As Benoit entered the glade, the borderman had mastered his emotions. Issuing quick orders, they got to work. The river was still distant, and any delay would allow their pursuers to draw closer.

Fortune had indeed smiled upon them. The cache was a treasure trove of supplies beyond imagining. Apart from the meat of the roasted stag, the small underground storeroom contained crude wooden shelves stocked with items ranging from hardened bread and mushrooms, to sturdy cloaks and decent clothing. A small weapons rack located near the back of the torchlit cavern also provided the men with a much needed upgrade of their arms. With glee, Angvald brandished a large double-bladed axe, the weapon finely crafted and well-balanced. Leoric and Auric found some common maces, and even Benoit found something that he was infinitely more comfortable bearing: a sturdy longbow and quiver full of arrows.

"I hunted with my brothers in my youth. I was a fair shot, but whether that still stands true remains to be seen," Benoit said with a rare smile.

Something in the easy manner in which his companion held the weapon brought a smile to Leoric's face as well. Even the man's slumped shoulders lifted, and a small glimmer of confidence, absent since their capture and subsequent exile to Shalo'k, had returned. Bolstered by their discovery, Leoric nodded with satisfaction. The company had executed their plan perfectly. If anything, the simple boost to their morale had been worth the risk of the attack. The supplies and weapons were an added bonus that would give them the strength to push onwards.

Leoric surveyed the small cave. "As much as we'd like to celebrate our victory, there are things that need doing. We need to separate what we've found here and take only what is required. Ben, I'll leave this task in your capable hands. Angvald, you and I need to dispose of the bodies and salvage what we can of the guard's armour. Auric, I need you to look to our meals and take a quick tour of the immediate area. Scout our back trail as well. Do your best to cover up our tracks, and keep an eye out for those who pursue us. We leave at first light, so let's make the most of our time here."

Leoric and Angvald dug a shallow grave to put the goblin corpses in using a pair of shovels Benoit had found among the supplies. The earth, still wet from the damp weather, easily gave way and in short order the bodies were hidden. Any tracker would have little trouble finding the site, but unless searched for, the unmarked grave would serve its purpose.

Sitting near the campfire and huddled close together for warmth, the four men talked sparingly as they devoured the venison; the giant Angvald consuming almost a double portion. The meal, accompanied by a barrel of watery ale found in the cave, was a veritable feast for the fugitives. Wiping away the juice dripping down his chin and into his thickening beard, Leoric believed he was eating what could only be the most enjoyable meal of his life.

With stomachs full, Angvald offered to take the first watch. As the three others lay down on newly acquired bedrolls, the Kaleenian began to hum a lively tune that had Leoric smiling happily.

"What's that you're singing, Angvald?" he asked, remembering that Angvald had shown some talent for song while at Darkenedge.

"'The Floating Flagon Barge of Ellan Reen'," Angvald answered with a chuckle. "It's an old favourite of mine. Would you like me to stop?"

"No, no, by all means continue. Sing the words if you'd like."

Beaming, Angvald cleared his throat and sang:

> *Was sixty years ago today,*
> *   that old barge went floating past.*
> *The merriment and drunken jests,*
> *   we thought would never last.*
> *Ellan Reen, slave to the spirits,*
> *   Yes, he was indeed!*

> *And on his barge, the Floating Flagon,*
> *   the barrels were piled high.*
> *Drunkards welcome and drinks poured,*
> *   What more did we need?*

So raise your glass and drink,
  a one, a two, a three, or four!
The Barge'll keep you floating,
  when you've hit the floor.
Oh, Ellan Reen, that man of legend,
  drank us all to shame.
The Floating Flagon, that rousing boat,
  no better one to name!"

As the tune ended, Leoric closed his eyes and fell fast asleep.

It was no surprise that upon being awakened for his shift, the tune still floated about his head. Humming the song, Leoric watched the sky lighten overhead. The peaceful night brought back memories of the outdoor nights spent in Kieri's company.

"I will return and find you..." he whispered in the dark.

At a moment such as this, hope seemed not so far away, the lingering promise no longer so unattainable.

For two days the small band continued to push their way westward. With stamina renewed, the four men covered much ground, the innumerable trees passing by in a blurry haze as they ran. After a short trek through broken ground, the area showing clear signs of having been the victim of a large fire, the far off sound of rushing water could be heard. Benoit noticed it first, the scholar visibly excited by the prospect of reaching their first goal.

Using Auric's maps, Leoric and Angvald guessed at where they may have crossed the previous winter. If they continued on their present course, they would reach the water further south, hoping in part to avoid the river guards both men had seen at the crossing. Although there was the possibility that the goblins had assigned no one to watch the eastern shore, Leoric deemed it unlikely after their encounter with the patrol. All they could hope for was a clear stretch of shore.

With the fire ravaged area now far behind them, they returned to the welcome cover of the trees. The land gently started to rise as the group pressed onward, becoming far rockier and with the dense underbrush thinning considerably. As with the brief jaunt across the treeless field, Leoric couldn't shake the feeling of being terribly exposed. Up ahead he could see the land continuing to rise, great boulders laying across their path. If anyone were to be standing guard within that natural cover, the four travellers could be spotted a league in advance.

With mounting concern, Leoric sent Auric ahead, Angvald taking up the man's heavily laden pack, map case and all, so that the old man could better maneuver. Watching his friend disappear up the slope, Leoric gazed backwards once more, his apprehension giving rise to a momentary sense of panic. Breathing deeply, he calmed his fears and scanned the forest.

Nothing... I'm just jumping at shadows.

Soon after, everything changed. Auric suddenly came bounding down the slope through the thinning brush, his arms frantically waving at the others. The man's features were enough to terrify Leoric. Racing upwards and into the jumbled set of boulders, Auric stood waiting, panting heavily from the exertion.

"Come quickly," he gasped. Reaching for his pack, he turned and sprinted back across the rocky ground.

He led them up onto a small shelf of rock that overlooked their destination. Down below flowed the mighty river, rushing forcefully southwards. Following Auric's outstretched arm, Leoric laid eyes on an incredible sight - an unguarded ferry lay docked on the shore.

"By the gods, fortune has truly blessed us!" Angvald breathed. "Blessed be Arne," Benoit sank to his knees.

Auric shook his head as he carefully placed his pack on the ground. "The ferry is good news, but I also have bad tidings to report," he said, clambering up a large boulder to his left.

With sinking hearts, Leoric, Benoit, and Angvald scrambled up to join their companion. Leoric's fears from that afternoon returned; from this distance, in such cover, a man could spot an enemy a league away.

Scrambling through the thinning woods near the river's edge were hundreds of goblins. They raced across the earth as though they had been traversing this untamed land every day of their lives. Unlike the wearied pace of the escaped prisoners, the goblins of *Lok'Dal hie* ran hard and at an astonishing pace. They were heavily armed, each soldier carrying a spear, axe, or sword on their belts, and a bow slung across their backs. The four men stood no chance against such odds; fleeing was their only option.

Assessing the dire situation, Leoric decided that they must move now. If they could reach the ferry, they might be able to survive. "Take only what is necessary. Angvald, uncoil the rope and tie it to that boulder," he motioned to a large rock nearby. "We need to get off this ledge. If we're to have any hope of escaping, we must be quick!"

The intricate and often complicated manipulation of Aer remains the
most guarded secret of the Silveryn Order. Each member of the Order
must swear a binding oath of fealty upon entry, a safeguard against
any perversion of their magical lore.
—*The Silveryn Doctrines, Volume I*

CHAPTER XLIII

The *Drayen* Plains, Protectorate

B ider felt strange in the soft leathers the *Drayen* had generously provided once
they realized that both he and Gavin wore almost everything they owned on
their backs. The leather was supple, far softer than his old company armour that
tended to chafe and irritate his skin. The tunic he now wore was light yet remarkably strong.

Gavin was amused by his obvious discomfort when first donning the new
clothing. Bider could say little in return as the captain seemed quite at ease in
the *Drayenmark* garments. That he had spent time living with the remnants of
Caledun's old ruling families was itself something of a surprise. It was no secret
that the clansmen of the east thought ill of almost all those living in the rest of the
shattered kingdom.

The wounds left behind by the slaughter after the Shattering simply refused to
heal. Visitors were rarely accepted, even in the outlying villages and towns of the
Drayen holdings. The Aeldenwood had grown so far out of control that the eastern
edge of the forest effectively cut off any safe land travel between the Protectorate,

the Northern Council, and the *Drayenmark*. Bider had no doubt that these circumstances were very much to the liking of the rightful heir, Serian Rhone.

Bider was grooming his horse when two of the *Drayen* approached him, their braided hair and ornamental feathers swaying gently in the breeze. With a smile and a nod, one of the men dropped a large sack slung over his shoulder to the ground.

"You carry only your crossbow?" the second *Drayen* asked.

Unsure of himself, Bider took a moment before answering. "Aye, that's correct."

"Tinaes and I don't believe that you're proficient with the weapon," he continued.

"I don't care much about your assessment," Bider snipped.

Laughing, the other *Drayen*, this one much younger in years, raised his hands and hastily replied.

"Remus meant no offence by his comment, friend. We are both scouts in the *Ca'lafi*, our Lord Prince's war party. It was obvious by how you surveyed the environment as well as your habitual glances to the surrounding countryside, that you are trained to be perceptive."

"You are a scout like us," Remus commented briskly.

Intrigued and impressed, Bider grunted. "Go on, I'm listening."

Smiling, Tinaes crouched and opened the large sack on the ground. "One of our companions would love to trade for your weapon. I have here an assortment of weapons that you may find more to your liking."

Bider watched as the bag was overturned and a number of weapons, ranging from small daggers to long swords, spilled out. Dropping carefully to his knees, the Fey'Derin fingered a black leather bandolier.

Lifting his eyes, Bider grinned. "I think we might be able to bargain."

The negotiations were lengthy but good-natured. Remus spoke little, whereas the younger *Drayen* scout debated each and every item in which he showed interest. In the end, the crossbow exchanged hands and Bider thankfully slipped the new bandolier across his chest and inserted six blades that he had worked hard to barter into the final exchange.

"Can I ask you a question, Coren?" Tinaes spoke, the weapons now returned to the heavy sack. The three men now sat quietly across from one another, sharing a large piece of hard bread and a cup of ale.

"Please call me Bider," he insisted with a shy smile. "And yes you may ask of me anything."

"You are a strange man, Bider," Tinaes hesitated when saying the name. "But I would like to know the truth of the tale we have heard circulating around camp this morning."

"And that would be?" Bider raised an eyebrow.

The young man leaned forward and whispered. "Is it true you fought a *Sciloc*? The legends of my people say it is a thing of darkness that can never be defeated."

"Oh it is a thing of darkness, friend," Bider answered seriously. "But it is also flesh and blood. It was Captain Silveron who defeated the creature. I was just there to lend a hand."

"Your Captain is also a strange man. He is someone with a purpose and a presence," Tinaes replied.

"He carries himself like a lord," Remus added sharply.

"He is fair and honest," Bider said. "And he's always treated everyone with honour and respect. He isn't a lord, Remus, but he often behaves much better than those who were born as such."

"He is a leader of men," the *Drayen* soldier declared.

"How long have you followed him?" Tinaes asked as he finished his ale with a healthy swallow.

"It has been almost three years now with the Captain, and I would never consider leaving the Fey'Derin," Bider replied.

"Never?" Tinaes asked skeptically. "Never."

CB

"I am not offering you a choice in the matter, Captain Silveron," Kaimon said for the third time, his tone attempting to dismiss any rebuttal. As far as the prince was concerned, the decision was final.

"You'll be in need of every soldier possible should you to find yourself in danger while crossing the Protectorate, Kaimon. Coren and I will be fine on our own, I beseech you," Gavin pleaded.

"The loss of six men would be of little consequence," Kaimon repeated. "And in any case, they will be travelling east after you arrive at the border to the Silveryn lands. My father needs to be briefed about this past month's events."

"Will it mean war for the *Drayenmark*?" Gavin pressed.

Kaimon was silent for a moment. The *Drayen* prince stared off into the sunrise as he contemplated his answer. "My father may raise our banners, but he won't act until he knows where Gadian Yarr stands in respect to the kingship."

"How do you mean?" Gavin frowned.

"If the Protectorate wants to avoid my father's wrath, Gadian Yarr has only to acknowledge Serian Rhone's legitimate claim to the High King's throne," Kaimon replied boldly.

A look of understanding swept across Gavin's face. "He would leave the south under Yarr's control if it meant having an ally who would proclaim him king..."

"For the moment, there are far too many outcomes to consider," Kaimon said. "It is impossible to predict the actions of someone in my father's *condition*."

"You speak the truth, Kaimon, but will your father look to the Northern Council for aid, or the Iron Shield for that matter?"

"My father will do what he thinks is best for my people. Unfortunately, I know he'll not hesitate to sacrifice soldiers in the name of his own glory," Kaimon replied mournfully.

"By the gods, then stand up to him!" Gavin exclaimed. "You are old enough now to speak for your people. Who, if not you, will do so?!"

Kaimon stared icily at Gavin. "He is my father, Gavin, and I am his son. While my father still breathes, it doesn't matter what I wish, but only what he desires. It is the curse of my people to have a leader who lusts only after power and kingship. For two hundred years we have somehow survived with such men and women as lords, and there's nothing anyone can do to help! Do you not think that I will be the same once Serian Rhone is dead? I too, Gavin, *will* go insane."

"No! I don't accept that!" Gavin replied angrily. "You are not your father!"

"Leave me, Gavin. I want to be alone," Kaimon said, turning his eyes back to the sunrise.

Seeing no other choice, Gavin turned and headed back to the camp.

In the end, six men were dispatched under Gavin's command. The *Drayen* soldiers were to provide an escort for the two Fey'Derin, and eventually turn back southeast towards the port city of Dragomere in the hopes of boarding a ship bound for the *Drayen* lands. Kaimon remained steadfast in his goal to first lead Lord Helmstead, the Dwarven emissary who had recently joined their party, all the way to Alerond. Afterwards, they would head north and skirt the edges of the Aeldenwood in the hopes of avoiding any patrols sent out by the new Protectorate general. With luck, they would arrive in Delfwane within a fortnight.

Gavin and the sons of Rhone spoke privately one last time, but little remained to be said. Kaimon had been properly informed as to the state of the south and Gavin wished him well. Soon after, he watched the large company of colourful *Drayenmark* stream off into the distance, the smaller *Sheves* trotting along beside the larger horses.

cß

"They're still gaining on us, Captain Silveron," Tinaes reported, his grey stallion trotting up next to Gavin's. The *Drayen* clansman looked nervous in the bright morning sunshine, his youthful face wrinkled with worry.

Scanning the horizon line, Gavin squinted into the sun. He muttered a curse when he realized the soldier had spoken the truth; their pursuers continued to gain.

"I need to know their numbers before I commit to any action, Tinaes. I need you and Remus to act as my eyes. Put some distance between us and see what you can discern from that cursed dust cloud that hounds us," Gavin ordered.

"And once we know how many?" Tinaes asked.

"Then get back to us swiftly. I'd judge them to number no more than two score. Either way, we may be in trouble if we can't reach some form of cover," Gavin replied grimly.

Tineas immediately spun his horse around and thundered to the southeast, Remus riding hard in pursuit.

Up until now, the days had passed with little incident as the small band had made their way north across the plains. Gavin had set a leisurely but steady pace, and the leagues had slowly passed beneath their mounts' steel shod hooves. With ample supplies and stomachs full, both he and Coren found themselves with renewed energy.

Coren was finding the going easier, but the travel was still draining. Gavin had noticed the scout favouring his injured ankle more than once. The healers at Dragon Mount remained the man's only hope for regaining a semblance of the same movement and agility he was used to. Nothing they had tried so far had helped guide the healing of the shattered bones. Without arcane help, Coren D'Elmark would never again walk free from pain.

Apart from young Tinaes and the tight-lipped Remus, Kaimon had attached four other men to the small retinue. All four were tough veterans of numerous battles along the frontiers of the *Drayenmark* lands, Gavin had been told. Rare were the years when selfish nobles weren't attempting to claim and usurp more of the vast land area that had at one time belonged to the ruling families of the *Drayenmark*. The frontier wars had been bloody and ruthless.

The senior most soldier was a tall man whose sun-browned face reminded Gavin of Caolte. Benias was one of Kaimon's most trusted men. It was a distinct honour for the clansmen to have been given the responsibility of reporting to Serian Rhone, but Gavin could sense that he was a man who wished to still be at the side of his liege lord. Benias was also a cousin to the Rhone family, and as such could never be ignored by the old monarch. Kaimon, Gavin thought, had made a wise choice.

Gavin sympathized with the veteran, but fretted more about the response that Serian Rhone would have concerning the events of the spring. Serian was erratic at the best of times, but the declaration of a new kingdom in the Protectorate could very well drive the man to actions beyond the advice of even his closest kin.

The first signs of pursuit had been detected nearly a fortnight from when they had first met Kaimon Rhone. The young *Drayenmark* scout had been the first to bring word, Tinaes' eagle eyes having caught sight of a slight disruption in his view to the south.

At first they had believed, or more appropriately hoped, that the sign of another band of travelers was nothing more than a coincidence. It was rare that caravans travelled this far north in the plains, for few traded now with the mage town of Dragomere, let alone the mountain fortress of Dragon Mount. But some merchants, those daring enough, still remained in contact with those connected to the Silveryn Order. It was the speed at which the other company moved that worried Gavin and the others. In one day their pursuers had quickly bridged the gap between the two parties. Merchants, they knew, would never travel at such a reckless pace.

Hoping fervently to put distance between both groups, Gavin had pushed his men hard, preferring to ride carefully throughout the night rather than resting and in turn risking a possible confrontation. The following morning saw no fading in the threat of those who dogged their steps. If anything, their pursuers had continued to gain ground. Without the benefit of any break in the barren plain, Gavin resolved that their only hope of escape was through the broken terrain to the north.

Already Gavin could make out the rough foothills of the *Erienn* range, the cracked and treacherous ground being the first line of defense leading to the sanctuary of the Silveryn mages. The rough countryside might give them the cover they so desperately needed.

As the morning passed, Gavin increased the pace of their march, alternating between fast trots and a slower canter in order to maximize the stamina of their mounts. It wasn't until Tinaes came riding at a full gallop back into their ranks that the young Fey'Derin captain knew that no choice was left; they would need to race for cover.

"How many?" he asked, the breathless scout reining in at his side for the second time that day.

"A handful over two score, just as you suspected, Gavin," Tinaes replied gravely. "They carry unfamiliar banners adorned with a hyena," the young man added between breaths.

"Khali..." Gavin swore.

As Remus came riding back into their midst, Gavin made his decision. Throwing an apologetic look towards Bider, he paused to survey the men entrusted with his safety. "The men who pursue us are known to me. They will offer no terms of surrender, and they will show us no mercy," he began with terrible conviction. "We ride now for the hills and broken ground of the mountains. If at any time it appears we will be overtaken, Cail you will ride east while the rest of us make our stand."

"By the gods, I won't!" the *Drayen* shouted defiantly. The veteran soldier, his feathers shaking madly in his fury, pulled hard on his horse's bridle, causing the mount to rear up.

"You will do as I say," Gavin interjected calmly. "Whatever my feelings towards your liege lord, Serian Rhone must be contacted. You are the most experienced soldier here, and whether you agree with my decision or not, you will follow my orders."

"I won't leave like a coward," Cail growled, turning to the *Drayenmark* veteran Benias for support.

Benias shook his head. "There's nothing else that can be done. You know the land and can survive where most of us could not. To you must fall this burden."

"You must reach Lord Rhone," Remus added.

In silence, Cail nodded in agreement, his face a dark mask.

"Then it is decided," Gavin announced. "Time is not on our side, let's be off!"

Without another word he spurred his mount into action and rode hard towards the northeast, the beckoning outline of the foothills still far off in the distance.

The jarring force of the prolonged ride was agonizing for Bider. His ankle throbbed unbearably as Gavin led the band towards the closest of the hills. With luck, Bider thought they might find a canyon or gully in which to hide or defend themselves, but staying conscious was proving to be the more pressing need at the moment. Clutching a handful of his horse's thick mane, he closed his eyes and gritted his teeth to fight the pain.

The sun rose high overhead as the chase wore on. Having already spent a portion of their strength in racing back to report their findings, both Tinaes and Remus found their steeds flagging noticeably. Unwilling to leave any men behind, Gavin gently eased the pace even though by doing so, Khali's Reavers would certainly gain ground.

As they neared the edge of the broken ground, Bider risked a glance at their pursuers. Unlike earlier that morning, Khali's men no longer resembled a simple dust cloud on the horizon. Clear figures on horseback, each man wearing the black and scarlet of the New Protectorate, were now distinguishable.

Tinaes had figured correctly; at least forty men tailed them. Without adequate cover there was little hope for the eight men. The numbers were simply too overwhelming. Not even Gavin Silveron's skill with a blade would be enough to help them in an open field battle.

The captain led them carefully through a smattering of crumbling boulders and steep canyon walls that rose up from the very edge of the flat plain. As they passed into a long but very narrow defile, the entrance partially blocked by large broken stones that had long ago fallen from the sloping sides of the canyon, Gavin slowed their pace. Beckoning Benias to his side, the two men bent their heads close and spoke privately. For Bider, those few minutes seemed to stretch out endlessly. For every moment they were delayed, Khali's Reavers drew ever closer.

Finally, Gavin nodded at the *Drayen* warrior and gracefully leapt from his saddle. Grabbing his longsword from over his shoulder he unsheathed the weapon and stabbed it point first into the ground.

"This is where we make our stand."

Cʒ

The thunder of hammering hooves echoed off of the cracked walls of the small ravine where Gavin and Benias waited with their small group. The sound seemed to come from everywhere all at once, and Bider could do little to hide his discomfort. The defenses behind which they now hid were barely adequate. Granted, the charging riders may very well lose a man or two as they roared around the sharp corner of the gully, but Bider surmised they could still be easily overwhelmed.

"Not such great odds, are they?" Tinaes whispered from his left.

A quick glance proved that he wasn't the only nervous man. "Being outnumbered almost six to one is never a bet I would take," Bider answered with a failed attempt at a smile. "But we have archers and the Captain, that's got to count for something."

"We place our lives in the hands of the gods," Remus added reverently. Try as he might, Bider still couldn't make hide or hair of the strange *Drayenmark* scout.

The noise increased and was now almost deafening. Bider found himself loosening the straps on his bandolier, patiently waiting with his hands ready to throw daggers at the first of Khali's riders as they came into range. How effective he would be in a fight considering his injuries still remained in doubt.

By the gods the noise is incredible!

Of the seven men, Cail had been dispatched east once they entered the foothills, only three stood on the ravine floor, the others were positioned on higher ground like Bider and his two comrades. Gavin Silveron stood foremost in the small line, his companions gripping their *Drayen* spears and preparing to block the impending cavalry charge.

"Hold tight, here they come!" Benias shouted, his braids dancing wildly. He tossed his head back and loosed a *Drayen* war cry. "*T'aheris ni feldnar!*"

"*T'aheris ni feldnar!*" the remaining *Drayenmark* echoed the cry.

It was at that moment, with the loose rocks and stones of the little gully shaking and sliding about, that the clear cry of defiance by the *Drayen* warrior inexplicably sounded from behind the small band of defenders.

"*T'AHERIS NI FELDNAR!!*" A voice cried out, and Bider turned towards the rear of the ravine just as the first of Khali's Reavers rounded the bend.

In awe, the Fey'Derin scout watched the tough, weather-beaten face of Caolte Burnaise charge up through the canyon with two scores of Fey'Derin and *Delan Fere* riding at his side. With jarring force, the lead elements of both companies collided, the powerful charge of the Fey'Derin forces slicing through the shocked Reavers.

On the valley floor, Gavin and Benias stood shoulder to shoulder as remnants of Khali's assault slipped through the carnage, most of the men immediately falling to the arrows released from both sides of the gully. But for those that reached the two soldiers, little hope remained for their survival. With calculated precision both warriors slew any that approached. Through it all, Gavin wore an expression of unwavering resolve.

Bider suddenly realized that he was shouting in triumph, his voice mingling with that of his companions. He could feel the blood rushing through him, and he was unsure of what to do with all his energy. He had been so close to death, and now suddenly the world seemed brighter than ever before.

The battle itself raged for only a short period of time. Khali's Reavers, outnumbered and outclassed, broke as easily as Caolte had expected. Within minutes of blunting their charge, those left alive from the group of forty former mercenaries scattered in the hopes of escaping the wrath of the Fey'Derin and the *Delan Fere*. Caolte ordered most of the men back instead of giving chase. Pursuit seemed of little importance. Only a small group of Eagle Runners ranged about the plain, the company scouts on guard and alert for any further signs of danger.

Bider was sitting quietly with Tinaes on the very ledge where they had been standing during the short-lived engagement, when he spotted a familiar figure among the assembled men. The man's unmistakable long black coat could be easily identified among the milling soldiers as Ethan Shade broke from the cluster huddling near Captain Silveron and approached the pair.

Bider limped painfully towards his company officer, offering his forearm to the man. "You're a sight for sore eyes, Sergeant," Bider grinned.

"Well, you look like you could use a drink or two of ale from my saddlebags, Bider," Ethan gripped the scout's outstretched forearm. "You're lucky Sergeant McConnal isn't here to greet you or he'd have had much more to say in the matter," the Fey'Derin officer laughed.

"I have no doubt of that!" Bider conceded.

"Are you well enough to travel?" Ethan asked, staring at the splint on Bider's lower leg.

"I can manage, sir," Bider replied with a shrug. "In any case, I'm not staying behind. There could be another *Sciloc* nearby," he added slyly.

"A *Sciloc*...?" Ethan uttered. "Bider, I believe you have a story to tell."

"And without some ale, I'll not be telling it, so you'd best get me headed in the right direction," Bider answered. "Oh and I'll need a drink for my new friend as well," he waved a hand at Tinaes.

"All right, all right, you win!" Ethan threw an arm around the smaller scout's shoulder, and the two men headed off towards the horses, Tinaes not far behind.

ꝏ

The manner in which Gavin had spoken of the promised healing should have been the first clue for Bider. The captain had always spoken of his shattered limb and the magical procedure in hushed tones, as if he never really felt comfortable broaching the subject. Bider had always assumed that Gavin's behaviour meant that some pain must be involved, or that the Fey'Derin commander had himself already been a beneficiary of a similar treatment.

Bider had had no idea that the pain would be so great.

Three robed women had placed him on a strangely warm, black wood table and warned him to expect only a 'slight discomfort' during the procedure. He now knew what those words truly meant. He would not even wish such torture on his worst enemies.

Upon their arrival in Dragon Mount, Gavin had immediately been ushered into council while Bider had been escorted by Ethan Shade to the lower levels of the Silveryn fortress. Bider had been fighting a fever for the better part of the journey, the harrowing chase across the plains at least partially to blame. His body ached all over, and his damaged ankle throbbed mercilessly. For days at a time sleep eluded the scout, but through all the hazy memories of the journey, familiar faces returned to lend him strength: Gavin, Ethan, Caolte, and even the *Drayen* scouts Tinaes and Remus.

Guided through the immaculate corridors of the Silveryn citadel, Bider was led into a large oval chamber with only one piece of furniture - an immense, black wooden table. Set at an angle, the strange contraption had restraints for his arms, legs, and head. Wondering if he had been mistaken for an enemy, he was worried about what was to come, but Ethan Shade never moved from his side, the hawk-nosed sergeant encouraging him even as the straps were tightened in place.

The three grey-robed women, mages no doubt, started to chant and his body had been filled with a wave of warm light that soothed his harried mind. The euphoric feeling lasted no longer than a heartbeat before it was replaced by the pain. It was as if every inch of his being was on fire; every vein, every fiber, every vessel, burned with a white hot heat.

He had screamed himself hoarse before the magical healing process was completed. He had passed out twice from the pain, but the second time he had been aware of his bones knitting themselves together. The effect was unsettling to say the least. Time soon lost all meaning to him, and he finally succumbed to the darkness.

Squinting at a slash of blinding light poking through a pair of thin white curtains, Bider gingerly opened his eyes.

"Good afternoon, Coren," a familiar voice sounded from beside him.

Turning his head slowly, as if in anticipation of more pain, Bider looked at Gavin Silveron. "I can't believe I'm still alive," he groaned.

"I can assure you, you are very much among the living."

"It hurt so much," Bider said.

"The process speeds up the natural rate of healing for a patient," Gavin explained, a guilty flush colouring his cheeks. "Unfortunately, tampering with the laws of nature brings with it a steep price. Your body, and more specifically your mind, cannot understand the speed in which your bones are knitting, your cuts healing or your bruises fading. What would have been a lengthy recovery time for your shattered ankle was amplified in your mind over the course of an hour. Our bodies simply don't know how to deal with such an event."

"You could have warned me," Bider retorted.

"I am truly sorry, Coren, but there was no time once your fever caught and the infections from your broken ribs spread rapidly through your system. You were nearly lost to us by the time Ir'Calen and her novices began their ministrations," Gavin said regretfully.

"I wish an explanation could make these horrid memories go away..." Bider lay quietly in the bed, a contemplative look on his face. Gavin remained seated in the high-backed chair for long minutes before finally speaking once again.

"It wasn't my intention to bring you to harm. I only wanted to help," he said.

"I know, sir... I know."

"How do you feel?" Gavin continued.

"I'm hungry, I guess, and apart from that I feel fine," Bider answered. "Almost..."

"Your ankle will always ache, especially in colder weather, but it has been fully restored," Gavin answered.

"I don't know how to thank you, Captain. I'm not sure if you can deduct the treatment from my wages, but..."

"I'll hear none of that," Gavin held up a hand in protest. "Without your well-fired crossbow bolt, neither of us would be here discussing this subject. Consider your healing treatment a recompense for time well served in the company of your commanding officer."

"How are the men?" Bider asked with some concern.

Gavin fairly glowed with pride as he answered the question. "Lieutenant Burnaise successfully led the company out of the Caeronwood and to Dragon Mount, as I knew he would. We took losses, but on the whole we've come out relatively unscathed. The men fought hard and we've no doubt given Gerald Armsmater something to remember us by," he smiled.

"And the *Delan Fere?*"

"Both the Sisters of the Sword and Herod's company reached the safety of the Silveryn Order with more significant losses, but regardless, they stand ready to continue the fight," Gavin replied.

"Thank you for everything," Bider bowed slightly at the waist. "I also feel well enough to fight once more," he added with a relieved sigh,

"Excellent," Gavin nodded in approval as he rose to his feet. "Then I'll expect you to report to Sergeant Shade immediately after you've found something to eat downstairs. Era Colwyn should have something boiling over the hearth."

"Any particular reason for the urgency?" Bider asked, slipping out of the large bed and reaching for his tunic and *Drayenmark* leathers.

"On the morrow the company will ride for Delfwane."

"So soon?"

Gavin chuckled. "You've been recuperating for almost a week."

"Alright then, why Delfwane?" Bider asked.

"Because that is where Gadian Yarr wishes to make war. I plan on being there to remind him of my views about his sovereignty," Gavin replied.

With a smile, Bider reached for his bandoliers.

*The river is immense. With such a mighty current, I deem it unlikely
the goblins cross the water without trepidation. That is, of course, if
they attempt to cross it at all. They are fearful of the water by nature,
are they not?*
—Lord Crispin, *The Explorers Vol. II*

CHAPTER XLIV

The *River D'Erlin*, Goblin Territories

Auric was the first to descend the rope. The instant he landed on the earth, Leoric ushered Benoit over the side of the cliff. Their survival depended on a speedy descent. As the moments slipped by, he kept a close watch on the approach of their enemies. It was as though they had sensed their prey was close, and now they moved with unbelievable speed and focus. Leoric had to grudgingly admit that the goblin soldiers were in excellent shape, their stamina far exceeding that of the weary fugitives.

"Can we fight them if need be?" Leoric asked his towering companion.

"It would be hopeless, Leoric. We'll take some to the heavens with us, but we've little chance against so many. They know we're here, and sometimes one's courage matters little in battle," Angvald answered.

"They are too many..." Leoric agreed and turned back to the task at hand.

He was the last to drop down below the ledge. Hitting the ground in a sprint, the others were already far ahead. Benoit and Auric were standing hip deep in the water trying desperately to drag the beached ferry off the shore. Unlike their first crossing of the River D'Erlin, this time the ferry wasn't tied to a dock. The heavy boat had been dragged partially up on the shore and tied to the nearest tree with a length of thick rope.

Auric had already sliced through the rope, but the ferry had barely budged, even when Leoric arrived to throw his weight behind the effort. Judging by the speed at which the goblin trackers were approaching, he estimated they had fewer than ten minutes to cast off. Leoric preferred not to consider the consequences if they failed to do so.

With an agonizing slowness, the boat began to shift on the sand. The four men made incremental progress, one slight movement at a time. At Auric's insistence, Benoit threw his bow and quiver onto the deck and scrambled over the side. Using one of the long poles, he was able to begin pushing off the shore as the others continued to shove the ferry along the sand.

As they struggled to maintain their balance while pushing the wooden barge into the deeper water, Benoit suddenly loosed a cry of alarm. From the trees near the shelf of rock where they had descended, a small group of goblins burst from cover.

"Ware, they come! And they aren't coming down the cliff!" Benoit warned, dropping the long pole and taking aim with his bow.

"Push, Angvald! Push!" Leoric bellowed, straining his muscles to their limit.

"There's no time!" Benoit screamed.

At his side, Leoric watched as Auric studied the oncoming attackers and reached for his belted mace. Then, the old man bolted across the sandy ground, raising his mace defiantly in the air as he closed the distance between himself and the goblins. "Get the ferry out into the water, I'll be fine," he called back over his shoulder.

As Auric sprinted to engage the four guards, the lead goblin fell to his knees, one of Benoit's black arrows lodged firmly in his chest. Shocked by the blow, the goblin sank wordlessly to the ground, hands twitching as he reached for the arrow.

Auric never flinched. He flew by the wounded soldier, his mace sweeping aside the closest attacker's blade and landing a heavy blow to the goblin's sword arm. With a cry of pain, the goblin dropped his weapon, clutching at the crushed limb. Only partially able to avoid the last guard's thrust, Auric stepped backwards and stopped, his eyes trained on the two remaining foes. A ragged gash where he had been struck on his upper arm started to bleed. The goblins had each moved to one side of the man, grudgingly showing respect for their adversary's agility and skill.

Standing on the ferry, Benoit notched a second arrow and sighted again down the length of the shaft. At the same time, Leoric finally felt the craft give way and begin to slide out into the water. Shouting with glee, he and Angvald leaned into the ferry and sent it moving even faster.

"Auric! We have to leave now!" Leoric hollered, reaching for the nearest steering pole and pulling himself onto the boat. On the opposite side, Angvald was doing the same. Already the current was pulling the watercraft forcibly into the violent, choppy waters.

Benoit loosed his second shot, and without bothering to chart its course, turned and grabbed a pole to help Angvald. Still on the beach, Auric danced about, the goblin attackers now reduced to one, a second guard incapacitated with Benoit's arrow imbedded in his upper thigh.

Leoric watched as the rest of the goblins suddenly burst from the trees only a scant hundred paces from Auric. If he didn't turn to flee immediately, he would be quickly overwhelmed.

"Auric!! Run!!" Angvald roared from the deck of the small ferry.

If he delays any longer, he won't make it! Leoric's mind screamed in panic.

Noticing the approaching soldiers, Auric leapt forward with a feint, his quick attack catching his attacker flatfooted. As Auric altered his speed, there was little the goblin could do in defense. With a loud crack, the mace came down hard against the goblin's helm. The creature staggered back from the blow and collapsed.

Auric didn't wait to finish his opponent. Instead, he whirled around and tore off back towards the water. Already the ferry was pulling away from the shore with astonishing speed. As Auric reached the water, a first arrow struck him hard in the back. Stumbling from the force of the blow, the old man fell into the water, his body quickly disappearing under the waves.

"No!!!" Leoric screamed, watching three more goblins raise their bows and take aim. He leapt into the water just as Auric was struck for a second time. Soaked up to his thighs in the fast current, Leoric felt an inkling of dread as his desperate jump nearly cost him his footing. Weighed down by his drenched leather armour and being a poor swimmer, falling would put him in serious jeopardy. With Benoit showering the goblins with arrows and Angvald fighting desperately to regain control of the craft, there would be no one left to save him.

Steadying himself, he waded towards where Auric had gone under. As he approached, the man surfaced only a few paces away, his eyes glazed over in obvious pain. A second volley of arrows hissed through the air as Leoric reached his friend.

In stunned disbelief, Leoric saw two more shafts sprout from Auric's side and shoulder. He drifted into Leoric's outstretched arms, his face constricted in a look of distress. Leoric barely registered the two arrows that grazed his own shoulder, one even lodging itself in his backpack, piercing the fabric.

He planted his feet and threw the wiry old man over his shoulder. Surprised by the lightness of his burden, the borderman drew on a reserve of endurance he never knew existed and began to walk back through the water towards the swaying ferry. Angvald had planted his long pole in the sandy bottom, and with a formidable effort, the Kaleenian's great strength held the large raft in place.

Benoit, seeing Leoric with Auric over his shoulder, jumped into the water as the pair approached. Together, with arrows now assaulting them ceaselessly, they managed to slide Auric's wounded body up on the deck of the craft. Leoric grimaced as he watched painful spasms wrack the old man's frame.

"Go!!" Leoric yelled as he and Benoit pulled themselves wearily out of the water. Ignoring the arrows landing all around him, and one in the pole he carried, Angvald ferociously raised the wooden shaft and allowed the powerful current to carry them away. On the shore, the distraught cries of their one-time captors could faintly be heard.

Angvald showed some skill in commanding the ferry, leading the small craft slowly but steadily across the wide river. Confident that the big man could handle the task, Leoric bent down and gently lifted Auric into his arms, cradling the man's wounded body. Unable to stop the flow of tears, he looked into his friend's eyes.

"I'm sorry, Auric..." he stammered.

Auric smiled weakly, "There was nothing you could have done. At a certain point in our lives, our destiny comes to claim us. That you risked your life for an old wounded man only confirms my belief that it is to you that I must bestow my sacred trust."

"What do you mean?" Leoric whispered. "I never understand what you are saying," he laughed through the tears that coursed down his cheeks.

"You will, Leoric... you will," Auric answered. Somehow, the old prisoner always seemed as though he knew something everyone else did not. "But you must listen to me now. Do you remember the night I spoke to you of a promise?"

"Yes," Leoric nodded.

"I knew that night that my time upon this earth was nearing its conclusion, and that I must begin your preparation," Auric gasped.

"You knew?"

"It is the curse that accompanies my gift. To know the manner of your death is no easy thing to live with, Leoric, but it is the burden my line endures in order to fulfill its destiny. I am the An'Dari, the last of a long line who have lived only to protect the kings of old."

"By the gods..." Leoric uttered, the words a barely audible whisper.

"Do you know what I am?" Auric asked.

"The An'Dari was the bodyguard to the High King; commander of the An'Darim, the King's Guard. But they say Druan Warder was the last; with his death, so too died the line," Leoric replied.

"History is written by those in power, Leoric. Not everything that you have been told is true, least of all the destruction of the An'Dari. If there is an heir to the kingdom alive, there will always be one to protect them," Auric stated, the words strangled by a cough from his bloodied lips.

"What do you ask of me, Auric? I am no leader of men, and there is no king."

"But there is an heir, a descendant from the line of Lordares. Have no doubt, Leoric D'Athgaran, you will one day be a great leader of men," Auric answered.

"Without a direct descendant, I must choose a successor so that the line remains unbroken. I choose you, Leoric. I did so the moment you came to *Lok'Dal hie*, though you would never have known. But you must accept my charge with your own free will."

"What does it mean?" Leoric asked.

"You will become the bearer of a sacred trust. You, and you alone, will bear the responsibility of keeping the heir alive. Your life will always revolve around that of the heir to Caledun, as mine did long ago although I failed terribly..." Coughing weakly, as though there remained little strength left in his body, Auric gripped Leoric's arm with sudden power, "Please... I will explain more when next I see you..." he gasped.

"I accept, Auric," Leoric whispered.

With a grateful sigh, Auric smiled and sagged in Leoric's powerful embrace. As the old prisoner breathed his last, free after so long a time in captivity, a sudden charge vibrated through the air. With his head bowed in sorrow, Leoric felt the shock travel through his body.

Crying out in pain, he fell backwards. Numbering in the thousands, visions flashed through his mind: battles, conversations, tragedies. A lifetime of experiences bombarded the stricken borderman. Overwhelmed, he could hear himself screaming, his voice eventually becoming hoarse as the images continued to race through his thoughts, imprinting themselves on his own experiences, intertwining with his own memories as though he had lived through them. In the space of a few minutes, Leoric lived the lives of hundreds.

ᙦ

He had no idea when he had blacked out, but now he found that that he was no longer sprawled prone on the deck of the ferry. His head throbbed painfully, and for some odd reason the distant beating of a heart pulsed in the back of his mind. The beat was incessant, yet somehow not intrusive. Confused, Leoric looked around at his surroundings.

He was encircled by trees, the faint sound of the river still audible. A small fire crackled nearby, the warmth of the blaze comforting him as he himself shivering inexplicably. Wrapped in a coarse blanket, he gingerly pulled himself up into a sitting position.

"You had us worried, Leoric," Benoit said from across the fire. "There was a moment there when I wondered whether you would return to us. Angvald, of course, never doubted that you would," he added quietly.

"What happened?" Leoric managed to say, his throat dry.

"When Auric died you were enveloped by a silvery glow. I tried to reach you but it was as though you were encased in a ball of lightning. Touching the light gave me such a shock I was almost thrown from the boat. Then you screamed until your voice gave out. Angvald and I were both hoping that you would be able to tell us what happened."

"It was Auric," Leoric replied. "He wasn't what he appeared to be."

"Did any of us truly believe he was one of us?" Angvald commented from the darkness. Stepping into the firelight, he held out the dangling length of a silver chain, a small falcon hanging from the end, its golden wings raised in flight. "I believe this belongs to you now, Leoric. It's the symbol of the Rhone family, is it not?"

Reaching out, Leoric took the necklace and held it gingerly in his hands. "This chain was a gift from the High Kings of old. It has been passed down through the years, worn by the one chosen as the An'Dari."

"How do you know this?" Benoit asked skeptically.

"I just do," Leoric answered with alarm. Tapping his temple with a finger he added. "I have the memories in my head. Somehow, when Auric died, his knowledge became mine. His memories are now my own."

"Incredible..." Angvald muttered. "You've been blessed, Leoric."

"No I haven't," he retorted angrily. "I'm not even sure what I've done, and for the moment I'd appreciate some time to think." As the words shot from his mouth, he was already filled with regret.

Benoit and Angvald turned away, the hurt clearly evident on their faces even in the shadowy light of the fire. "I'm sorry..." Leoric stammered with dismay. "I just don't —"

"We understand, Leoric. When the time is right you will speak to us about the path you chose. Until then, as your friends, know only that we will be ready to listen," Angvald replied solemnly.

"I never really knew much about him, but I miss him already," Benoit said after the silence that followed Angvald's words. "There was a calming influence in his demeanor that I never really understood."

"Where does he lie?" Leoric asked quietly.

"I built a cairn in the woods near the river. There was no time, and we didn't have the tools to dig a grave. Benoit sent him to the heavens with a blessing of Arne so that his soul will find its way quickly to the gods," Angvald explained.

"And our pursuers?"

Benoit frowned. "They headed north once we reached the midway point. If there is another crossing downstream, we may not be as safe as we believe."

"At first light we must press westward. Kelamyre lies to our south, Darkenedge to the west," Leoric thought aloud. "If you could, Angvald, would you show me to the cairn? I would like to pay my last respects."

"Aye. I'll do so gladly, Leoric."

The cairn lay nestled within a small natural grove of elm trees. Leoric approached the gravesite solemnly in the darkness, not wanting to disrupt the sanctity of the place. The various stones had been piled up in the center of the clearing, gathered from the ground where Leoric now stood. Angvald's attention to detail was touching; not a stone seemed out of place.

Leoric walked to within a few feet of the cairn and stopped. Alone with his thoughts, surrounded by the mysterious sounds of the Wilds, Leoric wished his friend well. Then reaching into his belt pouch, he retrieved the beautiful necklace Angvald had taken from their comrade's body. Leaning forward, he stretched a hand out to place the jeweled falcon atop the nearest rocks.

Angvald spoke truly, Leoric, that necklace belongs to you now.

Leoric's heart raced as the words drifted through the clearing. The voice was unmistakably Auric's. Scanning the trees, his heart pounded in his ears, the sound drowning out any ambient noise of the forest.

Turning to peer back behind him, Leoric gasped. Before him stood Auric, the old man's form illuminated in the darkness. He was dressed as he had been at the hour of his death, his leather goblin armour even sporting the very gashes he'd received at the river's edge. Only his eyes had changed. In them, there was now a look of peace that accompanied his gaze.

Why are you so surprised? I told you we'd meet another time, the apparition chuckled.

"I thought you knew not how serious your wounds were," Leoric answered. As the shadow of his fallen friend glided forward, he fought back a rising desire to flee the grove in terror.

Be at ease, Leoric. I cannot remain long here on this earth but I have been granted time to speak with you, to help you further understand what you have freely chosen to become. I swear to you no harm will come to you this night, nor will we meet like this again.

"I'm not afraid, Auric..." Leoric said nervously. "I am speaking to a dead man, though."

In a fashion, yes, the ghostly Auric smiled. *Do you feel the heartbeat yet, Leoric?*

Leoric nodded with apprehension. "I can feel it, but it's faint, sometimes I even forget it's there."

Good. That heartbeat represents the heir to the fallen Kingdom of Caledun. The High King of old, with the help of learned mages, fused a piece of his soul with the An'Dari, binding the lines forever. At no time will you be able to lose sight of that which you are sworn to protect. As you draw nearer to your charge, so too will the heartbeat increase.

"So I am to find Serian Rhone then?" Leoric swore under his breath. "That man deserves no one's protection."

You are mistaken. Look deeply within yourself, trace the heartbeat you can now sense and tell me where it leads, Auric replied.

Trying to maintain some semblance of normalcy in the midst of such strange proceedings, Leoric decided to sit down. Crossing his legs and resting his arms on his knees, he took a deep breath and focused on the strange pulsing sensation.

The beating pulled at his mind like a string. He followed the thin line and suddenly found himself speeding over the land, his corporeal body remaining behind. His mind soared over trees, mountains, and plains, through rolling hills and over fast flowing rivers. In the end, he came to rest atop a high-walled city. Examining the area below, he knew where he must be.

Opening his eyes, Leoric snapped back into his physical self, the jolt momentarily distorting his senses. "Serian Rhone is in Delfwane," he said confidently.

Not quite. Auric's smiled ruefully. *The heir is in Delfwane.*

"I don't follow? Kaimon Rhone then..."

The taint of madness in the blood of the heirs of Caledun blocks an An'Dari's power. Around the age of thirty, Serian Rhone's life force ceased to beat within my head.

"Serian Rhone was no longer seen to be a fit ruler?" Leoric suggested.

You are beginning to understand.

"Strange though, the taint..."

It is the land that is not being cared for. Just as we have a duty, so too did the High King act as the balance in nature for Caledun.

"You're speaking in riddles again. What connection lies between the two? There must be more." Leoric inquired.

The answers to the mysteries you seek are within your memories, Leoric. It is not my place to solve these riddles of the past, for that you must look to yourself. When I died, I transferred all of the memories of every man and woman who has held this unique distinction. In the coming years, your dreams will be visions of the past. Learn to use that information, the history of a kingdom lies within you, the true history...

"Why me?" he breathed. "And what of my death? Will I truly know when I shall die?"

A reoccurring dream will hint at your eventual end. I saw the river and flashes of other recent events. I tried to avoid my fate, for so long I tried... but your destiny cannot be altered, Leoric. In the end, your path will lead back to the road you must walk.

"But how could you live with such knowledge?" Leoric asked.

I didn't really. Remember the promise I asked of you?

"Yes," Leoric nodded.

Throughout the long years of our storied history, only a scant few An'Dari have ever passed on the gift to their own. Do not let your duty consume you, and in turn rob you of the happiness I know you seek.

"Like you did?"

Search my memories and find the answer to that question. But if you love her, Leoric, don't ever let her go...

Leoric could sense a change in the air. Rising to his feet, he felt a gentle breeze drift through the trees. The image of Auric began to fade as the wind swirled around the stones of his cairn. Leoric knew that it was time to say farewell.

"Auric, please, there is so much more I must ask..." he tried.

You know now where the answers you seek reside. I believe in you, Leoric D'Athgaran.

And with that, the ghostly apparition was gone, the silvery light that had spread though the glade like a soft mist dissipating within seconds.

"Goodbye," Leoric said, lifting the gleaming necklace and tying it securely around his neck.

He mentioned nothing of his experience at Auric's cairn to his two companions. Until he himself felt comfortable, the last thing Leoric wanted to do was worry his friends. Angvald pressured him to no end, the Kaleenian still in awe of the transformation that had transpired between Leoric and Auric. Leoric begged him to relax after the questioning persisted. Angvald wanted to know everything; from the names of each descendant, to specific battles and a detailed description of each one.

Leoric simply didn't know the answers. Many of his friend's queries mirrored his own. As Auric had warned, the knowledge would not appear overnight. Dreams and visions, he had said, would slowly help Leoric trace the history of those who had freely accepted the very same burden.

Benoit, on the other hand, remained relatively quiet, the thin man's dark eyes absorbing the information with keen interest. The scholar asked sensible questions, his voice calm and steady. It was the history of the long lost An'Dari that most intrigued him.

As the three men bedded down for the evening, Leoric found that sleep eluded him. *What would he see once his eyes were closed? Would he dream every night? What if he were to see his own death?*

The possibilities were endless and to consider them all was too much to take in all at once. Rolling on to his side, he pulled his bedroll tight around his thick frame and closed his eyes. As he drifted off, only Angvald's loud snoring and the distant drumming of a heartbeat invaded his thoughts.

In the end, as he should have guessed, he slept soundly, his slumber never once disturbed by visions of the An'Dari.

EPILOGUE

There was only darkness.

He had long ago given up on escaping the never-ending deluge of agony that wracked his body. From where his mind had retreated, the prisoner could no longer even be certain that his body still existed. No sensations remained except the pain.

At first there had been slight itches, small shivers that bore witness to the coming storm. Soon the tingles gave way to punctures, and if he yet maintained a physical body, he expected that it was likely riddled with holes. But as the sharp jabs lessened, the burning in his veins, the fire in his blood, the agony of his tortured mind pleaded for a return to such simpler measures of torment.

And there was no light and no sound other than his screams. He was losing his sense of self and he could not be sure if anything was real. Reality was slipping away. He floated in the darkness; a thing with no weight, no substance, and no form. On rare occasions when the pain mercifully receded, confused images and memories flashed in the blackness, visions of extravagance and wealth, of heartache and happiness. Although he strained to find some solid ground to hold, the blessed absence of the hurt would last so briefly that he doubted it completely.

And then finally came the cold; the freezing burn that had numbed all and left the prisoner free of everything but a dull ache pounding behind his eyes. He once again knew that he had returned to a body, his mind conscious of twitching limbs and weakened muscles.

With a ragged cough he drew breath. Feeling cold air burning his lungs, Corian Praxxus opened his eyes.

ABOUT THE AUTHOR

Emmet Moss lives in Canada with his family and cat. He is a sports enthusiast and an avid reader of fantasy and science fiction. *The Mercenary Code* is the first installment of his *Shattering of Kingdoms* epic fantasy series. Book two, *The King's Guard*, is set for release in the fall of 2019.

Printed in Great Britain
by Amazon